SPARROW AND THE MAFIA KINGS

MAGGIE ALABASTER

Cover design by Book Brander Boutique

Edited by Lily Luchesi

Proofread by Nora Hogan

POSSESSIVE

TRIGGER WARNINGS

Hi lovely reader. This book contains darker themes.

Assault
  Abuse
  Violence
  Mentions of sexual assault
  Mentions of child death

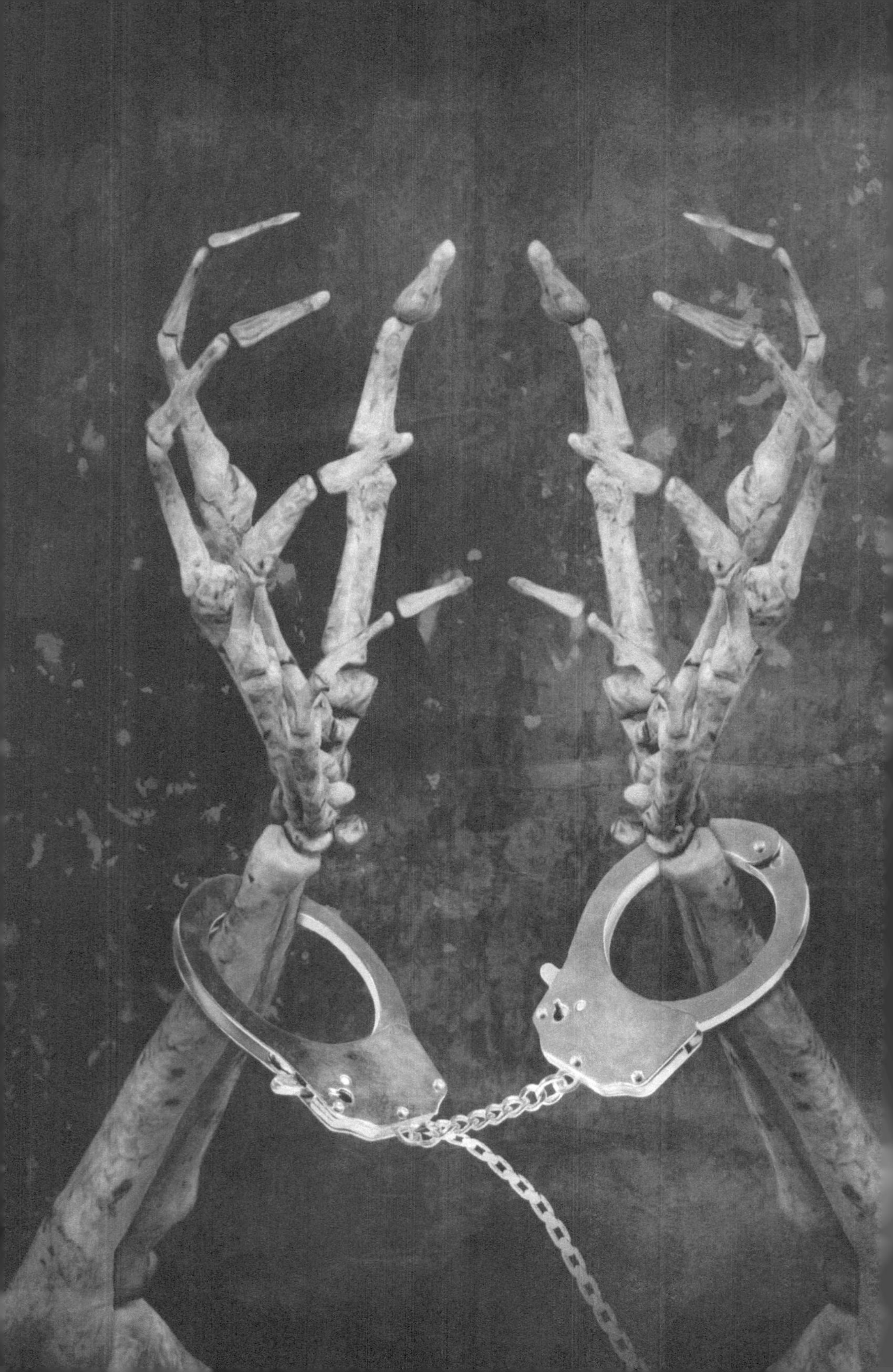

CHAPTER 1

MINA

I snapped awake. Froze, eyes half open in the gloom.

Shoving ragged, matted hair off my face, I pushed myself to an uncomfortable hunch. The rusty bars above me stopped me from sitting fully upright.

I pulled my legs closer to my body. The movement rattled the chain attached to the bars. Accustomed as I was to the strap chafing my ankle, I barely winced.

My attention wasn't on myself. It was on the barely visible outline of the door.

Every muscle in my body tensed, waiting. A minute past, then several more. Each punctuated by the dripping of water down the damp walls.

Just as I started to decide I'd heard nothing, and it might be safe to doze again, the door slowly opened.

"Miss me, bitch?" Kurt Lasalle strode into the dank basement. He crossed his arms and smiled, as though I should be grateful for his presence. Like he owned the place.

Owned *me*.

I didn't answer. Instead I focused on a patch of concrete floor in front of his feet.

Could it please open up and swallow him? If it couldn't, I wished it would do that to me.

The floor remained stubbornly solid.

He kicked the side of the cage, making it rattle and shake. "I said, did you miss me, bitch?"

I flinched and swallowed hard. Of course I didn't miss him. Every moment he was absent was a blessing. If there were blessings in a place like this.

Before I could answer, he dropped a slice of bread through the bars at the top of the cage. It landed near my knee.

My stomach pinched at the sight of it. How long was it since I'd eaten anything? The last time he was here at least. Two days, maybe three.

Not long enough, but too long at the same time.

"Eat it," he barked.

Before he could change his mind and take the bread back, I snatched it up and stuffed the whole piece into my mouth. I struggled to chew. With any luck, I'd choke on it.

Kurt laughed. "You look like a fucking animal."

Bit by bit, I swallowed down the stale bread. Parts of it tasted mouldy, but I couldn't bring myself to care. Focusing on chewing kept me from looking at Kurt.

Of course I looked like an animal. He treated me like one. He chained me in here, naked and filthy. He kept me on the verge of starving. My only source of water, most of the time, was the moisture that trickled down the walls and into the cage.

How long was it since I last saw sunlight?

I barely remembered how it looked, how it felt when it caressed my face. Maybe I dreamt that I used to walk in it, to skip around the garden with my sister and brothers.

Sometimes, when I dozed, I dreamt of that life.

Then I woke to this one. Hour after hour. Day after day. How long had it been? I had no idea. No way to tell night from day. All I knew was monotony, broken by dozing and visits from *him*.

I couldn't sleep here, not properly. Not deeply. I didn't dare.

Sleeping was for another life, one that was such a faded memory I wasn't sure if it was real either.

I swallowed down the last of the bread and huddled up against the side of the cage.

Kurt started to pace back and forth in front of it, putting me further on edge. Somehow, he knew what it did to me. That him moving around like he was caged put me further on edge. That was exactly why he did it. He got off on the power trip. On feeling like he had the upper hand on someone. Even if that someone was chained and caged.

"You should be grateful," he said, as though lost in thought about something specific. "After what you did, you should have had your throat cut. You know that, don't you?"

He stopped and crouched down in front of me. *"Don't you?"*

"Yes," I said. My throat was so dry, my voice was a hoarse whisper. The sound was strange to my ears.

I hadn't had reason to talk much for so long. I only did it answer his questions when he insisted on it. Usually 'yes' or 'no' was enough to satisfy him. He wasn't here for a conversation with me, he was here to remind himself he held the power.

Something must have happened to make him need an extra ego boost. I didn't give a shit what, only that I'd bear the brunt of it. I always did.

"Yes," Kurt echoed. "But here you are. Still alive. Because of me. Because I decided to have mercy on you."

I met his eyes for half a heartbeat before dropping my gaze again. His idea of mercy was fucked up. More than fucked up. He'd dreamt up a nightmare and I was living it.

"You're grateful to me, aren't you Mina? Because I was kind enough to let you live. Look at me." He gripped the bars of the cage and shook it. *"Look at me, bitch."*

I raised my gaze again and looked into his hateful face.

If he wanted gratitude, he should drive a knife through my heart. As I was dying, I'd thank him for it. But not for this. Not for this version of living. I wanted to spit at him, but my mouth was too dry. I resorted to looking back at him with cold eyes, expressionless.

His dark hair was cut close to his scalp. His stubble was as long as his hair. Brown eyes regarded me with amusement. I wanted nothing more in this world than to watch the light fade out of those eyes. For him to die slowly, painfully.

I didn't realise I'd curled my hands into fists until he looked down at them.

"You have some fight in you today, hmmm?" He raised an eyebrow.

No.

No. No. No.

He pulled a key out of his pocket and pushed it into the lock. He swung the door open and grabbed the end of the chain. He stood, dragging the chain with him.

I bit back a whimper of pain. The strap dug into my ankle as he pulled me across the floor of the cage on my ass.

The chain wrapped around one hand, he grabbed my wrist with the other and pulled me to my feet. He shoved me a handful of steps over to a basin on the side of the room.

"Wash yourself," he growled.

I grabbed hold of the side of the sink and held on to keep from falling. My legs could barely hold my weight. The chain was extended to the full extent of its length. I knew from past experience, it wasn't long enough for me to reach the door. Just the cage and the sink.

Before I could even pick up a washcloth, he grabbed the back of my hair, shoved my face under the tap and turned on the frigid water.

I struggled to breathe, but I managed to swallow a few gulps. It was fresher than what trickled down the walls. Not by much. It tasted like it passed through rusty pipes.

He pulled me back out of the water and laughed. "Refreshing enough for you? I should put in the plug, fill the sink and hold you under, but I won't. Not today." He sounded as though he was doing me a favour by letting me live.

He'd do me one if he carried out his threat and let me die. I wouldn't fight him.

He let my hair go and took a step back. "Hurry up."

I didn't want to obey him, but he gave me very few chances to get clean. I felt as though a layer of dirt coated every centimetre of my skin. If I could wash some of it away for now, it would stop being itchy and hard. For a while.

I grabbed the washcloth and wiped my face, before starting to wipe down my filthy body. I would have given almost anything for hot water and a proper shower or bath.

He snatched the washcloth from my hand and scrubbed it hard over my ass and pussy.

"That'll do." He turned off the water and tossed the cloth into the sink. From a hook on the wall, he pulled a towel and quickly ran it over me. The thin cloth was rough. Abrasive like a cheese grater on tender skin. It couldn't have been much cleaner than I was. Kurt had dried me with it several times already without taking it to wash it. It smelled sharp and musty.

Whatever the original colour was, was anyone's guess. It could have been blue, grey or maybe brown. Hell, it could have been bright pink for all I knew. Either way, it was old and worn. The kind people use on animals, rather than wasting the good, soft towels.

He stepped over to hang the towel back up on the hook. For those few seconds, he had no hand on me, or on the chain.

I stepped back towards the cage. If I was quick enough, I could scurry back inside.

He leaned over, grabbed a section of chain and pulled it, almost tripping me over.

I grabbed the outside of the cage to keep from falling on my face.

"Where do you think you're going, bitch?" He sounded amused. "You really are feisty today." He grabbed the back of my neck and pushed me forward until I was bent over the top of the cage. The cold metal dug into my chest and stomach, rough with wear and rust.

I pressed myself into it as though somehow I could slip between the bars and back into the cage. Hell was better than what he was about to do to me. What he'd done so many times before. I used to fight back, but I'd learnt the futility of that. The more I fought, the better he liked it.

I squeezed my eyes shut and hoped like hell he'd finish quickly.

The sound of a phone ringing echoed through the basement. It sounded so loud, I flinched. After spending hour upon hour in near silence, noises like that were a shock to my senses.

The ringtone wailed with the words to some rock song, the vocals sung by a woman, as far as I could tell.

"My love was a dark place,
Betrayed, denied, and broken.
I was shattered,
Over and gone.
Over and gone.
So gone."

"Fuck," Kurt growled.

He pulled his phone out of his pocket and pressed it to his ear. "What?" he snarled. He listened for a few moments before swearing again. "I'm on my way."

He shoved his phone back into his pocket and yanked me back upright. "Fun will have to wait until later." He pushed me back into the cage and slammed the door shut before pulling the key back out of the lock. "Try not to miss me too much." He smirked.

I'd miss him like I'd miss a bullet in my brain.

I scrambled back into the corner and curled up as small as I could. The cage was so filthy, I might as well have not washed myself at all. I couldn't avoid touching it, but I touched as little of it as I could.

I watched through slitted eyes as he hurried out the door and locked it behind him. It was a reprieve for now, but Kurt Lasalle was a man of his word. If he said he'd come back to finish what he started, then he would.

Tears were useless. Instead I let myself slip into my numb place, where I stopped thinking and feeling too much. I don't know how many times I'd been grateful to my training for allowing me to switch off like this. If it wasn't for that, I would have broken a long, long time ago.

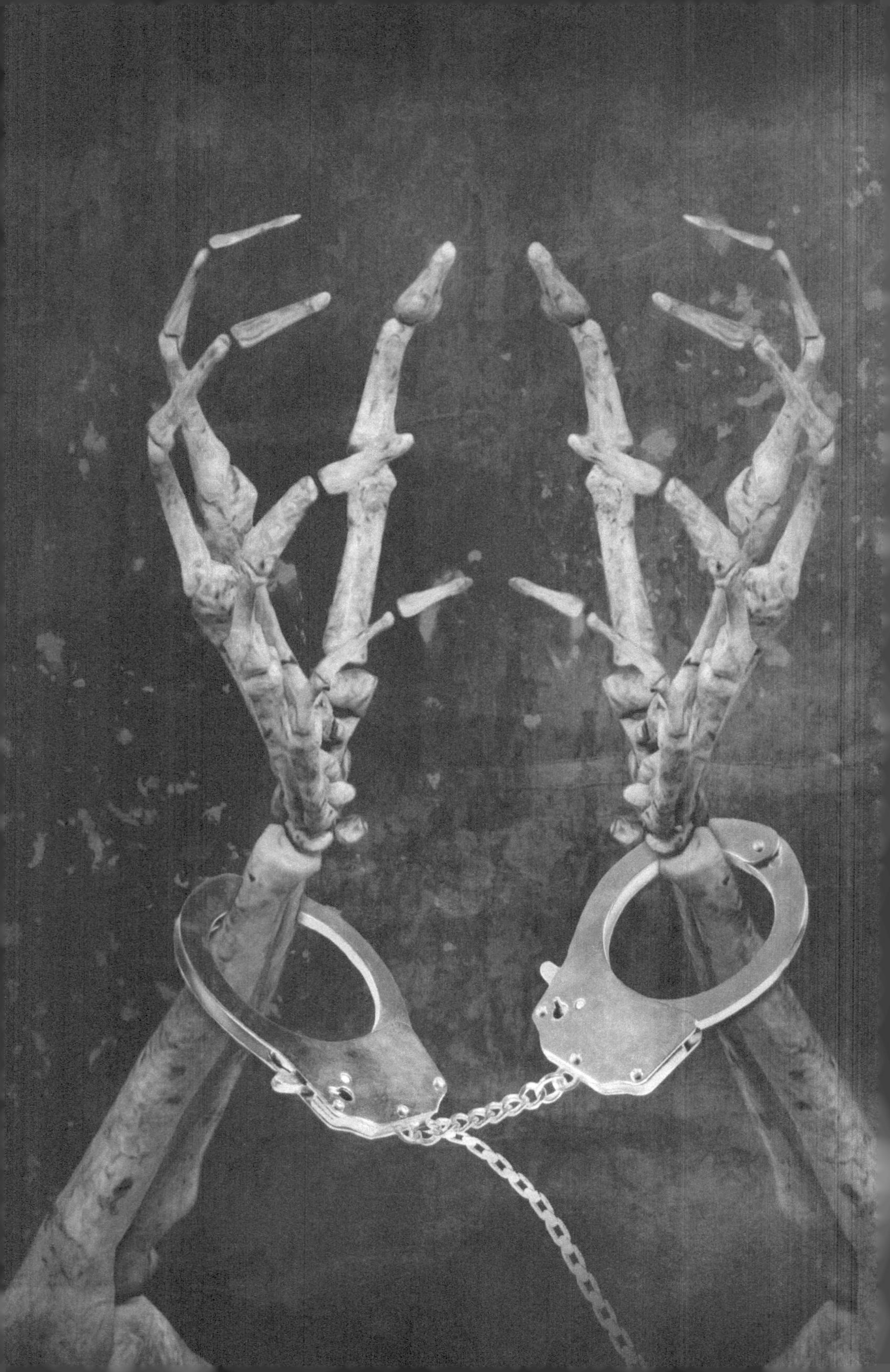

CHAPTER 2
MINA

I huddled with one eye open, watching the door while I let myself drift off again.

The doze wasn't deep enough to dream, not this time. Sometimes that was a mercy. The nightmares left me wanting to scratch my own skin off.

But the dreams were the worst. They helped me escape this hell, but when I woke here, I shattered all over again. Each time felt like a cruel joke. One my brain played on me over and over.

I couldn't blame my subconscious for wanting to take me out of here. It was trying to help me. I wished it would stop. All of it. The dreams, the nightmare and the reality.

Sounds from outside the room brought me fully awake.

Voices. Crashes and scraping from above my head. If I thought hard enough, I could remember being brought into the building and down some stairs. Upstairs was vague, a hazy memory seen through sedated eyes.

The murmur of voices filtered through the ceiling right above me. I couldn't make out a word they said. Didn't try very hard. I'd heard voices up there before. They never came down here. The one time I shouted, trying to be heard...

I shuddered at the memory. Squeezed my arms tighter around myself.

Heavy footsteps walked across the upstairs floor. Most likely Kurt or someone who worked with him, or for him.

I lay down on my side and try to get comfortable. There was no comfort here, just worse positions than others. I'd grown accustomed to that a long time ago. Deserved it. Maybe more than I deserved to have my throat cut.

What was the saying about the good dying young? I didn't deserve the peace, even though I craved it, more than anything.

The footsteps moved across the floor, down to the end of the upstairs. Slowly, deliberately they drew closer.

I pushed myself up to my elbows and stared at the door.

If I could raise the chain and wrap it round my throat, I would have. They say it's impossible to strangle yourself, but I would have tried. Anything to stop Kurt from touching me.

Whether or not I deserved everything he did to me, I hated it more than I hated myself. Hated him.

I squeezed my eyes shut and forced myself back into my numb, emotionless place. I had to lock myself in here. I couldn't let him get behind these walls anymore. He always found a way, but I had to keep him out. I had to cling to the last piece of sanity I had.

I asked myself why. Would it be better if I broke? If I lost myself completely. Maybe then I could switch off. Disappear to a place I'd never feel another thing again. Not death, but close enough.

The door rattled.

I frowned. Kurt would have unlocked it. Unless I'd finally lost my mind, whoever it was, they didn't have a key.

The murmur of voices was louder now, just on the other side of the door. Two distinct voices, at least.

"In my experience, people who keep things behind locked doors have something to hide," one of the voices said.

The others said something that sounded like agreement. "Open it."

A handful of moments later, something slammed against the door.

It held.

"Feels solid to me, boss," the first voice said. "Can I shoot the lock off?"

Apparently he was allowed to, because the question was followed by a gunshot, so loud it hurt my ears.

I clapped my hands over them and shrunk down, wincing.

The door swung open slowly.

"Ugh, it stinks in there, boss." In the gloom, I made out a figure waving a hand in front of his nose.

"You've smelled worse, Gianni," his boss said. He pulled out a phone and turned on the torch.

"True, boss," Gianni agreed. "I've probably *made* worse smells."

His boss grunted and stepped into the room, moving his phone around to illuminate the space.

I half closed my eyes against the sudden glare. They hadn't been subjected to light that bright in too long.

Gianni pulled out his own phone and waved the torch around the other side of the room. He stepped off to the side and stopped in front of the cage. He shone the light right at me. "Um, boss?"

I threw my arm up in front of my face to shield my eyes.

"What—" The second man turned. "Fuck."

"Fuck is right," Gianni said. "Is that…"

One of the men crouched down in front of the cage, not close enough to touch it with his expensive suit.

"Yes, I believe it is." He turned his face into Gianni's light.

My breath caught in my throat. I knew that face. Those cold, calculating ice blue eyes that saw everything. The strong chin covered in a layer of stubble. The strong mouth, often set in a line of disapproval.

He turned back to me, his voice a combination of gravel and honey. He never raised his voice. He didn't have to. When he spoke, people listened, before leaping to do what he said.

"Mina DiMarco, what are you doing here?"

"Reuben," I whispered.

He turned to Gianni and nodded.

I'd never believed in a higher power. No one was coming to save me from this hell. Not until now. Finally, I could get the one thing I craved so much.

Finally, I could die.

I ducked my head and waited.

"Get her out of there," Reuben said.

"On it, boss." Gianni nodded. "You might want to cover your faces." He slid out his gun and aimed it at the lock on the cage.

Reuben rose and stepped aside.

Elbows down to cover my chest, I put my hands over my eyes and tried not to wince at the second gunshot. The bullet slammed into the lock, blasting it into splinters. The cage door creaked ajar.

Gianni forced it open all the way, the hinges squeaking in protest.

Reuben slid off his suit jacket and offered it to me, along with his hand. The first I accepted and wrapped around myself. The other, I just stared at.

"I can't—" I tilted my head toward the strap around my ankle.

"I'm starting to hate this Lasalle prick," Gianni remarked. He put away his gun and pulled out a knife. "I'm sorry, sweetheart, this is going to hurt like a bitch."

He climbed into the cage and gripped my calf with surprisingly gentle fingers.

I flinched at his touch, but not enough to dislodge his hand. I didn't have the strength for that, even if I wanted to. I hated myself for my weakness, but I hated Kurt more.

Gianni and I had that much in common.

"How the..." He grunted.

"What is it?" Reuben asked.

Gianni directed the answer at me. "How long has this been on here? It looks like the skin has tried to grow up around it." His dark eyes looked angry, but not with me. There was a coldness about him, but a softness as well. The contract was too conflicting for me to figure out right now.

Reuben swore under his breath.

I could only shrug slightly and shake my head. "I don't know." I drew Reuben's jacket around myself tighter as Gianni searched for a place to slip the knife and cut the strap.

"Can you hold the light over here, boss?" He nodded towards my ankle.

Reuben stepped closer, holding his torch over Gianni's hands.

"It's lucky I like sharp knives." Gianni glanced at me and grinned before slicing through the leather of the strap like he was cutting an overcooked steak.

"This might suck." He put his knife away and gripped the two sides of the strap. Slowly and carefully he eased it away from my ankle. The leather stuck to my skin and the flesh underneath it.

He was right, it hurt like a bitch. The skin stung, trying to hold onto the strap like it was a part of itself. Every so often, he had to stop and push the skin down to pry the leather off.

"This has to have been there for... If I had to guess, I'd say years." He worked it loose and finally tossed it aside.

I blinked away tears of pain and forced myself to focus on what was more important. I was no longer attached to the chain. I could hardly grasp what that even meant. Was I free after so long, or was this a whole new level of hell?

I guessed Kurt hadn't invited them here. Otherwise they wouldn't have needed to force their way in, or break the lock in the cage. Unless this was some kind of sick game.

"Come on, sweetheart." Gianni backed out of the cage.

After a brief hesitation, I followed, crawling out and grabbing the side of the cage to pull myself to my feet.

"What the hell did he do to you?" Reuben asked softly.

"Where is he?" I peered towards the door. He said he'd come back. If he did, he'd find us all here.

"My guess is he saw us coming and ran," Gianni said. He seemed cheerful at the idea. Like he was amused at Kurt's cowardice.

"We'll deal with him," Reuben said darkly.

"Slowly and painfully," Gianni said. "If you want, you can watch."

I glanced at him. If anyone was doing anything slow and painful to Kurt, I wanted to do more than watch.

"We have some talking to do," Reuben said. He nodded towards the stairs. "Can you walk?"

I seemed to have three options: stay here, be carried or walk. I wasn't doing the first. The idea of either of them touching me gave rise to a spike of panic.

"I can walk," I said finally. "What are you going to…"

Reuben Brantley was high up in a huge organised crime network here in Australia. The Australian mafia, if you wanted to call it that. Before Kurt, our families were at odds. I couldn't rule out his intention to kill me, or worse.

"We're going to get you out of here." It was Gianni who replied. "Right, boss?"

I heard him referring to Reuben as boss several times now. Of course things would have changed since I was here, but the changes seemed to be bigger than I would have expected. I filed that thought away for later.

Reuben glanced at Gianni and stepped out of the room and up the stairs, leaving us to follow.

"I won't let anything happen to you," Gianni said. He made no effort to lower his voice. He wanted Reuben to hear what he was saying, whether he agreed with him or not.

Reuben grunted in response.

I grabbed hold of the handrail and strained to pull myself up the first couple of steps. I knew I was weak, emaciated. Until now, I hadn't realised how badly. I hadn't walked more than a few steps in…

"How long?" I asked softly.

Reuben stopped at the landing and turned around. "According to your father, you ran off to marry some nice boy and live in the suburbs."

Of course that was the line my father concocted. He would have had to tell people something.

"How long?" I asked again.

He pressed his lips together for a moment. "Five years. That was five years ago." He turned back around and continued up the stairs.

I put a hand over my mouth. If Gianni hadn't grabbed me, I would have fallen back down the stairs. Could it be possible? And yet, I knew it was. It felt like a lifetime and it almost had been.

I lowered my hand. "I was eighteen."

"Then you're owed a few birthday presents," Gianni said. "Five of them. You must be twenty-three. I really, really hate Kurt Lasalle right now."

My head was spinning so fast I had to let him help me the rest of the way up the steps.

I'd missed out on five years of my life. What else had I missed out on?

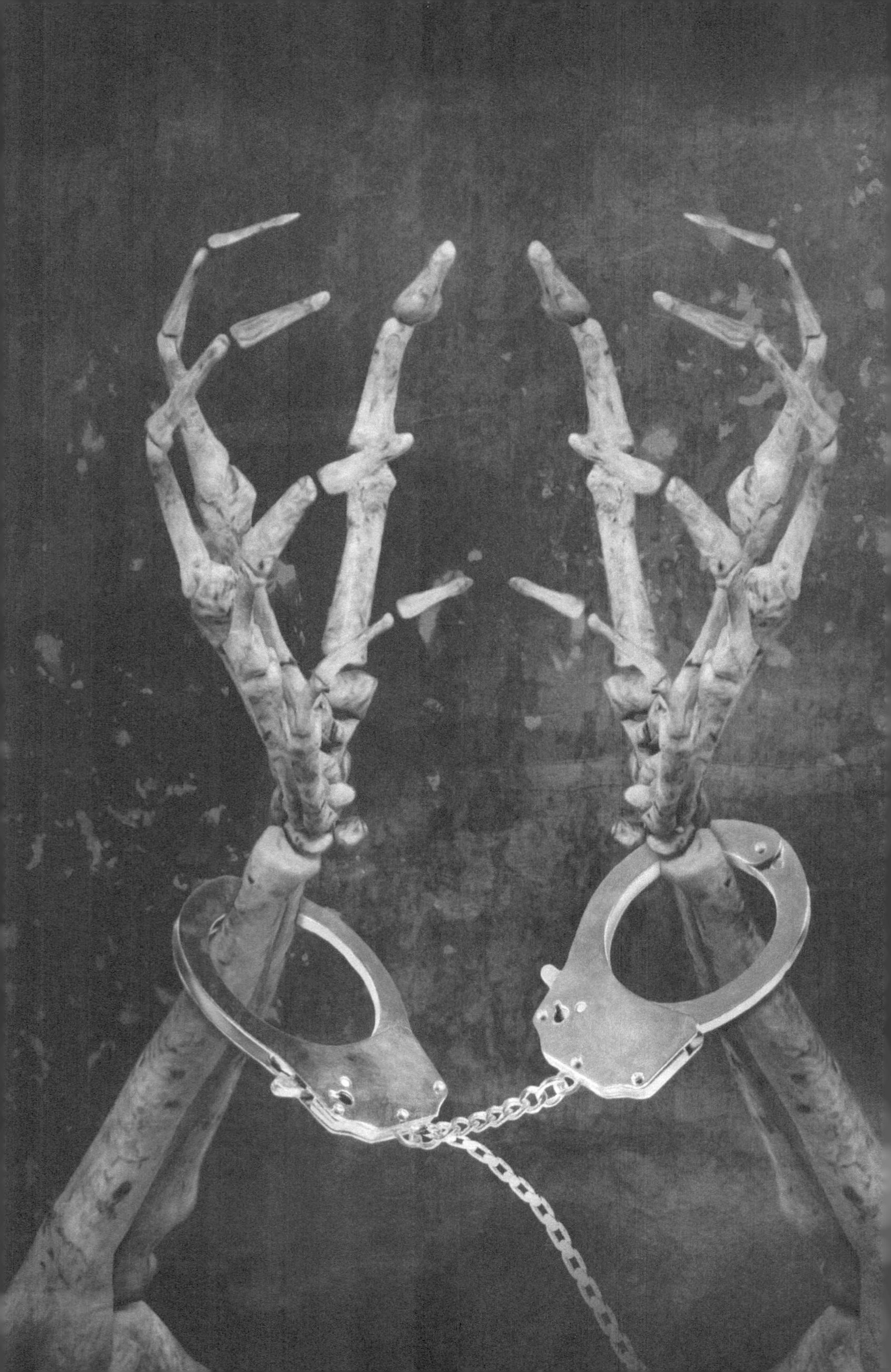

CHAPTER 3

MINA

Gianni lowered his hands from me when we reached the top of the stairs. He stayed close while we moved through the house, his whole body on alert.

Upstairs was a different world from the basement. Hardwood floors and expensive-looking furniture. Art on the walls. Hooks for them, anyway. Several paintings lay on the floor as if they'd been pulled down and left in a hurry.

Reuben's doing, I presumed. What was he looking for here? Not me. That was obvious from the shock when he first saw me. Had they found what they'd come here for?

The answer became evident when another man met us at the door. He was taller than Reuben and Gianni, with lighter hair and a tighter expression.

"Nothing, boss," he said briskly. "If Lasalle was doing what we were told he was doing, he's not doing it from here." His gaze slid to me. His eyebrows knitted and his mouth drew back.

Reuben nodded. "We'll find something in the other locations. I want everyone to keep looking." He stepped out the front door, toward a dark coloured sedan which was parked at the curb. "And Damon, tell them I want Kurt Lasalle alive."

"On it, boss." Damon took out his phone and sent off a quick text before making his way to the driver's seat.

I stopped at the threshold and recoiled from the glare. From the look of the light, it was late afternoon, but it was a brighter light than I'd seen in years. With the exception of the torches on their phones. Those were brief, this was overwhelming.

I wiped tears from my eyes.

"Boss," Gianni called out.

Reuben opened the passenger door and reached inside. When he stepped back towards the house, he held out his hand to me.

I had to blink a couple of times to realise he held pair of sunglasses.

I took them, opened the arms and slid them onto my face. They were much too big for me, but they filtered the worst of the sunlight.

"Thank you." That was something I hadn't said in a long time. Something I hadn't had a reason to say.

"We've spent enough time here," was Reuben's inpatient reply before he returned to the car and slipped inside.

That was an understatement.

I followed Gianni to the car and climbed inside, grateful for the tinted windows, comfortable seat and carpet under my bare feet. This felt like luxury after the cramped, filthy cage.

Gianni got in on the other side and sat far enough away to give me space, but close enough that I couldn't ignore his presence.

I felt like an injured bird he'd found on the side of the road and put into a cardboard box to nurse back to life. Just like me and my brother Asher did when we were kids. Our eldest brother, Dane, always told us we were wasting our time, but sometimes the animals lived. Usually with the help of our sister, Rose. She always seemed to know the right things to do.

"I'd ask if you're okay, but we both know the answer," Gianni said, his voice low to keep the conversation between him and me. "You will be."

The look I gave him should have conveyed my scepticism. How can I possibly, ever be okay? Did I deserve to be?

I clicked my seatbelt and curled my legs up on the seat beside me. I carefully arranged the jacket to cover as much of me as possible. For a piece of fabric, it felt like armour between me and the world. Like somehow I could hide behind it. It wasn't about modesty so much as it was about having a wall around me, however flimsy.

Damon glanced over his shoulder, frowned briefly, but put the car in drive and headed into the city traffic.

Pressed down as low as I could get, I watched flashes of the city go past. Nothing I recognised. Either everything had changed, or I wasn't familiar with the area to start with.

Whatever it was, I could have been on an alien planet. Other cars, other people, nothing felt real. Life had gone on without me. People had continued to live theirs while mine was on pause.

"You must be wondering how we came to be in that house today, of all days," Gianni said.

I turned back to him. I had wondered that. If I was honest, I wondered why they weren't there sooner. Maybe they were and never had cause to look in the basement.

"So, Kurt Lasalle works for Reuben," Gianni went on. "In theory. Obviously he didn't have permission to keep a girl in his basement. If we knew that, we would have gotten you out of there ages ago."

It hadn't occurred to me they might have known I was there and just left me there. It should have. Men like these, they had no loyalty to someone like me. Just to themselves and to each other. Even then, loyalty wasn't assured. Everyone has their price, as my father used to say.

"Lately he's been getting into things he shouldn't be," Gianni added. "Overstepping his authority. We've heard from a reliable source that he's been operating a few side hustles on his own. And not paying his dues. Reuben doesn't like it when people do that."

That was a lot to unpack. First of all, reliable sources were hard to find in their line of work. Secondly, was the suggestion Reuben was in charge now.

"What about Reuben's father?" I asked.

"Dead," Gianni said simply. "Both of his parents. But that's a story for him to tell." He nodded toward Reuben, who'd turned his head, indicating he was listening.

Of course they were. The Brantley family had their share of

enemies five years ago. It didn't surprise me someone took them out. It sounded as though there was more to it, but I didn't ask. Not now.

"So you came after Kurt?" I asked. "Thinking he was hiding something back there."

That would explain the paintings on the floor, and them breaking into the basement.

"He's definitely hiding something," Gianni said. "Apart from you, of course. Although, now we know about you, fuck knows how many other girls out there he has locked away."

That thought made the single piece of bread in my stomach threaten to come back up.

Of course at some point in the last five years, I'd wondered if I was the only one, but he never gave any indication there might be others. That didn't mean there weren't.

"We'll be searching all of his properties," Reuben said. "Thoroughly. And all of his contacts. Whatever he's hiding, we'll find it."

"I want to help," I said.

Reuben swivelled around in his seat to fix his ice blue eyes on me. "I'll consider it. When you're well enough."

Eighteen-year-old Mina might have argued with him, telling him she was perfectly capable of both helping and looking after herself.

The Mina of the present day, who could barely support her own body weight, just nodded slightly. There was little I could do apart from answer the questions if they asked any. Which they would. If it helped them to pin down Kurt, I'd tell them everything I knew. I was painfully aware that wasn't very much.

I leaned against the door beside me and closed my eyes. I didn't dare to doze here, but maybe someday I'd feel safe enough to sleep. Really sleep.

When I opened my eyes again, Gianni was watching me. He might give someone else the creeps with his intense stare, but he had an air about him. If I could trust anyone in this world, I could trust him.

Letting myself trust, that was another story. I was the little, broken bird in the cardboard box. Desperately wanting to fly, but needing to lie there under the old towel and gather my strength. Listening to kind words and careful gestures, but barely able to grasp that they could possibly apply to me.

I turned my gaze back outside the window.

"This must all seem strange to you," Gianni said. "It all seems strange to me too, and I haven't been through what you have."

I looked back at him, brow furrowed in question.

"You're wondering why I find it strange?" he guessed. "I suppose it's just that all of these people, living so close together, seems to me like a weird thing to do. People in general, I find their weirdness fascinating. I want to know why they do the things they do. Damon likes to tell me someday my curiosity will get me killed."

"It will," Damon said over his shoulder.

Gianni grinned. "See? But if there's any trouble, Damon is always the first to leap into it. Who do you think will get killed before whom?"

"Still you," Damon said. "I'm always careful."

Gianni cupped his hands around his mouth and whispered loudly. "No he's not. If he was careful, he'd stay home and knit."

Reuben snorted.

"Fucking *knit*," Damon muttered. "I don't know how to knit and neither do you."

Gianni chuckled. "It's so easy to get him going." He lowered his hands to his thighs.

"And that's why you'll get killed first," Damon said. "You'll piss off the wrong person and they'll shoot you."

"Are you threatening me?" Gianni looked completely unworried.

"Yes," Damon said. "Yes, I am. Can I shoot him, boss?"

"No," Reuben said simply. "Not today. Focus on what Lasalle is up to. Damon, have you spoken to his sister?"

"Ohhh, I wouldn't want to be Kurt when Daze finds out what he did to Mina," Gianni said. "We'll be lucky if she leaves his big toe behind for us to find."

When I looked questioningly again, he said, "Daisy Lasalle also works for Reuben, she's a bit of a badass, and she hates when men do bad things to women. When she learns about you, she's going to tear him a new one, brother or not. You're going to love her."

His description made me curious to meet her. Whether or not I'd love her remained to be seen. Was I capable of loving anyone? I wasn't sure but I was certain of one thing—it was impossible for anyone to love me. How could they after what I did?

Did they know about that? I supposed not, unless they left me alive so I could keep eating myself up with guilt.

"Not yet," Damon said, as if Gianni hadn't spoken. "You want me to go and see her, boss?"

"No," Reuben said. "Have her come to us. If she's working with her brother, I want to see it on her face. If she's complicit, she's dead."

"You think Daisy Lasalle is working behind your back?" Gianni asked.

"No, but blind trust gets people killed," Reuben said. He turned back to look at me. The message was clear. They'd been speaking very openly in front of me, but he wasn't sure if he could trust me to keep my mouth shut.

I looked back at him. Who would I tell? If he thought for a moment I was working with Kurt, he was out of his fucking mind. There was no one left for me to confide in.

Kurt had thoroughly enjoyed telling me when my parents and siblings died. He'd laughed while I sank further into despair. For a while, I thought one of them might come for me. When the last of them was gone, my hope went with it. I never expected to be found and freed by a Brantley. Especially not Reuben.

No, they could speak as openly as they wanted to. I wouldn't say a word to anyone.

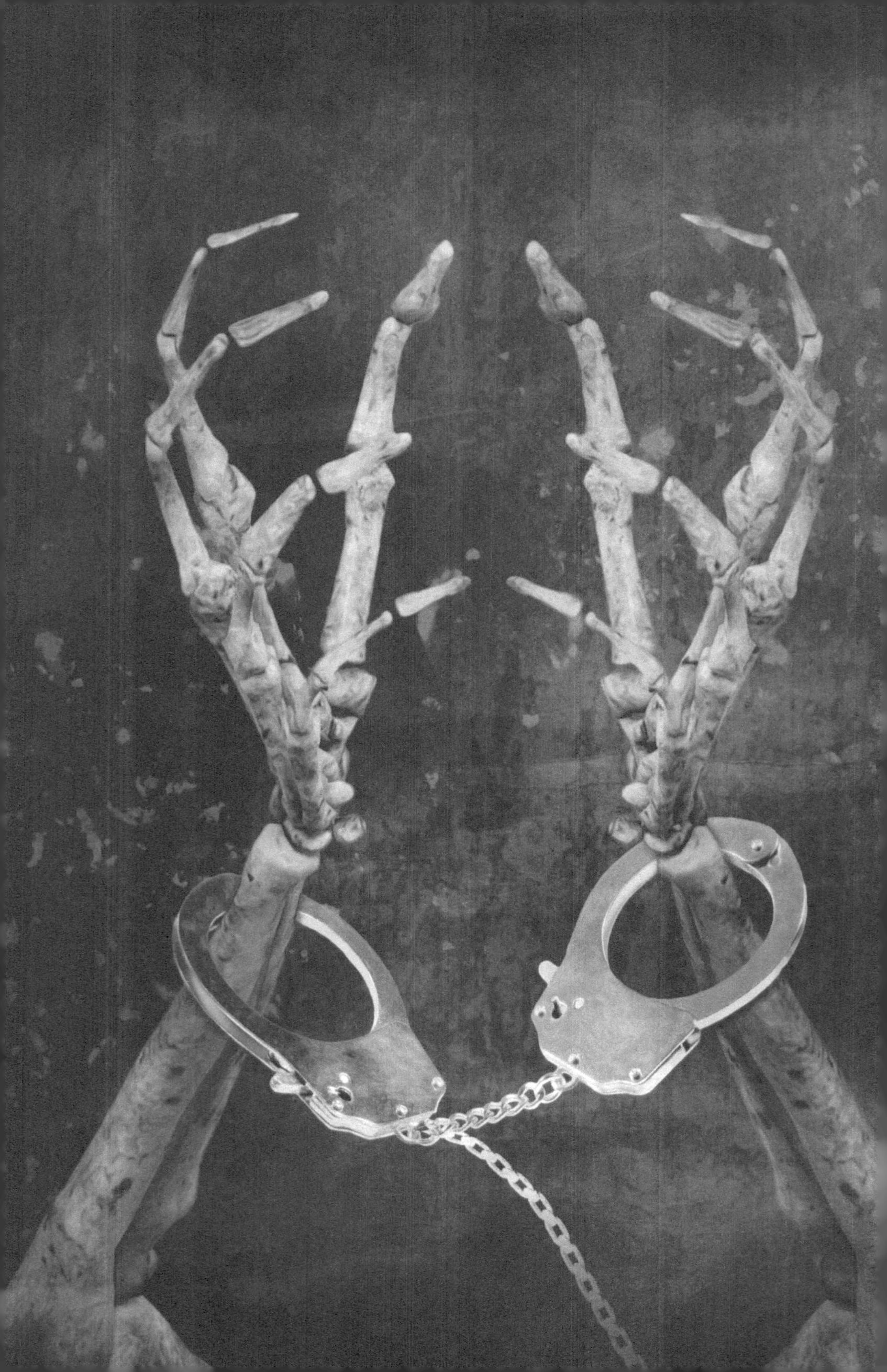

CHAPTER 4

MINA

Damon pulled the car into the garage of a large, but otherwise unassuming, brick house. A high, stone fence and a patch of land surrounded it, keeping the suburb around it at bay.

Reuben climbed out of the car and over to the interior door. "Gianni, take care of Mina." He disappeared inside, followed by Damon.

"You heard the boss," Gianni said. He waited until the garage door closed behind us, leaving us in dim light.

I undid my seatbelt and pushed open the door. Swallowed hard. I pulled the sunglasses off my face and held them in trembling fingers.

This isn't the basement, I told myself. *It's just a garage.* But I wanted to shrink back into the car and curl up on the seat. Let it be my cardboard box.

"It's okay," Gianni said softly. "I've got you. I'm going to snip off Lasalle's toes, one by one, when I catch up to him, but I've got you. Come on, step away from the car."

"I don't know if I can," I said. The walk to the door felt too far, too long. Too exposed.

"I can carry you," Gianni offered.

"No," I said quickly. I recoiled from the idea, and from him.

"It's okay if you want to stay here for a while," he said. "But there's a bath inside. Or a shower, if you prefer. And food. Terry made pizza last night, I bet there's some left over."

"Terry?" I asked in a quavering voice. I hated the sound of it. I was Mina DiMarco, I was stronger than this. I'd survived everything Kurt put me through. I wasn't going to break down now.

"He's Reuben's butler and chef and whatever the hell else," Gianni said. "He looks like a mountain, but he's harmless."

"The opposite of you," I said without thinking.

Gianni chuckled. "Something like that. I'm nice on the outside, but Reuben keeps me around because I know a variety of ways to get information from people."

"Torture?" I asked.

"If it comes to that," he agreed. "It's not my preferred method, necessarily. I don't hurt people for the fun of it, unless they deserve it. So, bath or shower?"

"With hot water?" I asked.

"As hot as you want," he agreed. "Unless you prefer cold?"

"I never want to feel cold water again," I said. I managed to push the car door closed behind me, but I leaned against the outside of the vehicle. Partly for physical support and partly for emotional.

How fucked up was I that a strange car felt like a safe place?

It was the first place in five years I could sit up and see daylight. The first surface I'd sat on that was actually comfortable. It was so small, but so big at the same time.

"Then you don't have to," Gianni said. He moved around in front of me and offered me his hand. "I understand being touched might be terrible. Just think of me as a crutch. Lean on me until you can lie down in the bath and get clean. Don't think of me as a person, if that helps."

I stared at his hand. "Why are you being so nice to me?"

The question made him frown. "Sweetheart, we found you in a cage, chained up like a wild animal. Don't you think it's time someone was nice to you? Also, Reuben told me to. But I would have anyway. You remind me of myself."

That statement made me blink. "How am I anything like you?"

"Some people think I'm an animal too," he said. "Like I said, I know a variety of ways to get people to talk, including torture. I don't flinch at blood, urine or screams of pain. Does that sound like a normal person to you?"

"In the world I grew up in? Yes," I said. He might be right that we were alike, but I didn't think he really understood how much.

He grinned. "I should have expected that answer. It sounds like your childhood was as fucked up as mine." His smile faded. "More so."

"Yeah." I pushed myself off the side of the car and started to slow walk to the door.

Halfway there, I had to grab his elbow to keep from falling. Through the fabric of his button down shirt, his skin was warm, reminding me he was definitely not just a crutch. He was a living, breathing person, and that was something I should be wary of. Whether or not I thought I could trust him, he was still a man. One who stood over a head taller than me. In my current state, it wouldn't matter what skills I had. I wouldn't be able to fend off him or anyone else.

That forced me to decide. I had to go along with them for now. I had to do everything I could to get fit and strong, until I could defend myself. Besides, the idea of pizza was enticing.

"That was what I thought," Gianni said.

I glanced sideways at him in confusion.

"You're stronger than you think you are," he said. "You're a fighter. I wouldn't expect anything less from a DiMarco."

"We're known for our stubbornness." I followed him inside the house.

He stopped in the middle of the dark hardwood floor. "There's no bathroom down here. I just remembered. Can you manage one more set of stairs?" He looked annoyed at himself.

"I can manage," I said. I let go of his elbow and made my way to the staircase leading upstairs.

It looked as though it had been there for a hundred years, along with the rest of the house. This must have been one of the first in the area, the suburbs growing up around it. The property had probably been in the Brantley family for a handful of generations. And now it belonged to Reuben.

I grabbed hold of the thick banister and pulled myself up step-by-step, while Gianni walked behind me. He made no attempt to touch me, or come too close. He just kept himself near enough that if I needed help, he'd be right there.

"You know mobsters aren't supposed to be nice," I said over my shoulder.

He chuckled. "I like to be different. Although, you're the first person who's ever called me nice. Usually it's something like 'that psychotic prick who works for Reuben.' Obviously they don't know me very well. I'm not psychotic, I'm creative."

I snorted softly. "I see how those two things could get confused." I had some experience in that myself. In another lifetime.

"Go to the right at the top of the stairs," he said.

I did what he said, and stepped into a large bathroom. The floor was covered in black and white penny tiles, and the walls with white subways. In the back corner, was a large shower. Beside that was a freestanding, clawfoot tub. Opposite the bath was a vanity with light timber doors and double sinks, with a marble countertop. Everything had a colonial look, but new, like it was recently remodelled.

"Looks expensive," I remarked.

"Nothing but the best for Reuben," Gianni said. He opened a cabinet that matched the vanity and pulled out a couple of towels. He set them down beside the bath and turned on the water. "Let me guess, you're a lavender kind of girl?"

"I'm a girl who probably smells like a week-old corpse, I don't really care," I said.

"I didn't want to be rude." Gianni winked at me. He pulled out some purple bath salts and sprinkled them into the rising water. "If you climb in, I'll work on your hair."

"You'll—" I stared at him.

"My mother was a hairdresser. If anyone can do anything with it, it's me. Unless you want me to get Damon. He'll just bring a knife and cut it all off." He made a hacking gesture with his hand.

I put a hand to my head. I hadn't given much thought to my hair.

Not for a long time. Every so often, Kurt would hack it shorter, but all I could do was run my fingers through it once in a while.

I stepped over towards the bath and caught sight of myself in the mirror. If I didn't know it was me, I never would have recognised myself. My cheeks were sunken in, my hair was tangled. My eyes looked huge in my face, greenish blue and haunted, surrounded by long lashes. I touched my cheek to make sure it really was me.

"I don't just smell like a week old corpse, I *look* like one," I said.

"Nothing a bath and trim won't fix," Gianni said. "Hop in." He turned his back and waved towards the bath.

He'd already seen me naked, but I appreciated the gesture. Especially given it was brighter in here than it was in the basement. In this light, I'd never hide all the scars.

I slipped off the jacket and stepped into the water. I closed my eyes and groaned at how incredible the warmth felt. I sank in, under the bubbles, and moaned again.

"It sounds like you're enjoying that," Gianni said. He turned around and hurried over to the vanity to pull out shampoo, conditioner and a pair of scissors. He knelt behind me and carefully started to wash my hair.

I flinched when his hands first touched my head.

He was still for a few moments, waiting for me to tell him to back off or keep going. Eventually, he started to slowly massage my scalp.

I grabbed up a bar of soap from the side of the bath and started to wash off years of dirt and grime from my skin. My ankle stung where the strap had been, as well as several other scratches and scrapes, but none of that detracted from how incredible it felt to be surrounded by hot water. Water that wouldn't stay clean for long.

"I'm going to rinse your hair," Gianni said. "Can you scoot down a bit?"

I slid down far enough to submerge the back of my head while he rubbed off the shampoo. I sat back up so he could apply the conditioner.

Using a wide tooth comb, he started to tease out some of the tangles. Every so often, he stopped to pick up the scissors and cut out a knot.

"He could have at least given you access to a hairbrush," he grumbled.

"If you have to cut it all off—" I started.

"Not all of it," Gianni said. He breathed out a frustrated sigh through his nose. "More than I'd like. Don't worry, you'll look adorable when I'm done with you."

"I'll settle for clean," I said.

"That, I can guarantee," he said. "There we go. Let's rinse off your hair again."

My head felt several times lighter when I lowered it into the water again. The rinsing took a lot less time.

"There we go. You'll feel like a whole new woman now." He stood and put everything away before picking up a towel and holding it out to me.

I could have stayed in there for hours, but the water was turning brown, so I stood while he averted his eyes, and took the towel. I wrapped it around myself and stepped out of the bath.

"I'll leave you for a few minutes," he said. "I'll ask Terry if he can find you some clothes." He hurried out the door and closed it behind him.

I pulled off the towel and quickly dried myself. A quick glance in the mirror showed my filthy, matted hair was now gone, replaced by a cute bob. Gianni saved more of it than I expected.

I still looked like a stranger to myself. How long would it take before the woman in the mirror looked like me?

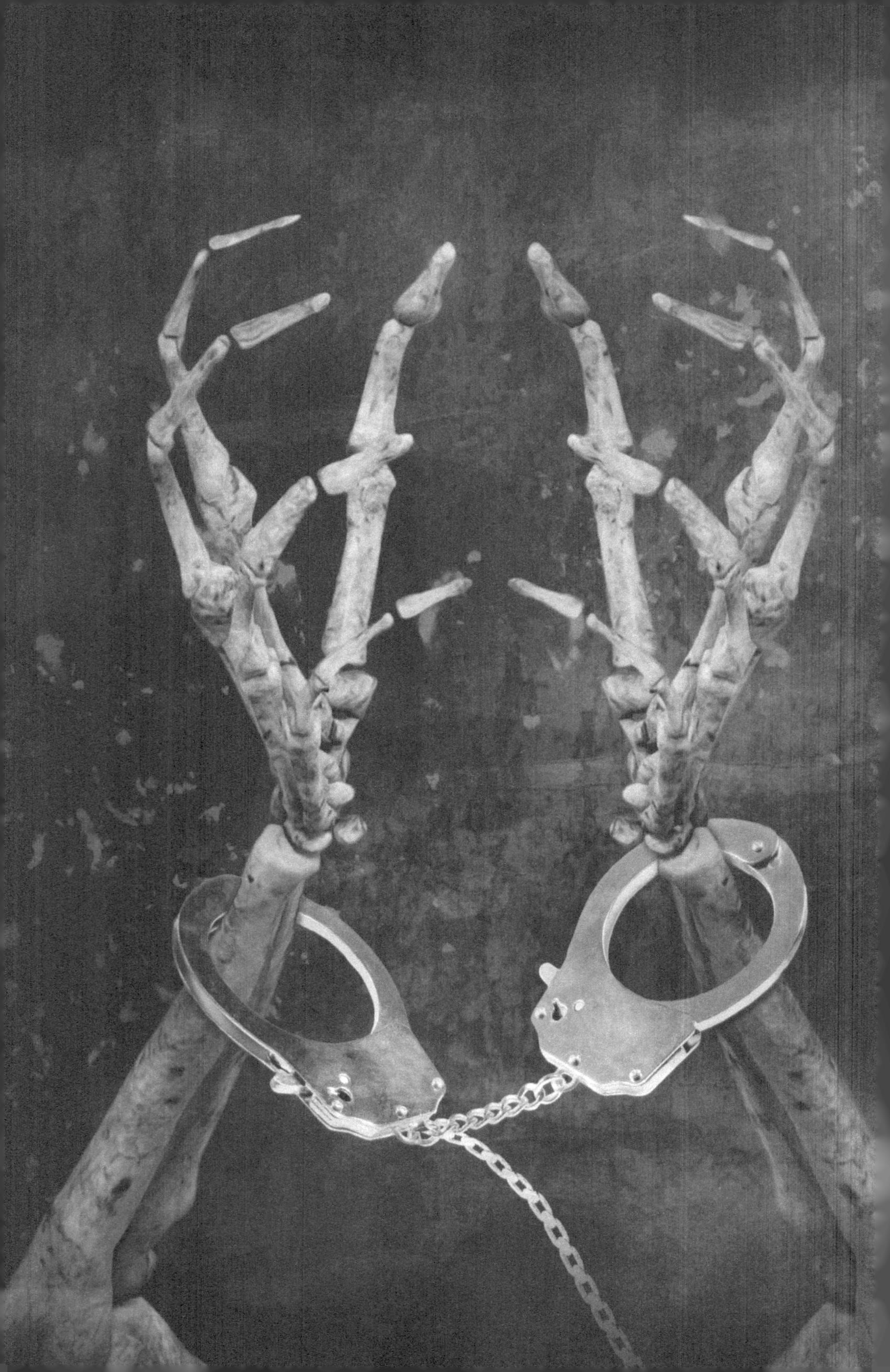

CHAPTER 5

REUBEN

I glanced up from my glass of whiskey as Damon stepped into the room. As always, his expression was guarded, closed. I trusted him more than most, but I gave up trying to read him a long time ago. He got the job done, that was what mattered.

He lowered himself into the leather chair opposite me and sat with his ankle resting on his opposite thigh.

"She wasn't what we were expecting to find," I said.

"No," Damon agreed. "Should we have?"

"I don't know." I scrubbed a hand over my face. "We've kept close track of all the members of the DiMarco family. Not close enough, apparently."

It wasn't guilt I was feeling, but rather irritation at not knowing something I should have known.

Men like Kurt Lasalle shouldn't be able to keep a woman chained up in their basements without my knowledge. Especially one I'd known all her life. What was that ridiculous nickname her family gave her? Mina Sunshine, because she was always happy and smiling. When was the last time she was either of those things?

I struggled to reconcile the girl I once knew, with the woman we found only a handful of hours ago.

"Wild guess the DiMarcos had no idea," Damon remarked. "Not unless there was something in it for them."

"What?" It was a pointless question, he had no more answers than I did.

"Are we going to tell them?" he asked.

"Not yet." I sipped my whiskey, savouring the way it burned down my throat. "I want to talk to her first. She may be able to shed some light on the situation. If any of the DiMarcos knew she was there, they may try to act against us if they learn we have her here."

Damon made an indeterminate sound in the back of his throat. He wasn't scared of them either.

"What are you planning to do with her?"

That was the question I'd had running through my head since I recognised the filthy woman with the big, blue-green eyes. Leaving her there wasn't an option, but I hadn't decided what happened next.

I'd speak to her and make my decision based on that conversation. No doubt Gianni would try to influence me. He was treating her like an abandoned kitten, in need of food and attention to nurse it back to health. But kittens grew into cats and cats had claws. Especially ones with the last name DiMarco.

"I'll decide that when the time is right." I didn't have to explain myself to him or anyone else. I hadn't had to for a long time. That was how I liked it.

"The boss is probably in his library." Gianni's voice came from just outside the doorway. That was followed by him looking in and smiling. "Here he is."

He stepped into the room. My breath caught in my throat as Mina followed him in.

She'd never been tall, but she was all but swallowed by the grey track pants and T-shirt she wore. Clothes that used to belong to the twins, if I had to guess. Neither Hunter nor Parker fit into them since they were ten or twelve, but they'd remained stashed away in a box somewhere until now.

Even in old, borrowed clothes, she was stunning. Even with the wary, on-edge look in her eyes. No one would blame her for that, least of all me.

"Sit down." Gianni waved towards a chair. "I'll see how Terry is going, heating up some food for you." He actually gave me a warning look before slipping back out the door. He was protective of our little stray. That better not cause a problem.

Damon looked at me questioningly, but I nodded for him to stay.

Mina stepped carefully into the room, looking around the shelves of books that covered the walls. Some of the shelves weren't filled yet, leaving spaces here and there that I tried to avoid looking at. They looked untidy. If there was anything I hated, it was mess.

She finally slid into a chair and tucked her feet up beside her. She wrapped her arms around herself in a classic, protective pose.

"You're looking better already," I said.

"It's good to be clean." She tucked a few strands of hair behind her ear.

I usually preferred longer hair on women, but it suited her better that way than tangled and matted.

"How did you end up with Kurt Lasalle?" I didn't believe in beating around the bush. I had questions and I wanted answers to them.

"My father gave me to him to settle a debt," she said softly. Did she always speak like that, or was she holding back because she was scared?

"What debt?" I asked.

She shook her head slightly. "I don't know. Just that there was a debt. I guess it didn't help, since my father was killed shortly after that."

"How did you know that?" I asked.

"Kurt told me." A frown furrowed her brow. "He told me when each of my parents and siblings were killed."

I ignored the strangled sound Damon made, and placed my whiskey glass on the table beside me. I leaned towards Mina, my elbows on my thighs.

"He told you your siblings were dead?"

She blinked a couple of times, those long lashes brushing her cheeks. "He said I didn't deserve to know, but he told me anyway."

I sat back. "He told the truth about your parents. Your father had mine killed, so I had them killed. But your siblings are very much alive." I watched as my words slowly sunk in.

She recoiled slightly, but then sat forward again. "Dane, Rose and Asher?"

"All alive," Damon said.

Mina turned towards him. She didn't look like she was sure she should believe a word we'd said.

"Dane teaches history at Brutham Academy," I said. "Rose is down in Melbourne doing whatever Rose does." She was good at solving problems, like disposing of unwanted corpses.

"Asher is…" I sighed. "A drummer in a band with my brother, Zeke." I hadn't given up on the idea of my brother quitting the band to come back to join the family business. One way or another, I'd convince him to stop wasting his time singing rock songs to sold out arenas all over the world.

Mina looked back and forth between us, her pretty mouth slightly open, plush lips quivering.

"It's true." Damon pulled out his phone and tapped on the screen for a minute or two before passing it over to her.

She took it from his hand and looked at the photo on the screen. Her blonde haired brother stood beside my younger brother, with the rest of the band.

"It says this photo was posted three days ago," she said. "He's really alive." She stared at the photo for the longest time, not moving, barely breathing.

"We can contact them if you like," I offered.

"No." She surprised me with her quick response. "I don't want any of them to see me like this. Not yet. They'd… I can't." She pushed the phone back toward Damon.

"You don't have to," I told her. "You can hide out here for as long as you need to."

Had those words come out of my mouth? Judging by the raised eyebrow, Damon was surprised to hear it as much as I was. We never took in strays. But now she was here, I couldn't bring myself to let her leave. Didn't want her to.

"Thank you," she whispered. "I don't know what to think."

"About what?" Damon asked.

She looked down in the direction of her knees, then back up again slowly. "I thought the reason they didn't come for me was because they were dead. But they weren't. Why would they leave me there? Why would they let him do the things he did to me if they were alive to stop it?" She closed her eyelids over her shining eyes and bit her lip.

"Why didn't they come for me?"

"My guess is they didn't know," I said, my voice quiet, even for me. "Asher, in particular, would have done anything to get you out of there if he was aware. Rose too."

Dane was a self-serving son of a bitch, who knew what his agenda might be?

"They didn't know," she echoed. "My father must have lied to them too."

"As far as anyone knows, you ran off to marry some nice boy and live in the suburbs," Damon said. "They say you kept in contact for a while before you didn't. They must have thought you were happier away from this life."

"I never contacted them," she said. "I couldn't. Kurt… Kurt had my phone. He must have sent messages, pretending to be me, and they never thought to question it. No one ever thought to try to find me."

"They might have tried," I said. "They wouldn't have been successful. If I had to guess, I'd say the only one who knew about the connection between you and Kurt was your father. Once he was dead, only you and Kurt knew, and he wasn't saying anything."

"And I couldn't." She chewed on her lip. "If you hadn't had my father killed—"

"I doubt he would have told anyone," I said. "I can't imagine your siblings would have taken it well if they knew. If I hadn't had him killed, they would have. Or someone else would have. He was good at making enemies." And giving his innocent daughter to a monster. My only regret was that he didn't die slower.

"He was," she agreed. "I'm glad he's dead. I don't believe in hell, but if it exists, I hope he's there. And I hope Kurt goes there soon."

"He will," I assured her. "I have a lot of resources on finding him.

The twins have assured me they are on his trail." Hunter and Parker were both pains in my ass, but they were useful in their own way.

"The twins are… I guess they grew up," she said.

"My youngest brothers got older, but I don't know about growing up," I said dryly. There were twenty years between me and them, so they had time. If they didn't get themselves killed first.

"I feel like I got left behind," she said. "Everything has changed. I don't know where to start to catch up."

"I recommend you start with pizza." Gianni stepped into the room and handed Mina a plate.

Her eyes huge, she started to eat.

"Don't eat too fast," Gianni warned. He crouched down beside her like he might snatch the food away again at any moment.

She moved the plate away from him, as though that might stop him from taking it, and bit into the pizza, a look of bliss on her face. Terry made the best pizza I'd ever had, but it must be just this side of heaven for her.

Watching her eat, the urge to keep her here grew stronger. I wanted to see her experience all of the things she'd missed out on in the last five years. Fresh air, sunshine and good food. Safety, security and stability.

Usually I wouldn't give a shit whether anyone enjoyed those things or not. But with her, things were different. I was drawn to her. The need to protect her was overwhelming.

Maybe I was getting soft, but I didn't give a fuck. If anyone lay a hand on her, they'd lose it.

I snapped out of my thoughts as she made a gagging sound. She pushed the plate towards Gianni, clapped a hand over her mouth and staggered towards the door.

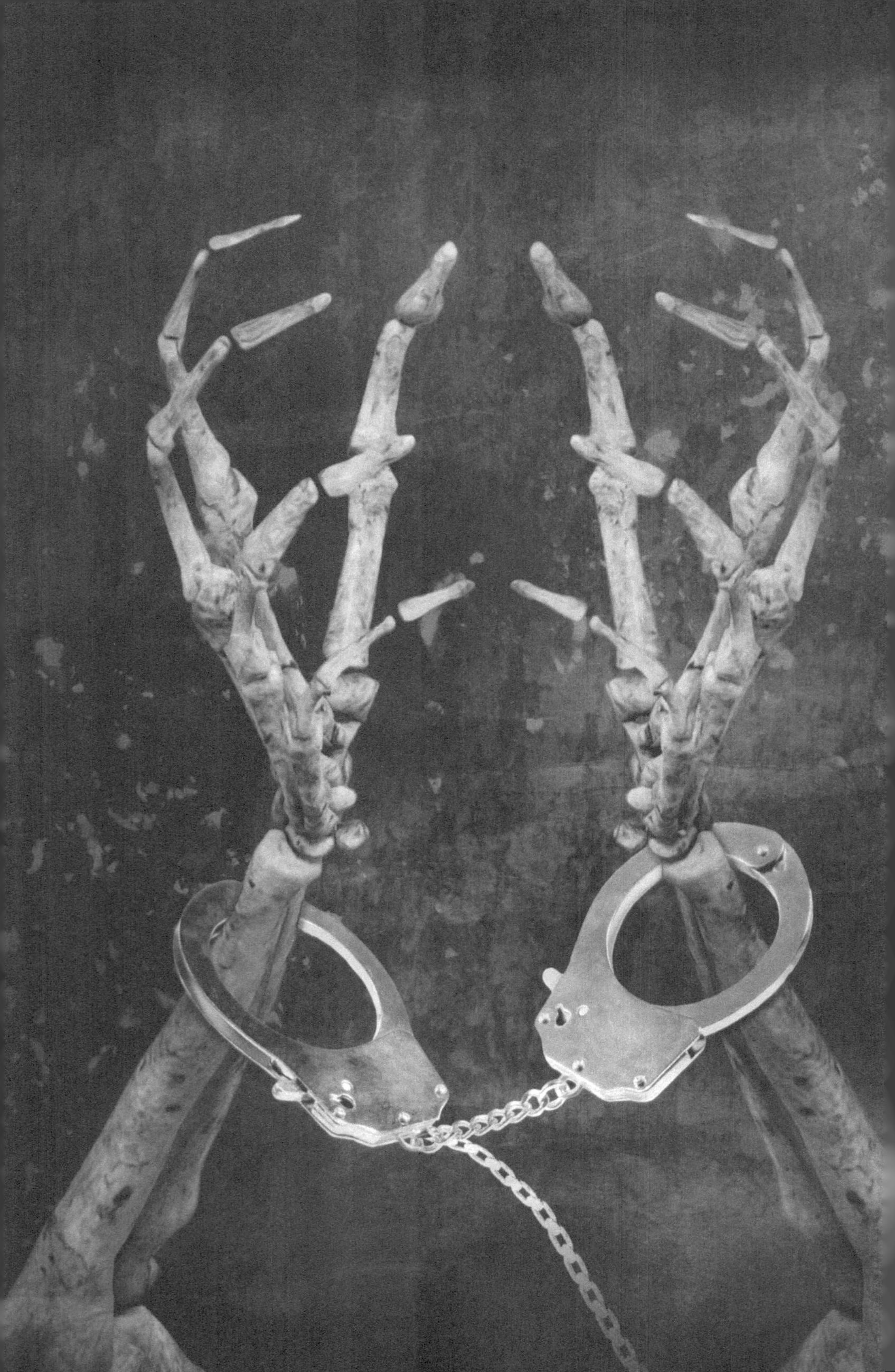

CHAPTER 6

MINA

I lay on my side, my hand on my bloated, sore stomach.

After throwing up the first few mouthfuls of pizza, I kept down some dry crackers and sips of juice. That meagre meal was more than I'd eaten in too long. The taste though…

Even watered down juice tasted like heaven. Clean and fresh and full of flavour. I could easily have ignored the pain and eaten a whole box of the crackers. If I did, I'd throw them back up. My stomach wasn't ready for that much food, even if the rest of me was crying out for it.

I flinched as a shadow stopped in the doorway. Surrendering to a spike of fear and panic, I curled up around my cramping stomach, even as I made out Reuben's silhouette in the light from another room. It illuminated the corridor and most of the room I lay in.

The bed under me was like a cloud after living on concrete. It was almost too comfortable, the blankets too heavy and warm. I'd pushed them aside and lay straight on the mattress.

"Better?" Reuben stepped inside, arms crossed as though he needed to defend himself from me. He had no reason to be physically intimidated by me, so I wasn't sure what was behind his posture. Something about me had him on his guard. Vice versa was true, so I'd lay no blame on him. Not yet.

Was I better? I wasn't sure. I hadn't thrown up for long, but it was long enough.

"I suppose so," I said. "I shouldn't have eaten so fast." I was lucky to have made it to the powder room in time. Otherwise I would have thrown up all over his hardwood floors.

"I don't blame you." He picked up a chair from the side of the bedroom and placed it down next to me. "For any of it."

I wanted to tell him he should, but I wasn't ready to explain why. The time for that would come when I was feeling stronger. When I was better able to defend myself against him and anyone else.

"I have a doctor on the way to see you," he said. "A discreet one. Anything you have to tell him won't leave these walls. If it does, I'll deal with him."

Of course he would. Someone like Reuben Brantley didn't like his orders being disobeyed.

"Like you dealt with my father," I said.

"Exactly." He sat forward, his elbows resting on his thighs. "I can't imagine how you survived those years. I'm not sure I would have." That was a surprising admission, coming from someone like him.

"I'm not sure I did," I said. "Maybe I'm dead and I haven't realised it yet."

He responded with a soft snort. "Does that make me the devil? Some would say it does."

"I don't think this is hell," I said. "Unless all those years were Purgatory and I've finally moved on."

"I'm no angel, so I'd suggest you're still alive." He didn't smile when he said that, but his words were slightly lighter.

Now I thought about it, I couldn't remember having ever seen him smile. Maybe that was something he didn't do.

"That's a possibility." I sucked in breath and held it for a long time before slowly letting it go.

"What is it?" he asked. It wasn't quite command, but he gave no apology for prying either.

I pushed myself to sit up against the headboard, my knees tucked into my chest.

"I'm scared of waking up," I whispered.

He took a moment to process that. "In case this is a dream and you're still in the cage."

"Yes." If I woke up and found myself there, the last shred of my sanity would shatter. I was certain of that.

He ran the tip of his finger across his lower lip, back and forth with mesmerising slowness.

"I won't offer to pinch you. I can assure you, this isn't a dream. Not, I think, a nightmare either. Your fear sounds rational. Expected after what you've been through."

"My mother used to say that people shouldn't make promises they can't keep," I said.

"That's good advice," he said. "I have a preference for operating the same way."

"Then I can believe you if you promise this is real," I said. Could I? I wanted to.

"I promise you, this is real," he said. "You're in my house. I can also promise you that Kurt Lasalle will never touch you again. He will be dealt with appropriately." There was a slight emphasis on the last word. It promised that when they found him, Kurt would suffer.

"I believe you," I said.

"This wasn't what you expected," he stated. "When you first saw me, you thought I'd have you killed. Why?"

I chewed my lip. "I believed Kurt when he said my family was all dead. He suggested you had them killed. I thought I was the last of us. Why wouldn't you have had me killed?"

Reuben inclined his head slowly. "Now you know that's not the case. I've had no reason to go after any of your family, after your father. Not your brothers, your sister or even your cousins." A brief frown creased his brow.

"What is it?" I asked. I hardly knew my cousins, but when he mentioned them he seemed troubled somehow.

"Gianni mentioned Kurt's sister Daisy," Reuben said. "One of her boyfriends is your cousin, Ric."

"Gianni said Daisy would have Kurt killed if she knew what he did to me," I said. "You think Ric knew?"

Reuben grunted. "No. He wouldn't have kept something like that from her. She'd rip his balls off and make him eat them."

I was starting to like her. She sounded like one hell of a woman. "You think there might be conflict between them because her brother did this to his cousin?"

"Conflict is bad for business," Reuben said. "If it becomes a problem, I'll deal with it. I assume you don't want your cousin knowing you're here either."

I unravelled myself a little, to relieve the pressure in my stomach. Eating would get easier, but it would take time. I'd have to be gentle with myself until then.

"No I don't," I said. "I don't want him to see me like this either." It was probably irrational to feel ashamed about the things Kurt did to me. No one said the human brain was completely logical.

"No one blames you for what he did," Reuben said.

"I do," I said. "I wonder if I could have fought harder. If I did something different, he would have let me out of there. Or maybe he would have stopped coming."

Reuben leaned forward a couple of centimetres, not close enough to touch, but looking like he wanted to. "You would have preferred to die down there alone."

"When I thought you'd kill me, I was relieved," I admitted. "I gave up on living a long time ago. I gave up fighting when he…" I swallowed hard.

"Forced himself on you." Reuben was always blunt, but he was pulling no punches tonight.

"Yes," I whispered. "He liked to toy with me. To see how long it would take before I cried or screamed."

I gripped the hem of my borrowed T-shirt and raised it up, above my stomach. It was too dark in the basement for him to have seen the scars, but from a sharp intake of breath, he saw them now.

He lifted a hand towards me, but stopped a centimetre or two from touching my skin. "What—"

"Cigar," I said simply. He'd sit beside the cage smoking one before pressing the hot tip against the sensitive skin of my stomach. Or my back.

Reuben swore under his breath. "Sadistic prick."

I lifted the T-shirt higher.

"Fucking hell," Reuben growled.

I glanced down at my bare chest. One of my nipples was perfectly normal, slightly erect in the cool air. The other was nothing but an angry, twisted scar. The skin melted around it was a testament to how long he'd held the tip of the cigar in place. He'd laughed while he did it. Laughed harder when I screamed in agony.

I dropped the shirt back down. "That was the first time I wished I was dead."

I thought I might break that night. Hoped I would. That was also the night I stopped fighting. I hoped he'd tire of me and stay away. Or better yet, kill me.

"He's going to wish he'd never been born." Reuben's tone was one I hadn't heard from him before. It sent a chill up and down my spine. If it was directed at me, I would have been terrified. But it wasn't. His fury was *for* me, on my behalf. I didn't know why, but it was.

"This is why I don't want my family to see me," I said softly. "I'm not me anymore. I'm a broken doll."

Ice blue eyes fixed sternly on me. "You are not broken. Nor are you a doll. You're a survivor. What you've been through would have destroyed most people. You have all the scars to prove that. But he didn't destroy you. You will get your strength back and we'll deal with Lasalle. Do you think those scars make you ugly?"

"They do." I turned my face.

"Mina," he said softly, making me turn back to him. "You've always been beautiful. Those scars make you even more beautiful. Every one of them shows how fucking strong you are. You said you stopped fighting. You didn't. You've never stopped fighting. You adjusted. You did what you had to do to walk out of there. I don't think you have any idea how fucking incredible that is."

I opened my mouth to say something, but he raised a finger and placed it right in front of my lips, close but not touching.

"I promise you this. I'm going to do everything I can to make you see how beautiful you really are. You deserve nothing less."

"You don't know—" I started.

"I know," he said firmly. "I know."

I leaned my head back against the headboard. "Why?"

He gave a laugh-grunt from the back of his throat. "I don't fully understand that either. I just know this is going to happen. There's a reason we were the ones who found you. I intend to discover that reason, but in the meantime you should get some rest. The doctor should be here soon. I trust him, but Gianni will be there too. If he crosses any lines…"

"You'll rip his balls off and make him eat them?" I asked.

"Precisely," Reuben agreed. "No one fucks with you and gets away with it. No one."

I believed him, but it was still strange. If you told me a day ago I'd be here, and that Reuben Brantley would say those things to me, I never would have believed it. I would have thought I'd finally lost my mind. Could I rule out the possibility he lost his?

"Thank you," I said softly. "I want to be there when you deal with him."

He nodded. "Of course. I wouldn't leave you out of it unless you asked me to." He pressed his hands to the seat on either side of him and pushed himself to his feet. "How much you're involved is up to you."

"Can I ask you a question?" I asked him before he stepped out of the room.

"You can ask," he said. "I can only say I'll try to respond."

"I haven't seen any women in the house since I got here." Just Gianni, Reuben, Damon and a glimpse of Terry.

"There are none," Reuben said. "None but you."

I nodded and lay back down on my side.

He gave me a long, last look before he strode out of the room.

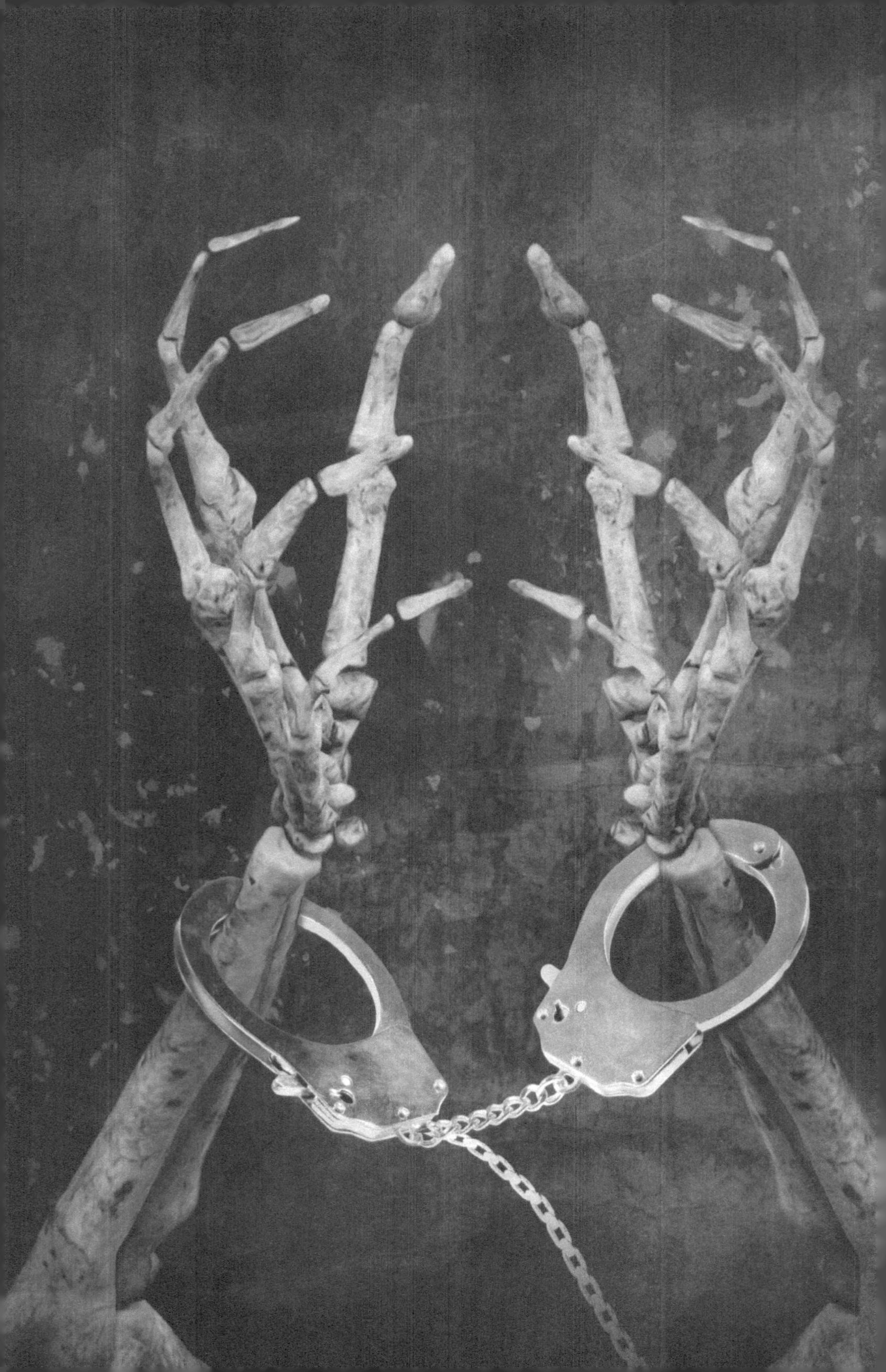

CHAPTER 7

MINA

"Later, Doc." Gianni walked Doctor Ryan out the door before sitting on the side of the bed. "You doing okay?"

"Yeah." I slid under the lightest of the blankets.

The doctor, he'd introduced himself as Oliver, was clearly shocked at what he saw, but he'd been professional. He checked my heart, blood pressure and ankle where the strap dug into the skin. Apart from needing a dose of antibiotics, a tetanus booster, and going easy on food, he said I was in remarkably good health. Physically anyway.

"That's the hard part out of the way," Gianni said. "Now you can focus on the other shit."

"Finding Kurt" I tucked my legs close to my body. "And anyone who worked with him."

"Did you ever see anyone there in the company of that asshole?" Gianni cocked his head at me.

"Saw, no," I said. "I heard them upstairs, but he never brought anyone down." I remembered a haze of faces from before the basement, but not once I was down there.

"Doesn't mean they didn't know about you," he said thoughtfully, but with a hint of anger. "We'll find them and we'll find out. And have some fun in the process." He rubbed heavily inked hands together.

I shrugged one shoulder. "I just want to find Kurt. Him and anyone else who knew and didn't do anything." I was happy for them to hang beside him.

"In my line of work, I see some shitty things," Gianni said. "This pretty much tops all of that. If there were other people in on what he did to you, that's even more fucked up. We're not known for being nice to each other, but when innocent women are involved, that makes me mad."

I pulled the blankets tight around myself. "Has it ever crossed your mind I might not be innocent?"

He chuckled. "Everyone is innocent if you look at them from the right angle."

"Even you?" I shifted uncomfortably. Between the softness of the bed, wearing clothes and the blanket, everything felt suffocating. I was tempted to throw everything off and sleep on the floor, but I had to regain some kind of normal. To me, that meant sleeping in a bed, with covers over me.

"Asking the big questions, I see," he teased. "In some ways I'm innocent. And by that I mean I'm not always guilty. Damon on the other hand…"

I forced myself to stop fussing and lie still. "What about him? He seems nice enough."

"For a mobster?" Gianni asked with another chuckle. "He's a good guy if he's on your side. If he's not, he's good at fucking people up. The best part, he's good at making people think he's on their side until it's too late." He made a slicing gesture across his throat.

"So I should be careful around him?" I asked. Truthfully, being around so many people was already overwhelming, and it was only three of them. Four if you counted Terry. I'd be more than careful.

Gianni rubbed his chin. "Good question. Damon is dangerous, but no more than Reuben. The difference is, if Damon double crossed you, he'd have me and Reuben to answer to. Does that mean he won't? If he does, he's going to cover his tracks pretty fucking well. There'd have to be a helluva payday in it from someone else, for him if he did that. So yeah, be careful, but don't be afraid to give him your trust either. He's one of the most loyal people I know."

"If he's loyal to you, then you're loyal to him," I said slowly. "What's to stop both of you from turning on me?"

"The fact I'm not an asshole," he said. "I don't hurt women unless I have to."

"Unless Reuben tells you to," I said.

"I've been known to disregard his orders when they go against my moral compass," Gianni said. "Yes, I have one. It mostly points north."

"So you keep turning until it suits you," I said.

He grinned. "Something like that. I've never been the kind of person to follow blindly. Reuben would have to have a very good reason for me to lay a hand on a woman before I'd consider it."

"Like what?" I was getting sleepy, but this was the most interesting conversation I'd had in years, and the least painful. I wasn't ready for it to end yet.

"Like being complicit in handing her daughter to a monster." His expression darkened. "Standing by and letting it happen. Knowing what was going on and saying nothing. Caring more about her own ass than her children."

I pushed the end of the blanket aside with my feet and lay with them sticking out. "You think my mother did that?"

He shrugged. "No way to know now. But if she did, she's the kind of exception I'm happy to deal with."

"How?" I asked. "What could you do that wouldn't make you as bad as Kurt?"

"I don't lay a hand on *innocent* women." He glanced down towards my bare feet.

"Which brings us back to people being innocent." Uncomfortable, I slid my feet back under the covers. "My mother might have been innocent of what you're suggesting. My siblings didn't know, she also might not."

"I hope she didn't." He looked back at my face. "Because that would be a really shitty thing to do."

He was quiet for a moment before jerking up straighter so suddenly I flinched.

"Sorry, sweetheart. It just occurred to me to ask if you wanted to hear some of your brother's music." He pulled his phone out of the back of his trousers. He knelt down beside the bed and tapped the screen to load a video. Holding it sideways, he turned the screen around to face me.

I read the text beside the video. "Wolf… Venom?"

"That's the name of the band. Look, here's where they come on stage."

I squinted at the screen. I recognised Zeke Brantley, who walked to the front of the stage where the microphone was set up. Behind him I caught a glimpse of blonde hair. My heart skipped a beat as my brother slipped behind his drums and picked up his sticks.

The rest of the band took their places. A couple of them looked familiar, but I couldn't put names to faces.

On some cue I couldn't see, they started to play. All of my attention was on Asher, who grinned as he played. He grooved at the same time, looking like he was thoroughly enjoying himself. Of course he did, he'd always enjoyed making music. And life in general. He was the one who should have been nicknamed Sunshine, not me.

"They're not bad, are they?" Gianni asked. "They're one of the biggest bands in the world right now. Living their best life and touring all over the place."

"They're a bit…loud," I said.

They finished playing and Gianni turned off the phone. "That's what Reuben always says too. That they're loud. He prefers his music soft and in the background. If he listens to it at all."

That definitely sounded like Reuben. I couldn't picture him rocking out to music like that.

"What about you?" I asked. "What kind of music do you like?"

"I like it louder than Wolf Venom." He tapped his phone against his knee. "There's a space under the house where we put people when we want to get information from them. It's soundproof. I like to go in there and turn up some metal as loud as it will go. Especially if I'm working with someone in there." He grinned. "When I've had enough of metal, I put on some Carrie Underwood. Or Abbie Hart."

"I've never heard of the second one," I said.

"You're in for a treat." He tapped on his phone again and held it in his palm until a song started.

From the first note, I couldn't contain my reaction. I all but leaped out from under the blanket, threw myself away from the sound and landed on the hard floor with a thump.

"Shit." The song was immediately silent. He jumped up and hurried around the bed to crouch in front of me.

I lay on the floor, pressed hard against the wall, curled up in the smallest ball I could manage. Every millimetre of me was trembling. I couldn't make it stop.

The world was folding in on me, pressing in hard, making it more and more difficult to breathe. My head was spinning, my stomach turning again. I had to swallow to keep from losing what little I'd eaten.

"I'd understand that reaction to some music, but…" Gianni looked confused and concerned. "If I thought you'd hate it that much, I wouldn't have played it."

He spoke lightly, but he knew as well as I did the song wasn't the problem. That was just the trigger. He was at a loss as to what to say to settle my racing thoughts.

I shook my head, my trembling so bad my teeth were chattering.

"What the hell is going on?" Reuben demanded from the doorway. His footsteps were heavy as he made his way into the room. Commanding attention and making me shrink in further.

"Sorry boss, I freaked her out," Gianni said. "I'm not sure what happened." He looked straight at me, brow furrowed, trying to figure out how to respond to me and to Reuben. That he blamed himself was clear from the expression on his eyes. He was worried he'd fucked up somehow and pushed me over the edge.

I needed to explain, to make them understand. Even if it made me sound like I was losing my mind. Who's to say I wasn't?

I sucked in a couple of rapid breaths, trying to put together the words as simply as I could.

"That song," I whispered. "It's Kurt's ringtone."

The moment I heard it, I was right back in the basement. Chained and scared. Terrified I woke up after all. I couldn't remember what happened after that. I just found myself on the floor, arms wrapped tight around myself, the hard floor a familiar comfort under me.

"Fuck, I had no idea," Gianni said. "I won't play it again. I'll even delete it from my phone." He held up his phone to do just that.

I closed my eyes and struggled back into my numb place. Shutting off everything and everyone around me. I wasn't in the basement, I was here. Safe, warm, clean and fed.

Get a fucking grip, I told myself.

"I'm okay," I said, half to myself. "I'm okay." My hands on the wall behind me, I pushed myself to my feet and sank back down to the bed. "If it's okay, I'd like to be alone now. Please."

"Of course," Reuben said. "We both have rooms just down the corridor. If you need anything." He waved for Gianni to precede him out the door.

Gianni stopped to give me another apologetic look before stepping out.

I slid back under the covers and pulled them up over my head. If I pulled them tight enough, maybe I could shut out the sound of the music that went around and around in my head.

I wasn't sleepy anymore. I was wide awake. With any luck, I might doze a little bit between now and dawn.

Kurt isn't here, I reminded myself. It was just a song. Just one song out of millions in the world. At least he hadn't chosen one of Asher's songs as his ringtone. That was the kind of fucked up shit he would have done, so he could laugh at the fact I had no idea.

I closed my eyes and willed my heart to stop beating so fast. I should never have freaked out so violently. I needed to be in better control of myself than that. I reminded myself that if I was, I wouldn't have ended up with Kurt in the first place. Somehow, I had to pull myself together, contain myself and keep my emotions and fears from getting the better of me.

I *had* to.

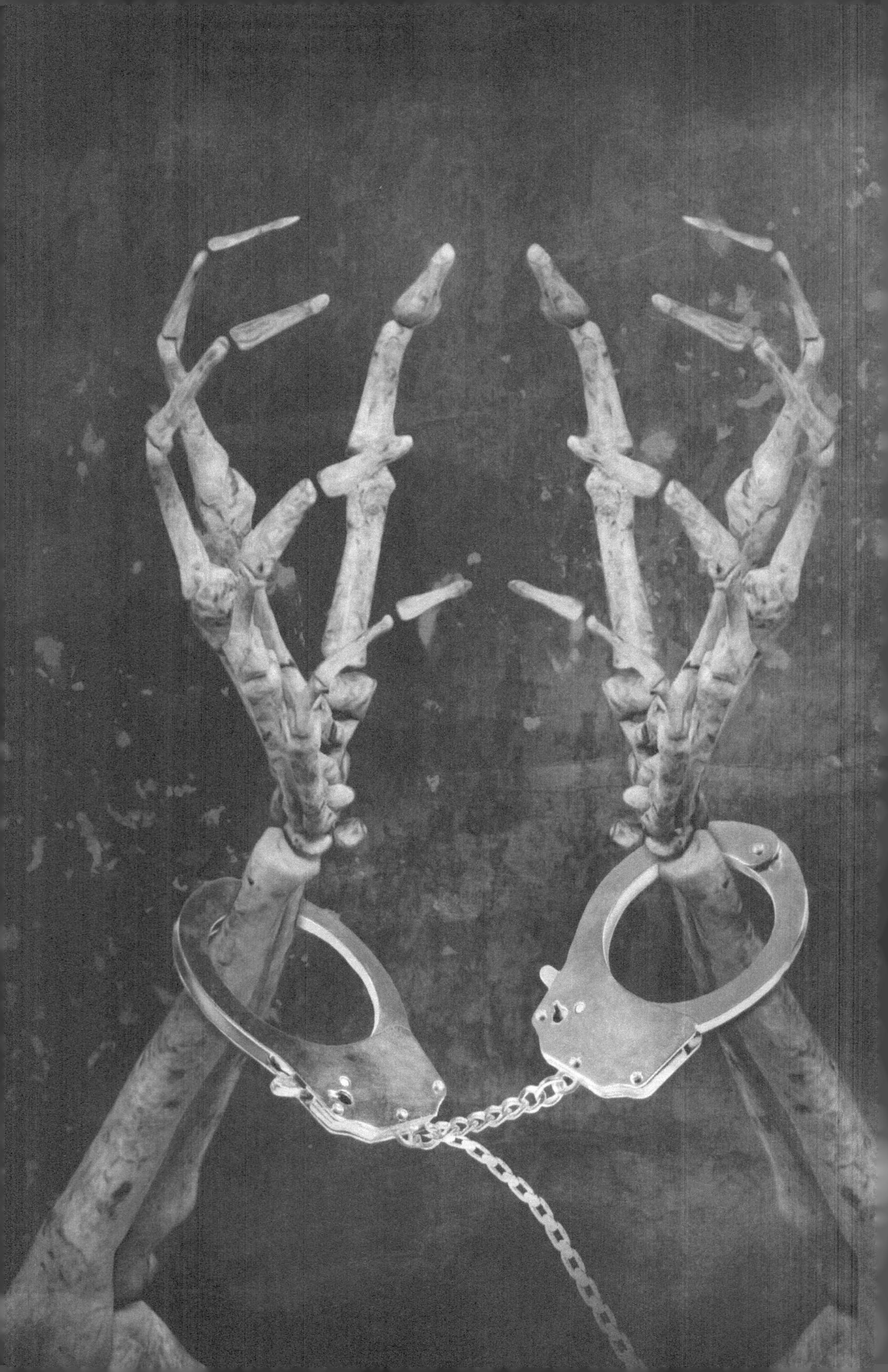

CHAPTER 8

REUBEN

For the last twenty or thirty minutes, I stared at the page without reading a word.

Finally, I slid the bookmark into place and closed the book. If anyone dogeared any of my books, they'd lose a few fingers. As they should. If I was obsessive over anything, it was the condition of my books. Meticulous, clean and with spines unbroken.

I placed the book on the table beside me and scrubbed a hand over my face. At the best of times, I couldn't sleep more than two or three hours a night. With Mina in the house, I was unlikely to get that much.

Gianni once suggested I was at least part vampire. I'd rolled my eyes at him. For his own amusement, he spent the next week with a scarf wrapped around his neck.

I ignored his attempts to goad me, and eventually he stopped wearing it. It might have been Damon's threat to use the scarf to strangle Gianni that did it. Damon was as quiet as I was and just as unpredictable. He may just as easily have carried out his threat on a whim.

Given how irritated I'd be if he killed Gianni, it was best he hadn't.

I suspected Gianni was safe from Damon's hands. They seemed to have some understanding that bordered on a fucked up bromance. Or at least, a mutual agreement not to take each other's lives. I didn't care as long as shit didn't get messy.

I looked up as Gianni slid into the room. Didn't say a word while he sat across from me, his hands steepled and pressed against his lips.

"I scared the shit out of her," he said finally.

"I saw." I heard a rapid shuffling, followed by a thump as she hit the floor.

I hadn't stopped to think, I'd just found myself at her door. Immediately, I wanted to soothe the expression of fear from her face. Fuck, I wanted to pick her up off the floor and wrap my arms around her. If I hadn't thought that wouldn't scare her more, I would have, so I kept my distance.

"I had no idea." Gianni's brow was as furrowed as I'd ever seen it. His dark eyes were troubled. "I showed her a video of her brother and I thought she'd like some other music."

"You couldn't have known," I said. "This won't be the last thing that triggers her."

"I know, I just figured if she could stand looking at my face, then a bit of music was harmless." His forehead smoothed and he smiled slightly.

I grunted softly. "Apparently there are things in this world more terrifying than your face."

He chuckled. "Reuben Brantley, did you just make a joke?"

My left shoulder rose and fell, barely more than a twitch. "I don't make jokes, just observations."

"I knew you secretly loved me." He laced his fingers together and placed them across his lap.

"So secretly I, myself, wasn't aware of it," I said dryly.

That made him grin more. "Ouch. I have knives gentler than you."

"I'm not supposed to be gentle," I said. "Gentle gets people dead."

He arched an eyebrow at me. "I saw the way you looked at Mina. There's gentleness deep inside you."

I arched mine back at him. "If you ever say that again, you'll be on the other end of one of your knives."

"You know what your problem is?" He tapped his hand against his thigh.

I gave him a flat stare.

As if I hadn't made it clear I didn't want to continue this line of conversation, he went on.

"Your problem is that you think being gentle is a weakness. Sometimes it's a strength. If you softened enough to let someone in, you might find it beneficial."

"I don't need to let anyone in," I said, my teeth gritted.

"Bullshit." He was unflinching. "Everyone needs to let someone in once in a while. Like I said, I saw how you looked at Mina. Like you wanted to tuck her into your pocket and keep her safe from the world. Or better yet, into your pants."

I gripped the arms of my chair and glared at him. "After all she's been through—"

He smiled with something that looked like triumph. "See what I mean? I've never seen you protective of anyone before. Not like this."

I worked my jaw back and forth, but couldn't summon the words to deny the accusation. Finally, I released the arms and placed my hands on my thighs.

"She was a fucking *kid*," I said softly. "What kind of monster hands a kid over to another monster? What debt did DiMarco have that he'd pay for it with an eighteen-year-old girl?"

"Is it because she was eighteen, or because she was Mina?" Gianni asked. "I heard you tell her she was always beautiful." He blinked a couple of times. "Is this why you don't let anyone in? You have a thing for her. For a long time by the sound of it."

"You're stepping very close to dangerous territory," I warned. I usually didn't allow anyone around me to speculate on my personal life, especially not to my face.

Gianni scoffed as only he could. "You're not going to have me killed because I figured out you have a crush. I don't blame you. I have a bit of a crush on her myself. I want to protect her from all the shit in this world. All the bad people who might want to hurt her."

"We are the bad people," I pointed out. "We're exactly the ones she should be protected from."

"Are you going to let her go?" He cocked his head, but he already knew the answer. He was nothing if not intuitive and he knew me better than most people. Sometimes it worried me that I'd let him get too close. Other times, having someone see through my stony façade was a relief.

"No," I said firmly. "She's not…well enough to leave here. Oliver Ryan was adamant about that."

"And when she is?" Gianni pressed. "In a week, or a month, or a year, when she's well enough to walk out the front door, are you going to let her?"

I averted my eyes. "No." It was as simple as that.

"Because?" He shot back. "Because you've already decided she's yours. Now you have her here, you want to keep her here."

"She's mine." I looked back at him, my jaw firmly set. "I'll make sure she knows that."

"And if I want her too?" His jaw was just as firm.

Gianni with his mind made up was insurmountable. He rarely needed to be so rigid, but when he was, nothing, and no one was moving him. Not a single millimetre.

I was just as stubborn, but I could have someone killed if they tried to get in my way.

"That's a conversation for the future," I said. I didn't bother to threaten him. If Mina wanted both of us, I wouldn't deny her. I didn't let myself think about what would happen if she didn't want either of us. She had too much healing to do to contemplate any of these possibilities yet. Healing we'd help her through.

"I'm going to have to find out what kind of music she likes," he mused, the tension leaving the conversation. "She didn't seem to be a fan of Wolf Venom."

"Then she has good taste," I said. My brother's band was not music I enjoyed. Another advantage when he quit and rejoined the family, was that I wouldn't have to hear any more of it.

"She might prefer Blazing Violet or Ice Blue Roses," Gianni mused.

I grimaced. Blazing Violet was at least as loud as Wolf Venom. According to the twins, both bands would be touring together soon. Along with Abbie Hart. She seemed to hold some influence over my brother. I made a note to have the twins bring her to me for a little chat.

"You should try listening to something that was released more recently than twenty years ago," Gianni said.

"I'd rather read books," I said bluntly. "Books aren't loud."

"Audiobooks can be loud," he pointed out.

"Have you ever known me to listen to an audiobook?" I asked.

He rubbed his chin with his thumb and forefinger. "Now I think about it, no I haven't."

"Because I don't," I said.

"Is this one of those 'audiobooks aren't real books' things?" he asked.

"No, it's one of those 'I prefer quiet,' things," I said. I couldn't concentrate on voices reading out loud to me. My mind wandered too much. Maybe if I had fewer thoughts fighting it out in my head to be noticed, I could focus on something like that. Right now, only reading a physical book shut out the noise. For the most part.

"Yeah, I guess you do," he said. "You tend to leave the room when the screaming starts." He wasn't accusing, just stating a fact. When the people he was slicing into started to shriek, I made myself scarce.

"I have better things to do than listen to you torture people." He was right though, I did leave the room before the noise became too much. One of the benefits to being the boss was that I didn't have to subject myself to things I didn't want to be subjected to. That included ear piercing sounds that gave me a headache.

"You don't know what you're missing." He rubbed the palms of his hands together and grinned.

"I know exactly what I'm missing," I said dryly. "Which isn't relevant. I pay you to do things like that so I don't have to." Just like I paid Terry to cook and the twins to do various odd jobs, and Damon to keep them in line.

"That's what I love about this job," Gianni mused. "I get paid to have fun."

"Maybe I shouldn't pay you," I said. "You might turn up and do it for free."

"If you didn't pay me, I'd have to go and work for the Bell family," he said. "I hear Samuel Bell has a—"

"I don't give a shit what Samuel Bell has," I said.

I wouldn't stop paying Gianni, because he might do just that. And if he did, I'd have to have him dealt with. He was too good an asset to let go like that. I wouldn't admit it to myself, but I was accustomed to having him around. He was good at what he did, including taking care of Mina. Scaring the shit out of her with a song, notwithstanding.

"Not even if it's bigger than yours?" Gianni teased.

I rolled my eyes. "Nothing he has is bigger than anything of mine."

The Brantley and Bell families had been rivals for as long as anyone could remember. So long, I wasn't sure anyone knew how it started. It didn't matter, it wasn't ending anytime soon, unless one of our families was wiped out.

Gianni chuckled. "That's what I like about you, boss. You don't pull any punches. You know who you are and you don't give a shit what anyone thinks about you."

That wasn't true, I cared what Mina thought. She was the only one since she got old enough for me to really look at her. I'd wanted her back then, but her father got in the way. If I had any clue what he'd done, I would have prevented it, no matter what it took to do that. I would have paid back his debt and taken her for myself. Her life and mine would have been very different.

Now she was back with me, it was time to put us back on that path. As far as I was concerned, it was inevitable. No matter what I had to do to convince her of that.

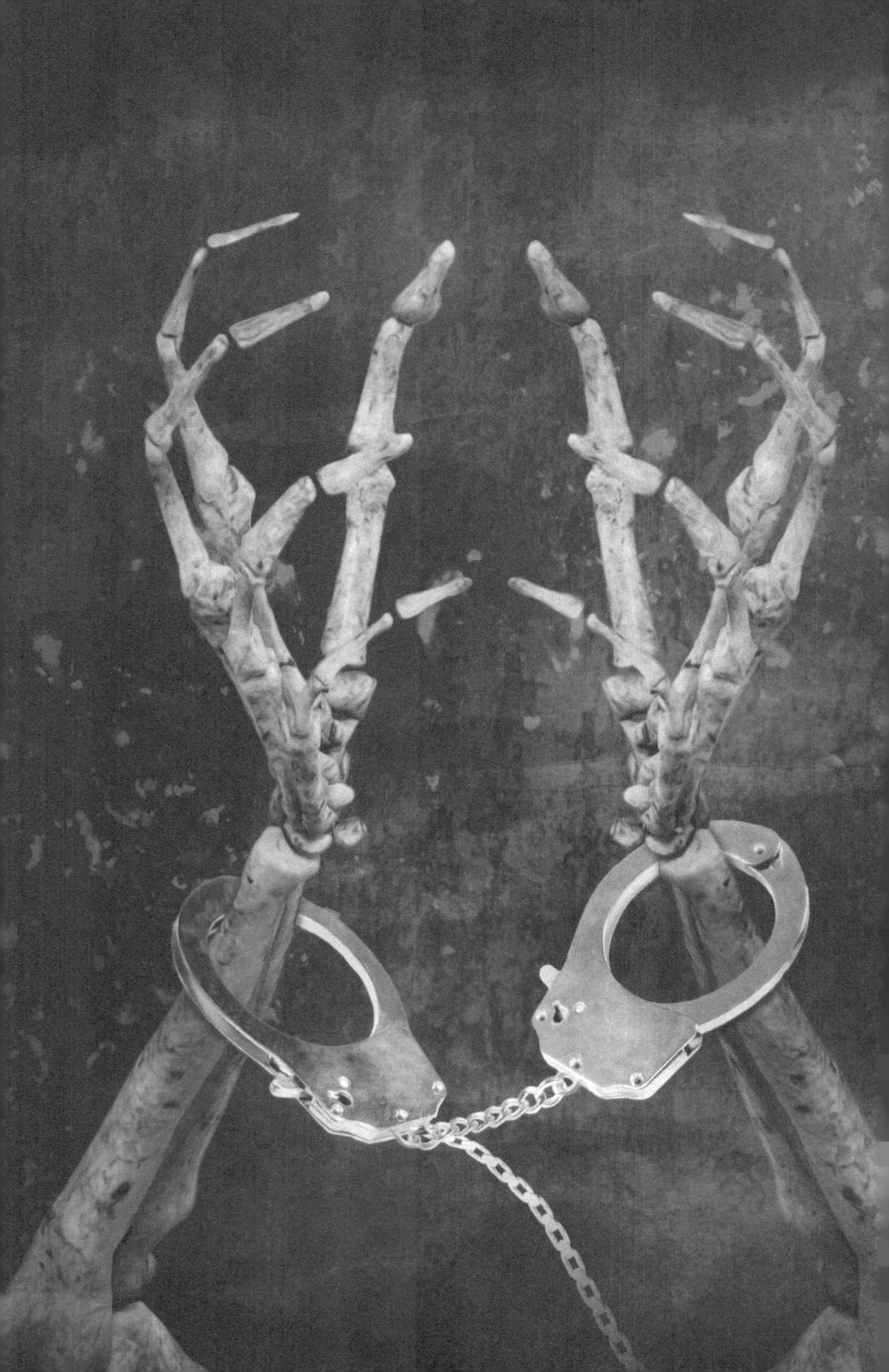

CHAPTER 9

MINA

I managed to get some sleep before dawn. When I awoke again, the house was in near silence. Someone, I guessed it was Terry, was in the kitchen. Every so often dishes rattled, or a pan or pot.

I pushed the tangle of blankets off myself and slipped downstairs and into the library.

Ever since I could remember, I found the company of books easier than that of other people. My mother used to say, you could tell a lot about a person by their books. I was intrigued by what books lined Reuben's shelves.

I wasn't surprised to find a section of classics, but many looked untouched. One or two were still housed in shrinkwrap. Another section contained non-fiction, mostly history.

The biggest sections were fantasy and adventure. All of the books were in good condition, but *Lord of the Rings* looked slightly more loved than the others. I wasn't sure what I expected, but it wasn't that. Maybe a worn copy of *Sixty-Nine Shades of Morally Grey*.

I flinched as someone walked past the door. Their footsteps stopped a metre or two past before they turned back and peered into the library.

"Hey." He stepped into the room, his hands pressed into his pockets.

It took me a few moments to recognise him. "Hunter? Or Parker?"

He grinned. "You were right the first time. Parker is bringing in some bags."

"Parker has bags, but is wondering why the fuck Hunter isn't helping," Parker's voice came from down the corridor.

"Hunter is wondering why the fuck Parker is talking about himself in third person." Hunter winked at me.

"You're doing it too," I said. I could hardly believe the guy standing in front of me was one of the Brantley twins. The last time I saw them, they couldn't have been more than fourteen. Awkward, gangly and full of mischief. The man standing in front of me now was tall and muscular. Still full of mischief, that much was obvious.

Parker stepped into the doorway, a bag in each hand. "Hey." He looked me up and down. "Little Mina DiMarco grew up."

If either of them were surprised by how thin I looked, they gave no indication. Given they weren't surprised to see me here, Reuben or Gianni must have filled them in.

"I was thinking the same about you," I said. "Are you still giving everyone hell?"

They gave me matching grins in response.

"We wouldn't be us if we didn't," Hunter said. "Some smartass, probably Zeke, decided to give us the nickname evil twins. We think it's hilarious."

I snorted softly. "I'm sure you do everything you can to live up to that."

Parker laughed. "I've always thought you were the smart one in your family. Not to mention the cute one." He hauled the bags over and placed them down on the floor beside me. "Reuben said you might need some new clothes. We did our best to max out his credit card."

"He trusts you with his credit card?" I did need new clothes, but I hadn't expected this. I probably should have, given that the twins' old clothes didn't fit that well.

"See, that's exactly what I think," Hunter said. "And yet, here we are." He spread his hands as though he was completely innocent.

"He's so full of shit," Parker said. "Reuben trusts *me* with his credit card, not Hunter."

Hunter turned to his twin and put a hand to his chest over his heart. "I'm shocked that you'd even suggest that, Park. Everyone knows I'm the trustworthy twin. As well as being the smartest and best looking."

"Keep telling yourself that, Hunter," Parker said.

I shook my head at them both and managed a smile. "I see you haven't changed a bit." They were still giving each other shit, but clearly adored each other. Whatever happened, they had each other's backs. What would it be like to grow up with someone you could trust implicitly?

"My cock is bigger," Parker said. He wiggled his eyebrows and grinned. "Hunter's stayed the same."

Hunter shouldered Parker hard enough to make him stagger a few steps. "What have I said about making unsubstantiated comments about my cock size?"

Parker shoved him back. "Fine, in the interests of accuracy, Hunter's got smaller."

"You're such an asshole," Hunter told him. He turned to me and said, "My cock is as big, if not bigger than Parker's. Any time you want to see, you only have to ask."

I cleared my throat. "Um, thanks. No offence but—"

They both groaned.

"Any time anyone says that, they're about to say something offensive," Hunter said.

"I was going to say that would be like looking at my younger brother's dick," I said.

They exchanged glances.

"I guess that wasn't so bad," Parker said.

Hunter nodded. "I can live with that. I mean, I don't *feel* offended."

I laughed softly. When was the last time I'd laughed? A very long time ago. Knowing I hadn't completely forgotten how, was a relief.

"Thank you for the clothes," I said.

"I hope they fit," Parker said. "And that you didn't want anything in pink. I didn't get any pink." He frowned. "If you want pink, I can go and—" He gestured towards the door.

"I don't want any pink," I said quickly. "I actually prefer darker colours like black."

Parker dropped his hand to his thigh and grinned. "I got lots of black things. Black goes with everything."

"Especially my soul," Hunter said. "And Reuben's heart."

"What about my heart?" Reuben stepped into the library.

"Hunter was just saying you have a black heart," Parker said.

Reuben raised an eyebrow at them both, but didn't deny it. Nor did Hunter deny saying that about him.

"Don't you have somewhere to be?" Reuben asked, eyeing the twins meaningfully.

"At this exact moment, no," Hunter said. "That's why we're here, talking to Mina." He glanced at me. "You like books too? There might be room on Reuben's credit card for more books."

"I can't ask you to buy me things," I said.

"We like buying things," Parker said. "Especially if Reuben is paying."

"If you want books, you can have books," Reuben said to me.

I got the feeling that if I asked for the twin's heads on a silver platter, he'd give them to me. Fortunately for all concerned, that wasn't something I wanted or needed. On the contrary, it was difficult not to like Hunter and Parker. With them, there was no pretence. What you saw was what you got. I appreciated that.

"I…like romance books," I admitted with a shrug. The old Mina, before Kurt, believed in happily ever afters. That was probably why everyone believed my father's story that I ran off to get married. Behind every good lie was a dash of truth.

What did I believe now? Did it matter? I just wanted to lose myself in the pages for a little while. No one could blame me for that.

"Get her romance books," Reuben said to the twins. "Whatever she wants."

"As if you won't read them too," Hunter teased.

Reuben looked back at him, a bland expression on his face. "My library is missing having books with covers made from the hide of human male twins. I could have that rectified, if you like."

Hunter and Parker both laughed.

"You wouldn't do that to us," Parker said. "You love us too much."

Reuben grunted. "Don't tempt me." He nodded his dismissal and turned his back to them.

They both made faces at him behind his back, then grinned at me before walking out of the room, their arms over each other's shoulders.

"Sometimes I wonder if they're adopted," Reuben said. "Then I remember, they're my half-brothers. It must be something from their mother's DNA."

"I envy them," I said softly. "They seem to love life."

Reuben sank into a chair and sighed heavily. "That they do. So should you." He pressed his lips together, then glanced down at the bags. "If you don't like anything in there, we can order more. Whatever you need."

I perched on the edge of another chair and reached for one of the bags.

"I need clothes, but if I open one of these and Kurt's head is inside…"

The sides of his eyes crinkled slightly, like he was holding back a smile. "We'd both thoroughly enjoy that. Unfortunately, we haven't found him yet. I have all of my resources on it. It won't be long. He can't hide from us forever."

At some point, I was going to have to use my own resources, but in the meantime I opened the bag and started to pull out various items of clothes. Mostly black trousers, black jeans, black skirts and lighter coloured blouses and T-shirts. Amongst those was lacy underwear in a variety of designs and sizes.

Every item looked expensive. The twins might not have exaggerated when they mentioned maxing out Reuben's credit card. Without access to my funds, I had little choice but to accept the extravagant gift. I'd draw more attention to myself dressed the way I was, than in the clothes stacked neatly in either of the bags.

"You didn't have to do this," I said, holding a black mohair jumper up to myself.

"You might prefer old track pants and T-shirts, but we'd soon run out of them," Reuben said dryly. "You'll feel more yourself in clothes of your own." His ice blue eyes regarded me intently, searching for my reaction, reading my response and taking note of everything.

For some reason, this was important to him, like he'd told the twins exactly what to buy. Like he'd chosen every item to make me look a certain way. The way he wanted me to look. This wasn't just about clothes, this was him making me into something. Moulding me into what he wanted. Claiming me in front of the world.

"I should try them on," I said. I stood and picked up both bags.

Reuben quickly rose too. "Do you need help?"

"I can manage," I said. Neither bag looked too heavy. If they were, I might have refused his help anyway. This was a small thing, but I needed to do it by myself. To prove to myself I wasn't a broken doll. "Thank you."

"It was my pleasure," he said, his voice smoother than silk. He'd be thinking of every centimetre of fabric as it slid against my skin, touching me in a way he wanted to, but couldn't. Not yet. If I was, *when* I was, ready to give myself to a man, he'd be ready. Ready to fill me, touch me. Claim me.

"Breakfast will be served soon," he said. "If you're up to eating."

He looked indifferent to the idea of food, as though he only ate because he had to, not because he cared about cuisine. What did he care about, apart from books and his family?

If the twins were open books, Reuben was one whose pages were shut tight and locked, the key hidden from the world. What would it take to break that lock? Why did I want to? He intrigued me. Many people found him intimidating, but I never had. To me, I saw a complicated man behind a stony façade. A mystery to be solved.

There was more to him than just a callous mobster, although he was undeniably that too. He'd have people killed without a second thought, but he's always looked at me like I was also a puzzle he wanted to figure out.

I hadn't realised until now that we were so alike.

"I am," I agreed. "I won't be long." Especially now I realised the smell of bacon was wafting through the house. It was good enough to make my mouth water, even as my stomach twinged in warning.

He sat back in his chair and nodded. "I'll wait for you in the kitchen in about ten minutes."

I nodded quickly and turned to make my way back up the stairs, one careful step at a time.

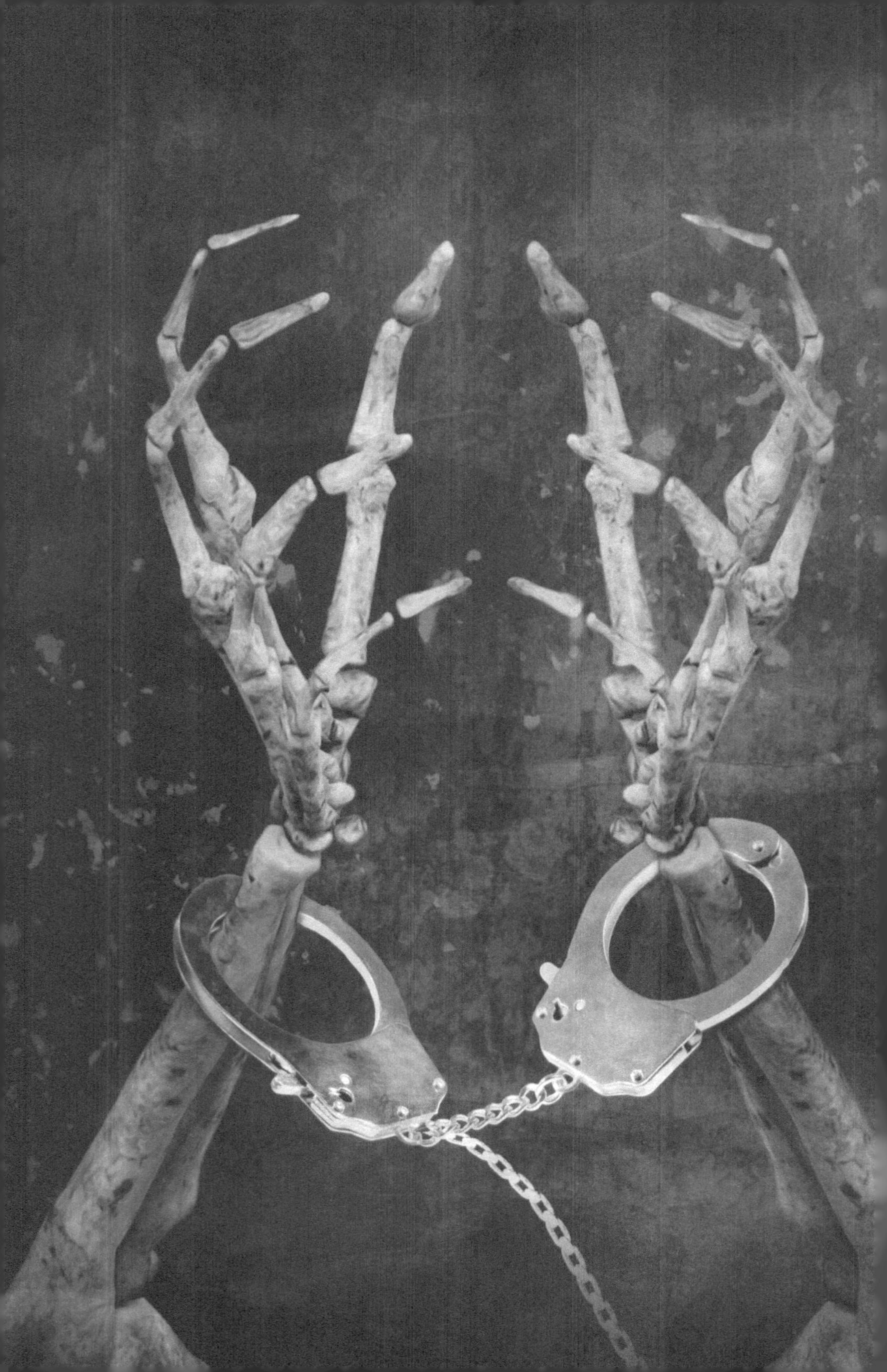

CHAPTER 10

REUBEN

If I was ever going to slam my fist down onto a tabletop, it would be now.

Inside, my blood was boiling. I kept it contained, kept my exterior calm, if tense.

"Even if Kurt Lasalle was dead, we should be able to find him," I said. "No one disappears off the face of the fucking planet unless we have a hand in it."

"It's possible Samuel Bell or someone else dealt with him," Damon said.

"If Bell did, he'd leave tracks in the sand deeper than his asshole," Gianni said.

I grimaced at that analogy. Bell didn't have the finesse we did, but the last place I wanted my thoughts to go was his asshole.

"Is there any chance he convinced his sister to harbour him?" I asked.

I didn't want to have to deal with Daisy, or Mina's cousin Ric, but if they were hiding Kurt, I'd have no choice. I suspected if they were, Mina wouldn't want me to be gentle with her cousin either. Not if he was complicit in what happened to her. It wouldn't matter if he was her cousin or a complete stranger. She'd want his head in a bag beside Kurt's.

Her comment about finding his disembodied head instead of clothes made my blood surge and my balls take notice.

There was something incredibly arousing about women who liked revenge. She was completely serious about wanting to see him dead in front of her. She wouldn't have flinched. At least, she wouldn't regret it if he was dead.

Seeing a part of him, without warning, may have served as a trigger. One that no one in this room would have blamed her for. No, we'd hold her close while Kurt's blood seeped into a puddle on the hardwood floor.

Damon shook his head. "I spoke to Caleb this morning. He said there's no way in hell Daisy would protect her brother. She was pissed when she found out what he did."

Caleb was probably pissed at getting a call from Damon instead of me. The second oldest in the family, my brother tended to believe in his own importance. He was useful, or he wouldn't have the responsibilities he did, but sometimes he came too close to overstepping.

I nodded slowly in response. "We have contracts out on Kurt?" I knew the answer, but I asked the question anyway.

"Every mercenary, hitman and assassin," Damon said. "All vying for a substantial amount of money." He'd questioned the need to offer that much, but I insisted. I would have offered double if it meant Kurt was found faster. Triple. I'd stipulated that he was to be brought in alive. His death was a last resort.

"I bet the Sparrow would have found him," Gianni drawled. "If anyone could, they could."

I grunted my agreement. When they were active, the Sparrow was one of the most skilled and feared assassins in the business. No one knew who they were, including me, which still irritated me after so long. No one knew why they'd gone inactive either.

They took a job a few years back, completed it and disappeared. Speculation was rife, as was to be expected. Maybe the Sparrow was dead. Maybe they made enough money to retire and were living quietly in a house beside a forest, where there were no people around for days.

If that was the case, I envied them. I owned a house like that, but didn't go there nearly enough. Maybe now I would, since I had more reason to spend time there. I could show Mina the place. I had a feeling she'd love the calm, the nature, the roaring fire in the massive fireplace. It was the perfect place to stop, think and just be.

"Given we don't have help from the Sparrow, we'll have to rely on what resources we do have," I said.

I glanced up as Mina stopped in the doorway leading into the kitchen. My breath left my body.

She was dressed in black jeans and a tank top in a shade of red so dark it almost looked black. Everything was slightly loose, giving her room to fill into it, but the sight of her still sent a surge of blood to my cock.

If I ever had a wet dream, it would feature her, just like this. I wanted to peel off every layer slowly, revealing her skin, scars and all.

I wanted to suck both of her nipples, the perfect one and the one Kurt tried so hard to destroy. I didn't care what they looked like, every part of her was mine. I wanted to touch her everywhere. To show her how beautiful she was, how strong.

"I'll get you food." Gianni leapt up from the table before I could finish taking a breath.

She turned to him and offered the smallest of smiles. "Not too much."

He picked up a plate and glanced back to grin. "Definitely no over-doing it this time."

He placed a piece of toast and a rasher of bacon on her plate before putting it down beside his spot. He poured her a cup of tea and placed it down before pulling out a chair for her.

I held back a growl. Not because I should have been doing those things for her, but because she seemed so determined to do those things for herself. He shouldn't be trying to undermine her. Lucky for him, she didn't seem to mind him helping right now.

She sat graciously and picked up her toast to nibble on the corner.

Gianni plonked himself back in his chair and resumed eating his own breakfast.

"We were just saying we haven't found Kurt yet," I told her.

"We're still looking," Damon said. "We'll find him." He seemed to take Kurt's continued ability to evade us, personally. Not for Mina's sake, but because he was one of the best. He hated to be shown up, especially by a prick like Lasalle.

"Hell yeah, we will," Gianni said. "Terry, this bacon is perfection."

Terry, who stood at the sink washing a pan, nodded to acknowledge that Gianni spoke. He was a man of even fewer words than me. He looked as though he'd punch the crap out of someone with one hand while sipping his coffee with the other. As far as I knew, the only thing he ever broke was eggs. Every so often, I'd send him out with one of the others to intimidate someone who deserved it. That usually got the job done quicker. They didn't know Terry wouldn't hurt a hair on their head. If anything, I think he found the whole thing funny.

I watched Mina as she picked up her own piece of bacon and bit off the end. She closed her eyes and sighed like it was pure bliss.

I pictured her mouth around my cock, the same expression on her face. I was a patient man, I'd wait until she was ready before I slipped my head between her lips and fucked her mouth.

My grip on my coffee cup tightened. If it wasn't for Kurt fucking Lasalle, we wouldn't have to wait. I could have her on her knees right now, licking, sucking, tasting me when I came down her throat.

Gianni made a sound in the back of his own throat like he was thinking the same thing.

Damon was staring at her too.

As if she suddenly became aware of the scrutiny, her eyes popped open. She looked around at all of us, shrinking back with self-consciousness.

"It's really good bacon," she whispered.

"It's the best fucking bacon ever," Gianni said.

"It's not bad bacon," Damon said.

Terry grunted.

Damon smirked. "Fine, it's great bacon, okay?"

"Lucky you said that," Gianni told him. "Terry has been known to stab people with a fork for less." He slid a sly glance in Terry's direction.

Terry gave him the side eye in return.

"No he hasn't," Damon said evenly.

"Okay, no he hasn't, but there's a first time for everything." Gianni shrugged and grinned.

I watched Mina as she listened to them banter back and forth. Her eyes were wide, but she seemed amused. What would it take to make her smile or laugh?

The answer to that was one reason I was willing to accept if she wanted to be with Gianni too. He could make her laugh and smile where I couldn't. Those were things that came easier to him than they did to me. I could buy her things, I could make her look the way I wanted, I could satisfy her in ways she hadn't begun to understand, but I wasn't the clown he and the twins were. I never would be. I didn't want to be. I wanted to give her everything I could offer, not the things I couldn't.

She looked back at me as she continued to nibble carefully on her bacon. From the look in her blue-green eyes, she knew exactly what was going on inside my head somehow. Or at least, on the surface and she wanted to dig down deeper.

I wanted her to do exactly that, but it would have to happen gradu-ally. As long as I could remember, I'd had walls up higher than those around a prison yard. No one had gone past them. Few people wanted to. Fewer people were *allowed* to. I couldn't take the risk of letting them in, I didn't want to.

The only person I ever wanted to see the real me was her.

Had I been so guarded for so long I didn't know how to let her in either? That was going to be my battle. That and making sure she knew she belonged to me. Whatever it took, I wouldn't step aside from her. The only way anyone would take her from me was if I was dead. Or she was. If anyone tried to kill her, they'd be the ones to end up dead. Slowly and painfully.

"I heard you say something about the Sparrow," she said. She finished her bacon and licked the tips of her fingers in a way that had all three of us staring again.

Fuck. This woman and her tongue. My cock was throbbing so hard it almost hurt. I wanted to feel that warm, wet tongue circling my tip, teasing me.

I cleared my throat. "That's right, we were," I said. "The Sparrow was an assassin. Or maybe a shadow."

She frowned at that. "A shadow?"

It was Damon who responded. "No one knew anything about them. They accepted a job, got it done and took the money. People tried to hunt them down, but never found them."

"Isn't that the job of an assassin?" she asked.

"The Sparrow got into places no one else could," Gianni said. "Places no one should have been able to get into. No one knows how."

"Precisely," Damon said. "People have spent years trying to figure it out. Some speculate the Sparrow used some special technology, and some suggest they were a ghost. Some people even say there was more than one. That it was two people who worked together."

"What do you think?" She picked up her tea and took a sip. There was no groan of appreciation now, but she seemed to enjoy the taste.

Damon shrugged. "I think they were very fucking good at what they did."

"Damon is jealous of their skills," Gianni said.

"So are you," Damon said flatly.

"Fucking right I am," Gianni agreed. "I'm too tall to sneak around like that. And too outgoing." He flipped his short ponytail.

"You mean too loud," Damon said. "You'd be playing metal music so loud, everyone would hear you coming from a week away."

Mina shuddered at the mention of music, but took another sip before putting her cup back down. "I think I've had enough for now."

"You're doing well," I told her. "Good girl." I didn't miss the way her eyes widened at that. Or the way my dick throbbed a little harder.

Waiting might be more difficult than I thought.

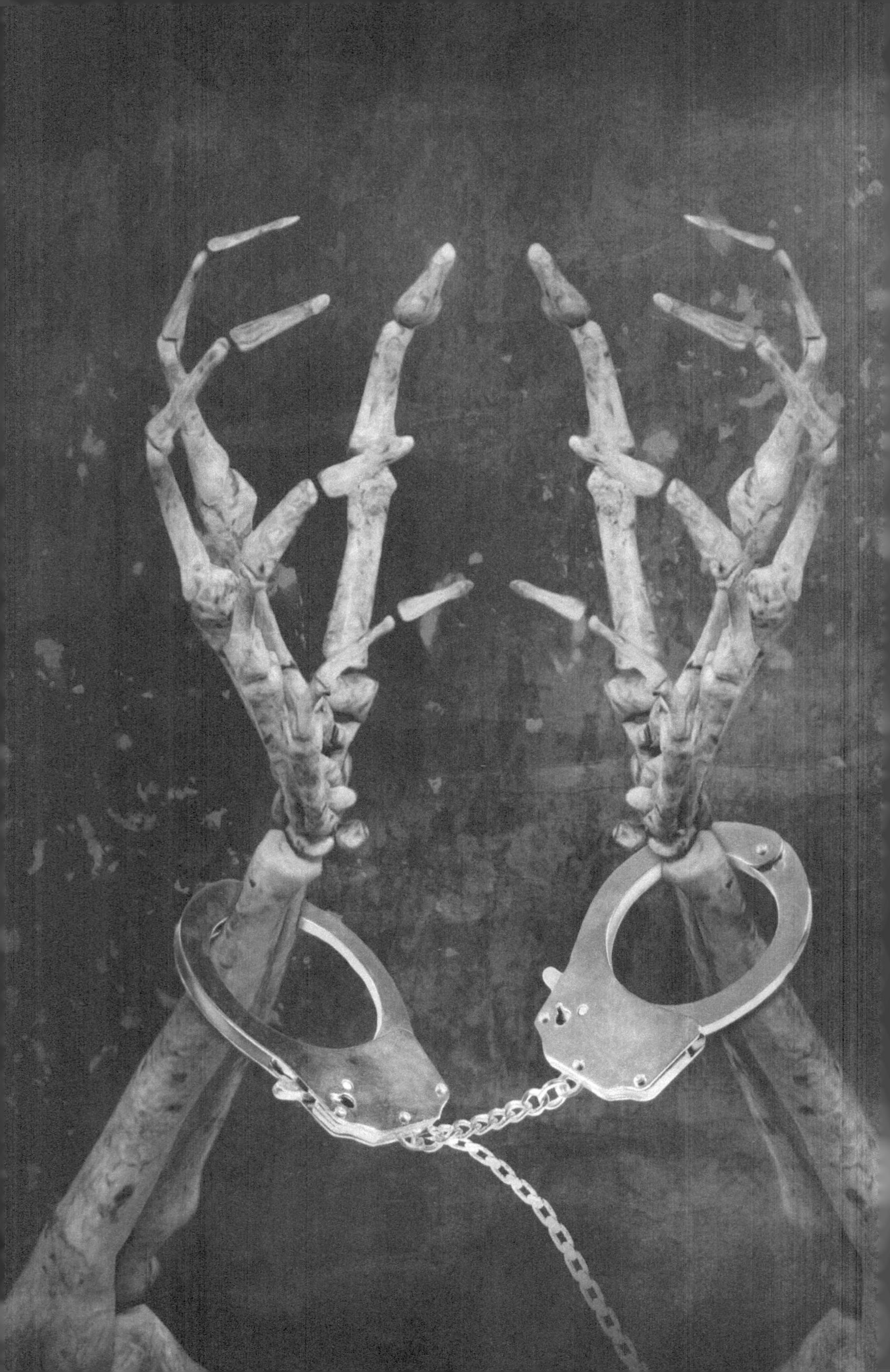

CHAPTER 11

MINA

I looked up from the book I was reading, a romantic comedy about ice hockey players, to see Gianni step into the room.

His gaze swept over me, followed by a smile. "Morning, sweetheart. Guess what?"

"Asher would have responded to that with, 'You're mad and I'm not.'" I closed the book.

Gianni chuckled. "He might have been right there. But no, that wasn't what I was going to say. We have a lead on Kurt." He looked like a kid who was let loose in a chocolate shop.

I stood up so quickly the book slid off my lap and onto the floor. I shook off a wave of dizziness and leaned over to scoop up the book.

"We found him?" I asked. I placed the book on the table beside the chair and clasped my trembling hands.

"Not yet," Gianni said. "But we found some associates of his. We're on our way to have a friendly conversation with them."

"I'm coming," I said immediately. I'd been here for a couple of weeks and felt a lot stronger already. My clothes fit better and I could move up and down the stairs faster. I could do this too.

He grinned. "I was hoping you'd say that. If Reuben or Damon say you can't come, I'll set them straight."

"Or I will," I said. The way he took care of me was sweet, but I was better able to stand on my own two feet each day. Literally and figuratively.

"Or that," he agreed, his smile unwavering. "Between us, we'll make sure you can come along." He offered me his hand.

I looked down at it for a few moments before slipping my hand into his. Touching another person didn't feel as uncomfortable as it had. The idea didn't make me break out into a cold sweat as easily. His respect for my boundaries led me to expanding them, bit by bit.

We walked down to the back of the house, to the door that led to the garage. Reuben was already there, dressed impeccably as always.

Damon stood beside him, checking over his gun.

They both looked up when Gianni and I approached.

"This isn't the time for—" Damon started.

"I'm coming with you," I said firmly. I slid my hand out of Gianni's and crossed my arms over my chest. They were all taller than me, but I wasn't going to let myself be intimidated. Not by them nor anyone else.

Reuben closed his eyes tightly for a few moments, before opening them and nodding. "If any of us tell you to do *anything*, including wait in the car, you obey. Understood?"

"Within reason," I said. "I'm not some sort of delicate flower."

He looked at me like he thought that was exactly what I was. Delicate anyway, if not a flower.

"I'll decide what's within reason or not." He nodded to Damon, who led the way out to one of the cars, a dark SUV.

Like when they brought me here, Damon and Reuben took their places in the front, Gianni and me in the back.

"It's been a long time since we've been on a road trip," Gianni said.

"We've never been on a road trip." Damon backed the car out of the garage and onto the road.

Gianni snapped his fingers, making me flinch slightly. "That's right. We should go on one sometime. Just for shits and giggles."

"Being in a car with you for hours on end would definitely give us the shits," Damon remarked.

"And giggles," Gianni said with a grin.

I shook my head at both of them. "Who are these people we're going to have a conversation with?"

Reuben sighed. "It seems Lasalle had his own network for running drugs and weapons. It's a lot more extensive than we suspected."

He sounded beyond irritated. Not just because Kurt was operating behind his back, but because somehow they missed the extent of it. He was the kind of man who didn't like to overlook anything. He wanted to be aware of everything that went on in his proximity, and way beyond it.

"How extensive?" I asked.

"Extensive enough," Reuben said. "We'll be making an example of them. After we learn what they know."

I leaned back and left it at that for now. What mattered to me was finding Kurt.

We sat in silence except for Gianni occasionally humming some random tune I couldn't recognise. Not the one he played for me the other night. He hadn't tried to play any more music for me after that. If I stepped into a room while he had any on, he quickly turned it off.

I didn't remark on it. No matter what I would have said, he would have done it anyway.

We drove for maybe thirty minutes, before pulling into a side road. Damon stopped the car in front of what looked like an ice cream parlour, and killed the engine.

"According to my sources, this was a front," Damon said.

"I like it," Gianni said. "No one would suspect an ice cream parlour." He steepled his fingers and pressed them to his lips. "Why didn't we think of this?"

"Because we already have a winery, several restaurants and a car wash," Damon said. "Those assets are sufficient and more profitable."

"But much less *fun* than an ice cream parlour," Gianni said. "Except the winery."

"If I ever decide to invest in one, you can run it," Reuben said dryly.

I wasn't sure if he was serious or not.

Gianni grinned. "Promise? Actually, I don't want to run it, but I will frequent it. Maybe the twins can run it. That sounds more like their jam."

Reuben smirked and pushed his door open to get out of the car.

I followed close behind, anxiety starting to get the better of me. I pushed it down. Reminded myself who I was. Chances were, Kurt wouldn't be here. He'd spent the last couple of weeks lying low, he wasn't going to stick around if he got wind of us coming.

What if he didn't? I asked myself. What if he had no idea we were here? We could walk right through the front door of the ice cream parlour and find him sitting there, eating a sundae. The kind with chocolate sauce and a sprinkling of nuts.

Before the anxiety became a full-blown panic attack, one of the twins stepped out of the front of the building.

Of course. Reuben wasn't walking through the front door without anyone knowing he was coming. The closer we got, the more of his people I saw inside, surrounding several men and one woman, who sat on the floor in the middle of the parlour. Each had a gun pointed at their head.

Reuben was the boss, he would have sent people here the minute he got word of Kurt's involvement. Possibly hours ago. They would have secured the area before he stepped foot out of his house.

That meant two things: I was safe here, and Kurt wasn't present. That didn't mean we couldn't learn his whereabouts.

I followed Reuben and Damon into the building.

Damon slid a side-eye glance at Gianni, when Gianni peered at the tubs of ice cream behind the glass panel.

Gianni grinned and turned his attention to the people who sat on the floor, taking in each one with interest.

It was an act, I realised. Pretending to be more interested in the ice cream than the people who worked for Kurt. He was letting them think he was harmless, nice even. For him, they might let their guard down. The truth was, he was more dangerous than Reuben and Damon. Subtler.

Reuben nodded for an older man to be brought forward. Two of his men grabbed him and dragged him closer.

"None of them have been helpful," Hunter said. At least, I thought it was him.

"Depending on your definition of helpful," Parker said. "A couple have promised to tell us everything, in return for keeping their toes."

"What Parker said," Hunter said. "But if any of them know where Kurt is, they're keeping their mouths shut."

"I swear on anything you want me to swear on, I have no idea where he is." The man at Reuben's feet looked up at him with begging eyes. "He hasn't been here in three weeks, maybe four." He glanced over his shoulder.

"Lionel is right," the woman said. She was the calmest of them all. "He rarely came here himself."

I took a step back. Gianni put out a hand to steady me. I shook my head. "I'm okay. I just…" I stared at the woman. I'd never seen her before, but I knew that voice.

"He didn't come here because you went to him," I said.

She turned a gaze on me that was so cold it was brittle.

Reuben's look was slightly warmer. "She went to him?"

"One of the voices I heard above the basement was hers," I said. "I heard it several times. She worked for him. She knew where that house was."

Damon had his gun out, aiming at her. The twins had theirs trained on her too.

"Did you know about the basement?" Reuben asked, an underlying warning in his tone. Warning of what, I wasn't sure. If she knew about the basement, she was dead. If she didn't…

I couldn't guess what he'd order to be done with her.

She looked confused. "What basement? All I know is that I went to one address to keep him updated with the operation here. Benny went too, at different times." She jerked her head towards another man, his hair cropped close to his scalp.

"You never went down into the basement?" Gianni asked. "I thought that was where Kurt kept all the weapons?" He spoke lightly, like maybe Kurt kept pinball machines down there or something.

"We were never allowed down there," Benny said.

All the guns were now pointed at him.

"Oh, you knew about the basement," Gianni said with a smile. "Did he tell you why you weren't allowed down there?"

Benny's eyes shifted back and forth. He swallowed physically.

Hunter cocked his gun. "Answer the question."

"He once said something about keeping someone down there," Benny said, his voice high. "He didn't say that to me, I overheard him talking to someone else. He laughed about it. I thought maybe…maybe he was trafficking women and kept them down there. It was none of my business."

"You never thought to check, in case there was something else going on?" Damon asked. "He might have had his mother down there."

"Like I said, it was none of my business." Benny raised his chin defiantly. "I wasn't paid to stick my nose into his personal business. If a guy wants to keep his mother in the basement, that's up to him."

I flinched at the sound of a gunshot and a spray of blood and brains. The back half of Benny's head was gone before he slumped down onto the floor.

"Oops," Hunter said. "My finger slipped."

"If yours hadn't, mine would have," Parker said. "What sort of asshole doesn't care if another asshole has his mother in the basement?"

"A dead one," Damon said. He looked around at the remaining prisoners, most of whom were cowering together. "Anyone else want to supply some useful information?" He raised his eyebrow at the woman who seemed to know more than the rest.

While silence fell, my eyes went to Benny. His eyes were open, staring. I should have been horrified, but I'd seen enough death that it hadn't bothered me, not for a long time. If anything, the idea of someone who might have been able to help me, but didn't, lying dead near my feet was arousing. Almost as much as if I'd done it myself.

I looked back up and locked eyes with the other woman. She tried to look away, but not before I saw something in her expression.

"You knew, didn't you?" I said softly. I was vaguely aware of everyone turning to me. "I don't just recognise your voice from hearing it above me. I heard it before that. When I was drugged and taken down there. People carried me and you were giving them orders to do it."

"Orders on Kurt's behalf," she said calmly.

"You still followed them," I said. I took a step towards her. "You knew I was there the whole time and you did *nothing*. You knew what he was doing to me."

"I had an idea," she said. She offered no further explanation.

"Fucking hell," someone whispered. I thought it might have been Parker.

"Damon—" Reuben started.

I put up my hand towards him. "No. Gianni." I held out my other hand until he placed a knife across my fingers. I curled my hand around the hilt, feeling the familiar, cool steel.

I took a step forward towards the woman.

The twins took steps back, but their guns remained trained on her head. They didn't need to. The woman didn't flinch as I sliced open her throat.

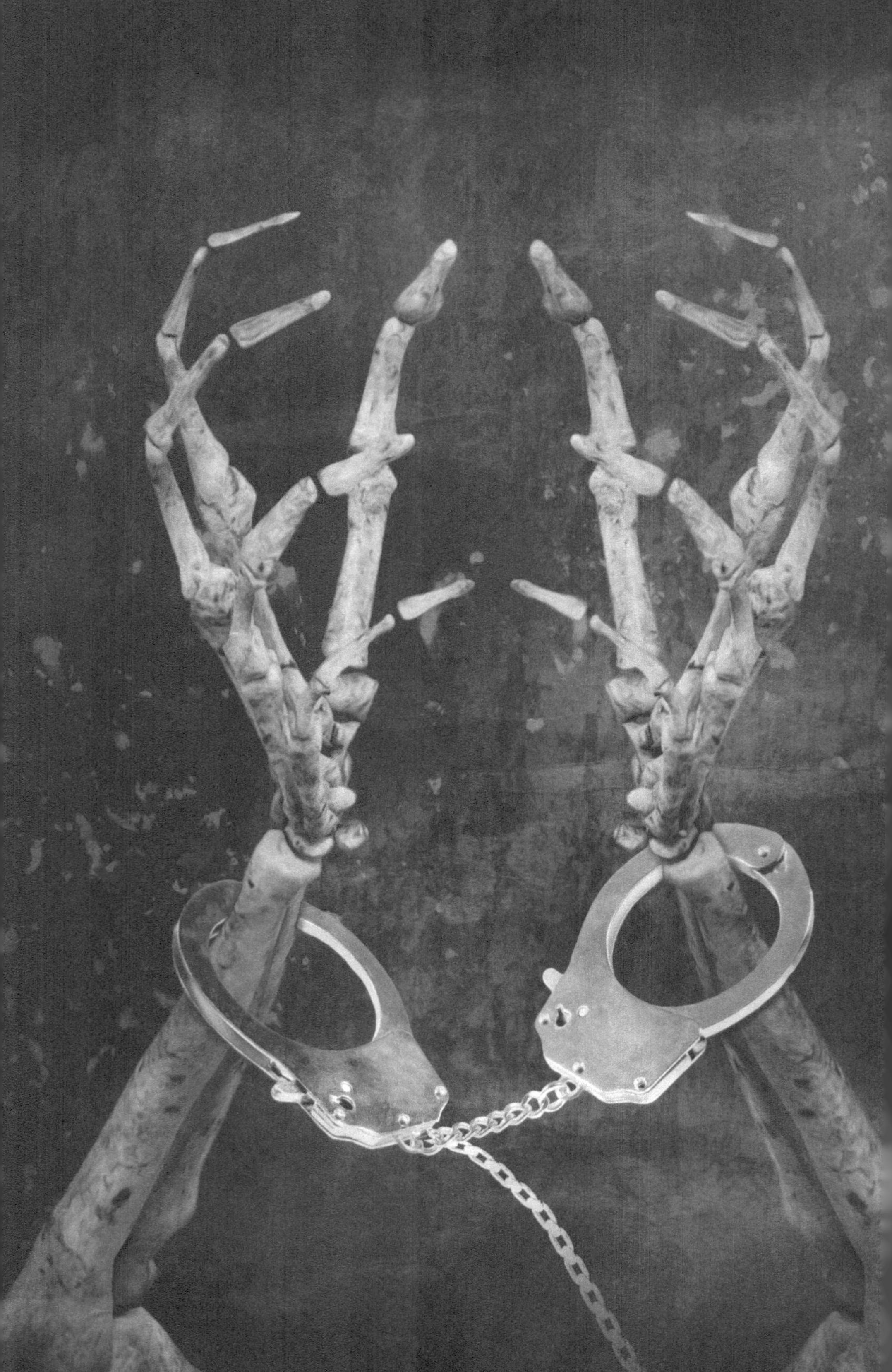

CHAPTER 12

REUBEN

"That was fucking hot," Gianni said softly.

I grunted my agreement. I was aware that Mina had some steel in her, but I hadn't expected her to use it to kill a woman. When she insisted Damon and I back off, I thought she was going to threaten her.

I should have known better. At the end of the day, she was a DiMarco. She was as much a part of this life as I was. And she was fucking angry at what they did to her.

Right now though, she looked small, her expression blank. She still had blood on her hand and up her arm. After killing the woman, she'd staggered back, the knife falling from her fingers. Her face was white, like she might faint. Instead, she sat in a chair and barely moved since.

I took the washcloth Parker handed me and crouched down in front of Mina to wipe away the blood from her fingers.

"I should have realised there was a chance someone like that might be here."

"I'm glad she was," Mina whispered. "She let me live down there for years, and didn't raise a finger. She probably didn't even think about me and what he was doing to me."

A frown crossed her brow. "Or maybe she did, and she didn't speak out because he might have put her down there instead. She'd rather let someone else suffer through that than go through it herself."

"She could have told me and no one would have gone through it." I turned her hand to wipe her palm clean. "She chose not to do that."

Mina looked down at me. "I had my doubts at first. That it was her. It could have been someone else's voice."

"Until she confirmed that she knew what happened to you," I said.

Mina nodded. "Until then. Before that, I wanted to kill her for working with him. I would have let one of you shoot her."

"And we would have," I said. "I would have ordered one of them to put a bullet in her brain."

"What if I was wrong?" Mina asked. "What if it wasn't her upstairs? You could have had an innocent woman killed."

I wiped Mina's wrist. "There are many adjectives for a woman like her. Innocent isn't amongst them. Whether or not she knew about you, she was still working with him. Any chance of her walking out of here alive were slim. Less than slim. I always intended to make an example out of the people here. I won't tolerate people working for Kurt or anyone like him. I won't tolerate rival operations, especially ones as big as his."

"Right," she whispered. "But what if you planned to let them walk away and I asked you to kill her, and then I was wrong?"

"Why are you asking this?" I asked. "If you asked me to kill her, you would have had good reason to do it." And if she didn't, I didn't give a shit. If she wanted someone dead, they were dead. Innocent or not.

"I just..." She glanced down at the floor. "I don't want to make a mistake." She looked like she was going to say 'again,' but didn't.

"What they did to you wasn't your fault," I stated. "It was your father's fault. Him and Kurt. And hers." I didn't so much as jerk my head towards the woman's corpse. She didn't deserve that much attention or recognition.

"And others. You mentioned several people carried you down there. Would you recognise any of them?"

She breathed in slowly through her nose and blew out through pursed lips. "I don't know. Maybe."

I finished wiping away the blood and tossed the washcloth aside. "How are you feeling?"

"About killing someone?" she asked. "If I'm supposed to say I regret it, I can't. I…" In a whisper she said, "I enjoyed it. They say violence isn't the answer, but…"

"Sometimes it's the only answer," I said. I noticed the way her eyes got darker when she talked about what she did. She more than enjoyed killing, she got off on it. She wasn't the first person to feel that way. Or the last.

I looked back over my shoulder. "Kill the rest of them," I said calmly. Even if they weren't working for Kurt, they saw Mina and Hunter kill. I wasn't leaving any witnesses behind.

I turned back to her, ignoring the pleas for me to change my mind. They were cut off by three gunshots. Quickly and efficiently, my people did as they were asked, before dragging the bodies out into the back of the building to be disposed of.

We'd done this so many times before, everyone knew their role and carried it out without hesitation.

"All of this death shouldn't be, I don't know…" Mina frowned.

"Loud?" I suggested. I was as uncomfortable with the sound of gunshots as I was with screaming. Not because I cared about the implications; because of the noise.

"I was going to say exciting," she said tentatively. "We got to decide who lived and died here today. We did that."

"Yes we did," I agreed. "That's one of the benefits of being the boss. You get to make those choices." I'd made them so often in the last few years I barely gave them a second thought. Speaking to her reminded me how much I enjoyed the power. I liked things done my way. My way made sense to me. Neat, orderly and organised.

"Some people would suggest we're fucked up," she said.

"What do you think?" I was genuinely curious as to how she saw herself and our lifestyle.

"I think it's who we are," she said. "Who we'll always be."

She understood. This was exactly what I'd been trying to tell Zeke for years now. This was who he was as well. He could try to put it behind him, but he never would. Not completely.

I'd never wanted to kiss her more than I did right then. I wanted to slam my lips down on hers and claim her right here, in front of everyone, beside pools of blood on the tiled floor. Was there a more appropriate setting?

I settled for placing a small kiss on the centre of her forehead. "You're so fucking beautiful."

"Because I'm fucked up?" she asked.

"You said 'perfect as fuck' wrong," Gianni said, crouching beside me. "I've never had the hots for a woman like I do right now. Seeing you kill that bitch was spank bank material."

I looked at him sideways and arched an eyebrow.

"Don't say you don't agree," he said.

"It was the wording I was questioning," I said. He sounded like the twins, using an expression like spank bank. Mina deserved better than to be talked about like that.

Admittedly, I didn't have a better term for it. I would be thinking about her when I curled my hand around my cock later tonight.

Gianni grinned. "What can I say, I'm classy as fuck. That's why you love me so much."

How could I respond to that but to roll my eyes and shake my head.

"Boss, the cleanup is finished," Damon said. "We just need to get someone in here to wash up the blood. I've already made the call." He stopped beside us to regard Mina. His expression was one of grudging respect, with a healthy dose of heat.

He'd be the last to admit it, but he felt the same way about her as Gianni and me. Right now, he was all professionalism as he pushed his expressionless mask back into place.

"Good." I rose to my feet, taking Mina with me, my hand gripping hers. "Keep an eye on this place. Kurt might return. If he doesn't, someone else who works for him will."

"Got it, boss," Damon said.

Gianni pushed himself to his feet. "I have to admit to being disappointed. Not only did we not find out where Kurt was, I didn't get to kill anyone. Although, watching Mina kill someone was almost as much fun. Maybe we can do it again sometime. A good date night isn't complete without a few corpses."

"Try to keep the killing to a minimum," I told him. "Unless they're involved with Kurt." Then he had free reign to deal with them however he saw fit. I knew I could trust him to be discreet and clean up after himself. And that he'd let me know whoever he killed, in great detail. He enjoyed giving those reports almost as much as doing the actual deed. His eyes always glazed like he was reliving the moment, step-by-step.

I also knew he didn't go around killing indiscriminately. It wasn't the death he enjoyed dispensing, it was the justice.

"I'll do my best," he said easily. He took half a step away before he stopped and frowned at Mina. "What's wrong?"

She stood with her back completely straight, frozen to the spot, staring at nothing in particular in front of her.

"If I hadn't acted so quickly, we might have been able to get her to tell us who else was with her that night," Mina said. "I screwed up."

Her face was paler again. Her blue-green eyes and dark hair were a stark contrast against her skin, almost making her look ghostly. Beautiful, but haunted.

I took the chance of putting an arm around her shoulders. When she didn't pull away, I squeezed lightly. "Chances are, she wouldn't have told you anything else. She already knew her time was done. I doubt she would have thrown anyone else under the bus."

"She was quick to point out Benny's involvement," Gianni said.

"I screwed up," Mina said again. "I screwed up. I screwed up." She put her hands over her face and pressed the heels into her eyes like she was trying to rub them out of her head.

I grabbed her wrists and pulled her hands down. "You did *not* screw up," I said firmly. "We will find the others if they're still alive. We'll make them pay for what they did to you. I promise you that. We'll find them."

Her eyes were wide as she looked back at me. A brief moment of confusion crossed her face before she blinked and stopped trying to pull away from me. I had the distinct impression she'd gotten lost in the past somehow. Whatever had her upset went beyond cutting the woman's throat today. Something happened that haunted her, something that had nothing to do with Kurt.

"We'll find them," she whispered.

"Yes," I said. "When we do, they'll get what they deserve."

She shivered. "What they deserve," she echoed. "Yes, they should get that. Everything that's coming to them."

I couldn't shake the feeling she was talking about herself.

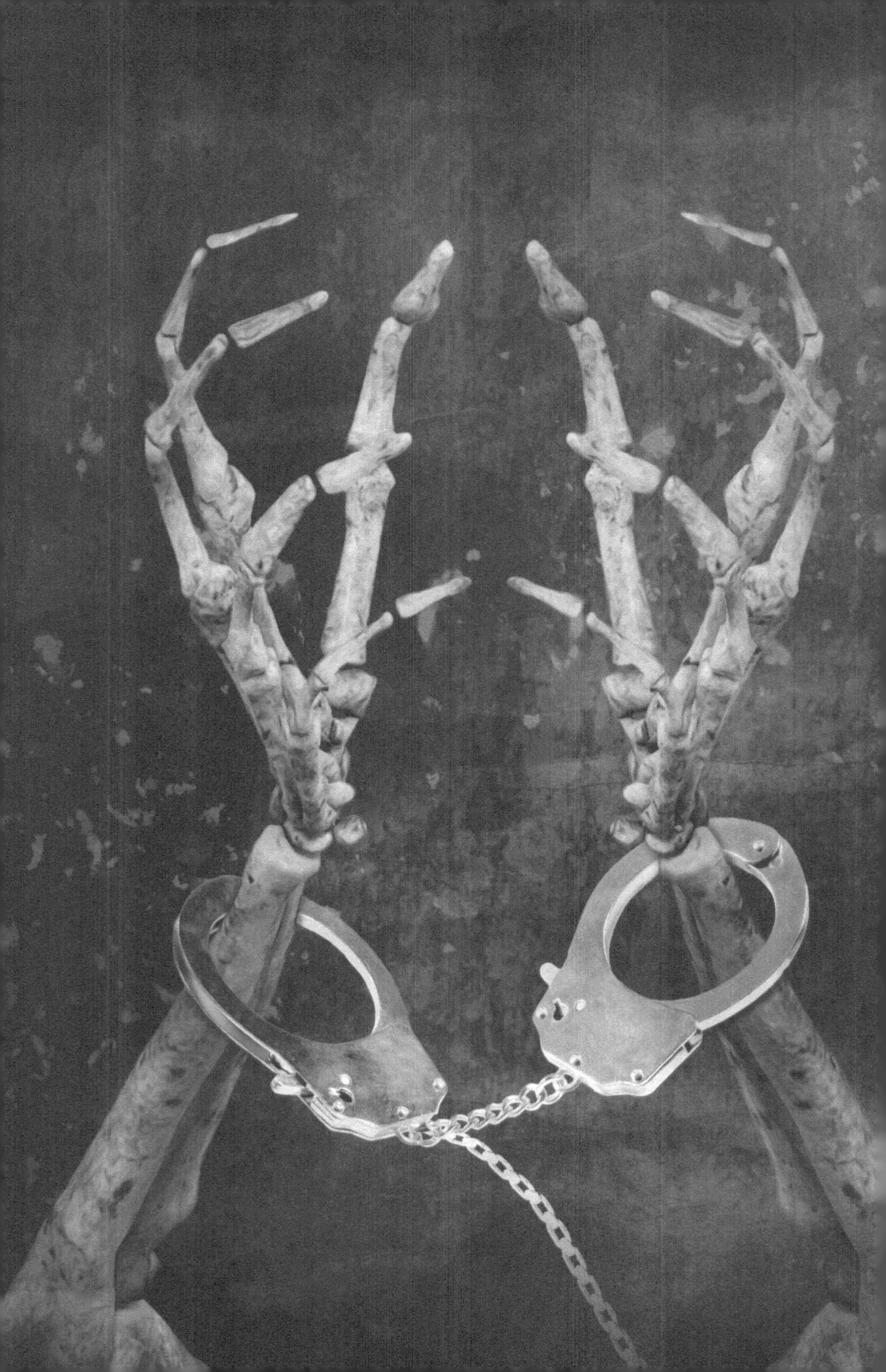

CHAPTER 13

I pulled on silky pyjama pants and a sleep singlet and sat down on my bed, my back against the pillows.

My hand still tingled from where Reuben cleaned the blood off my skin. I could still feel his touch long after the blood dried. So gentle and thorough, right before he ordered the deaths of several people.

Some would call him a monster, but my whole body throbbed in a way I hadn't felt in the longest time. Chained up in that cage, the last thing on my mind was intimacy or arousal. All of my attention was occupied with surviving.

Now, with time to think about other things, I could dwell on killing that woman.

I acted out of anger. That was the worst thing I could have done. I was trained to be cool, calm and rational. Not furious and rash. In spite of Reuben, Gianni and Damon's reassurances, I was regretful, my anger now turned inward to myself.

After a brief tap on the door, it swung inward and Reuben stepped inside. He wore black trousers and a dark grey button down, folded to his elbows. This seemed to be as casual as he ever got. I suspected he didn't own a pair of jeans or even a T-shirt. What would it take to convince him to try either of those?

He was handsome and compelling, especially with those intense, ice blue eyes. He also had the muscles to pull off a T-shirt and make women stare. Men too.

He didn't wait for an invitation. He closed the door behind him and stepped over to sit on the side of the bed.

"Have you come to tell me again that I shouldn't blame myself?" I asked. "Because you can say whatever you want I'm still going to—"

"I didn't." He spoke in a voice that was both deep and as compelling as his eyes. "I saw your reaction to killing that woman. And to Hunter killing that other man." He seemed to be hunting for his name, but couldn't remember.

"Benny," I supplied.

He hummed his agreement in the back of his throat. "They tend to blur together after a while. That's not important. What's important is you. What you were feeling at the time."

"Are we having a therapy session?" I asked lightly.

He choked back a soft laugh. "Fuck no. Not exactly."

"Then what?" I asked. "I wasn't bothered by seeing them die. I've seen enough death that it doesn't get to me anymore."

He tilted his head back and looked over at me. "I think we both know that's not true. It does get to you. You like it. Death turns you on."

His words left me breathless for a couple of heartbeats. Of all the things people ever said to me, this was the first time I felt as though anyone actually understood me. More than that, he looked at me with absolutely no judgement. No, whatever he thought about this, he wasn't judging me for it.

"I never said I wasn't fucked up," I said.

He made no move towards me. Or away. "You're not fucked up. Everyone has things that arouse them. It's what we do with them that matters."

"You've come to share what gets you off?" I asked.

One of his eyebrows twitched. "This isn't about me. This is about you and what you need."

"And what do I need?" I whispered. The idea of being touched was terrifying, but the way my pussy reacted to his presence, to the memory of warm blood all over my hand, I needed something.

"I'm guessing you didn't touch yourself when you were in that cage," he said.

"Not…not like that," I said. I glanced down at the bed covers.

"What about before that?"

I looked back up at him. "Before that I did. I mean, I was, you know…"

"A normal eighteen-year-old woman?" His jaw clenched, clearly furious at my father and Kurt for stealing those years from me.

"If you could call me normal," I said lightly. I didn't think there was much normal about me back then, but compared to now I supposed I was.

"What did you think about?" he asked. "When you touched yourself."

I thought back. "I don't know. Guys I knew. Book boyfriends. You."

A flicker of surprise crossed his face. "Me?"

Should I have said that? I couldn't take it back now. His raised eyebrow was a clear insistence that I explain.

"Why not you? You're strong, powerful and handsome. Dangerous. Like an open fire a girl shouldn't step into."

"But you wanted to?" His eyes darkened in a way that, under other circumstances, in another lifetime, I might have peeled off my clothes and begged him to fuck me.

"Yes," I said simply.

"Touch yourself," he whispered. "I want to see you."

I swallowed. "It's been so long."

"Exactly. You deserve to know your body belongs to you." He looked like he was about to add 'and me,' but held the words back for now. "Touch yourself."

I slipped my hand down between my legs and lightly ran the tips of my fingers over the front of my pyjama pants.

My eyes on his, I ran them up and down, barely touching the fabric, or my pussy underneath them. It felt good. Better than good. It felt as though a part of me was slowly coming back to life. That maybe I could put what Kurt did behind me. If I wasn't ready for a man to touch me, there was no reason I couldn't give myself pleasure. And give it to Reuben by doing this.

I slipped my hand down the front of my pants and over my damp pussy and throbbing clit.

"Are you wet?" Reuben asked.

"Very wet," I whispered. I traced circles around my clit with my fingertips before sliding my fingers inside myself.

"Fuck," Reuben said breathlessly. "Does that feel good?"

"So good," I murmured. I hesitated for a moment before I hooked my thumb around the waistband of my pants and pushed them down, exposing my pussy to him.

"Good girl," he whispered. "You have the most beautiful pussy I've ever seen."

I worked myself slowly, driving my fingers in deeper while I rubbed the heel of my hand against my clit. I slipped the other hand up the front of my singlet to roll my remaining nipple between my thumb and forefinger.

"That's my girl." He hadn't moved, but I saw his arousal tenting the front of his pants, his cock straining against the seams. He didn't touch me or himself, just watched while I drew closer and closer to coming.

"Reuben," I whispered. "I'm going to come."

"Good girl," he said again. "Let me see you come."

I moaned and drove my hand faster and faster before I came in a rush of sensation I hadn't felt in so long. It wasn't the most violent or intense orgasm I ever had. Instead, it was a gentle sweep of pleasure that curled my toes and made me cry out loud.

I slumped back against the pillows and pulled my fingers out of my wetness.

"You're even more beautiful when you come," he said. "So perfect."

Without thinking, I pulled my pyjama pants back up into place and rolled onto my knees. Slowly, and with my eyes still on his, I crawled towards him. I pressed my fingers, still wet with my juices, against his lower lip.

His eyes widened slightly, but he opened his mouth and took my fingers between his lips to suck them clean.

"You even taste perfect," he said as he slid his mouth along the back of my hand. "One day I'm going to taste your pussy for myself." He took my hand in his and kissed the centre of my palm.

"Thank you," I said. I seemed to have said that a lot in the last couple of weeks. "Thank you for reminding me I'm not his prisoner anymore. I can still live my life in spite of what happened. All of my life." Someday I could let him inside me. I wanted that, when the time came.

"I'm the one who should be thanking you," Reuben said. "Watching you come was a gift. One I won't forget. This first time between us will always be special." He didn't have to say it wouldn't be the last time, that was heavy in the air between us.

"Gianni—" I started softly.

"Also wants to be with you," he finished for me. "I'm well aware. I'm man enough to admit there are things I can't give you that he can. Damon too. As long as you don't choose them instead of me, then I don't see why we can't explore all our options. We want the same thing, what's best for you. That's the only thing that matters." He kissed my forehead and stood to adjust his pants.

"I hope you sleep well." Quiet as a ghost, he slipped back out the door and closed it behind him.

I lay down and drew the blankets over myself. I closed my eyes and did something I hadn't done in a long, long time. I fell into a deep sleep.

***

Reuben

I stepped away from Mina's room, grimacing at the steel in my pants. I couldn't remember being harder in my life. Watching her touch herself like that, was the single, most erotic sight I'd ever seen. I wanted to touch her. To fuck her. I would, when the time came. Seeing her get off, that was enough. For now.

I opened the door to my room at the back of the house, and stepped inside. I closed the door behind me, but didn't lock it.

If anyone entered my room, they had my permission to be inside my house. No one got past the security system. If they did, they wouldn't get past Gianni and Damon. Both knew better than to come into my private space anyway. Terry wouldn't bother.

That left Mina. She was welcome at any time, regardless of the hour, or if I was sleeping. She was one of very few people who'd survive the experience if she woke me up.

I stepped out of my clothes and left them in a neat pile on the floor. Terry would slip in and take them for washing in the morning.

My bedroom was the largest in the house, the most opulently decorated. It was also the one that looked the least lived-in. I only spent several hours a day here, mostly sleeping. There was no need to step through the door, otherwise. My library was my sanctuary and my office was for working. This was just a place to rest and store my clothes. And wash.

It was to the bathroom I headed. I closed the door behind me and turned on the shower, hot almost to the point of scalding. I stepped onto the black and white penny tiles, the same as in the house's other bathrooms, and under the water.

Washing took only a couple of minutes, but I didn't start on that yet. Instead, I leaned against the walls, the subway tiles cold against my back, and wrapped my hand around my thick cock. My erection under the water, I started to slide my hand up and down, from head to heavy balls.

My eyes closed, I pictured Mina, her legs spread to display her glorious pussy. Her hand moved over her clit, fingers pressed deep inside her. The more she worked herself, the more her fingers glistened with her own juices.

I pumped harder, remembering the way her breath came in pants and tiny moans. I didn't think she was aware of the sounds she made, but I committed each one to memory, seared into my mind like a brand.

I leaned my head back and pressed my eyes shut tighter. My lips curled back in a grimace as my orgasm rose so fast I couldn't stop it. It washed over me with the water, flooding my senses and forcing me to grit my teeth to keep from shouting out loud.

I didn't shout, ever, but I could have screamed her name in that moment. All I could think of was her. When cum exploded out of me in a rush, I wanted to spill myself into her body. I wanted to fill her so full she overflowed. I wanted to hear her scream my name as I pounded into her.

Puffing lightly, I sagged forward, my orgasm fading and leaving me exhausted and not completely satisfied.

I wouldn't be until I came inside her.

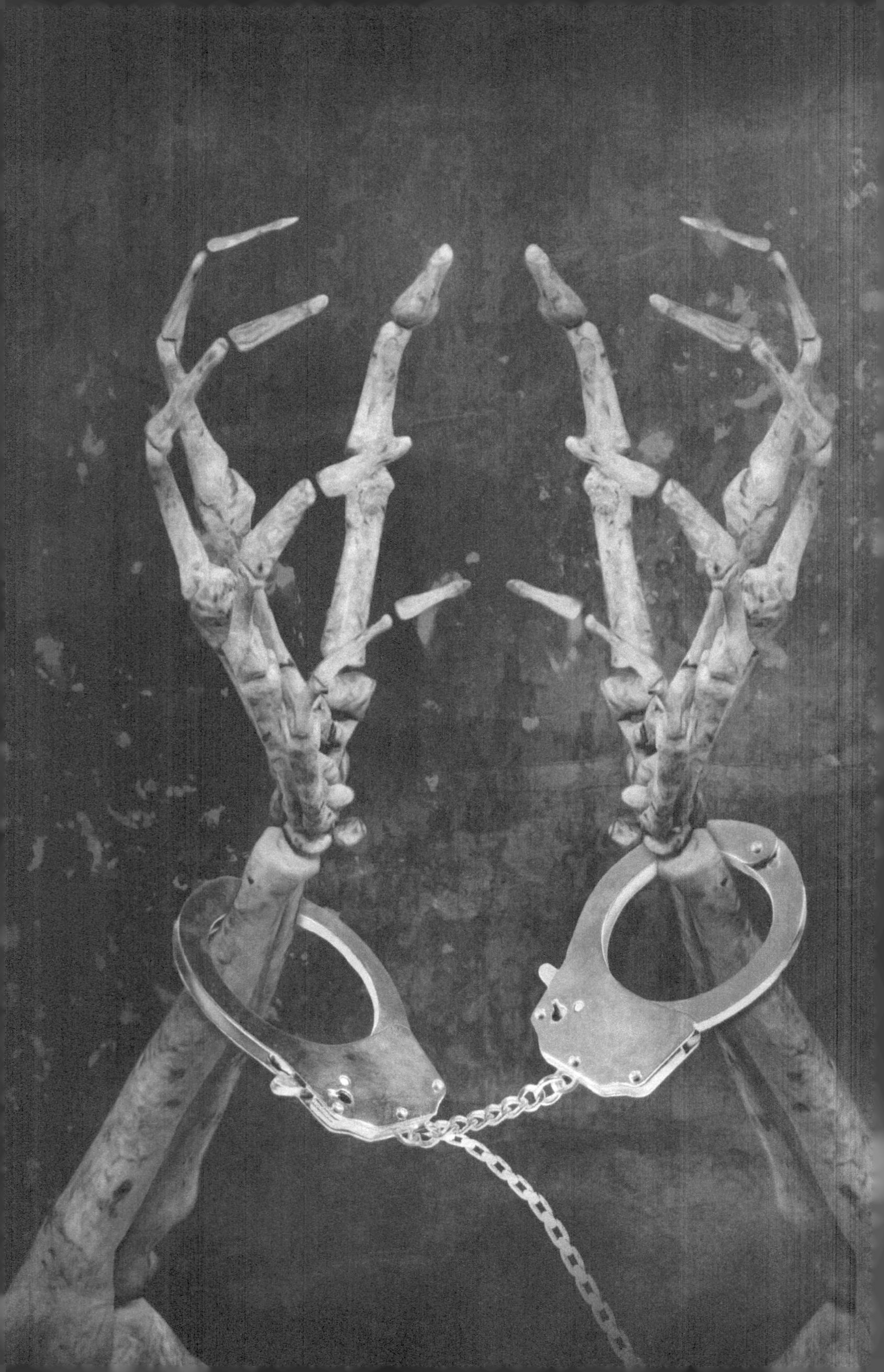

CHAPTER 14

MINA

"I am going to break his scrawny little neck." A female voice came from the kitchen. Not one I recognised.

"You're going to need to get in line," Gianni replied easily. "Your dear brother, Kurt, got himself onto a whole lot of shit lists. Especially mine."

"Fuck that," she said. "If I catch up to him first, he's fucking toast."

"I want him alive." That was Reuben's soft tone.

"So we can kill him slowly and painfully," Gianni added. He sounded very much like he was looking forward to it.

"You might as well go in." Damon spoke behind me, making me startle violently. He gave me a glance before walking past and into the kitchen. Not laughing at me, nor apologetic. He didn't seem to care one way or another if I stayed out in the corridor or joined the conversation.

I was torn between wanting to keep my presence a secret and needing to see Daisy Lasalle for myself.

With the full knowledge my cousin Ric might also be present, I stepped into the kitchen.

Several people sat at the table, including Reuben. Gianni leaned against the island, a coffee mug in his hand with the logo of the Dusk

Bay Demons ice hockey team on the side. From what I understood, Reuben's brother Caleb owned the team. Not because he cared about hockey, it was another front for the family.

Everyone turned to look at me as I entered the room. Ric looked at me with surprise, but it was Daisy who caught and held my eyes. She looked enough like her brother to give me chills, but she had the empathy he completely lacked.

She rose from her seat and came to put her arms around me. "If I had a clue what he was doing, I would have put a stop to it. You have to believe I never would have let you go through what he put you through. When I catch up to him, I'm going to kick his sorry ass."

I froze when she touched me, but gradually managed to relax enough to quickly hug her back before I pulled away again.

"I believe you." She wouldn't be here if Reuben didn't think she was sincere. Unless this was some kind of test. Presumably she passed or he wouldn't have allowed her anywhere near me.

"This is a surprise." Ric also stood, but made no move to step towards me. "You grew up, cousin."

"So did you." I wasn't close to him or his brother, but I'd seen him often enough to notice the difference. Only a couple of years older than me, he was barely more than a teenager himself the last time we met.

"Reuben tells me you don't want the rest of the family to know you're here," Ric said. Judging by the expression on his face, he was told something along the lines of, 'tell anyone and you're dead.'

I glanced over to Reuben, who watched everything with his usual measured interest.

"That's right," I said softly. "I'll tell them everything when I'm ready." I couldn't put it off forever, but I could put it off for now.

"They won't hear it from us," Daisy said. "Right, Ric?"

He sat back down and gave her an affectionate smile. "Daze already told me she'd kick me so hard in the balls they'd retreat back up into my body and stay there. Since I'm attached to their current location, I'll keep my mouth shut."

Daisy grinned. "I didn't actually need to threaten him. He already knows what I would have done." She sat back down beside him.

I slipped into a chair beside Reuben and nodded my thanks to

Terry who placed coffee in front of me. "I heard you talking about Kurt."

The mood of the kitchen dipped.

"I had no idea the extent of the shit he was up to," Ric said. "As you know, I've been tracking missing shipments for a while now, but haven't been able to pin down who was behind them. I came to the conclusion it was an inside job, but he was good at covering his tracks. Now we know where to look, it should be a lot easier. So far, I've uncovered at least a dozen redirected shipments of gems spanning the last two to three years. Some of those were believed to be intercepted by the cops."

"You think he was behind all of that?" Damon asked. He stood with his shoulder against the wall, legs crossed at his ankles.

Ric looked up at him. "Some of it. A couple of those shipments were stolen on the way to the police lock-up. Others, I suspect never made it into police hands. We were told what happened, but clearly that was a load of bullshit."

"You looked into it?" Reuben asked.

Ric's gaze swivelled to him. "On your orders or those of Caleb, we did. Kurt and anyone working with him was considered a trusted source at the time. This happens once or twice and you can blame outside sources, but after a while it became obvious someone working with us was working against us."

He let out a frustrated breath and shook his head. "If we'd figured it out sooner…" He shot me an apologetic look.

"Kurt was smart enough to spread out these redirections," Damon said. "At least, at the beginning."

"He got cocky," Daisy said. "He got away with it enough times to think he could keep doing that. He must have realised it wouldn't go unnoticed."

"It's likely he got desperate," Damon said. "He knew, or at least *sensed*, that Ric was onto him. It was only a matter of time before we figured it all out. And we did. He was probably as active as he dared to be, in preparation for fucking off and hiding."

"So he could be anywhere in the world," I said. "With enough money to hide for the rest of his life."

"He could hide for the rest of his life from honest people," Reuben said. "We have resources they don't have."

"Yeah," Gianni agreed. "And we don't care who we kill to get what we want."

I wasn't convinced it would be that simple. I wished I could believe it would be. Kurt knew exactly what he needed to do to evade all of us. With enough money he could change his identity and his face and never be found.

Reuben placed a hand over one of mine. "We will find him. There's nowhere he can hide that's out of reach."

I turned my hand around and laced my fingers with his. My heart actually fluttered. It had never done that before, not for anyone. I liked that it did it now.

"You can't put everything and everyone on this forever," I said. "Sooner or later, we have to move on from him and what he did."

Gianni chuckled. "When Reuben is determined to see something through, he will. It would take an army of tanks to stop him."

"There's nothing wrong with being driven," Reuben said.

"I didn't say there was," Gianni said. "Just like there's nothing wrong with fixating on a certain goal. Especially one like this."

"Women like a man who knows what he wants, right Mina?" Daisy smiled at me.

"Yes, they do," I said. I couldn't seem to tear my gaze from Reuben. The more I got to know him, the more he fascinated me. He was a stone cold killer, but he could be so gentle. I'd always found him attractive, but he was so closed, like a heavy door on a bank vault.

Now I realised he wasn't shut off because he was unfeeling, but because he was guarded. He was driven, yes, but he was also committed and loyal. When anyone tried to fuck with him or someone he cared about, he fucked back.

The fact he'd go to such an extent to find Kurt suggested he cared for me more deeply than I suspected. This wasn't just revenge for screwing with the Brantley family. He wanted to give me my own revenge and closure.

"No one else knows Mina is here?" Ric asked.

"Just the twins, Caleb, and everyone in this room," Gianni said. "No one else."

"That's as far as it goes," Reuben growled. "No one else needs to know. Not until Mina decides they need to." His gaze was also locked on me.

"No one else will hear," Daisy assured us. "We'll keep this all about Kurt stealing from the Brantley family. I think Ric is just curious what your brother Zeke will say when he sees Mina."

"I was thinking more of Asher, but yes," Ric agreed. "He's going to find all of this very…interesting."

"I don't care if he doesn't approve," I said softly. "It's not up to him." Trust my cousin to hit the nail on the head though. Yes, I didn't want my brother to see me looking starved and broken, but I also didn't want him to judge any of the choices I voluntarily made. Including being with Reuben.

"Can I be here when he finds out?" Ric asked. "Ouch." He glanced at Daisy, who jabbed him in the ribs with her elbow. "Don't say you don't want to see that too."

"Of course I do, but it's none of our business." She narrowed her eyes at him.

He responded by rolling his eyes playfully and making a face. It was clear that while she kept him in line, he wasn't intimidated by her. Not too much, anyway. What was her relationship with her other two boyfriends like? I didn't know Gunnar, but I'd met Hilton a couple of times. He seemed like the kind of man not to be crossed if people enjoyed living.

Like everyone else in this room, I supposed.

"Exactly," Reuben said. "Your business is finding Kurt and figuring out whatever else he was up to." He pressed his lips together. "I want to know if there are any other women hidden away."

The smile faded from Daisy's face. "You think there might be? If there are, I'm going to rip his fucking balls off."

"Did I mention that you need to get in line?" Gianni asked. "We don't know if there are others, but if he did this to Mina, he might just as easily have done it to someone else."

Reuben squeezed my hand. It wasn't until then I realised I was trembling. The idea of some other woman locked away, terrified, hungry, used and scarred, it got to me every time the subject came up.

So far, we hadn't found anyone, but that didn't mean they didn't exist. Even worse was the idea that Kurt ran, leaving them to die alone, not found until it was too late. That could so easily have happened to me. If they hadn't found me when they did, I'd be dead in that filthy cage. I might not have been discovered for years.

"I'm so sorry," Daisy whispered. "If there's ever anything I can do, please ask. I can't get my head around my own brother doing this to anyone. I knew he was an asshole, but I didn't know he was a monster." She sounded devastated. Furious.

"It's not your fault," I whispered back. "You're not responsible for what your brother did. He decided to be who he was. Not you or anyone else." Although my father gave him the opportunity. He was as guilty as Kurt, but Daisy wasn't.

"I know, I just feel like I should have seen it," she said. "Maybe there were signs and I missed them."

"We all missed the signs he was up to shady shit," Ric said. "Until we figured it out and got Mina out of there."

"We?" Gianni asked.

Ric shrugged. "I was the one who told you he was up to something. If I hadn't, my cousin wouldn't have been found. So yeah, *we.*"

"Touché." Gianni smirked. "You're a DiMarco all right."

Ric grinned. "We're all known for our awesomeness, right Mina?"

I wasn't sure about that, but I managed a small smile in return. "Absolutely. We're amazing."

"You definitely are," Gianni said. "More than amazing."

I wished I felt that way about myself, but it felt good to spend a little time with family. A little piece of normal would go a long way towards helping me heal.

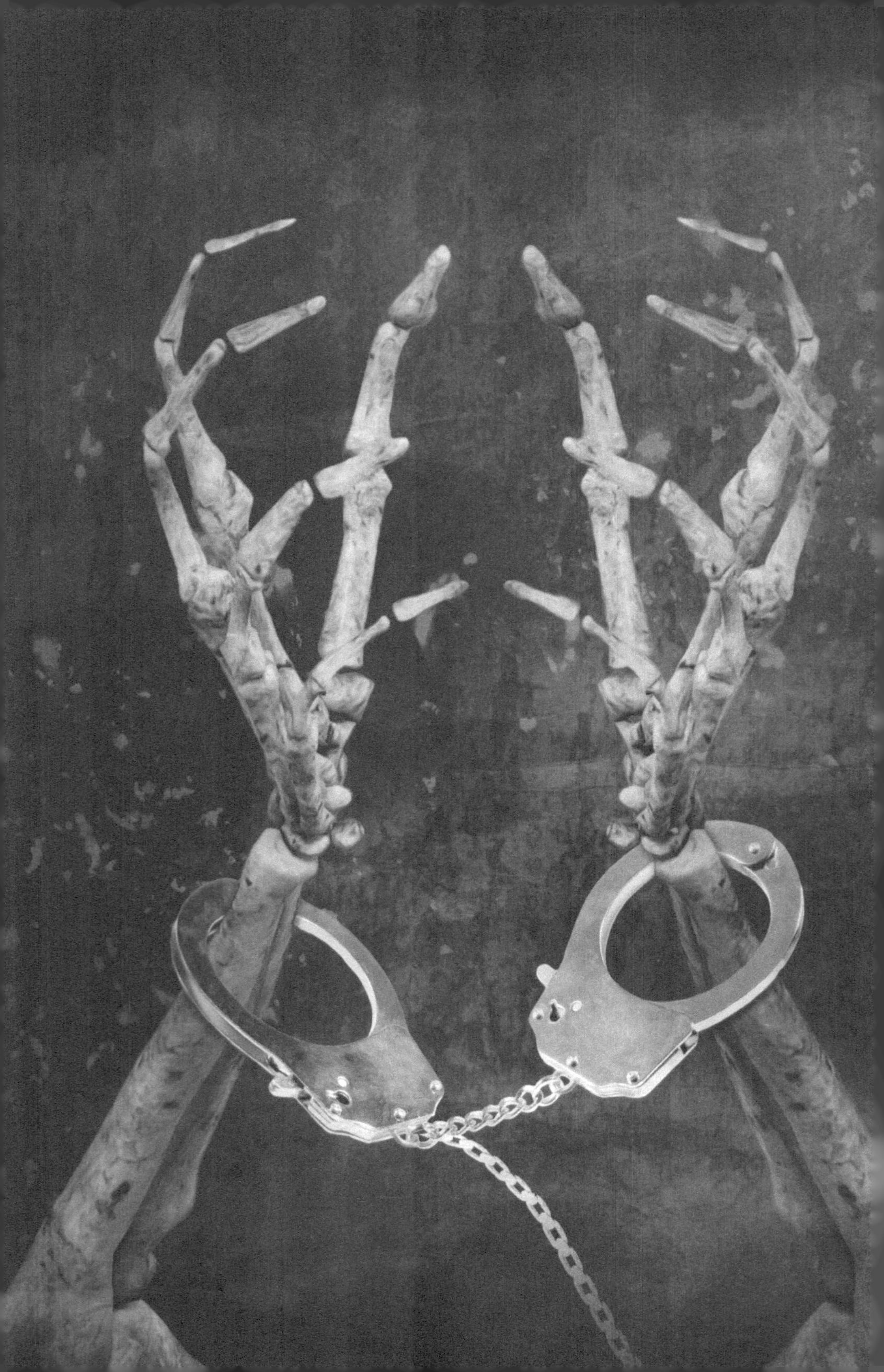

CHAPTER 15

MINA

"You can tell me to fuck off if you want to," Daisy said. She followed me out into the back garden, leaving Ric inside to talk to the other men. "I just thought you might like to have another woman to talk to. Men can be so testosterone-y sometimes."

I glanced over to the vegetable garden where Terry was tending to the plants, clearly not paying any attention to us.

Feet bare, I walked across the neat lawn to the back of the garden where the roses grew. Amongst the trees and fragrant bushes were a pair of stone benches.

I lowered myself down onto one of them. "Yes, they can. I appreciate it, but if you came to apologise again for—" She'd done enough of that as far as I was concerned.

There was nothing to forgive her for, therefore no need to keep saying sorry.

She sat on the other bench. "No. I mean, I won't now. You looked like you could use a friend. Someone who understands what this crazy life is like." She plucked a half-dead rose off one of the bushes and started to pull off the petals and scatter them on the ground.

"I tried to get away from all of this. To live a normal life away from crime, violence and death. Turns out, I kinda like those things." She glanced over at me and grinned. "The moment I saw Ric again, I was done for. I think I was in denial for all those years."

"So you went back," I said. I never considered walking away. I didn't know anyone who had done it successfully, unless you counted my brother, Asher. He seemed to be living his best life away from the craziness.

"I didn't just go back, I brought my daughter with me," she said. "Ric's daughter. I wanted to keep her out of it, but it's in her blood as much as it is in mine. I'm guessing it's in yours too."

I wondered how much she knew about me. Probably not everything. If she did, she probably wouldn't ask me that question.

"I can't imagine living any other way." I watched the petals drop from her hand and flutter to the ground. "I killed a woman the other day." I told Daisy about her.

She nodded and dropped another couple of petals. "Good for you. No one messes with women like us." She closed her hand over the last few petals. "I'm—"

"Don't say sorry," I interrupted. "You're absolutely right. No one will ever mess with me again. They'd have to kill me first."

"I wouldn't envy them if they did that. Reuben would rip them apart. I saw the way he looks at you. Like he'd go to the centre of hell for you. I've never seen him look at anyone like that. If I'm honest, I'd say I didn't think he was capable of those kinds of emotions. Men like him are — I don't know, they don't like being vulnerable." She opened her hand, turned it around and let the rest of the squashed flower fall to the grass.

"You think caring about someone makes him vulnerable?" I asked.

She glanced over and laughed once. "No, I don't. I just think that's how they see it. That if a big, bad man gives his heart to anyone, they might break it. All of my guys would have thought exactly that. Turns out, loving people makes us stronger and braver. And they get the added bonus of being with me." She grinned.

It was hard not to like her. She was strong and outspoken without needing to be nasty. Ric clearly adored her and the feeling was obviously mutual.

She was right, I needed another woman to talk to. Reuben and

Gianni were attentive, but after last night things were different. Reuben and I went past friendship. Whatever this was between us, we couldn't go back to that.

With Daisy, there was no such expectation. We could talk and share things we wouldn't share with any man. Experiences women had that men didn't. Fears and vulnerabilities. The need for constant vigilance against attacks from men like Kurt.

The fact she hadn't seen me in that cage, ragged and filthy, went some way to making me feel more comfortable with her. The woman sitting here now was the only one she'd seen, otherwise she might look at me with more pity than she had. Of all the things I might want from her, pity wasn't one of them.

"I'm not sure if giving his heart to me is something Reuben plans on doing," I said.

She laughed again. "Whether or not he planned it, you already have it. I'm guessing he hasn't said anything, but it's obvious to anyone watching. He's head over heels for you."

She shook her head. "I wouldn't have believed it if I hadn't seen it with my own eyes. Reuben Brantley madly in love with Mina DiMarco. It's like something out of a romance novel."

Was he madly in love? It seemed like a stretch. Caring about someone and being in love weren't always the same thing.

"Gianni looks at you the same way," Daisy added. "Damon keeps his cards close to his chest, but it wouldn't surprise me if you four ended up like me and my guys."

"They're just protective," I said. "And pissed off at Kurt for stealing from them. That's all it is."

She stared at me in a way that was disturbingly like her brother. "That's not all it is. They care for you very much. I know after what you've been through, you're not ready to rush into anything. I saw that they know that too, or they'd be wearing their balls as necklaces right now. Before I leave, I'll give you my details. If they ever overstep, you're welcome to contact me and I'll fly up and deal with them." She seemed completely sincere.

"Did I mention I killed a woman?" I asked flatly.

She grinned. "So you did. I'm sure you're capable of making them eat their own nuts, but if you need help, I'm here for you. So is Ric. He'd be hating himself right now for what happened to you. We trusted Kurt and his associates and we shouldn't have."

"You should be able to trust your brother," I said. I trusted both of mine, more or less.

Okay, I trusted Asher. Dane tended to look out for his own ass. He used to, anyway. Maybe he'd changed. Maybe he hadn't.

"If Ric hadn't looked into things, I wouldn't be here. I'm grateful to him."

"Still, it's his job to make sure shit like this doesn't happen. Caleb was pissed at him. If there's anything Caleb doesn't like, it's losing money. Reuben doesn't like it either, but Caleb is worse. I think it comes with being the second oldest brother. He always has to prove himself. Or maybe he just has a really small cock." She grinned.

I actually let out a small, choking laugh at that. "I suppose that's possible. I guess I should be grateful to Caleb too, for pushing Ric to keep looking."

"Do yourself a favour and never tell Caleb that," Daisy said. "If he thinks you owe him something, he'll hold that over you. He'll want something in return. Whatever that something is, it's bound to be a thing you don't want to give."

I recoiled. "He wouldn't want—"

She grimaced. "No, not sex. Who knows what it would be, but he wouldn't be stupid enough to try that with someone Reuben is interested in. He'd be too scared Reuben would take all his power away from him. Which is exactly what Reuben *would* do. No, Caleb would ask for something else. It's best you don't let him put you in that position. Trust me, I worked for Caleb for years. I see him all the time. He's always got an angle he's working. And he wants to use everyone around him to his own advantage."

"That doesn't sound different to anyone else in my life," I said. "Everyone wants something." Which led me to wonder what she wanted.

"Ain't that the truth," she said with a laugh. "Some of us just want what's best for you. Including me. I can't even imagine the things you've gone through. Hearing about it was enough to make me want to puke." Her smile had faded to an expression of regret.

"You must be a lot stronger than me, because there's no way I'd survive five minutes down there, much less five years."

"You might have found a way out," I said. I'd tried more times than I could count but failed and eventually gave up. In the end, the only hope I had was for death. Even that seemed like too much to wish for.

Daisy fixed me with a firm look. "If there was a way out of there, you would have found it. I know Kurt, he wouldn't have left even the smallest opportunity. He was always like that. He thought everything through, every scenario, every possibility. That was exactly why he got past us for so long. He's intelligent and meticulous. I'm coming to realise he might be a sociopath. The point is, not being able to get away from him is not a reflection on you or your abilities. You did what so many other people wouldn't be able to do. You survived and walked away. I don't think you have any idea how incredible that really is."

"I just…" I didn't know how to respond to that. All I did was take it one minute at a time. Count the bars around me and the lines on the ceiling. Survive when Kurt came to give me what meagre food he bothered to drop into the cage. Switch off as best I could when he used my body. Was that really so incredible?

"I did what I had to do," I said finally. "I switched off my feelings and focused on breathing and not what was happening around me. I listened to my heartbeat and counted them to calm myself. I took myself out of there, in my head." I curled and flexed the fingers of one hand as I spoke.

Daisy gave me a searching look, but nodded. "See what I mean? You're stronger than you think you are. Switching off the world around you and focusing on one thing is difficult to do without practice."

In that moment, I felt like she could see right through me. Like she fully understood me and all my darkest secrets.

I lifted my chin. That was all. Not a word of warning, no threats. Just a short, silent motion.

She lowered hers. She understood and wouldn't say anything to anyone. This was between us and us alone.

"My friends call me Daze." She held out a hand to me.

I took it without hesitation and squeezed before letting it go again. "Mine used to call me Mina Sunshine, but now I'm just Mina." I used to go by another name, but we wouldn't talk about that. Not now. Maybe not ever.

CHAPTER 16

MINA

"I have a surprise for you," Gianni said. "I was thinking about the way you sliced that woman open the other day."

He picked up the plates from lunch, took them into the kitchen and gestured for me to follow him outside.

"Don't damage the roses," Damon called out after us. "Terry will be pissed."

Terry grunted his agreement and continued to slice potatoes to throw into a pot. The knife in his hand was huge and, judging by the way the blade sliced effortlessly through the potato skin, sharp.

"*I'll* be pissed," Reuben said as he finished his coffee.

"No roses will be harmed in the making of this surprise," Gianni said. He rolled his eyes at them playfully and closed the door behind us.

"What about the woman?" I asked.

He hadn't brought me a group of people to practice on. That was probably for the best. Instead, a couple of large targets were set up in the centre of the lawn.

"It's less about her and more about using a knife." He picked up a box from beside the door and opened it. Inside, several small knives lay on black velvet. Sun glinted off the steel like a wink, or a challenge.

"You want me to throw those?" I guessed.

"I think knife throwing is a skill every girl should have." He picked up a knife and set the box back down. "Have you done this before?"

I opened and closed my mouth.

He pressed the heel of his hand to his forehead. "Of course you haven't done it *recently*. I'm such a fucking donkey sometimes."

I snorted a laugh. "You're not a donkey. I have done it, but like you said, not recently. I'm probably rusty as hell." I leaned down to pick up another of the knives. Picturing the blade right in the centre of Kurt's forehead made me smile.

"This is going to be torture on my dick," Gianni murmured. "Okay, watch me and that might help it come back to you. If not, there's plenty of time to practice."

He turned to face the target, aimed and sent the knife flying from his hand. It landed just to the right of the centre of the target.

"Apparently I need to practice more too." He shrugged. Even if his aim was slightly off, he still would have killed the person he was aiming at. "You try."

I regarded him for a moment before leaning over to pick up two more knives. I eyed the target, cleared my mind and let the knives loose, one at a time. The first landed dead centre of the target. The second landed to the right of his and the third directly above.

He stared at me, then burst out laughing. "I should have known you'd be good at this. I bet you could hit the target blindfolded."

"I was aiming to put them all in the centre," I said regretfully. "I'm rusty."

"You're fucking amazing and my cock is hard as hell now." The front of his jeans were tented, his expression strained. "I never could resist a woman who knew how to handle a knife."

"Maybe we should stop," I suggested. I admit to being curious to see what was under the denim. He looked so big. My clit pulsed in agreement, but I couldn't tell if my trembling was from fear or desire. Possibly both.

"I definitely think we should keep going," he said. He adjusted the front of his pants and walked to the target to pull the knives free.

He handed me two and kept two for himself before stepping in front of the other target. "Who taught you?" He aimed and hit closer to the centre of the target.

"My sister, Rose," I said. "She's a big believer in women taking care of themselves and each other." My first knife hit the centre of the target, but the second went too far to the left again. I wouldn't be satisfied until they were both lodged in the same hole.

"I've heard that about her," he said. "She seems almost as badass as you."

I walked over to pull the knives out of the target. "She's much more badass than I ever was."

"You miss her?" He seemed to have forgotten to practice and was standing looking at me, a knife held loosely in his hand.

"I miss her a lot," I said. "Her and Asher. Dane too, I guess. Do you think I should contact them?"

"If you're ready." He remembered the knife and turned to throw it. "No one is going to pressure you into anything. Least of all me. I haven't spoken to my family in years."

This was the first time he mentioned a family. Until now, I hadn't wanted to intrude by asking.

"Why haven't you spoken to them?" I asked.

He rubbed a hand over his chin. "It's a long story. Mostly they're assholes and I'm better off without them." There was clearly more to it than that. I decided not to push. He'd tell me if he was ready.

"Their loss." I threw again, this time getting the blades closer together.

"Very much so." He adjusted his pants again. "What other skills do you have that are hot enough to almost make me come in my pants?"

I walked over and spoke softly in his ear. "I can pick locks."

He groaned. "Fucking hell, woman. You really want to see me make a mess, don't you?"

I laughed softly. "Is this where I say I'm sorry?"

"You can try, but I wouldn't believe it for a moment. You seem to enjoy torturing me." He was grinning as he said it.

I was close enough to reach out and touch the front of his pants with the tips of my fingers lightly. I swallowed at how hard he felt. How big.

"Sweetheart," he said softly. "I won't ask you to—"

"I want to." This was all about me taking back my power. I knew he'd let me go as far as I was comfortable and wouldn't say a word if I pulled back.

I worked the button of his jeans out of the hole and slid down the zipper. I wasn't surprised to find brightly coloured boxers, decorated with cartoon characters. None I recognised, but very Gianni.

I pushed them down to free his massive erection. A piercing glittered in the tip. Three or four more decorated the underside of his cock.

"Jacob's ladder," he said. "For the pleasure of my partner. When she's ready."

Intrigued, I ran the tip of my finger across each of the steel bars and the warm skin between them.

"Did they hurt?"

"Yeah, but I like pain," he replied easily. "Giving and receiving it. Don't worry, I only give it without consent to people who deserve it. I know how to be restrained." He swallowed hard, clearly holding back the urge to thrust himself into my hand.

"I thought you might," I ran my finger up and down his length, enjoying the feeling of hot, throbbing pulse beneath thin, blood-darkened skin.

He moaned softly. "Can I ask you something?"

I glanced at his face, then back down to his cock. "That depends what it is."

He chuckled softly. "I guess it would. I'm wondering if you were ever with anyone. By your choice."

I stopped stroking to look back up at him. "No," I whispered. "There was never anyone I wanted to…fuck. None that wanted me, too." None I knew of anyway. It wouldn't have crossed my mind that Reuben might have. He seemed so far out of reach, we might as well have lived in different worlds.

"Anyone who doesn't want you is out of their mind," Gianni said. "But I promise when that happens between us, it will be fully with your consent. No pressure from me. No obligation."

"When?" I ran my whole hand up and down his length before curling my fingers around him.

"When," he said firmly. His eyes half closed. "There will come a day when I slide my cock deep into your sweet pussy. But for now, this is enough." He rolled his hips as I started to slowly pump his cock. "You have magic hands."

"I don't know about that." I watched his face while I worked him, revelling in how responsive he was. Everything he felt right now was because of me. Because of my touch. Because my hand was wrapped around his cock. I was the one in control. I decided how fast or slow we went.

"I do," he said with a groan. "Fuck, sweetheart, I'm going to... Come." He gave me time to pull away before he gritted his teeth and thrust his hips faster. He slid in and out of my hand until he stilled. Hot, pearly cum squirted out of his tip, onto my fingers like the blood from the woman's neck.

He sagged forward, puffing lightly. "Shit, that was good. Better than good."

I uncurled my hand from him. My fingers were coated with his release, thick and warm.

"You did that to me," he said softly. "Just looking at you makes me want to come. You let me do that and I thank you. No one ever got me off that hard before. I bet your pussy is even better."

My pussy pulsed in response to his touch, his orgasm, my power over his body. I'd never felt anything like it before. I felt more powerful than I had when I killed that woman.

I looked up at him, raised my hand to my mouth and started to lick my fingers clean.

Gianni's eyes widened. "Just when I think you couldn't get any hotter, you fucking do. One day, I'm going to come in your mouth and watch you swallow every drop, but this is almost as good. How do I taste?"

I hadn't reached my pointer finger yet. It was still covered in a thick layer of cum. I lifted it to his mouth and, when he opened for me, pressed my finger inside.

He closed his lips around and sucked. "Mmm, delicious," he said around my fingertip. "I taste good on your skin."

He sucked for a while longer before pulling his mouth back with a wet pop. "This just cements what I already knew. We belong together."

I was starting to think that too. I couldn't deny my attraction to him and Reuben, and my curiosity about Damon, but it went deeper than that. They seemed to understand me in a way no one else had before. They let me be me and take my time to settle back into life outside the cage. No coercion, no pressure, no judgement.

All of those were reasons I wasn't ready to see my family yet. Dane in particular would judge me for being here and probably try to manipulate the situation to benefit him in some way. He'd encourage my relationship with Reuben, but only because he'd hope to gain power for himself from it. He was always the most ambitious in our family. The one most likely to throw the rest of us under a bus if it helped him in some way.

I placed enough pressure on myself to put the past behind me without having someone like him making things more difficult.

"Those look like some deep thoughts," Gianni said. He'd pulled up his pants and fastened them, and was now looking at me like he wasn't sure if he should offer to get me off or not. He clearly wanted to, but would let me take the lead in that too.

"I was just thinking about my family," I said. Before he could respond, I stood on my toes and brushed my lips over his. He tasted of coffee and cum, with a touch of salt. A delicious combination.

He placed a hand on my upper arm and deepened the kiss in a way that let me pull away when I was ready. When his tongue pressed against my lips, I opened them to let him slide inside. Tentatively, I slid my tongue against his.

My body throbbing, I eventually drew back. "I've never been kissed like that before."

He smiled. "Neither have I. Your mouth is even more perfect than your hand."

I laughed softly. I wanted him to touch me more, but not yet. The huge steps I'd already taken were enough for now.

"We should get back to practising," I said. "You might be able to concentrate now."

He chuckled. "With you next to me, never."

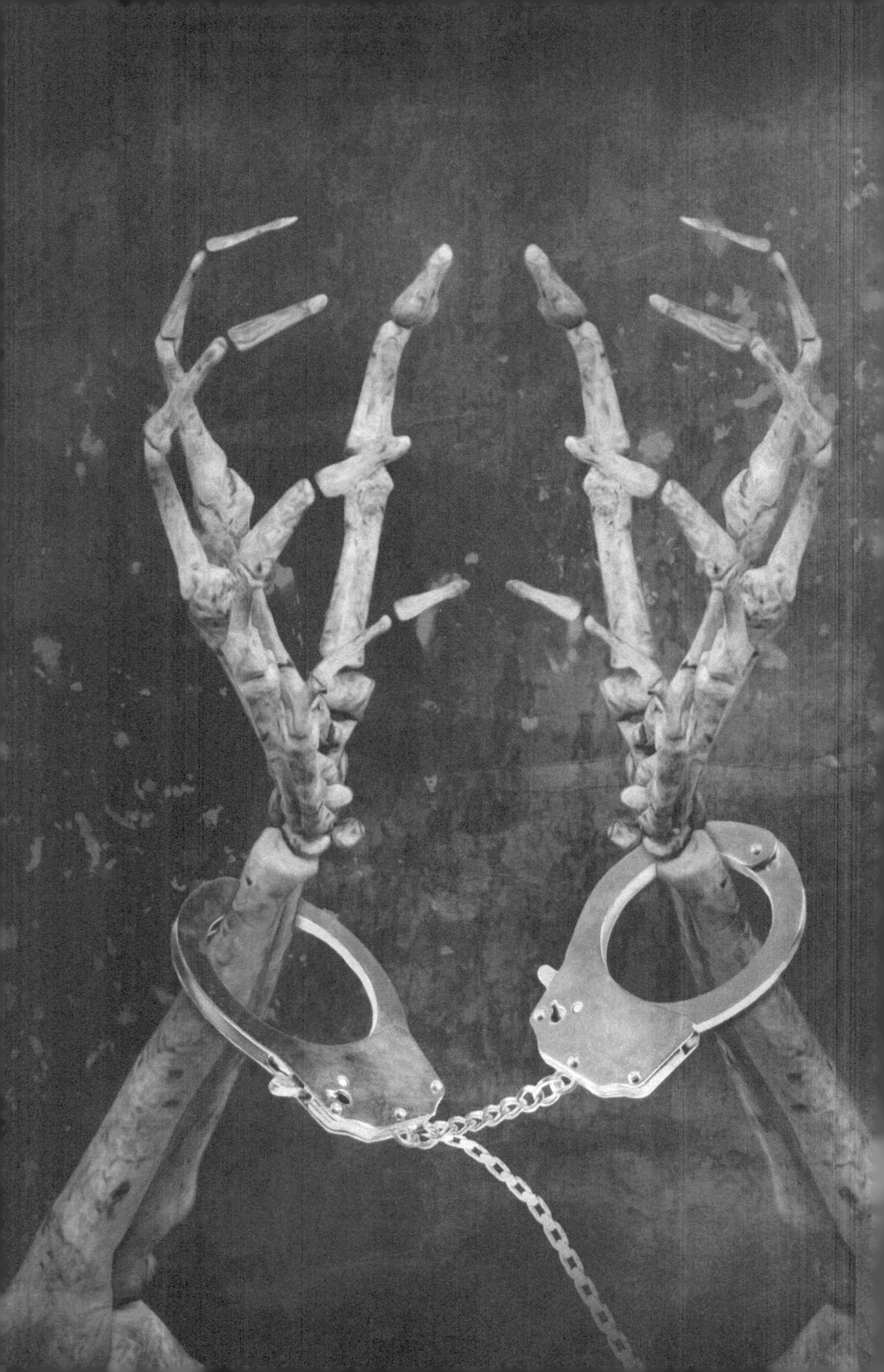

CHAPTER 17

REUBEN

I stepped away from the window as Mina and Gianni resumed practising throwing knives. Her skill didn't surprise me. Watching her hand stroke Gianni's cock did. I'd watched as he thrust and came on her fingers, my cock aching to do the same.

"She's a distraction," Damon said.

I glanced over to him. "Perhaps. That changes nothing. I'm not sending her away."

"I didn't expect you would." He eyed the bulge in my trousers, which I was trying hard to ignore and deflate. I didn't look at his. I didn't need to; I knew it was there. We'd both watched.

"What do you expect then?" I walked past him to place my empty cup in the kitchen.

"I don't know. Since you found her, you've been obsessed with finding Kurt Lasalle. Killing him won't change what he did to her." Damon leaned his hip against the island and crossed his arms.

"It'll make me feel a whole fuck ton better. Knowing he's out there is pissing me off," I growled.

"Me too," he said easily. "I want to make an example of him as much as you do. He spent long enough going behind our back. It's past time he paid for that, regardless of what he did or didn't do to Mina."

I wanted to tell him he had his priorities backwards, but the point wasn't relevant right now. The fact was, Lasalle operated behind our backs and we needed to send a message that it wouldn't be tolerated.

"This is personal," I stated. "You feel responsible for not seeing what he was doing sooner."

Damon took pride in keeping a tight leash on our businesses. And on the people who worked for me. If they put a foot out of line, he was the one who either pulled them back, or cut it off. Often literally. This level of betrayal was something else.

His expression suggested I was exactly right. He looked ready to grind his teeth.

"I should have seen it. Ric and Caleb didn't, but I fucking *should* have. You're right it's fucking personal. That prick must have been laughing at us while he was trying to build an empire to rival the Brantley family."

He curled his hands into fists.

"Should I punish you for missing it?" I asked, my own tone deadpan as ever. "I could have Gianni remove a few of your toenails. It's not his usual method, but I'm sure he'd make an exception for you. Or he could lock you in a room and play some of his music at full volume for an hour or two."

That sounded like torture to me.

"You probably should punish me," Damon grumbled. He exhaled out his nose in frustration. "I fucked up. Since when do you tolerate failure?"

"Since I need you to find him," I said. "You have skills and contacts. The moment he pops up, you'll know." Damon's network was enviable. With my money and backing, he'd grown it into something both impressive and valuable. His network, and him, were assets I wasn't going to let go, whatever the cost.

"Which is exactly why I'm pissed off: I didn't know what he was up to. All those contacts and skills and the fucker still got past me." He ran a hand over the back of his hair. "What the fuck did I miss? I've gone over everything for the last three or four years and there's nothing. Not one thing to indicate what he was up to."

"He was a sneaky prick," I said. "Smart enough to pull it off and low-key enough to stay under the radar."

"I should have been smarter," Damon insisted. "If he got away with shit, fuck only knows who else is out there getting away with other things."

"We've increased our eyes and ears," I said. "Nothing else is getting past any of us. You said word is already out on the street about what happened in the ice cream parlour?"

Damon dropped his hand against thigh, a sure sign he was winning against his annoyance.

"It has. It's set a few people on edge. Anyone twitchy, I've put extra people on them. If they have a reason to be twitchy, we'll find it. I've also found two more fronts for Kurt's businesses. One was a pet shop. The other was a pub."

"Hiding behind the pussies," I remarked.

Damon chuckled. "If I didn't know better, I'd think Gianni is rubbing off on you."

My mind was immediately back on Mina, rubbing him. My cock twitched in response. Ached to feel her hand on me. Stroking, caressing, coaxing.

I cleared my throat. "Just making an observation. You dealt with both premises?"

"Most of the staff were oblivious," Damon said. "The ones believed to be working for him are being followed. People are watching both establishments. If Kurt turns up at either of them, we'll know. Hopefully he'll get thirsty at some point soon."

We both knew he wouldn't turn up anywhere so obvious, especially if he did the smart thing and left the country. This wasn't a complete waste of time. Reminding people they wouldn't get away with trying to fuck me over was worth the effort.

I nodded. "Good work. We could use someone who's ready to turn on him. Someone who knows enough about him but is willing to spill everything for the right price."

"There must be someone out there like that," Damon agreed. "I've been looking, but so far nothing. If Kurt trusted anyone to that extent, they're hiding as well as he is. He didn't even trust his sister enough to fill her in."

"Good, because Daisy Lasalle working with him would be fatal to her," I said. Not to mention devastating for us. I much preferred to have her on our side, than working against us. Especially given that she and Mina seemed to have formed a friendship. I'd allow that to continue for Mina's sake.

"One thing I have been able to ascertain," Damon said. "Whatever Kurt was up to, he didn't seem to be working with Samuel Bell. If anything, we may have a mutual enemy in the prick."

"He stole from Bell too?" I shouldn't have been surprised by that. Someone like Kurt would have known to spread out his movements. It was unlikely Samuel Bell and I would compare notes, and put two different events together.

Damon shrugged. "At this point, it's hearsay. It's unlikely we'll get the truth from the Bell family, but a contact of a contact spoke about several missing shipments over the last few years. It could have been Lasalle or it could have been someone else. It wasn't us. Not unless the twins are getting up to things you didn't endorse."

"I wouldn't put it past them," I said. I wouldn't be pleased if they went behind my back, but stealing from the enemy wasn't something I gave a shit about, endorsed or not. I had no sympathy for any member of the Bell family. Animosity yes, in abundance, but not sympathy.

"Do you ever worry those two will get out of control, boss?" Damon asked.

"That question assumes they were in control to start with," I said dryly. "No, I don't. They have their moments, but I don't question their loyalty. No more than I question yours. Or Gianni's. They're outrageous sometimes, but they have the family interests at heart."

I'd never tell anyone how fond I was of Hunter and Parker. They probably wouldn't believe it anyway. I was, after all, the coldhearted prick who headed the family. Incapable of emotion, even anger.

I felt all of that and more, I just hid it better than most.

"Should I worry they might come after my job?" Damon asked, looking completely unworried.

"Without a doubt," I replied, with no inflection. "I didn't say they weren't ambitious. They're probably plotting how to take my job as well as yours."

"They better not," Damon growled. "Unless you plan to retire someday."

Before Mina, I would have scoffed at that suggestion. I wasn't even forty and the family business was my whole life.

Now, I found myself with different priorities. Priorities I never expected to have. The women I was involved with in the past were nothing but brief flings. A fuck or two to release tension. Usually, they worked for me and knew I wasn't looking for anything more. I always made that extremely clear.

Mina changed all of that. Around her, I could be someone more than Reuben Brantley, mob boss. I could admit I had feelings I'd put aside for so long I was surprised to find I still had them. They hadn't withered away and died from lack of use. No, they'd lain dormant until the moment I saw her face again.

In that second I understood I'd put them aside to wait for her. She was it for me. She had been for the longest time. I had no idea when I'd fallen for her, but I had and there was no going back.

That realisation made me even more determined to find Lasalle and fuck him up. He'd pay for all the years he kept me from her. He'd pay fucking dearly.

"Someday," I echoed. "Not any day soon, but eventually. I might retire to that nice cottage beside the forest where I can put my feet up in front of a fire and read a book."

"Three days," Damon said.

I frowned questioningly at him. "Three days?"

"Yes. That's my guess on how long it'd take before you got bored and wanted to get back to work." He actually looked slightly amused, which for him was the equivalent of hysterical laughter.

I smirked. "Give me some credit. It would be four and a half days minimum. Maybe four and three quarters." Then I'd be looking for gems to traffic, politicians to bribe and ways to make even more money. I was addicted to power almost to the extent as I was addicted to Mina.

No, I didn't want help to recover from either of those addictions.

"Maybe even five," Damon said. "I guess you won't be going anywhere anytime soon then."

"Probably not," I agreed. Realistically, men in my position rarely lived long enough to retire. There was always someone plotting my death. Someday they might even succeed.

As if he read my mind, Damon said, "I'll do my best to make sure you live long enough to change your mind. Reading in front of a fire sounds relaxing. Not as much fun as fucking in front of one."

"I can always do one, then the other," I said. "That would keep me from being bored."

Now I was thinking about Mina's pussy and the way it glistened with her juices as she touched herself. I wanted to slide my cock into her so much it hurt. I'd waited this long, I could be patient for a while longer. No matter how much it hurt. Having blue balls was better than losing her forever by forcing her to do something she wasn't ready for. That would be unforgivable.

"I'm sure you—"

Whatever Damon was going to say, his phone ringing interrupted him. Not with an Abbie Hart song as his ringtone. Not Wolf Venom either, thank fuck.

He pulled his phone out of his pocket and pressed the screen before putting it to his ear. While he listened to the person on the other end, he frowned, deeper and deeper.

"Shit."

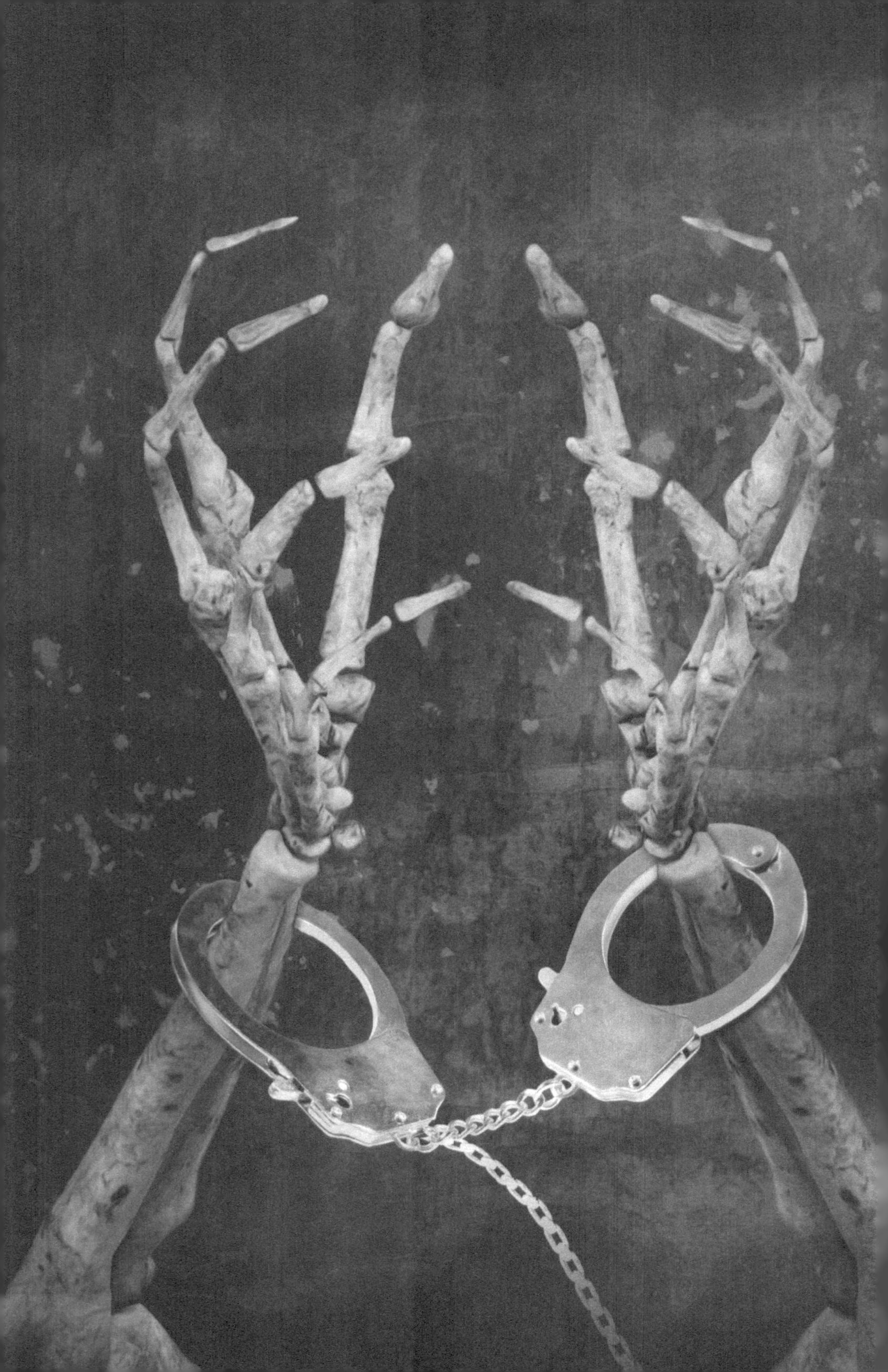

CHAPTER 18

MINA

"Shit."

I followed Gianni into the kitchen in time to hear Damon on the phone. He looked pissed off. The moment he noticed me standing near the door, his expression closed down tight. He ended the call and lowered the phone from his ear.

"What is it?" Gianni asked. "Don't tell me they've sold out of your favourite brand of chocolate again?"

Damon gave him a look that would have withered anyone, but Gianni grinned.

"He's a real bitch when he doesn't get his chocolate," he whispered loudly.

"Fuck off," Damon told him. He glanced at Reuben, then at me.

"If it's about Kurt, she should hear it," Reuben said.

"I'm not sure if it is," Damon said. He rubbed a hand over the back of his neck. "Someone matching his description just flew into Sydney from Hong Kong. It could be him or he could be completely unrelated."

A chill passed all the way through me. Was the room this cold a moment before? It felt icy right then.

Gianni raised a hand to touch my arm.

I flinched. I hadn't forgotten about Kurt, but I'd packed him into a box in my mind and pushed him aside for the last hour or so.

Now, Damon's words brought everything back in a rush. I knew I'd have to see Kurt in order to kill him, but the idea of being face-to-face with him, looking him in the eyes, him looking back at me with his usual contempt, made my stomach heave.

"It's okay, sweetheart," Gianni said gently. "You don't have to see him."

"It might not be him," Damon said. "The twins followed him to the location about twenty kilometres from here. They're keeping an eye on him. They'll let us know if he leaves."

Reuben nodded. "Get the car ready. We'll see for ourselves." His gaze lingered on me.

"I'm coming with you," I said firmly. "If it's him, I need to know. And if it's not, I want to know that too."

"If it is him, chances are he'll be ready for us," Damon said. Again, he looked at me, eyes unreadable.

"We won't let any harm come to her," Gianni said. "I won't let anything happen to her." He sounded ready to take on an army single-handed. "She can bring a couple of knives."

Reuben pressed his lips together, his blue eyes contemplative. "She can come with us. I'd prefer that to leaving her here."

Damon looked irritated, but turned on the heels of his leather shoes and stalked towards the garage.

"I'm guessing he didn't have his quota of chocolate today," Gianni remarked.

"I've never known him to eat chocolate," Reuben said.

Gianni nodded. "That's exactly my point. If he ate some once in a while, he might lighten up."

"Fuck off," Damon said over his shoulder.

"You know you love me," Gianni called out after him.

Without looking back, Damon flipped him off. He wrenched open the garage door and disappeared inside.

Reuben shook his head slightly and rolled his eyes before following Damon.

"Should you antagonise him like that?" I asked.

"Definitely," Gianni agreed. He made no move to touch me or step closer. "I meant what I said."

"About taking care of me, or about me bringing knives?" I asked.

He smiled. "Yes." He grabbed up the box we'd taken outside and tucked it under his arm. "Unless you'd prefer a gun."

"I can shoot." Of course I could. That was a skill we learned from an early age. Both my parents insisted. My father used to take us to the range to practice regularly. "But I prefer knives." They were easier to hide and quieter to use. Subtle and discreet. Until someone had the blade embedded in their brain.

"I sensed that about you," Gianni said. "I thought to myself, *she doesn't seem like a gun person.* Neither is Reuben. Don't get me wrong, he can shoot a man between the eyes from a distance, but he prefers to leave pulling of the trigger to people like me and Damon. And the twins."

That sounded about right. Why get your hands dirty when someone else could do it for you?

I walked behind Gianni to the garage. "Why do you think he came back?"

"Why does anyone do anything?" He opened the back door of the SUV and gestured for me to climb inside. "Unfinished business or money. People are often motivated by one or the other."

I slid in and he closed the door behind me.

"Or desperation." Damon drove the SUV out onto the streets which were surprisingly quiet for this time of day. Quiet enough to make me shiver again.

"Or for a good cup of coffee," Gianni added. "People can do a shit load of dubious things for one of those. Look at Damon, for example. You know he doesn't do this for the money. Not just for my attention either."

"Give the woman a knife so she can shut you up," Damon growled.

Gianni chuckled. "She'd never use a knife on me. Well, not unless I ask nicely." He glanced over at me and winked.

In spite of my anxiety at the idea of seeing Kurt again, my heart fluttered. Thinking about his cock, the way he came in my hand, and the kiss we shared, was a better use of my thoughts. A healthier one. I would have liked to focus on that, but Kurt was too dominant over my mind right now. I'd spent five years with him occupying my thoughts. It was a difficult habit to break. Was it impossible? I hoped not.

"Is that something you ask often?" I managed to ask. He'd mentioned enjoying pain, did that include knives and blood?

"Only if my partner is someone I implicitly trust," he said. "I'd prefer not to be stabbed mid-fuck if I can help it. A few nicks and slices, on the other hand…"

"If anyone was going to be stabbed mid-fuck, it would be you," Damon said.

"Are you offering?" Gianni asked.

"To stab you? Definitely." Damon glanced at the rear view mirror.

"He means with his cock," Gianni whispered loudly. "I told you he loves me."

"And I told you to fuck off, but here you are," Damon said.

I leaned forward as far as my seatbelt would allow and said to Reuben, "Are they always like this?"

They reminded me of the playful arguments my brother Asher had with Reuben's brother Zeke. They'd been friends since school, practically brothers. Thick as thieves, my mother used to say. When it came to each other, they had no filter. The nastier the words, the harder they laughed. I'd forgotten about that until now. Listening to them slinging insults back and forth always made me giggle.

He sat around to look back at me. "Probably. I tend to tune them out."

Gianni clutched his heart. "Boss, you wound me."

"You'll live," Reuben told him. He offered me the faintest of smiles.

"He really loves me too," Gianni said, lowering his hand back into his lap. "Obviously he does, or he wouldn't share you with me."

"Don't make me change my mind," Reuben said.

"That's up to Mina," Gianni said.

Reuben turned around further and gave him a look that said otherwise. That I belonged to him and he would decide on my behalf if anyone tried to force his hand.

"Like I said, she's a distraction," Damon said. "You two shouldn't be disagreeing over a woman. With all due respect, boss."

Reuben grunted and turned back around.

If I didn't already have the impression Damon didn't like me, I did after that comment.

Did he expect me to walk away from them both or for them to walk away from me? Maybe he thought they should cut my throat and leave me to die by the side of the road.

I eyed the box of knives. I could snatch a couple of them out there before Gianni could move a muscle. I could slice open his throat while he was still thinking about doing the same to me. His blood could coat my hand the way his cum had, thick and hot. I could watch the light fade from his dark eyes as his life slipped away. I could press my hand against his chest and feel the last of his heartbeats, before he fell still.

My hand twitched.

"If you're a distraction, I'm happy to be distracted," Gianni said softly. He was looking at me with half-lidded eyes, as though completely aware of the thoughts churning in my mind.

Of course he was. He acted silly at times, but it was a cover for the man underneath. He was clever, observant and read people the way Reuben read books. He hadn't lived as long as he had without knowing exactly what was going on with the people around him.

I folded my hands over each other. "I'm not a distraction. I'm just a woman trying to reclaim her life from a fucking monster."

I kept my voice low, but loud enough for everyone in the car to hear. Damon in particular. I spent enough time laying blame on myself, I didn't need it from him.

"I didn't ask for what happened to me." No matter how deserved I felt it was, my punishment could have been less extreme. Less traumatising.

"No one said you did," Damon said coolly. "I don't want the boss or Gianni getting killed because they're too busy thinking with their cocks." He glared at a driver who tried to change lanes without indicating.

"Them or you?" I retorted.

Damon didn't respond.

Yeah, that was what I thought.

Gianni chuckled and even Reuben snorted softly. Neither seemed worried about any feelings Damon or his cock had for me.

I sank back into my seat and closed my eyes. During my darkest days back in the cage, right after Kurt left, I pictured what life outside would be like. I knew better than to picture rainbows and unicorns or any of that bullshit. I pictured my family hating me and wanting nothing to do with me. I imagined them turning their backs on me. Maybe not Asher or Rose, but the rest. They'd give me pitying looks and shake their heads.

All of those thoughts were bleak, but realistic to my troubled mind. My mother used to tell me never to dream beyond what we can actually achieve. She expected all of us to achieve a great deal, and never make excuses when we didn't succeed. If we worked hard enough, we didn't need to have frivolous dreams. Everything was within reach, we just had to believe in our abilities. When we fucked up, it was always our fault. Everything was a lesson in doing better the next time.

Never in a million years would I have expected to end up here. The sky above me was bluer than I remembered. Food tasted better. Being touched wasn't as terrifying as I'd become accustomed to. But everything was so much more fucking complicated than I would have dreamt. It was hard to believe any man would care about me, or want me, much less three of them.

Damon was right, they could get killed if they let me distract them. He'd never forgive me and I'd never forgive myself. Maybe I should walk away while I still could. Before I fucked up their lives as well as my own. For their sakes, because I cared about them. Because I'd caused enough damage in the past that I didn't want to pay for any more.

Could I walk away? It would take some time and planning. But one thing I knew for sure. I wasn't going anywhere until I knew Kurt was dead. I needed these three men and their resources to make sure he, and anyone working for him, was gone for good.

Unless…

I chewed my lip and toyed with my options. The first of those was seeing if the man the twins were watching was Kurt.

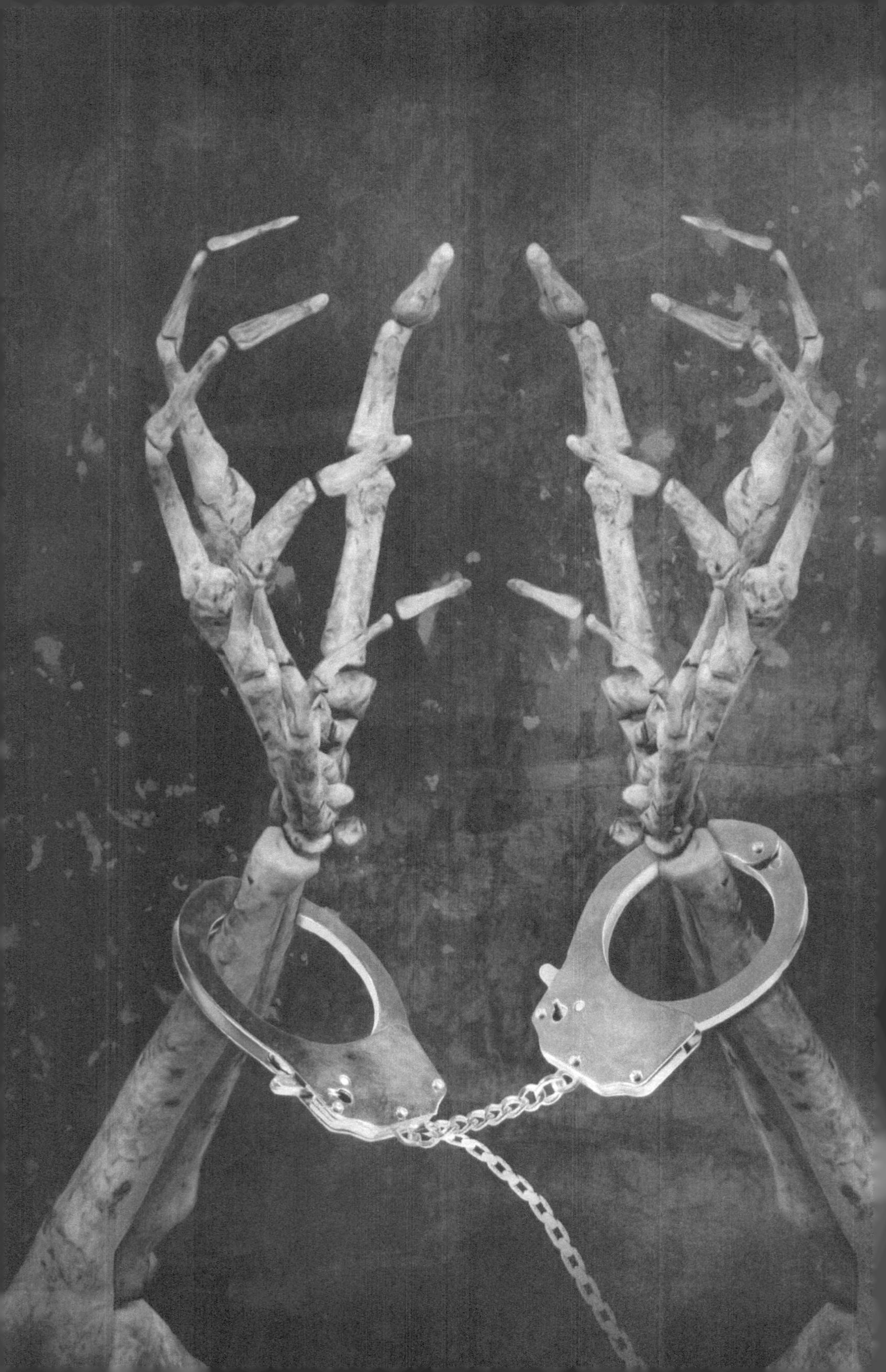

CHAPTER 19

MINA

"Asshole is in there." Hunter leaned closer to a streetlight and jerked his head towards the house at the end of the street.

A light was on, but I couldn't make out anyone inside.

From the outside, the house looked no different to any other in the area. Small, single story, driveway big enough for one car. The bushes at the front were neatly trimmed, as was a short section of grass between the house and the road.

"We didn't get close enough to confirm whether or not it's him," Parker said.

"That's right," Hunter said. "When the notification popped up, we picked him up from near the airport. He matches the description of the asshole on the security camera."

"So he could be anyone?" Damon asked.

"He could be, but my spidey senses tell me otherwise," Hunter said. "And the fact he tried to throw us off his tail three times on the way here. If that doesn't say guilty as shit, nothing else would."

"Sounds guilty as shit to me," Gianni agreed. "I see he didn't manage to lose you."

Parker grinned. "You have to be smarter than this guy to outsmart us."

"Kurt is smart enough to have eluded us up until now," Reuben said. He leaned against the side of his car, his gaze intent on the small house as though he could look right inside.

"Until now, being the key words here," Hunter said. "He wasn't going to be able to do it forever."

"What are you thinking?" Gianni asked me softly.

I blinked a couple of times. "The same thing you're thinking."

He nodded. "This is much too easy."

"Tracking that dickhead here wasn't easy," Parker said. He didn't exactly bristle, but his tone was this side of offended.

"For someone who got away with what he did for so long, it was," Gianni reasoned. "Something about this is off."

"You think this is a trap," Damon stated.

Gianni glanced at him. "You don't? This isn't what you'd do if you were Kurt?"

I shuddered. Damon was prickly, but he was nothing like Kurt.

"If I was that shithead, I'd stay as far away from us as I could get," Damon said. "I'd be well aware my days were numbered. I wouldn't bother trying to lure us into anything."

"Unless he believes he has something up on us," I said. "Some way to convince us to stop hunting him." I wouldn't be surprised what depths he'd sink to in order to get what he wanted.

"Nothing exists that would stop me," Reuben said. "There's nothing he could say, do or threaten."

"What if he was holding Parker and me hostage?" Hunter asked.

Reuben arched an eyebrow at him.

Hunter winced. "Ouch. Thanks a lot, big brother. We love you too."

"Since it's clear he isn't holding you ransom, you're being offended for no reason," Reuben said. He seemed particularly unimpressed.

"It was hypothetical," Hunter grumbled.

Parker put an arm around his twin's shoulders. "You know Reuben would do whatever he had to do to get us free. He just likes to play with us and piss us off. It's his favourite pastime. Maybe it's our fault for telling him to get a hobby. He made this his."

Reuben grunted, but didn't take the bait any further. "Get closer and see if it is Kurt." He nodded to the twins and Gianni, before gesturing for Damon and me to stay with him.

"I can go too," I argued. "If it is him, I need to see." I wouldn't be surprised if Gianni or the twins killed him on sight. I wanted to see him before they could. I wanted to be the one to kill him.

"Mina," Reuben said, his voice even lower than usual.

"Nothing is going to happen to me," I said. "Not with Gianni, Hunter and Parker there too."

"We'll be fine too," Parker said. "Thanks so much for caring."

Reuben glanced at him and smirked.

Parker just grinned and shrugged in response.

Reuben closed his eyes and exhaled, his breath reluctant at best. "If anything happens to you—"

"The twins better be dead first," Gianni finished for him.

"Hey," Hunter protested. "Not you too, Gianni. I thought we were friends."

Gianni grinned. "I'm just saying, that's all. The only way anyone gets to her is through us. For what it's worth, I'd be dead too."

I caught Damon glowering in my direction. Clearly he hadn't changed his stance that I was a distraction. This whole conversation was a perfect example.

I reached into the back of the car, opened the box and pulled out two knives. Without another word, I headed through the darkness, toward the house.

"Shit." Gianni hurried to catch up. The twins weren't far behind.

"Just remember it might not be him," Gianni said as we stepped past the other houses and slowed. As tempting as it was to break down the front door, it wasn't subtle and he was right.

I didn't want another innocent person to get hurt or killed because of me.

"At this point, I don't give a shit if it is him or not," Hunter said. "I'm enjoying myself. The expression on Reuben's face was fucking priceless." He offered his twin a fist bump.

"Enjoy it quieter," Gianni said. "Both of you go around the back. See if you can find a window to look through." He took my hand and pulled me down into the shadows near some bushes.

I forced myself not to flinch, or squeeze his hand for reassurance. I needed to be cool, calm and rational right now. Anything else would be dangerous for all of us.

The twins nodded before slipping away into the darkness.

"Call me crazy, but this shit is the most fun part of the job to me," Gianni whispered. "The anticipation of what might come next is next level."

"I like knowing exactly what's coming next," I whispered back.

I preferred careful planning and a flawless execution, to running into a situation and hoping for the best. Sometimes the latter was all you could do, but the former was easier to control.

Admittedly, it was almost impossible to control every aspect of anything. With that in mind, I was always flexible and watching for unexpected variables.

"I like coming," Gianni said lightly. "Especially when you're involved."

I snorted softly. Everything had to come back to sex, didn't it?

"It's not my fault if situations like this turn me on," he added. "With you next to me, it's even hotter." He adjusted the front of his pants and looked pained. Judging by the tenting, he was ready to go again.

"You're not planning to sneak off and fuck are you?" Parker asked. He slipped back through the shadows and crouched beside us. "He's still in there, but I can't make out anything more than a shape moving around. There's blinds on the back of the house that don't have convenient peepholes in them. So inconsiderate."

"I knew this guy was an asshole." Hunter crouched beside Parker. "He could have left one of the blinds open."

"How thoughtless of him to want privacy," I said sarcastically. Kurt didn't deserve any, but if it wasn't him, then we shouldn't be peeking in. There might be an innocent woman or child on the other side of that blind. The twins hadn't mentioned seeing anyone else, but that didn't necessarily mean they weren't here.

"She gets it." Hunter offered me a fist bump.

I brushed my fist over his before quickly pulling it back. "I guess we're going to have to do this a different way."

"The direct route," Gianni agreed. "We walk right up to the front door and knock. I know, it's an old-fashioned thing to do, but I think we can pull it off."

"Knocking on the front door is so lame," Parker complained.

"Yes, it is, but that's what we're going to do," Gianni said. "At least, that's what I'm going to do. The three of you are going to stay here."

Before anyone could argue, he rose and strode toward the door like he had every reason to be there.

Without hesitating, I rose and followed him.

"I told you to stay back there," Gianni said conversationally.

"So you did," I said. "I decided not to. Kurt knows what you look like."

"He knows what you look like too," Gianni said. "If he tries anything, you should be far enough away to be able to run."

"I want to be close enough to stop him," I said. "You know what I can do with a knife."

"I also know you're traumatised by what he did." Gianni stopped short of the front steps. "Trauma and fear can make people hesitate."

He was right, but not in this situation. I couldn't let myself freak out. If I did, Kurt won. Fuck that.

"I won't hesitate," I insisted. "I can do this. Not to mention, there's nothing you could say that would make me back away now. We're doing this."

He sighed out his nose. "Woman, you're making me hard as fuck again. Fine, just be careful, okay? The longer this goes on, the more desperate Kurt will be. The more desperate he is, the more chance there is that he'll do something stupid. The stupider it is, the more likelihood we die. The more dead we are, the better chance I haunt his ass. No one wants that because I will be noisy as fuck." His teeth flashed white in the darkness.

"I'll be careful," I promised. "I don't want either of us to end up dead." The reality of that surprised me. At some point during the last few weeks, I'd started wanting to live again. I had things to live for now. Hope that my life wasn't a complete cluster fuck. I also really, really didn't want Gianni to die. The idea made my heart hurt.

"Okay, let's do this." He slipped his hand into mine and we took the front steps together, side-by-side.

A single light illuminated the front door. Painted off-white, it looked fresh, as though the whole house was recently renovated.

Gianni tapped on the door.

A shuffling came from inside the house, followed by footsteps.

"If you're looking for Courtney she's not—" The door slid open smoothly.

My heart bottomed out. The man standing just inside the door wasn't Kurt, but the resemblance was strong enough to knock the breath out of my body.

"We're not looking for Courtney," Gianni said easily, like they were having a pleasant chat. "Although, she's a lovely person. Really sweet. No, we were looking for someone else. A guy named Gustav. I know he lives around here somewhere. Do you know which house is his?" He twisted his upper body and gestured back toward the street.

The man looked confused. "I don't know no Gustav. I only just moved in here, I don't know anyone in the area. How do you know Courtney?" His eyes narrowed like he was trying to figure out what Gianni's angle was. And if he could get the door closed fast enough.

Gianni grinned. "I don't, I was just guessing. You seem like the kind of guy who likes his women sweet. I mean, don't we all?" He glanced over at me.

I smirked in response. I wouldn't consider myself to be sweet. Anything but.

"I guess so," the man said uncertainly. "Like I said, I can't help you."

"That's a shame," Gianni said. "That's okay though, we'll keep looking. He must be around here somewhere. A guy like Gustav is difficult to hide. He's the kind who stands out in a crowd, if you know what I mean." He turned away from the door and back towards the steps.

Before I followed, I pinned the man with a look. "Do you know Kurt Lasalle?"

His brief moment of hesitation was all the answer I needed.

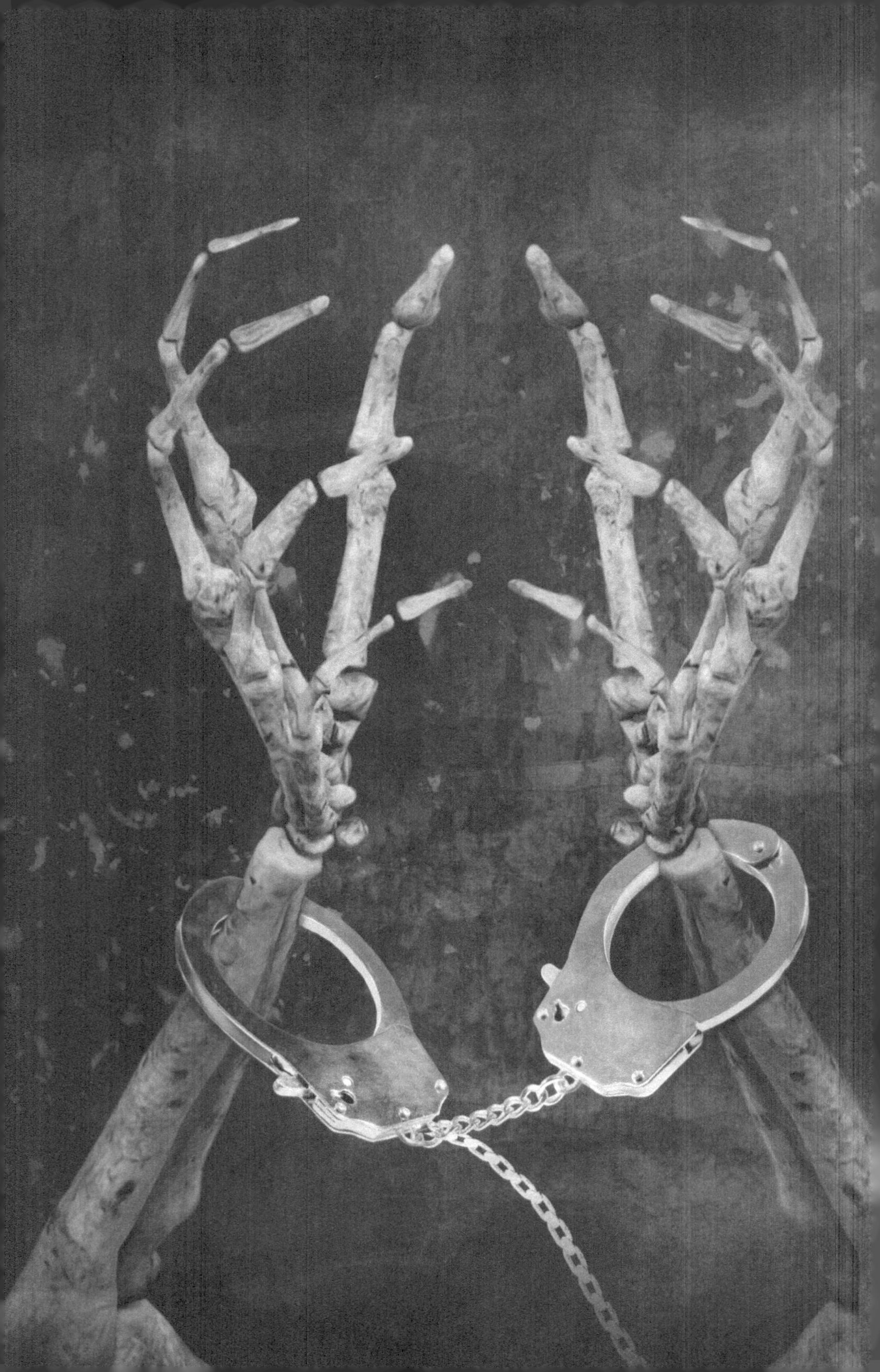

CHAPTER 20

MINA

Before he could take another breath, I had a knife to his throat and was pushing him back into the house, my fingertips barely touching his chest.

He stepped back so fast he almost tripped and fell. He spread his arms to either side to balance himself and lunged for a gun that lay on a table beside the door.

"Don't fucking touch it," I said. The tip of my knife was right against his jugular. It would be a simple matter to slice it open.

He froze, his hand hovered over it before he pulled his arms back in.

"Where is he?" I snarled.

"I don't know," he stammered. "I swear. He contacted me through a mutual acquaintance. Offered me ten grand to come here. That was all. I never met him and I don't know why he wanted me to come here."

His voice was high. He seemed ready to piss his pants.

"Who is this mutual acquaintance?" I asked.

"Let me guess." Gianni followed us inside. "Courtney?"

"I never met her either," he insisted. "She was some chick I met online. For all I know, she doesn't even exist. I needed the money, that's all I fucking know. I'll swear on anything you want. My phone is over there, on the table. You can see all the conversations I had with her." He jerked his head to the side.

"Pick it up," I said. If this was some kind of trap, the phone could be hiding a bomb or who knows what else.

He inched over, scooped up the phone and offered it to me.

"Open it," I said.

He hesitated.

Gianni scooped up the man's gun from the table and aimed it at his temple. "You heard the woman."

The man swallowed, but tapped on the screen to open the phone and enter the message app. He offered it to me, but Gianni took it first.

"Let's see what this motherfucker has to say for himself."

"Are you having fun without us?" Hunter stepped inside the house, Parker behind him.

"It looks like it," Parker said. "I like a woman who knows how to handle a knife."

"Don't even think about it or you won't be able to handle anything ever again," Gianni said pleasantly. "You'll find life more difficult without hands."

Parker chuckled. "Chill out, I was just making an observation."

Gianni grunted and returned his attention to the phone. "Dick pics? Really? You're old enough to know better."

"I thought she was legit," the man whined.

"Well, StudMuffin69, I think you've been had," Gianni said. "Or should I say, Frank."

"Stud muffin?" Hunter cracked up laughing. "He wishes."

I ignored him. "Is there any indication of where Kurt is right now? Some reason why he set this up?"

"My guess is he hired Frank here as a distraction." Gianni tossed the phone back on the table. "I don't think he knows Jack shit."

"I really don't," Frank said frantically. "All I know is what you saw there. I was told to take that flight to Sydney, make sure those two noticed me and come here." He tilted his head towards the twins, the movement subtle and nervous.

"Was he supposed to contact you with more instructions?" I directed the question at Frank and Gianni.

"If there's anything else, he deleted it," Gianni said. "Or Kurt hasn't contacted him again yet."

"Parker and I will report to Reuben," Hunter said. "He'll want to know if this has something to do with us and not Mina."

I watched Frank's eyes for any reaction to Hunter saying my name, but discerned nothing. If this was anything to do with me, he didn't know about it.

"Now, what do we do with Frank here?" Gianni asked. He picked the phone back up and tucked it into his pocket. "If Kurt tries to contact him, he can go through me. But it seems to me that if Frank doesn't know anything, he's no use to us."

"Please," Frank groaned. He swallowed hard. "I don't know anything, I swear. You have my phone, I can't contact him again. I don't know where he is. Fuck, I don't even know *who* he is. He might not be real either."

I wished he wasn't, but he was, and the reality was that he'd want to speak to Frank about this whole incident. After Kurt ran, he might have assumed I died in that cage. Frank seeing me would be proof that didn't happen.

But only if I left him alive.

I pressed the blade more firmly against his throat.

"Daddy?" A small voice came from the back of the room.

I looked away from Frank, to see a girl of five or six years old, standing in what looked like a bedroom doorway. She wore pyjamas that covered her feet, so she was head to toe in pink and purple unicorns. Her dark hair was messy, her eyes looked heavy with sleep. We must have woken her up.

"What the hell?" Gianni whispered, echoing my thoughts.

"It's okay, Holly, go back to bed. Everything will be okay." Frank slid a smile in her direction, trying to be reassuring while clearly scared out of his wits.

It was my turn to freeze. My mind went back to a night a bit over five years ago.

A tangle of dark curls. Huge eyes that looked back at me with no hint of understanding.

She shouldn't have been there.

She wasn't part of the plan.

I should have known.

I should have anticipated.

I should have been able to stop myself.

The blood on my hands was hers. I never meant to spill a drop, but I had. She died in my arms. I felt the life slip away from her. Bit by bit, drop by drop. There was nothing I could do or say to stop it from happening. The second our lives intersected, hers was over.

Her body went still and cold while I held her. So tiny. Small and innocent and gone. Her pale yellow pyjamas turned sickly orange with her blood. The smiley faces on the fabric grinned at me in accusation. Mocking me.

I fucked up.

I fucked up badly and she paid the price.

I stepped back from Frank and lowered the knife. "No one said anything about a kid."

"Her mother had to work late," Frank said. "She brought her in through the back so she wouldn't be seen. This wasn't about her."

"No it wasn't," I agreed. "She shouldn't be here." Like that other little girl wasn't supposed to be there that night. She was dead because of it. Like Holly would have been if Kurt set a trap for us all.

"I'll take her home," Frank said. "I don't need to be here either." He stepped backward towards the little girl. Held out his hand to her.

"Word of advice," Gianni said. "Stay away from creeps on the Internet. There's a lot of shady people out there. You got paid?"

"Yeah," I did," Frank said. Holly slipped her hand into his.

"Then take it and get out of here," Gianni said. "Don't talk about what happened here and don't look back."

Frank picked up Holly and rested her on his hip. "No one will hear about this from me. I swear that on my daughter's life." She clearly meant everything to him. He wouldn't say anything to anyone, if only because we knew she existed too. Some people wouldn't hesitate to use a child to further themselves. Especially someone like Kurt. I didn't want to think about what he might do to her if he got anywhere near her.

I put the knife away and watched while they hurried to gather Holly's things and slip out the back door.

"You okay, sweetheart?" Gianni asked. "You look like you saw a ghost when that kid appeared."

"I didn't expect to see her there," I said. That much was true. The rest was something I wasn't ready to talk about yet. What would he think of me if he knew? My own father sent me to Kurt when he found out. If someone who was supposed to love me would do that, then there was nothing I could put past anyone, no matter their feelings for me. I may find myself back in that cage, or dead.

No, that was better kept to myself.

"I'll be having words with those twins about missing that piece of vital information," Gianni said. He twirled the gun around his middle finger.

I might have a few with them myself. In the meantime, I had more questions than answers. Why had Kurt wanted Frank to lead the twins here? I remembered what Daze said about him being smart and meticulous. There was no way in hell he'd do all of this for no reason. If he wanted to distract us, then there was something he wanted us to be distracted from. What the fuck was he up to?

"Come on, Reuben and Damon will want to know you're okay." Gianni took a step towards the door.

Before he stepped outside, he stopped and turned around. "I might not be the handsomest or smartest guy around, but I know when something is up. I saw the expression on your face when you saw that kid. Something happened. I don't give a shit what it was but I'll tell you this."

He pointed a finger in the direction of my nose. "It wasn't your fault. All of this, it might just have been some kind of set up. Some way for that prick to fuck with your head. If that's all it was, don't let him get to you. He doesn't deserve to live rent-free in your head. He deserves a fucking bullet in his."

He lowered his hand and nodded once like that was that, end of story.

I pressed my lips together and rolled them a couple of times. "You might be biased."

He didn't know the circumstances and he wasn't going to hear them from me tonight.

He was guessing, based on his feelings for me. Feelings that were sweet, but were they misplaced?

Seeing that kid standing there tonight brought everything back into painfully sharp focus. Maybe Kurt was fucking with me, but he'd succeeded in rattling me. He'd gotten right back into my head. Reminding me of who and what I was.

I wasn't sweet little Mina anymore. I hadn't been for a long time. Longer than most people knew. Everyone except my father, and a couple of other people, including Kurt.

"If I'm biased, I don't give a shit," Gianni said. "I meant what I said. Whatever the fuck went down, I don't blame you for it. Not even if anyone else does, you've more than paid the price. I'll fucking tell them all that too."

He fixed me with a look like that was that, whether I liked it or not. His determination was endearing, as was his blind faith. He'd made up his mind and no one and nothing was going to change it for him. Or so he thought. The reality might end up being very different. He might end up being the one with his heart torn clean out of his chest.

"Yeah," I said softly.

We stepped out the front door of the house and back down the steps.

We reached the street as Frank bundled Holly into a small hatchback. The vehicle looked old enough to back up his story about needing money. It had definitely seen better days.

He glanced over his shoulder at us before quickly jumping into the driver's seat. The door slammed behind him with a thud before he roared off down the street and was gone.

A heartbeat later, the house beside us exploded into flames.

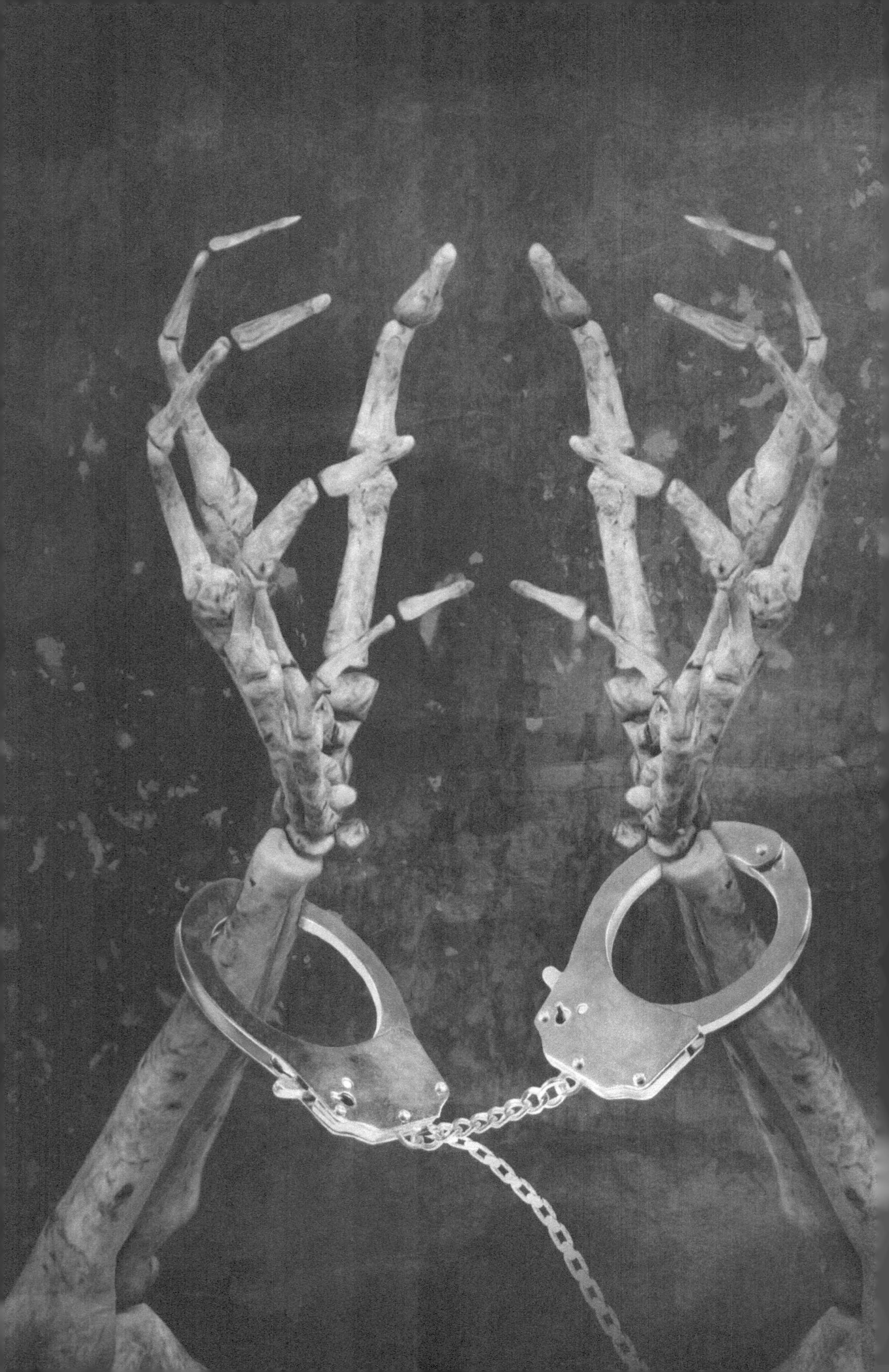

CHAPTER 21

MINA

Gianni pushed me off my feet and threw himself over me, arms wrapped around me tight.

I landed on the footpath with a thud, forced my eyes shut, and curled up as small as I could.

He let out a grunt of pain. His ragged breath was hot on the side of my face. Fingers dug into my hip, holding frantically while hell rained down behind us.

I heard a shout, but couldn't make out the words past the ringing in my ears.

Gianni's body pressed against me was overwhelming. Conflicting. Both comforting and terrifying at the same time.

Finally, everything fell. Everything but the pounding in my heart and the roaring of blood through my veins.

"Mina?" Reuben's voice sounded distant, like he was talking through a tunnel.

Someone helped Gianni to his feet. His weight was suddenly gone from me.

I opened my eyes and squinted.

Reuben crouched beside me.

"I'm okay." I rolled over and sat up. "Gianni?"

Gianni waved me down. "I'm all good. The back of my shirt might be a little singed." He grabbed the hem and pulled it around to frown at it.

"I'll buy you another shirt," Damon told him. He stood between Gianni and the burning house, flames dancing in the night behind him.

"I knew you cared." Gianni gave him a quick hug before he too crouched down beside me. "You okay, sweetheart?"

"I'm fine," I said vaguely.

My eyes were on the destroyed house. "He did this." I was both horrified and more furious than I ever remembered being. "He knew I'd be here."

"He was probably hoping we'd still be inside," Gianni said.

"The prick seemed to be targeting us." Hunter approached from the shadows, appearing unhurt.

"It does seem a bit personal." Parker was right behind him. "I'm officially offended."

"Me too," Gianni agreed.

"Get out of here," Reuben told the twins. "Gianni, Mina, back in the SUV. I want to be gone from here before the police arrive. Damon, have people move into the area and keep an eye out for Kurt."

"Good idea, boss," Gianni said. He stood with a wince of pain.

Reuben offered me his hand to help me to my feet. His usual closed expression was laced with concern and anger.

"He's fucking with us," I said.

"Or he misjudged," Reuben said quietly. "He might have expected you to be inside for longer."

"Possibly both," Damon suggested. He had his phone to his ear, his expression tight.

Once again, I had more questions than answers. Was he somewhere nearby, deliberately waiting until we were clear before setting up the explosion? Or had he timed it wrong? Did he have any idea a child would be in the house tonight? If he did, he must have known how I'd respond. Was it aimed at me or, like the twins suggested, they were the target?

My lips pressed together, I followed Reuben to the SUV and let him help me inside.

Gianni grimaced, but settled down beside me. "I should say thank you again," I said. "For protecting me. You could have been killed."

"Better me than you, sweetheart," he said. He seemed a lot less cheerful than he usually was. If anything, he seemed rattled. I wouldn't have thought it was possible if I hadn't seen it for myself. Nothing seemed to get to him like this had.

"I'm not that easy to kill." The smile he gave me was forced.

"If we were still inside, or a metre or two closer, we would have been," I said. "Five minutes earlier and he would have killed a child." I watched Gianni's expression carefully.

"Lucky for her he didn't," Gianni said.

"What would you have done if he had?" I asked.

Gianni shrugged. "If she was dead, chances are I would be too."

"But if you weren't?" I pressed. "If you were alive and she was dead, what would you do?"

"In this particular case, we're already hunting him down and want him dead. That hasn't changed." He looked curious as to why I was asking. Enough so that I decided to back off before he was the one with the questions.

"I guess we can't kill him twice," I conceded.

"Technically, we can," he said with a grin. "I have a friend who brought a guy back to life three or four times, just to see how many times he could. But he's a sadistic fuck if I ever met one. On the other hand, that comes with the territory."

"Some people get more enjoyment out of it than others," Damon said from the driver's seat.

"I'd suggest Damon was talking about himself, but I've never known him to get off on other people's suffering," Gianni said.

"Did you just say something nice about me?" Damon asked.

"I guess I did, in a roundabout way," Gianni agreed. "Did you like it?"

"I could get used to you not being an asshole," Damon said.

I leaned my head back against the seat and watched the city lights flash by as we passed.

This whole night was a lot to process. Was Kurt nearby, watching us? I sensed that he wasn't, but no more than that. Without doubt, he'd engineered all of this, but whether things went to plan or not, I had no idea.

I couldn't discount the idea he hoped Reuben and Damon would step into the house with Gianni and me. If that was the case, why not set off the explosion before we left? He would have caught at least two of us if he had.

Although, he'd had five years to kill me if he wanted to. He hadn't. He preferred to toy with me. If that was his plan, then he'd try something else to get to me. If we didn't get to him first.

"We're being followed," Damon said, breaking through my thoughts.

Gianni and I both swivelled around in our seats and looked out the back window. The traffic was light, and the dark vehicle made no attempt to hide the fact they were tailing us.

When Damon turned down a side street, they turned too. When he steered the SUV back onto the main road, they stayed right with us.

They made no attempt to get closer to us until a couple of streets from home. There, they manoeuvred themselves so close the front of their car almost touched the rear of the SUV.

"Hang on," Damon said. He slowed the SUV right down, before pressing his foot hard on the accelerator and jumping forward. He took a bend so fast I thought the tyres on the right-hand side of the car might lift off the road.

I grabbed hold of the handle above the door beside me and held on tight.

Gianni had his gun out, but made no attempt to use it. "Bullet-proof glass," he explained. "Works both ways."

Damon slowed the car down again, and Gianni lowered the window beside him. He stuck his hand out and got off a couple of shots in the direction of the sedan. One hit the side of the windscreen and left a crack, but the sedan didn't slow.

Gianni pulled his hand back in and closed the window. "Fuckers have bullet-proof glass too. I guess they mean business."

"We're not usually followed by people who don't mean business," Reuben said. He sounded as though this happened regularly.

I glanced forward to see him quickly shooting off a text message. A few moments later, his phone flashed with a return message.

"Keep driving," he said. "The twins can be here in three minutes. They're still in the area."

"Got it, boss," Damon said. He resumed driving at a normal speed, weaving through traffic.

I didn't know Sydney well enough anymore to know where we were going, but the traffic and houses gradually thinned, leaving us in a more industrial part of the city. Somewhere less likely to contain crowds or innocent people. Somewhere with less chance of collateral damage. Or, maybe, more places for us to hide.

Reuben's phone lit up again. "The twins are on their tail." For a moment I thought he might leave this to them, but then he said, "Find somewhere to pull over."

"Got it, boss," Damon said again. He didn't question the orders, just drove past a handful of cars and into an empty parking lot in front of a tyre shop.

The car that was tailing us followed us in, another dark sedan right behind them. They must have realised the twins were there, because they turned a tight circle and drove right out of the car park, past the twin's car.

"That was anticlimactic," Gianni remarked.

"You spoke too soon," Damon said.

The sedan stopped sideways across the exit leading out of the car park. The doors opened and several figures stepped out.

"Looks like party time after all," Gianni said. He turned to me. "Is there any chance we can convince you to stay in the car?"

I smiled slightly and pulled out my knives. "Nope."

He sighed dramatically. "That was what I thought. Boss?"

"Keep her safe," was all Reuben said before he opened his own door and stepped out of the SUV.

I slipped out but stayed near the car, using the vehicle as a shield. Just because I'd spent five years living out of the world, didn't mean I was oblivious to the futility of having knives at a gunfight. If I had an opportunity to use them, I would. Otherwise, I'd stay out of the way.

Reuben stayed beside me, Damon and Gianni on either side of us, guns trained on the approaching figures.

In the corner of my eye, I saw the twins get out of their vehicle, guns in their hands.

"This is an interesting place for a chat," Gianni said, loud enough for everyone to hear.

"This isn't a chat." The first of the strangers, a man in his forties with a long chin, said.

"I thought not." Gianni raised his gun and shot him in the centre of his forehead.

The other three dropped back, crouching on the other side of the SUV.

"We came to deliver a message," one of them called out.

"Why can't these motherfuckers learn to text?" came from the direction of the twins. "Even Reuben can text."

"What message?" Damon asked.

"Kurt Lasalle said to back the fuck off."

"We have no intention of backing off," Reuben said coldly. A heartbeat later he said, "Kill them."

Apparently he wasn't in the mood to follow the suggestion of whoever said not to kill the messenger.

Before anyone could move to follow his orders, another two dark sedans stopped behind the first, further blocking the exit.

"Shit just got real," Gianni said.

Damon hummed his agreement. "Too fucking real."

CHAPTER 22

REUBEN

I rubbed a hand over my forehead. A headache threatened. They usually did on nights like this.

I reached into the SUV to pull out a gun for myself. Reluctantly, I handed one to Mina.

I should insist she stay in the car, but under the circumstances, we needed her, and knives would not be enough. Not unless they got a lot closer. None of us had any intention of them getting anywhere near her.

She eyed the gun, but slipped the knives away and took it. As I would have expected of her, she checked to make sure it was loaded and the safety was off. Old, well-learned skills were hard to forget. Impossible with our lifestyle.

I turned my attention back to the new vehicles. Two people stepped out of each one, all on the opposite side, keeping their vehicle between us and them.

Unless others hid in the back, then it was six against seven. Three crouching on the other side of the SUV and four out on the street. We'd faced worse.

Gianni dropped down low and crab-walked silently to the end of the SUV. After a moment, Damon followed. They slid around the front, their movement followed by a painfully loud gunshot, then another.

They threw themselves back behind the SUV.

"One down," Gianni grinned. "One of them almost took a couple of hairs off my head."

Lucky the shot wasn't lower than that.

Without a word, Mina dropped to her stomach on the concrete. For half a second, I thought she'd been shot. That was until the gun in her hand flashed once, twice.

Shouts of pain came from the other side of the vehicle.

"My fucking foot!"

Laughing, Gianni darted back around the front of the SUV and finished off the last two attackers with a shot each.

Damon grunted his approval of Mina's tactic. Injuring them by shooting them in the feet or ankles was the perfect distraction. Unorthodox, but perfect.

She stayed down on the ground, her gun trained on the last two sedans. They were too far away to get a good shot under them, but if the attackers stepped out from behind them, they'd be fair game.

"I told you she was fucking hot." Gianni joined us behind our vehicle. "Foot shot. I'm going to remember that one."

She glanced up at him, but her expression was unreadable. Half a shrug and her attention was back on the car park in front of her.

"We need to draw them out," Damon said. "Can you make it over to the twins' car?"

I nodded. They were a handful of metres away at most, probably growing irritated that they hadn't killed anyone yet. Or at least maimed them. They weren't the kind who got off on killing either, not exactly, but if anyone attacked any of us, they'd want to make them pay. They were a pair of clowns at times, but they had zero tolerance for enemies.

All of us Brantley men had that in common. Even Zeke, although he wouldn't admit it.

"Mina," I said.

She glanced up like she might argue.

"Go with them," Damon told her. When he took that tone, not even I would bother to argue with him. He wouldn't budge.

With a sigh, she rose. She and Gianni bolted a few metres to the other car.

I followed along more slowly. Confident if anyone stepped out to shoot me, they'd end up dead first.

"Nice of you to join us," Hunter said with his usual smug grin. "We were getting lonely over here."

"Hunter was getting lonely," Parker said. "I was getting bored."

"Sorry to disappoint you with the lack of excitement tonight," I said sarcastically. "Next time, I'll organise three explosions and twice the amount of enemies."

Both twins laughed and Gianni chuckled. Mina's expression remained unchanged. She was completely focused on those other two sedans. Laser focused like nothing else in the world was happening right now. I'd only seen her look like that on— I shook my head. That was something I'd have to think about later.

I turned back to my SUV as the engine turned over. Damon put the car into reverse and backed up to the edge of the car park. He revved a couple of times before the car surged forward, flying across the concrete towards the two sedans.

"Holy shit," Gianni said in disbelief.

I silently agreed with them. When Damon suggested a distraction, this wasn't what I thought he had in mind.

The engine roared, the SUV not slowing a hair as it drew closer to the sedans.

At the last second, all four attackers leapt out from behind them, scattering in different directions.

The SUV slammed into the sedans, driving into the gap between them. The front of one and the rear of the other crumpled. They were forced apart with a squeal of steel and the smell of burning rubber.

I was still trying to process what Damon just did when Gianni and Hunter darted out from behind the vehicle and shot two of the attackers before they could flee.

"Reuben," Mina said in warning.

I turned.

One of the attackers had run around and came up behind us. They barely raised their gun before a knife appeared in the centre of their forehead. Blood blossomed on their skin and their eyes widened before they slumped to the ground.

Mina stood with the other knife in one hand, gun in the other, her hair caked to her temples with sweat. She looked fucking beautiful.

"I don't know where the last one is," she said, eyes scanning the area.

"A long way from here if they have any brains," I said.

She shook her head, the movement so brief I almost missed it. "They're still here."

I knew better than to question instincts when it came to things like this. Instincts kept us alive. Her instincts saved my life. If she said they were here, then they were.

I stayed perfectly still, also scanning the area. Whatever she sensed, I felt nothing, but I was better at giving orders than I was at this. I had no trouble admitting that. My skills were different, not flawed.

"Stay there," she whispered.

"I don't—" I started to say.

She cut me off with a look. "I can do this. Stay here."

If anyone else spoke to me that way, I'd growl at them. Her tone and the look on her face convinced me to nod and stay back near the car.

"Be safe," was all I could say.

She nodded in return and slipped away into the darkness.

"Where did she go?" Gianni asked. He had one eye on me and the other on the SUV. Clearly torn between protecting me and staying near Mina, and seeing if Damon was okay.

"I don't—" I was interrupted by a grunt from several metres away. That was followed by a thud. "There, I think. Go check on Damon." It was clearly not a female grunt. Not Mina's anyway. That should account for all of them.

Gianni hesitated, then nodded. "On it, boss." Gun still in his hand, he trotted to the SUV, followed by the twins.

I waited until Mina returned a minute or two later. She looked exhausted.

"That's the last of them," she confirmed. "He was trying to sneak up on you. Or on me." She shrugged. "Either way, he won't be sneaking anywhere again."

She made to trudge past me towards where the others were helping Damon out of the SUV. As far as I could tell, he was unhurt, apart from a few bruises.

In spite of the impact, the front of the SUV protected him. Of course it did, I paid good money to have vehicles that would stand up to anything we put them through. Bullets, crashes, explosions. That was money well spent.

I reached out and grabbed Mina's elbow. Even when she flinched, I didn't let it go.

"Take a moment," I said softly. "Damon is okay."

"I'm not—" she started to say.

"You're as tired as the rest of us," I said. "More so. You're still recovering."

She stopped and turned back to me. Her focused, professional mask eased somewhat, if it didn't melt away completely.

"Everyone is okay." She blinked as though suddenly realising that.

"Everyone is fine, thanks to you," I said. "And Damon." And Gianni too, but she and Damon were exceptional tonight.

She seemed to crumble a little. Her throat bobbed as she swallowed hard.

Taking the chance that I wouldn't freak her out, I wrapped my arms around her and pulled her to my chest.

She hesitated for a moment before leaning into me and letting herself be held.

I rubbed a hand up and down her back and held her as tight as I dared. If she was anyone else, I would have expected her to cry, but she didn't. She just let me hold her while she composed herself again.

She fit perfectly into the circle of my arms, like she was made to be there. The scent of her was more addictive than anything I'd ever experienced before. I wanted to inhale enough of it to imprint it on my mind forever.

She finally pulled back and looked up at me. "Just another regular Tuesday?"

I snorted softly. "Fuck no. This is more like a regular Thursday. Tuesdays are usually quieter."

She grimaced but managed a short laugh. "Remind me to stay in the library and read on a Thursday night."

"And miss a chance to see Damon crash a car like a fucking rally driver?" Gianni had his arm over Damon's shoulders as they approached us. "That was fucking epic. I don't know who made me harder tonight, Mina or Damon. It might be a tie."

"We all know it was me," Hunter said from behind them. "I have that effect on everyone."

"You don't have that effect on me," Parker told him.

Hunter made a face. "Thank fuck for that."

I rolled my eyes at them. "Both of you can get out of here now."

They gave me identical, meaningful looks.

I sighed. "Thank you for coming to help. Even though it's what I pay you for. And neither of you did what Damon did. Or what Mina did. Or—"

"You're welcome," they both said before I could finish. They high-fived each other before getting back into their car and driving the car up a section of gutter, over grass and back onto the street.

I shook my head. If anything in my life was constant, it was those two and how ridiculous they could be. But they were here when we needed them and that was what mattered.

I made a mental note to give them both a pay raise. In a week or two, when all of this was forgotten.

"I'll drive," Gianni said. "Damon can sit in the back and relax."

"I should be grumpy about the scratches on my SUV," I said. "But, good work. That took some balls." I didn't really give a fuck about scratches or dents on a piece of equipment. They were easily replaced. The people I could trust were not. They were few and far between as it was.

Damon nodded. "I had to prove mine were bigger than Gianni's somehow." His expression was perfectly deadpan.

"If you wanted to compare ball size, you only had to ask," Gianni said. "I'd happily show you mine." He patted the front of his jeans.

"Maybe later." Damon trudged back to the SUV and all but fell into the back.

"That wasn't a no," Gianni pointed out. "Maybe I could rub your back for you when we get home. We'd hate for those muscles to tighten up after crashing a perfectly good car."

He grinned and opened the other back door for Mina.

She let me walk over with her and help her into the back. I didn't want to let her go, but I had to step back and let Gianni close the door. The feeling of holding her like that was going to linger on my senses for a long time.

I was going to need a long shower and my hand on my cock to get any sleep tonight.

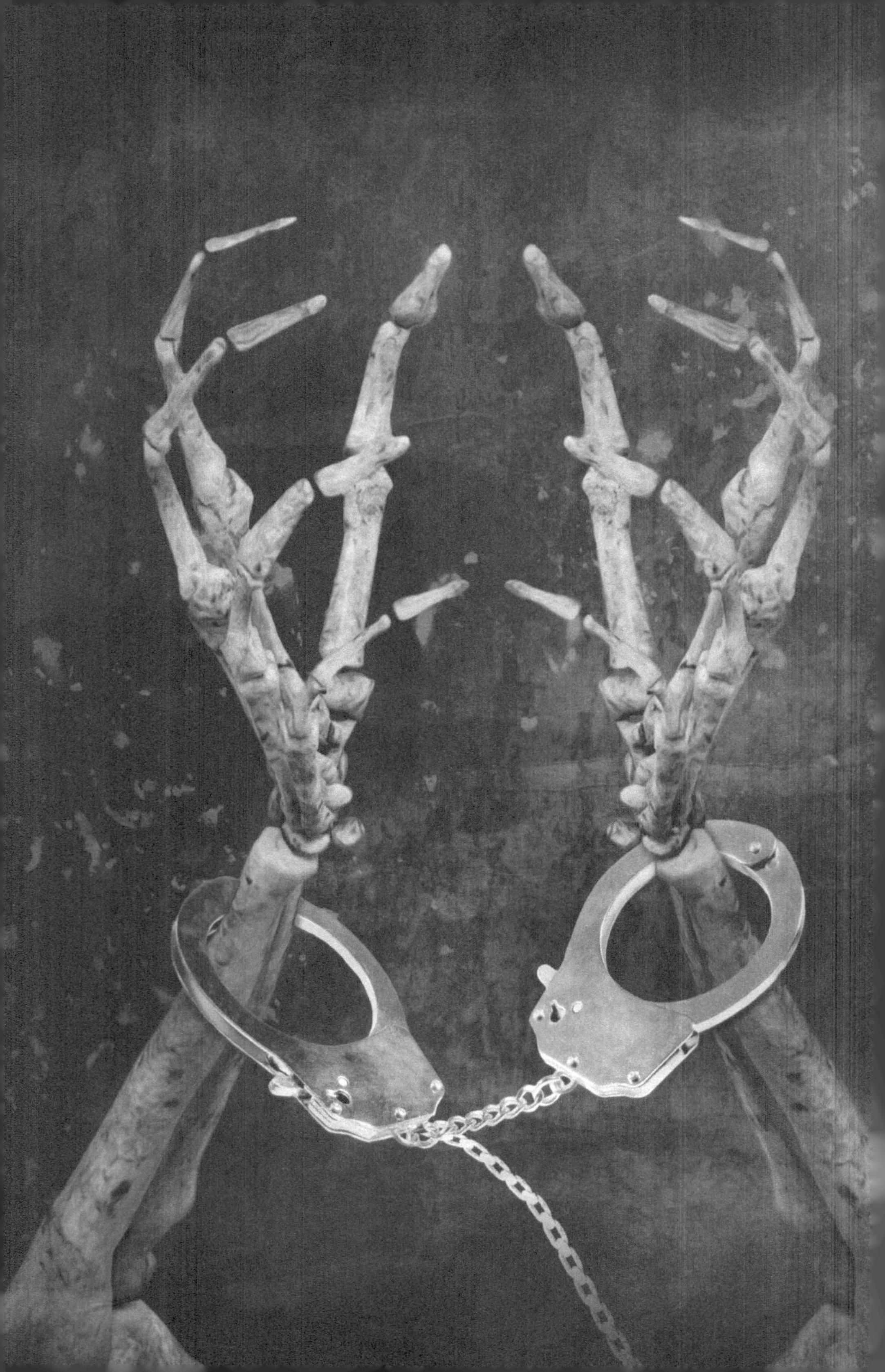

CHAPTER 23

MINA

I held my mug in both hands, half-watching the steam rise off my tea.

"That was a hell of a thing you did." I glanced over to Damon, who sat hunched over the table.

He shrugged one shoulder. "I knew the SUV was up to it." He sipped a drink which was more alcohol than coffee.

"You could have been wrong," I pointed out.

He looked back over to me and scoffed before turning back to his drink. "I wasn't."

"If you were, you'd be dead now. Or worse." I blew lightly on the steam and watched it dance away.

I hadn't been able to sleep, so I figured I'd come down here and have something that might relax me. It seemed he had the same problem.

"I'm sure you wouldn't have minded too much," he said. "If I was dead, I mean."

"It helped us to get out alive," I said lightly. Of course I didn't want him dead, or injured, but if he was going to play the grumpy asshole, I'd play along.

He turned back to me and smirked. "That's what's important. Princess Mina walking away unhurt."

I rolled my eyes. "Please, I'm no more a princess than you are. We both know why you did what you did."

He swivelled around and propped his elbow on the table. "Why don't you enlighten me? Don't try to paint me as some fucking hero."

"Why not?" I asked. "Is there something wrong with doing a brave thing? Whether or not you thought the SUV was up to smashing head-first into another two cars, it's above your pay grade." I stopped and crinkled my brow. "You're right. Now I think about it, it was a dumbass move. You could have gotten yourself killed and wrecked a perfectly good car."

He arched an eyebrow at me.

"But you did it because you care," I said slowly. "Because, at the end of the day, this is a family. Reuben is more than a boss to you. Gianni is more than a co-worker. The twins too, I'm guessing." I sipped my tea and watched his expression.

"Could be," he said. "Or I'm a reckless dumbass who gets off on driving fast and smashing shit up."

"Maybe both," I said. "I didn't say you weren't a dumbass that cared."

He grunted. "You're making me out to be something I'm not. Someone had to do something and I did. That's all there was to it. Nothing fucking more and nothing fucking less."

"If you say so," I said lightly.

"I do say so." He turned away again.

"Why is it so difficult to accept that someone appreciates something you did?" I asked.

"Reuben told me you went off by yourself to kill the last of the attackers," Damon said, his voice low. "What did you do? Cut their throat like you did with that woman?"

My pulse sped up, blood thudding through my ears like it had when I walked through the darkness, hunting before I struck.

"Yes, I did. It was the quickest and cleanest thing I could do at the time. The most efficient."

"Why did you do it?" He turned back around to face me. "You could have let them come to you. Reuben or Gianni would have shot them. You didn't have to do a thing."

He was trying to bait me. To make me admit that I did what had to be done. As if somehow that would lessen what he did. I wasn't going to take it.

"I did it because I didn't want anyone else getting hurt," I said. "Because this is my family too."

"Even though you could have been killed," he said. "You don't think that was reckless?"

I didn't think that in the slightest. I knew what I was capable of. Dealing with one attacker who didn't see me coming was almost effortless.

"I wasn't thinking about myself," I said. "The same way you weren't thinking about yourself. We did what we had to do to protect the people we care about. They did the same for us."

He made an indeterminate sound in the back of his throat and picked up his drink to take a gulp. It looked like half of it went down in one swallow.

"You don't think they care about you?" I asked. "Because I can tell you, they do. Gianni will tell you that himself. Reuben is more… reserved. He doesn't trust easily, but he trusts you. Even when you're being a grumpy asshole. Which, as far as I can tell, is most of the time."

He responded with a side eye. "You think I should be more warm and fuzzy like Gianni or the twins? That's not who I am. No more than it is who you are. Not anymore."

He took in my look of surprise. "I met you before. At least, I was present. Reuben went to talk to your father and you came into the room. It was like the fucking sun rose in the middle of the night. But not anymore."

He might as well have taken a needle and stabbed me right in the heart with it. His aim was perfect, the target hit dead on.

"We all change," I murmured. "I had to grow up sometime. Even if Kurt wasn't—"

"But he was," Damon interrupted. "Do you know why everyone bought the story about you running off to marry some nice guy and living in the suburbs? It wasn't because your father was convincing. It was because we thought it was the truth. Because a girl like you doesn't belong in *this* world. You should be baking birthday cakes for sweet little babies who grow up never knowing how to use a gun. You should be going to school plays and ballet recitals. Soccer games on Sunday morning and watching Disney movies a hundred times over.

"You shouldn't be sneaking around in the dark and cutting throats, or trying to find some asshole who locked you up in hell and tortured you until you became the shadow instead of the sunshine. I've seen some fucked up stuff in my day, but what he did to you is by far the worst. And to the person who deserves it the least."

For the first time in years, I found tears trickling down my cheeks. He was so wrong and so right at the same time. Everyone had the impression I was sweet and innocent, but it was a façade. It was a role I played so well no one thought to look for me. No one thought anything bad could happen to that sweet girl.

"I'm not the sweet person you think I am," I managed to say.

His lips moved as he thought about how to respond to that. Finally he said, "Probably not. You know how to throw a knife and use a gun. You don't flinch when Reuben orders us to kill. It's possible that if it wasn't for Kurt, you would have become as jaded as me in time."

I stepped over to lower myself into the chair beside him. "It's also possible the girl you think you saw never existed. You've had years to build her up in your mind and make her something else."

"I know what I saw," he said with a grunt. "What I don't understand is why your father handed you over to that fucking prick. It was clear for everyone to see that he adored you. You were his favourite. His princess."

A knot in the table became absolutely fascinating for a minute or two. I focused on it and let his words rattle around in my brain.

"He had a debt," I said eventually. "He had to pay it."

"He had money," Damon insisted. "What could be so big or important that he had to give up his favourite daughter?"

"You might be wrong that I was his favourite," I suggested. "Have you met Rose? He adored her. And Dane and Asher. Just like tonight, he did what he had to do."

Damon shook his head. "I don't buy it."

"It doesn't matter whether you do or not," I said, sharper than I intended. I didn't want to break this fragile truce between us, but he couldn't keep pushing the way he was. I couldn't give him the answers he needed. Not tonight. No matter how much I wanted to tell him everything. I couldn't guarantee he wouldn't turn on me the moment I stepped foot out of the kitchen. Or before.

He sat back. "I guess it doesn't. " His stony expression was back in place. "All those years is enough time to trick myself into thinking someone is different to how they really are." He clearly didn't believe that either. If he did, that would mean questioning his own memory and judgement. In his line of work, that was a dangerous slope to get onto. One that was difficult to get off again alive.

"It's nice to know you were thinking of me," I said lightly. "I must have made quite the impression."

That wasn't the point he was making here, but I couldn't resist the gentle dig. It seemed as though he'd given me a lot of consideration over the years. Now I thought back, I remembered seeing him with Reuben. He was sullen and stayed in the background, much like he was now. Much like many of my father's visitors were.

He smirked. "Short skirt, cute tits, fuckable mouth, it's hard to forget. Don't flatter yourself too much, I just pictured you riding my dick, that's all."

I returned his smirk. "If you say so." That was not all and we both knew it.

Although, that may have been part of it. I *was* cute and confident back then. Happy and comfortable in my skin. As comfortable as anyone could be at eighteen.

Now— Calling me a shadow wasn't inaccurate. I was a shadow of my old self. If you showed me photos of me back then, I'd probably struggle to recognise myself. Especially if I compared them to my reflection in the mirror.

"You're still a distraction," he said.

"You're still an asshole," I retorted. If he wasn't going to give me a centimetre of leeway, then I wasn't giving him any either. Although, there wasn't as much animosity behind either of our words as there was before.

The sides of his mouth tugged up just a fraction. "Yes, I am. Don't forget it. I'm a reckless asshole who likes to drive too fast and smash perfectly good cars. I missed my calling. I could have done that professionally."

"I'm guessing this pays better," I said. "And you get to be surrounded by family."

"There are worse ways to live," he conceded. "Or die."

I raised my mug and toasted him. He raised his and tapped it against mine.

"I propose we don't die anytime soon," I said. "In fact, I refuse to die until I know Kurt is dead." However long that took, I didn't care. Until I saw him dead with my own eyes, I wouldn't fully relax, and I sure as hell didn't plan to die. After everything, I wouldn't give him the satisfaction.

Damon hummed. "That sounds like a good ambition to me. I think I'll do that too. Although, I might add Samuel Bell to that list. And maybe those daughters of his. They're a pair of snakes, both of them." He pressed his lips together and rolled them a couple of times.

I toasted him again, then took a sip. "To outliving our enemies."

He nodded and gulped down the rest of his drink. "With that goal in mind, I need to get some sleep before the actual sun rises."

I nodded and watched as he stood and stepped out of the kitchen.

I finished my tea and put the empty mugs in the sink. Now the adrenaline from the attack had finally subsided, I was exhausted. Hopefully enough to get some sleep myself.

With the house in silence, I slipped up the stairs and into my room.

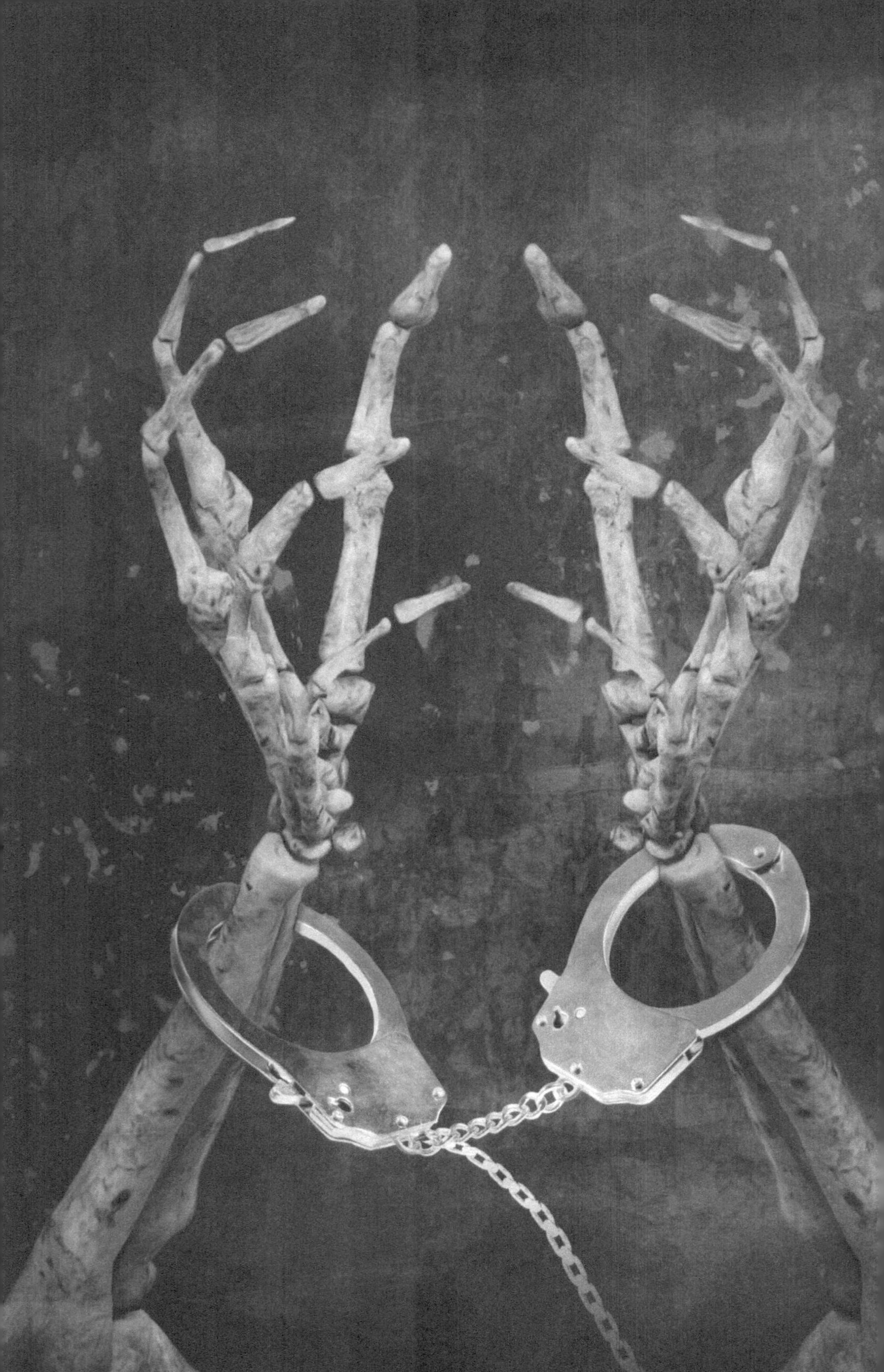

CHAPTER 24

MINA

"I don't like it when people attack me." Reuben's gaze scanned the office.

I stood near the door, Gianni beside me. Damon and the twins were near the window.

"None of us does, boss," Gianni said. He leaned against the corner of Reuben's desk, his palm on the dark wood.

"None of us like being attacked, or none of us like it when Reuben is?" Hunter asked. "Just for clarification."

"Both," Gianni said. "I'm sorry I didn't make that clearer for you."

Hunter grinned. "No problem."

Reuben cleared his throat. "I don't like it when people attack any of us."

"There's been no further sightings of Kurt," Damon said. "Not before we saw Frank and not after the attack. To the surprise of no one, Frank has disappeared off the face of the earth. Whatever his real name is, is anyone's guess."

"I'm guessing it's not Gustav," Gianni remarked. "When I said that name, he gave me a blank look. If he was actually Gustav, he would have at least twitched."

"That narrows it down," Damon said sarcastically. "We can rule out a couple of thousand men."

"Does it matter who he was?" Parker asked. "He was probably just a random dude in the wrong place at the wrong time."

"I don't think his resemblance to Kurt was a coincidence," I said softly. "It might be, but they might be related."

"We should check with Daisy Lasalle to see if they have a relative with a resemblance to that prick," Damon said.

Reuben nodded. "Do it."

"I find myself conflicted," Hunter said. "Frank might be his twin. On one hand, twins are cool. On the other, Kurt is an asshole."

"It's possible to be a twin and an asshole at the same time," Damon said pointedly.

Hunter turned to Parker. "I think he's talking about us."

Parker squinted at Damon. "I think so too."

In unison, they flipped Damon off.

He flipped them off in return.

Both twins grinned.

"I don't think Kurt has a twin, but I can speak to Daze," I offered. I'd welcome the chance to spend more time with her. Even if it meant talking about him.

"All right," Reuben agreed. "You and Gianni go to Dusk Bay and speak to her. She should know about the attack. Kurt clearly has more resources than we previously assumed. But wait a few days. Let things simmer down. We'll give Damon's contacts time to keep looking for him and how he organised the attack. I don't want you going anywhere without me being sure you won't be ambushed."

"I don't want that either," Gianni agreed. "Not that we can't take care of ourselves, but I'd prefer not to be dealing with eight attackers when there's only two of us. Six or seven maybe." He gestured his hands back and forth. "But not eight. Especially not without Damon and his car smashing skills." He jerked a thumb towards the other man.

"You could crash a car if you had to," Damon said. "Knowing you, you'd enjoy it."

"You're so sweet," Gianni told him.

Damon rolled his eyes.

"They should just kiss and get it over with," Hunter whispered loudly.

"Maybe I should shoot you and get it over with?" Damon suggested.

Hunter grinned. "We all know you won't do that. Parker and I are too useful."

"Is that what they call it these days?" Damon asked. "Useful?"

"I think he's insulting us again," Parker said.

"Enough." Reuben's voice was low, but forceful. "In case you've forgotten, we could have been killed last night. Let's focus on the matter at hand. You can insult each other on your own time."

All three of them fell silent. The twins even looked slightly apologetic. Reuben was right, we could have died. Kurt was the enemy here, not each other. There was no animosity in the banter, but it wasn't going to help us find him any faster.

"I'll keep in touch with my contacts," Damon said. "Someone has to have seen something, even if they got paid not to see. We have people looking at the financials of any of his known associates, or anyone who might have come in contact with him in the last few years. If he's paid any of them to pretend they didn't see him, we'll pin them down."

"I don't care who you have to bribe, threaten or kill, I want him found," Reuben said. "That is our priority. That and keeping our interests running. No doubt he'll try to fuck with them in some way, at some point. If he's getting desperate enough to send people after us, there's no telling what shit he might try to pull."

"Consider everyone bribed, threatened or killed," Damon said. "He can only hide from us for so long. At some point, he's going to make a mistake and we'll be right there, ready to pounce."

Reuben scrubbed a hand over his face. "We may have to consider approaching Samuel Bell. If we pool our resources, that should make it easier to find Lasalle."

"That's a good idea," Hunter said surprisingly quickly. "I definitely think the Brantley and Bell families should work together. Don't you Parker?"

"Definitely," Parker said with just as much enthusiasm. "I mean, the two families have been at each other's throats for so long. And for what?" He spread his hands. "No one even knows anymore." He gave an awkward laugh.

Reuben narrowed his eyes at him. "If you're so enthusiastic, you can talk to him."

The twins exchanged a glance.

"He'd probably have us killed on sight," Hunter said.

"That sounds accurate," Parker agreed. "A phone call might be safer."

"I'll consider it," Reuben said. He clearly thought they were up to something, but it wasn't something he was going to get into right now. "You all have jobs to do. Go and do them. Mina, stay here."

I stood aside to let them all out the door before closing it behind them. I caught a glimpse of Gianni grinning before it clicked shut.

Reuben stood and moved around to the other side of the desk, ice blue eyes on me. At first, he said nothing. He was silent for long enough to make me uneasy.

"Is something wrong?" I asked. Apart from all the other things I already knew were wrong in my life right now.

"No, nothing," he said, his gaze still intense. "I like to understand everyone and everything around me. It helps me to keep things in order. But you… I can't figure you out."

I struggled to remain still and calm. "There's not much to figure out. I'm just Mina DiMarco, sister of a famous rock star, a university professor, and a woman who knows how to dispose of suspicious body parts. You've known me for most of my life."

"And yet, I don't think I know you at all," he said. He shook his head and stepped back. "I think I underestimated you. Of course you know how to use a knife and gun, and stay calm in a crisis. We were all raised with those skills."

"You thought maybe I was going to wilt after what I've been through?" I asked.

That was a logical assumption. Alone at night, I did wilt, but I forced myself to keep going when the sun rose. I had to. If only so I could see this through to the end.

"People have gone through less and been thoroughly destroyed," he said. "Gianni has broken people by threatening to torture them. The suggestion of a few horrific methods has them begging for mercy and telling him everything they know. Some people are stronger than that. But you, you're stronger than any of them."

He slowly raised his hand and touched the back of my head, his fingers tangling in my hair. I didn't move while he lowered his mouth, lightly brushing his lips over mine.

Gradually, he deepened the kiss, his tongue dipping into my mouth, holding my hair in his fist.

Reluctantly, he pulled back and let his hand slip from my hair.

"You're mine," he whispered. "One day, I will show you how much."

"One day I'll be ready," I whispered back.

"Don't take too long," he said. "I want you." His eyes were dark, his expression heated. At the same time, fully in control. Contained. He wanted me, but he needed me to be ready to give myself fully. I needed the same thing.

I would have liked to be able to assure him I wouldn't, but I had no guarantees. No timeline.

I took both of his hands in mine and laced our fingers together.

"I'm yours." That was the only promise I could make right now.

The whole house was silent and in darkness.

I slipped past everyone's bedrooms and down the stairs. At the bottom, I took a moment to be sure no one knew I was up. I heard no sound, no indication anyone was awake. Nothing but Gianni's distant snores.

Smiling to myself, I slipped over to press the buttons on the keypad which would turn off the alarm system for a short time. I'd be back before it re-engaged.

I eased the door open and slipped out into the predawn gloom. It wasn't far, just a five or ten metre brisk walk.

My mind turned over and over with each step. There was no guarantee everything was still in place. Someone might have found or destroyed everything at some point in the last five years.

To my relief, the small house was still present, empty as far as I could tell. Just the way I left it.

I slipped around the back and counted the bricks just above ground level.

"Five. Six. Seven. Eight." I crouched down and eased the eighth brick out of its slot. I slid my hand inside and felt around. My fingers connected with cold metal. I grabbed onto it and pulled out a long, wide box. I placed it on the ground and opened it.

Smiled.

Everything was still here.

I pulled out the phone and connected it to the portable charger I borrowed from Gianni. It took several minutes for the phone to charge enough to turn on.

I pressed in my passcode to enter the home screen. It took a few moments longer to remember my bank password, but I entered that to check my funds.

"Nice," I whispered. Interest had accrued over the last five years.

I closed the bank app and opened another to reach out to my contacts. It would take time to hear back from them.

I opened a third app, and followed a series of prompts and pass-words to reach the area I wanted.

The screened read, 'Sparrow,' in red.

Underneath that, I changed 'inactive' to 'active.'

'Sparrow' turned to green. A few minutes later, job offers started to pop up on the screen. Some I'd accept, others not. The first job was finding Kurt and ending him.

Then I'd get back to work doing what I was good at.

The Sparrow, one of the most efficient and deadliest assassins in the world, was reactivated.

I slipped everything but the phone back into the box and back under the house. Carefully, I put the brick back in place and stood.

I needed to get home before my family woke.

. . .

If you've like to read about how Mina dispatched the attacker in the darkness, you can read that in the bonus scene here

RUINED

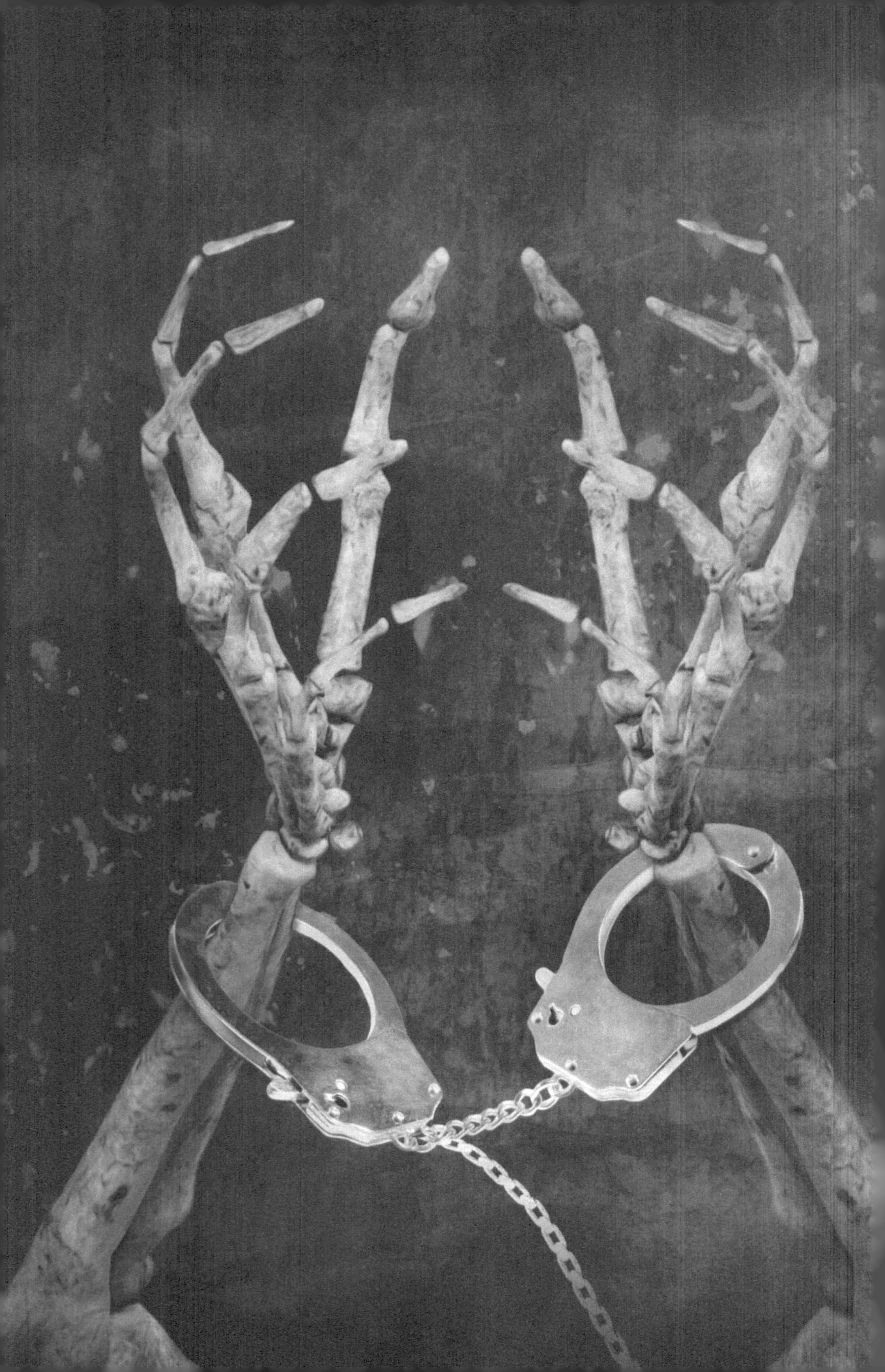

CHAPTER 1

MINA

The dream was always the same.

I stepped through the darkness, silent as a ghost.

The layout of the house was seared into my memory. I'd gone over the map more times than I could count, making sure it was embedded tight. Every room, every door, every corridor.

The only variable was the placement of furniture, and that was predictable. The couch under the window, dining table near the kitchen. 'Standard for today's living,' as those home design shows on TV called it.

The room where my target should be sleeping was at the other end of the house.

Some people in my line of work like to wake up their targets before they kill them. I didn't. It was a waste of time, and added another unknown variable to the situation. The target might wake quickly and set off some kind of alarm. Worse than that, they might offer more money than the hit out on them. That created conflict and uncertainty I had no time for.

Once I took a job, I saw it through until the end.

No, they'd never know I was coming.

I placed my gloved hand on the doorknob and started to turn it.

"Who are you?" a voice said behind me.

I turned.

What happened next was always a blur. I don't remember the knife going in, or… much of anything. I went from standing beside the door, to finding myself on the floor, holding the girl until long after she died.

"You shouldn't still be here."

Even in my dream, hearing Kurt's voice, looking up to see him, gave me chills. He loomed over me, dressed like I was, all in black.

"What did you do?" he demanded.

I had no answer. This was not what I'd come here for.

"Mina," he hissed. He grabbed my arm and tugged me to my feet. "We need to get the fuck out of here."

I let him pull me to the door and out into the night. The moment the cold air hit my face, I stopped.

"I need to finish what I started." I turned to go back in but froze at the sound of a scream from inside the house.

Kurt's grip tightened on my arm. "Too late." He huffed out a frustrated breath. "You fucked this up. Hell, Mina, you were trained better than this."

"It was an accident." But he was right. I had fucked it up. Badly. I was better than this. I'd never been sloppy before. Never killed anyone who wasn't my target. Especially not…

"Cry about it later," he snapped. "We need to go."

I nodded vaguely and followed him through the dark, to our waiting car. We just got inside when the front of the house lit up. Sirens wouldn't be long.

Kurt started the engine and drove away like we weren't in a hurry. Even if we were seen, we'd soon ditch the car and use another. We'd have to, to be sure we weren't caught.

"What the hell, Mina?" He glanced over at me.

"I don't know," I said, vague and numb. "I don't know what happened." I ran through it in my head, over and over, but all I found was a blank space between her seeing me, and her dying. I didn't remember moving toward her, but obviously I had. Her death was evidence for that.

"I'll tell you what's going to happen next," he said. "The Sparrow is going to have to disappear for a while. We'll put it out there that someone else was behind this tonight. With any luck, they'll buy it. Fortunately, at least one of us did the job they were there for tonight." He lifted a hand from the steering wheel and rubbed his chin.

I pressed myself down, smaller against the seat. I'd had a bad feeling about this job from the start. I was used to working alone. Kurt was there to hack into the computer system and get some information. I was there to take out my target.

I'd failed.

"We'll get past this," he said. His voice was a fraction milder now, his attempt to soothe me after what I'd done. Him and me against the world. That was what he wanted.

We were never going to happen. Not like that. He was too short-tempered and aggressive for my taste. Too much of a hothead. I preferred men who weren't rash and snappy. Sooner or later, he'd realise I meant it when I said I wasn't interested. Not in him.

Not in anyone except the one man who was completely out of my league. There was no way he'd look twice at me, but my heart ignored my attempts to tell it that. Either way, Kurt Lasalle wasn't my future.

"Are you listening?" Kurt snapped, reminding me again why I should keep my distance from him.

"Yeah," I lied. I'd tuned him out for the last couple of minutes.

"Good, then we understand each other. You know why I need to do what I need to do next."

***

"Mina?"

I awoke so violently, I almost threw myself off the side of the bed. The covers were tangled around my legs. My body was slick with sweat. I wasn't in the car with Kurt, and I wasn't chained in a filthy cage in a dank basement.

The mattress underneath me was comfortable, the room clean and tidy. Like everything else in Reuben Brantley's house.

It took a moment to register that someone else spoke. I wasn't alone.

As if he knew he occupied a place on the edge of my dream, Reuben sat on the side of the bed. He was dressed only in a pair of black, silk pyjama pants. The early morning light that slipped between the curtains illuminated the frown etched on his brow.

"You were dreaming," he said. "Or having a nightmare."

I pushed myself up to sit back against the pillows. "I'm sorry if I woke you."

"You didn't." He rested his weight on the palm of his hand, and made no move to touch me.

He seemed to know when I'd be more likely to freak out. Clearly uncomfortable at the prospect, he held himself back, more tightly controlled than usual. Which was saying something, given how controlled he generally was.

"I was already awake," he added.

I glanced at the clock on the bedside table. One of those old-fashioned ones with an analog face and little feet.

"It's not even six o'clock in the morning yet." My eyes lingered on the grooves of his abs and the light sprinkling of hair on his chest. Unless he had one hidden under his pants, he had no tattoos. That didn't surprise me. There weren't too many people he'd trust to go anywhere near him with a needle. Besides, his body was a work of art without one.

"Is it?" he asked. "The day is half over then."

I snorted softly. He wasn't given to joking overtly, but he had a sense of humour, even if he wouldn't admit to it.

"Do you want to talk about it?" he asked quietly. Like everything else about him, his voice was understated and controlled. I wasn't sure if he knew how to shout, even if he was inclined to. He didn't need to. If Reuben Brantley spoke, people listened.

"I don't remember it," I lied.

Parts of it were vague, like they always were. The bits that lingered in my memory… I couldn't explain. Not yet. I wanted to. I *needed* to. But I needed to find Kurt first and kill him. Before that, I couldn't risk Reuben not understanding what happened that night.

Then there was the additional concern that he might not want an assassin living under his roof. No, his response was a variable I couldn't control, even though he made it clear how he felt about me. That I was his.

I was sure he must see right through me, into my thoughts, but he nodded.

"I can have a therapist come to the house," he offered. "A discreet one."

I appreciated his offer. I even considered it. Five years of being chained up, tortured and used, would fuck anyone up. Five years of dwelling on what happened that night and being so sure I deserved everything Kurt did to me.

I fought him at first, or at least, I tried to. Between the chain, the cage, the lack of food and guilt, fighting was difficult. Once I realised it got him going, I stopped. All he got from me were occasional bouts of anger or frustration. Most of the time, all I really wanted was to die so it could end.

"I'll think about it," I said.

He rolled his lips a couple of times. "You can talk to me anytime. There's nothing you could say that would shock me." A hint of a smile played around the corners of his mouth. "Bear in mind, I've had nineteen years of listening to the twins. I'm desensitised to shock value."

That got a smile from me.

"I'll bet. They seem to get great pleasure from trying to push the buttons of everyone around them."

"Especially mine," Reuben agreed. "Lucky for them they're both useful. Otherwise, I wouldn't keep them around."

"They would say otherwise," I said. "They'd probably say you keep them around because you love them or something." I couldn't resist the gentle tease.

"They *would* say that," he said. "I'll neither confirm nor deny the accusation."

He wouldn't, but I was certain he loved his brothers, and that was reciprocated. It was hard not to like Hunter and Parker. They could charm the pants off almost anyone. Anyone but me. They were also too wild and hotheaded for my taste.

Reuben placed a hand on mine and laced our fingers together. "I understand how difficult it is for you to trust anyone. Between our lifestyle and what that asshole did to you, I don't blame you for being guarded. Anyone would be. I hope someday you can come to trust me."

"I want that too," I said softly.

I knew what he was asking. It wasn't just about trust. He knew I was keeping secrets and he'd prefer I tell him before he found out some other way.

I'd do whatever I could to make sure he didn't find out from anyone else. As far as I knew, the only person alive who knew what I was, was Kurt. That was another on a long list of reasons why he needed to die. Not only because he might tell Reuben, but because he might reveal my identity to the world.

How many people would believe sweet Mina DiMarco was really an assassin?

Perhaps more than I'd like. Once everyone knew, I'd never get another job.

I was anxious to get back to work. I needed the money to help fund the search for Kurt. For that, I'd take on anything.

Almost anything. I'd never take a job that meant killing anyone who lived under this roof. Or any of my family members. Anyone else was fair game.

"Would you care to join me in the gym?" he offered. "I was headed down there when I heard you cry out." He squeezed my hand lightly.

"I'd like that," I said. "I need to build my muscles back up."

After so many years of disuse, I was weaker than I liked to be, my reflexes slightly slower.

I knew from the two people I killed a few weeks ago that I still possessed the ability to take a life, but I wanted my body to be quicker and sharper, like a knife. I had to be able to rely on it as well as any tool. I could not, *would not* screw up again. I needed to be even better than I was five years ago. If they thought the Sparrow was daunting then, they'd seen nothing yet.

"I'll see you down there." He leaned in to swipe his lips over mine.

Electricity crackled between us, so tangible I could almost see it. It could have set the whole city on fire.

He wanted more. If I let him, he'd press me down on the mattress and slide his cock into my pussy. He'd fuck me long and slow and thoroughly. When I was ready, that's what he'd do. As long as it took, he'd wait for me.

If I wasn't careful, I might just fall for him the way he'd already fallen for me.

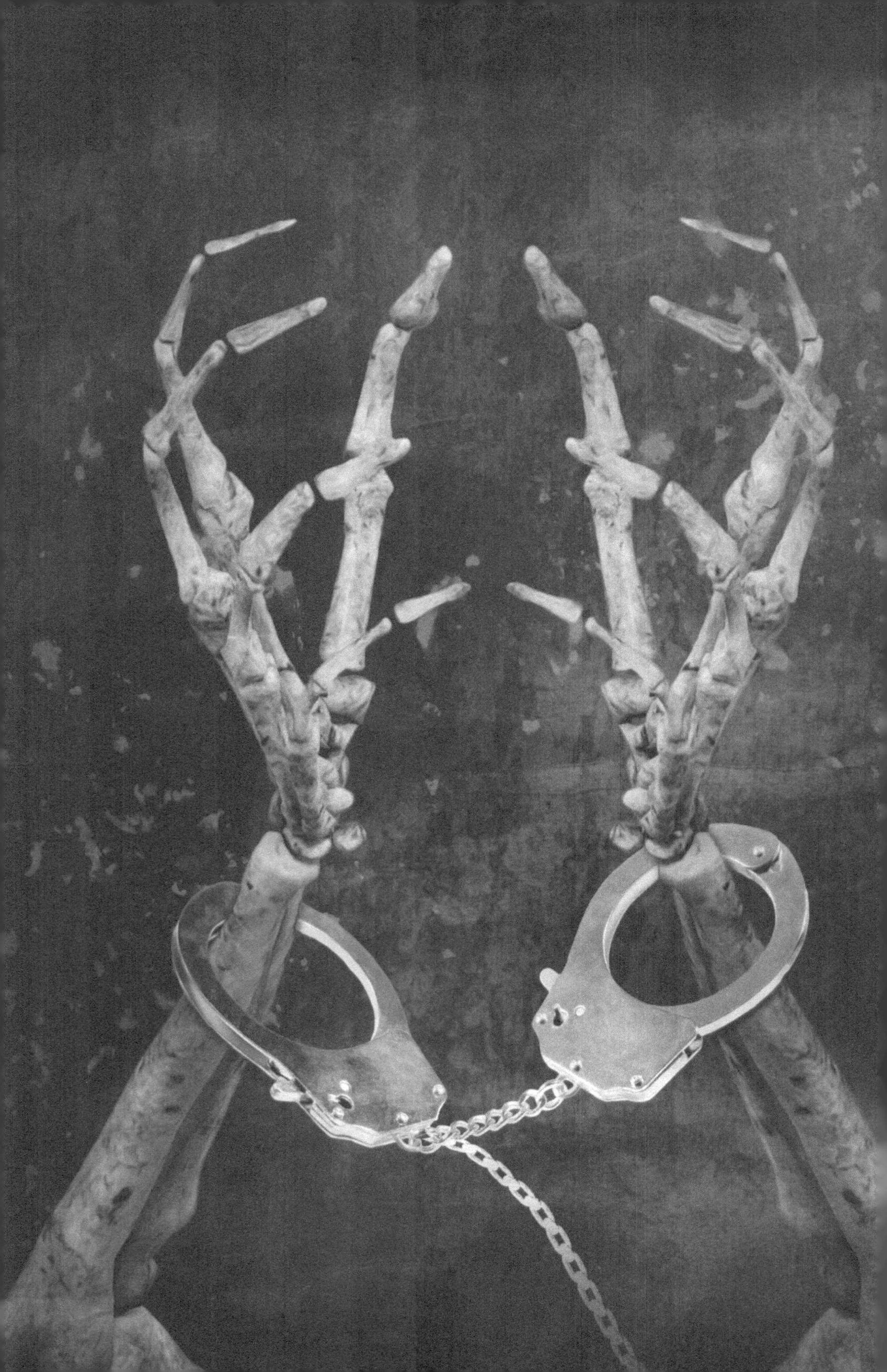

CHAPTER 2

MINA

Damon entered the kitchen, his eyes on his phone. He managed to navigate his way around the chairs and over to the electric kettle, without looking up.

"I know that face," Gianni remarked. He sat beside me, eating fruit loops and sipping coffee.

Damon glanced at him and frowned. "Yeah, it's the same handsome-as-fuck face I've always had."

Gianni grinned. "I meant the expression on your face, but that's true too."

"That he's a fuck face?" I said, deadpan.

Damon scowled at me, but looked over to where Reuben sat watching us while chewing on toast. "You're not going to believe this, boss."

Reuben lowered his toast. "You'd be surprised what I might believe."

Damon shrugged one shoulder to concede the point. "This might be an exception. The Sparrow is active again."

My heart skipped a beat. I'd expected this conversation. Anticipated it. I was ready with my mask in place.

Sweat still broke out on my hands.

Reuben placed his toast back on his plate. "I believe you, but you're right, I'm not surprised. Just like that?"

"Just like that," Damon agreed. "The notification popped up on my phone sometime in the middle of the night. I've spent the last hour confirming that it's legit. As far as anyone can tell, it is. The Sparrow is operating again."

"Cool," Gianni said around a mouthful of cereal. "Maybe I can meet them this time."

Damon looked over at me, slightly smug. "The Sparrow is—"

"An assassin," I interrupted. Clearly he'd expected I wouldn't know that. "I've heard of them from before."

"Not just any assassin," Gianni said. "One of the best. They could get in anywhere, anytime. If anyone could get in here and take out Reuben, it would be them."

Reuben arched an eyebrow. "You might be overstating slightly. However, that's reasonably accurate. The Sparrow had impressive skills." He turned to Damon. "Is there any chance it's someone else stepping into the role?"

Damon placed his phone down on the kitchen island and poured himself a coffee.

"After all this time? Why now? It's been years. If someone was going to take on their persona, wouldn't they have done it by now?"

"They might have been honing their skills," Gianni suggested. "It would take a lot of work and practice to be that good."

"I'm still not convinced it's one person." Damon leaned back against the kitchen counter top, his long fingers curled around his mug.

"What makes you think that?" I asked. "Maybe they were just that good." I was, apart from that one major fuck up, but I was interested in his theory.

"It would take more than one person to break in here," he reasoned. "They couldn't just walk through the door."

I'd done exactly that, because they brought me here after they found me in Kurt's basement. Of course, that wasn't what he meant, but still. Knowing how wrong he was gave me a certain, possibly petty, satisfaction.

"Some people suggested the Sparrow was dead," Gianni said, but his tone was dismissive. Clearly he didn't think so. "If that's the case, maybe one died and it took this long to find someone else good enough."

"You don't believe that," I said. "What do you think happened?" How well had Kurt and my father covered my mistake? Well enough to avoid rumours?

Gianni shrugged. "They could have gone on a really long holiday."

"It's possible their cover was compromised," Reuben said. "Or they thought it was going to be. They might have thought it wise to step back and let things blow over. And now, apparently, they have."

Damon was watching me intently over his coffee mug. "What do you think happened?"

I tapped the tip of my finger on the table top and frowned while I thought. "If I was an assassin, why would I disappear for years?"

"You don't have to—" Gianni started.

"It's okay." I couldn't avoid talking about it forever. "Kurt ran when he was found out, before you could get to him. It's possible that happened to the Sparrow too. They thought someone was coming after them. Or maybe someone turned on them. Forced them to hide out. Or they made a mistake."

I tried not to look as if I was searching for information in their responses. Some sign of what they knew, or thought they knew.

"This is all conjecture," Reuben said. "Whatever the reason, they're active and we can make use of them. If anyone can find Kurt, it's the Sparrow. I prefer he be found alive, but if that isn't possible, dead will have to do." He nodded to Damon, who picked up his phone and tapped on the screen.

"I've sent the message," Damon said after a minute or two. He lowered his phone back down again. "I'll let you know when I hear back."

Reuben picked up his toast and went back to eating. "Gianni, in two days time I want you and Mina to go to Dusk Bay to see Daisy Lasalle. Try to find out if Kurt has made contact in any way. If he has, I want to know. And see if he has a twin named Frank."

"You don't think she's working with him behind our back?" Gianni asked.

"No, I don't," Reuben agreed. "But someone who works for her might be. Keep your eyes peeled. Someone out there knows where he is. Sooner or later, they'll make a mistake and we'll be there to deal with them. In the meantime, keep reminding everyone I don't tolerate people operating behind my back. If any of them think they can get away with it, we'll remind them they can't. Painfully or fatally, whichever is appropriate."

I loved it when he got authoritative like that. My clit throbbed in appreciation.

"Got it, boss," Gianni said. "Consider everyone threatened. If I was working against you, I'd be shaking in my shoes right now."

"If you were working against me, you'd have a bullet in your brain," Reuben said.

"Courtesy of me," Damon said.

"Lucky for all of us I'm not," Gianni said. "Especially Damon. He'd really, really hate to have to kill me." He winked at me.

"I'd hate to have to use up a perfectly good bullet," Damon said dryly.

"He'd cry over my grave." Gianni grinned.

"You said 'dance' wrong," Damon said.

"You dance?" I asked.

"No, but I'd make an exception for his grave." The sides of Damon's mouth twitched up in a hint of a smile. As far as I could tell, that was his equivalent of a grin.

"He really does adore me," Gianni said. "We'll probably be buried in adjoining graves. Side-by-side. In death as we were in life."

Damon grimaced. "Remind me to change my will so it says I have to be buried on the other side of Sydney."

"That's still close enough for me to haunt your dead ass," Gianni said.

I exchanged glances with Reuben, who looked amused at their banter.

"It's like having the twins around, but they're older," he said wryly.

I choked back a laugh.

"I think I'll have it revised to say I need to be buried on the other side of the *world* from all of you," Damon said, smirking at us.

"That sounds lonely," I said.

"It sounds quiet," he insisted.

"Quiet is overrated," Gianni remarked.

"No, it's not," Reuben said. "Damon might have a point."

"Says the man who has a family mausoleum that's nice and quiet," Gianni said.

Reuben shrugged, but looked smug.

I didn't much care what happened to me after I was dead, as long as no one haunted me. Then I'd be pissed off. Honestly, my life was haunted enough now as it was. By Kurt and by that girl.

"Where are my parents buried?" I asked. It hadn't occurred to me to wonder until now.

"On the other side of the city," Reuben said. "Did you want to pay them a visit?"

"We could dance on your father's grave," Gianni offered.

I thought for a moment before shaking my head. "No. I was just curious. My brothers and sister, how did they react? Were they upset? Did they know what happened?"

"All three of your siblings know your parents killed my parents," Reuben said softly. "I told them myself. They had the option of joining your parents or staying the hell out of my way. Rose works for me once in a while, but otherwise they took the second option. I didn't want to have to kill any of them."

"Why?" I asked. He didn't seem reluctant to kill, when and wherever necessary.

He gave me a lingering look in response.

"You thought someday I'd come back and I wouldn't forgive you for killing them?" I guessed.

He really had thought of me a lot more than I would have expected him to. Thinking he was out of my league seemed silly, now I was looking back at the past. What would have happened if I'd gone to him when I had the chance? He might have saved me from going through hell.

No, there was no 'might' about it. He would have.

"I hoped you'd come back. If what your father said about you being married and living in the suburbs was true, I would have kept my peace, but this is your place."

He gestured around himself and the house. "If your siblings chose to make trouble, I would have done what I had to. But not without considering the potential consequences."

"The only one who looks like he has any potential of causing trouble is Dane," Damon said. "He's ambitious and he's always looking for a way in. He'd be right here at the table, if he could, but none of us would turn our backs on him."

"I wouldn't turn my back on him either," I said. For a while, I'd wondered if Dane knew what I was. It was possible he did and thought the Sparrow was inactive because I was living life as a suburban wife and mother.

That thought gave me a moment of panic. If he knew I was active again, he might wonder why. He might come looking for me.

Let him try. He probably wouldn't think to look for me here. If he did, he wouldn't get past the front door without me knowing. I'd have plenty of time to make myself scarce. No one would enlighten him unless I wanted them to. Someday I would, but not yet. Not until Kurt was dealt with.

"Family are the people you choose," Gianni said, his eyes intent on me.

"That's deep," Damon said.

"It's true though." Gianni was unruffled. "You three are family to me. More than anyone I'm related to by blood. The twins too. They're more like my younger brothers. Except my actual younger brothers are assholes."

"Does that mean I'm like a sister?" I teased.

I remembered the way his cock felt in my hand, running my fingers up and down his length and over his Jacob's ladder. The way he came in my hand. The way his cum tasted when I licked my fingers clean. Yeah, there was nothing sisterly about it.

"I hope not," Gianni said. "Because if we're related, I'm in all kinds of trouble. There's nothing brotherly about the things I want to do to you." In a loud whisper he added, "I don't want to do brotherly things to Damon either."

I glanced over to see Damon's reaction. His face was as tightly masked as ever, but his eyes darkened slightly.

In the corner of my eye, I caught Reuben watching us, his whole body rigid. I knew he wanted me, but he spent a lot of time with these guys. Did it go beyond work and brotherhood? If it hadn't, could it?

A shiver of heat passed through me at the idea of these men kissing each other, touching each other. For a few moments, I let my imagination run wild.

Finally, Reuben cleared his throat. "Gianni, make the arrangements to travel to Dusk Bay. Don't let Daisy know you're coming, or anyone else there. I'd rather catch them unaware. If they have anything to hide, we'll find out sooner if they're not expecting you."

"Got it, boss," Gianni said. "If they're up to something, we'll bust it wide open."

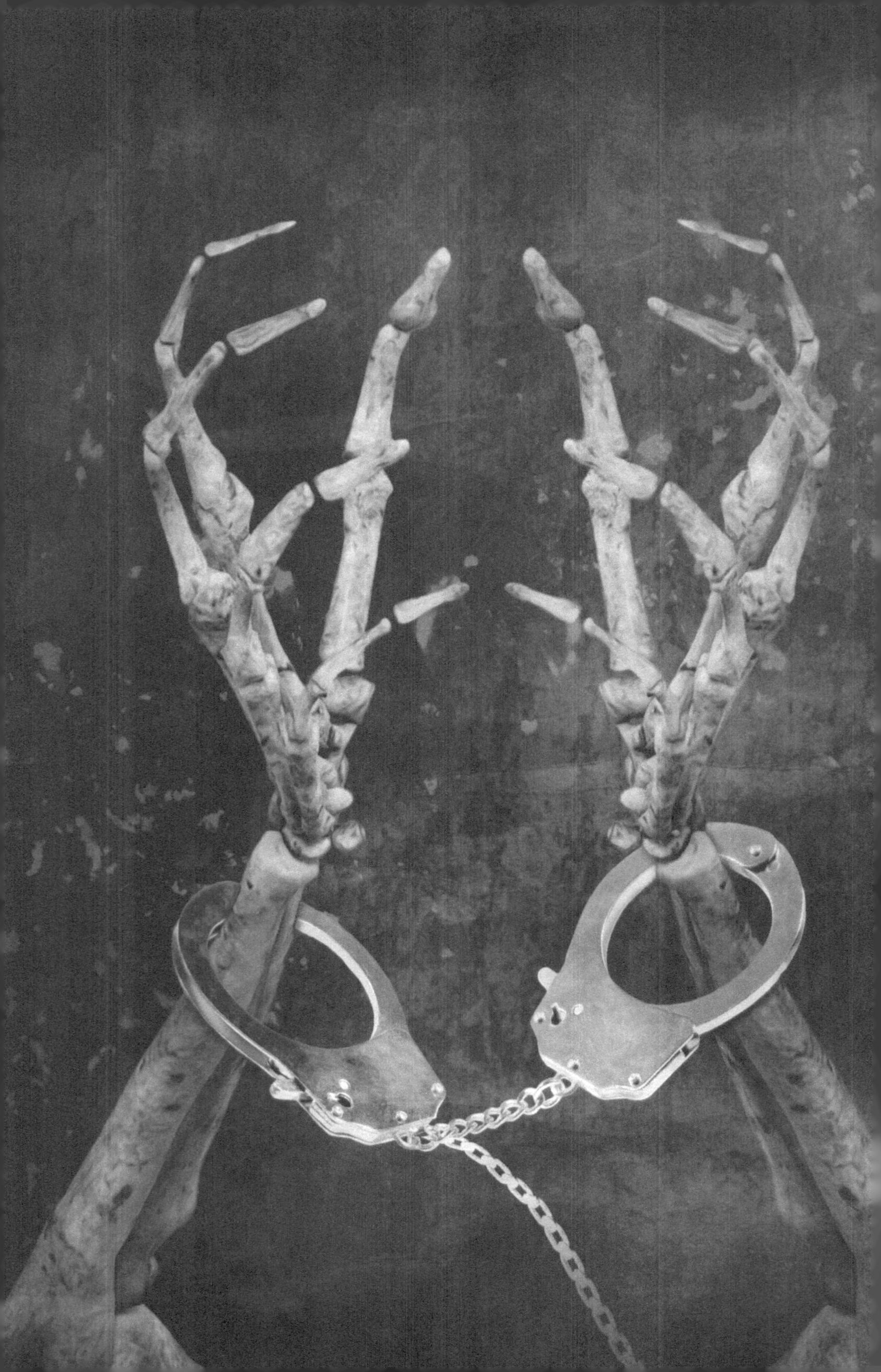

CHAPTER 3

MINA

"I had no idea Reuben owned a private jet." I trailed my fingers along the back of a seat before lowering myself onto the soft leather.

Gianni flopped sideways onto the seat facing me, feet dangling into the aisle.

He grinned. "When he realised Zeke and his band were still flying commercial, he bought this bad boy." He patted the leather beside his thigh. "No one said he couldn't be petty once in a while."

I was smiling as I fastened my seatbelt. "So he bought this to get one up on his brother? Does he ever let him use it?"

Gianni sat around and clicked in his own seatbelt. "There's only one way he'd let Zeke fly in this. If he quits the band and comes back to the family."

"Where would he fit in?" I adjusted the armrest and propped my elbow. "I mean, he wouldn't take the place of you or Damon."

"Fuck no," Gianni agreed. "No one could replace us. Zeke is a good guy, but he's not going to go around crashing SUVs, or killing on Reuben's orders."

"Then why does Reuben want him to come back so badly?" I asked.

"Because he's family." Gianni shrugged. "He's also good-looking and charismatic. Everything I'm not. He could talk people into doing things without needing to threaten them. By the time they realised what was going on, he'd be long gone."

"I can see the value of that," I said. "What about Asher? Does Reuben want him to return to the fold?"

"He'd be welcome, if he brought Zeke back with him. As far as I can tell, they're a package deal. You can't get one without the other."

"That sounds like them," I said. It didn't seem like that changed at all since I was away.

"Also," Gianni continued, "if you wanted Reuben to welcome Asher, he'd do it. Rose or Dane too."

I wrinkled my nose. "Dane would love that. He'd do everything he could to make himself Reuben's right-hand. Or better yet, his heir."

Gianni smirked. "That would be an interesting picture. Dane DiMarco, the new head of the Brantley family. Over the twins' dead bodies. Not to mention Caleb, Joshua and Lucas. He better make sure they're good and dead first, or they'd be coming for him."

"I think it's better not to encourage him then," I said. That would result in a lot of bloodshed. When things escalated, innocent people tended to come under fire.

"If Dane starts to get too big for his boots, Reuben can always have the Sparrow deal with him."

Gianni had glanced out the window as he spoke and missed seeing me twitch in response. Even an assassin had to draw the line some-where. I drew it at killing my own family, but to avoid all that blood-shed, I may have to consider it.

"I'm sure that won't be necessary," I said, my voice tighter than I intended.

Gianni's gaze swung back to me. "Sorry, I shouldn't make light of killing members of your family. You must miss them."

"I do," I agreed. Seeing my cousin Ric a couple of weeks ago felt surreal. At some point I'd be ready to see my siblings, but right now I had to focus on the job at hand.

"It's better they keep thinking I'm happily living a suburban life for now." The truth was going to shock the hell out of them.

Unless Asher changed a lot since I saw him last, it would rip his heart out. Rose too.

"You mentioned your family," I said carefully. "If you don't want to talk about them…"

He shrugged and steepled his fingers before pressing them to his lips. "My family is Italian. You probably figured it out from the look of this mug." He pointed a finger at his face. "They're up to their eyeballs in mafia shit. They'd prefer I worked with them than Reuben."

"Why don't you?" I asked.

He exhaled, long and slow. "I've never gotten along with them. They…" He searched for the words. "They don't give a shit who they step on to get what they want. They'll happily step on each other. If you can't even trust your family, then who the fuck can you trust?"

"The family you choose," I said.

He grinned behind his fingers. "Exactly. So I choose Reuben, Damon and you. And not them. Lucky for me, they don't live in Australia, for the most part. Also, Reuben was happy to sponsor me to join the Brotherhood."

I grimaced. "I shouldn't be surprised they're still around."

"The Brotherhood of Kings has been around for a few hundred years; they aren't going anywhere anytime soon," Gianni agreed.

"The Brotherhood, owning governments since the dawn of time," I said sarcastically. Although, that was the truth of it. "Are they letting women join yet?"

"Only as fillies." Gianni's smile was teasing, knowing he'd get a rise out of me. No woman was allowed to join the Brotherhood, but they could become a filly, offering sexual favours in the hope of catching the eye of a powerful man. My parents met that way. Reuben's parents too, probably.

I'd never been interested in hunting for a powerful husband, especially after what I heard about the Brotherhood. They tended to hand women around like they were a bag of chocolate pieces, to be shared, used, and degraded.

To me, that seemed like a high price to pay for money and power. As far as I knew, my brother Asher wasn't a member. I wasn't sure about Dane, but if he could join, he would have.

"Misogyny is alive and well I see," I remarked.

"Running the world has to come at a price." He shrugged. "Would it be better to leave it to politicians?"

I snorted. "No, it would be better to leave it to women."

Gianni grinned. "When you become Queen of the world, can I wash your feet?"

I pretended to consider the matter. "I'll think about it. It depends who does it best: you, Damon or Reuben. Or maybe the twins."

Gianni chuckled. "Don't make me kill the twins to keep them from muscling in on my territory."

"The day I'd be interested in either of them…" I shook my head. "They're too young for me anyway."

"They're closer in age to you than you are to me," Gianni pointed out. "Or Reuben, or Damon."

"Just the way I like it," I said lightly. I glanced out the window as we taxied down the runway. "I've always preferred men who have their shit together."

"I've always had a thing for women who know how to use a knife," Gianni said. "Who don't let the world hold them back. Who stand on their own two feet. The opposite of the kind of women who fraternise with the Brotherhood. Although, every now and again, there'll be a firecracker. I'm mostly there for the parties and world domination."

"World domination does seem to be a good excuse to hang out and get drunk," I said.

"It's the best excuse," he said. "Let other people have good looks and fame, I prefer power and money. Or to be close to it."

"Who says you don't have good looks?" I asked. He'd said several times now that he was the brains or the brawn, while other men were the attractive ones.

"When I was born, my mother cried," he said. He gave me a lopsided grin.

"I don't believe that for a minute," I said. "I think you're cute." He wasn't as classically handsome as Reuben or Damon, but he had his own charm.

"That's the first time anyone has called me cute," he said. He placed his hands in his lap and cocked his head in contemplation. "I think I like it."

"I'm glad you do," I said. "But I'm sure you've been called that before."

"I tend to think that's a word that applies better to you, but we can share." He reached over to take my hand, his smile replaced by earnestness. "Can I confess something?"

My heart skipped a beat at his touch and the expression on his face. Was there a chance he knew what I was and was about to tell me? If it wasn't that, then when was it?

I forced myself to say, "Of course you can." I wasn't oblivious to the fact we were now in the air. He couldn't shoot me, but I couldn't run. Was I strong enough to defend myself against him if I needed to? I'd have to be, if it came down to that. What then? The pilot might have orders to take me to fuck knows where.

He took a deep breath and looked from side to side before locking his gaze back on mine.

"I hate flying," he admitted. "I know, big badass guy like me shouldn't be scared of anything. But we're a long fucking way up and it's a long fucking way down. I hate heights."

I pushed out a breath of relief and reminded myself to be sympathetic. I didn't need him to wonder why I was on the verge of freaking out. Although, the enclosed space around us *was* unnerving. I could always say it reminded me of the cage.

"There's nothing wrong with being scared of heights or flying," I said. "Everyone is scared of something. Heights, snakes, marshmallows."

He looked surprised, then grinned. "Marshmallows?"

"Yeah." I grimaced. "They're all squishy and sticky." I mimed pressing one of them between my thumb and the rest of my fingers. Imagined the way they felt, soft and sugary. Like flesh, but sweet. I couldn't understand why anyone would want to put one of them in their mouth.

"I like sticky." He chuckled.

Of course he did. Our conversations came down to sex more often than not. The memory of slipping my finger between his lips and letting him suck his own cum from my skin made my skin tingle and my clit throb.

I rolled my eyes. "Not that kind of sticky. I just don't like them, okay?"

He held up his hands in surrender. "Noted. If I make you a hot chocolate, I won't put them in."

"And I won't insist you fly anywhere unless Reuben tells you to," I said. "Although, this is a lot more comfortable than flying commercial."

"It really is." He sank back against the seat and crossed his arms. "I should take a selfie and send it to Zeke. Remind him of what he's missing."

"I bet the twins would do that," I said. I pictured them with identical smug grins, taking several photos and bombing their brother with them. Laughing the whole time.

"They definitely would," he agreed. "Anything to get a rise out of anyone. There's nothing they wouldn't do for shits and giggles."

"They haven't changed either," I said. "Sometimes I think five years changed everything and sometimes I think it changed nothing."

"It changed you," he said softly.

I closed my eyes and sighed. "Yes, it did. What he did to me would change anyone."

What would I be like if I hadn't gone through that? Would I be as carefree as Hunter and Parker? Or would I have been fully consumed by the persona of the cold-blooded assassin? Unfeeling and uncaring.

Either way, sweet, innocent little Mina DiMarco was dead. The woman who sat in her place was a lot more ruthless and driven. I wouldn't kill my family, if I could help it, but I'd destroy anyone who got in my way. Anyone who got between me and killing Kurt.

Let their blood coat my hands; I wouldn't feel a thing. Not until I drove that blade through his heart and watched the life drain away from him.

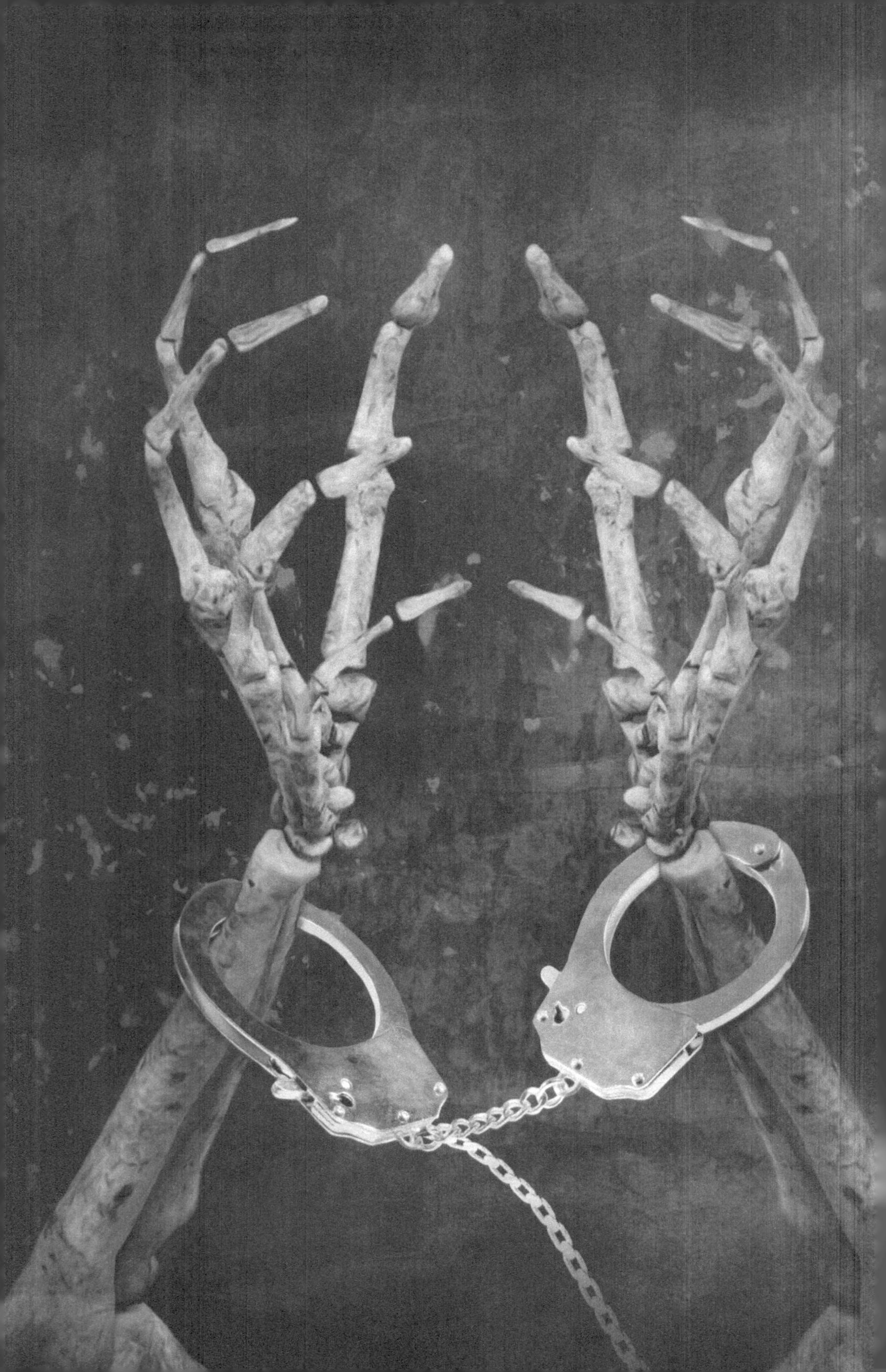

CHAPTER 4

MINA

"Mina." Daze hurried into the room and gave me a hug. If she was disconcerted about Gianni and my sudden appearance, she gave no sign. If anything, she seemed happy to see me.

I hugged her back quickly before stepping away again. Physical contact with another person was still difficult for me. Chances were, it always would be. That was another item on the long list of reasons why I hated Kurt. I wanted to be able to touch, hug and fuck. Not flinch and pull away.

"Sit down." She waved towards a couch in the centre of the room. The walls were lined with bookcases, overflowing with books.

The mess would give Reuben anxiety, but I found it easier to trust people who had lots of books.

She flopped down beside me. Gianni slipped into a chair opposite.

"What brings you to Dusk Bay? Let me guess, this is about Kurt?" Her smile quickly faded. "We haven't found him. I assume you haven't come to tell me you did?" She looked tentatively hopeful.

"Not exactly." I told her about finding the man who called himself Frank, after the twins followed him from the airport. Her eyes widened when I described the house that exploded just after we stepped out of it.

"Fucking hell," she whispered. "You're right, that sounds like Kurt, but at the same time, it doesn't. He's not usually messy like that. He'd lure you there, then set off a bomb while you were still inside if killing was his end goal. If it was, he swung and missed."

"Twice." I told her about the gunfight on the way home. "Apparently they were sent to tell us to back off from trying to find him."

She snorted loudly. "Good luck with that. None of us is giving up now. I'm guessing Reuben is more pissed off than ever."

"About that and other things," Gianni agreed.

I rubbed my palms together absentmindedly. "Does Kurt have a twin? The man who called himself Frank looked a lot like him."

Daze frowned. "No, he doesn't. We don't have any other siblings. At least, not that I know of. I suppose it's possible we have a half brother, but if we do, his existence was kept from me."

"Who would dare to keep anything from you?" Ric stepped into the room and closed the door behind him.

"Only someone with a death wish." She gave him a fond smile.

He stepped around behind her and started to massage her shoulders. While he worked out her knots, she filled him in on the conversation.

"One Kurt is bad enough," he said. "The world doesn't need two."

"The world doesn't need the one it has," Gianni said.

"We're doing the best we can to rid the world of him," Ric said. "But if he's hiring people to attack Reuben, that's concerning."

"We're starting to think his operation is bigger than first thought," Gianni said. "If he can afford to go around setting off bombs and sending mercenaries after us, then he's doing better than we knew about."

Ric's hands stilled. "That's why—"

The door opened. "This is where you all are."

I froze like a proverbial deer in headlights when my sister, Rose, stepped through the door. She looked around the room before she noticed me sitting there. Her lips dropped apart.

"Mina?" She blinked a couple of times like I was a mirage that might disappear at any moment.

On unsteady feet, I stood.

"Yes, it's me." My lips moved, but I couldn't think of another thing to say. Then she moved towards me and wrapped her arms around me.

Unlike the hug from Daze, I melted into this one. I put my arms around my older sister and held her firm, like I could have five years worth of embraces in one.

"What in the world are you doing here?" she asked without letting go. "I thought you were…"

"I know what you thought." I rested my head against her shoulder. I'd forgotten how much taller than me she was. I was the shortest in my family, hence the nickname, the Sparrow. I'd always been dainty. I could fit into spaces others couldn't, and sneak around more silently than bigger people. Not to mention, who would suspect a tiny woman of killing people? It was the perfect ruse.

Daze scooted over to make room on the couch for Rose and me. My hands in my sister's, my voice soft, breaking occasionally, I told her everything. Not the part about being the Sparrow, but everything else.

She listened with growing horror, her blue eyes filling with tears for me. Every so often, she stopped me to give me a hug, before sitting back to listen.

"I had no idea," she said finally. She shook her head, her blonde ponytail swishing back and forth. We shared some facial features, but in colouring and body shape, we couldn't be more different.

The expression of fury in her eyes matched the one I saw in the mirror.

"I assume there's a long line to kill this prick?" she asked. "If so, I want in. I never liked him very much, but to do this to my baby sister…" She wiped away tears from under her eyes.

"There's definitely a line," Daze growled. "For the record, I had no idea what my fuckhead brother was doing. None of us did."

Rose glanced at her. "I know you better than to think you'd let it go on a second after you found out about it. No more than I would."

Daze nodded, but looked slightly relieved. There was always a chance Rose might have blamed her.

"I didn't know either," Ric said. "Not until…" He grimaced. "A few weeks ago."

Rose's scowl reminded me so much of our mother. "A few *weeks* ago? You knew what happened to my sister and didn't tell me?"

"I asked them not to," I said. "I wasn't ready to see any of you yet. I'm still not ready to see Dane or Asher."

"But they—" she started. She stopped when she saw the expression on my face. "Okay, when you're ready. What do you need from me?"

"Same as you've been doing," Ric said. "Keep your eyes and ears open. Make sure your contacts know we're looking for that asshole. The minute you do, we want to hear about it."

She nodded. "I can do that. That's not enough though." She shook her head. "No one gets away with doing what he did to my little sister. I'll put everything onto this and I'll be wherever Mina needs me to be."

She wiped away tears again. She'd already cried more than I had in years. She was efficient, and dangerous in her own way, but evidently she wasn't as cold-blooded as me.

Did I have a dark heart or was I dead inside? Possibly both. That would explain my attraction to Reuben and Gianni. Damon too. Like-minded people coming together.

"Thank you," I said softly. What else could I say? I glanced over to Daze. "You had no idea I was coming?"

It was Ric who answered. "If we did, we would have made sure Rose wasn't here." He ignored the way she bristled in response.

"Why *are* you here?" I asked her.

"Taking care of a few things for Ric and Daze," she said vaguely.

I decided not to press the issue. I had some idea of what my sister got up to. I didn't need too many details.

"It's just as well I was here," she continued. "If I wasn't, who knows when I would have seen you and found out what happened. As it is, I was only supposed to be here for a few hours before heading back to Melbourne. I don't suppose I can convince you to come with me? Now I've seen you, I don't know if I can let you go again."

"I have things to take care of in Sydney," I said. "But now you know about me, maybe you can come and visit?"

I felt as though I barely knew her. She was my older sister, by six years as it was, and we'd missed so much time. She must have changed during the last five years.

Did she like any of the things she used to like? I had a feeling she'd want the answers to the same questions and I didn't have them.

Apart from reading, I hadn't paid much attention to the world outside Reuben's house. I hadn't watched TV, listened to music or touched a device that wasn't my phone. None of that interested me. Right then, I was focused on taking things one day at a time.

"Of course I will," Rose said. "Are you sure I can't say anything to Dane or Asher? They'd really want to—"

"No," I said firmly. "You never saw me. As far as you know, I'm off living my best life. When I'm ready, I'll tell them everything." I exhaled softly. "Do you see much of them?"

She shook her head. "I see Dane once in a while and Asher a few times a year. We always get together when he's in town for a gig. Or when I'm in Sydney."

"Is he happy?" I asked in a whisper.

She smiled softly. "He's Asher, he's always happy. He's living the high life doing what he does with his closest friends. Sometimes I envy him. Only sometimes. What I do is fun too. In its own way."

"I'm sure it is," I agreed. In the corner of my eye, I caught the expression on Daze's face. She was looking at me speculatively. I could almost hear her thinking.

"Is there any chance Mina and I could have a few moments?" Daze asked. "It's almost time for dinner. We could meet you in the dining room."

They all hesitated, Rose and Gianni looking at me, Ric looking at Daze.

"It's okay," I said. "We won't be long." If Reuben thought she was a threat to me, he wouldn't have let Gianni bring me here. I was certain I could hold my own if I needed to anyway. Daze wasn't that much bigger than me.

Gianni gave me a long look, but reluctantly herded the others out of the room and closed the door behind us.

I turned to Daze and gave her an eyebrow arch worthy of Reuben. "I'm guessing they won't give us long."

She snorted. "Probably not." Her tongue slid over her lips. "I saw the Sparrow is active again."

"I heard the same thing," I said.

"Interesting coincidence they disappeared right around the time you did," she said.

"It's very strange," I agreed. "What are the chances?"

She smiled. "No one is going to hear about it from me, but I have to tell you I'm a big fan. I've heard so many stories about the Sparrow."

"You can't have a selfie with me," I said deadpan. "At least, not in that capacity."

She laughed. "Of course not. The boys should watch out though. You, me and Rose, and a couple of others, could take over the world."

"The Sisterhood of Queens," I said.

She grinned. "I prefer goddesses, but sisterhood works. Lucky for them, we need some muscle once in a while. And some cock."

"We have to keep them around for something," I said with a slight smile.

Hers faded when she realised what she said. "I'm sorry, I didn't mean to…"

I shook my head. "I can't live the rest of my life dwelling on what he did to me. Neither can you. Please don't try to tiptoe around me. I get that enough at home."

I understood and appreciated it there, but I didn't want it from her.

"You really are a badass aren't you?" she asked. "Thank fuck we're on the same side or, frankly, I'd be scared of you."

I snorted. "I can't imagine you being scared of anything. Or anyone."

She spread her hands. "I didn't think it was possible either, but here we are. Now, shall we go and join the others?"

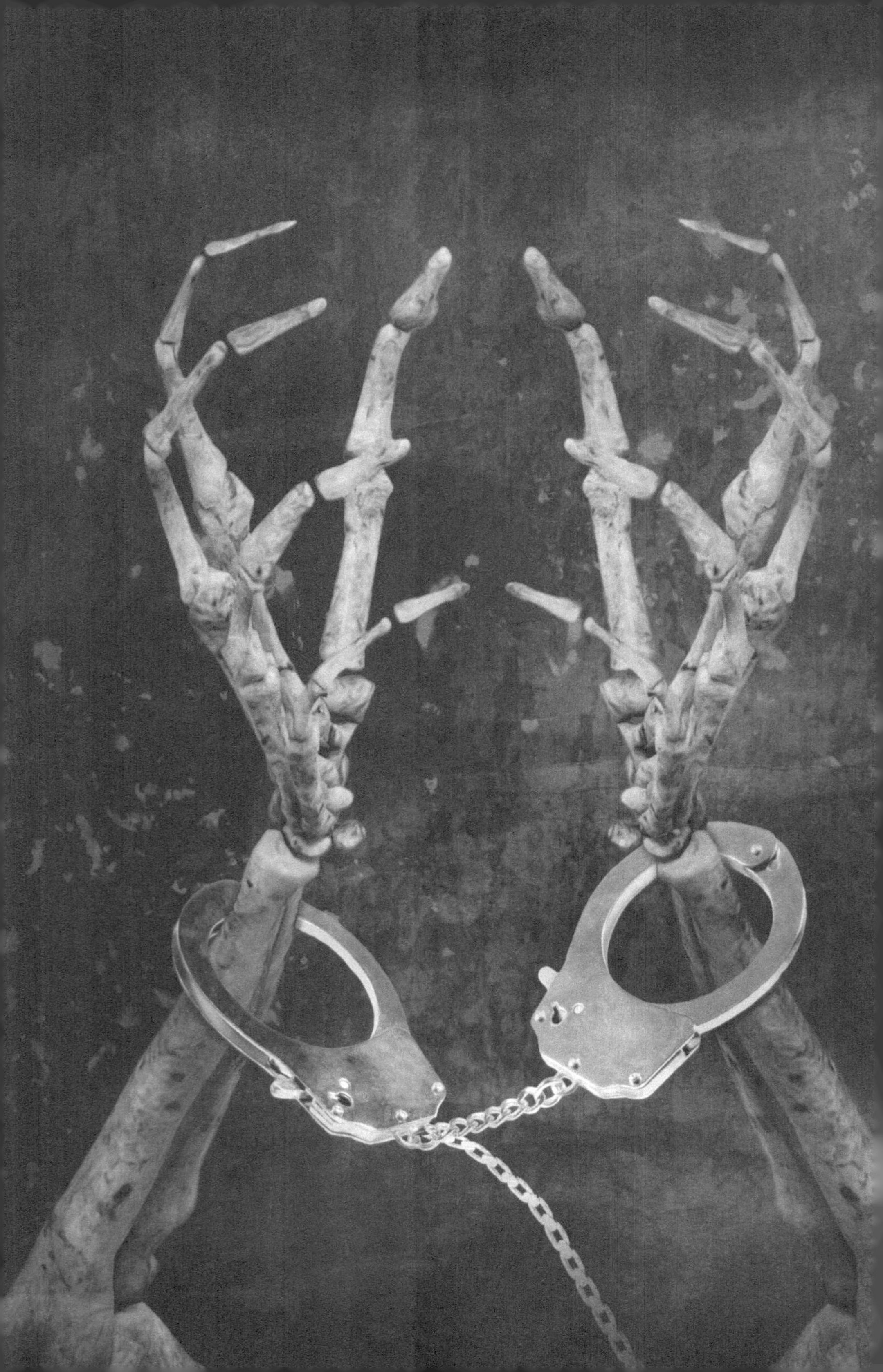

CHAPTER 5

DAMON

"I fucked up." Gianni rubbed his cheeks with the heels of both his hands and grimaced. "I should have looked into where Rose was before we flew out of Sydney."

Reuben looked at him over the top of his desk. "How did she respond?" He seemed more interested in Mina's reaction to seeing her sister than in Gianni screwing up.

Right here was a prime example of why I kept insisting she was a distraction. Not because I didn't care about how she felt, but because Gianni making a mistake should have been a higher priority. He didn't make mistakes like that. Neither did I.

Except on this occasion. I hadn't looked into Rose's whereabouts either. My attention was focused on searching for Kurt. And keeping an eye out for any sign of trouble in Dusk Bay. The city was a cesspool at the best of times. Mostly under Reuben's control, but a cesspool nonetheless. I didn't envy Caleb having to keep a close eye on it. Although, fuck knows if the man fit in better than the rest of us would.

Gianni looked at Reuben through his spread fingers. "Surprised, but happy to see her, I guess. They sat together after dinner and had a long chat. Rose was as pissed off as you'd imagine. She went all mother tiger over what happened to her baby sister."

"That sounds like Rose," I said. Both of us were good at fixing things. I would have brought her in on this earlier if it wasn't for Mina's insistence. Rose had contacts I didn't and vice versa. Between us, we could have Kurt screaming down in the basement by now.

"It doesn't sound like too much harm was done," Reuben concluded. "Have you—"

"Dane is still at Brutham Academy," I interrupted. "Asher is on tour. As of two minutes ago, Rose is back in Melbourne."

Ric contacted me before Gianni and Mina returned from Dusk Bay. I'd anticipated Reuben wanting to know the whereabouts of her other siblings.

Reuben nodded. "They're easier to keep track of than Kurt."

I held back a grimace. The comment wasn't personal, but it was difficult not to take it to heart.

If anyone should be all over finding him, it was me. This was literally my job. I didn't appreciate Kurt making a laughing stock of me, or my network of contacts. I wasn't even one of the first five people in line to kill him slowly, but I'd happily watch.

"I have everything and everyone on this," I said smoothly. "Lasalle is like a ghost. Or a slug. He's left a trail behind, but no one seems to know where he is. If he's paid people to say they haven't seen him, he's paid them well. Not even threats or torture have uncovered anything. If I didn't know better, I'd think he doesn't actually exist."

"Is that possible?" Gianni frowned. "He was in the building where he kept Mina just before we found her. Maybe he ran out onto the road and got hit by a car. He could be a John Doe lying in the morgue somewhere. His face might be so smashed in he's unrecognisable. His teeth all broken up and his ugly face ruined."

He waved his hands in front of his face. He didn't find himself attractive, but he had the kind of face people couldn't help looking at. Intelligence burned in those dark eyes, along with a good amount of deviousness. He fascinated people and in turn, was fascinated by people.

He fascinated me, but he wasn't the only one who held my attention.

"I think you're projecting," I told him. "You want to smash his ugly face in and ruin it."

"Hell yeah I do," he agreed. "So do you."

I shrugged one shoulder. "A bullet between his eyes is quicker and cleaner." I knew Reuben's preference for neat and tidy over messy and sloppy. Truthfully, I shared that preference. Mess got out of control too quickly.

"I don't care how he dies, as long as he dies." Reuben steepled his fingers and pressed them against his lips. His voice was low as ever, a rumble that made my balls tingle.

As long as I'd known him, he'd had that effect on me. Something I barely admitted to myself, much less to him. He was my boss. That was one of many reasons why I had to push those thoughts aside and focus on the conversation.

"I was thinking we could set a trap for him," I said. "Something that will ensure he comes out of the hole he's buried himself in."

Reuben turned those ice blue eyes on me and arched an eyebrow in question. "You have something in mind?"

"We can start by hacking his bank account and draining all the funds," I said.

Until now, we'd been keeping track of them, watching for money to be withdrawn. Hoping the transactions would give away his location. So far, he hadn't touched any of his accounts. Not the ones we knew about anyway.

He may not even notice us empty his accounts, but it would be fucking satisfying.

"Can I have a Maserati?" Gianni asked. "I mean, Kurt's money should go to something useful."

"His money should go to Mina," Reuben said. "She can decide if you should have a Maserati."

Gianni punched the air and grinned. "That wasn't a no."

Reuben smirked at him.

Gianni, as always, was unapologetic.

"Have the twins hack his accounts," Reuben said to me. Parker was studying cybersecurity to prevent anyone from hacking us, but that skill was useful in reverse. "Make sure they don't drain the money into their own accounts."

That was definitely something they'd do, given half a chance.

I glanced over at Gianni.

He looked back at me. "What?"

"I'm waiting for you to wonder out loud if the twins would buy you a Maserati." I leaned against the wall, crossed my arms and cocked an eyebrow at him.

He chuckled. "They probably would, but if that money is meant for Mina, and they tried to take it, I'd have to smash their kneecaps. Then we'd have to transfer the money to her and, voilà, we're back to me asking her for a Maserati."

"I see you've thought it all the way through," I said.

"I always do." He grinned. "To be honest, I thought you would have too."

I rolled my eyes at him, then turned back to Reuben. "If that gets no response from him, we may need to think bigger."

His eyes narrowed slightly. "If you're suggesting what I think you're suggesting…"

"If Kurt knows Mina is alive and well, and with us, that's going to elicit some kind of response," I said.

"Prick," Gianni snapped. "We're not using her as bait."

Reuben bristled too, but waited for me to continue.

"I'm not suggesting we use her as bait. Sooner or later people are going to need to know she's alive and what he did to her. We could let everyone know. Eventually, word would get back to him. People who are loyal to him might turn on him. This might be exactly what we need to draw him out."

"Mina isn't ready to—" Gianni started.

"It doesn't fucking matter what she's ready for," I said. "The fact is, this might be the only way to get to him. I'm not suggesting she walk around the streets waving a red fucking flag. I'm just saying we can let people know she's here and let the rumour mill do the rest."

"You're a red fucking flag," Gianni muttered.

I choked back a laugh. "Pot, meet kettle."

"What's that supposed to mean?" He rounded on me.

"I mean, you're not exactly a middle-class, suburban working guy, are you? We break the law for a living. We kill people. Threaten, bribe and coerce. What's that if not a red flag?"

"Sounds like a green flag to me." He jutted his chin out in defiance. "Women, and men, are attracted to powerful people like us. You need to read one of Mina's mafia romance books. I'm telling you, we're fucking hot. Some more than others." He pretended to fluff the back of his hair.

"Yeah, some are." I resisted the urge to look at Reuben. If he was in a book, he'd be the character readers were drooling over. Him and Mina.

I forced myself to not think about her on her knees, his cock between her lips. I would also not think about me on my knees doing the same thing.

Reuben cleared his throat. "I'll think about it. That's something we'll need to discuss with Mina before we proceed. I'm not going to do that behind her back."

"I wasn't suggesting we should," I said. "She should know the plan before we execute it."

Having her upset after the fact was another distraction we didn't need. She should be told what we were doing and deal with it. She wanted Kurt dealt with even more than we did. She'd understand the need for this.

"If we do," Gianni said firmly. "There has to be a better way."

"You could walk around Sydney waving a red flag," I suggested. "Maybe with the words, 'Where the fuck are you, Kurt?' written on it."

"That would be subtle," Reuben said dryly. "If I thought it would work, I'd send Gianni out right now."

"If I thought it would work, I'd go," Gianni said. "On the other hand, Damon is better looking than me. He'd be much better at something like this."

I ignored the comment. "If I thought Kurt would actually reveal himself for his sister, we could try that. It doesn't seem like there's much love lost between them." Since Daze was one of those top five in line to eviscerate Kurt, I doubted he'd care what happened to her.

"Is there anyone he cares about?" Reuben asked. "A wife? Children? Friends?"

"None," I said. I thought for a moment. "Mina said something about her being given to Kurt as payment for some debt. I've always had a feeling there was more to it than that. I haven't found any evidence of financial debt."

I'd gone through every record I could find from five years ago, and further back. If Mina's father owed Lasalle anything, there was absolutely no record of it. That didn't mean it hadn't happened. Some transactions still took place with cash. That was exactly why the Brotherhood of Kings was pushing for a cashless society. It was much easier to track funds electronically than it was to trace notes and coins.

"That might have been a lie Kurt spun," Gianni said.

"Then how did she end up with him?" I asked. "I don't get the impression he randomly snatched her off the streets. Have either of you dug down deeper?"

"She hasn't been—" Gianni started.

"Let me guess, she hasn't been ready," I interrupted. "She might have to be ready. Anything she can tell us might be the key to leading us to him."

I understood she needed to heal, but we couldn't sit around and wait forever. If we did that, she may never be ready. Kurt could elude us until the day he died of natural causes. I had no intention of letting that happen. Whatever the cost.

Gianni looked like he was going to continue the argument, but exhaled and nodded. "I'll speak to her. If that's okay with you, boss?"

Reuben inclined his head. "Do that. Damon is right. She might have the answers we need."

CHAPTER 6

MINA

Terry making crème brûlée was mesmerising. One of those little blow torches in his large hand, he leaned forward, careful to let the flames lick the top of the desert, browning them.

"It's hard to believe someone so big can do something so dainty, isn't it?" Gianni asked.

I was aware of him stepping into the kitchen, and over to stand beside me. I didn't need to look to know who it was, even before he spoke. He moved differently from anyone else here. His footsteps were lighter, like a cat.

He made no effort to be quiet, but he was anyway. Like he made it his life's work to be unassuming. Physically anyway.

Terry gave him the side eye, but didn't look away from his work.

Gianni chuckled. "He's a master of making desserts. Fortunately for my stomach, he doesn't make them too often." He patted his flat stomach. "When he does, they're sublime." He mimed a chef's kiss.

"They smell incredible," I said. Everything he cooked did. To be fair, he could have made toast with butter on it and it would taste like paradise after five years of stale bread and the occasional apple.

"Can we talk for a minute?" Gianni asked.

I looked over to him. "That sounds ominous. Was Reuben pissed off about me seeing Rose?" I was tired after our flight back and the drive through the city, so I'd opted to take a nap instead of attending that meeting.

My continued lethargy was frustrating, but slowly easing as I got stronger. I could spend longer in the gym now, working out. Soon, I'd be back to my full fitness.

Not soon enough, as far as I was concerned.

"Nothing I couldn't handle," Gianni said lightly. He laced my fingers in his and led me out of the kitchen.

"I'm not feeling reassured." I followed him into the library and let him close the door behind us. Was there a chance they figured out who I was? Had Daze told them, even after promising not to?

I decided that was unlikely. The vibe I was getting from him was different to that. He seemed apprehensive, but nothing to suggest he was processing a bombshell that big.

He waved for me to sit down and pulled over a footstool to perch in front of me. "Damon has some...ideas." He grimaced as if he'd tasted something nasty in the past and was now remembering how unpleasant it was.

"Judging by the look on your face, you don't like them," I said.

His expression relaxed slightly. "I like one of them." He explained the plan to drain Kurt's bank accounts. "Reuben thinks you should have the money."

"I suppose so," I said unenthusiastically.

I couldn't explain why I didn't really need it. Not without telling him why. It wouldn't hurt to have extra funds to put into finding the asshole, I supposed. Anything left over after that could go to charity. I didn't want Kurt's dirty money. I didn't have to fake that. I wanted nothing from him.

"What was Damon's other idea?" I asked.

I listened while Gianni told me quickly and briefly what Damon proposed.

My first instinct was to give in to a spike of panic. If they did what he suggested, Dane and Asher would know where I was and what happened to me. That couldn't happen, not yet.

"I told him this was a bad idea," Gianni said. "I'll tell them both to fuck off." He placed his hands to either side of him on the footstool and started to stand.

Without thinking, I grabbed his wrist, my hand snapping out so quickly I surprised myself.

"What if we put out word someone was found down in the basement?" I said slowly. "We don't have to say who. We don't even have to say I'm alive. Knowing he was keeping a woman chained up down there, in a cage, would be enough to make people think twice about supporting him. They may not turn on him, but they might get sloppy."

Gianni lowered himself back down. "Now I know who the brains of the outfit is. We should have thought of that. I was busy being pissed off at Damon."

"He doesn't like me, does he?" I asked. "He'd happily throw me to the wolves."

"Damon doesn't like much of anyone, including himself," Gianni said. "He has some shit in his past to overcome." He hesitated. "Speaking of the past…"

The subtle change in his tone immediately had me on edge.

"What about it?" I asked carefully.

"Damon can't find any sign of a financial debt between your father and Kurt," Gianni said. "You said you don't know what the debt involved, but I don't remember if you said whether or not you knew Kurt before all of that. Did you?"

I hesitated. This would have come up sooner or later, but was I ready to respond?

"Did you know him before he put you down in that cage?" Gianni asked, gentle but insistent.

I sat back and rubbed my forehead with my thumb and fingers. "Yes I did. My father hired him to teach me self defence." Other skills too, but that explanation would do for now. "I guess he paid him in cash, if there's no trail. Or they found a way to hide the transactions." That wasn't my area of expertise.

Gianni's wide lips dropped apart. "He taught you self defence?"

"And he used everything he taught me against me," I said. "He could anticipate what I'd do."

That only helped him in the moments I tried to fight back. Mostly, he used words, reminding me of what happened that night. Breaking me down, bit by bit, with my own guilt.

"Shit," Gianni breathed. "He really is a prick."

I glanced down at the hardwood floor under my bare feet.

"He said he had a thing for me. I told him I wasn't interested. He decided he didn't want to take no for an answer. I don't know what happened between him and Dad." I shook my head. "But somehow Kurt forced his hand so he'd give me to him."

"That's fucked up," Gianni said softly. "It sounds like he was obsessed. I'm obsessed with you, but my obsession is much healthier than that."

I looked back up at him and managed a small smile. "I never said Kurt wasn't unhinged as fuck. Normal people don't lock people down in basements. They don't starve them until they're too weak to stand. They don't…" I didn't need to elaborate. Gianni knew what happened to me.

"By the time we're done with him, the biggest part of him anyone will be able to find will be his little toe," Gianni growled. "I plan to keep him alive until that point. I don't know how, but I will."

"I believe you," I told him. I wished I could tell him everything else. I hated lying to him. Was I as bad as Kurt for doing it? The line was too fine, too blurred, even though I reminded myself I wasn't doing it to be cruel.

"How old were you when you met him?" Gianni asked.

I swallowed to keep the contents of my stomach from coming back up. "I was fourteen. He was about eighteen. Full of anger and arrogance."

I remembered the way he used to throw me, then pin me to the mat and look down at me, like he wanted to devour me. I quickly learned how to throw him off me.

Down in the basement, he'd looked at me the same way, so many times. Usually right before he forced himself on me. Did he ever see me as a person? I doubted it. He thought of me as his possession. A toy he could do whatever he wanted to. As if I had no thoughts or feelings of my own.

"I'm so sorry." Gianni cupped my cheek lightly with his hand. "I wish I could take all the hurt away." He leaned in to brush his lips over mine.

I hesitated for a moment. Pushed my dark thoughts aside to kiss him back. I wanted to think about anything else right now but Kurt. No, I didn't even want to think. I just wanted to feel. I needed a connection to another person that didn't involve fear and violence. I wanted that connection with Gianni.

I wanted more. My body and soul both ached for it.

I took his hand and guided it down between my legs. "Can you… touch me here?" I whispered. "I want to know how it feels to be touched gently."

"Of course I can, sweetheart," he said. He rubbed his knuckles over the front of my jeans, light and tender. My clit throbbed, yearning for more.

I sucked in a breath. Could I do this? I'd be exposing myself literally and emotionally.

It was the latter that had me terrified. With some effort, I forced myself not to switch off and retreat into the back of my mind. Doing that would be an injustice to us both.

I managed to work the button loose on my jeans and draw down the zipper.

After another breath, this one more shallow, I lifted my hips to push my jeans down to my thighs. A thin layer of pale pink lace was the only thing between his hand and my pussy.

His eyes were huge, but reverent, very much aware of what I was asking of him. Very much determined to give me exactly that, what and how I needed it.

He rubbed the tips of his fingers across the gusset, with increasing firmness, until I was rolling my hips, increasing the friction.

"Sweetheart—" he whispered.

"Don't stop," I whispered back. "I want more."

He pulled the gusset aside and slid his fingers against my bare pussy.

I shivered at his touch, but this was nothing like… I didn't want to think his name right now. I'd never been touched like this before. This was gentle and sweet. At the same time, hot as hell.

"Are you okay?" he asked.

"More than okay," I said. "Please—"

"Can I taste you?" he sounded tentative, like he wasn't sure if he was overstepping boundaries. Worried he'd scare me away.

My tongue swiped over my lips. "I— Yes."

He dropped from the footstool, down to his knees in front of me. With gentle fingers, he gripped my thighs, opening me out to him. His eyes on mine, he lowered his mouth to my pussy. Letting my reactions guide him, he started to lightly tease me with the tip of his tongue.

When I didn't freak out, he carefully pressed a finger inside me, then another.

I was trembling, ready to come faster than I ever would have expected. I found myself looking down at him through a glaze of tears, surprised at myself for not freaking out or wanting to run away. For being able to let him touch me without flinching violently.

I blinked away the tears and watched him fuck me with his mouth and hand. Every lick and stroke brought me closer and closer to coming.

I let out a soft moan and pitched over the edge, into the first orgasm I ever had that I didn't give to myself.

I arched my back and ground myself against his mouth, wanting to enjoy every second, every moment for as long as I could. This was what I'd been missing all this time. A pure, loving connection between two people. Sweet touches from a man who wanted nothing more from me than to see me enjoy myself.

He went on lapping at my pussy until I came all the way down from my orgasm and my vision cleared. My pulse raced like crazy, but the rest of me felt like blissed out rubber.

He pulled his head back and grinned. "Sweetheart, you taste like pure heaven. Sound like it too. I've never heard a woman come like that."

He slid his hand out of me and, with a cheeky smile, licked my release from his fingers.

"Thank you," I said softly. "No one has ever done that for me before."

"I should be thanking you," he said. "For letting me do that for you. I could lick that sweet pussy of yours all day long. And all night. You're so fucking perfect. So fucking mine."

When he said it, there was nothing creepy about it. Nothing to suggest he wanted to hide me away from the world and use me. His tone was one of love and genuine appreciation and respect for me. When he said I was his, he meant I was his to cherish, not to possess. At least, not in the way Kurt wanted to possess me. They couldn't be more different.

"If I'm not careful, I could fall for you," I told him.

He grinned. "That's great, because I've already fallen for you. What's that fishing analogy? Cook, line and sinker?"

I laughed softly and lifted my hips to help him put my panties and jeans back into place. "I think it's hook, line and sinker. But yours is good too."

"Mine is more likely to include food," he said. "I've had my dessert, I'm sure you'd like to have yours. They're probably ready by now." He offered me his hand, just as my stomach rumbled.

I took it and stood. I chewed my lip for a moment before saying, "I want to taste you some day."

"Any time, sweetheart," he said. Judging by the tenting in the front of his pants, he was ready right now. I wished I was too, but we had plenty of time.

I hoped.

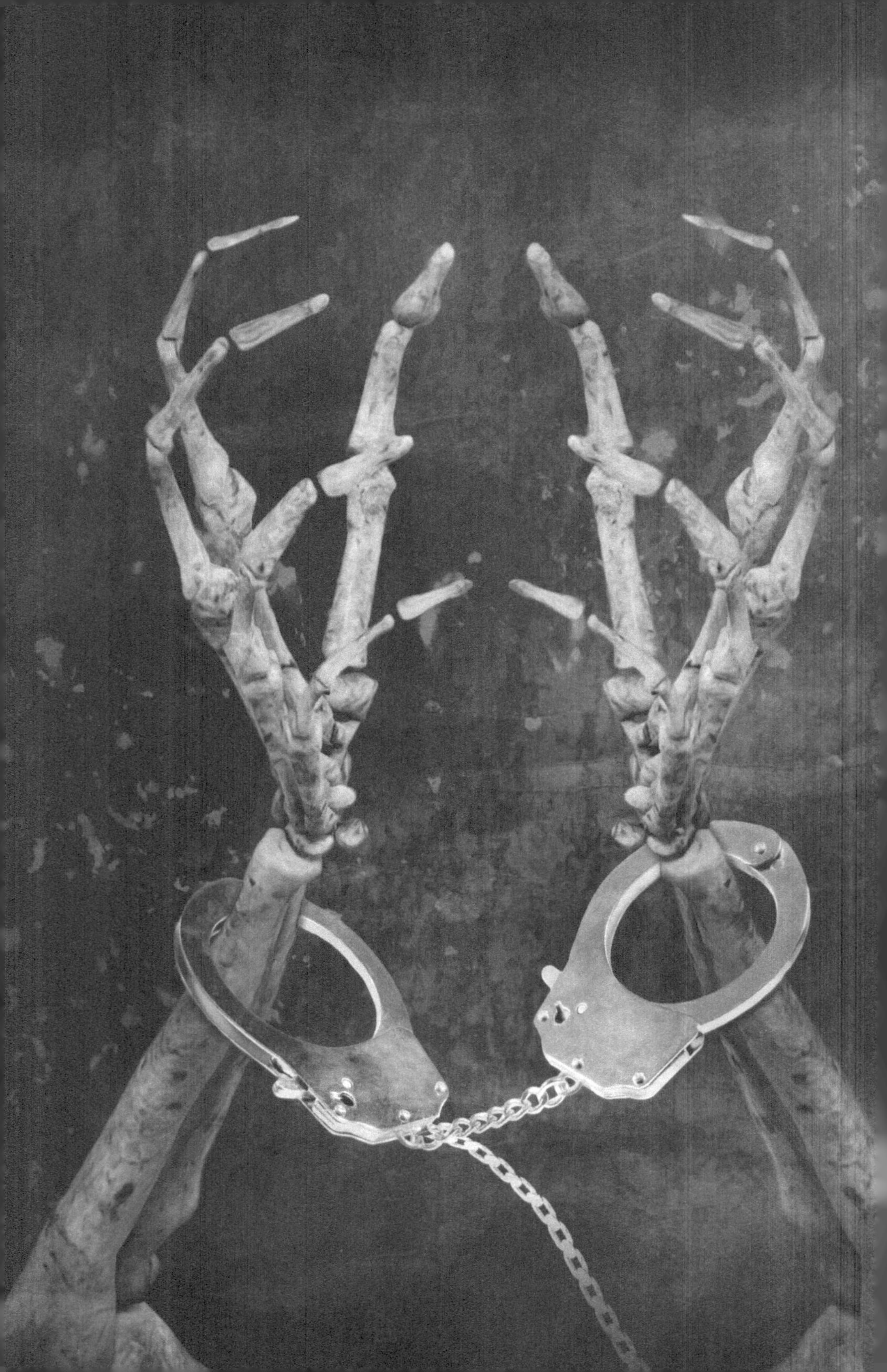

CHAPTER 7

MINA

I double and triple checked the address. Double and triple checked the layout of the building. Moved around it slowly, taking in everything.

The building looked old and tired, but it was a façade. The security system was state-of-the-art. Unable to be disabled or hacked.

Unable, my ass. There was no such thing as a security system that couldn't be bypassed. You just had to know how.

Ignoring the fact it was Kurt who taught me, I pulled a small device out of my pocket and held it up to the touchscreen beside the door.

I pressed my fingers against the front of the device, letting it read my thumbprint. A screen on the front turned on, dark enough that it wouldn't alert anyone to me standing outside in the shadows.

A tap on the screen and it started to run through numbers and symbols. One by one, it deciphered the pass code. The keypad flashed green and the door unlocked with a faint click.

I shoved the device back in my pocket and opened the door wide enough to slip inside. Silently, I closed the door behind me.

The corridor in front of me was in darkness, but a room at the end was well lit.

I grimaced at the sound of groaning that came from it. It was loud enough that I could have stomped down the corridor and not be heard.

I shook my head and eased forward, stepping carefully across the polished concrete floor. I passed two closed doors and an open one. I glanced in, but saw nothing but darkness and the outline of a bed. No one was in there.

I stepped to the room at the end of the corridor.

A man sat on a couch in the middle of the room. His track pants were pushed down his thighs, his hand curled around his cock.

The groans came from a huge TV on the wall. On the screen, three or four guys were railing a woman who looked as though she was thinking about her shopping list, while they thrust in and out of her pussy, ass and mouth.

"Fuck yeah." He worked his cock harder, oblivious until I stepped behind him, leaned over the back of the couch and pressed a knife to his throat.

He stopped mid-beat, eyes wide. "The fuck?"

"Hi, Stefan. I see nothing has changed. It's just you and your hand." I pressed the blade in slightly. Not enough to make him bleed, but to let him know I meant business.

"Mina fucking DiMarco," he growled. "You scared the shit out of me." His hand was still tight around his cock, like he didn't dare to let go. Just in case I cut it off.

Fair call. I was tempted. Not that I wanted to touch his cock.

"If you have nothing to hide, you have nothing to fear," I said.

He raised his spare hand. "I'm an open book."

"Where's Kurt?" I asked.

He lowered his hand, bringing it down over the other one for additional protection. "I have no idea."

"Mmm." I pressed the knife in a little more, barely breaking the skin. "Wrong answer."

"I can't give you what I don't have," he said. "I swear, I don't know where he is. But—" He exhaled reluctantly.

"But?" I prompted.

"But I have a number to contact him," Stefan said quickly. "Not directly. I send a message and someone passes the message on to him. It's on my phone." He nodded to the table in front of him.

"What happens then?" I asked.

"After a day or two, he sends a message back via, I dunno, whoever the fuck it is. The last I heard was to lay low and play it cool. Seems one of the big heavies is on his ass. Reuben Brantley or Samuel Bell. Kurt was fucking them both over, so I'm not surprised. Dickhead likes to live dangerously."

"You worked with him," I said.

"Indirectly," he argued. "I'm just a fence. People bring me their shit and I sell it for them. Get a nice tidy profit on top of it. Getting involved in things too deeply is above my pay grade. I'm what they call a petty criminal, but you know that."

"I think you're underselling yourself," I said. "Rumour has it you're Kurt's right-hand."

He laughed-grunted. "Not me. He didn't trust me enough for that."

"Who did he trust?" I asked.

"I don't—" Stefan started.

A bead of blood rose where I pushed the knife in a little more.

"Let's try this again. Who did he trust?" There was no doubt in my mind he knew.

That was why I was here tonight. Why I'd snuck out of the house again to deal with him. I had to take the chance he'd speak to me. We weren't friends, but he knew who I was. More or less.

He sat perfectly still, probably weighing his options. If he talked, he was dead. If he didn't talk, he was dead. If he told me everything, he might just have the chance to run and hide before shit hit the fan.

"There's a dude named Leon Graves, he's an old friend of Kurt. He ran a lot of Kurt's operations. If anyone knows where he is, it's him. If I had to guess, I'd say he was the one receiving and relaying the messages."

"There, that wasn't so difficult, was it?" I asked.

"If he finds out I said anything to you, I'm fucked," Stefan whined.

"I have no reason to tell him you said anything to me," I said. "And I know *you* won't."

"Of course not." He took the chance to raise his left hand, as if to promise he wouldn't say a word.

I smirked and sliced open his throat. "You might have misunderstood what I was saying." His blood squirted out onto my fingers, warm and sticky. Better his blood than his cum.

His hand dropped back down with a soft thud. He slumped back against the couch, his hand still wrapped around his cock.

"Sucks to be you," I said with no sympathy. I walked around the couch to pick up his phone. After a couple of attempts to guess the passcode, it opened.

"Sixty-nine, sixty-nine, sixty-nine." I rolled my eyes. "You shouldn't have been so predictable."

His glazed eyes stared back at me. He looked regretful, but I doubted it involved his pass code.

On the screen, one of the men grunted as he came, spilling cum all over the woman's face. I snatched up the remote and turned it off. I dropped the remote back on the table and scrolled through his phone.

His photos contained various candid shots of women. They all looked like they were taken through a window, or under the door of a public toilet. Their faces weren't visible in most of them, just a breast here, leg or pussy there.

"Looks like I did the world a favour," I said. "One less pervert." I tapped out of the photos and went in to read his messages. As I expected, there weren't many. One or two with a vague address or a thumbs up symbol. The rest were deleted, or he didn't get many.

His contacts were likewise sparse. The pizza place down the street, the number of a ride share, and a couple that might be Leon Graves, or another of Kurt's associates.

I pulled out my phone, copied the numbers and wiped down his phone with a cloth before placing it back on the table.

Leon would change his number if he knew someone took Stefan's phone. If I just had the number, I stood a chance of being able to use it.

"I'd like to say it's been fun, but I hope this was worthwhile," I told Stefan. "Don't worry, someone will find you in a couple of days. If you're lucky."

The man was a snake and always had been. He was also one of the men who carried me down into the basement. I recognised his voice as soon as he spoke. Was Leon Graves another of them? I'd met him a couple of times, and two of the men didn't say a word that night. All I had was vague memories of their faces in shadow, my mind muddled by whatever Kurt drugged me with.

From my phone, I sent a tipoff to one of Damon's contacts, giving them Stefan's name. They'd pass that on to Damon. He could come by and find him like this.

Reuben would be pissed off if he knew I wasn't telling them any of this directly, but I couldn't explain how I got into this building without telling him everything. He'd insist on knowing how I got past impenetrable security.

I wasn't ready to share that yet. Not even with him or Gianni. Not with Damon either, although I still had no idea where I stood with him. He seemed to want me as much as he disliked me.

I respected him, but I wouldn't push. There was no hurry to take things any further. Not yet. When this was over, maybe we'd find time to work things out.

I tucked my phone away and took a few minutes to search around the building. I found a locked room, but no sign of the key. I looked back at Stefan and grimaced.

His pants were down around his ankles. One side looked heavier than the other.

"Really?" I asked, not knowing if I directed the question to him or myself. Either way, I had no choice.

I had to crouch to feel around in his pockets. The heavier one contained a small ring of keys. One said Mercedes on the fob. The others looked like house keys, or keys that unlocked filing cabinets.

Stepping away from him and his now flaccid cock, I tried each of the keys until the door opened.

I half-expected to find a woman caged and chained, but the room was full of boxes.

Guns, gems, phones and cash. One contained what looked like bricks of cocaine. The street value of everything here would add up to several million, at least. This, Reuben would be happy to recover.

I left everything untouched and closed and locked the door behind me. Grimacing again, I replaced the keys in Stefan's pocket and went to rifle through his bedroom. I found nothing but the usual: clothes, shoes, an unopened box of condoms. I picked it up and checked the expiry date.

"Three months ago," I said with a smirk. "That tracks." Stefan was a slimy bastard. The women of the world wouldn't miss him. Neither would the men, for that matter.

I knelt down beside his bed and shone my phone light underneath.

"What do we have here?" I said to myself. I set my phone aside and pulled out the box. Metal and maybe thirty centimetres wide and just as long, it was fitted with a basic padlock. The kind quickly unpicked with the lock pick I kept in my pocket.

I eased open the lid and looked inside.

In the centre lay a phone. The battery was flat, but I decided I could spare a few moments to charge it until the screen turned on. The passcode was simple. There was nothing on the phone but a single app.

I pressed on the screen to open it.

My stomach turned. I felt as though my whole world was tipped upside down. My entire body started to tremble. In my mind, I was right back in the cage, the chain on my ankle.

I slammed the box, shoved it back under the bed and fled out into the night, right before I threw up my last meal.

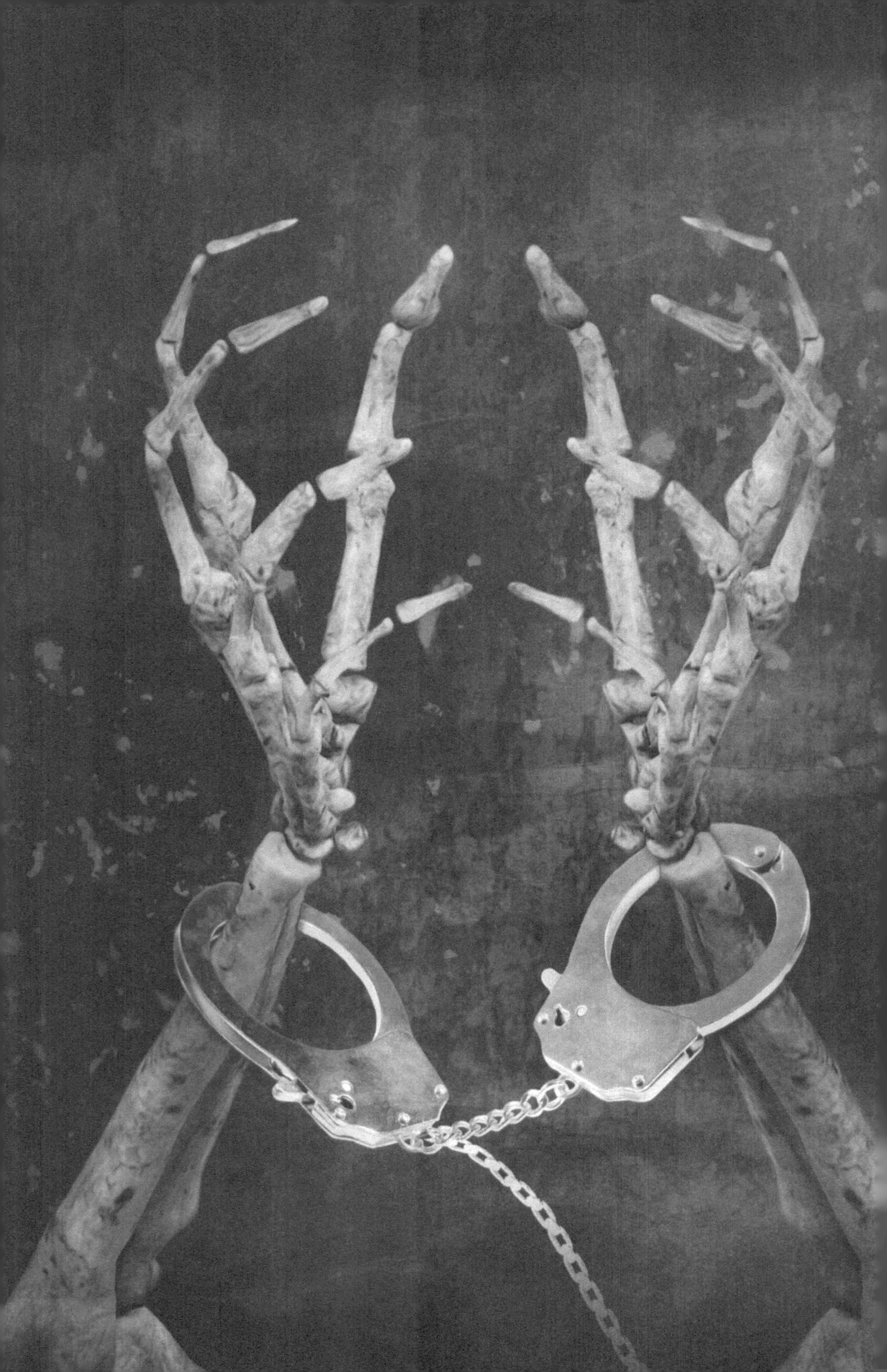

CHAPTER 8

DAMON

I frowned at my phone as I stepped past Mina's room. It was only a matter of time before Reuben or Gianni moved her into theirs, or stayed with her.

The idea set off a flare of anger inside me. Not just because she was a distraction, although she was.

The real reason… I wasn't ready to admit it to myself. My feelings for Reuben, Gianni and Mina were complicated.

I didn't do complicated. I didn't *like* complicated. I liked my life straightforward, carefully planned.

The message on my phone threatened to disrupt that planning.

A sound from inside her room did the same.

The door was ajar, as it often was. I presumed she didn't want to sleep in a fully enclosed space after what she'd been through.

I peered through the gap. A hint of light shone between the curtains, illuminating a single form on the middle of the bed, wrapped in blankets.

Also nothing new. She was fucked up. Who wouldn't be?

I shoved my phone into my pocket and pushed the door open.

"Mina?" I whispered. If she was asleep, I didn't want to wake her, but I sensed she was awake already. That was confirmed when she startled so violently she almost rolled off the bed onto the floor.

I lurched forward and grabbed her at the last moment.

She whimpered and flinched away, pushing the blankets off and retreating to the head of the bed, where she curled into a tiny ball. Her whole body shook, eyes wide, staring at me as if she'd never seen me before.

"Hey." I sat down far enough from her to give her some space. Close enough to… I didn't know what.

I considered calling for Reuben or Gianni, but couldn't bring myself to move. "Rough night?"

She'd had nightmares since we found her, some nights screaming in her sleep. Others crying out and thrashing before falling still. This felt like something else entirely.

"What happened?" If Reuben or Gianni did anything to her…

I mentally shook my head. If they did, it wasn't on purpose. They were both gone, as far as she was concerned. They'd cut their own throats before they lay a hand on her in a way she didn't want them to.

Who then? The twins weren't here and they wouldn't touch her either. Reuben wouldn't hesitate to put them both in a shallow grave. Blood ties only went so far.

Her face was as pale as the first time I saw her. In the light, her freckles would stand out. In the gloom, she looked like death.

"Bad dream," she said softly. "I was back in the cage."

"The thing about spending all my time around criminals and liars is that I can pick a liar from days away," I said slowly. "Something else happened. What was it?"

She slid a hand under the blanket near her foot. For a moment, I thought she was going to pull out a weapon.

My body tensed, ready to defend myself.

Instead, she pulled out a phone.

"The pass code is four, three, two, one." She handed me the phone.

I frowned at her, then at the phone. "Okay." I tapped on the screen and entered the pass code. An app was already open on the phone. One that contained photos and videos.

I felt the blood drain out of my face. "Fucking hell, where did you get this?"

She shook her head and curled up again, the blankets up to her chin.

I shook my head and looked down at photo after photo of her. She couldn't have been more than eighteen.

A few candid ones showed her smiling and laughing with her siblings.

After those, were at least twenty of her lying naked, eyes closed. The bars of the cage were around her, the strap on her ankle. She looked peaceful, unaware she was about to wake up in hell.

I found myself clicking on a video, and immediately wished I hadn't. She was still unconscious, but Kurt was laughing, opening her legs and climbing on top of her…

I closed the video and turned off the phone. No wonder she'd unravelled. This would have brought everything back to her like a blade in her heart. Tore open wounds that were finally starting to heal.

"How did you get this?" I asked again. "Did someone send it to you? Let me guess, Kurt." He'd do anything to mess with her mind. He knew all the buttons to push to drive her over the edge. "How long have you had this?"

She didn't answer. I wanted to shake it out of her, but that might be the thing that broke her completely. None of that mattered as much as what we needed to do next.

I tossed the phone onto the bedside table and scooted over closer to her. "I saw you kill a woman. I know you killed that attacker the other night, before they could get to Reuben. You shot those other assholes in the foot. You might be the shadow, but you're a badass. Those photos, that was the old you. You survived all of that. None of that is your life anymore. You're here now, with us."

I placed the tips of my fingers on her shoulder. She twitched, but didn't flinch away.

"Someone took those photos," she whispered. "That video. Someone took them and didn't stop him. They stood there with that phone filming him while he…" She swallowed audibly.

"Do you know who?" I asked. Whoever they were, they'd be missing every finger they used to hold that phone if I got a hold of them.

She shook her head slowly. "I remember one of the men. A friend of Kurt's. His name is Stefan Lowe."

"He won't be a problem anymore," I said. "I just got a message from one of my contacts that he was killed tonight. It seems like someone took a contract out with the Sparrow to end him. I don't suppose you sent the Sparrow after him?"

I was joking, but something about her demeanour shifted slightly. Something that drew both my attention and my suspicion.

"Mina?" I tightened my grip on her shoulder slightly.

"People like Stefan make lots of enemies," she said, her voice empty. "He got what he deserved."

I frowned. "You didn't tell me how you got that phone. No one has been in or out of the house all night. I'd know if they had. They would have set off the alarm. Unless they turned it off. Was it Gianni?" He was known to slip out every now and again, for reasons of his own. Reuben was aware of his movements, so I never questioned it.

"Was it you?" I asked. "You went somewhere in the middle of the night?"

She didn't answer, but I knew I was right. "Where did you go? Did you kill Stefan? That's where the phone came from." I was missing something, but I couldn't figure out what.

"You can't tell Reuben," she whispered.

"The hell I can't." I started to stand.

She grabbed my wrist and held on with a grip that was surprisingly firm. "You don't understand."

I lowered myself back down, pulled my wrist away from her and crossed my arms. "Then make me understand. What the fuck were you doing leaving the house in the middle of the night by yourself? Did you kill Stefan?"

She closed her eyes. "Yes. I remembered him from before and tracked him down. I thought he might know where Kurt was. He gave me the name of someone who used to work for Kurt. Leon Graves.

Then I killed him." She told me about the locked room and finding the phone in the box under the bed.

"I don't understand why you thought you needed to do that alone," I said, while still trying to process everything. "We would have gone with you. You're the one who calls this a family, but you felt like you needed to do that by yourself?"

Her tongue darted over her lips. "I wanted to face him myself. I wanted to look him in the eye and know he was another piece of the past I was putting behind me."

"You could have done that with us there," I insisted. I ran through the conversation in my mind and sat back.

Realisation struck me like a hammer.

"I should have seen it," I said, trying to maintain my composure. "Now I think about it, it's fucking obvious. You were gone for five years. So was the Sparrow."

If realisation was a hammer, it hit right on the head of the nail. She didn't move. Didn't breathe.

"You didn't need to hire an assassin to kill Stefan Lowe," I concluded. "You are one. Or you were."

"I still am," she said softly.

I couldn't understand why the hell that was hot, but it fucking was. Mina DiMarco was the Sparrow. Of all people in the fucking world. She was right here, in Reuben's house, where I also lived. Lying on a bed wrapped in blankets, cracked but not broken.

No wonder she survived all those years. She would have learned a variety of techniques to control her emotions, all of which she would have used, possibly daily.

"You're the fucking Sparrow," I said. My brain spun. "You know Reuben has to know. Gianni too. We can't keep this from them. If you don't tell them, I will."

"Or I could kill you to keep you from saying anything, and make it look like an accident," she said. Her expression was so mild, I wondered what else she got away with.

She might be the best actor I ever met. Sweet on the outside, deadly on the inside.

The perfect woman. Fuck, apparently Reuben and Gianni weren't the only ones who were gone.

"You wouldn't do that," I said.

She cocked her head at me. "Wouldn't I?"

"No, you wouldn't," I said. "First of all, you would devastate Reuben and Gianni. Secondly, you still need me to find Kurt. Third, I know you have a thing for me. Just like you do for them."

She straightened her head and hummed, before replying to each point, one at a time. "They'd get over it. That's an assumption, and that's also an assumption."

I lowered my hands to my thighs and smirked. "No they wouldn't, and both of those are correct. Right now, you're thinking of kissing me."

I'd kiss her if I hadn't found her in a huddle of blankets. Those photos would set her back. Freaking her out would do even worse.

Fuck Kurt fucking Lasalle. And fuck Stefan Lowe for keeping that phone. And fuck him harder for taking that video in the first place. They were both sick. She was right, Stefan got what he deserved. I just wished I'd been there to see it.

"How do you fit that ego inside this house?" she asked.

"It's not ego, it's fact," I said. "I'm actually very humble."

She snorted softly. "You're full of shit."

"You wouldn't be the first to say that," I replied. "Probably not the last either. None of that means I'm wrong."

"You're right," she whispered. She wasn't talking about her attraction to me. "You would have gone with me. If you had, I wouldn't have seen those photos. Not if one of you found that phone first."

"No fucking way we'd let you look," I agreed. I wanted to bleach my eyeballs after seeing the video of Kurt. All of this must be a million times worse for her.

"He doesn't get to win," she said in a shaky voice. "I won't let him."

"*We* won't let him," I corrected. "Family, remember? Even if we are dysfunctional." That was an understatement.

"Right." She raised a hand tentatively and pressed the tips of her fingers against my lips.

I kissed her soft, warm skin. A jolt of electricity passed all the way through me, but I made no move toward her. This intimacy was enough, for now.

"You're still a distraction," I teased.

She managed a faint smile. "You're still an asshole."

"Absolutely correct," I said. "I hear Terry in the kitchen. Reuben and Gianni will be up soon, if they're not already. If you're not down in the kitchen for breakfast, I'll tell them without you."

CHAPTER 9

MINA

Reuben flipped through the photos, his expression quietly thunderous. He seemed determined to look at every one of them. Not because he wanted to see them, but because he needed to know what I went through. So I wasn't alone in this. He needed to understand, no matter how difficult it was to see.

Finally, he rose from his seat far enough to hand the phone to Gianni, who nodded.

Gianni carried the phone over to the kitchen benchtop beside the stove. He opened a drawer, pulled out a meat mallet and smashed the phone screen with it.

Terry, who stood stirring a pot, grunted. I presumed he approved. He met my eyes for a moment, inclined his head slightly and went back to his cooking.

"You could have deleted the photos," Damon pointed out.

"Chances are, there's a tracking chip in here," Gianni said. He went on smashing the phone until it was nothing more than a mess of plastic and broken glass.

There wasn't, I'd looked. There was nothing useful on the phone, just the photos and video. Seeing Gianni destroy it was almost as cathartic as doing it myself. He would have let me if I asked, but I didn't want to touch the phone again. Not even the scraps of it.

"Damon was right," Reuben said. "About you being a distraction. I was so distracted, I didn't see what was right in front of my fucking face. You're an assassin."

His whole body was tense with anger, but much of it was directed at seeing those photos. The rest, I suspected, was directed at himself. None at me.

"That's the point of me being the Sparrow," I said softly. Part of me was relieved all of this was out in the open, but in some ways, it complicated the situation even further. "Who would have thought I'd be a cold-blooded killer?"

Gianni raised his hand. "I thought it was possible. Not necessarily cold-blooded, but a killer. All the best people are."

Damon snorted softly. "And some of the worst."

Gianni pointed a finger gun at him. "Good point. But in this room, it's the best."

Reuben ignored them both and kept his eyes on me. "You didn't mention this until you had to. Until Damon figured it out."

"No, I didn't," I agreed. I wanted to look away, but I forced myself not to.

"How did Kurt Lasalle end up with the Sparrow chained and caged?" Reuben asked. "You have skills."

I took a few moments to collect my thoughts and figure out the best way to articulate them. In the end, I decided the best was to jump right in.

"As far as I can tell, my father slipped something into a drink he gave me. When I woke up, I was in that house. Kurt was there with the woman from the ice cream parlour, Stefan and a couple of others. I remember them talking, then Kurt jabbed a needle into my arm. When I woke up, I was in that cage."

Sticky and sore, with no doubt of what Kurt did to me.

"He left me there for three days before he came back to give me something to eat."

He'd taunted me, laughed at me and told me how much he enjoyed fucking me. Reminded me of what I did that night and why I deserved to be there. Guilt kept me from responding, or accepting any food. He'd thought that was hilarious.

"Fucking asshole," Gianni muttered.

"He was obsessed with you. He took the opportunity to have you in a place he could keep you," Reuben said.

"I gave him the opportunity," I said reluctantly. They had most of the story, they might as well have the rest of it. If they turned their backs on me now, I'd manage on my own. I had money and contacts and, like Reuben pointed out, skills.

"I was on a job," I said slowly. "There was a kid. She shouldn't have been there. I saw her standing in the doorway and then, she was dying in my arms." I shook my head. "She had nothing to do with any of this. She was supposed to be with her mother, not her father. He was the one who was supposed to die that night."

"That explains why you looked so upset when you saw Frank's kid," Gianni said.

All I could say to that was, "Yeah"

"I don't understand," Damon said. "You said you saw her, and then she was dying. You killed her?"

I shook my head slowly. "I had to have. I don't remember doing it, but it was only me and her there. Kurt was in another room." I briefly explained his mission was to find information.

"Think back," Reuben said. "Is it possible he did it?"

I frowned. I'd thought about that night a million times. It lived in my nightmares. Her blood, my guilt, were the only things I was certain of.

"If he did, I should have been able to stop him," I said finally. "If I just gave him what he wanted, he wouldn't have forced my hand like that. She'd still be alive now."

"You'd voluntarily sleep with him in return for the life of a child?" Damon asked.

"I'd do *anything* to erase that night," I said quietly. "What happened to her was my fault. What Kurt did to me, I deserved every moment of it."

"Sweetheart." Gianni slid into the chair beside me. "You did *not* deserve any of that. The only one to blame for this was Kurt. He's a fucked up monster who used a kid to get to you." He carefully slipped his arm around my shoulders. "Her blood is on his hands."

I shook my head. "I should have seen the extent he'd go to. I should have insisted I do my job alone. He could have come in afterward. He shouldn't have been anywhere near there. I misjudged him and she paid the price."

"The only one responsible for his actions is him," Reuben said darkly. "He let his obsession take hold of him and he did something unspeakable."

Damon cleared his throat.

Reuben's gaze slid to him. "There's a difference between distraction, and obsession to the point of imprisoning a woman to keep her." He returned his gaze to me. "Who was this girl?"

"I don't really know. The daughter of my target. He was some kind of politician. He upset someone and they decided to take him out."

My guess was one of his ex-wives, possibly all three of them, if they could afford me. He had a reputation as a massive asshole. Not to mention a serial cheat.

"Kurt was supposed to find information on his whereabouts on a few nights in question. And details about bribes from some construction company."

I guessed his ex-wives wanted to pin his death on them. That was their business. I was just there to carry out the job I was paid to do. There was no benefit in getting too nosy. It wasn't as though I needed the money I get from bribing them. Killing people for money was lucrative enough.

"Did he end up dead?" Gianni asked. "Sounds like he deserved it."

"According to Kurt, someone finished the job a year later," I said. "Unless that car crash was really an accident." Stranger things had happened.

"That seems unlikely to me," Reuben said. "Once someone takes out a hit—"

"It's seen through until the end," I finished for him. "Unless the client withdraws the job. But that's a rare occurrence. Once people are committed to having someone killed, they tend to follow through."

"Have I mentioned recently that you're hot?" Gianni squeezed my shoulders. "An actual fucking assassin. I knew you were a badass. I just fucking *knew* it. You're the baddest of the badasses."

I managed a faint smile. "Yeah, but what happens now?" I looked back to Reuben. "Now you know what I am, and what I did."

"It changes nothing," Reuben said. "You expected us to turn on you?"

"A child died because of me," I insisted. "I expected you to agree that I deserved what Kurt did."

Deafening silence followed my words. Heavier than a thundercloud ready to break apart and release a flood, accompanied by thunder louder than a Wolf Venom concert.

I'd spent too many years convincing myself I was a terrible person. It was so ingrained by now, I didn't expect any other response. I'd readied myself to defend against them. I'd die or kill them all before I let that happen. The idea of being locked away again was my own personal hell. Whatever I had to do, I wouldn't allow that. Even if I stabbed a knife into my own heart.

I hadn't pictured understanding. Words or looks of concern. Of love.

The anticipated waves of hate and threats of violence didn't come. No suggestion I should go back down into the basement.

"Kurt deserves what we're going to do to him," Reuben growled. "Nothing you've said makes you any less ours. Any less *mine*."

His expression was more intense than I'd ever seen on him. He was the thundercloud, but he wasn't coming for me.

This was the man people were scared of. The one who decided who lived or died with barely a second thought. The one whose absolute certainty that I was his made my clit throb and my heart flutter.

What was it Gianni said? Some people thought love made us vulnerable, but it made us stronger. We were a family, no matter what any of us did.

"If anything, it says you belong here even more than we thought you did," Gianni said. "You're a fucking assassin. You fit in perfectly."

I finally let myself lean into him and start to relax. "Then you'll understand I have contacts I've reached out to. Contacts who are looking for Leon Graves as we speak. He's next on my shit list. When I find him, I should be that much closer to finding Kurt."

"When *we* find him," Reuben said. "You're not doing this alone. Between us, we have the resources to find both of these pricks and deal with them appropriately."

"I don't know," I said lightly. "Damon might be a distraction."

Our conversation and connection were surprising, as was the intimacy of his kiss on my fingers. They were all distractions, but they were distractions I needed. For their resources and for them. They'd become my safe harbour in an ocean of crazy.

Damon barked a short laugh. "Fucking touché. Doesn't matter though, you need us. Who else knows who you are?"

"Just Daze and Kurt," I said. "My father did. And the people who trained me. If anyone else knows, I'm unaware of them."

"That debt." Damon's forehead creased.

"I still don't know what it was," I said. "Why my father would drug me and give me to him." I was relieved to get all of this off my chest, but that still hung over me. Would I ever get an answer as to why he did that to me? If I didn't, it would linger in my mind for the rest of my life.

"I'm glad I had him killed," Reuben said darkly. "All right, Leon Graves. Anyone else?"

"Not that I can remember, yet," I said. "I'm hoping Graves will shed some light on them." I explained how I got the information on him from Stefan. Including the way I'd surprised him, literally with his pants down.

Gianni laughed. "Taking out a guy while he's jacking off. That's fucking awesome. I love you, Mina 'The Sparrow' DiMarco."

"My middle name is actually Jasmine," I said. "But I love you too, Gianni Covino."

He pulled me closer and wrapped his arms around me. He nestled his face into my hair and laughed softly. "A fucking assassin."

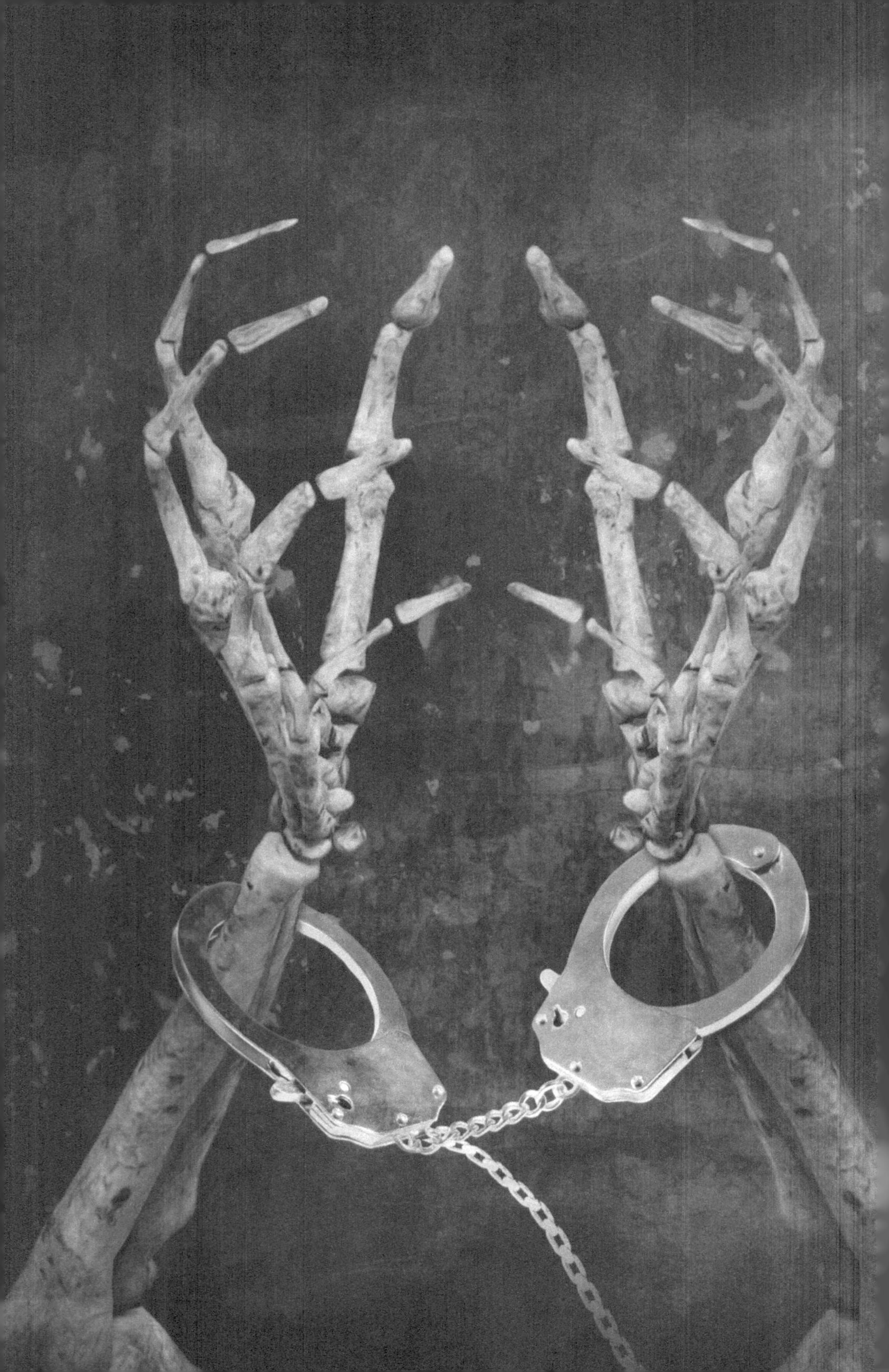

CHAPTER 10

MINA

I sat down on the bench beside Reuben and looked back at the house.

The light was on in the kitchen, Terry moved back and forth every couple of minutes. The night was still, except for the distant hum of traffic, the rustling of birds and sounds of crickets somewhere in the bushes.

"Why aren't you angrier that I lied to you?" I kept my voice low, not wanting to disturb the quiet.

"Because I understand why you did it," he replied after a few moments of pause. "Self-preservation is one of our strongest instincts. The ability to trust is difficult. It often leads to disappointment."

He turned to me. "You trusted Kurt? Before all of this happened. When he was training you to defend yourself."

"I suppose I did," I said reluctantly.

I placed my hands in my lap and leaned back against the trunk of the tree behind us.

"My father trusted him to teach me. Kurt gave me the creeps, but I never had much reason to question my father's decision. Back then, I was still under the misguided belief that parents do what's best for their children. I trusted my father to do that."

"Two people you trusted, betrayed you," Reuben said. "It would be an inconceivable stretch for you to trust me after we'd just found you. Why would you? After everything you went through, why would you trust someone like me? No one who endured that, would be immediately forthcoming. I wouldn't have. That's why I'm not angry. However…"

Of course there would be a caveat.

"If I lie to you again, you'll be furious," I guessed.

"Precisely," he agreed. "I don't expect to know all of your secrets, but never look straight at me and lie, and I'll extend the same courtesy to you."

"I won't," I promised. "I'm not keeping anything else from you, that I can think of. Except…"

In the light coming from the kitchen, I saw his eyebrow arch.

"I've always had a thing for you," I confessed. "You were imposing and so many people were intimidated by you, but I felt drawn to you. I figured a man like you wouldn't be interested in a girl like me. Partly because of the part I played as sweet innocent little Mina, and partly because of what I really was behind that mask. I don't think 'assassin' is in one of the top ten most trusted professions."

"Neither is mob boss," he pointed out. "Although, it should be. Both of us are loyal, driven and ruthless. I consider those to be positive attributes."

He draped an arm over my shoulders and rubbed the pad of his thumb across the side of my upper arm.

"We're more alike than you might think. Including the attraction between us. I was waiting until you were old enough, but with the expectation you'd reject me. Which does come back to the sweet façade. You played that role to perfection. If I knew exactly who you were, I would have made a move sooner. Before Kurt got to you. It's his fault I missed out on all those years with you."

"He has a lot to answer for." So fucking much. "For the record, I never would have rejected you." I leaned against him, enjoying his warmth and masculine scent. "Things could have been very different."

"They could have," he agreed. "You might have been the key to keeping the twins in line."

I snorted softly. "I don't think I have that kind of influence over them. That might have gone the other way though. They could have led me astray." If anyone would try, it'd be them.

"Not if they wanted their heads attached to their bodies," he growled. "I think their survival instincts are too strong to cross that line."

"If not, you could have taken out a hit on them," I said. "Which I wouldn't have taken, because they're basically family to me too."

"Don't tell them that, it'll go to their heads," he said dryly. "Although, I'm not sure they can get egos bigger than the ones they already have. But let's not talk about them."

He turned his face and brushed his lips over mine. The kiss was tentative at first, the memory of those photos weighing heavily between us.

I'd freaked out when I saw them, but, like everything else, I was determined to put them behind me. If I held back too much, more than I wanted to, then he won.

Fuck that.

I deepened the kiss, tasting his lips and the inside of his mouth with my tongue.

He turned me to him and placed his other hand on my hip.

"Mina…" He said against my mouth.

"Reuben." I pulled back and whispered, "I want to…taste you."

I moved my hand down to the front of his suit trousers. His cock was already hard, straining against the fabric.

"I don't want you doing anything you're not ready for," he said. He seemed like he was about to pull away from me, for my own sake.

"I'm ready for this." I slipped away from him and knelt down on the cool grass in front of the bench.

Hands trembling slightly, I undid the front of his pants and pulled the sides apart. Only his black silk boxers were between his cock and the tips of my fingers.

I touched him carefully, stroking my fingers up and down his erection before I was brave enough to pull down his boxers, letting it spring free.

I ran the tips of my fingers around his head, brushing my thumb over the bead of pre-cum that glistened on his tip.

He quivered under my touch. "Fuck, Mina," he whispered. His expression was strained with the effort to keep from pumping himself into my hand. He wanted this to happen on my terms. There was time later for him to be dominant. Right now, I was the one in charge.

This was the first time in my life I had my face, voluntarily, this close to a man's cock. There was no persuasion, no force. If I stepped away right now, he'd be frustrated, but wouldn't press.

I swallowed and tentatively touched his head with the tip of my tongue.

His skin was warm and smooth, salty and inviting. I ran my tongue all the way around his tip, marvelling at the way he felt in my mouth. He must be going wild, but he let me take my time and explore every centimetre of him before I took more of him between my lips.

He groaned softly and placed his hand on the back of my head, his fingers stroking and tangling in my hair.

Again, there was no force. He held me in place, but I could have knocked his hand away if I needed to. Instead, he encouraged me to take him in deeper, to close my lips around him and gently suck.

"Your mouth..." he said breathlessly. He kept still while I moved, bobbing my head back and forth, sucking and sliding.

I reached up with my hand to lightly cup his balls. Those too were hot, the thin skin over throbbing flesh and blood.

Throbbing because I did that to him. Me. He was hard as steel because I aroused him. Because I was touching him and making him feel this way.

I looked up at him and sucked harder and faster, then softer and slower. Every drop of control was in my hands. And in my mouth. I knew I had him right on the edge and that was where I kept him for as long as I could. I held him there, deciding when he'd come. If he'd come.

The expression of rapture on his face was all because of me. The control he gave me made me feel powerful. As powerful as I did when I took a life.

I couldn't decide which of those turned me on more.

I decided I'd teased him enough. I sucked him harder and faster, while firmly massaging his balls.

"Mina…" His breath was ragged. His lips moved, but the words wouldn't form.

I kept my eyes locked on his and went on sucking, silently communicating an answer to his unspoken question. Whatever he could give me, I'd take it. All of it.

I was Mina fucking DiMarco and I wasn't going to be anyone's victim anymore.

Kurt could fuck himself, he wasn't going to stop me from being fucked. Or from being loved.

Reuben's grip on my hand tightened as he came. He let out a low cry.

His cum exploded into my mouth, hot and salty. It slid across my tongue, tingling my tastebuds.

I managed to swallow down his release before he sagged, puffing lightly.

"You're incredible," he said once he caught his breath and slid his cock out from between my lips. "I imagined what it would be like to fuck your mouth, but that was so much more." He took my hand and pulled me up beside him, before fixing his boxers and pants back into place.

"It was more than I expected too," I admitted. "Reading about it in romance books is one thing, but I liked it more than I thought I would."

"I have another confession." He pulled me onto his lap. "I've never let go like that with anyone. Never let them take the lead. I'm usually the one who's in control."

I gave him a bland, but teasing look. "I'm shocked," I said, deadpan. "Reuben Brantley, in control?"

He surprised me by chuckling in response. The sound wasn't as carefree and uninhibited as Gianni, but it was just as pleasant. That was another win for me. Making a man who rarely laughed, chuckle.

"I know, it's a difficult concept to grasp," he said, equally deadpan. "I'm usually so passive and in the background."

"No one could ever describe you like that," I said. "You only have to walk into a room to command the attention of everyone in it. Even the twins."

"That might be overstating it slightly," he said. "Those two like to pretend they can ignore me."

"Pretend being the key word here," I said. "They can no more ignore you than I can."

I leaned over and kissed his mouth. My clit throbbed with the knowledge he'd taste himself on my lips.

I'd actually sucked him off. He'd come in my mouth. This was something I could do because I wanted to and he wanted me to do it. Not because anyone was holding me down or telling me lies. Filling my mind with heartbreak.

"I want to do that again," I said.

"Kiss?" he asked, one eyebrow slightly raised.

I poked him in the chest with my fingernail. "You know what I mean."

He leaned in and rested his forehead against mine. "You want to suck my cock again. Consider it all yours. If you want to put your beautiful mouth around my cock, you can. Any time, anywhere."

"Anywhere?" I echoed.

"Anywhere," he agreed. "I will never not want to fuck your mouth. In the meantime…"

He kissed my mouth. Lightly, gently with more intimacy than we'd ever kissed before. If I ever doubted his feelings for me, I didn't now.

I hoped I conveyed the same to him. I'd been in love with him for as long as I could remember. We'd missed so much time, but we could make up for it.

Someday, it might feel like those five years never happened.

I caught a hint of movement near the back door, leading into the house.

How long had Damon stood there, watching us? I sensed he was there for a while as I sucked Reuben off.

I got a vibe from him. If he could have taken either of our places, he would have.

Apparently, I wasn't the only one with secrets.

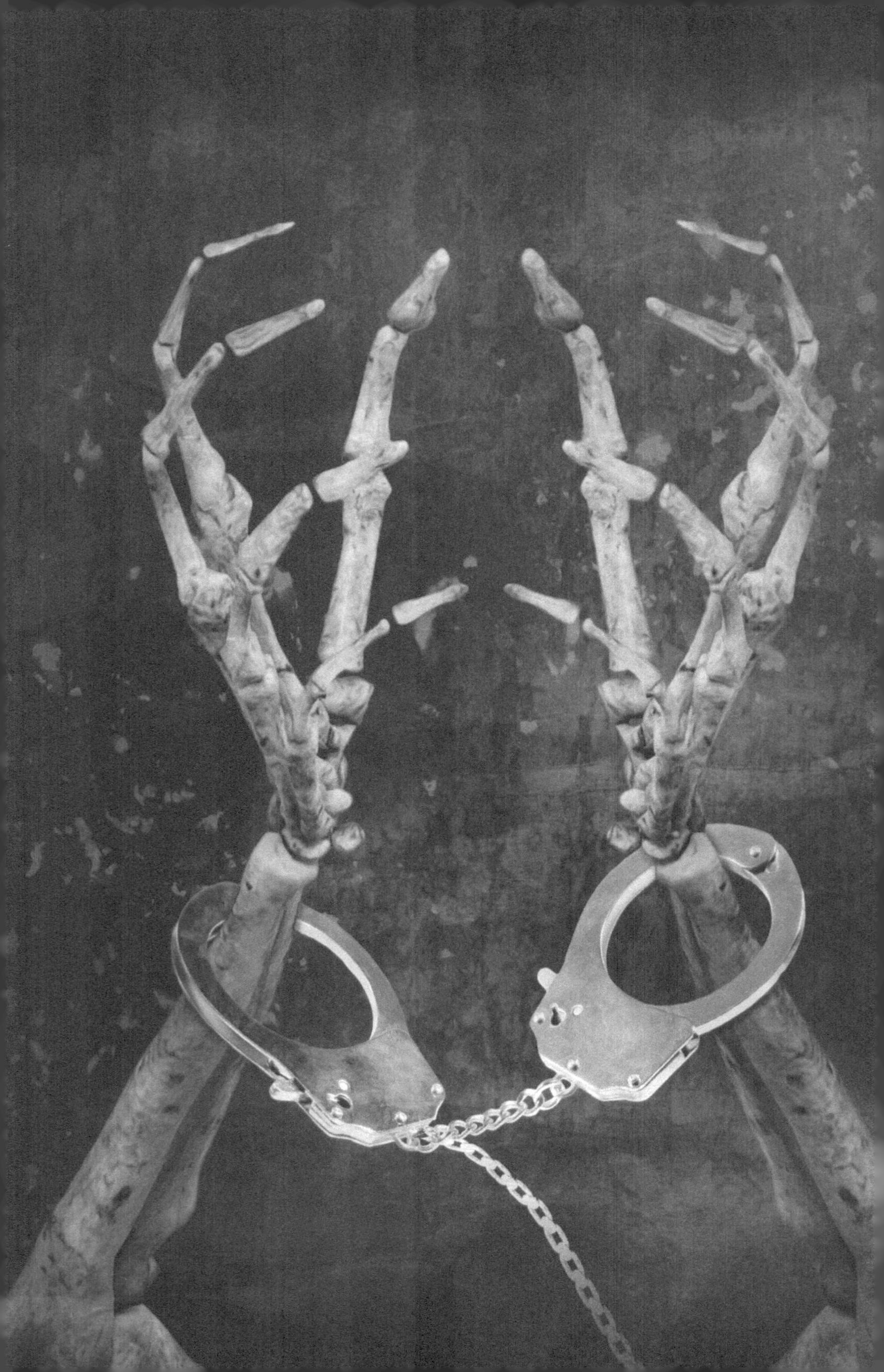

CHAPTER 11

MINA

"You know this is confidential information, right?" I glanced back as Gianni peered over my shoulder.

He grinned, but didn't move away. "I figured I could help. Give you some advice as to which job to take next."

His face was centimetres from mine, close enough for me to breathe in the warm, unique scent of him. He always smelled of lavender, leather and danger.

I turned off my phone screen. "What makes you think I need advice?"

I followed him with my gaze as he walked around the back of the couch and plopped down beside me.

He was completely undeterred. "You probably don't, but there's a shit load of suburbs that didn't exist a year or two ago, much less five. Besides, you might need someone to drive the getaway car."

He raised his tattooed hands to either side of his face, to gesture at himself. He wore a gold ring on his right hand, which shone in the light that came through the library window.

"I'd suggest you watch too many movies, but I suppose that's Damon's job." I placed my phone down on my lap and leaned against the arm of the couch. "I could ask him to come with me." I couldn't help trying to see if I could get a rise out of Gianni. Naturally, I didn't.

"We could all go." He spoke as if he was suggesting an afternoon out, maybe with a picnic.

"Nothing says 'stealthy assassin at work' quite like a car full of people," I said dryly.

Now I was picturing us turning up in a bright red car, with bright clothes and maybe a neon sign or two. Fun, but it wouldn't go unnoticed.

"What I really need is a current driver's license and a car." Some of these jobs were close, but others were on the other side of Sydney. Many were in different states and a handful were in different countries.

Being an assassin was not only lucrative, but it was a great way to see the world.

If you liked to see cities at night, and didn't mind missing all the things tourists got to do. If I kept turning up in interesting places, people might start to notice. Especially if they coincided with the deaths of influential people.

I might look sweet, but at the end of the day, I was a DiMarco. Anyone who knew our family would wonder what I was up to.

"Too easy," he said with a wave of his wrist. "We just need a photo and we can sort the license. And Reuben has lots of cars. You could borrow one of his. Or ask him to give you one. If you told him you needed a black Maserati with hot pink seats, he'd have that here in a day or two."

"I prefer black seats," I said. "And something less obvious than a Maserati. Something more inconspicuous, like a small hatchback."

"Does anyone drive small hatchbacks anymore?" He frowned. "You'll be noticed less if you drive an SUV. Everyone seems to have those these days. Preferably bullet-proof and crash proof. And electric. Can you drive?"

"Electric?" I frowned.

That was one of the many changes I was still trying to come to terms with. That and people delivering food on the back of a bike.

Personally, I thought that was a perfect front for an assassin. I made a mental note to get a bike and a uniform. It might come in useful.

"I'm a bit rusty, but how hard could it be to pick it back up again?" I shrugged. "I got my license before…"

I didn't need to finish that sentence. We both knew what I was referring to. I didn't want to sugarcoat it, but I didn't want to keep saying Kurt's name either. There really were no good ways to say 'chained and stuck in a cage in a basement.'

"My sister Rose taught me to drive." Asher was too young, Dane was too impatient, my parents too busy or disinterested. Rose took it upon herself to make sure I knew how.

"You two were close," Gianni said. He pulled my feet onto his lap and started to massage one of them.

I fought the instinct to pull them back away from him, and let him touch me.

If a day was coming when I wouldn't automatically flinch, I wished it would come sooner. Now they knew who I was, I felt compelled to live up to my badass persona.

Assassins weren't supposed to be human. We were supposed to be something else, something *more*. The monsters under the bed our parents warn us about.

Sitting in a library, surrounded by books, while one of my boyfriends gave me a foot rub was definitely outside that stereotype. Maybe I should give myself a break and remind myself I was a person first, and my job second.

"We are as close as we could be with so many years between us," I said. "She was just as likely to tell me to get lost as she was to do things with me. Asher and I were closer. We were always spying on the other two, and doing things like waiting behind a tree to throw a water balloon at them."

We'd hurl them, wait for them to connect, then run away laughing. Asher would always make sure I was out of reach of either of our older siblings, even if he had his ass kicked once in a while.

"Dane used to get so angry. He was the one who'd run off and tell our parents what we did." I rolled my eyes. "I think he liked it when we got in trouble, but it was more than that. He wanted us to look bad and for him to look good, like the dutiful son. The one who kept us in line, as if he could actually do that."

Asher and I were more inclined to laugh at him, flip him off, then plan another prank. Not where our father could see.

"Dane wanted to be the golden child. The head of the family. He wanted to be like Reuben."

I doubted Reuben was a snitch the way Dane used to be. He would have given his siblings a glare before slipping off to be by himself and read.

"Who doesn't?" Gianni massaged my toes, one by one. His hands were warm and firm, but gentle at the same time. "Reuben is a powerful man. If I was going to aspire to be anyone else, it would be him. But I don't, because I like being me. So you'd say Dane was the most ambitious one out of you all?"

"Not necessarily," I said thoughtfully. "The rest of us were ambitious in different ways. Rose wanted to be the best at what she does, and so did I. Asher wanted to take over the world with his music. Dane was the one who craved power. When he was at school, he always sought out the popular kids. If he couldn't be the leader, he wanted to be as close to them as he could."

He snitched on the other kids the way he did with us, but only if that was in line with his friends. He wanted to ruffle only the *right* feathers.

"Why do you think he went into teaching?" Gianni asked. He didn't seem as though he was judging Dane, he was just curious about him. Dane was a part of the childhood that helped to shape me. Another piece of my complicated puzzle.

"That's a good question," I said. I wondered that myself. If you'd asked me which of my siblings would be interested in teaching anything to anyone else, he probably would have been at the bottom of the list.

"I'm not sure I know the answer. Maybe he was hoping Brutham Academy would give him contacts, the same way so many men want to join the Brotherhood. Maybe it's something for him to do while he waits for his opportunity. Maybe he just likes teaching."

I laughed slightly. My oldest brother liked ambition more than he liked people. Unless there was something in it for him.

"Everyone has an angle," Gianni said. "I'm surprised he hasn't come knocking on Reuben's door, asking for a job. Unless he has and I don't know about it."

His expression suggested that was unlikely. He had a way of knowing about almost everything that went on around here. He watched, he listened and he learned. He observed and absorbed everything. Like I did. Missing even a small detail could get me killed. Or get someone else killed.

I glanced in the direction of the door, as though he might suddenly turn up outside. When no one knocked, I turned back to Gianni.

"That's what he'd do if he knew I was here," I said. "If he thought I had any influence with Reuben, he'd be right here, looking for scraps."

"Is that why you don't want him to know about you?" Gianni asked. "You don't want him putting you in that position?" He rubbed the ball of my foot. "What about Asher? He's off living his life. I don't get the impression he'd need you to do anything for him."

"No, but Asher, being Asher, he'd be devastated about what happened to me. You know what they say about ignorance being bliss." I didn't want to break his happy, rock star bubble.

"I've heard something about that, but I also know people don't like having other people make up their mind for them," he said. "Whatever you decide to do, I support you one hundred percent. Just think about it, okay?"

His expression wasn't judgemental at all, just offering an alternative perspective. One I had considered, but had to dismiss for now. When the time came, I'd see both of my brothers. In the meantime, I'd let them live their lives.

"Can I ask you something?" I glanced toward the door, but no one seemed to be around.

As far as I knew, Reuben and Damon were in Reuben's office working. Terry was in the kitchen making something that smelled wonderful. The scent of meat and vegetables wafted through the house.

"Of course," Gianni said. "I'm as open as any of these books." He jerked his head towards the shelf closest to the couch. A lot more books were housed there than there used to be. Many I'd read, but lots I hadn't.

"Damon and Reuben," I said carefully. "Have they ever…"

A brief frown flitted across Gianni's brow. "Been intimate? Fucked?"

I swallowed at the mental image his words conjured. "Either of those things. Both. The other night, I got the impression that Damon might want to."

Gianni looked thoughtful. "To my knowledge, no, nothing has happened between them. Unlike me, Damon is a closed book. Reuben too. I won't say I haven't noticed chemistry between them, but whether or not they'd act on it is another thing. Would that bother you?"

"Not at all," I said.

A sly grin crept onto his face. "Would it turn you on?"

My face heated. "It might. I wouldn't ask them to if they weren't interested."

"I would," Gianni said with a grin. "Now you've put that idea in my head, I'd pay money to see it. Just imagine…"

He was interrupted by the sound of my phone ringing in my lap. The sound was so unexpected, I startled.

The screen lit up. No contact or location, just a number I didn't recognise.

"Who knows your phone number?" Gianni asked.

I shook my head. "No one." My first instinct was to ignore the call, but I picked up my phone and glanced at Gianni before accepting and pressing the screen to put it on speakerphone.

Before I could say anything, a voice spoke.

"Miss me, bitch?"

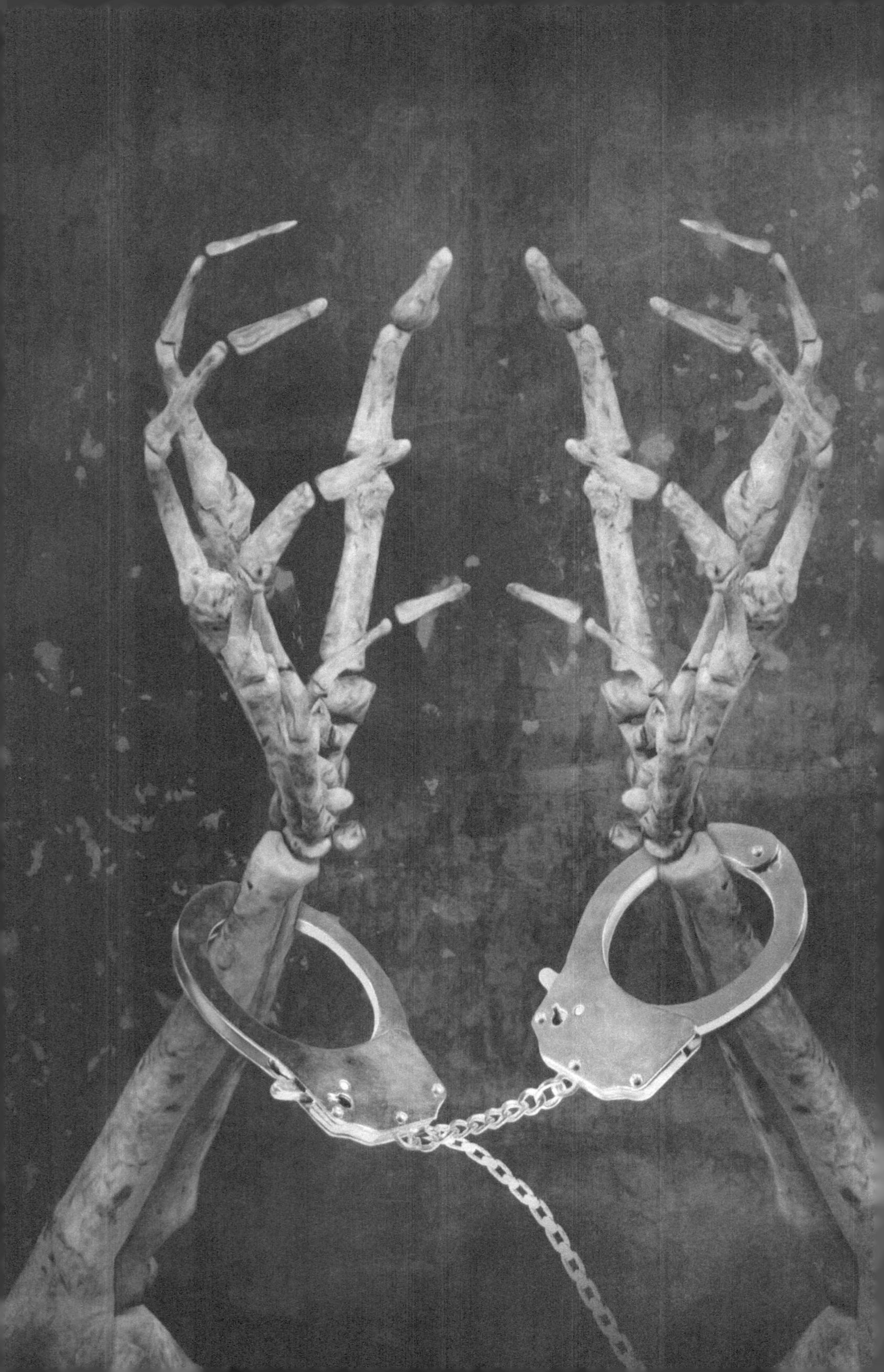

CHAPTER 12

MINA

I almost dropped the phone, but managed to hold on in spite of trembling fingers.

Hearing Kurt's voice again brought everything back in a flood that threatened to swamp me harder than the photos had.

His voice haunted my sleep and waking hours for so long, it was stamped in an endless round of nightmares.

He continued before I could formulate a response.

"You're so fucking predictable, Mina," he said. "Did you think I wouldn't have this number? That I wouldn't know the moment the *Sparrow* was reactivated? The second that happened, I was notified. You think I don't keep track of my property?"

He emphasised my codename, probably hoping someone was in the room with me and didn't already know. He'd be more than happy to expose me. Whatever it took to drag me down. To get under my skin.

Gianni fumbled with his phone and sent off a message. I was vaguely aware of it in the corner of my eye.

I didn't know who he was messaging, or why, until Reuben and Damon all but thundered into the library.

"Did you want something, prick?" I asked coldly.

He laughed. "Is that the best you can do, bitch?"

"I don't know, it's more original than 'bitch,'" I replied.

How I managed to keep my voice even, I didn't know. I drew strength from the three men around me. Every single one of them would have torn Kurt apart if he was here.

They'd hold me if I wanted to lose my cool and cry for a while. They'd also hand me knives if I wanted to carve my initials into Kurt's forehead.

If it wasn't for them, I might well have unravelled on the spot.

"Bitch is appropriate," Kurt said. "Like a female dog, you belong in a cage." He chuckled. "That was why I kept you in one. Don't tell me you didn't enjoy being on all fours in front of me while I—"

Reuben growled. A literal growl. His face was red, eyes flashing with pure fury, as though he might rip Kurt's throat out through the phone.

Silence came through the line, followed by another laugh. "Sounds like the bitch found another dog. I heard a rumour about you being seen with Reuben Brantley. I'm surprised he'd want anyone's sloppy seconds. Then again, he's a Brantley. None of them are known for being discerning."

"I'm going to enjoy rearranging his face," Gianni whispered.

"If I don't do it first," Damon snapped.

"I don't mind sharing," Gianni told him.

"I bet you don't," Kurt said. "Mina has three holes. I'm sure she's told you all about how I've had all of them."

"Did. You. Want. Something?" I ground out. "If you called to remind me what a piece of shit you are, you could have saved us both some time. I have better things to do than think about you."

"Right," he drew the word out. "Like getting back to being an assassin. Does Reuben know about that?"

"Yes, he does," I replied. "He knows what happened to that girl. He's seen the photos of what you did to me. They were on the phone I found at Stefan's place before I killed him."

The silence on the other end suggested Kurt hadn't known his associate was dead. Good, it was about time I got the better of him.

"He was very helpful," I continued. "He gave me all sorts of interesting information about you. It's funny how much people like to talk when they have a knife to their throat."

"You never were a good liar." He sounded uneasy.

I clearly hit a nerve. He wasn't sure what I knew. I could be right outside his door, waiting to step inside and slice him open. Like all cowards, he went on the defensive.

"That's bullshit, and you know it," I said. "Like everything else that comes out of your mouth. Let me tell you, you will regret everything you did to me. We will find you and—"

"Fuck you up," Gianni said helpfully.

"Yes, that," I said.

Kurt chuckled, his ego back in place. "That's where you're wrong, bitch. You won't find me before I find you. Then we'll see who fucks whom up. I know you. You can't and won't hide behind Reuben Brantley forever. The minute you step out, I'll have you. In every sense of the word. I'm going to make that cage look like a holiday. When I'm finished with you, you'll beg for forgiveness and for my cock. Just like you used to."

Before I could respond, he ended the call.

"I hate telemarketers," Gianni said, his expression perfectly serious.

I managed a faint smile before turning off the phone. "Looks like I need a new phone number." Although, he'd likely find a way to get that too.

"These days, most people don't answer their phones," Damon said. "It saves talking to someone they don't want to talk to."

I gave him a funny look. "What's the point of phones then? Don't tell me, people are still watching funny cat videos on social media."

"Exactly," Gianni said. "They also come in useful for texting and letting the boss and Damon know that prick was on the line."

"I should have realised he'd try to contact me when I switched my status back to active." The rest of the conversation played on my mind, going around and around on repeat. Most of it made my stomach turn.

"Unless he was dead, there was no way to keep that information from him." Reuben lowered himself down into a chair opposite me. "He's smart enough to keep an eye out for any sign of you."

"How did he know I was here with you?" I asked. That was at the forefront of my mind, more than Kurt's threats and reminders. "He said someone told him. The only people who have seen us together work for you or they're dead."

"It wasn't me," Gianni said immediately.

"It wasn't anyone in this room," Reuben said. "It better not be anyone who works for me." The fury hadn't completely evaporated from his expression. He looked like a bomb about to explode.

"What would any of them have to gain by telling him?" Damon asked slowly. "We know Rose wouldn't say anything. Neither would Daze. She'd skin her boyfriends alive if they did. That leaves the twins and Caleb."

"The twins wouldn't," Gianni said. "They may be as morally grey as the rest of us, but they also don't like men who abuse women. Which narrows it down to…"

"Caleb," Reuben said darkly. "If he's working with Kurt, against me, it will be the last thing he does."

I didn't know Caleb well, but I remembered Daze warning me about him. That he was ambitious and would grab any opportunity that arose. How loyal was he to his oldest brother?

"I'll tell Caleb to come here for a little chat," Damon said.

Reuben nodded. "Do it. Better yet, send the jet to pick him up. I don't want to give him an opportunity to run, and if he's done nothing wrong, sweating for a while won't hurt him."

Damon pulled out his phone and stepped out of the room.

Reuben scrubbed a hand over his face. "Are you all right?"

"I don't know," I admitted. I let Gianni take the phone from my hand and look through it.

He tapped on the number Kurt used to call me, but it was already disconnected, if it wasn't fake to begin with. "I suspect it might be impossible to trace him through this, but we can ask the twins to try."

"It can't hurt, but he'll probably be long gone from wherever he is now by the time they figure it out," I said. He was proving to be slipperier than a snake.

"We know one thing for sure," Gianni said. "He's still alive. And while he's still alive, we can find him and remedy that."

"That was a mistake," I said slowly. "If he really was smart, he'd find a way to convince us he was dead, so we'd stop looking for him."

"I wouldn't stop," Reuben said darkly. "But you're right, he let his arrogance and his obsession for you do the talking. That will be to his detriment."

"We also know he's still in the country," I said.

They both looked over at me sharply.

Reuben frowned. "How do you—"

"I recognise the bird in the background. It's some kind of cockatoo. I only heard it once, and only briefly, but it was clear enough." I shrugged.

Gianni's lips dropped apart. "Not gonna lie, I'm impressed."

"When you have to rely on being stealthy and observant, you tend to notice even the smallest thing," I said. Anything you miss could get you dead, or worse.

"Anything else?" Reuben asked, his eyes intent on me.

I frowned and thought back. "Maybe a car. It was in the background though. Like… He was outside, some distance from the road. Everything else was just him and his bullshit. I wish I could narrow it down further."

"Still in the country is narrower than we had before," Reuben said. "Judging by the way he sounded, he wouldn't have travelled far from Mina. He might well be on the outskirts of Sydney."

"If he is, we will find his sorry ass," Gianni said. "And we'll make it even sorrier."

"You have any idea if there was anywhere he liked to go?" Reuben asked.

I ran everything I knew about Kurt from before through my mind. "He frequented a gym. He was obsessive about fitness. He taught self defence classes there too. And boxing. He also liked to go camping. A couple of times, he wanted me to go with him, but I refused."

"Who trained you to become an assassin?" Gianni asked. "Was it Kurt?"

"No. It was Zara Levin and her sister, Paola. My father wanted me to learn from the best."

"Ohhh, the Sisters of Death," Gianni said in appreciation. "I've always wanted to meet them, but you know what they say. You only meet them once and they're the only ones to survive the experience."

"Only if someone hires them to take you out," I said. "Then your chances of survival are approximately zero percent." If I was scared of anyone in my life, it was the Levin sisters. They were card-carrying badass bitches, if they ever were any.

"They're almost as deadly as the Sparrow," Gianni said. "And now I'm as hard as hell." He made a face and adjusted the front of his pants. "There's something about women who know how to kill that just gets me going every time."

"Is there any chance the Levin sisters are working with Kurt?" Reuben asked softly.

"I doubt it," I said. "They didn't like him and he didn't like them. I think he was concerned they'd influence me against him." Not that I needed any convincing.

"They were quick to take me up on my request to hunt him down. For a fee, of course." They did nothing for free. Including getting out of bed in the morning. Why should they when they could ask anything they wanted in return for a job?

"That answers the age-old question," Gianni mused. When we both turned to look at him he said, "I'd always wondered who the assassins hire to assassinate someone the assassin wants assassinated. Now I know. The Levin sisters. I bet they hire you too."

"I think people are too scared of them to piss them off. So they wouldn't need to hire someone to kill them," I said. "But that's a job I'd accept."

I owed them everything for all they'd taught me. They'd kept me from losing myself. That was a debt I doubted I could ever repay.

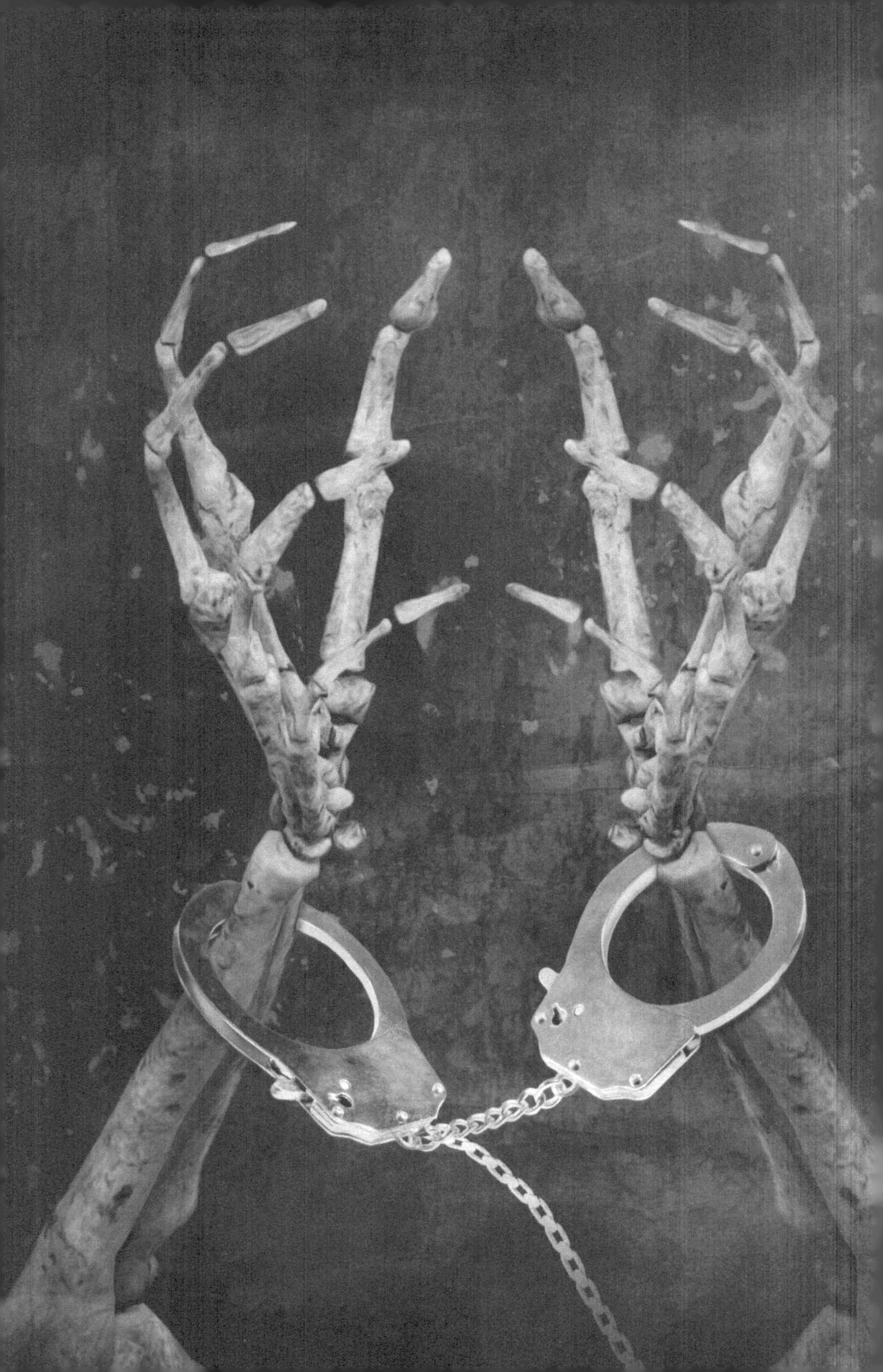

CHAPTER 13

DAMON

"You brought me all the way here to question my loyalty?" Caleb stood with his palms pressed against the top of Reuben's desk, his upper body leaning forward as though he might loom over his older brother.

He was taller, around the same height as me, but he lacked Reuben's presence. Caleb was commanding, but compared to Reuben, he might as well be in the background.

No, I wasn't biased. Much.

"You're always looking for an excuse to borrow my jet," Reuben drawled. "We thought you might enjoy the ride."

"Bullshit," Caleb snapped. He pushed himself back from the desk and turned around, a hand on the back of his head. He stood with his eyes closed for a few moments before turning back to Reuben.

"You think I'm working against you? With a lowlife piece of shit like Kurt Lasalle? Why the fuck would I do that? I've worked hard all these years to build our family into what it is. You think I'd throw that away? For what?"

"If you thought you could replace me, you might take the opportunity," Reuben said evenly.

Caleb's jaw clenched, but he didn't deny the suggestion. If he thought he'd succeed, he might well step out of line. But if he was going to take that bet, he'd have to be very sure he'd win. Otherwise, he'd be stepping out of an aircraft without a parachute. Literally.

Caleb dropped his hand to his thigh with a slap. "I'm not working against you with Kurt fucking Lasalle."

"Who are you working against him with?" Gianni leaned against the door frame, his head cocked.

Caleb looked like he might lunge at Gianni and punch him in the face, but managed to restrain himself.

"I'm not working against Reuben," he growled. "I have my people looking for Kurt, as requested." He shook his head. "Why are we even having this conversation?"

"Because someone told him Mina was here," I said. I reclined in one of the chairs to the side of the room, my ankle resting on the opposite thigh. A subtle reminder that I was more trusted around here than Caleb. A reminder that didn't go unnoticed, from the glare he gave me.

"Who told him?" Caleb demanded. "You said she was—"

"Yes, I did," Reuben said. "But Kurt had that information anyway." He didn't explain how he knew. Caleb didn't need to be privy to that. Unless Reuben thought he did. He wouldn't hear it from me or Gianni.

Caleb frowned and sank down into a chair, elbows propped on his thighs, where they threatened to wrinkle his perfectly tailored suit. He exhaled, long and slow. "What are you thinking?"

"Either we have a leak, or he was watching on the occasions we left the house," Reuben said.

"We checked the ice cream parlour for cameras," I said. "The only one present was CCTV and we destroyed the footage. The car park was the same. If the house where we found Frank had cameras, we'll never know, since the place exploded."

"If I was going to keep a woman against her will, I'd have cameras on her," Caleb said slowly.

"Sounds like you're speaking from experience," Gianni said. "But there were no cameras in the basement. Not in the rest of the building except outside. We dealt with that one too."

"I know you don't want to hear this, but is there any chance Mina is working with him?" Caleb asked.

I wasn't aware I was about to move, but I leaped out of my seat and grabbed Caleb by the front of his suit to haul him out of his.

"If you ever fucking say anything like that again, you'll be breathing out your ass," I growled.

To his credit, Caleb looked unruffled. He was fully aware I wouldn't kill him unless Reuben ordered me to. No matter how tempted I was.

"Like I said, you wouldn't want to hear the suggestion, but that doesn't mean it didn't need to be said," Caleb said evenly. "I'm no student of psychology, but Stockholm Syndrome is a thing. We both know people can be made to do all sorts of things with the right level of brainwashing. Isn't that Gianni's specialty? Convincing people that what they think is true, isn't it?" He grabbed my wrists and pulled them off the front of his suit.

I glared at him before stepping back to the other side of the room. If I was too close to him, I might do something I'd regret.

"I have considered the possibility," Reuben admitted. "If that's the case, then she wouldn't be acting on her own choice. What Kurt did to her left her traumatised. Every time she's reminded of him, she looks ready to slice off her own skin and step out of it. When she first saw me, she thought I was going to have her killed. She was *relieved*. She would have preferred to die than stay there."

Caleb nodded and reclaimed his seat. "I trust Daisy Lasalle when she says her and her boyfriends aren't involved. She worked for me for years. She's never spoken highly of her brother. Now, she seems more inclined to make him breathe out his ass." He nodded at me to acknowledge his use of my wording.

"I trust the twins," Reuben said. He steepled his fingers and pressed against his lips. "What are we missing?"

His brow was furrowed with measured thought and a dose of annoyance. He didn't like it when he didn't know things. When he wasn't fully in control.

"It's possible Kurt was guessing," Caleb said. "You know he was operating behind your back. He would have known you'd come for him at some point. Someone got Mina out of that basement. He might have put one and one together and actually managed to come up with two."

"He could have been fishing for information," I conceded. "But I don't think so. Everything he said seemed calculated. Like he knew exactly what he was going to say. He was sure he knew all the right buttons to press."

"He was very sure one of us would be in the room with her," Gianni said. "I know for a fact there aren't any bugs or cameras inside this house. Not unless we control them."

His words bounced around in my mind for a few moments before they bumped into a firm idea.

I stood up straighter. "Can you excuse me please, boss?" I slipped out of the room before Reuben could even acknowledge I'd spoken.

I slipped down the corridor and down to the last place I saw Mina. The place she seemed the most comfortable, apart from her bedroom.

I stopped in the doorway of the library. Sure enough, she was sitting on a chair in the corner, reading some kind of sports romance. I didn't realise rugby romance was a thing, but then again my knowledge of the romance genre was limited.

"How do you get into buildings undetected?" I asked.

She looked up at me and frowned. "How do I—" My question sank in. She seemed reluctant, but finally said, "I have a device."

"Where is it?" I asked. "Where is this device?"

She slipped the bookmark into her book and set it aside. "In my bedroom, why?"

"I need to see it." I should have guessed it was something like that. After years of speculation, I had an answer to one of the more interesting mysteries. I'd take some time to think about it later. In the meantime, there were more pressing matters.

Still looking uncertain, she stood. "Okay."

I followed her upstairs, vaguely aware Gianni, Reuben and Caleb stood outside Reuben's office watching us in confusion.

In spite of that, they were behind us when she reached into a drawer, pulled out a jumper and unfolded it.

Inside was a small, black device with a screen on the front.

"This disables alarm systems." She placed it on my outstretched palm.

"Mina is the Sparrow," Reuben said to Caleb, his voice low and reluctant.

Shit.

I probably should have thought of the consequences before I bolted out of the room, but I got an idea and ran with it. If there was a chance waiting might get us killed, then I had no choice.

"How does it work?" I asked.

"It hacks into the Wi-Fi that security systems are run on these days," she explained. "It reads the code and switches the system off."

"So if it hacks, it can be hacked," I reasoned.

"If technology has changed since it was invented," she agreed. "It was supposed to be hack proof. At least, as hack proof as anything could be."

I turned the device over in my hand. In the back were four, small screws. "I don't suppose you have a—"

She reached into the drawer again and pulled out a small screwdriver. She held it out to me with the handle facing me.

I nodded my thanks and accepted it. She really was prepared for almost anything. How many knives did she have hidden in those drawers and around the room? If I was her, I'd have several, in case anyone got past the security system.

The device balanced on my palm, I carefully unscrewed each of the screws and handed them to her. I had to use the screwdriver to pry off the back of the device, but it eventually came off with a pop.

"Bingo." Sitting in the back of the device was a tiny bug. The kind used to listen in and track people. The kind that crunched satisfyingly under my heel.

"He said I was predictable," Mina said, her eyes glazed as she spoke. "I thought he meant coming here, but he didn't. He knew exactly where I kept my phone and that device. He knew if I ever got out of that basement, I'd go back for those things. That could have been inside the device for years. Waiting."

Her face was pale again. That asshole really knew how to get to her. Fuck only knew what else he'd done that we hadn't uncovered yet.

"Mina DiMarco is the Sparrow?" Apparently it took Caleb a few moments to process that information. "How long until Kurt tells the world that?"

Or maybe he processed it immediately and moved quickly to the implications, conjuring scenarios in his mind. His tone wasn't panicked, or even concerned.

His brow was creased as he made calculations in his head. Planning like someone plans moves in a game of chess. Reuben was commanding, but Caleb was the strategic brother. Often several moves ahead of everyone else.

I turned to glare at him.

He shrugged and raised his hands. "Don't say it hasn't occurred to you, because it would have. If this prick has gone to such lengths to track her, then what's keeping him from pulling the pin on this?"

"What would he have to gain from telling everyone?" I asked. "People would want proof. The only way he could give them that would be to throw himself under the bus."

"I wish he would throw himself under a literal bus," Gianni said.

"People like him don't give away information like that," Caleb said. "They sell it to the highest bidder. Can you imagine the amount of zeros information like that would go for? That device Damon is holding in his hand is almost as valuable." He gestured at me.

"The price governments would pay for retribution against her for assassinating their officials would be eye watering. Or better yet, finding out who hired her. Information like that could bring down whole administrations. Hell, countries could collapse. You know the kind of people she was hired to target. I'm not fucking exaggerating." His jaw was set tight.

"We're not letting them torture Mina," Gianni said, his low voice a thinly veiled threat.

"Then we better find Kurt fucking Lasalle before he can offer her up," Caleb said. "Because people aren't going to let any of us stand in the way when there are millions of dollars involved."

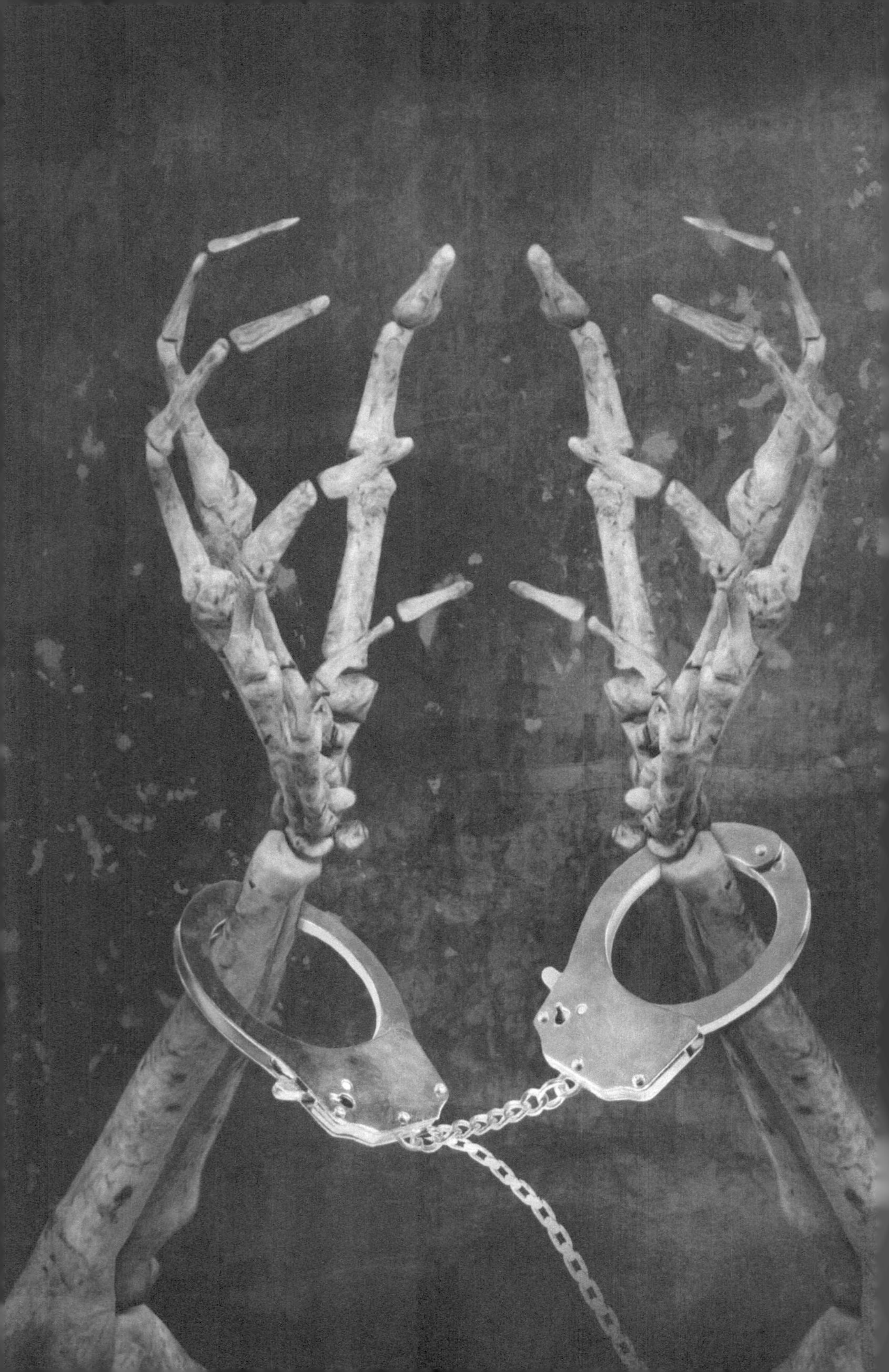

CHAPTER 14

MINA

"Pack as much as you can, " Reuben said. "I want to be out of here within the hour."

"Where are we going?" Gianni followed him to the door.

"Dusk Bay," Reuben said briskly. "My house there is more secure than here. Damon, Caleb, have your connections be on the lookout for any information regarding the Sparrow, especially any offers to sell her identity." Evidently he'd decided to take Caleb's words seriously.

Unfortunately for me, Caleb was right. Kurt would sell that information to whoever would pay for it.

"We could stop him from getting rich," I said softly.

They all stopped to stare at me.

"I could sell that information myself," I said. "Or I could give it away for free."

"No." The word was simple, the delivery soft, but Reuben's expression was firm. "Start packing."

"Listen to what she has to say," Caleb advised. He crossed his arms and nodded to me.

Reuben glared at him, but didn't contradict him. Instead, he leaned against the door frame and looked back at me while I spoke.

"If we release the information, we can control what people hear," I said. "And who hears it. If we leave it to Kurt, he gets to make millions, and he controls who he speaks to and what he gives them. I can't freely disclose information about past clients. Just enough information to satisfy people. They can do whatever they want with that. We can carefully choose what we share for minimal impact on us and our interests. And innocent people. Kurt won't have that kind of restraint."

Reuben looked thoughtful. He didn't dismiss the idea, but he didn't agree with it either.

"I'll consider it," he said finally. "We now leave in fifty-five minutes." He turned and walked out of the room.

"For what it's worth, I think it's a good idea." Caleb nodded and stepped away himself.

Damon waited until he was gone, grimaced and said, "I hate to agree with anything Caleb said, but it is."

"Technically, we're agreeing with what Mina said," Gianni pointed out. "You need help packing, sweetheart?"

"I don't have much," I said. "You should go and pack your things."

"I'll go and organise the jet," Damon said. "And speak to my contacts about putting your plan into action."

"You think Reuben will agree to it?" I asked.

Damon shrugged. "I don't see how he'd have a choice. This is the best way to stop Kurt from having control over this. It might also help to flush him out." He tucked his hands into his pockets and strode out of the room.

I glanced at Gianni.

He looked back at me and frowned. "What?"

"I was expecting you to say something like you wanted to flush Kurt down the toilet."

I grabbed the handle of the suitcase Reuben gave me and pulled it out of the top of the wardrobe. I set it down on the bed and started to toss things inside.

Gianni laughed. "I must be losing my touch if I missed that one."

"Or you thought it was low hanging fruit and weren't going to bother," I offered.

"When it comes to Kurt, there's no such thing as too low." In spite of my assurances that I didn't need help, he started to pull my underwear out of the drawer and place it neatly in the suitcase. "Not even toilet humour."

"I suppose so." I tossed my jeans in beside my underwear.

"So, you can pick locks and have a device that disables security alarms," Gianni said. "What other tricks do you have up your sleeve?"

"Is that why you offered to help?" I asked, half teasing. "So you could get the gossip?"

"It's mostly because I like your company, but colour me curious," he said. "Caleb was also right, that device would bring in millions, maybe billions, of dollars. Imagine the places we could get into with a few of those."

I cocked my head at him.

"Right, you don't need to imagine. Have you ever been tempted to rob a bank, just because you could?" He matched the angle of my head and smiled.

I scoffed. "I prefer a challenge." My lips moved as I considered adding to that, but I pressed them together and smirked at my own thought.

"What? Where did kid-Mina sneak into?" He pressed his palms to his hips and lifted his chin expectantly.

"Nowhere I wasn't paid to go," I said evasively. I stepped around him to pick up a couple of books from the table beside the bed.

"Where did you *want* to go?" he asked.

"You'll think it's silly." I placed the books down on top of my jeans.

"Have you met me?" He looked at me sideways. "I like silly. I don't think you could say anything sillier than the thoughts that go through my mind on an hourly basis." He raised his hand and gave me a 'give it to me' gesture with his fingers.

I sighed and straightened up. "I had a crush on a popstar once. I thought about breaking into his house and… I don't know. Stealing his underwear or watching him sleep. Something stupid like that." I shrugged.

Gianni smiled. "That's adorable. If he had half a brain cell, you could have just knocked on the door. I wouldn't have turned you away if I was him."

"There's no challenge in knocking on the door," I said. "It doesn't matter anyway, because I didn't know where he lived, or what his real name was. It was just a childish fantasy."

"Those are the best kind," Gianni said. "The problem with growing up is losing things like that. What was his name?"

I made a face. "Bobby Starlight. Like I said, I was young." He sang songs about love, relationships and corny things like dancing under the light of a full moon.

His lyrics and upbeat tunes were a sweet counterpoint to the rest of my life back then. They helped to balance out all the death and gave me a place to escape to. It didn't hurt that he was ridiculously good-looking, with washboard abs and tattoos to spare. He was the fantasy of teenage girls all over the world. The one time I could have seen him on tour, I'd had a job all the way in London. I was gutted, but work always came first. Especially when I was still building a reputation.

"I love him," Gianni enthused. "He hasn't released anything in years, but I bet we could find him." He looked as though he might pull out his phone right now and send a message to his own contacts to find out the real name and address of Bobby Starlight. For all I knew, Asher might have been one of those contacts. Didn't people in the music industry know each other, or something like that?

I shook my head. "We should focus on the present and the shit that matters." I closed my suitcase and zipped it up. That part of my past was so long ago it didn't matter anymore. We had more pressing things to do, like find Kurt, and Leon Graves.

Gianni stepped over to me and placed his hands lightly on my shoulders. He looked me straight in the eyes, knowing I could step away from him at any time, but wanting to get his point across, because it was important to him.

"There's no reason why you can't have childish fantasies if you want to. If I'm too young to give them up, then you are. I know Kurt stole them from you, but I want to help you get them back. Everyone deserves to have some fun once in a while. Especially you. I'm not saying we should break in and steal a person's underwear. Although, I'm not ruling that out either, but we could do other things."

"Don't steal his underwear for me," I said.

I'd be deluding myself if I didn't think he'd do exactly that if I asked him to. I wasn't sure there was anything he'd say no to if I wanted it. He was sweet, but I wasn't going to take advantage. Especially not when I was struggling to find my own independence again.

"I won't steal his underwear for you, but I might do it *with* you," he said with a grin. "Seriously, what did you used to do for fun?"

"Kill people," I said flatly. "I read books and I killed people."

"As hot as that is, you must have done other things," he pressed. "Did you go out and dance all night? Go to the movies? Lie around with your friends, giving each other facials while you gossiped about boys?"

I glanced away from him and let my eyes glaze as I thought back. All of that seemed like a thousand lifetimes ago. It could have happened to someone else, or in my imagination.

"Used to play the guitar," I said finally. "I thought maybe I'd be in a band with Asher some day. Or tour with Bobby Starlight." I snorted at the ridiculous idea. "Can you imagine an assassin touring the world as a guitarist?"

It would be a nice cover, but it sounded like something out of a mafia rock star romance book. Was that such a thing? I'd have to look it up.

"As a matter of fact, I can," Gianni agreed. "You would have been amazing. You still might be. I'm sure Reuben wouldn't mind buying you—"

"I can buy my own guitar," I said, slightly more snappy than I intended.

I exhaled softly. "I'm sorry. I just feel like…that dream passed me by. There's no point in trying to pretend it's going to happen. For one thing, Asher's band already has a guitarist."

"That doesn't mean you can't get a guitar and play it for fun," Gianni said. "I could play with you. We could jam."

"You play the guitar?" I squinted at him. I couldn't quite imagine him doing that.

He grinned. "No, but I can play the triangle. And believe it or not, I'm not too bad on the flute." He mimed playing one, his lips pursed as he blew into an invisible instrument. "You never heard this from me, but Damon is pretty good on the saxophone."

"Don't tell me, Reuben is secretly an accomplished drummer?" I asked.

Gianni chuckled. "I don't think Reuben would be caught dead playing a musical instrument. Besides, I think he's more the bass player type." He mimed playing one of the four stringed instruments, leaning backwards as though he was rocking out to an audience.

A laugh slipped out from between my lips. "That's an interesting visual image. I'm not sure I'll be able to get that out of my head."

"You're welcome," Gianni quipped. "Maybe you can work on him to learn to play. He could use another outlet to let himself relax."

"I might start by getting my own guitar first," I said. He was right, I should give myself the chance to enjoy my life. As much fun as killing and reading were, I enjoyed making music. Even if I was the only one who ever heard it.

"Do you need help packing?" I pulled out my phone and glanced at the time.

I had no reason to believe Reuben wasn't completely serious when he said we'd had an hour. If that was the case, we used up half of that already.

"I'm still packed from when we went to Dusk Bay," Gianni admitted. "Never got around to unpacking. You're going to love the house there. It overlooks the beach. There are stairs that lead right down to it. It's the only way to get there by land. The view is absolutely fucking beautiful."

He grabbed the handle of my suitcase and led me out the door.

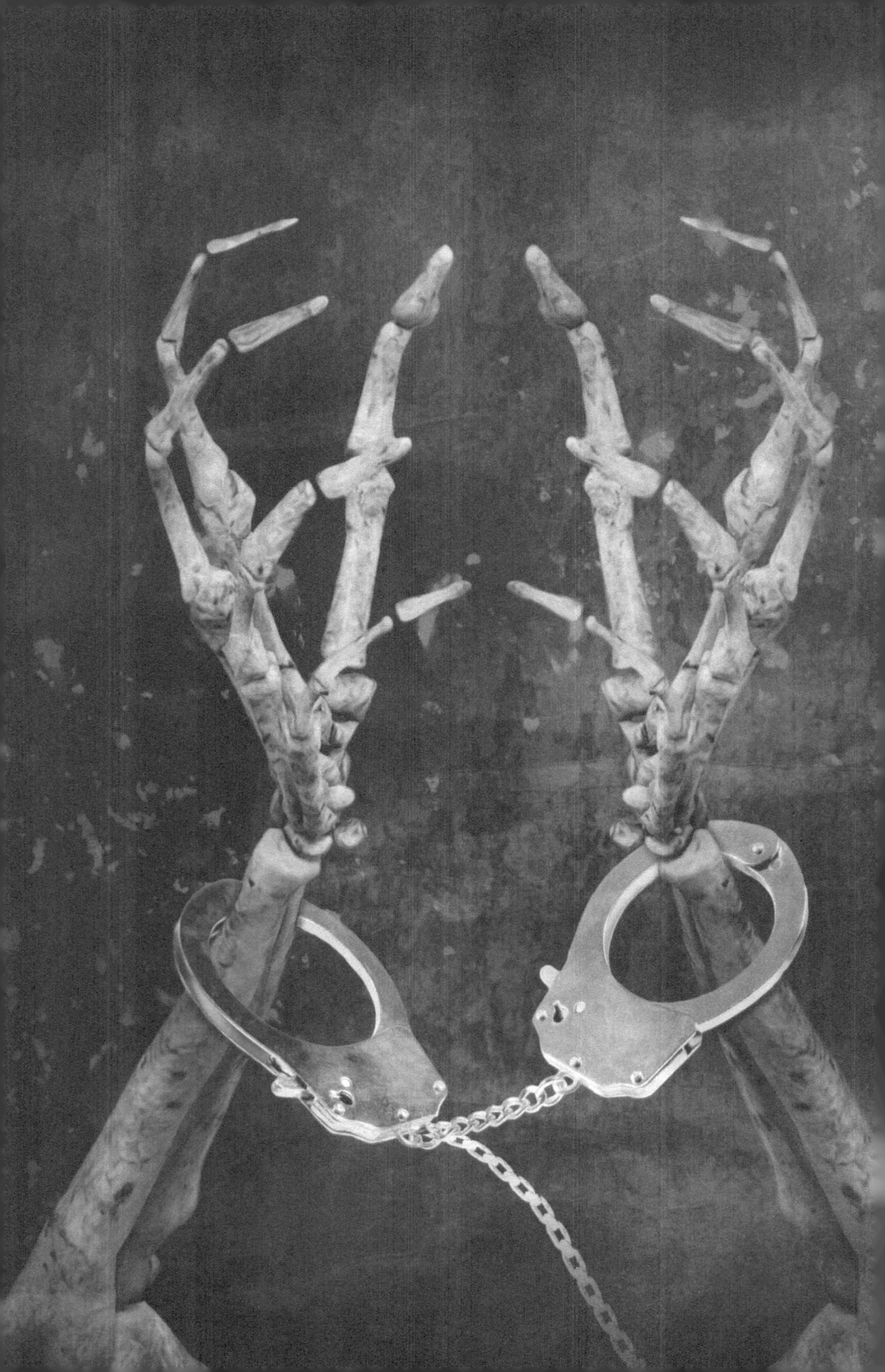

CHAPTER 15

MINA

Gianni was right about the house in Dusk Bay. From the moment we stepped through the front door, the house opened up to the expansive view of the Pacific Ocean.

Easily three or four times the size of the house in Sydney, it was just as tastefully decorated, with light wood, creams and blue-greys. Coastal without looking cliché. Decadent and elegant, but comfortable at the same time.

The rear of the house was a bank of windows that framed the sunlight glittering on the waves.

"This is incredible," I breathed.

I felt as though if I spoke too loud, I'd disturb the peace in this place. "Do you come here a lot?" I stepped over to look out at the water.

Reuben stopped beside me and placed a hand on my shoulder. "A couple of times a year. Not enough."

"It's empty the rest of the time?" I asked.

"Except for the staff, yes." He shrugged. "They keep it clean and well-maintained."

I pictured the expression on his face if he found dust in his house and held back a smile. "It's amazing."

"It's a waste not to be here more often," he said. "Sometimes I consider letting someone else watch over things in Sydney while I live here." He looked contemplative. "There are several rooms for you to choose from, unless you're ready to share."

I expected him to bring that up at some point, but it still knocked the breath out of me for a few moments. Was I ready? Could I do more than share a room, or a bed? I knew what all three of them wanted. I wanted that too, but the idea still left me in a cold sweat.

"You know I won't pressure you—" he started.

"I know," I said quickly. "I think I'd like to share a room. Being by myself at night is lonely and I get into my own head. If someone else was there, it might help." I held my lower lip with my teeth.

"It doesn't have to be me," he said reluctantly. He clearly wanted it to be.

"It's not that," I said. I glanced around to see we were alone. Gianni and Damon must have taken their bags and mine upstairs. I appreciated them giving us some space. "Damon…"

"Cares about you too." A faint frown creased his brow, uncertain as to whether we were on the same page.

Honestly, I wasn't sure we were in the same book.

I cleared my throat. "He cares about you too."

Reuben's brow smoothed. "Ah."

"You know?" I asked.

"I suspected." He inclined his head.

"And?" I prompted. "Can I ask if it's reciprocated?"

"How would you feel if it was?" he asked carefully.

"Happy for you both," I said without hesitation.

"It wouldn't be about us picking each other over you," he said, frowning again. "We both want you as well."

"I was hoping you'd say that," I admitted. "I didn't want to make things any messier than they already are. I mean figuratively messy, not literally." My face heated.

A slight smile tugged at the corners of his mouth.

"But I wouldn't have stood in the way if that was what you wanted," I added quickly. "You haven't said what that is."

"I'm not sure what the answer is to your questions," he said carefully. "There's an attraction there, but we've never acted on it. I wasn't sure if he wanted to, or what it would do to our working relationship. And I thought maybe he and Gianni might have a thing."

"I don't think Gianni would object to anything and everything," I said. "Me, Damon, you. Any combination of the above. But I'm certain Damon wants you as much as I do." I stood on my toes and lightly kissed his mouth. The idea of seeing those three men together was enough to set my panties on fire. How would it feel to be in the middle of all that testosterone and muscle?

Reuben placed a hand on my hip and deepened the kiss. His tongue delved into my mouth, tasting my lips and brushing over my teeth.

"I can't stop thinking about the other night," he said against my lips. "The way your mouth felt on my cock. I've been hard as a rock ever since. All I can think about is tasting you."

His words made me wet before he finished speaking. His voice was a low, compelling rumble that sent my pulse racing.

The only thing I could say in response was, "Please."

He hooked a hand around the back of my neck and kissed me while walking me over to the massive couch that sat facing the view.

Giving me a chance to pull away, he guided me until I was lying on my back, my ass on the edge of the couch. He worked the buttons on my jeans loose and pulled them down to my ankles.

I pushed off my shoes and kicked my legs until my jeans fell onto the floor.

He knelt in front of me and looked at me, his eyes dark with need. "I don't want to go too fast for you."

I swallowed hard before grabbing the hem of my shirt and pulling it up over my head. I tossed it aside and lay back, dressed only in a red lace bra and panties.

My blood was on fire. My body ached to be touched, but my scars made me self-conscious. I wanted to curl up around myself.

I forced myself to lay still and try to relax. He wasn't going to hurt me, I knew that. He was looking at me like he'd never seen anything so beautiful in his life.

He gently traced a line up my thigh and across my stomach,

circling the scars with the tip of his finger like he was worshipping each of them.

"I know you hate these," he whispered. "But they're a sign of how strong you are. After everything you went through, you didn't break. I have scars too, some on the inside, some on the outside. Every one helped to shape us into the people we are today. They say we can be beaten but not broken. They say 'fuck you' to anyone who dared to try."

He pulled down the cup of my bra that covered my ruined nipple. Slowly, he leaned forward to trace circles around it with his tongue. For the longest time, that was all he did, tasting my skin and my scars, like nothing in the world was more important, beautiful or delicious.

Finally, he pulled down the other cup and suckled on my nipple until I was quivering and my self-consciousness was forgotten.

With gentle fingers, he parted my knees and kissed his way up one thigh and down the other. He kissed his way back up and grabbed onto my panties with his teeth.

With a playful expression I'd never seen on his face before, he pulled them down my legs with his mouth before opening his lips and dropping them on the floor. He looked pleased with himself.

I smiled at him before I sat up just high enough to unhook my bra and slide it off my arms. I swallowed back another wave of self-consciousness. I'd never been naked in front of anyone in daylight before.

"Mina, you're absolutely fucking gorgeous," he said breathlessly. "Every centimetre of you is perfection."

His eyes on my face, he lowered his mouth to my pussy and slowly started to explore with his tongue.

I pressed my palms to the couch on either side of me and let myself enjoy the way it felt to have him tease me, dipping first his tongue inside me, then a finger.

Every so often, he'd look up at me to make sure I was all right before returning his attention to my pussy. He looked fascinated, like he'd never seen anything so incredible in his life.

I heard footsteps on the stairs and glanced over to see Damon and

Gianni walking toward us. They both stopped a few steps from the bottom before continuing on.

Eyes dark, they stepped over to the couch and sat down on either side of me to watch.

The expression on their faces pushed the last drops of self-consciousness out the window and into the ocean. They saw my body, with all of my scars, and still looked at me like I was some kind of goddess.

I rolled my hips slowly, adding to the friction I already got from Reuben's tongue. He expertly worked my clit like he knew exactly what I wanted. Like he understood every centimetre of my body and how to give me what I needed.

"Fucking beautiful," Gianni whispered.

Damon hummed his agreement and lightly touched my skin where my nipple used to be, with the pad of his thumb. He ran it up and down as if he wanted to memorise every millimetre, every bump, every bit of red, ruined skin.

Anger flashed in his eyes at how this must have happened, but, like Reuben, this was just a part of me. He leaned over and gave my other nipple the same treatment, making the inferno in my body rise even higher.

Gianni kissed my cheek, then my lips, moving slowly and carefully so he didn't overwhelm me. Having all of this attention from three incredible men could easily have done exactly that. It had the opposite effect. I felt both liberated and loved. Appreciated in a way I'd never been before.

Safer than I'd ever been before. More alive.

Reuben slipped another finger inside me and fucked me slowly with his hand and his tongue. Damon lavished attention on my breasts, while Gianni left me breathless with his kisses.

Gianni broke off and smiled at me, a hint of mischief lurking in his dark eyes. He scooted down until he was almost face-to-face with Damon.

Damon lifted his mouth off my nipple and sat still, close enough that their noses almost touched. Their chins hovered my chest.

I held my breath until Gianni moved forward, brushing his lips over Damon's.

Fireworks went off inside the room. Electricity snapped and crackled.

They deepened the kiss, a clashing of lips and teeth and tongues. Their stubble must have grazed each other's faces, rough but sensual.

Between the sight of the two men kissing and Reuben's mouth and fingers, I couldn't hold back anymore. I arched my back and surrendered to an orgasm that washed over me bigger than the waves outside the window.

I dropped my head back and cried out, while every millimetre of me was engulfed in flame. Instead of burning, it was an inferno of pure pleasure. I held back absolutely nothing, and neither did Reuben. His tongue flicked over my clit. His fingers were firm on my G spot, pushing me to heights I never thought possible.

When I finally floated back down to earth, it was to see three sets of eyes on me, each as hot as the next. Damon and Gianni with their faces just above my nipples and Reuben with his head still between my legs.

"That was fucking hot," Gianni said. "I'm officially rock hard."

Damon grimaced in agreement and shifted his position on the couch.

"It was," I agreed. "Everything."

Damon and Gianni exchanged glances, while Reuben lifted his shining mouth and sat back on his heels.

Damon broke the silence by clearing his throat and pushing himself to his feet. "I should be working on making sure security is in place."

"Right," Gianni agreed. "I should be checking we have all the weapons we might need, just in case." He rose too and they hurried off in opposite directions.

"I'll show you to your room." Reuben offered me my clothes and his hand. "Before any of the staff appear. It would be inconvenient to have to have them killed because they saw you naked." There was no hint that he was joking. Not even slightly.

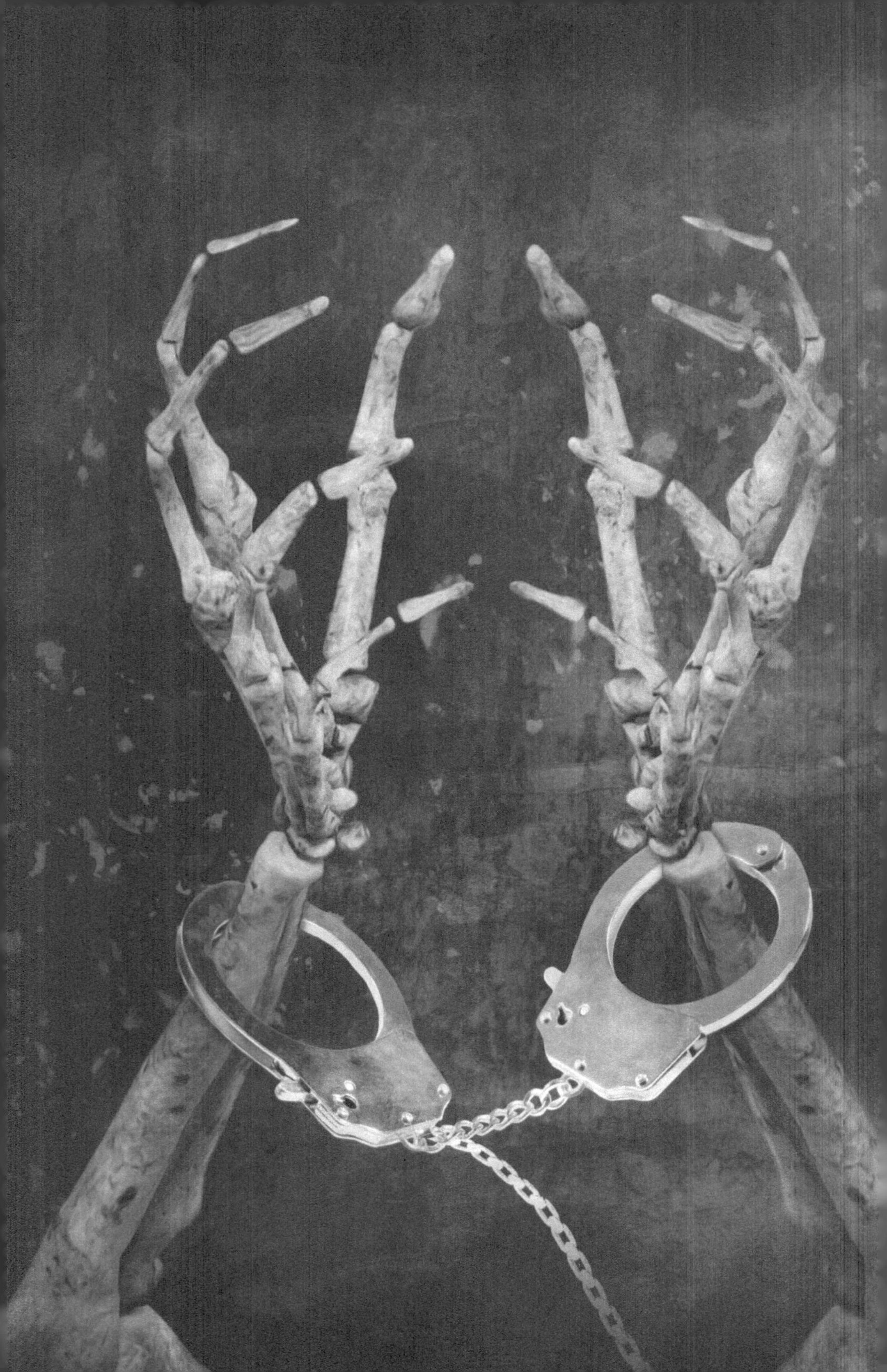

CHAPTER 16

MINA

Caleb put on a pair of reading glasses and looked toward his phone screen. "As far as my contacts have been able to determine, Kurt hasn't made any move to sell Mina's information. Any attempt to trace the phone number he used to call her led nowhere."

"He hid his tracks too well." Parker looked annoyed, as if him not being able to trace Kurt either was personal. "He needs to use more modern technology. Then we'd be all over him. Not literally." He stuck out his tongue in disgust.

"No one thought you meant it literally, Park." Hunter patted him on the shoulder. "If I was him, I'd be going through someone else anyway. Let someone else hang on his behalf. Possibly literally."

"Definitely literally." Reuben sat behind his desk, rubbing his forehead with his fingertips like he had an impending headache.

Hunter and Parker lounged on a couch against the wall. Caleb sat in a chair, his back ramrod straight.

Damon and Gianni both leaned against the wall near the door, glancing at each other occasionally, but looking more comfortable than they had right after they kissed.

I sat perched on top of Reuben's desk and listened, one eye on the view of the ocean behind Reuben, the other on the room. To anyone who didn't know better, I wasn't paying attention.

No one in this room would make that assumption. Even here, surrounded by high walls and abundant security, we were all on alert.

"We have a lead on Leon Graves," Damon said.

Caleb didn't try to hide his scowl. Not because he particularly cared about me, but he clearly prided himself on what, and who, he knew. He didn't want to be bettered by someone like Damon.

Regardless, everyone's attention was immediately on Damon.

"He made contact with one of my contacts two days ago," Damon said, undeterred by the scrutiny.

"We're only hearing about this now? Why?" Caleb asked coldly.

Damon ignored him, his gaze on me and Reuben. "I was just informed about this. She didn't know you were looking for him."

"She, huh? Is she hot?" Hunter asked. He glared at Parker when he elbowed his twin in the ribs. "I was asking for Caleb. He clearly needs to get laid." He gestured towards his older brother.

Caleb turned his glare on both twins. "I suggest you mind your own fucking business. The cliff outside is high. I don't think either of you would survive the fall."

Neither twin looked particularly ruffled, but for once, they didn't respond. Possibly because of the cold death glare all three of them got from Reuben.

His gaze slid from them to Damon. "Where is this contact of yours?"

"Right here in Dusk Bay," Damon said. "I thought we could pay her a visit."

Reuben nodded. "Take Gianni with you."

"I'm going too," I said. "Sometimes a woman will open up to another woman." In the corner of my eye, I saw Parker open his mouth to speak. "Not that kind of open up."

He closed his mouth, but grinned. "A guy could hope."

I rolled my eyes at him but smiled. To be fair, I couldn't blame him. I got off on seeing two men kiss, so why wouldn't he fantasise about two women being together? Or want to watch?

Reuben looked as though he wanted to refuse to let me go, but he finally inclined his head. "Take the twins with you, in case everything goes south."

"We'll be sure to put them between us and any trouble," Gianni said teasingly.

Both twins smirked.

"That would take care of two problems," Caleb muttered.

"He really loves us as much as Reuben does," Hunter said to the room in general. "We're useful to him."

"Occasionally," Caleb said. "I'll keep monitoring the dark web for any sign of Lasalle. There's a lot of chatter about the Sparrow. Mostly curiosity about why they suddenly returned and where they were. I'll keep looking for people asking who they are, or offering that kind of information."

I chewed my lip and looked back at Reuben. He'd still given no indication he'd let me offer up the information myself. I could do it without his help, but I didn't want to go behind his back with this. Besides, it would be easier with him and the other men helping me.

I was tech savvy five years ago, but so much had changed since then. The act of logging onto social media was more complicated than it used to be. Just as toxic though, from the sound of it.

Reuben looked back at me, obviously knowing what I was thinking. He was hoping we'd find Kurt before I had to put myself out there.

I appreciated that on a personal and professional level. Once the world knew what I was, it would be difficult to keep working. Not impossible. The Levin sisters never hid their identity in the way I had. People knew who they were, if not what they looked like.

I didn't even know. They worked and trained with masks over their faces. Zara spoke occasionally, but Paola never said a word in my presence. I could have passed them both on the street and never recognised them.

I supposed I could do that if I was outed. Get myself a mask and a new codename. I'd have to rebuild my reputation from scratch. That would suck, but it wasn't insurmountable.

Reuben seemed to see all of that pass through my mind. Like it or not, we were on the same page on this. For now. If Damon's contact couldn't lead us to Leon Graves, then we might be back to square one.

"I'll bring the SUV around," Damon said. He slipped out of the office, followed by Gianni.

"Be safe," Reuben said to me.

"I will." I dropped down off the desk and walked around to kiss his mouth. I didn't care that Caleb and the twins were still in the room, watching. Let them see. I wasn't ashamed of the relationship between me and their brother.

Fortunately for them, they'd arrived after Reuben tongue fucked me on the couch. I had a feeling there'd be three bodies at the base of the cliff if they saw me naked.

Reuben hooked a hand around the back of my head and deepened the kiss before reluctantly letting me go. "If anything happens to you, Damon, Gianni and the twins better be dead already."

"We'll take good care of your woman," Hunter assured him. He looked like he was about to add something, but after exchanging glances with Parker he closed his mouth.

"Make sure you do," Reuben said.

I stepped back, offered him a smile and followed the twins out of the room.

"How is the—"

Caleb closed the door before I could hear the rest of Reuben's question.

"In case you were wondering, yes, Caleb is always like that," Parker said. "Every now and again, I wonder who is more uptight, him or Reuben. Then we'll get together and I remember, it's Caleb. If you ask me, I think he tries too hard. He's always trying to impress Reuben."

"I got that vibe," I said. "He seems to be good at what he does."

"He is," Parker agreed. "He wouldn't dare not to be. His reputation, and job with the family, count on it. In his universe, those two are the most important things. In that order."

"He really, really needs to get laid," Hunter said. "I mean, we take our jobs seriously…ish…but we know how to have a good time too. Life is way too short to walk around with a stick up your ass. Where's the fun in that?"

"If you're talking a literal stick, not fun," Parker said. "There are other things I'd rather have up my—"

Hunter interrupted him. "Too much information, bro. I don't need to know what you want up your ass."

"As if we don't share a sex life," Parker said.

He looked Hunter up and down, a mock frown on his face, as if he was actually offended in any way. It would obviously take a lot more than that to really get to him. Especially when it came to his twin.

"Yeah, but Mina doesn't want to hear it. Right, Mina?" Hunter asked.

I shrugged. "It doesn't bother me, one way or another. In fact, it's refreshing that you're not shy about shit like that."

Sex wasn't discussed in my family, unless you counted Asher's penis jokes. None of which he ever would have told in front of our parents.

"We've never been shy about much of anything," Parker said. "That's another thing life is too short for. We like to grab every day by the balls and ride that motherfucker for all she's worth."

Hunter nodded. "Accurate. Not literal, but accurate."

I couldn't hold back a smile at their obvious enjoyment of life.

It faded when I wondered if I'd be like that if not for Kurt. I had a vague memory of being more outgoing and bubbly when I wasn't sneaking around assassinating people. I might still be like that. I'd never know for sure.

"If we didn't say it before, we're sorry for what happened to you," Hunter said, in a rare moment of seriousness and sincerity. "That was fucked up. This might sound weird, but you're kinda like a sister to us. If someone does something to anyone in our family, we take it personally. Whatever it takes to deal with Lasalle, we're both in."

"Balls deep," Parker agreed. "Once again, not literally. If I meant that literally, Reuben would probably tear mine off. Since I'm attached to my balls, I will stick to speaking figuratively. But like Hunter said, you're like a sister to us, so that would be fucked up."

"You two are crazy, but you're sweet," I said.

They both grinned.

"That's what we keep telling everyone," Hunter said. "It's about time someone believed us." He offered his twin a fist bump.

Parker bumped, then offered him a high five.

I cocked my head at them. "I'm surprised you don't have a secret handshake."

"Who says we don't?" Hunter asked. "If we showed you, it wouldn't be a secret anymore. Although, if we were going to show anyone, it would probably be you. You're the cool, big sister we never had."

"No one has ever called me that before," I said. Tears prickled in the corners of my eyes.

"Which one?" Parker asked.

"Both," I replied. "Cool, or big sister. I'm the youngest in my family."

"You *were* the youngest," Parker corrected. "Now you're our family and we're the youngest. As far as we know."

If we kept talking like this, I was going to get choked up with emotion. That wasn't something any of us had time for right now. But I admit, this conversation made me feel warm inside. I'd be happy to have the twins as my younger brothers. From now on, I had their backs and they had mine.

I cleared my throat. "If we don't hurry, Damon and Gianni might leave without us."

They'd do exactly that if Reuben told them to. Honestly, I half expected to step out of the front of the house to see the SUV driving through the gates and away.

Instead, Gianni and Damon sat in the front of the dark vehicle, waiting for us with various levels of patience. Gianni looked relaxed, Damon looked on edge. So, the usual for them both.

I slid into the back and the twins walked around the other side to climb in with me.

Hunter clicked his seatbelt and rubbed his hands together. "It's party time."

"We're just going for a chat," Damon reminded him.

"That's where it starts," Hunter said. "We'll see where it ends."

I hoped a chat was all it would be, but I wasn't naïve enough to think anything would be that simple.

Nothing was yet.

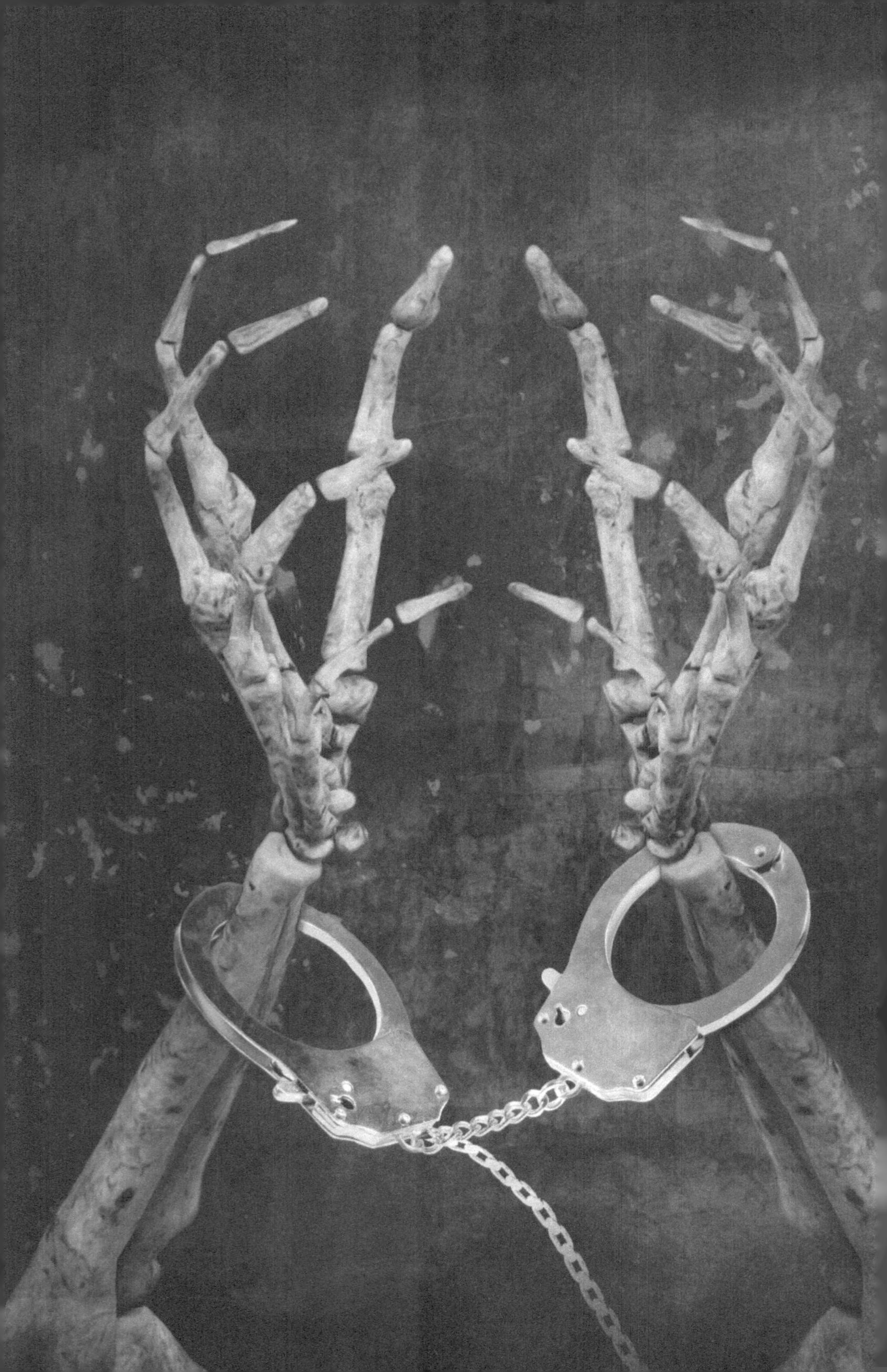

CHAPTER 17

DAMON

"Try not to look too conspicuous." I addressed the remark to Gianni and the twins. I didn't have to tell Mina that. In spite of being stunning, she knew how to blend into her surroundings. She held herself with a casual alertness that wouldn't draw excessive attention.

Gianni and the twins on the other hand, did nothing to disappear into the background.

Hunter and Parker walked behind Mina, and Gianni beside her, looking like a guard of honour. Somewhat appropriate, given she was a queen, but in no way subtle.

"Have you forgotten this is Dusk Bay?" Hunter asked. "Everyone knows us here. They know who we are and what we do. At least three people have crossed to the other side of the road instead of walking past us, and we've only been here for a handful of minutes."

He wasn't wrong about Dusk Bay. Reuben controlled most of the city. Almost everyone who lived here worked for him, directly or indirectly.

Still, strutting around would draw further attention to us and that would have people talking. We didn't need the scrutiny or speculation. Reuben's presence in town would generate enough of that.

"Maybe you stink?" Gianni teased. He ducked to the side as Hunter took a playful swing at him.

I rolled my eyes and turned my back on them.

"Who is this contact?" Mina caught up to me while the other three were joking around. Her gaze seemed to be everywhere, taking everything in, while focused on me at the same time. How much of that was training and how much was a result of the trauma?

She was hyper-vigilant all the time. I suspected she slept with one eye open.

"Her name is Clarissa, but I don't think that's her actual name," I said. "She runs a vegan grocery store." I waved in the general direction of her business. "We're meeting her out the back."

I led them through an alleyway and around to the rear of the block of shops. In the back was a car park and several large skips. Heavy iron doors indicated entrance to each of the businesses.

The vegan grocer itself was nestled between a gymnastics school, and a shop selling musical instruments and music lessons.

The back door was open and Clarissa herself leaned against the door frame. As tall and sturdy as me, she regarded us all, unflinching. If I had a fistfight with her, I wasn't sure I'd back myself.

"Look what the cat dragged in," she drawled. Her voice was a deep rumble. "Damon Riviello and…friends."

She glanced around me, curious but not intimidated. She offered her hand and shook mine in a grip that made me wince.

"Nice to see you too," I said sarcastically. I shook out my hand and briefly introduced Clarissa to everyone.

Her eyes lingered on Mina before taking in Gianni and the twins.

"I've heard about you two," she said to Hunter and Parker. "Don't touch anything." She waved a thick finger at them.

Both twins raised their hands.

"We wouldn't dream of it," Parker assured her.

She squinted at him, but stepped back inside, gesturing for us to follow.

Mina glanced at me, but followed me over the threshold.

"Nice place," Gianni said.

The storage area was neat, lined with shelves and shelves of boxes.

Most would contain stock for the grocery store, but it wouldn't surprise me if some contained guns or other contraband. Where better to smuggle things like that?

Clarissa grunted and picked up a phone from the desk in the corner. She turned on the screen and held it out in front of her. "I got this message two days ago."

Even before she started playing it, Mina's body stiffened.

Instinctively, I moved closer to her, as did Gianni and the twins. A protective wall of muscle between her and the ghosts of her past.

A male voice echoed through the space, tiny from his surroundings and ours.

"Hey, Clarissa, it's Leon. I have a delivery arriving in Dusk Bay in three days and need you to intercept. I'll text you the details." The call ended.

Mina's face was drained of colour. "That's him. I know that voice."

"Did he send you the details?" I asked.

Clarissa's gaze lingered on Mina again, but she tore her attention away and tapped on the phone again. "Just a time and location." She held the phone out to me.

"Any chance he's sending some bacon?" Hunter asked.

The look Clarissa gave him was drier than the Simpson Desert. "Chances are it's bacon, attached to the rest of a person. They're coming here to Dusk Bay. Leon doesn't want anyone to know. He's expecting me to pick them up."

"You work closely with Leon?" Mina asked, her tone this side of dangerous. Any associate of Leon was a potential enemy of hers.

If I thought Clarissa was tight with him, she'd be dead right now.

Clarissa shrugged her broad shoulders. "On and off. He's done me favours and I've done him favours. All within the umbrella of Brantley business. So he claimed. If he was working with Kurt Lasalle against you, I was unaware. I would have told him to fuck off. That's why I'm here telling you about this. I don't want anyone to think I'm not loyal. I like breathing."

"Has he given any indication who he wants you to pick up?" I asked.

"Nope," she said lightly. "What I've shown you is all I have."

I rubbed my chin. "I want you to follow through with the pickup. Don't let on to anyone else that we know. Once we have some idea who it is, we'll move."

Mina swallowed audibly. "You think it's Kurt?"

"Why else go so hard to hide it?" I asked. If anyone was going to arrive like this, it would be him. Trying to sneak in the back door without being noticed. Like the snake he was.

"I'll do whatever you need me to do," Clarissa said. "I've heard some disturbing rumours about Lasalle." Once again her gaze was on Mina. She knew better than to ask and we weren't going to enlighten her, but that wouldn't keep her from being curious.

"We'll be right there with you," Gianni assured her.

"You better, because if he suspects I'm working with you, shit might get ugly," Clarissa said. "I have a feeling you want to get your hands on him before I stab him in the throat."

Of course she hadn't meant that he'd try anything with her, or that he'd succeed. People fucked with her to their own detriment. Personally, I would have paid good money to see her eviscerate him, but that honour went to Mina first.

"Yes, but we don't mind if he loses a few fingers," Gianni said. "Just leave a couple for us."

Clarissa punched him on the shoulder hard enough to make him wince. "I like you."

He grimaced and rubbed his shoulder. "I'd hate to see what you do to people you don't like."

She grinned. "Stay on my good side and you never need to find out."

"I'll keep that in mind," he said. He took a moment to glare at the twins who were both laughing, but keeping a safe distance.

Mina was the only one who didn't look amused at the exchange. If anything, she looked slightly green.

"Stay in touch," I said to Clarissa. I took Mina's hand and guided her back out to the street.

"If it's really Kurt..." She sat down on the curb beside the car park.

"He'll be dead this time tomorrow," I finished for her. I lowered myself down beside her and put my arm around her.

"It doesn't seem real," she said, her tone hollow. "After all those years, he'll finally be gone. I can put all of this behind me."

My heart ached for her. The fact he continued to breathe was starting to piss me off more and more. It was past time for that to stop, and for her to get on with the rest of her life. While he was out there, she'd be in some kind of limbo. Always looking behind her and wondering if he'd appear. Wondering if she'd wake up in that filthy cage, the strap around her ankle. Her naked body dirty, hair matted. Living through hell day after day. Treated like some kind of wild animal.

She deserved so much better than that. She deserved to be spread out on the couch and worshipped the way we'd worshipped her. The sound of her coming rang through my ears like the most beautiful music I ever heard.

The taste of her skin still lingered on my lips. That and the way Gianni's mouth felt on mine.

I was still trying to get my head around having kissed him. Thinking about it and doing it were vastly different things. I never expected to act on feelings I'd suppressed for so long. My attraction to him and to Reuben were best kept under wraps.

Or so I thought.

Now, I was conflicted, but that was something I needed to think about later. Right now I needed to focus on Mina and tomorrow's pickup.

"Why would he come here?" she asked.

I was wondering the same thing. "I'm guessing he has business here."

"Or he knows Reuben is in town," she said. The wheels in her mind seemed to be turning over, considering all the possibilities.

"Leon sent that message before Reuben decided we'd come here," I pointed out. "He wouldn't know that at the time." Even if he was listening in to all of our conversations, he couldn't have known what our plans were before we even made them.

"I suppose so," she said reluctantly. Her blue-green eyes were slightly glazed, her thoughts clearly dark and troubled.

I wished I could take every one of them out of her mind and give her back the sunshine she used to radiate. The carefree warmth.

"He won't go anywhere near you," I assured her. "If he so much as looks at you, I'll poke his eyes out. We don't need him to have eyes or fingers. Just a pulse. He needs to live long enough to experience the pain he put you through."

"I think to have a pulse, you need a heart," she said. "I don't think he has one of those."

I couldn't disagree with that. People with hearts didn't keep women prisoner. Unless they were the enemy. Reuben wasn't inclined to give leniency to anyone based on sex.

"Whatever he has in his chest to keep him alive," I said with a shrug. "It won't be doing it for much longer. Twenty-four hours and he'll be dead as a slab of bacon."

"Vegan bacon," Hunter said as he sat down on the other side of Mina. "Never with a beating heart, but still kinda dead."

"Don't ruin bacon for me," Parker complained.

"I think it's already ruined for me," Mina said. "Every time I see it, I'll think of him."

I squeezed her more firmly. "The way Terry cooks it, none of us will be able to resist eating it anyway. Even if it was vegan bacon. Is that actually a thing?"

"Absolutely it is," Hunter said. "Along with vegan cheese, vegan hamburgers and vegan leather. It's a growing industry. Literally." He grinned.

"Anyway, we should get going." I glanced over to see a red haired woman look at us before unlocking the gymnastics studio and disappearing inside. "We don't want to draw too much attention to ourselves, remember?"

"Before we go back home, I want to show Mina something," Gianni said.

I waited for cock jokes that didn't come, before helping her to her feet and following her and Gianni.

CHAPTER 18

MINA

"The 'don't touch anything' rule applies here too," Damon said to the twins.

They grinned and headed over to the drums in the corner of the music shop.

I looked at the drums wistfully. If Asher was here, he'd be right there with them, trying them out.

"I figured this would be a good time to get that guitar you talked about," Gianni said. He gestured towards a selection of instruments that hung on the wall.

In spite of the growing feeling that Kurt was going to pop out of thin air right in front of me, I let myself walk over and take a better look.

In the corner of my eye, I saw Damon appraising the saxophones. I had no trouble imagining him playing one. Which led to me remembering Gianni miming Reuben playing the bass guitar. A small smile crept onto my face.

"See any you like?" Gianni asked.

I returned my attention to the guitars before reaching for a black Fender Jazzmaster, and holding it carefully in my arms.

"I used to have one just like this." Where was it now? Had my siblings kept it after I left, and my parents died? Rose hadn't mentioned one, but it wasn't something we discussed when we stepped aside from everyone else. For all I knew, they'd thrown it away or sold it. If Dane went through our parents' things, it was definitely gone. He wasn't known for being sentimental.

I plucked at the strings a couple of times before automatically tuning the instrument and plucking again. It felt so natural, like I'd never stopped. My ear was probably off, after all these years, but it sounded better than it had.

I played a couple of bars of *Good Day Sunshine,* one of the first songs I learned to play. Ironic now, but that was the song that came to me first.

"You're good," Gianni said once he finished giving me a clap. "Musical talent must run in the family."

"Unlike some." Damon grimaced in the direction of the twins, who were tapping at the drums with dubious rhythm.

I suspected they were doing it on purpose to get a rise out of him. If they weren't careful, he'd shoot them for being too annoying.

"We're very talented, thank you very much," Hunter called out. "Remind me later to give you a pack of Kink Or Drink cards. They might help you to lighten up." He punctuated his sentence by hitting a drumstick on a cymbal, making it ring out.

Damon rolled his eyes. "I don't need your help to be kinky."

Gianni's eyebrows shot up.

Damon's lowered. "We're not having that conversation here."

Gianni raised his hands in surrender. "I can wait until later." His intention was clear. As long as they had that conversation, he was content to be patient.

I couldn't help being curious. I'd barely started to explore my sexuality, but I wondered how far they'd be willing to take it. Apart from being tongue fucked, sucking Reuben off and letting him and Gianni lick my fingers, I didn't know what I was into. I knew for certain I didn't want to be tied up in any way. Anything else, I had no idea.

Damon pressed his lips together and rolled them a couple of times. A sure sign of his annoyance. "Will you be buying that?" He nodded toward the guitar I was still holding.

I glanced at the price. That was another thing that changed a lot while I was away. The price of everything had gone up so much I couldn't get my head around it. The idea of paying that much for a bottle of milk or a bag of apples seemed crazy, but Reuben didn't blink when time came to pay for them. Of course, he could afford to, but still.

"I don't know," I said slowly. "It seems like an indulgence."

"That's a yes then," he said firmly. "You should have some indulgences. Hell, buy three of them. And a few picks, songbooks, a stand and a good quality amp."

"This quick shopping trip to get a guitar just got real," I said, half-joking. I hadn't even thought beyond the instrument himself. Yes, all of my guitars were a he. I didn't know why, they just were.

The sides of his mouth twitched upward ever so slightly. "If you're going to do it, you might as well do it properly. Why bother doing anything half-assed? Life is too fucking short for that."

All of them had said that to me at some point during the last few weeks. That life was short. They certainly seemed to believe in living each day to the fullest. That was understandable when we could step back out onto the street and get shot, or run over.

Hell, we might get struck by lightning, even though it was sunny outside.

"I'm going to buy it," I said definitely. "And all the other things too. The best of everything."

"That's my girl," he said softly. "Get some of those headphones so only you can hear yourself play. When Reuben is in a mood, you'll need them." He seemed to be speaking from experience.

I nodded and placed the guitar on the counter before walking through the shop to gather up all the other things.

I finished paying for all of my new purchases when I heard an excited rumble from the street outside. While we'd been in the shop, a crowd gathered. I'd kept half an eye on them, but now they had my full attention.

"What's going on?" Damon snapped to the shop assistant.

She was standing behind the counter, bouncing on her toes. "Wolf

Venom is in town to do some promotion. They usually drop in here for a meet and greet with fans."

It was my heart that dropped. Asher was coming here?

"We need to go," I said quickly. I grabbed my guitar and the bag with the smaller items, while Gianni picked up the amp.

"We'll never get out the front," Damon said.

The assistant looked as though she might try to stop us from going through the back, but she thought better of it. With wide eyes, she stepped aside and let us pass.

"What's the hurry?" Hunter drawled. "Their music isn't *that* bad."

I shot him a look and stepped over boxes and packaging material that was spread all through the stock area at the rear of the shop. Past him, I caught a glimpse of the door opening.

I recognised the dark-haired man who stepped through first. Zeke Brantley, lead singer and brother of Reuben and the twins. He grinned and usherd fans to come inside too. He'd changed a lot since I saw him last. Matured.

My gaze only lingered on him for a few moments before a blonde haired man stepped into the shop behind him.

Asher was also grinning, joking around with his bandmate who followed him in.

Judging by the expression on his face, his bandmate didn't appreciate his humour. That seemed to amuse Asher even more. His grin was so broad he lit up the room.

My heart raced. Part of me wanted to drop everything I was carrying and run over to him. Instead, I was frozen on the spot for a minute or two, watching my brother interact with adoring fans and the other guys in the band, completely oblivious to my presence and scrutiny.

Like Zeke, Asher changed and matured. He kept his hair short, but his chin was covered in a couple of days' worth of stubble. His eyes were still the same brilliant blue, but he had crinkles around them. He wasn't a gangly boy any more. He was tall and muscular, his biceps thick from hours of drumming.

He wore a black T-shirt, tight over what was clearly a fit body. No wonder women were drooling over him. My brother had grown into the perfect rock god he'd always wanted to be.

I could hardly reconcile the man I glimpsed through the crowds was still the same person I used to share finger paint with, and make plans in whispers to annoy the shit out of Dane. He could have been a completely different person. Why wouldn't he be, I was. A

"Mina?" Gianni said in my ear. "We can stay if you want."

I blinked away the moisture in my eyes and shook my head. "Not today. This is his moment."

He looked so happy, so content. I wouldn't be selfish and steal that from him. I couldn't steal his time from his fans either. They were hanging on every word he said, taking photos and videos while he signed everything they put in front of him.

He leaned in to whisper something in the ear of a cute brunette, who giggled and tugged down the front of her dress so he could sign her breast.

His scowling bandmate scowled even deeper, but didn't hesitate to sign her other breast when it was offered.

"Then we should go," Damon said. He placed his hands on my shoulders and guided me towards the door and out to the street.

Apparently word of the band's presence had got out. People were coming from all directions, going around to the front of the shop, chatting with excitement. Some were even singing what I assumed were their songs. Some stopped to look at me, as if I might be someone famous, being quietly bundled out the back door.

They hurried on when they realised I was no one. Not one of their favourite rock star idols. Just a regular woman out shopping for a guitar on a Wednesday afternoon, who just happened to get caught in a throng of adoring groupies.

Lucky for them, they realised that before they took any photos of me, otherwise things might have gotten ugly.

"I'll bring the car around here," Damon said. "Stay here and stay out of trouble." He strode away, hands in his pockets. He tried to pretend he wasn't hurrying, but his steps were quick and short.

Gianni adjusted the amp he was carrying. The expression on his face was pensive. I hadn't seen him look uncertain before. It took me a while to realise what the cause of that was. It wasn't that he thought my brother would follow us out at any moment, there was more to it.

"You knew, didn't you?" I asked. Not accusing, just wanting him to be honest with me.

"I had an inkling," he admitted. "I didn't realise they'd come inside, but I thought maybe you could catch a glimpse. You weren't in any danger. I made sure of that. We had a lot of security in that crowd."

How should I feel about him going behind my back like that? I didn't like surprises at the best of times, but he meant well and obviously took precautions to ensure my safety. There was absolutely no malice behind his planning.

That didn't automatically make it all right. If Kurt found out, he would have taken full advantage. He could have killed me and my brother. He still might.

"It was nice to see he's living his best life, but never do anything like that again," I said, struggling to keep my voice even.

His face fell. "Of course not. It was dumb."

We didn't say another word until we got back to the house and the gates clanged shut behind us.

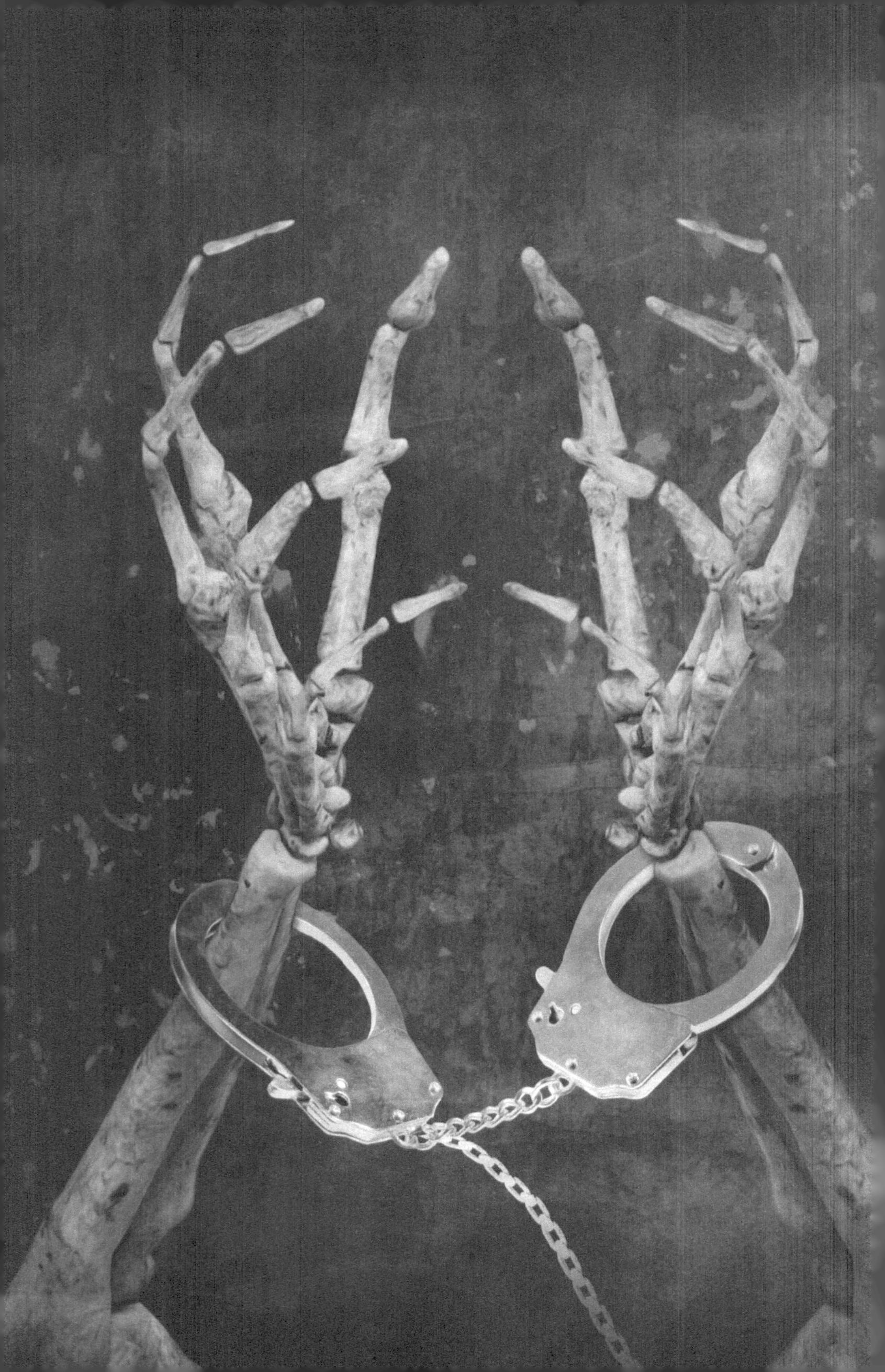

CHAPTER 19

MINA

"You did fucking *what?*" Reuben's voice was low as usual, but laced with a heavy dose of absolute fury. His ice blue eyes snapped with lightning that could have burnt Gianni to a crisp.

Gianni stood his ground. "I had everything under control. I just thought Mina would like to see her brother."

"With cameras and press everywhere," Reuben said. "One image of her would have told Kurt exactly where she was. If she decided to talk to Asher, or he'd seen her, that would have gone viral. Things could very quickly have gotten completely out of control."

Gianni still didn't flinch. "It didn't. Everything went exactly as it was supposed to. She got to see him and the world is none the wiser."

Reuben's gaze slid to me. His expression softened. "Too much could have gone wrong. Risks like that aren't ones I'm willing to take. Not when it comes to Mina." He propped his elbow on the desk and rested his head on the palms of his hands. "Did you get what you needed?"

"Potential information on Kurt arriving in town tomorrow, and a guitar," I said. "You could say I did. And I got to see my brother."

Reuben was right, so much could have gone wrong, but it hadn't. Seeing Asher was soothing in a way I hadn't expected. Knowing he was doing well and seeing it with my own eyes were two different things.

"See, everything worked out perfectly," Gianni said. "Tomorrow we'll get to pin down Lasalle and deal with his ass. For all we know, Asher will still be in town and we can invite him over for a few beers. Or go and see them live. I'm sure they'd have a few tickets left for us."

Reuben grimaced. "Let's deal with one thing at a time. Kurt first."

"I have everyone organised," Damon said. "We'll have people in place hours before the pickup time. If anything looks suspicious, they'll deal with it. When the time comes, we'll be right there. Clarissa will let us know if anything changes."

"Good." Reuben nodded. "I don't want any unexpected surprises tomorrow. No one goes off on their own and does anything rash." He looked directly at Gianni.

"Me, do something rash?" Gianni smiled. "You're thinking of the twins."

"Hey, what did we do?" Hunter protested. He and Parker reclined on the couch, coffees in their hands. "We had no idea what Gianni planned. We didn't even run off and say hi to Zeke."

"No, we didn't," Parker agreed. "We got the hell out of there when Mina said she wasn't ready to talk to Asher. No one ever knew we were there."

"This time," Reuben said. "Which I appreciate. Otherwise we'd be having a different conversation. Tomorrow, I want everyone on the same page. Follow Damon's plan to the letter. If anyone steps a toe out of line, we could be screwed. We could lose this chance at Kurt. I won't allow that to happen because someone feels the need to be a loose cannon."

"My cannon is never loose," Gianni said. He grinned at me.

I rolled my eyes, shook my head and smiled back at him. Nothing ever kept him down for long. Not even been chewed out by Reuben.

"I feel like one of us should have said that," Hunter said. "If Gianni is going to start stealing our one-liners, we might have a problem."

"Not my fault if I'm quicker than you are," Gianni said.

"Being too quick isn't a good thing," Parker pointed out. He grinned and offered Hunter a fist bump.

"Ha fucking ha," Gianni said sarcastically. "I'm never too quick when it matters."

The twins smiled unapologetically.

"That's what they all say," Hunter teased.

"As fascinating as this conversation is," Damon said slowly but meaningfully, "can we get back to the matter at hand? In case you need a reminder, Kurt fucking Lasalle. Remember him?"

I shuddered. I wished I didn't. Remembering him was one of the worst things about waking up in the morning. I wished there was a way I could forget. He still haunted my dreams and nightmares. When I closed my eyes, I could picture him leering at me through the bars of the cage. Looking down at me as he…

"We all remember him," Gianni said as he stepped closer to me. "He's the prick who brought us all together here today. If he was right in front of me, I'd thank him by punching him in the face. Or stabbing him in the dick. Maybe one, then the other." He mimed doing that.

He had a way of making a situation lighter, even when we were talking about someone who, to me, embodied pure evil. People thought of Reuben that way, but he was a pussycat compared to Kurt. Hell, I'd rather be alone with Samuel Bell than Kurt. He was an asshole, but he could be reasoned with. Sort of.

"We all feel that way," Damon said. "But let's not allow our need for revenge to cloud our judgment. The best thing we can do right now, is focus and be cool and calm. Rational. Not rash. If we let our anger guide us, he has a better chance of getting to us. We can't let that happen."

"You missed your calling," Hunter said. "You should have been a motivational speaker."

Damon smirked at him. "I'm not saying anything that isn't accurate. We've all done things in the heat of the moment that could have made a situation worse, or gotten us killed."

"Like driving an SUV into a couple of other cars?" Parker asked.

"That was a completely rational thing to do," Damon said. "I'm sure you'll recall I saved your asses."

"I don't know, it sounds like a heat of the moment thing to me,"

Hunter said. "Sometimes you have to be flexible, especially when the stakes are high."

"Flexible is good, just don't be stupid," Reuben said. "Any of you. I don't want anyone in this room getting killed."

"I told you he loves us," Parker said. "Not wanting us dead is Reuben's love language."

"Or it might be my way of saying your death would be inconvenient," Reuben said flatly.

"We can read between the lines," Hunter said. "Our deaths would be inconvenient and heartbreaking."

"I'd be heartbroken if I died," Parker said. "As well as inconvenienced."

"Me too," Hunter agreed.

I leaned against Gianni and listened to them banter back and forth. This family I'd found was a little crazy, but they adored each other, in spite of what they might say. If we lost anyone here, we'd all be devastated.

"Maybe we shouldn't go after Kurt," I said softly.

The silence that followed my words was heavy. If I turned into a giant, purple dinosaur, I couldn't have taken them by surprise more than I just had. The only sound in the room for at least a full minute was the pounding of my heart. It beat so hard it almost hurt, but I meant what I said. Like it or not, we had to consider everything.

"What are you saying, sweetheart?" Gianni asked.

"I'm saying he's not worth risking any of you," I said. "It won't change what he did. It won't give me back those five years. It won't erase the memories. I'd rather build new ones with all of you, than take the chance."

"You don't want revenge?" Damon squinted at me.

"I do," I said. "I want that very much. But at what cost?"

"If it costs us our lives, we'll pay that price," Gianni said. "He can't be allowed to walk around, doing fuck knows what to fuck knows who. Not to mention double crossing all of us. We all want our own revenge on him. Whatever it takes, we'll do it. Right guys?" He glanced around Reuben's office.

"I will," Damon said.

"I will too," Reuben agreed. His gaze was so intense my heart skipped a beat or two.

The twins were right, not wanting any of us dead was his love language. If anything or anyone threatened one of us, they'd have him to answer to.

I already cared about him, but those feelings were getting deeper every day. I couldn't imagine living my life without him. Without any of them.

"Us too," Hunter said. "No one fucks with our family and gets away without us fucking back. That's our love language. Like we said, you're our sister now. Your revenge is our revenge. Besides, screwing with people like Kurt is fun."

"It really is," Parker said. "We basically live for shit like this. Some people jump out of planes for fun, we hunt down assholes."

"We'd also jump out of planes though," Hunter said. "And bungee jump. And rappel." He nodded with each new addition to his extreme sport list.

I could imagine him and Parker doing every one of them on a nice relaxing Saturday afternoon.

"You certainly repel me," Gianni laughed.

Hunter flipped him off.

Gianni just grinned. "Bro, you walked yourself right into that one. Don't offer up the opportunity if you don't want me to take it. Because I will, every time."

"Exactly how attached are you to him?" Hunter asked me, clearly joking around. "If you ever feel the need to rid yourself of him, let me know. I'll be happy to oblige."

"That's sweet of you," I said. "I'm capable of getting rid of him myself if I need to. Which I don't foresee happening," I added quickly.

Hunter leaned over to Parker and whispered loudly, "She thinks I'm sweet."

Parker loudly whispered back, "She doesn't know you very well."

Hunter frowned at his twin. "Fuck you too, bro."

Parker chuckled and gave Hunter a hug. "We have to keep you on your toes."

Gianni wrapped an arm around me and spoke softly in my ear.

"That was really hot. You saying you could kill me yourself if you needed to. My cock is so hard right now."

I turned my face to him. "I'm not sure how I feel about you getting aroused from death threats."

He wiggled his eyebrows at me. "I can't help being fucked up, but it's more the idea of you killing, in general, than killing me in particular. I'd get just as hard if you threatened the twins or even Damon or Reuben."

"I'll bear that in mind," I said. I wasn't sure under what circumstances I'd threaten to kill any of them. As long as they never tried to restrain or cage me, then I'd have no reason to. If they did, they could expect a blade across their throat, not threats. I wouldn't hesitate if it meant avoiding being locked away again. I couldn't afford to. I wouldn't survive being back in there.

I didn't want to.

"I think we can all agree there's something attractive about a woman who can take care of herself," Damon said.

"And a man who can do that," Gianni said. "Which reminds me about your remark in the music shop. About being kinky." He cocked his head at Damon and looked expectant but hopeful, like he wasn't sure he'd get an answer, but he wanted one. And if he didn't, at least he got an opportunity to get a rise out of Damon. Although, I suspected he'd prefer his curiosity be satisfied, than teasing Damon. I wouldn't have minded knowing, myself.

Damon cleared his throat. "Can I be excused, boss? I have a few last-minute things I need to check over before tomorrow."

Reuben nodded. "Go. Keep me posted."

Gianni made a disappointed sound in the back of his throat as Damon opened the door and slipped out. "We can have that conversation later then. Good talk."

"I'm sure you all have places to be," Reuben said. He gave us all meaningful looks, but lingered longer on the twins and Gianni. His anger had cooled, but the message was clear. If any of them thought to go out on their own, he'd be pissed off at them. He expected them to stick to Damon's plan and bring Kurt in to be dealt with.

No one said anything about me following his plan.

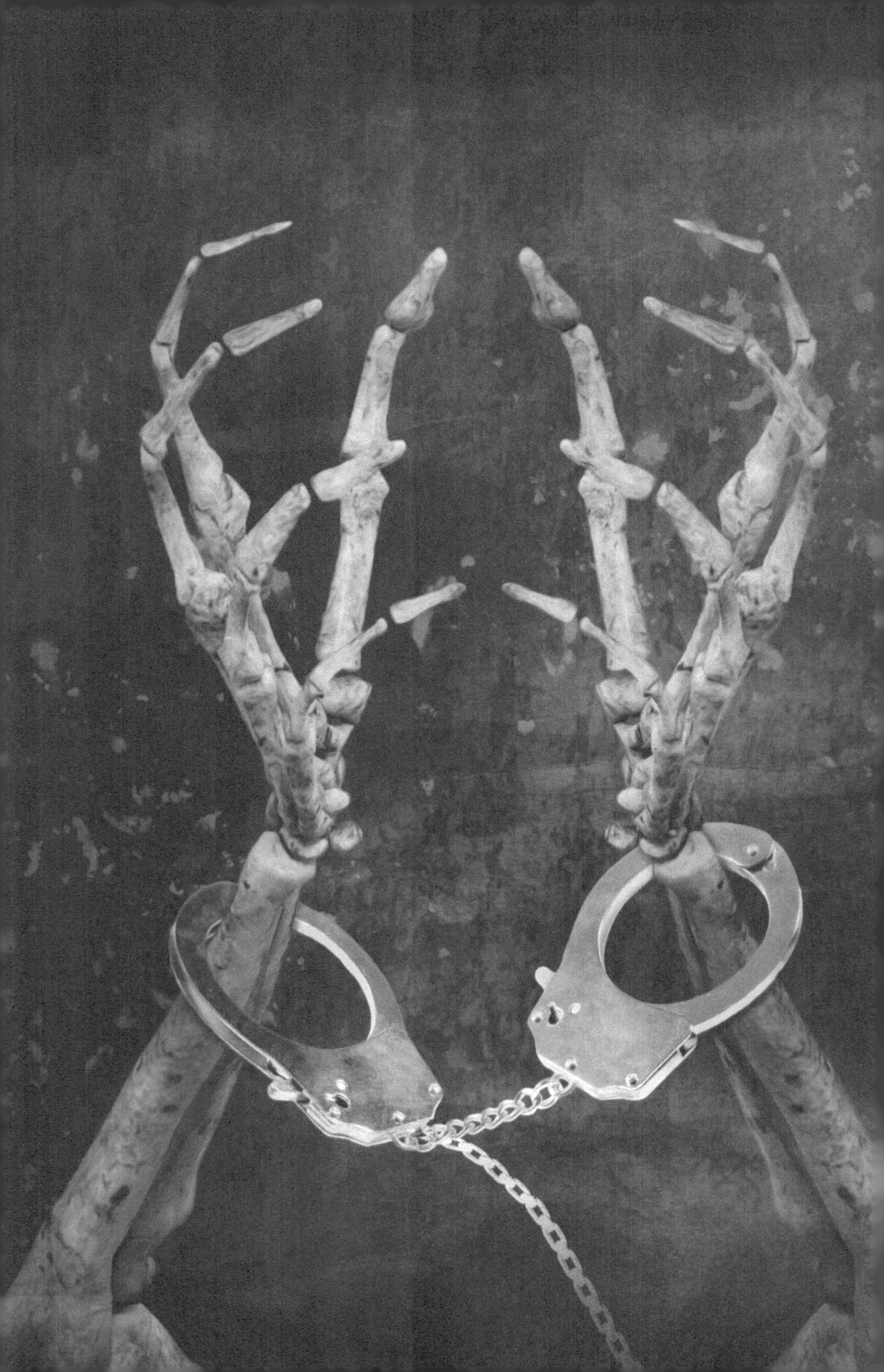

CHAPTER 20

MINA

"Reuben is going to kill me for this." Daze drove the car away from the house. She only turned the lights on when we were out of sight.

"I won't let him kill you," I said. "You're only doing what I asked you to do."

"Which I'm only going along with because it was my brother," she said. "I still feel responsible for what he did. I mean, how did I *not* know?"

"My siblings didn't know either," I pointed out. "Don't beat yourself up about it. Save that anger for him." I had plenty of people I could blame for what happened. She wasn't one of them. She reminded me a lot of my sister, but wilder and more outspoken.

"I will, don't worry," she assured me. "I'm going to need some anger to spare, to deal with my guys too. They are going to be pissed off I left them out of this. Ric in particular. He hasn't stopped talking about you and the fact he should have figured things out sooner. I think he's waiting for Reuben to have him executed for failing him, and you."

"If Reuben has my cousin executed, I'll kick him in the balls," I said. "He wouldn't do that. He knows what family means to me. It means the same to him."

She glanced over at me. "I hope you're right. Killing Ric would create all kinds of trouble. It would irritate the hell out of Caleb and put a bunch of our operations back by a long way. Not to mention I'd miss him."

"All good reasons for Reuben not to do it. He'd be shooting himself in the foot. And annoying both of us." I checked the side of my boot for my knife, as well as my hip. If I was right, I needed to be ready. If I was wrong…

But I wasn't wrong. I knew Kurt and the way he thought. He said I was predictable. So was he.

"Reuben wouldn't want to do that," she agreed. "He's always been the pragmatic one. Always the one thinking with his head, not his heart, or his cock. Well, usually. When it comes to us women, they tend to let their body parts do the talking."

"That's why I asked you to help me tonight," I said. "I don't have to worry about you thinking with your dick." I also didn't have to worry about her feeling the need to sacrifice herself for me. She'd look after her own skin, as she should. That made her more impartial than any of my… Could I call them my boyfriends? I supposed I could.

She laughed. "I'd never be accused of that, that's for sure. Lots of other things, but not that."

"I'm sure you would," I agreed. "Mostly by people jealous of you."

"Does that include you?" she asked. "Because I'll be the first to admit I wish I was more like you."

I snorted. "Me? You're gorgeous, strong, smart and powerful. You're exactly the person I wanted to be when I was a kid."

"You're all of those things too," she said. "Especially strong. You're also an assassin, which is the absolute coolest thing I can possibly think of. I couldn't do it. I'd probably trip over my own feet and let everyone know I was there."

I choked back a laugh. "I'm sure you wouldn't. You don't seem like the clumsy type. Besides, it's all a matter of training."

"It's more than that," she said insistently. "You're also dainty, with a face that screams 'I'm innocent, I'd never hurt a fly.' If anyone saw you walking around their house, they'd probably assume you got lost."

I shrugged. "Maybe." That was why I was chosen for the training, but I couldn't have done my job based on looks and build alone. It took years to learn how to move silently, to kill and slip away without looking back.

It was definitely not for the faint of heart.

One of the boys I trained with carried out one kill and then couldn't continue. I vividly remember the first life I took. They never knew I was there. They went to sleep one night and never woke up. Apparently his mistress found him in the morning on blood drenched sheets, his throat cut.

I felt nothing, but a fleeting moment of arousal. The power of having taken a life. The rush of slipping away right after he took his last breaths. Triumph at having a plan executed flawlessly.

After that night, I was forced to accept that part of me was wrong. Twisted, fucked up, whatever. I could have run from it, but instead, I embraced it.

"Definitely," Daze said. "Can I ask you for a favour?"

"Of course you can," I said. She was doing me a big one, I owed her after this.

"I have a daughter, Nova," she said slowly. "I wonder if she'd be a suitable candidate to train as an assassin. She's only five, but I thought maybe…"

"They're never too young to start," I said. "I'm happy to teach her self defence and some of the basic skills, and see how she develops." I couldn't promise more than that. She might not be suitable, but what I could teach her would help her to survive in Dusk Bay in particular, and the world in general. They were skills every girl should have. Skills that might keep her out of the hands of someone like Kurt.

"That would be fantastic," Daze enthused. "Thank you. Nova is going to be so excited. She loves learning new things, especially things that make her more independent. I'm sure she'll be driving the day she's old enough. You know what they say, they grow up so fast."

"I've heard that," I agreed. I'd never given much thought to having children of my own. What would my boyfriends think about it? Assuming I could get pregnant at all.

In that cage, I was too malnourished to menstruate, thank fuck. Having Kurt's baby would have made the hell so much worse. No one deserved to enter the world like that.

The only saving grace was the possibility I would have died giving birth. That was offset by the chance the baby might have survived. That was further nightmare fuel, as if I needed more.

No, thank fuck that never happened.

"It's absolutely true." She slowed the car and stopped where I indicated.

"You should stay in here," I said.

"Fuck that," she replied immediately. "I've come this far. You're not leaving me out now. It's the best way to avoid Reuben kicking my ass later. If you're dead, I better be dead too. Besides, this might be fun." She flashed me a smile and pushed out the driver-side door.

I sighed softly to myself and climbed out of the car. I hoped like hell I didn't regret not insisting she stay behind. I would have left her out of all of this if I thought I could take one of Reuben's cars and not be noticed.

Since that wasn't going to happen, I'd asked her for a ride into the city, and some help. She's eagerly agreed, saying she hadn't had a girls' night out in too long.

"This is the place," I whispered as we approached the vegan grocery store. We kept to the shadows, moving silently in the darkness.

I glanced down at my phone. "By my calculations, he should be here in a few minutes."

We crouched down near the doorway to the gymnastics studio and waited.

The city was quiet at this time of night, just the sound of passing cars and the occasional shout. The air was cool and laced with the smell of exhaust fumes and Chinese food. Most sensible people were at home, watching the Dusk Bay Demons ice hockey team on TV, or still at the Wolf Venom concert. Not sneaking around at night like a pair of criminals.

"This is where you got to." I heard footsteps right before Gianni spoke. Lucky for him he did, or I would have stabbed him in the neck. As it was, I had my knife in my hand without realising I'd moved. The hilt was cool on my palm, reassuring and familiar. Like holding onto an old friend when you need them the most.

"What the fuck are you doing here?" I whispered. I grabbed his hand and pulled him down into the shadows with me.

"I went to check up on you and you weren't in your room," he said. "Or Reuben's room. Or Damon's room. Or mine. Then I saw you sneak out the door, so I followed you. It's a real prick to drive all this way without headlights on."

"You shouldn't have followed us," I hissed. "Who's with you?"

"Just me," he whispered. "Who's with you?" He seemed to be searching and squinting, but he couldn't make out who crouched beside me.

"Daisy Lasalle," Daze said. "You're interrupting our girls' night." She sounded a little disappointed, if glad it was him and not someone else that found us here in the darkness.

Anyone else, and things could be messed up already. Someone would be dead, and it wouldn't have been either of us, if we could help it.

His teeth flashed white in the darkness. "Sorry, but I wasn't going to let you be out here by yourself. Unless you're working, in which case you could have asked me to give you a ride, or borrowed one of Reuben's cars."

"I'm not working," I said. "Not exactly."

I gave him a quick rundown of why we were here. I couldn't see the expression on his face, but I heard the change in his breathing as I spoke. I could almost feel his pulse racing faster and his mind turning over with possibilities. Including wondering if he should contact Reuben or Damon.

"I'm definitely not leaving," he said when I was finished. "First of all, you can't make me, and second of all, you might need my help."

"We can make you if we have to," I said. "But now you're here, you might as well stay. But I expect you to do what I tell you to do."

I had a plan. I could adjust it to fit him, but I didn't have time to rethink everything. If he followed what I told him to do, everything should go smoothly.

'Should' being the key word. It had to; I had no room to fuck this up. This might be the best shot I got. I was taking it and I wasn't going to miss.

"Sure thing, boss," he said easily. "I live to serve."

"I'm sure you do," I said. "Now, be quiet. We don't need anyone to hear us and find us here."

"Got it," he whispered.

I slipped my knife away and crouched, scanning the surrounding streets and listening carefully.

What was the time? I was certain only a couple of minutes had passed, but I didn't dare to turn my phone on again. The light would give us all away. That was probably how Gianni found us in the first place. One little glance was all it took.

Of course, he knew to look, others might not, but I wasn't taking the chance.

A car roared past, then another. A fourth car was quickly followed by a fifth.

It was the fifth that slowed down and turned into the car park behind the block of shops.

My whole body stiffened with anticipation and a dose of anxiety bigger than I was comfortable with.

I forced them both down. Adrenaline was bad at times like this. I needed a clear head, precise thinking and exact action.

I took a deep breath, and another, regaining my calm. Forcing my mind to the state where I didn't simply react. I needed to act on instinct and training, with careful precision, not recklessness.

Gianni would have called it assassin mode, or something similar. Whatever it was, I needed it right now.

The car stopped in a parking space and the engine was turned off.

Clarissa stepped out of the driver's side. "I wasn't expecting you until tomorrow morning. I'll have to give myself a few minutes to have a bed ready. I have an apartment above my shop." She gestured vaguely in that direction, her movements illuminated by the light inside the car. The look on her face suggested her passenger was not a welcome surprise.

From inside the car, a male voice responded. Slowly, the passenger side door was pushed open and a man stepped out.

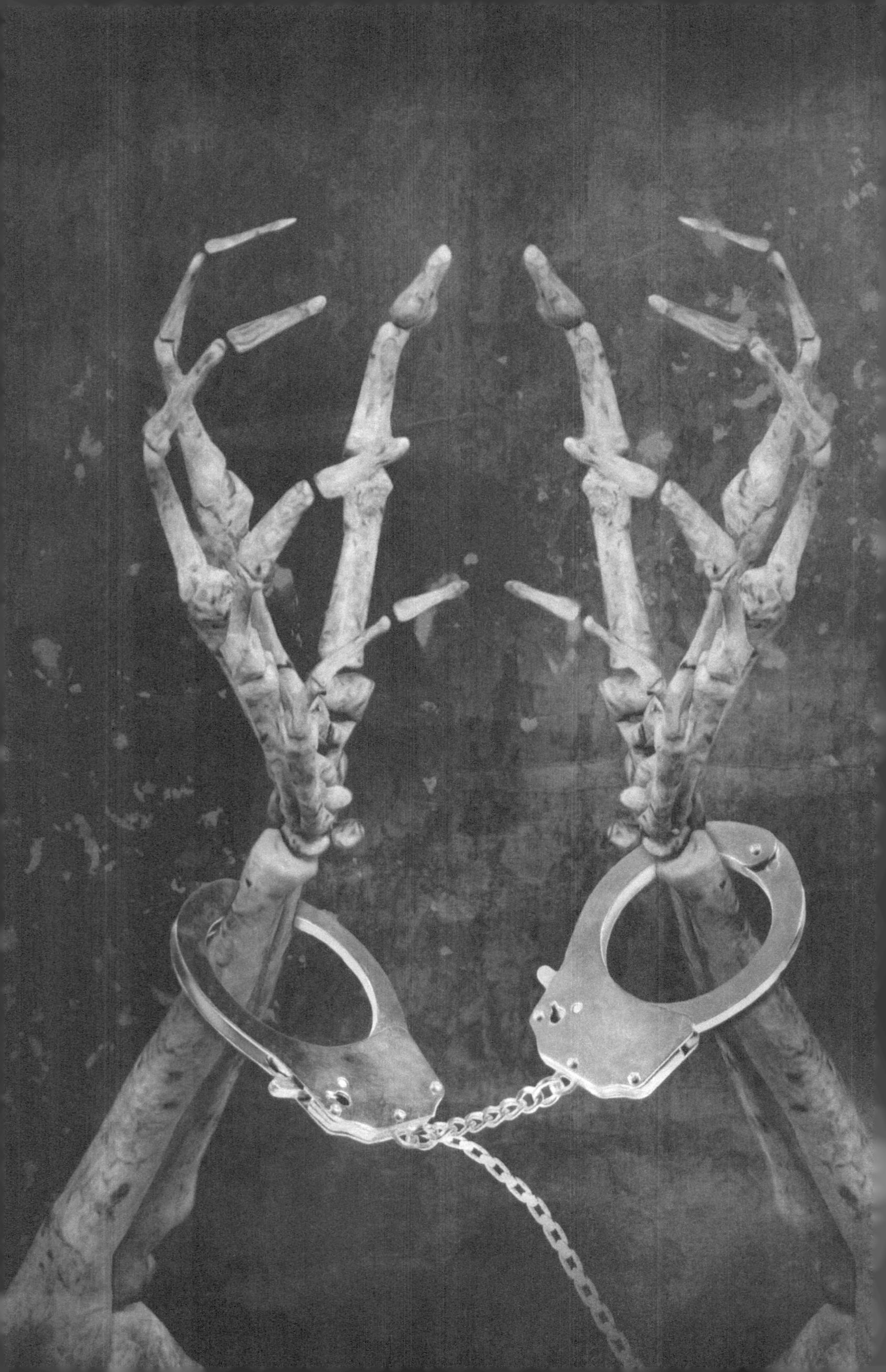

CHAPTER 21

DAMON

I stopped outside the door to Reuben's room. Even this close to midnight, the door was open and a light was on inside. I didn't hear any groaning, so I decided it was safe to push the door open a little further and peer inside.

Typical of Reuben, he was still fully dressed, sitting on a chair near the window reading a recently released, thick epic fantasy.

Not my kind of thing, but they kept him engaged for hours. I'd bet that when he was a child, if he was quiet, it wasn't because he was up to something. He would have been sitting in a corner reading. When he wasn't learning to take over from his father.

I glanced around the room. "Mina isn't in here."

He looked up, his brow creased. "No. I thought she was with you or Gianni."

"She might be with Gianni, but I can't find him either," I said. "Neither of them are in their rooms, or anywhere in the house as far as I can tell. I tried ringing Gianni, but there was no answer. It's possible his phone was on silent and he didn't hear it."

Reuben slipped his bookmark into his book and set it aside. He sat up straighter, hands on his thighs.

I ignored the way my pulse ratcheted up. This was not the time for that.

"What else?" he asked. He knew me too well.

"One of the cars is missing. According to the tracker, it's in the city."

"It didn't get there by itself," he stated.

"No, and the staff are all accounted for. It's only Gianni and Mina I can't find." I shoved my hands in my pockets to keep from showing the worst of my frustration and concern.

"Fuck," he said softly. "Gianni wouldn't have…"

"No," I agreed quickly. "If they're together, she's a willing participant."

"You think they're together," he said.

"They better be." I couldn't think of another scenario. "I have a theory that Mina thought Kurt might come to Dusk Bay earlier. She might have decided to confront him. Gianni went with her."

"Why wouldn't she come to us?" Reuben asked. He shook his head slightly. "It doesn't matter. You have the location of the car? Wake the twins, we're all going." He pushed himself to his feet.

I nodded. "Yes, boss. I'll get them and the car ready."

"We'll get to her in time," he said half to himself.

"Of course we will, boss. Knowing her, she'll have him pinned down by the time we get there. Tied up and ready for us to bring him back here." I wished I could be so sure.

"Without doubt." He stopped beside me and placed his hand on my shoulder.

If I thought my pulse was going faster before, it was doubled now. My heart was beating so fast I could barely catch my breath. His face was so close to mine, his breath would have brushed my lips if he turned just slightly.

My balls throbbed. Time stopped while we stood there side-by-side, his skin burning a hole in the fabric of my T-shirt.

Moments passed, like a clock ticking slowly.

"We should go," I managed to grind out.

His throat bobbed as he visibly swallowed. "Yes." He dropped his hand and stepped past me.

The moment contact was broken, time started again. My shoulder felt colder than ice, but I shook myself out of my stupor and went to wake the twins.

All of the Brantley brothers must be night owls, the twins weren't asleep either. Fortunately for everyone concerned, because I suspected when woken up they came out swinging. Or stabbing, if a knife was close to hand.

I gave them a brief explanation and they were hurrying down to the car behind me. I had to give them credit. They'd fully accepted Mina as one of their own. If she ever needed them, they'd be there for her. At this rate, she'd have her own army.

Reuben was waiting patiently beside the car, with one of the staff who'd sorted guns for each of us. Usually Gianni's job.

I was going to tear him a new one when I saw him next. He should know better than to go out on his own, even in Mina's company.

If anything happened to either of them, I was going to be... I'd have to finish that thought later. Right now, I needed to be cool and clear-headed. I'd leave being rash to everyone else.

"The car is near Clarissa's store," I said. The comment was more or less redundant. Where else would Gianni or Mina have gone?

"I'm surprised," Hunter said. "Knowing Gianni, I thought he would have taken her to tonight's Wolf Venom concert. No one would have recognised her up in the nosebleed seats."

"It was sold out." Reuben looked unimpressed with that suggestion.

"And you know that, how?" Parker leaned forward from where he sat in the back seat.

"It's my job to know things," Reuben said. "Unless people go behind my back like this." He appeared to be perfectly calm and composed on the outside. We all knew him better than that. On the inside, he was a cauldron of cold fury.

Like I was.

"Just remember, Mina cares about Gianni," Hunter said. "Try not to shoot him too much."

"I'm not going to shoot him," Reuben said. What he left unsaid was clear. If Gianni did anything to her, including encouraging her to leave the house without us, he'd be a lot worse off than if he was dead.

No one asked what would happen if Mina was the one who coerced him.

"Who said Reuben doesn't have a heart?" Parker asked.

"I might have said that in the past," Hunter said. "I'm pretty sure Zeke said the same. And Caleb, Joshua and Lucas. I'm as surprised as anyone to find out he actually does. Much less that it beats for Mina DiMarco."

"Don't make me shoot *you*," Reuben said darkly. "If either of you so much as look at her in a way that's not brotherly…"

"We wouldn't dream of it," Parker said. "Mina is sweet, but she is not for us."

"Fucking right she's not," I growled. She belonged to Reuben, Gianni and me. No one else. I didn't let myself think about us belonging to each other. That was something we'd have to think about later. Assuming we got a later.

I focused on driving, while the others fell silent.

The drive from the house in Dusk Bay Heights, to the city, wasn't far, but it felt like it tonight. It could have been a hundred kilometres instead of twenty. The traffic was heavier than usual for this time of night, with people heading home from the concert.

Personally, I wouldn't have minded going, but I knew how Reuben felt about his brother's band. That was a conversation not worth having, just to go to a rock concert.

"Still no answer on either of their phones." Reuben sounded frustrated.

That didn't surprise me. If they were up to something, they'd want to keep them silent.

Mina always did now, after that call from Kurt. She had little reason to accept incoming calls anyway. Anyone who had her number, could either text or speak to her in person. The rest of her communication was done via some app on her phone I'd only gotten a glimpse of. Something, I presumed, was only for assassins, not everyday people like me.

"We'll get to her in time," Hunter said. "If there's anything I know about Mina and Gianni, it's that they have each other's backs. They won't let anything happen to each other."

"They better not," Reuben growled.

I'd never heard that much emotion in his voice before. If anything happened to either of them, he'd be as gutted as I would. He'd burn down the whole world in retribution.

I'd hand him the matches.

"Park around the corner from where the car is," Reuben said as we drove into the city. "We don't want anyone to know we're here."

"Got it, boss," I replied automatically.

I ran through the best places to park, finally settling on a side street around the corner from the vegan grocery store. It was empty at this time of night, apart from a darkened delivery truck and a couple of wheelie bins.

I killed the engine and was the first out of the car. My shoes barely touched the ground before my gun was in my hand.

"Just making sure you're all aware this might be a trap," Hunter said carefully.

"Of course it might," Reuben said. "Be alert for anything."

"Okay, just checking." Hunter nodded and made sure his gun was loaded and the safety off. "Wouldn't want to walk into anything fatal."

"We won't," I said. I'd considered the possibility Gianni and Mina had. There was a chance they might both be…

I wouldn't let myself finish that thought.

I led the way down Riley Street, all the way to the corner, where I stopped. I raised a hand to indicate that the others should wait, then peered around the corner.

The street that stretched out in front of me was quiet. The other of Reuben's cars was parked by the side of the road, engine off, in darkness. Intact, as far as I could tell. And empty.

"I'm not seeing anyone," I whispered. "Living or dead."

A light was on above the grocery store. Clarissa's apartment. I squinted, but if anyone was inside, I couldn't tell.

"Have you tried communicating with Clarissa?" Reuben asked.

"I sent her a text to confirm there were no changes from the plans we made earlier today," I said. "She replied that everything was under control."

That was when I started to suspect something was wrong. I started searching the house for Mina and Gianni, and any missing cars. Only when I was certain did I take the information to Reuben. He didn't appreciate people going off half-cocked and making assumptions without looking for the evidence. No, I had to be sure before I bothered him with it.

After all, Mina and Gianni could have been out in the garden practising knife throwing, or fucking.

"That's a weird way of saying yes," Parker said.

"Sounds like a thinly veiled no to me," Hunter said.

"Funny, I was thinking the same thing," Parker agreed. "That sounds like something I'd write if I was under duress, with someone looking over my shoulder. Someone like Kurt."

"Exactly," I agreed. I rubbed my chin with my thumb and pointer finger.

The stairs leading up to Clarissa's apartment were narrow. Only one and a half people could walk up them at the same time. Anyone at the top could pick us off one by one. If he was there, we might have a hard time reaching him.

If Mina was up there with them, we'd fucking try. I didn't care if I died, as long as she didn't, and wasn't taken by him. Those options weren't even on the table.

The question was, where did Clarissa fit into all of this? Had she double crossed us? I didn't want to believe that, but right now, all possibilities were up in the air.

I ducked aside as a car slowed and came around the corner. If they saw us in the shadows, there was no sign from inside the vehicle. They didn't stop to look or turn the headlights on us. They drove on until they reached the car park behind the grocery store.

With practised precision, the car slid into a parking space. The engine was turned off and the driver's side door pushed open. Clarissa stepped out.

I gestured the others forward and moved around the corner silently as the passenger door opened and a man stepped out.

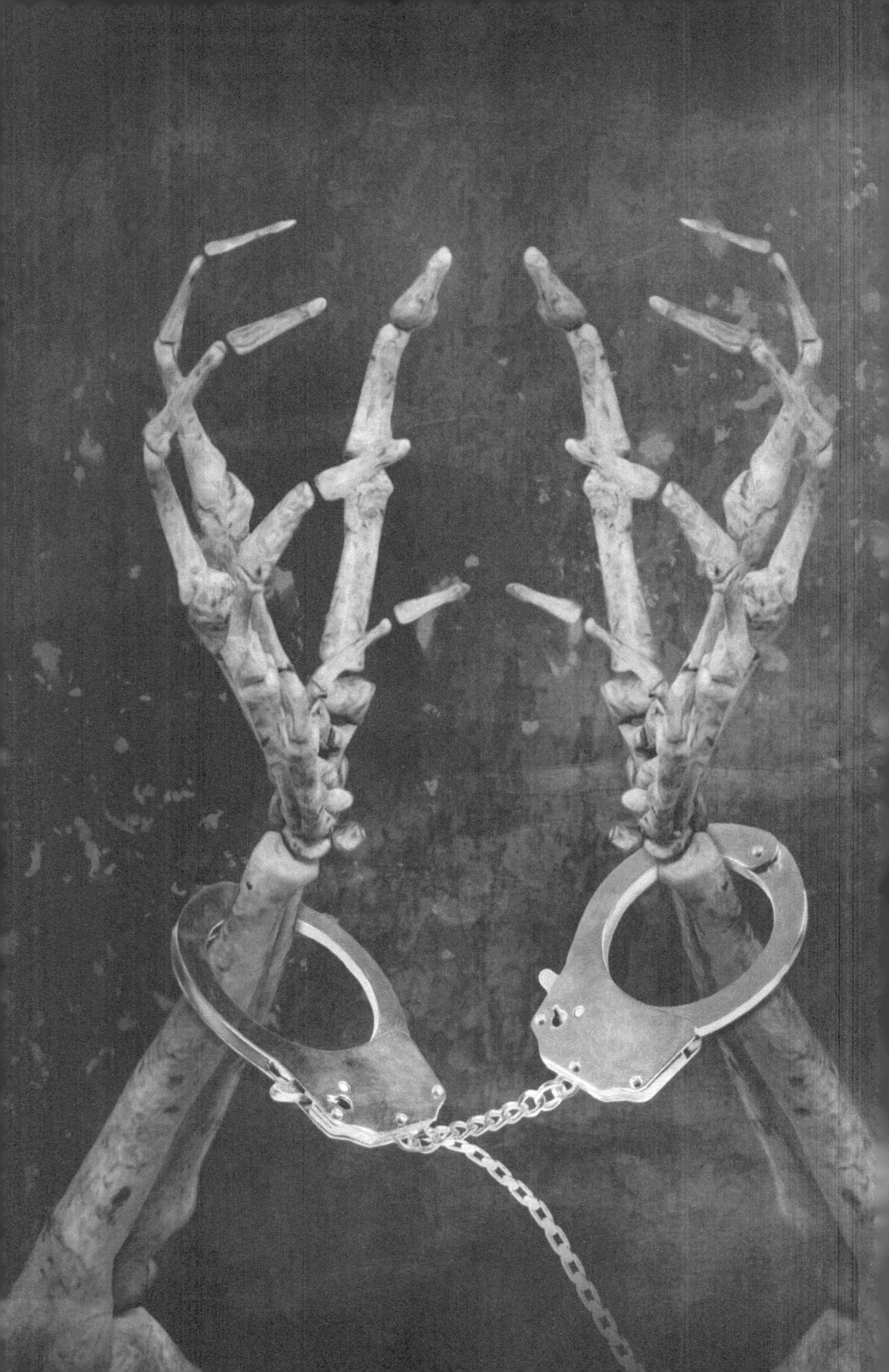

CHAPTER 22

MINA

"That's not Kurt," Gianni whispered.

"No, it isn't," I agreed. "It's Leon Graves."

Fuck.

Fuck.

I knew there was a possibility it would be someone other than Kurt. That Leon had contacted Clarissa on behalf of himself. I'd wanted to assume it was Kurt so I could end this. If he was standing right in front of me now, I'd lodge my knife in his brain. Or somewhere lower, to give him a slower, more painful death.

It was some consolation that I was right about one thing. Leon arrived earlier than originally planned. The question was, why?

Clarissa's eyes swivelled from side to side, as though certain we were waiting in the shadows. She looked nervous, anxious.

So she should. If he'd contacted her to change plans and she hadn't told Damon, she might be taking her last breaths herself.

"I guess you can come on up," she said reluctantly. She didn't seem to want him near her any more than I did.

"Relax," Leon said. "I'll only be here for a couple of hours to put some things in place. Then you can drive me back to the airport."

"Great," she said flatly. "So you won't need a bed then?"

"Just a chair, coffee and Wi-Fi," he said. "As always, you'll be rewarded for your discretion."

"Yeah." Her expression suggested that was what she was worried about. She rattled the keys in her hand and walked over to unlock a door I presumed led up to her apartment. "After you."

Yeah, I wouldn't turn my back on him either. Apparently he had no such reservations where she was concerned. He nodded and headed inside.

Clarissa lingered near the door, her hand on the handle. Eventually, she stepped inside and closed the door behind her.

"Unless that locks automatically..." Gianni started.

"Then it's unlocked," Daze finished for him. "That could make life easier."

I hummed my agreement. "Let's give her a couple of minutes to get him settled, then we'll pay them a visit."

The hairs on the back of my neck rose. My skin prickled. Someone else was here. I hadn't heard them, but my instincts were screaming at me that we weren't alone.

I'd considered the possibility this was a trap, but until now I hadn't seen any sign to back that up. Of course, they'd wait until Leon was safely inside before converging on our position.

"I feel that too," Daze whispered. She must have felt me stiffen. "Behind us. On the corner. I saw a movement."

"There might be people in front of us too, trying to pin us in," I said. "We need to get out of here before that happens."

I cast a long look at Clarissa's apartment. Shadows moved past the blinds. Her and Leon. If he knew where to find Kurt, I couldn't let him slip away. But if this was a trap, I had no choice.

Fuck. I didn't like being pushed into corners.

"I'll lead them away from you," Daze said. "I'll try to give you enough time to confront Leon."

"Me too," Gianni agreed. "We can hold them off."

I wanted to tell them no, but I saw no other way. I could handle Clarissa and Leon by myself if I had to. If she wasn't on our side, it would be more difficult, but not impossible.

I sighed softly, but nodded. "Stay safe." I reached out to find Gianni's face and kissed him quickly.

"You too, sweetheart." He crept away, moving at right angles to whoever was at the corner.

Daze was right on his tail.

I waited until they were a few metres away, before I slipped through the shadows toward Clarissa's door.

As I'd hoped, it was unlocked. I winced at the slight creak of the hinges as I eased it open. It was only audible this close, but it sounded as loud as a gunshot to me.

Calm your tits, I told myself. *No one heard it but you.*

Lips pressed tight together, I slipped inside and closed the door behind me without making another sound.

The stairs were in near total darkness, broken only by a light that peeked under the door, at the very top. I paused to listen.

When I decided no one was waiting to ambush me, I headed up the steps, one at a time.

"The best thing about Dusk Bay is the fast Wi-Fi," Clarissa was saying. "One of the fastest in the world. Of course, the city is also a beautiful place to live, but the Wi-Fi is a bonus. I've lived in some places where it was barely better than dial-up. It's ridiculous, I know. In this day and age, we should all have decent Internet. But here we are."

Leon's response was mumbled, something along the lines of, "Good to know."

"I know, right?" she responded. "That's one of the reasons I moved here. That and the fact people are mostly nice here. For a bunch of criminals. I mean, not everyone is a criminal here, but you know that. Oh, sounds like the kettle has boiled. Excuse me for a minute, I'll make you a coffee. I might even have one myself, even though it's late. Wouldn't want to fall asleep when you want me to drive you. How do you have it? White with two sugars? Okay I'll just be a moment or two. I might even have some biscuits around here. You must be hungry."

"Yeah, whatever," Leon replied vaguely. Apparently he wasn't impressed with her hostess skills. Or maybe he was an ungrateful prick.

I pictured him hunched over a table, laptop in front of him while she hurried around the kitchen, making him a coffee and hunting around for a snack. She seemed to be making as much noise as she could.

She knew I was there, or at least suspected. She was talking to cover any noise I might make.

I smirked at the idea. I made mistakes, but never noise, not when I didn't want to. Who was she expecting, if she wasn't expecting an assassin?

She might assume Reuben would send the twins to collect Leon. A fairly accurate assumption to make, most of the time. If Reuben knew Leon was here, Hunter and Parker would be knocking the door down by now. Me, I preferred to catch Leon unaware.

That meant continuing to move soundlessly, like the shadow Damon once told me I was. At the time, his remark hurt, but I embraced it now.

I was part of the shadows. Darkness inside and out. I didn't need the sunshine to feel whole. I needed this. To be the cunning predator moving through the night, ready to claim my prey.

Like the door at the bottom of the stairs, the one at the top was unlocked. I pushed it open slowly and stepped through.

Damon

"Graves went inside with Clarissa," I reported.

What game was she playing? She'd sent me a message that would raise my suspicion. She must be hoping we'd turn up to take him off her hands.

We'd done the first. We could do the second, but it was too easy so far. If Kurt was thinking a couple of moves ahead of us, this was just about to go south.

If Clarissa was working with him, she'd also go south, to an early grave.

Although, was it really early, in our line of work? Now I thought about it, it was probably about average.

Either way, she'd end up dead, which would be unfortunate. Up until now, she'd been invaluable and trustworthy. Maybe she still was. There was time for her to prove herself yet. If she could.

She'd know as well as I did, once the seeds of suspicion were planted, they tended to take root and grow. Coming back from this would be difficult.

In the corner of my eye, I caught a hint of movement. Then another. There were two people on the opposite corner. No, three. Four. I couldn't make out any more, but fuck only knew who else was hiding in the dark around here.

Across from them I caught another hint of movement. Someone walking up the street toward them. Someone making no effort to avoid being noticed

Gianni. And someone else. Someone taller than Mina. Daze? What the fuck?

Neither of them were usually that sloppy. Given they were now, they were doing it for a reason. They wanted to be seen. They were trying to draw them away.

As far as I could tell, they didn't know we were there yet, so they weren't trying to distract attention from us.

Where was Mina then? She didn't seem to be with them. They were trying to lead any potential attackers away from her.

Was that brave, stupid, or both? It was classic Gianni. He'd take risks others wouldn't, especially when family was involved.

I made a mental note to throttle him later for trying to do this. Daze too.

Across the road, someone spoke. A light flashed on, aimed directly at Gianni. He threw himself to the side as a shot rang out. It must have missed him by a hair.

The bullet hit the wall instead. This was Dusk Bay, no one would notice another one lodged in the side of the building. Eventually, someone would come along and paint over it.

I didn't think.

I aimed for the light and squeezed the trigger. The gun recoiled in my hand. The gunshot echoed, followed by a cry of pain.

The phone dropped to the ground, offering a faint glow from the screen. It wasn't much illumination, and it'd turn off quickly, but it was enough.

Taking a leaf from Mina's book, I aimed for the visible feet.

"Fucking hell!" a male voice called out. He slumped to the ground, hands on his ankles until Hunter put a bullet in his head.

Parker took out another with a shot through his chest, but the last of the would-be attackers turned and ran.

"Go after him," Reuben told the twins.

"On it, boss." They both sprinted across the road and disappeared into the shadows.

Gianni emerged from them, followed by Daisy Lasalle. What the fuck was she doing here anyway?

Gianni picked up the phone and shone it across the two bodies. The third person lay a couple of metres away, groaning in pain.

It was a woman who held the phone; she was now missing a hand. A moment later, courtesy of Gianni's knife, she was missing a whole lot more. Bleeding out onto the footpath before dying quietly.

"Perfect timing," Gianni said cheerfully. He wiped his knife clean on his black T-shirt and tucked it back away, out of sight. "I'm guessing you have a few questions for me. Let me start by saying—"

"Where's Mina?" Reuben interrupted.

"She went inside." Gianni gestured. "It wasn't Kurt that turned up tonight."

"We know." I clapped him on the shoulder. "It's good to see you, but if you sneak off like that again, I'll put a fucking bullet in your knee."

"I love you too," he said lightly. He drew me in for a quick hug.

I stiffened for a moment, before hugging him back. Later, I'd have time to think about how right it felt to hold him, but right now, we had work to do.

"Have you seen anyone else around?" It was possible Kurt only sent four people to ambush us, but none of us would rule out anything at this point.

"Just you reprobates," Daze said. "And these dead ones." She gestured towards them. "And Clarissa and Leon Graves. It's been pretty quiet apart from that."

"Right," Gianni agreed. "If Wolf Venom was still playing, we'd be able to hear them from here."

"Too quiet," Reuben said.

"Boss?" I asked carefully. He was visibly as torn as I was. We both wanted to go up those stairs to Clarissa's apartment. To Mina. If there were others around, they could pin us all in. Including her.

"Search the area," he said finally. "We need to make sure it's not—"

"Full of people who look like they want us dead," Hunter interrupted. He and Parker trotted back toward us, guns still in their hands. "There's another four on the next corner over and four on the opposite one. Now might be a good time to call for some help."

Reuben grunted in annoyance. "Do it. We'll deal with them and then we'll go for her."

"Got it, boss," I said with some reluctance. I pulled out my phone and started to make the call.

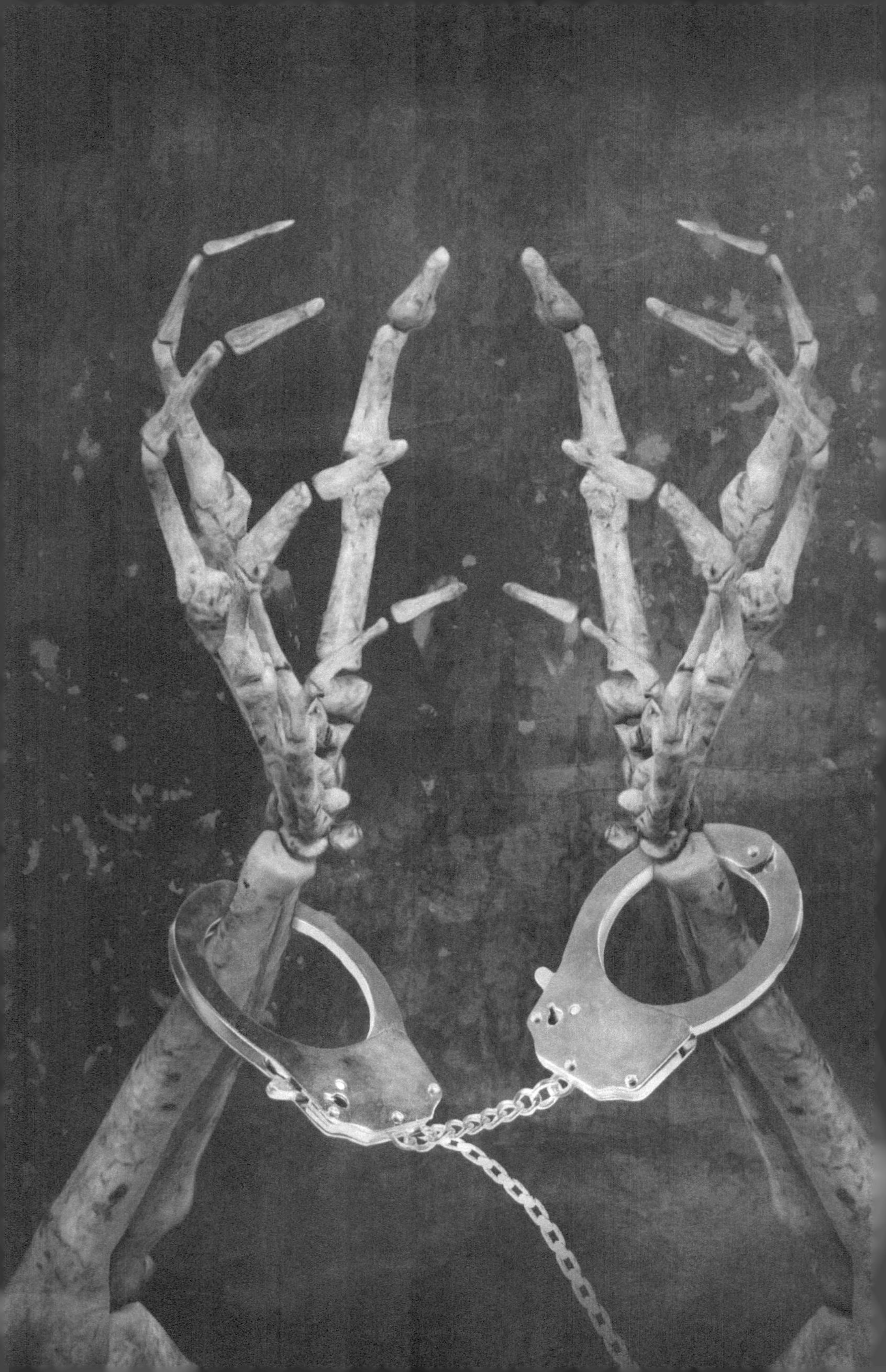

CHAPTER 23

MINA

Leon was engrossed in something on his screen when I stepped through the dark entry hall, towards the living room. He didn't look up, but I knew he was aware of my presence. His body language was too relaxed, one leg draped over the side of the chair. His face was turned towards the laptop, but he wasn't seeing anything on there.

"Kurt said you were predictable," he said slowly. He swivelled around in his seat and looked over at me.

I lounged against the door frame, knife held loosely in my hand. "Not as predictable as him. Or you. You might as well have taken out an ad to say you'd be here tonight instead of tomorrow."

"That was the point, silly girl," he said, looking down his substantial nose at me. "He knew you'd figure it out and turn up. He has lots of people outside waiting for your friends. When they're done with them, they'll be up here for you." He leaned forward. "Lots of them. Too many for one little girl to deal with."

He sat back and took a sip from his coffee.

Smug prick.

"For a little girl, it took four of you to carry me down into that basement," I pointed out. "And a cage and a chain to keep me there. But you know all of that. Because you were there. Were you the one with the camera, filming Kurt violating me while I was unconscious? So brave of him that he couldn't even deal with me when I was awake."

I snorted softly and ran the tip of my knife up and down the side of my finger.

"It was Stefan who took the photos and video," Leon said easily. "He thought it was hilarious. So did Kurt, Hammer and Jase."

Apparently he had no trouble throwing his associates under the bus. People like him never did. At the end of the day, he was nothing but a coward. One who thought he had the upper hand. He was absolutely certain of it. Otherwise he wouldn't dare to taunt me. Even if he didn't know what I was, I still carried a knife I knew how to use.

"And you, no doubt," I said. It was taking all the restraint I had not to throw my knife, and put it through his eyeball. From there, it was a quick trip into his pathetic brain.

Watching him die would be as satisfying as hell, but that would be too quick. He had to at least live long enough for me to twist the blade.

Leon shrugged. "It was just a job. I was paid well to help Kurt to get you down there. What he did to you after that was not my business."

"So you're okay with women being raped?" I asked coldly. "You were happy to see him cage me? You walked away and never gave me a second thought, as long as you got paid? That's fucked up."

It was way beyond fucked up. It was psychotic, disgusting, and made my stomach turn. What kind of man does the things he'd done? I didn't know how he slept at night. He deserved the nightmares I was tortured by.

He shrugged again. "Like I said, it was just a job. When it came to you, he was unhinged as fuck. I wasn't going to get in his way. The one person who tried ended up dead."

I couldn't help the surprise that flitted across my face.

Leon smirked. "You didn't know that, did you? Some guy named Prior, or something like that. He told Kurt he was fucked up and should let you go. He tried to stop him from touching you, but Kurt put a bullet between his eyes. The rest of us, we weren't going to argue."

I didn't remember anyone named Prior, but I respected his attempts to help me. If there was an afterlife, I sent him my thanks, along with a dose of regret that he died trying. And that he failed.

"He had bigger balls than all of you put together," I said. "Where's Kurt?"

"It doesn't matter." Leon shook his head. "There's two ways this goes down tonight. One, people are about to walk through the door, take you and give you back to Kurt, or two, you die. You don't need to know where he is. Just stand there and wait and they'll take you to him."

"And you're going to sit there and let it happen," I said darkly.

If he was right, and people were coming for me, I'd choose death. But I'd fight like hell first. "Don't tell me, you're paid well to do nothing."

"Exactly," he said. "You're finally catching on. Personally, I never understood what he saw in you."

I snorted. "Am I supposed to be offended by that? The last thing I want to be is your type. Besides, someone with balls as small as you wouldn't be able to handle a woman like me."

"Ohhh, your insults sting, little girl," he sneered. He picked up his coffee and downed the rest of it.

"Not as much as my knife will," I said. "Maybe you're right, and there are people coming for me. But I can't think of a single reason why I should leave you alive to see it."

I tapped the tip of my finger against the tip of my blade. Not hard enough to break the skin, but enough to make his eyes widen.

He glanced backwards slightly, in the direction of the kitchen. Presumably this was where he expected Clarissa to come out and do something. Maybe help him pin me down until help arrived.

Clarissa didn't appear.

He blinked a couple of times, like his eyes were becoming heavy.

"Is it too late for you, old man?" I taunted. He couldn't have been more than in his late twenties. "Do you need a nap? I'm sure Clarissa can find you somewhere to lie down for a little while."

He blinked again and shook his head. "I'm fine."

He was clearly not fine. He was struggling to keep his eyes open.

His body swayed to the side. He grabbed the table to keep from tumbling over.

"Are you sure?" I asked sweetly. "You look like you're about to pass out. I'd be very careful about doing that, if I were you. You never know what might happen to you while you're unconscious."

"You wouldn't fucking dare," he snarled, but there wasn't much force behind his words.

"No, I wouldn't, because I wouldn't want to touch you," I said. Unless it was to open a vein or two.

I moved towards him, my knife still in my hand. There was always the possibility he was faking.

If he was, he was doing a good job of it, especially when he toppled to the side and hit the floor with a painful thud. His head rolled back and he lay still.

Clarissa stepped into the doorway that led to the kitchen. "Oops. I might have accidentally-on-purpose slipped something into that coffee. My bad." She grinned.

I managed a small smile back and slipped my knife away. "I had a feeling you were a badass."

"Through and through," she agreed. "If there's people coming for you, we better get him out of here quickly."

She stepped around him and locked the front door. "That'll slow them down," she said before grabbing his feet and dragging him towards what looked like a bedroom.

"What are you—" I started.

"There's more than one way out of here," she said. "Give a girl a hand?"

I leaned over to grab Leon's wrists and heft him up off the ground. Together, we carried him into the bedroom and over to a wardrobe.

"Wild guess what my favourite books were when I was a kid." She opened the wardrobe door and pushed the clothes aside to reveal a trapdoor in the floor. She pulled a key out of her pocket to unlock it and tugged the door up and out of the way.

Under the trapdoor was another set of stairs leading down.

"Motherfucker is gonna have some bruises when he wakes up." Her smile suggested she was pleased by the idea. She grabbed his feet again and started to drag him down the stairs, his head bumping on each as they went.

"I'm struggling to feel bad about that," I said. If all he got was bruises, he was getting off lightly. "Where does this end up?"

Wild guess it wasn't Narnia. Although, I could use some Turkish Delight right about then.

"Down to a tunnel that goes under the street," she said. "Up some more stairs to the back of the next block. I may keep a spare car there."

"I want to be you when I grow up," I told her.

She laughed and waited until I was at the bottom of the stairs, and could grab up Leon's wrists again. We carried him through a dimly lit tunnel that smelled of moisture and disuse, and strained to lug him back up another set of stairs.

We set him down beside a door and I pulled out my phone.

"We could use some help." I sent off a quick text to Daze and Gianni to meet us outside, if they could.

A few moments later, Daze texted back that she was on her way.

I frowned at the lack of response from Gianni, but he might be busy dealing with Kurt's minions. There was no way in the world he could be dead. He was too smart for that.

I rubbed my forehead with my fingers. I was starting to get a headache. I was also starting to wish I told Reuben of my plan.

I hadn't wanted to put any of my men in danger, but that was exactly what I'd done. I knew Kurt had something like this planned and I'd walked into it anyway. If it wasn't for Clarissa, I might be well and truly fucked.

I startled as a knock sounded on the door right beside Leon's unconscious body.

"I'll get it," Clarissa said. "In case it's not anyone friendly, I can pretend I'm working with them. I'm just trying to help Leon escape from the clutches of the enemy." She pressed the back of her hand dramatically to her forehead and grinned.

I nodded and stepped back out of sight.

She must use these tunnels more than I thought, because the bolts slid free easily and the door opened on almost silent hinges.

"Hey." Daze's voice echoed through the space. "I see you brought a friend."

Relieved, I stepped back, but grimaced at her wording. "He's no fucking friend of mine. We need to get him out of here, to Reuben's. It won't be long before..."

I caught the look on Daze's face. "Reuben is here."

"He's somewhere around here," she agreed. "He and the other men are dealing with a few bad guys. Nothing they can't—" A gunshot rang out. "—Handle." The first gunshot was followed by a second and a third.

"Just another night in Dusk Bay," Clarissa said. "Let's get this asshole into my car. He should be asleep for another few hours, but it's always a bit of a hit or miss, because it depends on their body weight and whatnot." She moved her hand back and forth, before grabbing Leon's ankles once again and dragging him out the door.

Daze and I exchanged glances before taking a wrist each and helping to throw him into the boot before Clarissa slammed it shut.

"I hope he doesn't vomit in my car," she remarked. "I hate when they do that."

I made a face and leaned against the car to send a text to Reuben. And then one to Damon. Leon better have some good answers as to where Kurt was, because I had a feeling I was going to get bawled out very soon.

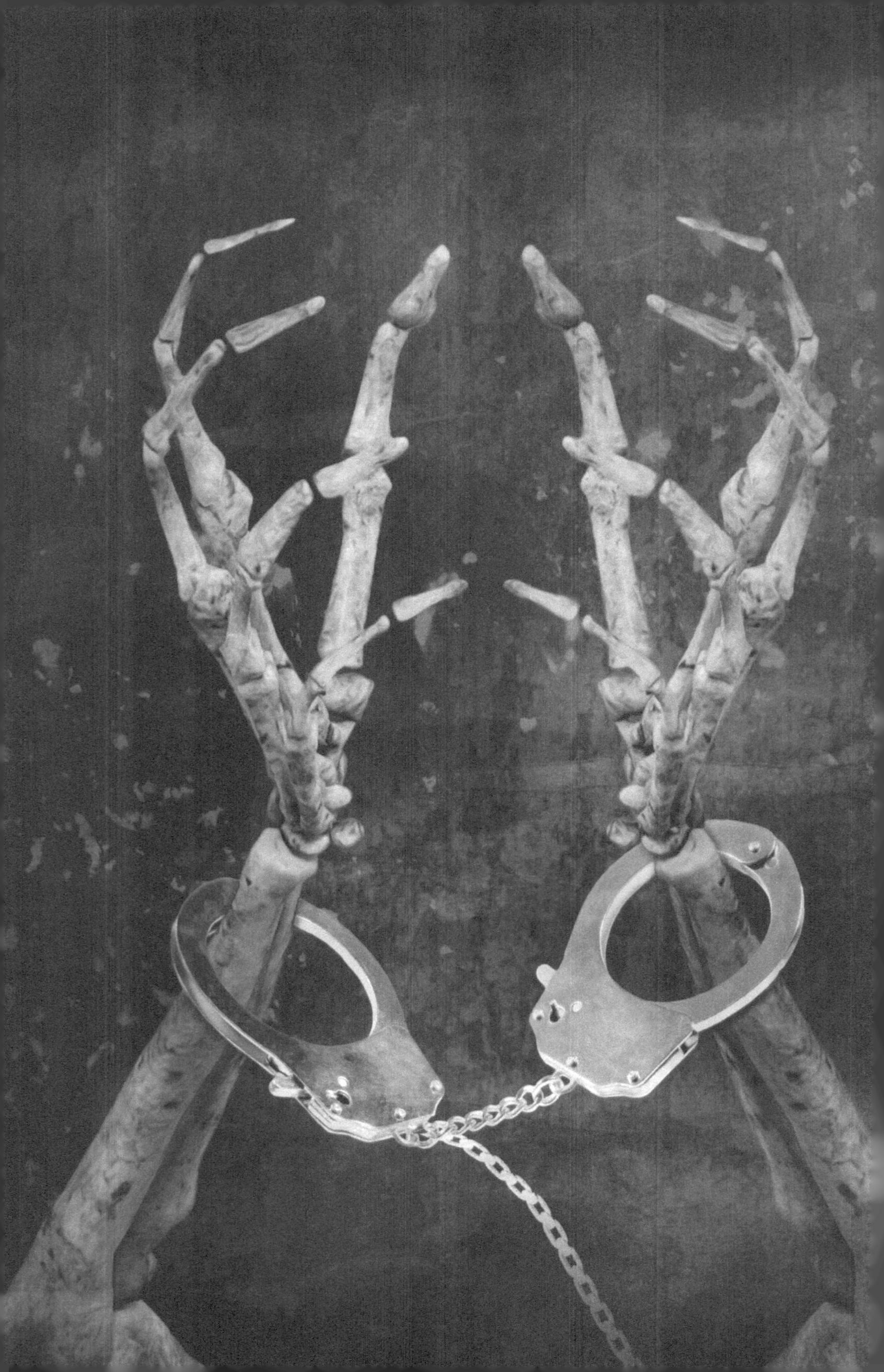

CHAPTER 24

DAMON

We'd barely finished dispatching the last of the attackers, when my phone vibrated in my back pocket. Impatiently, I tugged it out and glanced at the screen.

"It's Mina," I said. "It seems she's taken care of Leon Graves and would like to meet up with us if we're not otherwise occupied." Those weren't her exact words, but close enough.

"So I see," Reuben said dryly. He looked down at his own phone. "I trust Daze is with her."

At some point during the last hour, she'd said she was needed and darted off into the night.

She was going to be hearing about that from me and from Reuben. She was supposed to be following our orders, not hers, or even Mina's.

"That's what my message says," Gianni said. "Daze is with Mina and Clarissa. Just over…" He turned a slow circle, eyes on a map app. "Two blocks in this direction."

"Hunter, Parker stay here and wait for cleanup," Reuben said. "I want all of these bodies gone before morning. The rest of you, let's go."

"Later, bro." Hunter saluted Reuben before we turned away from them and headed away down the street.

"This has been an interesting night," Gianni remarked.

"That's one word for it," I agreed. "Except the evening part." I nodded to the east, where the sun was starting to peek above the horizon. Morning wasn't far away. Chances were, the cleanup crew would be working in daylight.

"It's been a while since we've pulled an all-nighter," Gianni said. "Does that mean we're getting old?"

"Probably." I rubbed the heel of my hand on my forehead and blinked away the weariness that began to descend. Between being up all night, running around the streets being shot at, and killing, I was exhausted.

Far from old, but feeling it right now.

"It means we have other people to do this, most of the time," Reuben said. "People we would have left this to if not for Mina." He narrowed his eyes on Gianni.

"For what it's worth, I followed her," Gianni said easily. "If I knew what she was doing, I would have stopped her and we could have done just that. Sent someone else to pick up Leon." He spread his hands to either side. "But don't tell me you didn't have fun. At least a little bit."

The glance Reuben gave him would have withered anyone else, but Gianni just grinned. "It's not like you sleep anyway."

Reuben grunted.

I shouldn't have found that sound hot, but even in my state of tiredness, I did. Maybe *because* I was so tired. I was done fighting how I felt.

"Took you long enough," Daze drawled as we rounded the corner of the building to see her standing beside a car, Clarissa nearby. "We've been waiting for ages."

"For the record, when I told Ric you were here, he said something about putting you over his knee and spanking you," I said.

She grinned. "Don't threaten me with a good time."

I smirked.

"He knows better than to think he can keep me in line anyway," she added.

The door to the back of the car was open. Mina slipped out, looking as weary as the rest of us, but more beautiful than ever.

"Thank fuck," Reuben said softly.

She trotted over to him and threw her arms around him, before dragging me in for a hug. Gianni invited himself, until we were all embracing each other. Hard bodies pressed against hard bodies. The smell of guns and blood clung to all of us. Heady, but all too real.

"Speaking of spanking," I growled.

"Any time," Gianni said. "If that's your idea of kinky, I like it."

I should have expected him to respond like that. He'd always be himself. Irreverent and possibly crazy, but always charming and, if I was going to admit it to myself, compelling.

"Be careful what you wish for," I muttered.

"If that's on the cards, I'm there for it," he said. "I have a thing about pain. I'm happy to let Mina and Reuben watch."

"I don't want to interrupt the reunion, but we only have a few hours before our guest wakes up again," Clarissa said. "I assume you're going to want him tightly under wraps before then. Not that you can't deal with anything, but…"

"Yes," Reuben said, his voice strained. "Let's get him out of here and back home."

"Is it wrong if I say I don't mind seeing him chained?" Mina asked. "I wouldn't object to him being in a cage either. He didn't mind it happening to me." She scowled in the direction of the boot of the car. I presumed Leon was safely stashed inside.

Telling my cock to behave, I made a mental note never to piss her off. I had a feeling if she served up revenge, it would hurt like hell. She really was the perfect woman.

"Whatever you want, sweetheart," Gianni said. "We can make it happen. Even if you want him hung upside down by his balls. It'll be icky, but I volunteer to touch them."

"I don't think they'll be big enough for you to fasten anything to them," she said dryly. "I'll settle for him being restrained and scared."

"I like a woman who holds a grudge," Gianni said.

"She holds one with good reason," I said.

I made another note to myself. This time to do some searching online when we got home. I had an idea for something that would make her feel much better.

"Gianni, travel with the women," Reuben said. "Damon and I will be right behind you."

"I'll try not to run into the back of your car," I said. With the right amount of force, Leon Graves would be a dead man.

"Only if you want to pay to replace it," Clarissa said. "I don't take kindly to having people…" She paused to choose her words carefully. "Ramming their car into the back of mine."

Gianni grinned.

I rolled my eyes at him before turning back to Clarissa. "I'll try to restrain myself. For the sake of your vehicle."

"I appreciate that." She opened her door and climbed inside.

I waited until all three women, and Gianni, were in the car before nodding to Reuben and trotting down the street to get ours.

Mina

I managed a few hours of sleep, but couldn't linger in bed for long. Especially when I realised I was alone.

I pulled on a pair of track pants and a singlet, and headed downstairs.

That was where I found Reuben, sitting on the couch, facing the view. He held a cup of coffee in his hand. His eyes were glazed, lost in thought.

I didn't say anything. I just lay down and placed my head in his lap.

He went on drinking slowly while running the pad of his thumb up and down my cheek.

We stayed like that, in silence, until Damon and Gianni came down the stairs.

"Morning," Gianni said cheerfully. He wasn't showing any signs of suffering from a lack of sleep. "Is anyone else looking forward to having a little chat with our guest? I'm sure he's ready to be helpful."

"He will; he's a coward." Damon said, his phone in his hand. He still looked weary, but better than he had a few hours ago, when he was all but dead on his feet.

"That seems to be the criteria for being an asshole," I said. I would have sat up, but I was too comfortable where I was. Too secure lying here with Reuben's fingers on my face, Damon beside me, and Gianni sitting in a chair opposite.

Reuben made a sound of agreement in the back of his throat. "They usually are. Any further information on Kurt?"

"Nothing yet," Damon said. "If Mr Graves is forthcoming, we'll pin him down soon." He tossed his phone down on the table. "*When* he's forthcoming. If anyone knows where Lasalle is, it's him."

"Assuming he's still there," I said. "By now, he'd know we dealt with a lot of his minions. He may disappear."

"Then we go back to Leon. He'll tell us where to look," Gianni said. "He won't be going anywhere for a while. He's too useful."

"We will find him," Reuben said firmly. "He knows we're closing in. He'll make a mistake."

"He already did," I said. "He thought Clarissa was on his side. If she was, I wouldn't be here now."

"Yes, you would," Damon said. "No way in hell we would have let Kurt take you anywhere." He locked his gaze on me, solid, unflinching and rapidly growing darker.

I didn't move while he lowered his mouth to mine and kissed me. I wrapped my arms around him, holding him to me, while Reuben continued to stroke my face.

I slid my tongue across Damon's lips and into his mouth.

He pressed a hand to my hip and stroked my tongue with his. His touch had my body on fire. I should have been exhausted, but I was energised all over again.

After a brief hesitation, he peeled up the front of my singlet and kissed his way down my cheek, across my neck and down my chest.

My eyes on him, I pulled my singlet off the rest of the way, and raised my hips to let him pull off my track pants.

Fingers trembling slightly, I touched the front of his pants, where his erection was straining, begging to be let out.

"Damon," I said breathlessly.

"Mina." He slipped his hand between my thighs and over my pussy, lightly teasing my clit.

I rocked against his hand while one of Reuben's moved down to stroke my nipple.

Damon slid a couple of fingers inside me, hooked his hand around and stroked my G spot. The heel of his hand created the perfect friction on my clit.

I arched my back, pressing my head deeper into Reuben's lap as I came.

"Good girl," Reuben said softly. "You come apart so beautifully."

That made my orgasm last longer, reaching peaks I never knew existed.

Panting, I finally came back down to earth. Damon's hand must have been drenched from my release.

I caught my breath and undid Damon's pants. I pushed them down far enough to free his erection. My tongue darted over my lips and I swallowed.

"I... I want you." I said tentatively.

I glanced up at Reuben as he said, "Only if you're ready."

"I'm ready," I said firmly. "I want Damon to fuck me."

Damon hurried to push his pants off the rest of the way, and tossed them aside.

"Anytime you want me to stop, I'll stop," he said. Eyes on mine, he carefully knelt between my legs and pushed the tip of his cock against my entrance. He stopped there, waiting for my reaction.

I swallowed again, but nodded. "Please." I was done being scared of being intimate with them. I wanted this. I wanted it with all of them, but him first.

I needed to know I wasn't too broken to let them in fully.

Damon nodded and pushed in further, slowly, slowly easing in until he was fully seated inside me.

"Are you okay?" he asked.

"Better than okay," I assured him. "You feel good. Amazing." He filled me up so perfectly, like we were made to fit together.

As slowly as he slid inside me, he started to move, thrusting carefully, watching me the entire time. This was no wild, frantic fucking. He was gentle, tender and holding back. Just what I needed for my first time.

"You take him so well," Reuben said. "Good girl."

I looked up at him and smiled. I could feel his erection behind my head, but he made no move to satisfy his own needs. This moment was all about me. I was the centre of their world, and I loved every minute of it.

Gianni moved over to kneel beside the couch and slip his hand between my body and Damon's. Eyes slightly wider, he circled my clit with his fingers, while the rest of his hand would have felt the slide of Damon's cock as he moved in and out of my body.

"Fucking hell," Damon whispered. "This is…" He shook his head, at a loss for words.

"Perfect," I said. The way all three of them were touching me had me closer to the edge again already.

"Come for us again," Reuben said. "I want to see you come around Damon's cock."

"Okay, boss," I said, half-teasing.

I dropped my head back, matching the rhythm Damon set, rocking my hips harder and faster until I pitched over the edge again, coming harder than the first time.

My muscles squeezed Damon's cock, drawing an orgasm out of him too.

He went still, eyes half closed in focus, an expression of bliss on his face. Finally, he let out a ragged breath and sagged forward.

"Holy hell, that was incredible," he said. He leaned down to kiss me. "Thank you. Thank you for letting me be the first."

I smiled up at him. We still had a lot to deal with, but these three men were helping me to feel whole, for the first time in years.

Damon slowly slid out of me and rolled off, almost landing on Gianni who had to hurry to get out of the way.

"Bro," Gianni complained.

Damon smirked and snagged up his pants to throw over his shoulder. "I don't know about anyone else, but I need some sleep."

"Me too," Gianni agreed. "By the time we're awake, our guest should be too. But first, let's get Mina cleaned up. After-care is important."

They both offered me their hand to stand before we headed up the stairs, Reuben right behind.

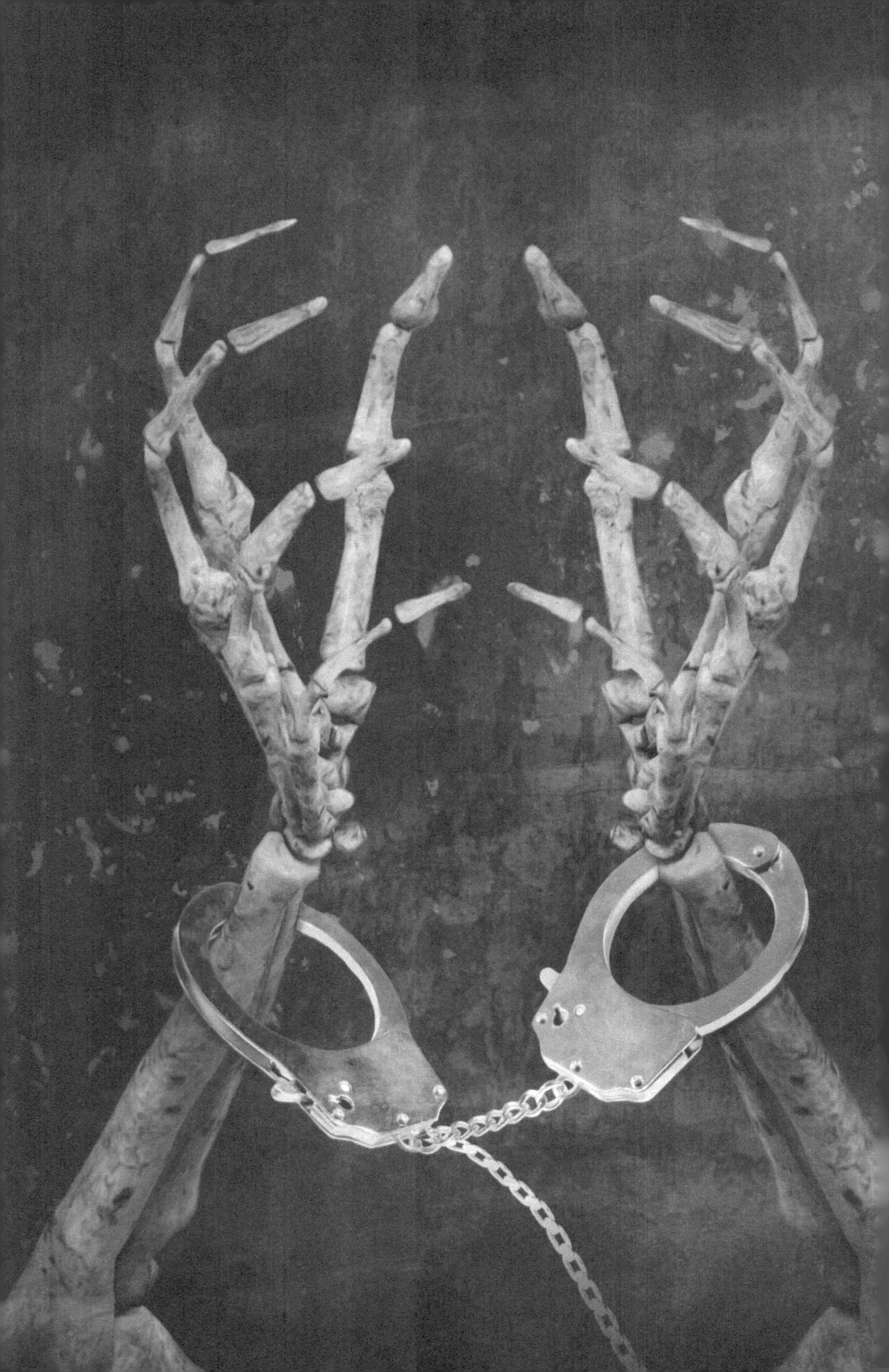

EPILOGUE

DAMON

"Well, isn't this cosy?" Gianni said. He stood with his arms crossed, looking at Leon who was on the floor, his arms raised above his head. On his wrists were manacles, attached to a chain which was, in turn, attached to a ring in the ceiling.

Leon was just beginning to wake up. His head hung to the side. Finally, he roused, straightened his head and looked around himself.

"Fuck," he grunted.

"Sucks to be you," Gianni said. "Welcome to your new home away from home. All you need to do in order to get out of here is tell us exactly where Kurt is. It's that simple."

"If I tell you that, you'll kill me," he whined. He looked ready to piss his jeans.

"You might prefer that to sitting down here for days on end," I said. "I know you have some idea what Kurt did to Mina. You were there."

Fucking piece of shit.

"You saw the conditions she was kept in. After all that time down there, all she wanted to do was die, and she's a shit ton stronger than you are. How long do you think you'll last before you beg to die? A day or two? A week? A year?"

Leon groaned. "If I tell you I don't know where he is, you won't believe me."

"That is a correct fact." Gianni pointed a finger at him. "Because we know that you know. And if you don't, we know that you know how to find him. All you have to do is tell us and this will be a lot easier on you. Personally, I don't think you deserve it, but Damon is nicer than I am."

I glanced over at him. "Since when?"

"Since I suggested I pour some acid into a bowl and place his hand into it, and you said no," Gianni said.

"I said no, put his *foot* into it," I said. "Starting with his toes. Toes are a lot more sensitive than fingers."

We hadn't had that conversation until now, but none of that mattered. The only thing that did was that Leon was listening, and his eyes were getting bigger and bigger. He had no reason to think we wouldn't follow through with everything we mentioned. Because we would, if necessary.

"Right," Gianni dragged the word out. "I guess that means I'm nicer than you then. Hmmm, interesting. What else did you have in mind?"

"After we burn off his other foot with acid?" I asked. "Then I guess we start with his stumps. All the way up to his knees."

Leon groaned. "Please."

I leaned forward, towards him. "Please, what? Like we said, we can make this easy for you. Just tell us where Kurt is and none of this has to happen. At least..."

Leon jerked his face up towards me. "At least what?"

"I think it's only fair that we leave some of this up to Mina, wouldn't you say Gianni? She might not want to go easy on him, since apparently he didn't give a shit about what happened to her. All we can do is try to convince her that you're not a bad person. You're just a guy who got caught up in some stuff, a long time ago. What were you supposed to do? Let Kurt kill you?"

He should have done exactly that.

"Yes, yes, exactly," Leon said eagerly. "I was in the wrong place at the wrong time. I didn't want what happened to her to happen. I mean, I didn't do anything to her. I couldn't stop him, he was determined to do those things. Kurt is fucked up. He's wrong in the head. He probably should have gone to therapy or something. I mean, who locks a woman in a cage for..."

Gianni crouched down in front of him. "Five years, Leon," he said, his tone icy. "It was five fucking years. That's how long she went through all of that. That's how long Kurt did those things to her. Things I couldn't even bring myself to do to you. You're right, he is fucked in the head. But are you any better? Did you ever go to anyone and tell them she was there? Did you try?"

"Nnnn... No," Leon stammered. "But I should have. I was scared. I knew if I did, he'd... He'd know. He'd come for me. He thought of her as his property. If anyone tried to take away his property, he'd—"

Leon screamed in pain as Gianni stabbed a knife into his calf.

"Oops, I slipped," Gianni said sarcastically. "Women. Are. No one's. Fucking. Property. Especially not his. You could have come to us and told us, and we would have got her out of there. We might have even protected you. Got you a new identity and made you disappear. You could have gone off and lived your best life, instead of hiding in the shadows like a fucking coward."

Gianni gripped the hilt of the knife and twisted it.

Leon screamed again.

The sound grated on my last nerve. No wonder Reuben left stuff like this to us. The noise was painful. So much so, he'd insisted Mina sit out. To the surprise of everyone, she'd agreed and went off to have a long soak in a hot bath. That sounded like fucking heaven right now.

After this, I might even join her. If she'd let me. Fucking her was addictive. I wanted to do it again, over and over, until she was so comfortable with my cock, I could stop holding back.

Right now, I wasn't going to think too much about the spanking Gianni mentioned. That was too enticing, I needed to take time to get my head around it.

"We'll ask you again," I said calmly. "Where is Kurt Lasalle? If you don't tell us, this is going to get a whole lot worse for you."

I didn't feel too bad about that. Even if he told us everything we wanted to know, I might let Gianni continue for a while. Just for shits and giggles.

"Okay, okay," Leon pleaded. "I'll tell you everything."

I leaned against the wall and listened, my phone in my hand to record every word.

"Fucking hell," Gianni whispered when Leon was finally done.

If you'd like to know what Mina and Rose talked about in Daze's house, when they went off alone, you can read that in the bonus scene here.

CORRUPTED

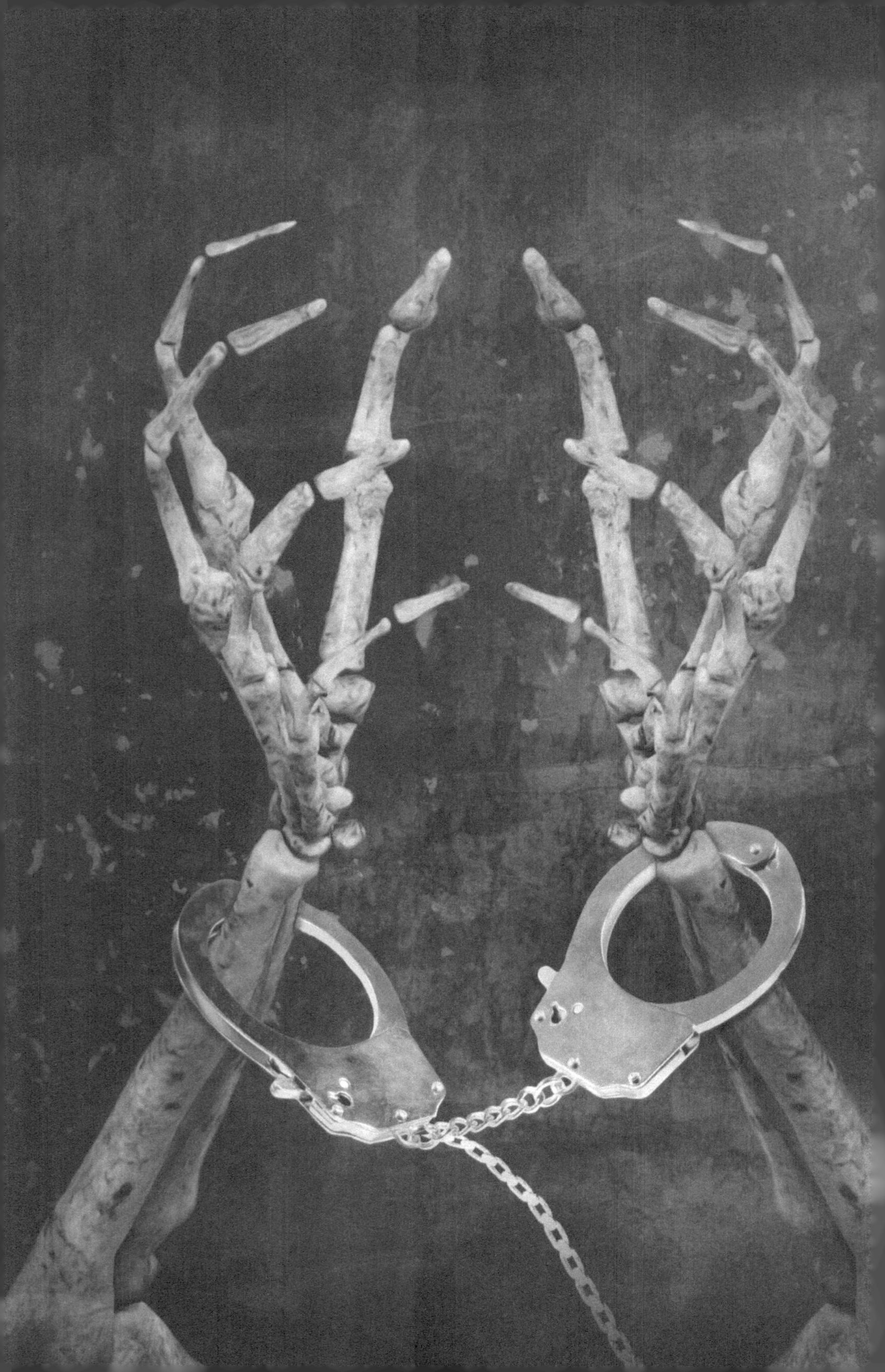

CHAPTER 1

MINA

The door that led down to the basement of the house in Dusk Bay swung open.

I snapped my attention from the view and looked over the back of the couch.

Typically, Gianni's expression was jovial, while Damon's was guarded. The two of them were like night and day. An open book and a closed one.

I adored them both.

"Did you learn anything?" Reuben asked before I could. He was seated at the head of the large dining table, laptop in front of him. He looked every part the successful businessman he was. As well as being a successful mob boss.

"You could say that." Damon leaned against the door frame, crossed his arms and closed his eyes. He looked weary. We all were. The hunt for Kurt Lasalle was taking a toll on all of us.

"Bitch ass prick sung like a bird," Gianni said. He flopped down beside me and put an arm around me. With only a moment of hesitation, he leaned over and kissed my mouth.

I was getting better at not flinching when anyone went to touch me. I'd even let Damon fuck me while the other two watched.

I was still getting my head around that. It was wonderful, special. Especially given I wasn't sure I'd ever be comfortably intimate with anyone. It was gratifying to know I wasn't as broken as I'd thought I was. Healing.

"What did he say?" I leaned against Gianni, inhaling his warm scent, drawing comfort from his closeness.

"He said that Kurt prick-of-the-year Lasalle is right here in Dusk Bay. Apparently," he drawled the word, "he's been here all along." Gianni gestured behind him, roughly in the direction of the city.

My heart skipped several beats. "He's right here?"

What the absolute, ever loving fuck?

"According to Leon Graves, he left Sydney after we found you in the cage and came here." Damon's tone was dark, laced with both thought and irritation. "He's been laying low ever since. He was waiting for his people to grab Mina and take her to him."

He opened his eyes and settled his gaze on me. Even for someone as guarded as he was, rage burned just below the surface. Fury at the idea of Kurt, or anyone else, touching me.

"Of course he is," I said absently, the possibilities tumbling around in my brain.

"No," Reuben said as though reading my mind. "There's no way in the world we would have let him take you, even if it meant leading us to him." He turned to Damon. "Did he say exactly where Kurt is?"

It was Gianni who answered.

"He passed out right before he got to that. Something about a knife in his calf being painful or something." He grinned and shrugged.

"He says he doesn't know," Damon supplied. "He was 'following orders'. Going where he was told to be."

Gianni made a sound of disbelief. "That's what they all say. I'll give him a few minutes, then try again. Otherwise we'll be searching for a needle in a haystack."

"It's a much smaller haystack than the one we had," Reuben observed. His gaze slid to me. "I don't suppose he ever said anything about having a house here?"

"He wasn't particularly forthcoming about his life," I said dryly. He was too busy taunting me, torturing me and forcing himself on me.

Conversation wasn't part of the equation most of the time. Not unless he was telling me lies, like my siblings were all dead.

"I know we don't want to consider the possibility…" Damon said slowly.

"We have to," Reuben said. "If there's any chance Daisy Lasalle knew her brother was here in Dusk Bay, we have no choice but to find out."

I shook my head. "If she knew he was here, she would have dealt with him, or at least told us."

I trusted her almost as much as I trusted anyone not already in this room. She was as angry about what her brother did to me as my men were.

Unless she was an incredible actor.

"While it's even a possibility, we need to consider it," Reuben said. "Gianni, persist with Graves. Damon, tell the twins to go and collect Daze. Have them bring her here for a talk. Mina, you will *not* go off by yourself again. What we do, we do together."

His expression was firm. Set in granite. He'd take no arguments from any of us, not even from me.

"I was trying to protect you." I raised my chin, just as stony, even though I had no intention of going off alone. Not right now anyway.

"I was hoping it was Kurt who was going to turn up at Clarissa's. If it was him and only him, we'd be having a very different conversation." And Kurt would be dead.

"It wasn't." Reuben's expression was unchanged. "It was an ambush, designed to trap you. If it wasn't for Gianni following you, and Damon working out where you both went, we *would* be having a very different conversation. The three of us would be trying to figure out how to get you back."

"Which we totally would," Gianni said.

"Only if she was still alive." Reuben's expression softened. "I can't tie you down or lock you up, but I can insist you don't risk yourself like that again."

The love in his tone was obvious, even if he didn't say the words. He didn't need to. We both knew the way we felt about each other.

"You're right," I said reluctantly. "I'm so used to being alone. Before that,

I was doing things by myself and *for* myself. For a long time, I was the only one I could rely on. The only one that was keeping me sane." Or close to it.

"You can rely on us, sweetheart," Gianni said softly. "We can be clowns sometimes, but we love you. We'd do anything to protect and help you. That's what relationships are for. We take care of each other."

"What Gianni said," Damon grunted. "Except the part about being clowns. He can keep that description to himself."

Gianni flashed him a grin. "You know it fits. We just express it differently."

Reuben smirked. "Speak for yourself."

I flinched slightly at the sound of the door that led to the garage opening. It was all the way down the back of the house, but it got me every time. Someday, I'd grow used to it.

I hoped.

My shoulders relaxed when the twins stepped through the door. Both looked exhausted, but cheerful. Nothing seemed to hold either of them down for long. I envied them that.

"Cleanup is done," Hunter reported.

"Speaking of clowns," Damon said under his breath.

"We didn't see any of those," Parker said. "Thank fuck, because I hate clowns." He gave a full body shudder.

Damon snorted. "You're just in time, Reuben has a job for you."

They both groaned when he told them what it was.

"I was hoping for a nap," Hunter said. He exhaled, loud and dramatic. "Just for Mina, we'll do this one thing first. But we expect overtime for it." He clapped his twin on the shoulder and they turned to head back to the garage.

"They usually complain more," Reuben said. He arched an eyebrow at me. "This was exactly what I was saying. We look after each other. Including those two."

I raised my hands in surrender. "I promise I won't go off by myself again, unless I have to."

He arched the other brow.

"I can't promise more than that," I said. "I don't know what might happen in the future. I might have to work alone to save your ass. Or

Gianni's, or Damon's. Or even the twins'. But I'll only do it if it's absolutely necessary."

Honestly, part of me was tired of working alone. Not in my job as an assassin, but when it came to the hunt for Kurt. This whole situation was easier, more tolerable, with them to support me.

"We'll make sure any circumstances that would force you to work alone, don't happen." Reuben was nothing if not stubborn. He very much liked things done his way. Or else.

"Yes, we will," Gianni agreed. "We're a team and you know what they say about teams."

"You're not going to say 'teamwork makes the dream work,' are you?" Damon groaned.

Gianni chuckled. "I wasn't going to, but it's not wrong." He snuggled in closer to me.

Silence fell for a few moments, broken by Damon's frustrated sigh. "Fine, what were you going to say?"

"I don't know," Gianni admitted. "I was going to say something off-the-cuff. Like, teams get shit done."

"I should have known better than to ask," Damon said. He scrubbed his face.

"You really should," Gianni agreed. "I think we've left our guest alone for long enough already. I should go and check on him, see if he's enjoying my music."

"I'll come with you," I said. "I want to see what this asshole has to say for himself."

I didn't need Reuben's permission, but I glanced over at him anyway.

"Keep me informed," was all he said.

He stayed out of the torturing of people as much as he could. Especially, from what I could gather, if Gianni had his music playing down in the basement.

Reuben was a badass in his own right, but he didn't deal well with loud noises like music and screaming. He was a complicated man, but I loved that about him.

"Will do, boss," Gianni said.

"Gianni can keep you informed too," Reuben said before I stood. "You don't have to face Graves if you don't want to."

"I want to," I insisted. "Ever since I heard him speak, bits and pieces of the past keep coming back to me. He mentioned Jase and Hammer. I can almost picture their faces. If Leon Graves knows where they are, I want him to tell me." I wanted to find Kurt more than I wanted to find them, but they were still a priority. Which reminded me.

"Do either of you know someone named Prior?"

"It rings a bell." Gianni cocked his head at me. "Why's that, sweetheart?"

"Leon mentioned someone by that name," I said, playing the scene back in my head. "Apparently he tried to stop Kurt from caging and hurting me. He said... Prior told Kurt he was fucked up. Kurt shot Prior for it. It was one of the reasons Leon did nothing to stop Kurt from doing what he did. He figured Kurt would shoot him too."

Which was no excuse, but he was paying for that decision now.

All three men frowned in thought.

"I'll look him up," Damon said. "If he's someone who used to work for us, there should be a record. We tend to keep those for a long time. Bear in mind though, we may never be able to find him to give him a decent burial."

Trust him to understand why I wanted to know what happened to the one person who stuck their neck out for me. He deserved better than a shallow grave, or to have been tossed in the harbour for the sharks to eat. Or incinerated, which was more likely.

I nodded. "I appreciate that." We could at least try.

"If we can't find him, we can do a nice memorial in the garden," Gianni said.

"I'll go and see to it, and a few other things," Damon said. He pushed himself off the door frame and disappeared in the direction of the stairs that led to the upper level.

"I don't know about you, but I'm ready to have some more fun with our friend." Gianni offered me his hand.

I took it and rose. "He's no friend of mine." Gianni's hand was warm in mine, large and reassuring. He got off on the fact I was an assassin and enjoyed killing, but he could be surprisingly gentle when he wanted to.

"To be completely fair, people like him rarely have friends," Gianni said. "So, he's not mine either. That's what makes it funny. It's ironic."

"It certainly is that," Reuben said. "I don't think anyone will miss him when you're finished with him." He rubbed a hand over his eyes and turned his attention back to his laptop screen.

"I will," Gianni said. "He's been a ton of fun already." He smiled happily and we walked to the door that led down to the basement.

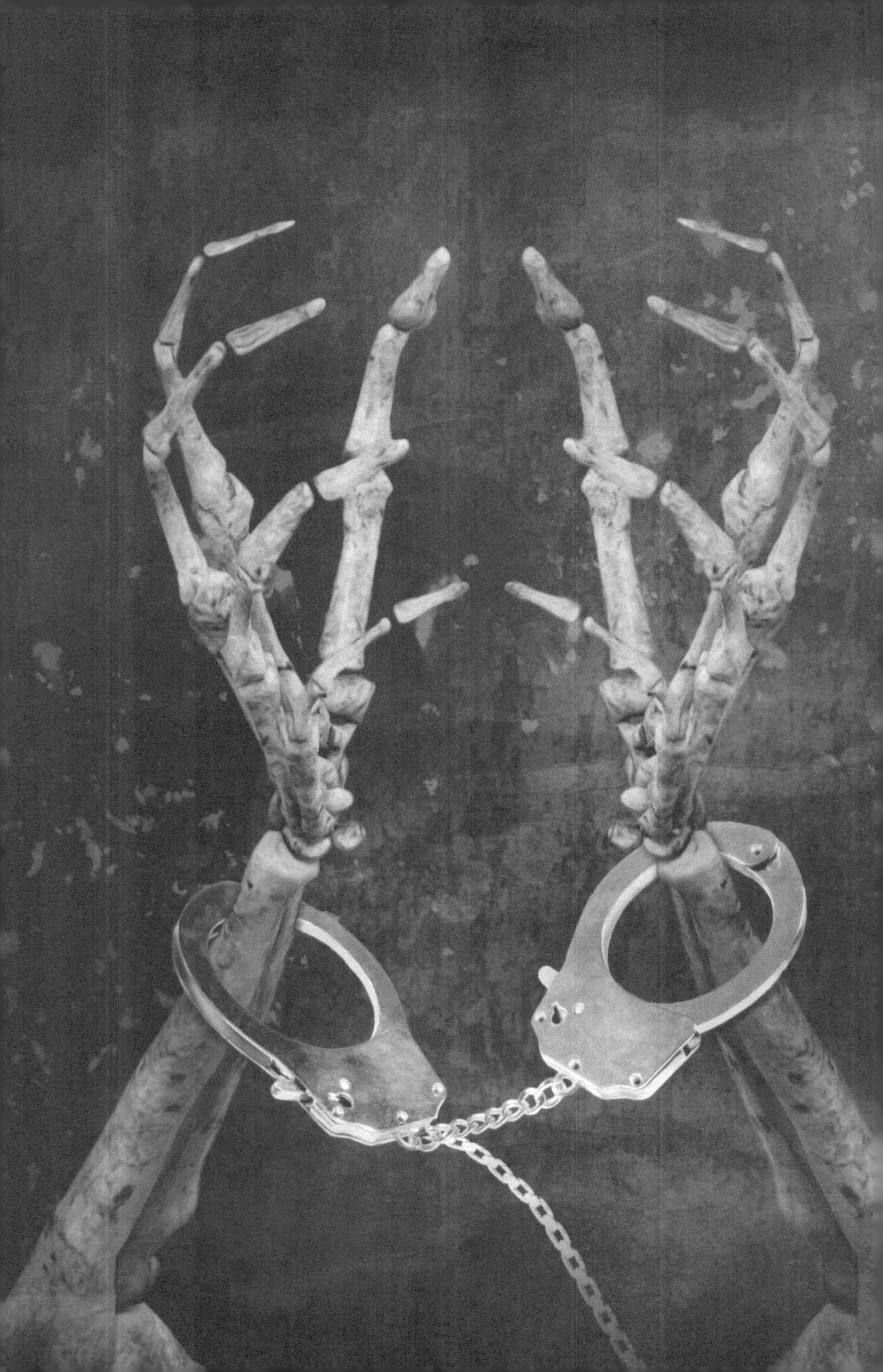

CHAPTER 2

MINA

The volume of the music made me wince the moment I stepped through the door at the bottom of the stairs. The room below was soundproofed, so until now, I hadn't heard a hint of the pounding drums or ear-splitting vocals.

Gianni grooved to the sound for a few moments before pulling out his phone and tapping the screen. The music stopped immediately.

The ringing in my ears would last longer.

Leon Graves was chained to the ceiling, his arms above his head. He lolled to one side, the chain holding up all of his weight.

"Thank fuck," he groaned. He raised his face to look up at us. His eyes were bloodshot, the exhaustion obvious. Apart from the knife sticking out of his calf, he seemed physically unhurt.

I wrinkled my nose at the smell. He knelt in what looked like a combination of piss and vomit, mixed in with a bit of blood. Not enough blood, if you asked me.

"People often say that when they see me," Gianni remarked. "It must be my charm."

Leon snorted. Apparently some of his sense of humour was still intact.

"I think he misses your music," I said. "Don't worry, Leon, he'll turn it back on when we leave."

He looked at me like he was considering begging me to kill him so he didn't have to listen to it anymore. Noise that loud would grate on anyone's nerves after a while.

Which, of course, was the point. This wasn't a pleasure dungeon. Well, not for him.

Pleasure came in a variety forms, including seeing someone who had a hand in your personal hell chained to the ceiling.

Leon managed a venomous look before dropping his head back to the side. "I told you everything I know. Kurt is somewhere here in Dusk Bay. If I had more to give you, I would. Anything to get out of here."

I stepped closer to him. "You know you're not getting out of here alive, right?"

"Don't care," he groaned. "Get it over with." He raised his face until his stubbled throat was exposed, begging to be sliced open.

"Tempting," I admitted. "But too easy. Do you think Kurt would have killed me if I begged him to?" I had, but never when he was around. I'd managed to cling on to that much dignity.

"Kurt is an asshole," Leon said. "You can be better than him."

Gianni crouched beside him, gripped the hilt of the knife and twisted it until Leon screamed.

"We *are* better than him, *dickhead*," Gianni snarled. "We don't plan to keep you down here for five years. Not that you'd last." He twisted the knife again. "You'll die of cowardice long before that."

Tears poured down Leon's cheeks. "I will, but you could make it quicker. Please, for fuck's sake."

Gianni pulled the blade from Leon's leg and stood. "You haven't even been here for five hours yet and you're already begging to die. That must be a record. Most people last at least..." He held out his other hand, palm up. "Six or seven hours. The best last two or three days."

"He's far from the best," I said. "But maybe we can make this easier on him."

Leon looked up, suddenly hopeful. "Please..."

"You mentioned Jase and Hammer," I said slowly. "Where are they?"

His hope faded. "I don't know. I haven't seen Jase since that night. He might be dead. Hammer, I don't even know his real name. He could be anywhere. He might be dead too."

"You know where to find them," I said. "You have contacts. Tell us who we can ask."

"You're so hot when you're assertive like that," Gianni told me.

I glanced over at him and smiled before returning my attention back to Leon. "It's that simple."

"There's a woman named Martina," Leon confessed. "She deals in information like that. I can give you her number. You have my phone, it's in there." He nodded, then winced as though his head hurt. It probably did. Gianni's music would have given him a killer headache.

"We'll track her down," Gianni said. "With any luck, she'll tell us where they are. Hopefully they're still alive so we can kill them."

"If anyone will know, it's her," Leon agreed. He looked from me to Gianni and back again.

"When we have them, we'll deal with you," I said.

"But... But," he stammered, "I told you what you wanted to know."

"You gave us something for a start," I agreed. "But that's all it is, a start. For all we know, you might be lying through your teeth."

He wasn't. He was desperate enough to say anything, to get us to kill him or let him go. I suspected he was still clinging to some shred of hope we'd remove him from the chain and kick him out the door. Or better yet, help him disappear before Kurt caught up with him. I had to give him some credit for clinging to hope while there wasn't much of it to cling to. The moment he helped Kurt chain me up, he signed his own death warrant.

"I swear," he groaned, "if I knew anything else, I'd tell you." He swallowed hard. "Martina might be able to tell you where Kurt is. Or Clarissa. She works with him too, you know."

"Nice attempt to throw her under the bus," Gianni said. "You know she drugged you, right? She's the reason you're here."

His eyes flashed with anger, although he must have known what she'd done. One minute he was having a conversation with me, the next he was tumbling to the floor. Any bruises on the back of his head were from her dragging him down a set of stairs.

She was definitely not on his side.

"That won't go unpunished," he said.

Gianni laughed. "By you? Good luck with that, asshole. In case you forgot, you're chained up in here, kneeling in a puddle of your own vomit, and she's out there, living her best life." He jerked his thumb towards the door. "And she's going to go on living, because she works for us, not the prick who pulls your strings. That was your first mistake, Leon. You chose the wrong fucking side. What did you think working for Kurt would get you, anyway? It was only a matter of time before we figured out what he was up to and put a stop to it. And put a stop to *him* and anyone who works for him."

"I can give you details of his business dealings," Leon said, his voice strained. "They go way back before..." He glanced at me, obviously unsure as to how to word what happened to me. It was best he didn't articulate that. I didn't need a reminder and neither did Gianni.

"He was screwing Reuben over even before then?" Gianni asked. His apparent interest seemed to have given Leon an extra spike of hope.

"He was trying to screw the Brantley family over, yes," Leon said. "Indirectly." He exhaled painfully. "He stumbled upon a plan of old man DiMarco's. He was going to dispose of Reuben's father and take over his empire and assets. Kurt was going to go to Brantley and tell him everything. DiMarco begged him not to. He knew if he did, he'd be worse than dead."

My blood went cold. "So to stop Kurt from going to Reuben's father, he gave me to him. To keep him quiet." I glanced at Gianni. "That was the debt. Kurt was bribing my father. He gave me to him to save his own ass."

Gianni's lips pressed together in sympathy and anger. "That's fucked up."

That was one way to describe it. I was nothing but a pawn in my father's game. A game he ultimately lost after killing Reuben's parents. Reuben, in turn, had him and my mother killed. An act I didn't blame him for. Especially now.

"Shit," Gianni said. "So Kurt's business interests and influence go further than we thought. Who knows how much of DiMarco's he gained."

"A lot of it," Leon said. "DiMarco built an empire almost big enough to rival Brantley's. He'd spend years building up all of that, ready to make his move. When Kurt found out, he panicked and brought his plans forward. Then everything went to hell. And Kurt stood back and reaped the benefits."

"He's an opportunistic prick," Gianni said. "But this explains a lot. Why it's been so hard to find him, and how he has the funds to finance everything he's been doing. And why Leon here is shit scared of him."

"His reach is further than you might think," Leon said. "Not as much as the Brantley family, but significant. He's arrogant and thinks he's smarter and better than everyone else. Between you and me, I don't think he's all there."

"Some of the best people aren't all there," Gianni said. "But he's not one of the best people."

"He's the worst," I said. My brain was still turning over with what Leon said. Why my father drugged me and handed me to the devil.

I'd always thought he was brave and strong, if somewhat harsh, ambitious and distant. Now I knew he was a coward. As big a wimp as Leon. He had to be, to hand over his eighteen-year-old daughter to save his own neck. He'd preferred that, than owning up to what he was doing, and wearing the punishment for the betrayal.

Better yet, he could have been loyal to the people he worked for. He got everything he deserved, and more, for the things he'd done. I hope he suffered when he died, knowing what I was going through.

He was a monster like Kurt.

"One of the worst," I amended. "Reuben doesn't know any of this?"

"If he does, he never shared it with me," Gianni said. "All I know is that your father killed his parents and he acted in retribution. He may have his suspicions as to what went down, but no one was alive to confirm it. At least, not that we knew of."

"That explains why Reuben doesn't trust Dane," I said. I had my own reasons for not trusting my brother too much, but our father's betrayal would have reflected on him. The son of a betrayer might prove to be one himself.

"Dane is a snake," Gianni said. "That's why Reuben doesn't trust him. He trusts Rose and tolerates Asher. And he loves you. He doesn't hold your blood against you."

For that, I was grateful. When he found me in the basement, I thought he'd kill me. After what Kurt said about the relationship between our families having soured, I expected nothing less. At the time, I didn't care. I wanted to die.

Now, all I wanted to do was live.

"We should tell him all of this," I said.

"So, I've been helpful?" Leon looked hopeful once more. "I don't know what more there is to tell you."

"You'll think of something," Gianni said. He pulled out his phone and smiled.

"No, please, I swear I'll—" Leon's pleas were drowned out by the sound of the music flooding the room again.

"Enjoy!" Gianni shouted. He took my hand and we stepped out of the room before the sound became overwhelming.

I sighed in relief as the door closed behind us, blocking off the noise.

"You're not feeling sorry for him?" Gianni asked.

I snorted. "Fuck no. I'm just glad it's not me."

"Would you prefer to kill him?" Gianni waved back toward the door.

"I think I'll savour the idea for a few days," I said. "I've waited this long to feel his blood on my hands. I can wait a little while longer."

He groaned. "Fuck, that's hot. Probably for the best too. I suspect he'll remember some more important information if he tries hard enough."

"Can I ask you something?" I asked, suddenly shy. "You mentioned you like… Knives?"

Gianni's hand in mine, we slipped upstairs to the room designated as mine. I hadn't actually slept in it, but my things were here, rather than cluttering Reuben's space.

"So, knives, you say?" Gianni stepped inside and let me close the door behind us. He was letting me take the lead in this, every step of the way.

"I do say." I stopped short of engaging the lock. Closed doors were one thing, as was locking the world out of the house. Being inside a locked room was another. Even if it was locked from the inside.

"I don't want to—" I stopped a metre or so from the door, uncertainty seeping in.

"Whatever you want to do, sweetheart. I'm here for it. If you've changed your mind, and just want to talk, that's okay. Or if you'd prefer me to leave?" He stepped toward the door, but I put out a hand to stop him.

"No, don't leave. Please. I want…this. Us. You." So eloquent, but it was all I could manage right now.

I crouched down in front of my suitcase and pulled out a jumper. The black garment was wrapped around one of my favourite knives. The one I'd used the most often to kill.

If blades absorbed blood, it would have been soaked.

"She's beautiful." Gianni crouched beside me and looked admiringly at the cold steel. "Beautiful and deadly, just like you." He leaned over and kissed me.

I kissed him back before finding myself placing a hand on his chest and pushing him back onto the cool, hardwood floor. I straddled him and pressed the knife to his throat.

His eyes widened, but he smiled. "Hello there."

I smiled back. I could have taken his life then and there, but he knew I wouldn't. He trusted me completely to hold a sharp blade to his throat and not drive it into his vein, or slice him open.

Would I trust anyone else to do the same? Didn't know, but this was both gratifying and arousing.

With my spare hand, I pushed up his t-shirt, only lifting the knife to push the fabric up over his head.

His upper body bare, I was free to run the tip of the knife over his rock hard skin. Light, so I didn't break it, not yet.

He half closed his eyes and smiled. "Fuck, that feels good."

I licked my lips and undid the button of his jeans before sliding down the zipper. I pushed them down far enough for his erection to spring free. He was already hard and ready.

I glanced at his face before carefully sliding the side of the knife down his length and back up again.

"Holy shit." He swallowed audibly. "Sweetheart, that is…" His hips rolled, equally careful, obviously mindful of the damage I could do to him right now.

I replaced the knife with my tongue, licking him from tip to balls and back again.

He quivered. "Mina…"

I set the knife aside and pulled my singlet off over my head and onto the floor. He gripped the waistband of my leggings and tugged. I half stood to pull them off, before lowering myself back onto him, dressed only in a bra and panties.

I picked the knife back up, and once again brought it to his throat. While I pressed lightly, he snuck a hand between us, over the gusset of my panties.

It was my turn to quiver.

Taking that as his cue, he tugged my panties aside and rubbed the pad of his thumb over my clit.

I swallowed down a ball of nerves and positioned my pussy over his cock. Blade poised in one hand, I slowly lowered myself onto him.

Until now, I was acting on instinct, and having read a lot of smutty romance books. I'd never imagined doing this myself, much less taking the lead. But the knife in my grip gave me confidence like nothing else could. It made me feel both safe and powerful.

Nothing and no one could touch me, unless I chose to let them.

"Don't be scared to draw blood," he said, rubbing more firmly on my clit.

My tongue slid over my lips. I nodded. I pressed down until a bead of blood formed on his throat. The sight was almost enough to make me come on the spot.

"Mmm, yeah," he groaned. He thrust up slowly, taking his time to enjoy every moment.

I moved to a different spot, a centimetre from the first, and pressed down until blood sprang from the small incision. It trickled over the tattoo on the side of his neck, and onto the floor.

Once, twice more, I cut into him, always gentle, always shallow, my desire rising with every stroke of his thumb.

"I'm going to come," he said, sounding pained with the effort from holding back. "Come for me first."

With one last incision, I came, bucking slowly, holding my hand steady so the blade only went exactly as deep as I wanted it to.

He came a few moments later, eyes shut, expression one of total bliss as he spilled himself inside me. Cum flooding warm and wet like the blood that dripped onto the hardwood.

I sagged down over him and pulled the knife away. I breathed in heavily, inhaling the scent of sweat, blood and him. The most heady combination I ever remembered smelling in my life.

"See, I like knives," he said finally.

I laughed, deep and husky in the back of my throat. "So do I."

He chuckled. "I thought you might. That's why we fit so well together. We both like blood, death and sharp objects."

"Three of my favourite things," I said.

He wrapped his arms around me. "Mine too. After you. You're on top of me and my top four."

I rested my head against his chest and exhaled softly. Content to lie there for a while and be alive.

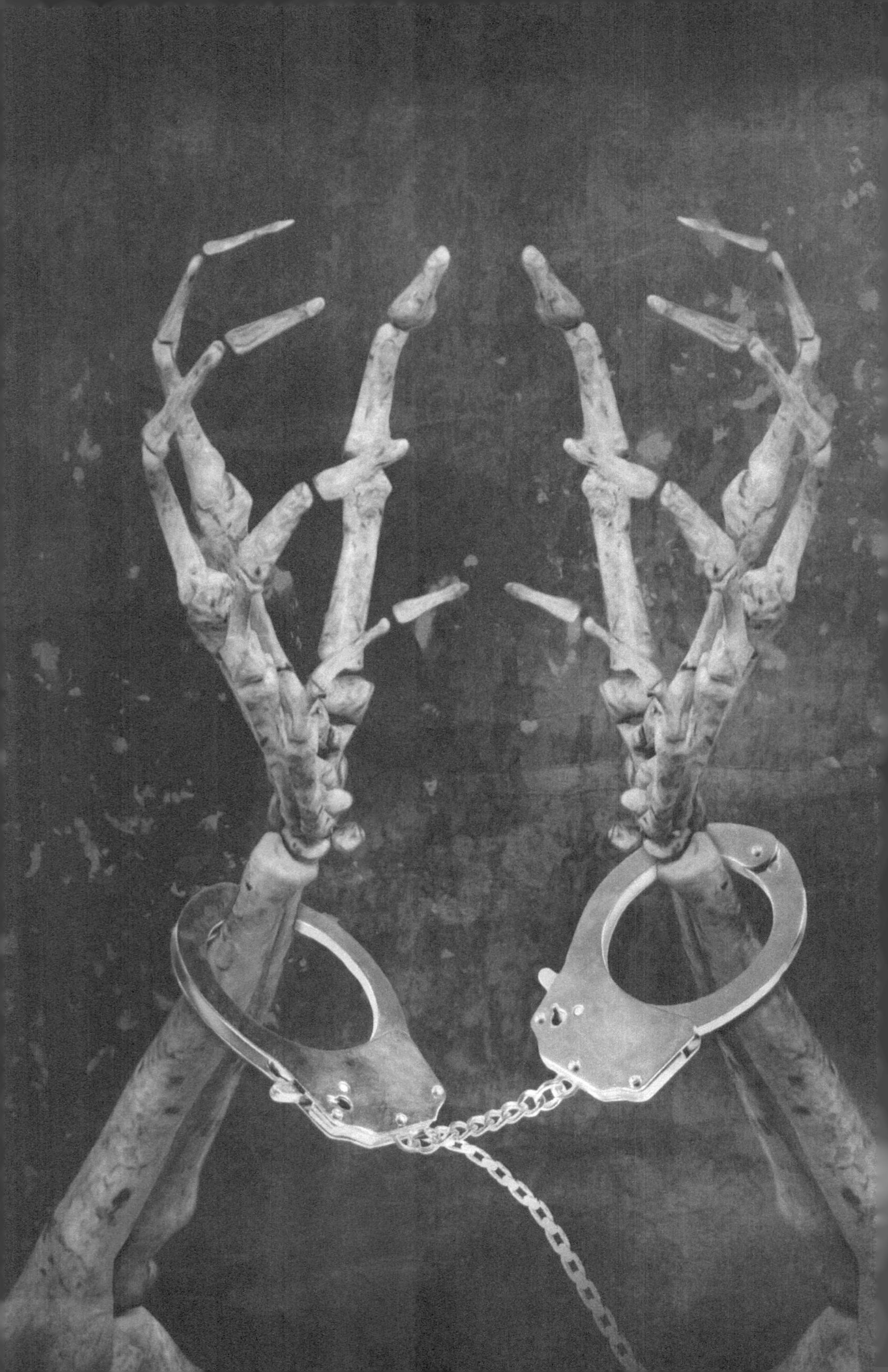

CHAPTER 3

MINA

Reuben sat behind his desk, hands in front of him, fingers laced together. To anyone who didn't know him, he'd appear calm and composed.

To those who did, he was filled with barely contained rage. His knuckles turned white. The vein in his forehead throbbed. He didn't say a word while Gianni and I told him what Leon said.

Everyone else in the room was equally silent, apart from the occasional mutter from the twins and gasps of surprise from Daze.

Damon and Caleb both sat in chairs, each as stony-faced as the other.

"That's horrendous," Daze said when we finished. She leaned against Ric, who insisted on coming with her, and closed her eyes. "If my father tried anything like that with me…" She shook her head.

Ric wrapped his arms around her and held her as if he could protect her from what she just heard. "This explains a lot. Including why we didn't know any of this. He had the funds to keep us from finding out." He glanced at me apologetically. Just because it made sense didn't make it right.

"He shouldn't have," Caleb snapped. "This shouldn't have gotten past our father. It shouldn't have gotten past *us*."

He looked at Reuben with an expression laced with accusation, but also with a touch of annoyance and fear. If anyone should have known what was going on after their father died, it was Caleb. If their father hadn't told Reuben anything, that was unfortunate. Caleb had five years to figure it out. He wasn't alone in that, but he clearly took it on his own shoulders. Or at least suspected he'd be blamed.

"It shouldn't, but it did," Reuben said simply. "Now we know. We can take steps to ensure it doesn't happen again. That isn't the most pressing concern at the moment." His gaze went to Daze and Ric.

"You didn't bring us here to fill us in on that, did you?" Daze asked. She glanced over to the twins who clearly hadn't given her or Ric a choice. That made her visibly nervous as hell.

"According to Leon Graves, Kurt is in Dusk Bay," Reuben said. "Do you know of his whereabouts?" He wasn't pulling any punches today.

Daze stared at him, then at me. "Of course not. You can't really think I'd... *We'd* keep that from you?"

"We don't want to think that," I said. I hated this. We were supposed to be on the same side, not accusing each other. I wanted to believe her and my cousin. I needed to, if only for my own sanity.

"Then don't," Daze replied. "We don't."

"But your concerns aren't with us," Ric said slowly. "You think someone who works for us might have some idea."

"Has anyone been behaving particularly twitchy lately?" Gianni asked.

"Apart from Caleb?" Hunter said. "But then, he's always twitchy."

Caleb gave him a dark look.

"Not that I can think of," Ric said. "That is to say, everyone's been on edge since we started digging into what Kurt was up to. We all feel responsible for everything. Me, Daze, Gunnar and Hilton, in particular."

Daze nodded her agreement. "We haven't been able to tell our people much, just that we're looking for him. Our concern might be somewhat contagious."

"Keep an eye out," Damon told her. "Someone knows something."

"Do you know anyone named Jase or Hammer?" I asked.

Ric looked contemplative, but ultimately shook his head. "I can't say either name rings a bell. That doesn't mean we don't know them."

"Did they…" Daze started carefully.

"They were there," I said simply. I didn't need or want to explain any further. Nor did I feel the need to explain that we got Martina's number from Leon's phone. We'd deal with her on our own.

Silence hung heavy in the air, finally broken by Caleb clearing his throat.

"From what I've been able to ascertain, Kurt either hasn't noticed, or doesn't care, that the account balance of most of his accounts is approximately sixty-nine cents each."

Parker grinned at having done that, transferring the money into different accounts Kurt couldn't access.

"Yes!" Gianni pumped the air. "Maserati, here I come."

"Can I have one too?" Hunter asked. "Parker and I would look good in matching Maseratis."

"If you can afford to buy them out of your own pocket," Reuben said.

All three of them sagged with playful disappointment.

"Spoilsport," Parker muttered.

Caleb cleared his throat again, clearly becoming impatient. "There's the matter of the information Kurt has, that he might decide to sell." He carefully avoided looking at me.

Everyone else did instead, including Ric, who looked confused.

I sighed. "He might as well know too."

"Know what?" Ric asked. He looked around the room, then at Daze.

She shrugged, then looked over to me.

"I'm the Sparrow," I said.

He stared at me in disbelief for a few moments before my words sunk in. "I see." To Daze, he said, "You knew?"

"I guessed," she said. "We're all sworn to secrecy. That includes you now."

"Yes, it does," Reuben said, his tone a thinly veiled threat.

"No one will hear it from me," Ric assured me. "Does—"

"Rose doesn't know," I said. "Neither do Dane or Asher, as far as I know. I'd like to keep it that way. For now."

"Because we need to sell the information," Caleb said. "To keep Kurt from doing the same thing."

"We talked about this," Reuben said.

"And we came to no conclusions," Caleb reminded him. "If I recall, Mina was in favour of this plan."

"As opposed to giving any more power to Kurt," I said. "We also talked about spreading the information that a woman was kept in his basement. Without naming me."

"We're happy to do that," Hunter offered. "Parker and I have many skills. Spreading gossip is one of them. We can make it sound as bad as you want, but keep your name out of it."

Reuben glanced at me before nodding. "Do it. But Caleb is right, we need to address the issue of the Sparrow. We need to take that information out of his hands and stop him from capitalising on it."

"By capitalising on it ourselves," Caleb said.

"Is it really necessary to mention Mina?" Ric asked.

Silence fell again while everyone processed his words.

"How difficult would it be to convince everyone Kurt is the Sparrow?" I asked finally. "We give out that information and he'll have people going after him, right along with us."

Hunter burst out laughing. "That's fucking awesome. Like throwing him in the centre of a shark-feeding frenzy."

"Right where he belongs," Parker agreed.

"Easier if we can find Kurt," Damon said. "Or better yet, have him turn up at a location where the Sparrow is expected. The second part will be easier than the first."

"We need to draw him out," I said. "We need to offer him something he won't be able to resist."

"No," Reuben said. "You're not putting yourself out there as bait. We've had that discussion."

I shook my head. "We already know that won't work. He didn't come for me in person when he used Leon as bait for us. There has to be something else."

"Like what?" Hunter asked.

"I have no idea," I admitted. "What does he care about more than me or his money?"

"Power," Ric said. "The same thing that drives most of us. If we can whittle down his power, he'll have no choice but to show himself. If we tell everyone he's the Sparrow, who…abducted a woman he met while he was working, people will start to turn on him."

"Definitely," I said. "That goes against the assassin code of conduct. But we can go one further. We can tell everyone he murdered an innocent child. They only need to look into it to learn the truth. We give them the place and the dates and they can confirm it."

Her face flashed in my memory, small and perfectly innocent. Another pawn in Kurt's fucked up game, like I was.

"I can provide the logs of my movements that night."

Reuben rolled his lips before he said, "Do it."

"Are you sure, sweetheart?" Gianni rose and came to put his arms around me.

The nicks in his neck had stopped bleeding, but my pulse ratcheted up at the sight of them. Each one of them. I had to push the thoughts aside before my panties ended up drenched again.

"Once the name of the Sparrow is tarnished, it's going to be hard to clear that," Gianni said. "Once people believe it's really Kurt, that's what they're going to keep believing. They're not going to want to hire the Sparrow when the rest of it comes out. You may never work under that name again." His brow creased, dark eyes worried for me, and the implications of the idea.

I appreciated his concern for me and the reputation I'd worked so hard to build. He was always first to think of me, and make sure I was all right, no matter what was happening.

I leaned into him and inhaled his masculine scent. Today he smelled like cinnamon and leather, and satisfaction. Maybe with a tiny hint of blood.

"I'm starting to think that persona is my past," I said. "I can build a new one. If this is the only way we can get him, I'll gladly give it up. It was a part of me, but not all of me. Not my entire identity."

"No, you're Mina fucking DiMarco," Gianni said. "My badass woman."

"Our badass woman," Reuben growled.

Damon grunted his agreement.

"Our badass woman," Gianni corrected himself. He kissed my forehead.

"I'll start to put out hints that we have this information to sell," Caleb said. "I doubt it'll take more than a day or two to get a few bites."

He looked satisfied at this compromise. That was fortunate, because I'd wondered if his intention was to throw me to the wolves. Evidently, he was more interested in the same agenda as the rest of us. Putting an end to Kurt Lasalle.

"I found references to a Gage Prior," Damon said, his blue eyes on me. "Apparently he worked for Reuben's father. As far as I can tell, he was investigating something, but there's no mention of what. If I had to guess, I'd suspect there were suspicions about Kurt and he was trying to uncover what he was doing. He disappeared around the same time as Mina. They never found his body." He looked regretful.

Caleb, on the other hand, looked shaken. "Gage Prior was investigating Kurt?"

"You knew him?" Reuben asked. There was more concern in his tone than I'd ever heard from him when he addressed his younger brother. He appeared genuinely concerned at Caleb's response. Even the twins were staring at Caleb like they might actually be worried about him.

"He... We were..." Caleb swallowed. "Yes, we knew each other. I was aware he disappeared, but never knew why. I always thought..." He looked rocked to his core.

"We only have Leon's word for it that he's dead," I said. "It's possible he's...somewhere else. I was." I briefly explained what Leon said.

Caleb swallowed, his skin slightly green. "That sounds like Gage. He was always trying to be a fucking hero. Like he could save everyone. He never understood some people couldn't be saved." He seemed to be talking about himself.

"Everyone can be saved," I said softly. "They just have to want to be."

He gave me a sharp look, and a curt nod. "I should get to work. The sooner this is dealt with, the better."

I got the feeling the matter had become personal to him. I also got the impression I'd never get the truth out of Caleb, but at least he had answers about his… Friend.

Although, maybe it gave him more questions than answers. That might be cold comfort.

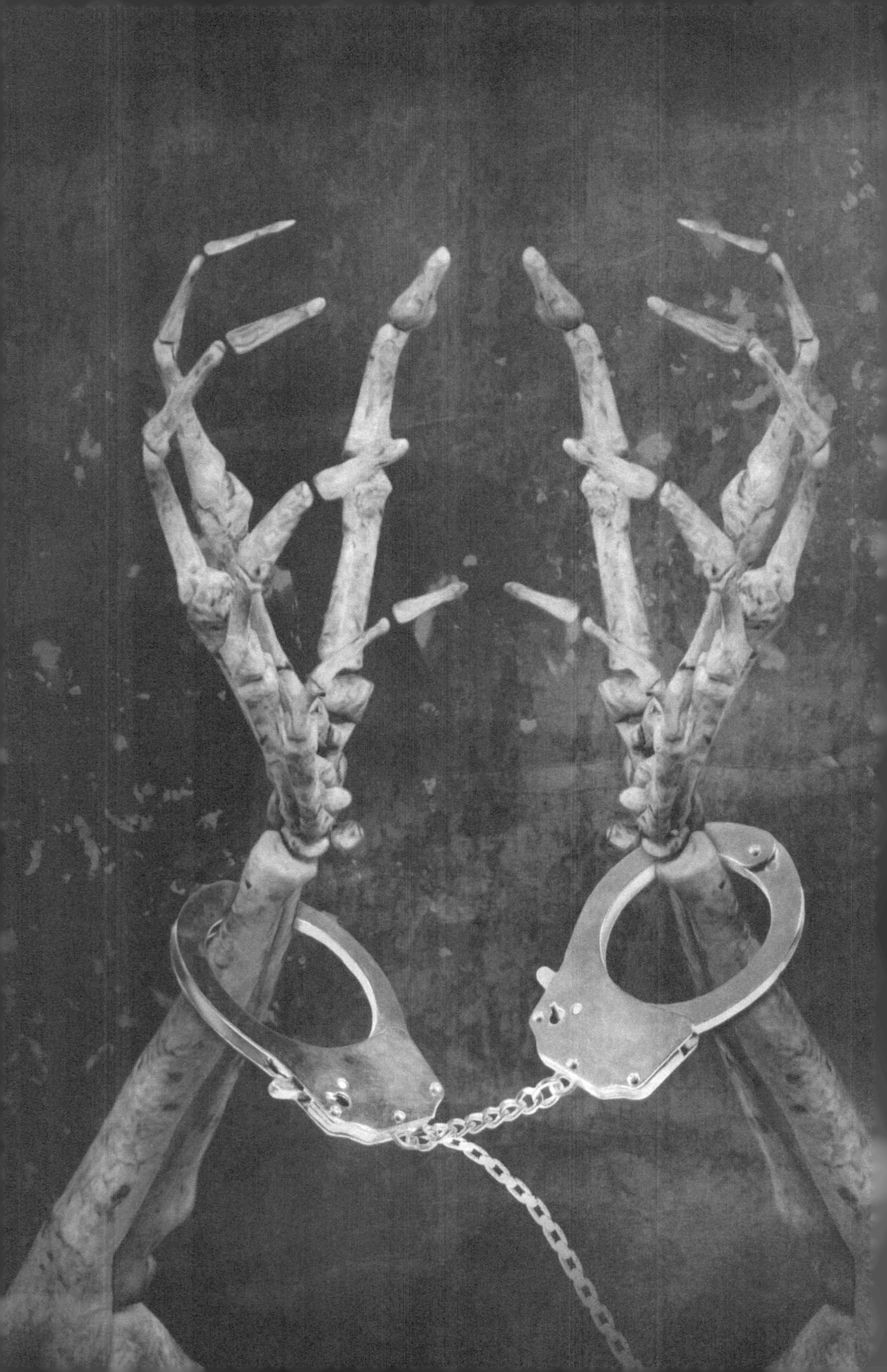

CHAPTER 4

GIANNI

"Are you sure this is the place?" I peered through the front windscreen at the small cottage.

"This is the address my contact gave us," Damon replied. "He's always been reliable before. No reason to think any different now." He didn't look as convinced as he sounded.

"No offence, but we have every reason to think other people might not be reliable right now," I said. "Including your contacts."

I thought about adding, 'especially your contacts,' but didn't. Judging by the expression on his face, he knew what I was thinking. That was enough to get a rise out of him. Or at least a scowl.

I grinned at him. He was adorable when he scowled.

"This is the place," Damon said with more certainty. There was nothing like having his professionalism questioned, to make him double down. "Do you really think I'd bring Mina here if I hadn't sent people ahead to check it out?"

"Of course not," I said. I glanced over to where she sat in the front passenger seat, beside him. She was even more adorable. In a deadly, kick ass kind of way.

The moment I saw her in that cage, I was head over heels for her. Seeing her change from a frightened, malnourished bird, into the confident woman she was becoming, was a delight. She was a bud then. Now she was a flower. The kind that thrived in the face of chaos and death. Not unlike me.

"What do you know about her?" Mina directed the question to Damon.

"Not a lot," Damon admitted. "I guess we're going to find out." He placed his hand on the door handle. "You can stay here if you want to." He knew he had as much chance of her staying behind as night becoming day, but he wouldn't be him if he didn't say the words.

His love language was reminding people they didn't need to throw themselves into the fire. He'd wade in for them.

She rolled her eyes at him, then got out of the car.

I followed right behind her. I wasn't going to let her out of my sight if I could help it. If this went south, I'd put myself between her and any shit that arose.

Yes, I'm fully aware she didn't need me to do that, but it's who I am. I protect the people I love, as much as Damon and Reuben do.

"We could have sent the twins to do this," I remarked. "It is basically their job to be lackeys."

If they were here, they'd give me shit for saying something like that. Lucky for me, they weren't. Although, it was nothing I couldn't handle if they were. The pair were like younger brothers to me. In fact, they were better younger brothers than my actual brothers. Which I'd never tell them, because they'd get huge heads. Given their already healthy egos, they didn't need the boost.

"I want to talk to her in person," Mina said. "If she knows anything, I want to hear it."

"Fair enough, sweetheart." I took her hand and tucked her in to my side, where she fit like we were made to go together. Two pieces in a complicated and sometimes crazy puzzle. "Damon and I understand that, right Damon?"

He pressed his kissable lips together in a line and gave half a shrug, but didn't disagree. He didn't agree either, because he was Damon. He never could, or would make things that easy.

Including our relationship.

I would happily have kissed him again by now, but I was giving him time to process how wonderful the last time was. The electricity that sparked between us was unexpected, in spite of the attraction we'd had bubbling between us for a long time. He'd deny it, but we both knew it was there.

Just like our attraction to Mina was there. And Damon's attraction to Reuben. I can't deny I admired the man, but Reuben was like a brother to me. He was the one person who saw what I could be, when my family turned their backs on me, and no one else gave a shit. I owed him for that, but Mina and Damon held my heart.

Also, watching Damon fuck Mina, and the idea of him and Reuben together was the stuff of fantasies.

I touched my neck, where she'd drawn blood while riding me, my cock deep inside her. Seeing her surrender to the woman she always wanted to be was indescribable. Incredible.

Mina and I followed Damon up to the front door of the cottage and waited while he tapped.

"I can't help remembering the last time we approached a house like this," I remarked.

Mina gave me a look. "If this one explodes, I'm going to be really pissed off."

"Be pissed off at Damon, he's the one who sent people ahead of us. If we die, it—"

"Won't be my fault," Damon interrupted. "They checked the place out thoroughly. There are no bombs here."

"There are guns though," I said as the cottage door opened and a hand emerged, finger on the trigger, barrel pointed at Damon's temple.

"What do you want?" a female voice came from behind the door.

"Just some information," Damon said as though not even slightly concerned she might be about to blow his brains out. "We're willing to pay for it."

"Information about what?" The gun didn't move.

"Just the whereabouts of a couple of people," Mina said.

"We have cash," I said.

The gun dropped and the door opened to reveal a woman in her mid thirties, with bright pink hair. "Why didn't you say so? Come in." She stepped back to let us enter the cottage.

Like her, the cottage was brightly coloured, with an array of mismatched furniture, rainbow coloured rugs and cushions everywhere. On one wall hung a huge painting of what looked like a cow skull on a bright blue background. On another wall was a similar one with a purple background.

"She must really have a thing for dead cows," I said in Mina's ear.

She choked back a laugh and gave me a pointed look that suggested she prefer I didn't make fun of our hostess's decor. And that I shouldn't say anything that might end with one of us shot.

Damon gave me a similar look before turning back and saying, "You're Martina?"

"That's what they call me," she agreed. "You're Damon Rivello and Gianni Covino. And…" She looked at Mina.

"Yes we are," Damon said before Mina could introduce herself. "We're looking for people named Jase and Hammer. They both used to work for a man named Kurt Lasalle."

The moment Damon said his name, Martina looked disgusted. If we were outside, she probably would have spat on the ground.

"If you're friends of Kurt…"

"We're not," I said quickly. Ewww. We had better taste than that.

"Far from it. If you happen to know where he is, we'd appreciate that too. Obviously we'd pay for it."

"Obviously," she agreed. "I have no idea where that son of a motherfucking prick is. If I did, he'd be running for the hills. Backstabbing, two-faced piece of crap he is."

"I see you've met him," I said. "That's a very accurate description."

"I heard some disturbing as fuck rumours about him." She sat down on the middle of a bright orange couch, which happened to be the only place in the room to sit. "Something about keeping a woman chained in a basement?"

I squeezed Mina's hand, but glanced at Damon, deliberately not looking at her. I could tell what he was thinking. Caleb and the twins' gossip had started to spread already. Quicker than I thought it would.

"We heard something to that effect," Damon said. "It seems as though Jase and Hammer had a hand in that too. Which is another reason why we'd like to get our hands on them."

"What's the main reason?" She squinted and looked at us with suspicious, hazel eyes.

"The usual," I said. "Double-crossing the men they're supposed to be working for. And, believe it or not, Jase might have knocked up my sister and run."

Martina again looked like she was going to spit. "Cowardly piece of shit. I hate men like that. Did you know one hundred percent of babies are caused by cum? That only comes from one place. Men need to take responsibility for where they nut." She shook a finger at me and Damon.

I held up my hands to either side. "I would never get a girl pregnant and run." The first bit, yes, not the second. Like she said, every baby was caused by a man ejaculating. I'd always take responsibility for it, if it happened.

"She looks like she knows how to hunt you down." Martina looked over to Mina and nodded approvingly.

Mina smiled. "That I do," she agreed. "But like he said, he wouldn't run." She glanced over to Damon meaningfully.

He sighed. "Neither would I. Can we get back to the reason we're here? I realise it's not much to go on, but if you know anyone by those names, and where they might be, we'd be grateful."

"How grateful?" She held out her hand, palm up.

I pulled out my wallet and peeled out a pile of hundred dollar notes. I handed half of them to her and kept the other half. "Very grateful."

"I'll see what I can find out," she said. "Anyone named Jase is going to be difficult, obviously. But most men don't have the level of insecurity you need to refer to themselves as Hammer."

I grinned at her assumption, which was probably correct. Why would you use a nickname like that unless you were trying to compensate?

"I doubt too many people with that nickname worked with Kurt," Damon said.

"Probably not," Martina agreed. "It sounds like a match made in heaven to me. A pair of gutless men."

"They are also associated with Leon Graves," Mina said.

"Sounds like the Triad of Tiny Dicks to me," Martina said. "Leon is as gutless as a jellyfish. Not as smart though. He does like to throw his cash around, I'll give him that."

"Can I ask what Kurt did to you?" Mina asked. "You seem to hate him as much as we do."

"Before or after I found out about the woman in the basement?" Martina asked. She exhaled loudly. "He's the kind of man who uses people until he doesn't find them useful anymore, then he'll give out our identity to people who shouldn't have it."

She pointed a finger at us again. "I know what you're thinking. A woman with bright pink hair isn't trying to hide. I don't mean that he told people about what I do for a living. I have people in my past I don't want in my present. Or my future. He thought it was wise to swap my whereabouts for money. Or favours, or... Whatever. They came after me and I had to deal with them. Because of him. He thinks he's above the rest of us. The truth is, he has his own agenda and he doesn't give a fuck who he steps on to get there."

"What agenda is that?" I asked.

"Fucked if I know." She shrugged. "He'll do anything to get ahead. Fuck over anyone. Apparently he was fixated on some woman who rejected him. He seemed to lose it after that. If he ever had it."

I looked sideways to Mina, whose gaze seemed to be locked on a spot on the floor.

This couldn't have been easy for her, listening to us talk about him. I wished I could erase every memory of him that resided in her head, to take away all the pain he'd inflicted on her. And, preferably, give it all to him.

"That sounds like Kurt," Damon agreed. "So, you'll get back to us on finding Jase and Hammer?"

"Oh, I already know where, or rather, who Hammer is," she said. She cocked her head at Damon. "And so do you."

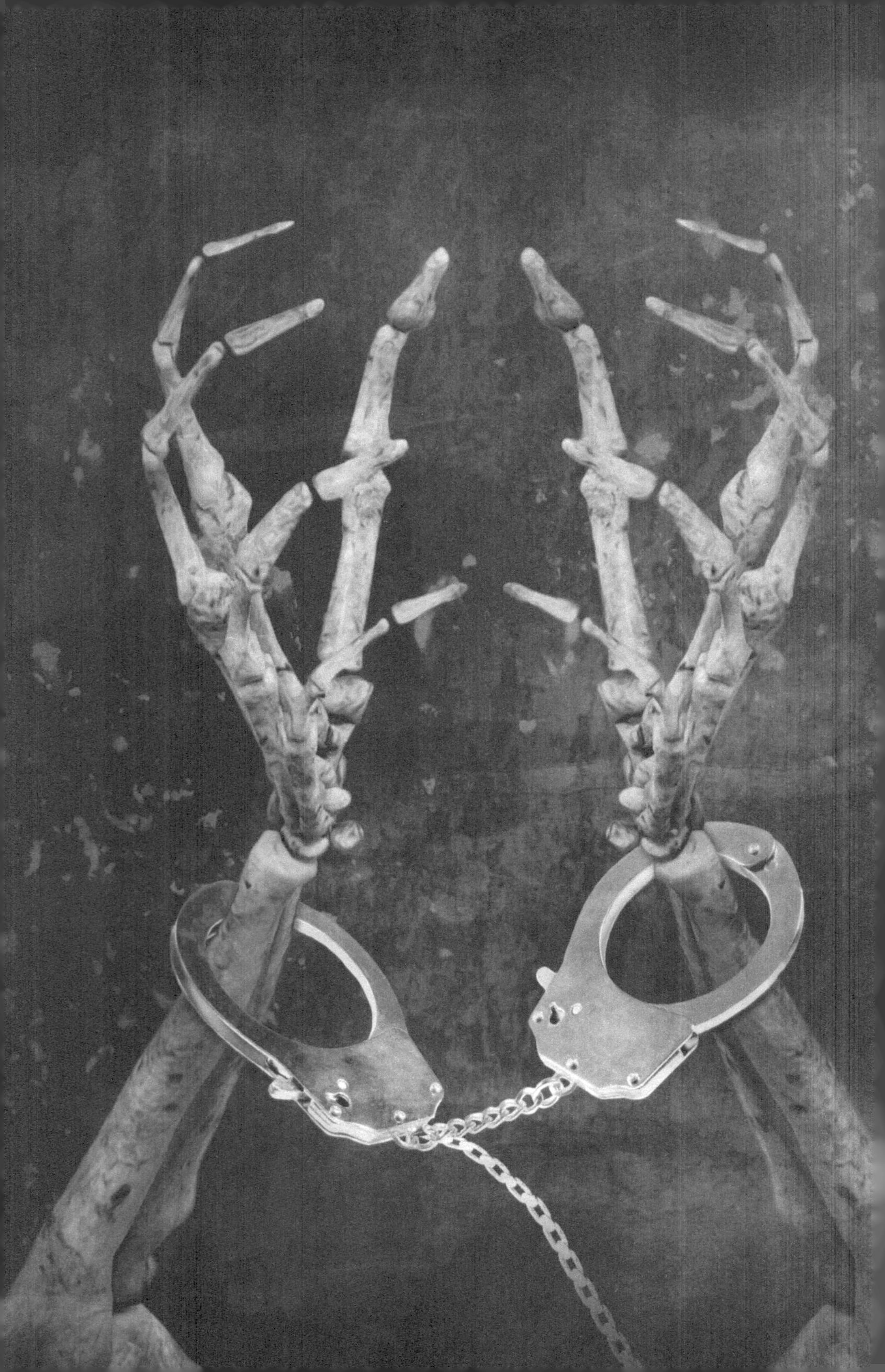

CHAPTER 5

MINA

I stepped out the back door of Reuben's house and headed toward the cliff. The breeze whipped my hair around my face. I pushed it back and turned my face into the wind.

Damon stood at the edge of the cliff, arms crossed, staring out at the ocean. His back was dead straight, eyes glazed like he saw nothing.

"What he did wasn't your fault," I said once I was close enough for him to hear. "You know that, right? You're not responsible for the actions of anyone else."

Damon spoke without turning towards me, his expression unchanged. "He's my brother. I should have been keeping track of him better. Enzo was always a hothead. Always the one getting into trouble. I'm his older brother, I should have…" He trailed off.

"Do you blame my older brothers for not knowing what happened to me?" I asked.

He was determined to take responsibility, but as far as I was concerned, it wasn't his to take. From what I remembered of Hammer, or Enzo, he knew what he was doing.

"Honestly?" Damon said. "Yes I do. Dane in particular. He was the oldest son. He's ambitious. If anyone should have known what your father was up to, he should. And if he didn't know, then he shouldn't have believed what your father said about you running off and getting married. Fuck, Rose should have known. *I* should have known."

I put a hand on his shoulder. "Is that what this is about? If you happened to be keeping track of your brother's whereabouts on one particular day, you might have stopped them from caging me?"

"I could have," he agreed.

"You could have tried," I said. "But it didn't get Gage Prior anything but dead."

I thought back to Caleb's reaction. I wouldn't have thought he was capable of being rattled until then. He must have had a close relationship with the other man.

Damon grunted. "I'm harder to kill. And I wouldn't have been alone."

"You might have gotten Gianni killed too," I said lightly.

"I'll deny ever having said this, but he's harder to kill than I am," Damon said grudgingly.

"Why do I think you know that because you tried?" I teased.

That drew a faint smile from him, which was about as much smile as anyone ever saw on him or Reuben. Gianni seemed to have enough for the three of them.

"I'll deny that too," Damon said before exhaling softly and turning back towards the view. "Enzo was the wild one in the family. He was always getting into trouble. He got suspended from school and thought it was hilarious. More time to run around with his friends and get up to shit. He was back for two days before he got expelled. He lasted a week or two at a new school before they kicked him out too. He was sixteen when Dad threw him out of the house. I let him live with me, but I couldn't control him either. In the end, I gave him two choices. Work for Reuben, or go to jail."

I slipped an arm around his waist. "I guess he chose to work for Reuben?"

"He did, and for a while he was…better. He seemed to enjoy what he was doing. He got paid to break the law, and beat the shit out of people. He always struggled when it came to taking orders, but I tried to be sure he was doing things that fit with his—for want of a better word—skillset."

"It sounds like you did everything you could," I said. "If he was determined to be an asshole, that's on him. That's his choice. There's only so much you can do for people who don't give a shit."

"Yeah, but I should have tried harder. I could have kicked his ass more often. I could have done more to make sure he didn't end up working for Kurt instead." He dug the tips of his fingers under his opposite armpits.

"Correct me if I'm wrong, but Reuben would only have put up with so much bullshit before he lost patience with Enzo. His father seemed to have even less than he does."

From what I remembered of Reuben's father, he had a short temper and a world class scowl. Reuben was a pussycat in comparison.

"That's right," Damon said grudgingly. "Enzo wouldn't have lasted unless someone got him under control. I should have been able to do that. He's my fucking brother."

"You're right," I said. "It's totally your fault. You should have fit him with a shock collar and an ankle monitor. Then, the moment he put a toe out of line, you would have known. Hell, you should have kept him on a leash. Maybe one of those backpack ones people use with kids who like to run off."

Damon glanced at me, blue eyes narrowed.

"There's nothing you could have done that would have stopped him from doing what he did," I insisted. "He made the choice. He woke up that morning and decided to work with Kurt. He went along with everything he was told to go along with. Him, not you. Just because you're related doesn't mean you have any control over him, or any obligation to blame yourself for his decisions. Even if you did, it's in the past. Nothing that happened back then can be changed now. The only thing we have any control over is ourselves and the future."

He regarded me, his expression softened. "You're going to want to kill him, aren't you?"

"For his part in that day, yes," I said simply. "Leon could have come to you and told you about me, and so could Enzo. But he didn't. That was another choice he made." I exhaled through my nose. "When was the last time you saw him?"

For a moment, I thought he might not tell me. Damon might have a brotherly need to protect his younger sibling. Even if that came between us.

"A few months ago," he said finally. "At our father's funeral. I didn't think he'd come, because they hated each other, but he turned up and stood at the edge of the crowd. He was only there for a few minutes, then he left. I think he just wanted to make sure Dad was gone."

"Were you close?" I asked gently.

Damon grunt-laughed, the closest to a sound of amusement I'd heard from him.

"No, he was an absolute prick. His idea of raising boys was to belt the shit out of us when he decided we did something wrong. That's also the kind of husband he was. It took years for me to ask Reuben to have him killed. He was dead the next day."

"Sounds like the world is a better place without him," I said.

"Accurate," he replied. "Enzo got his temper. I got his charm."

I leaned my head against his shoulder. "You're an asshole, but you're not as big an asshole as him."

"You sure about that?" He wrapped an arm around me. "Gianni might disagree with that."

"Gianni adores you and, as far as I can tell, he's a good judge of character," I said firmly. "But don't let that go to your head or anything."

"Not a chance," Damon said.

We stood in silence for a while, staring at the ocean as the wind whipped past us.

Finally, reluctantly I asked, "Do you know where he is now? Or his friend Jase? Would either of them know where to find Kurt?"

"I have no idea who Jase is," Damon said. "As for Enzo, I can think of a couple of places he might be. Places I prefer you not go."

"Because I might accidentally kill him?" I asked coolly. There'd be nothing accidental about it, but we both knew that.

"No, because I don't want to take you into the snakes' den. There are far worse people out there than us. If he's where I think he is—The Vipers are a ruthless cartel. They receive drug and weapon shipments from us. Other things too, from time to time." He didn't elaborate on that and I didn't ask.

He continued, brow lightly creased. "They're just as likely to kill you on sight as to welcome you in the door."

"But they won't shoot *you* on sight?" I asked. "Surely they won't shoot anyone in your company?"

Okay, I wasn't that naïve. People like that always had their own reasons for doing the things they did. They may kill me just to remind Damon not to bring anyone next time. Or for a lesser reason.

"I wouldn't take that bet. Their only allegiance is to themselves. They wouldn't kill me because we have an established network. If I was dead, that would inconvenience them. So much so, they'd probably kill whoever killed me. Like I said, they're ruthless."

"They don't sound like anything I can't handle," I said easily. "I'm also not easy to kill, remember?"

"I'm aware," he said softly. "I'll think about it. Reuben will also have an opinion. If he orders me not to take you anywhere near them, then I won't." The set of his jaw said that would be an end to the matter.

I nodded. That was as far as I'd get right now. Arguing the matter wouldn't change it.

Until now, I'd managed to stay clear of most of the known cartels, unless I was doing a job for them. Which was rare. They tended to do their own killing. The only time they needed an assassin was when they wanted to eradicate competition within their own cartel, and wanted to avoid all-out war.

In those circumstances, I had to make the hit look like an accident. That way, those who wanted to could pretend they didn't know anything. If anyone objected, they'd have a hard time proving who was actually behind it.

If I was honest with myself, proving it would be more than difficult. It would be impossible. I was good at what I did. Too good to make a mess with those jobs, or leave evidence. They were always a challenge, but I enjoyed them for exactly that reason. They gave me the chance to push myself to try new things.

"So, how brave are you?" he asked. He unwound his arm from around me, took my hand and stepped closer to the edge of the cliff.

I followed him carefully and peered down into the water below. "Depends. How deep is it?" I couldn't see sand or rocks, just relentless waves that struck the rocks over and over, wearing it down bit by bit.

"Deep enough." He dropped my hand and pulled his shirt off over his head. He tossed it aside on the grass. His shoes and pants followed, until he was down to his boxer briefs.

"You've jumped off here before?" It was a long way down, and if he was wrong about the depth of the water, the landing would suck. Only for a moment, because it would probably kill us.

Caleb hadn't threatened to throw the twins over for nothing.

"Nope," he said easily. "Never."

"You're not just an asshole, you're a crazy asshole," I told him. In spite of that, I stripped down to my underwear and walked right to the edge, until there was nothing under the tips of my toes.

"You know what they say. What doesn't kill us makes us stronger." He actually seemed to be enjoying this.

"If I die, I will haunt you." I grabbed his hand and pulled him close to me. If I was going, he was definitely going with me.

"Deal." He actually smiled right before we both jumped off the cliff, plunged down and landed with a splash in the ocean.

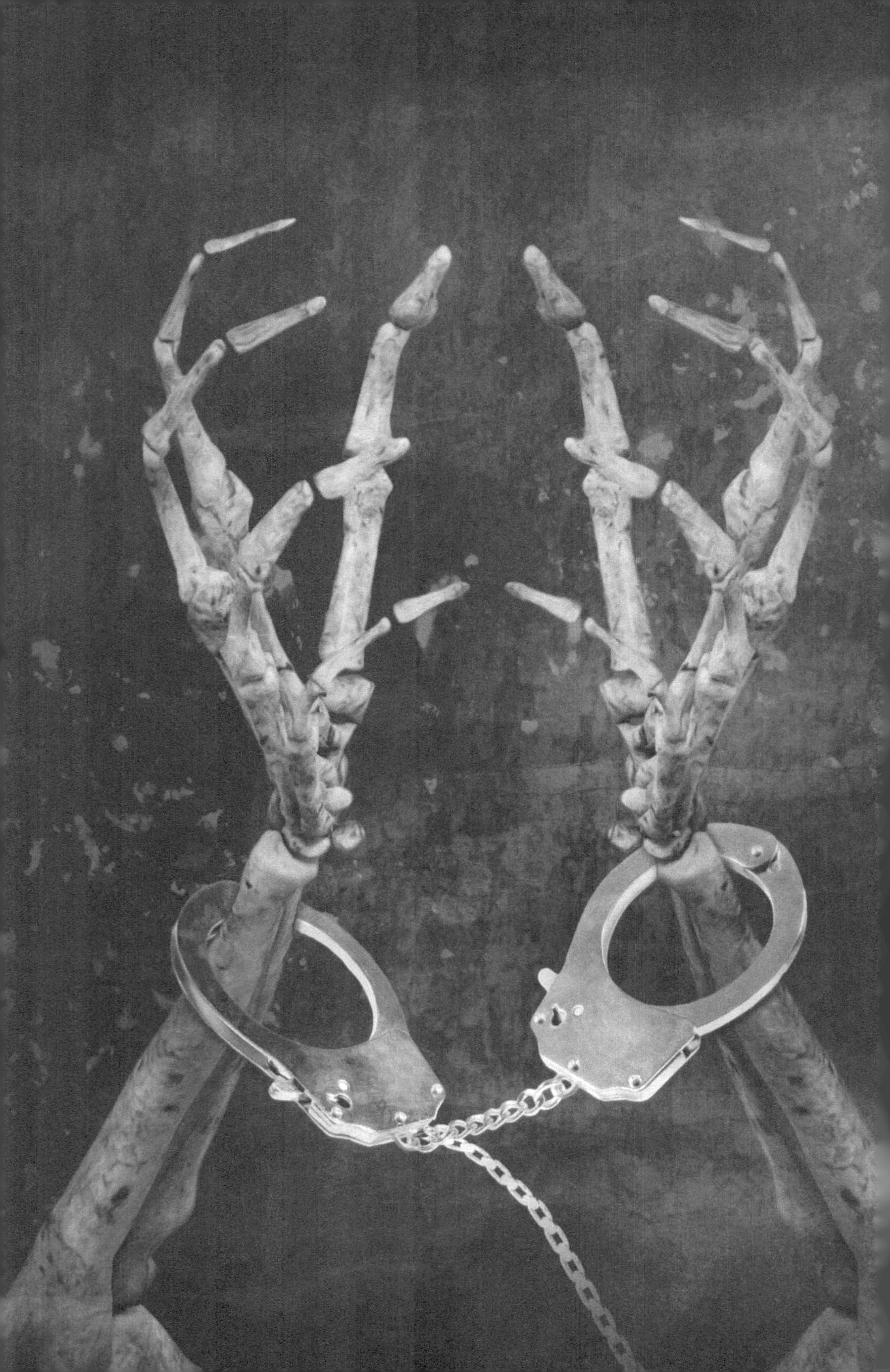

CHAPTER 6

MINA

"That was exhilarating," I said as we walked up the track that led to the house.

After a moment of terror that we might actually die after all, the water was more than deep enough. I'd plunged in hard before swimming back to the surface and popping out between the waves.

My heart was still racing. I couldn't remember the last time I did something like that. Something that wasn't planned, that had my adrenaline spiking like crazy. The pure rush made me want to do it over and over.

That faded when we reached the top of the track and saw Reuben was waiting, his expression a cross between stone and thunder.

"What the fuck were you doing?" He didn't snap or snarl, he didn't need to. His icy tone was enough to chase the smile from my face.

"Just jumping off the cliff, boss." Damon draped an arm over my shoulder, as though he needed to protect me from Reuben's anger. He was more likely to need protection from it himself. The majority of Reuben's fury was directed at him. Especially when he added, "You should try it."

Reuben's jaw twitched. He looked as though he was trying to form the correct response, but there wasn't one for this situation. We hadn't died, but we'd obviously given him a nasty shock.

Finally, he started to relax.

"When I saw you jump, I thought..." Apparently not caring that I was wet, he stepped towards me and placed his hands on my shoulders.

"We're fine," I assured him. "The water was deep and the tide's in. We wouldn't have jumped otherwise."

Did he really think we wanted to take our own lives? Evidently, he did. Or at least, assumed, when we disappeared over the side.

He wrapped his arms around me and held me tight, like he might keep me from jumping again.

I pressed my head against his chest and listened to his heart beat rapidly. Gradually, it began to slow to a normal pace. Strong, like everything about him.

"Don't do that again," he whispered. That was as close as he'd ever come to admitting he was scared of anything. "I lost you once. I'm not losing you because you jump off a fucking cliff."

"We didn't mean to worry you," I whispered back. "It was spontaneous." I tilted my head back and looked up at him. "We'll warn you next time."

Instead of answering with words, he brushed his lips over mine. Feather light, with a hint of stubble.

In that moment, I realised I was standing outside the house in the fading light, dressed only in my underwear. Rather than feeling vulnerable, I was aroused. My nipples, already hard from the cold, became harder still.

I deepened the kiss and wound my arms around his neck.

I sensed movement behind me before Damon placed his hands on my waist and stepped up to let his erection graze the side of my hip. I found myself pressed between both of them.

My pulse ratcheted up. If my panties weren't already wet, they'd be dripping now. I was surrounded by so much hot muscle. At the same time, I knew if I stepped away, they'd let me go. If I felt uncomfortable, they'd stop.

I didn't want them to stop.

One by one, I started to slide the buttons on Reuben's shirt out of their holes.

"Mina…" he said softly.

"I want this," I said. "Please."

It was Damon who unhooked my bra. I dropped my arms from Reuben long enough for the straps to slip down my arms, onto the ground.

Damon pressed the palms of his hand to my belly, then up to cup my breasts. He palmed my nipples until I groaned softly.

I pushed off Reuben's shirt and ran my hands up and down his rock hard abs and chest.

"We shouldn't do this here," Reuben said, his voice as strained as the front of his pants.

He swallowed audibly and led us over to a covered patio, surrounded on three sides by lattice and vines. The fourth was open to the ocean. In the centre of the patio, was a plush outdoor rug and a massive daybed.

He laid me back on the daybed, him on one side, Damon on the other.

Damon placed his thumb and forefinger on my chin and turned my face to him so he could kiss me.

Reuben hooked his fingers on the top of my panties and pulled them down my legs and off my feet. He scooted down, parted my legs gently and, eyes on mine, dipped his face down between them. Gripping my thighs with gentle hands, he started to explore and tease my pussy with his tongue.

Damon used his own tongue to taste mine, my lips, my throat, my neck, down to my breasts. He traced circles around my ruined nipple with the tip of one finger, while gently suckling the other.

I moaned, long and low with the sensations of pleasure already washing over me deeper than the waves. Pushing me to heights bigger than the cliff.

"You like that?" Damon asked, around a mouthful of my sensitive flesh.

Reuben chose that moment to graze his teeth over my clit. My response was another moan and a full body shiver of delight.

"I asked you a question," Damon said more firmly. He lifted his face from me and looked at me like he expected a coherent response.

"Yes," I gasped. "Yes, I like all of it."

"Good girl." He went back to sucking, like my nipple was the most delicious thing he ever had in his mouth.

Any time any of the guys called me that, it got me going like crazy. I couldn't remember anyone having ever said that to me before and I loved it.

"Are you close?" Damon asked after a couple of minutes of spoiling my sensitive nipple, while not ignoring the other one. He seemed to like both of them equally, like Reuben did. Like Gianni did, too.

"So close," I panted. "So… Close… So…ahhh…" I arched my back as I came against Reuben's mouth.

I came so hard I might have caught a glimpse of stars in some distant universe. A universe where nothing existed but orgasms, and the stroke of his tongue on my clit.

I didn't ever want to leave that paradisiacal universe, but gradually, I floated back down to this one.

"You're so fucking perfect when you come," Reuben said. "Good girl."

I blinked a couple of times to clear my vision. "I want you," I said. "Please."

"She asks so nicely," Damon said.

"She does," Reuben agreed. He shed his pants and black silk boxers and tossed them aside. Eyes on me, he crawled up the daybed and kissed my mouth, so I could taste my release on his lips.

He gripped my hips and rolled us over so I was straddling him, his erection nestled between my thighs.

"Be a good girl and ride the boss," Damon said.

I glanced over at him and kept my eyes on his as I lowered myself onto Reuben's cock. "Be a good boy and take your pants off. Let me taste you."

Damon's eyes widened, but he hurried to do what I told him to. He knelt beside me and stroked his hand up and down his cock a couple of times before I opened my mouth to let him slide inside.

In the corner of my eye, I was aware of Reuben watching us both. I wasn't sure if I imagined him getting harder inside me. I was certainly aroused again.

I placed my hands on Reuben's chest and pushed myself up, sliding almost all the way off his cock, then down again.

He gripped my hips with his large hands and helped to guide me up and down, while he thrust up into me at the same time.

"You feel like heaven," he whispered. "I knew you would. I've waited so long… You're more than I imagined."

He had. He'd waited patiently for years for this.

I couldn't think of a more perfect place for our first time together. The waves crashed against the cliff, in time with his thrusts. The breeze blew off the ocean, cooling the sweat on my skin as it rose. The setting sun turned the water and the sky pink and orange, like it was celebrating with us.

I could only smile in response and massage Damon's balls while I sucked and teased him with my tongue. His cock was warm, smooth but hard, throbbing between my lips. Salty and sweet at the same time.

Reuben's cock was thick in my pussy, filling me like he too was made to fit inside me.

"Good girl," Damon soothed. "You take both of our cocks so well. You suck so beautifully. So fucking perfect."

Reuben hummed his agreement. "So fucking ours."

So fucking yours, I agreed silently.

I closed my eyes and focused on keeping the rhythm of sucks and thrusts, my breasts bouncing each time I rolled my hips.

"Do you want to taste Damon's cum?" Reuben asked.

Without stopping, I nodded.

I opened my eyes and locked them on Damon as his crossed and he started to pound harder into my mouth.

Finally, he grunted and his body went still. He squirted a mouthful of salty cum so hard and fast, I had to swallow before it went down my throat too quickly.

Puffing lightly, he slid his cock out of my mouth and flopped down beside us, his head right beside Reuben's.

They were both aware of that fact. They kept side eyeing each other without quite looking.

Would they act on their attraction? Did I dare to ask them to? I didn't want to push them into anything they weren't ready for, but I was aching to see them touch.

"If you wanted to…" I started tentatively.

"Tell us what you want," Reuben said, his voice low and husky.

Fuck yes, but I was still tentative. Still not wanting to press too hard.

"I want you to kiss each other," I whispered.

They turned and locked eyes. As if some kind of dam broke, they moved their faces until their lips met. Their first kiss was light, barely more than a brush of lips.

Then Damon cupped the back of Reuben's head and kissed him like he'd been aching to do it for his entire life. Like he was scared he'd never get another chance, so he might as well make this count.

But then, Reuben was kissing him back with lips and tongue. The only sound apart from the waves was the wetness of their kisses. They went on kissing as Reuben came inside my body, thrusting hard, and moaning against Damon's mouth.

I felt the warmth of his cum flooding inside me, like Damon's had in my mouth. I savoured every drop, knowing I did that to him. My body gave him pleasure, the way he gave it to me. The friction we created together, gave him an orgasm, moments of bliss he'd waited so long to experience.

That drew another orgasm from me, more intense than the first. I tipped my head back and cried out with pure pleasure, every sense tingling throughout my entire body. This time, it lasted and lasted, until I could almost reach out and grab that other universe.

With a gasp, I finally plummeted back down to reality, which was almost as incredible as a pleasure universe.

Only then did they pull apart and sag against the mattress of the daybed.

I slumped over Reuben, one hand his chest and the other on Damon's. They were both panting slightly, their hearts racing, skin damp with sweat in spite of the breeze. At the same time, rock hard and mine.

"That was…wonderful," I said between breaths. "Thank you."

"We should be thanking you," Damon said. He looked like he couldn't quite believe what had happened. Any of it.

Reuben had a similar expression on his face. Not regret, but something else. Relief, but with a hint of concern that this might change everything forever.

It probably would, but we'd figure that out together.

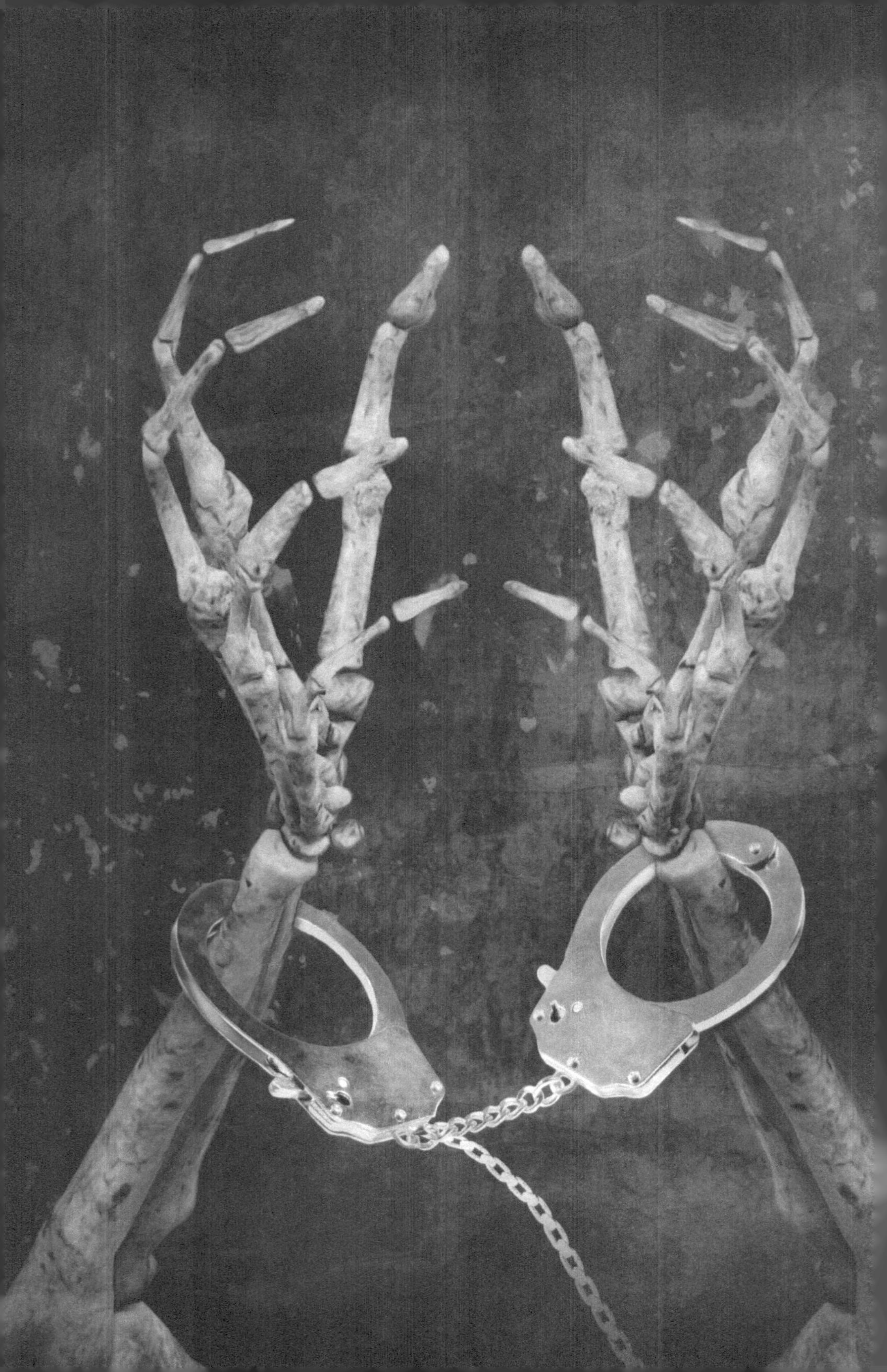

CHAPTER 7

GIANNI

Terry moved around the large kitchen, grumbling to himself under his breath. Every so often, he'd glance at us, Reuben in particular, with disapproval in his eyes. Not at anything we were doing, or talking about, but at him being uprooted from Sydney to come to Dusk Bay. He knew, as well as we did, that we couldn't function without him, but he was very much a creature of habit. That included knowing where everything was. Every time he came here, he had to rearrange everything in the kitchen to suit himself.

Ultimately, that was the prime source of his annoyance. The staff who worked here in our absence didn't leave things where he put them.

I patted him on the shoulder on the way to grab a fresh cup of coffee. "Maybe we should lock the cabinets when we leave."

He grunted his agreement and trudged off with a stack of plates.

I smiled to myself, picked up my coffee and carried it into the office. The air between everyone inside had changed since we were here last.

Reuben and Damon kept glancing at each other awkwardly. In between that, Reuben looked at Mina like he'd won the lottery. Considering he didn't need to play, because he had plenty of money, I assumed they'd fucked.

Good for them. It was about time.

I slipped into a chair just as Damon said something about the Vipers.

"If he's there, we need to speak to them," Damon was saying.

It took a moment for my brain to catch up to what he was saying. "You think Enzo is working with them?"

When it came to Damon's brother, I was as conflicted as everyone else in the room. I wanted to kill him on Mina's behalf, or at least hold him down while she did it. I also didn't want to cause a rift between either of us, and Damon by killing his brother.

"He has in the past," Damon said. "They'll know where he is, if anyone does. They're his kind of people."

"Riffraff?" I suggested.

Not that I was perfect, but the Vipers were a special breed of asshole. The kind that left their morals at the door. I was aware that we took part in human trafficking from time to time, but the Vipers put in orders for the kinds of people—usually women—they wanted to receive. I tried not to think too much about what happened to them after that, but I knew they had a lot more freedom than Mina was afforded.

Usually.

"Exactly," Reuben remarked. He rubbed his chin. For the first time in a long time, he actually looked relaxed. For him, that meant slightly less wound up than usual. Definitely the look of a man who got laid.

I glanced over to Mina, who sat on the couch near the window which was usually occupied by the twins. Her legs were crossed at her knees, eyes half closed as if she wasn't paying attention.

I knew better. She was listening to everything we said and everything we didn't say. Taking in every nuance and every movement. If things went to hell, she'd move in a heartbeat. Faster than a heartbeat.

I let my gaze linger on her, appreciating the sight. She was so fucking gorgeous, she sucked the breath out of my body.

I raised my hand to my neck and brushed the pad of my thumb across the healing wounds around my throat. Picturing her with the knife while she rode me made me harder than diamonds in a heartbeat. Just when I thought she couldn't surprise me, she went and did something like that. I had a feeling I'd still be uncovering layers of her until the day I died. She was fascinating and complex. I loved that about her.

My attention returned to Reuben as he spoke.

"We'll all go," he said finally. "They won't kill me, that would be too messy."

"If they know Mina is looking to kill Enzo, they might—" Damon started to push himself up from his chair.

"Then we don't tell them," Reuben interrupted. "You're looking for your brother. That's all they need to know."

Damon sank back down with a gusty exhale. "I don't trust them with her."

"That's why we're all going," Reuben said. "They won't get past us."

"Let them try," I said. I wasn't afraid of a bunch of street thugs. "I don't mind handing them their asses."

"This would be better if I went by myself," Damon said. One last attempt to change Reuben's mind, albeit a weak one. He was defeated and he knew it, but he wasn't going down without a final swing. "I can talk to them."

"They won't say no to me," Reuben said, effectively ending the conversation.

***

"No." Carlos Jones looked Reuben right in the eyes, arms crossed over his burly chest, chin jutting out like a dare. "I cannot give out the whereabouts of anyone who works for me."

"You mean, you will not," I said.

Carlos' eyes barely moved. "Same thing."

We'd been given a cool welcome to the Vipers' headquarters, which was little more than a warehouse beside the Dusk Bay docks. Several members of the cartel gave us dubious looks and a wide berth, as a young man led us to the cartel's leader.

A short, stocky man in his mid-forties, the only place he had no visible ink was his face. He didn't need it; the scars across his forehead and cheeks were enough decoration. They made him look exactly like what he was. The kind of man women should cross the street to avoid.

Like me, but with less class.

"Enzo is my brother," Damon said. His tone was as icy as Carlos. "I know the cartel rules."

"Don't quote my own rules to me," Carlos snapped. "I wrote them."

I decided that vocalising my surprise at his ability to write was low-lying fruit, even for me. I also strongly suspected that Carlos wouldn't care whose company I was in, if I insulted his intelligence.

Unless he was really, really big, then that was a gun in his pocket. If it wasn't a gun, I was impressed.

"So you're going to ignore them?" Damon asked. "The cartel is supposed to protect brothers. That's what I'm trying to do here."

Beside me, Mina stiffened slightly. I could almost feel her thinking, wondering if that was Damon's agenda. If anyone else was aware of a response, I saw no sign. They were too busy trying to out testosterone each other.

"In the cartel, brother doesn't mean blood," Carlos said. "It means we protect the brothers of our allegiance. Our brother Vipers. Blood means shit." He spat on the concrete floor beside Reuben's shoe.

"Name your price," Reuben said. He seemed completely unruffled.

Carlos' jaw moved in irritation. Of course, this was just part of the game. The harder he made it look like we wouldn't get what we wanted, the higher the price.

I doubted there was anything in the world that wasn't for sale if we offered enough. Men like this would sell their own mother if it benefited them and their bank account.

Finally, Carlos jerked his head towards a room to the side of the headquarters that he used for his office. The space was makeshift at best. Trestle tables and folding chairs, a locker to one side that probably contained guns and knives. None of the finesse of our lifestyle.

Which begged the question, why would Enzo prefer to work here than for Reuben? Each to their own.

Carlos sat on one of the tables. It groaned under his weight, but held.

"How much do you want to know where Enzo is? It seems to me you want that a lot. The question is, why?" His gaze slid to Mina, taking her in like she was a piece of meat.

To men like him, women were nothing more than a commodity. A place to put his cock when he needed release.

He jerked his chin toward her. "That's why you brought her? You want to exchange her for him?"

We all anticipated the question, so none of us reacted. None of us even killed him.

Yet.

"That wouldn't be a fair exchange," I said easily. "She's worth more than six or seven of him."

That got Carlos' attention. He looked at her more intently. "You think so?"

"I know so," I said. If he looked at her like that for much longer, I was going to have to relieve him of his eyeballs. Didn't he know it was rude to stare?

"She's not for sale," Reuben growled softly. "We can double your next shipment in return for Enzo."

Carlos failed to contain his surprise at the generous offer. "You really do want him, don't you? If he's worth that much, maybe I should hold out for more."

"Maybe we should kill you and deal with whoever takes your place," Damon said mildly.

Carlos barked a laugh. "You think you'd walk out of here in one piece? I fucking dare you to try." He raised his hands to either side. He was beyond smug.

I would be too if I knew no one would kill me, even if I provoked them. Not openly, anyway. He wasn't stupid enough to turn his back on us, or anyone we might send to kill him later. Which we wouldn't do. Probably.

As long as he served our needs, he could keep breathing. He should be careful not to get too self-important though. That was when people started to make wrong moves.

"Do we have a deal?" Reuben said, clearly impatient.

"I'll take triple," Carlos said. "For four times that, I'll throw in my sister." He chuckled. "You look like you could handle a wildcat like her."

"Triple," Reuben said. "Keep your sister. I have no interest in buying women."

Carlos smirked. He was smart enough not to point out that Reuben didn't seem to have too much trouble selling them. A comment like that would see the price drop back to double. Or the regular price of shipments Carlos bought from us, would suddenly skyrocket. He couldn't afford that and we all knew it.

"Enzo first," Damon said. "Then I'll make the arrangements for the next shipment."

Carlos nodded. He jumped down off the table and sauntered over to the door. "Hades! Get your fucking ass over here."

I couldn't see who he was speaking to, but a male voice responded, followed by the sound of heavy footsteps heading out of the head-quarters.

Damon's expression was tense. The muscles in his face were going to hurt later if he kept them as tight as they were.

I gave him a smile, which he responded to with a nod. That was as much comfort as he was going to accept right now.

Mina appeared less apprehensive, but she was getting better at containing her emotions.

Having only been around Kurt for so long, she'd had to relearn how to interact with other people. Including not flinching when the instinct told her to.

Honestly, I wished I had half of her self-control. Whenever she was in assassin mode, she was as closed a book as Damon or Reuben. Only the slightest twitch of her right hand gave away any hint of what she was feeling. Poised, ready to pull out a knife and use it.

I couldn't see one, but I knew she'd have several on her, within easy reach. Reuben would have insisted before bringing her here, but he wouldn't have needed to. She would have stashed them on her with as little thought as pulling on clothes.

The Vipers weren't given to being welcoming towards women.

I was tempted to suggest we take Carlos' sister, to save her from whatever might happen to her. Chances were, he'd sell her to a rival cartel to make an alliance. If she was the wildcat he suggested she was, she'd be pissed off at him for doing that.

Mina must have sensed my scrutiny. She looked over at me and offered a small smile. I gave her a bigger one in return.

Carlos stepped back into the room. "Seems you're out of luck. Enzo met with the wrong end of a bullet last night. He's dead."

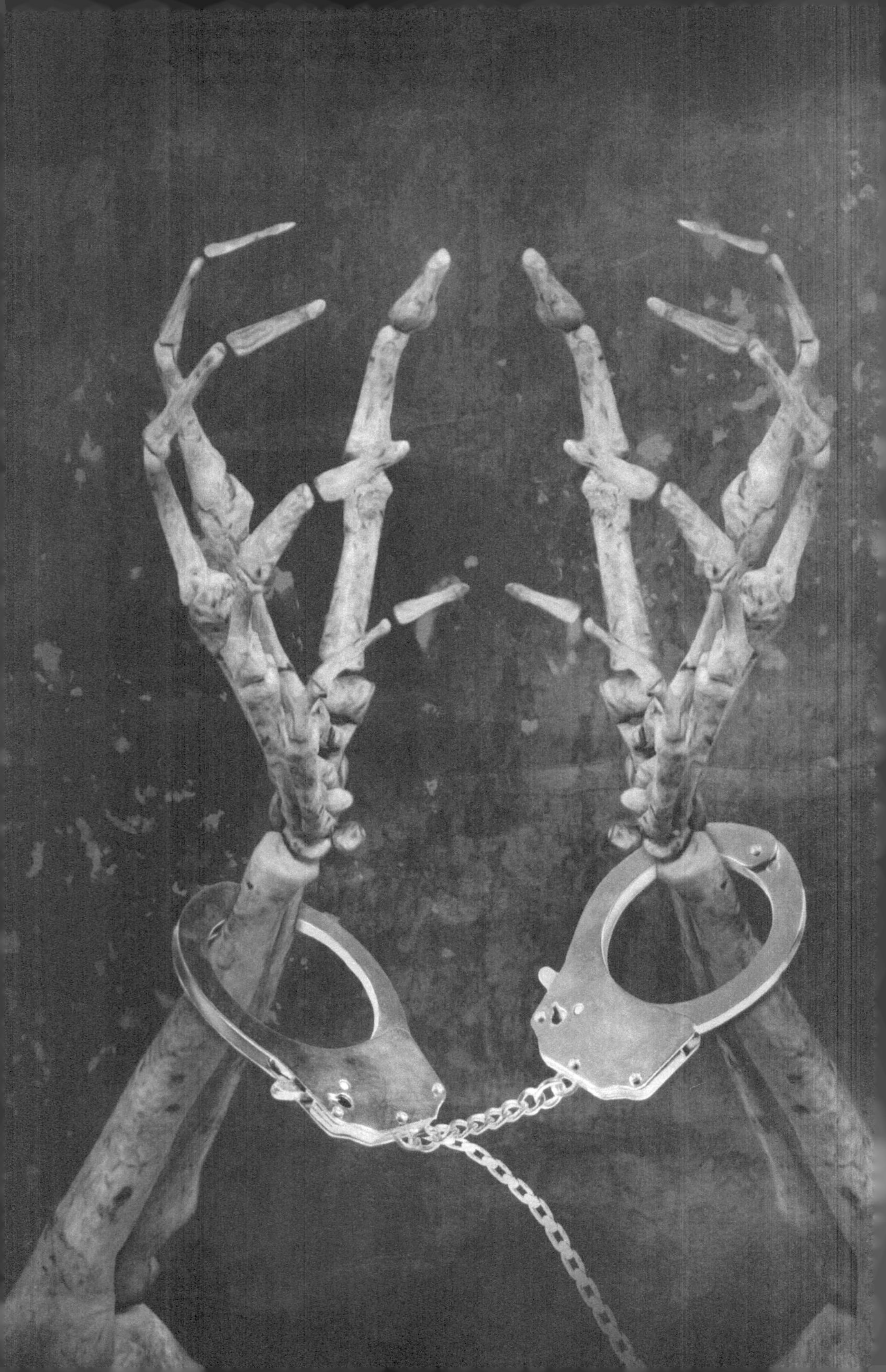

CHAPTER 8

MINA

"Do you believe him?" I asked Damon as we stepped out of the warehouse and toward the ocean. Reuben and Gianni walked ahead of us, both quietly furious on my behalf. How did I feel about being robbed of my revenge? In some ways, this was easier. If Enzo was already dead, Damon couldn't blame me for killing him.

If he was dead.

"Not for a minute," Damon said. "Either he doesn't know where Enzo is and doesn't want to admit it, or he's expecting a bigger payday than we can offer." He looked ready to chew rocks.

"Who from?" Gianni asked over his shoulder. "You don't think Kurt would bother, do you?"

"I don't know," Damon admitted. "It might be that he doesn't know, but I can't see him giving up triple the shipment unless the stakes were really high."

"Maybe Enzo ran off with his sister," I said dryly.

Damon snorted. "She might be better off away from Carlos, but with Enzo…"

"Do you know her?" I asked. I was in no way jealous, but I was curious.

"Angelina Jones? Yeah, I've met her a couple of times," he said.

"Wildcat is accurate. She doesn't take shit from him or anyone. If he'd suggested he'd sell her, she probably would run off. If he survived the night. She's as headstrong as they come."

"It sounds like you admire her," I remarked. Maybe there was a little jealousy there, but they all had a life before me, I knew that. Relationships, lovers. That was the past. It couldn't hurt me now, except to remind me of everything I'd missed out on. That would always sting, no matter how much time passed.

"He's scared of her," Gianni said.

"Fuck off," Damon told him. "I'm not scared of Angie. She's more likely to get a man killed than kill them."

"Carlos would kill Enzo if he ran off with her," I said.

"Very likely," Damon agreed. "He's probably planning to have Enzo meet the wrong end of a bullet as we speak."

I put a hand on his bicep. "I know this isn't how you want things to go."

"He was going to end up dead either way." He shrugged. "At least, this way, I don't have to kill him. And neither do you."

"I would have killed him to save you from doing that," I said.

I'd hesitate, because he was Damon's brother, but when it came down to it, I'd spill his blood if necessary. If it helped me to put the worst of my demons to bed.

"Doesn't she say the sweetest things?" Gianni said. "For the record, I'd kill him for you too."

Damon nodded in response to his offer. "I thought you might."

"I'm sweet that way too," Gianni said. He dropped back to walk on the other side of me.

"You want to find him, don't you?" I asked softly. "You want to find Enzo."

Damon hesitated. "If I don't, I'll never know the truth of what happened. Why did he work for Kurt? Why didn't he try to stop him? He could have convinced Gage Prior, Leon Graves, and Jase to overpower him. Lasalle wasn't a match for four other people. Five if you were conscious." Regret flashed through his eyes. "He also might know where Kurt is."

"Is there any chance he ran because he was scared he'd be associated with Kurt after the rumours we spread?" I asked. "When people hear what Kurt did, they'll start pointing fingers at anyone who worked with him. Especially those who worked *for* him. Or, they might go after Enzo because they want to hunt down the Sparrow."

"Both are possible," Damon said. "That being the case—"

"Carlos is trying to put us off his trail so he can find Kurt himself," Reuben said. "He must know Enzo worked for Kurt and how to get to him. Once he has Kurt, he can make more money than triple the shipments."

"He's a crafty bastard," Gianni said. "Smarter than I gave him credit for."

"Never underestimate Carlos Jones," Damon advised him. "He didn't get where he was by being stupid and making mistakes. He got there by being smart and ruthless."

"We need to find Enzo before Carlos does," I concluded. "I know we're only guessing about Angelina Jones, but—"

"She'd be a good place to start," Damon said. "I have a feeling if we find her, we'll find him."

"I have the same feeling," Gianni said. "If you were a cartel princess, where would you be?"

"Probably as far away from the cartel as I could get," I said. "Before my brother could sell me."

What was it with men? When Carlos said that, I had to resist the strong urge to kick him in the balls. I didn't give a fuck if the cartel did things differently, there was nothing I hated more than men thinking women were possessions. Angelina could end up the same way I had.

"Neither of your brothers would have dared," Gianni said.

I raised my eyebrows at him. "You really think Dane would have hesitated if it was worth it to him?"

"I think you, Rose and Asher would have torn him a new one," Gianni said. "I would have helped them."

"So would I," Reuben said. He paused for a moment. "I would have outbid everyone else. I wouldn't have let anyone else buy you."

"If it was you, I would have gone along with it," I told him.

If only that was what happened. I would have preferred to be sold to him than given away like a used doll. I might even have insisted

Dane take whatever offer he made. He would have had money and I would have had a completely different life.

"That might be the most romantic thing I've ever heard," Gianni said. "Would you buy me too, Reuben? Or Damon?"

"I pay you," Reuben pointed out. "I don't need to buy either of you."

"Good point," Gianni said. "I think I prefer that to being bought and sold. So, where do we find Angelina Jones?"

"We start by speaking to her mother," Damon said.

"What is my son up to now?" Bianca Ramirez looked unimpressed. She was even shorter than me, but very much the kind of woman you would never underestimate. Her side eye alone would make the average man think twice about fucking with her. Her full on glare almost intimidated me.

Almost.

"Probably a fuck ton," Damon said. "Including trying to sell Angie."

Bianca swore under her breath in Spanish.

I expected her to curse out her son, but instead she said, "That girl will be the death of us all. I said to her, if she doesn't behave, no man would want her and you know what she did? She laughed and said no man could handle her anyway." She threw her hands up in the air. "It would take an army to control her."

"Just like her mother," Gianni said, unflinching.

She said a few more words in Spanish. None of them sounded flattering.

Gianni grinned and replied in Spanish. Whatever he said had her cheeks turning red.

She waved a finger at him. "You, you're trouble. No sensible woman would let you near her daughter." She turned the waving finger on me. "Are you with this man?"

"Yes," I replied. "I'm with all of them."

"Madre dio!" she exclaimed. "Loco."

Now *that* I understood. Sometimes I agreed that I might be crazy. "Do you know where your daughter is, by any chance?"

Bianca grunted with annoyance. "Probably off with that boy. I told her, Angelina-Maria Marguerite-Rosa Ramirez-Jones, you stay away from that boy! Did she do what I said? Of course not? I should have told her to go with him. She would have done the opposite, like she always does."

Bianca crossed her arms and rolled her eyes toward the ceiling.

"If I recall correctly," Reuben said slowly, "your father was trying to negotiate a marriage for you and you ran off with Anthony Jones instead."

Bianca sniffed. "That's right. Tony had more brains in his little finger than the man my father was trying to sell me to. He was bad. No bueno. We would have killed each other. No, let me correct myself. I would have killed him. Before I let him put his greasy fingers on me." She shuddered.

"So you think women should be free to choose who they're with," I stated.

As I expected, she saw right through what I was trying to imply. "Unless they are a no good, two-bit troublemaker like Enzo."

I grabbed Damon's wrist before he could respond too strongly.

"Where is he?" he asked, his voice barely contained. "When did you see him last?"

"This morning," she replied. "Climbing out the window of Angie's bedroom. As if I wouldn't notice." She scoffed.

"Carlos said he was shot last night," Reuben said.

"He might have been shot, but it wasn't last night," she said. "I chased him away and Angelina left maybe an hour later. Wherever they are, they're together."

"If Carlos tries to kill him, he might accidentally hurt her," I pointed out. "If you can tell us where you think they might be, we can stop that from happening."

I wasn't sure if Carlos wanted Enzo dead, but if Bianca thought that, she might help us. At this point, it was all we had to go on.

Bianca looked reluctant, but sighed. "I can give you an address. If they aren't there, then that's all I have." She grabbed a notepad from a side table beside an ancient couch and scribbled with a blunt pencil.

She tore off the paper and handed it to Reuben. "If you weren't with her, I'd insist you take me out. I've been lonely since Tony passed away."

Reuben carefully folded the page and tucked it into his pocket. "Thank you."

I suspected he was thanking her for the address, not the flirtation. I couldn't remember having seen him with another woman other than Daze and some of the staff, but he wasn't the flirtatious type. That was Gianni's wheelhouse.

"You could always ask Carlos to find you someone," Gianni said. "I bet a woman like you would go for a shit ton."

She gave him the stink eye. "If you don't get out of my house, I'm going to put a curse on you."

He grinned. "You wouldn't do that. You secretly like me. I can tell."

"So secret I don't even know," she said dryly. "Did you hit your head too many times?"

"Probably." Gianni chuckled. "That would explain a lot."

"Pretty much everything," Damon agreed. "I should have thought of it."

"You really should," Gianni agreed. "How did you miss something like that?"

Damon rolled his eyes at him.

"I'm starting to think you're all trouble," Bianca said. "Except Reuben. If she ditches your fine ass, you know where to find me." She winked at him.

He looked back at her, clearly uncomfortable.

"I don't plan to ditch his ass," I said. "Sorry, his *fine* ass." I put an arm around him. "But if I do, I'll remind him of your offer."

He gave me the same look he'd been giving her. If things didn't work out between us, he was not coming back here for her. He looked as though he'd prefer to swallow a whole echidna. Spines and all.

Lucky for everyone, I couldn't imagine life without him and I knew he wouldn't let me go without one hell of a fight. Unfortunately for Bianca, she was out of luck when it came to him. I doubted they'd be a good match anyway. Although, a woman her age might teach him a thing or two.

"If you find my daughter, tell her that if she takes off again, I'll let

Carlos choose a husband for her," Bianca said. She led us to the door and opened it before hanging on to it as though she wanted to be certain we actually left.

"Will do," Gianni said. He made kissing faces at her before leading the way out the door.

My arm still around Reuben, I shook my head and followed him out.

If Angelina was anything like her mother, she'd marry Enzo today if we gave her that message. I had a feeling I'd like her, but she wouldn't like me if she knew I'd leave her a widow.

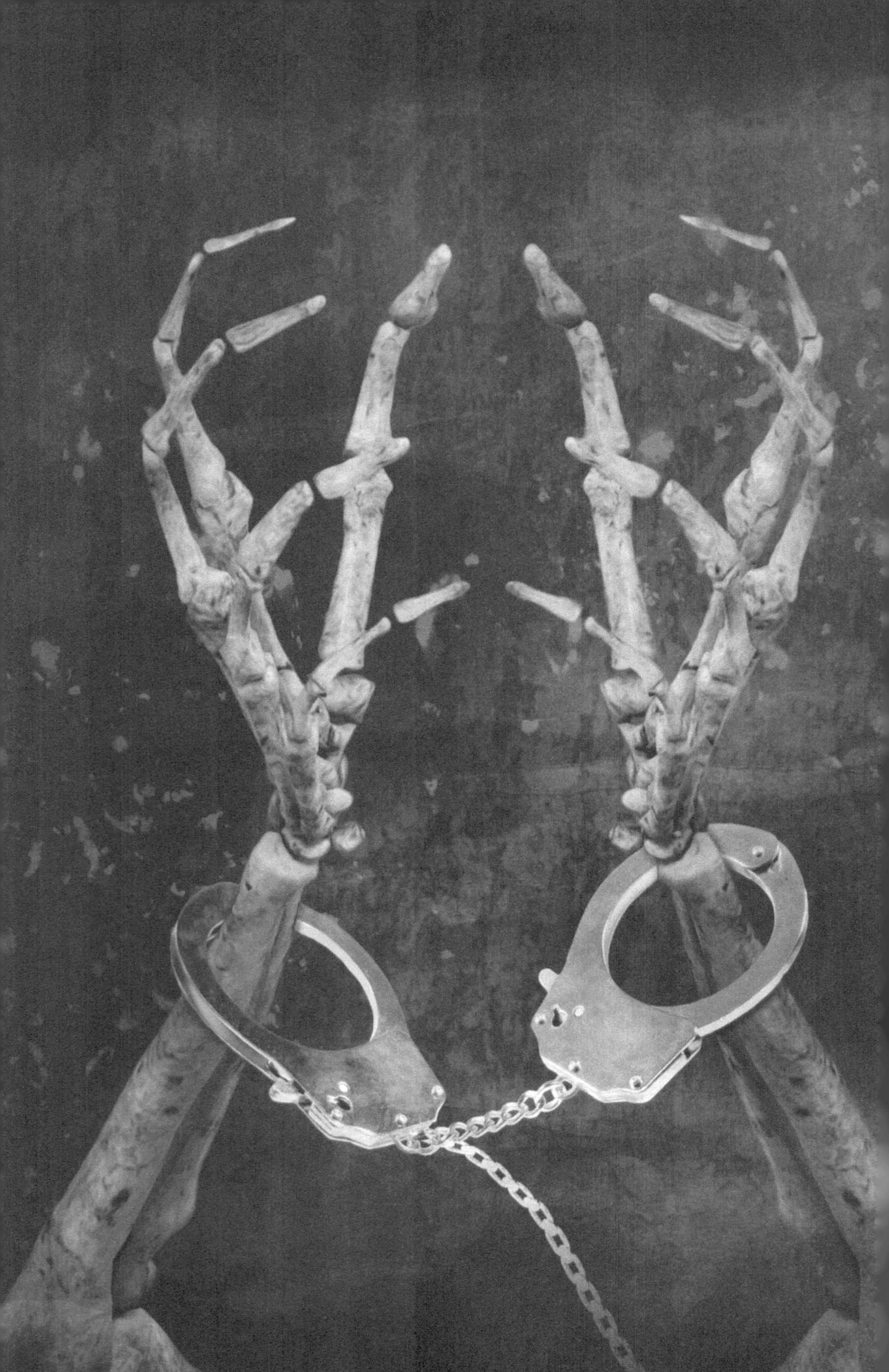

CHAPTER 9

MINA

"How many languages do you speak?" Gianni hooked his arm through mine and walked beside me to the car.

He shrugged. "Four or five. Italian, Spanish, French, English, and of course, bad."

I laughed. "I think we can all speak bad language."

"Fuck yeah we can." He grinned. "How about you?"

"I can definitely speak bad," I said. "Also, Italian and French, but I'm rusty. I learned French at school and Italian at home. And bad from Asher and Zeke."

Reuben grunt-laughed. "That sounds accurate."

"You learned all your naughty words from your younger brother?" Gianni teased.

"Who else?" Reuben asked. He shot us a playful look of mock innocence, but it only lasted a moment.

Those flashes fascinated me. The insight into the man under the stony exterior. I suspected we'd never see more than flashes, but those he displayed were endearing. Every time I saw them, I fell in love with him a little more. They made him seem more human, and reminded me that he also had vulnerabilities. None he'd admit to, but he had them.

"My guess would have been the twins," I said.

I glanced over at Damon, ready to tease, but the expression on his face made me hold my tongue.

He was clearly not listening to us, his mind elsewhere. On his brother, I presumed. In a mood like that, he might be inclined to shoot first and think about what he was doing later. Not that he was a hothead, usually, but he was wound up tighter than a spring, ready to burst. Now was the time to step lightly around him.

I wanted to reassure him we'd find Enzo, but I had no idea what would happen after that. Carlos might kill him or we might.

I considered suggesting we put my vendetta aside, but I sensed Damon wouldn't stop until he found his brother, regardless of what he'd done. Regardless of what I might do to him.

Damon unlocked the SUV and we all climbed inside without another word.

"Is it far?" I asked to fill the silence.

"Nope." Damon started the engine.

Gianni scooted over closer to me and fastened his seatbelt. He took my hand and squeezed.

"No one will blame you for what you have to do." His tattooed fingers were warm around mine, reassuring.

I looked over at him and pressed my lips together. "I might. Damon will."

Nothing quite says 'I love you' like killing his brother. Even if he understood, some part of him would always resent what I did. He'd always wonder if maybe he could have found a way for Enzo to make up for the past.

But this wasn't a romance novel, and no amount of grovelling from Enzo could undo his part in everything. His death wouldn't take away the pain either, but it would help to give me some peace.

Was it worth the risk of starting a war with Damon? I didn't want to lose him, especially not like this.

I tried, but I couldn't remember a time when I was more conflicted than I was right now. I might have been about to rip us all apart, just for revenge.

What did that say about me? Was I as bad as Kurt for wanting to burn down everyone who burnt me? I reminded myself that if I didn't, and another person suffered because of it, that would be my fault. Their blood, their suffering, would be on my hands.

That, I couldn't, *wouldn't* tolerate. If I could help it, they wouldn't touch another person. I owed that little girl that. I owed younger Mina that. I owed it to Daze's daughter, to make her safer.

No matter the price.

"Damon understands what's at stake here," Gianni assured me. "So does his brother. You can't be responsible for his actions. That would be like blaming Damon for them."

He raised his voice to make sure everyone in the car could hear. "And anything Enzo did is not Damon's fault."

Damon tensed, but didn't glance back or respond. He was clearly not finished blaming himself. What would it take?

I spent five years hating myself for something I didn't even do. I blamed myself for her death, but I was starting to accept that everything which happened was Kurt's fault. Not mine.

Someday I may forgive myself and hopefully, so would Damon. Otherwise, we'd spend the rest of our lives eating ourselves up from the inside out, with remorse for things we didn't do.

"Give him time," Gianni said. "He knows the score, even if he's busy beating himself up right now." His tone was soft, gentle with affection for Damon.

At some point, they'd gone from working together to being something more. At least, as far as Gianni was concerned. I was almost certain it was reciprocated. They weren't rushing into anything, but the feelings were there, like they were between Damon and Reuben.

I remembered the way they kissed and my blood suddenly became hot. Being fucked by two guys at the same time wasn't something I would have dreamt of, but it was incredible and I wanted to do it again. Next time, with Gianni present too, and taking part. What would it be like to be with all three of them at the same time?

Fuck, now my panties were wet. Good. I deserved to enjoy intimacy with my three incredible mafia kings. Sparrow and the mafia kings, who would have thought? Certainly not me, but here we were. If I didn't break us all apart, we could be together forever.

Plenty of time for us to explore each other and all the possibilities.

All I could do in response to Gianni's words, was nod and lean against him while we wound through the streets of Dusk Bay.

The address on the piece of paper Bianca gave to Reuben, led to a large house a block or so from Demons' Arena, where the ice hockey team played their home games.

"They're actually a front for a lot of Caleb's smuggling operations," Gianni said. "As a team, they kinda suck. In a loveable losers kind of way." He nodded towards the arena.

I'd watched a game or two on TV with Gianni and he wasn't wrong about that. I didn't know much about ice hockey, but they lost both times I watched. Their goalie was my cousin, Phoenix. As far as I could tell, he was good at what he did, saving more goals than letting them through, but the team still lost. What would Phoenix think if he knew I watched him play?

I hadn't seen Ric's brother since the guys found me, but I would eventually. He was on the list of people who weren't allowed to know about me yet. Although, he was lower on the list, because we were never close. Not in the past, anyway. In the future, I hoped we could form a bond of some kind. The frustration he showed every time the puck got past him was pure DiMarco. We hated losing. He must be irritated as hell at doing it all the time.

I couldn't imagine Caleb giving a shit about the team's performance on the ice, although he technically owned them. Honestly, I felt sorry for them. Professional athletes worked hard and deserved better than to be an afterthought in the life of Caleb Brantley. Just another part of the business.

I made a note to suggest to the twins that maybe they could take over the team. Between them, they'd run it better than he did. Without a doubt, if I suggested it to Caleb, he'd tell me it was none of my business. This was a handy sidestep, and the twins would, if nothing else, get a hoot out of it. Anything to get under Caleb's skin.

I turned my attention to the house, and shivered. It reminded me of the last job I did.

The house where the girl died. I tried not to think about her blood seeping into my clothes. Her eyes, staring at me…

Two stories, brick painted cream, black windows and a roof that slanted across the top of the structure. The look was too modern for my taste. Judging by the look on his face, it was too modern for Reuben's taste too.

"Who owns this place?" I asked.

Damon was on his phone, searching for exactly that information. "Not us, or the cartel. Or the brotherhood, as far as I can tell. It seems to be privately owned. Someone by the name of Karrie Levine." He shrugged.

"Hopefully we won't get too much blood on Ms Levine's house," Gianni remarked. "Although, if you rent houses to dubious people, you get dubious things happening."

"Gianni and Mina, you go around the back," Reuben said. "Damon and I will check out the front."

"On it, boss," Gianni said. He grabbed my hand and we slipped over to a side gate that led to the back of the house.

"How inconsiderate of them to lock it," Gianni remarked.

"How considerate of them to have such a simple lock." I pulled out my lock picking tools and had it open in about ten seconds flat.

"I've always said locks only keep honest people out." He grinned and pushed the gate open.

"Considering we could have climbed over it, yeah," I agreed. We might have been seen by the neighbours, so that would have been a last resort. Why risk what could be done with a turn of my hand?

We walked slowly across paved ground, past raised gardens with the kind of plants that didn't need any attention. The kind that were planted for decoration, not because the owner enjoyed getting their hands dirty.

Terry would have hated the place.

We walked past windows with curtains drawn over them, to the back door. Beside it, a keypad was attached to the wall, a light flashing at the top.

"I've been looking forward to this," Gianni whispered.

From my pocket, I drew out my device and placed it beside the keypad to turn off the security. The screen turned on, numbers tumbling over numbers, letters over letters until they hit on the combination and the light turned dark.

"That was fucking awesome," Gianni whispered. "I want one."

"If I can find out how to get one, I'll give you one for Christmas," I assured him.

"Fucking yes, please." He tried the door, but it was locked. With an elaborate gesture, he stepped aside for me to pick that too. "No wonder you could get in anywhere. Is there anything that could keep you out?"

"Not that I know of," I said. "But no job ever included a moat and crocodiles. Yet."

He laughed softly. "If anyone could get past those, it would be you."

I didn't know about that, but the vote of confidence didn't hurt my ego.

I eased the door open and listened carefully.

Grimaced.

Unless there was someone else in the house, Angelina and Enzo wouldn't hear us coming. By the sound of it, they were too busy coming themselves.

My hand in Gianni's, we moved slowly through the darkened house, towards the source of the sound.

I caught a hint of movement at the front of the house. Reuben and Damon must have entered when I turned off the security system. I estimated that the pair were between the four of us. With that in mind, I slowed slightly.

Let Damon find his brother first.

I caught a glimpse of them moving down the corridor towards us, illuminated in the light that came from a single room. It shone across the floor, glowing on pale hardwood.

Damon stepped into the doorway and stopped.

I moved to stand beside him.

Sure enough, a dark-haired woman around my age was riding a man who bore a striking resemblance to Damon. Her head was back, eyes closed, her hair long enough to brush her ass. Her breasts bounced with every roll of her hips.

"That's Enzo," Damon said.

They didn't realise we were there until he spoke. Angelina let out a squeak and threw her hands over her breasts.

Enzo turned to stare at us, squinting in confusion and disbelief.

I gave him the same look. "I've never seen him before."

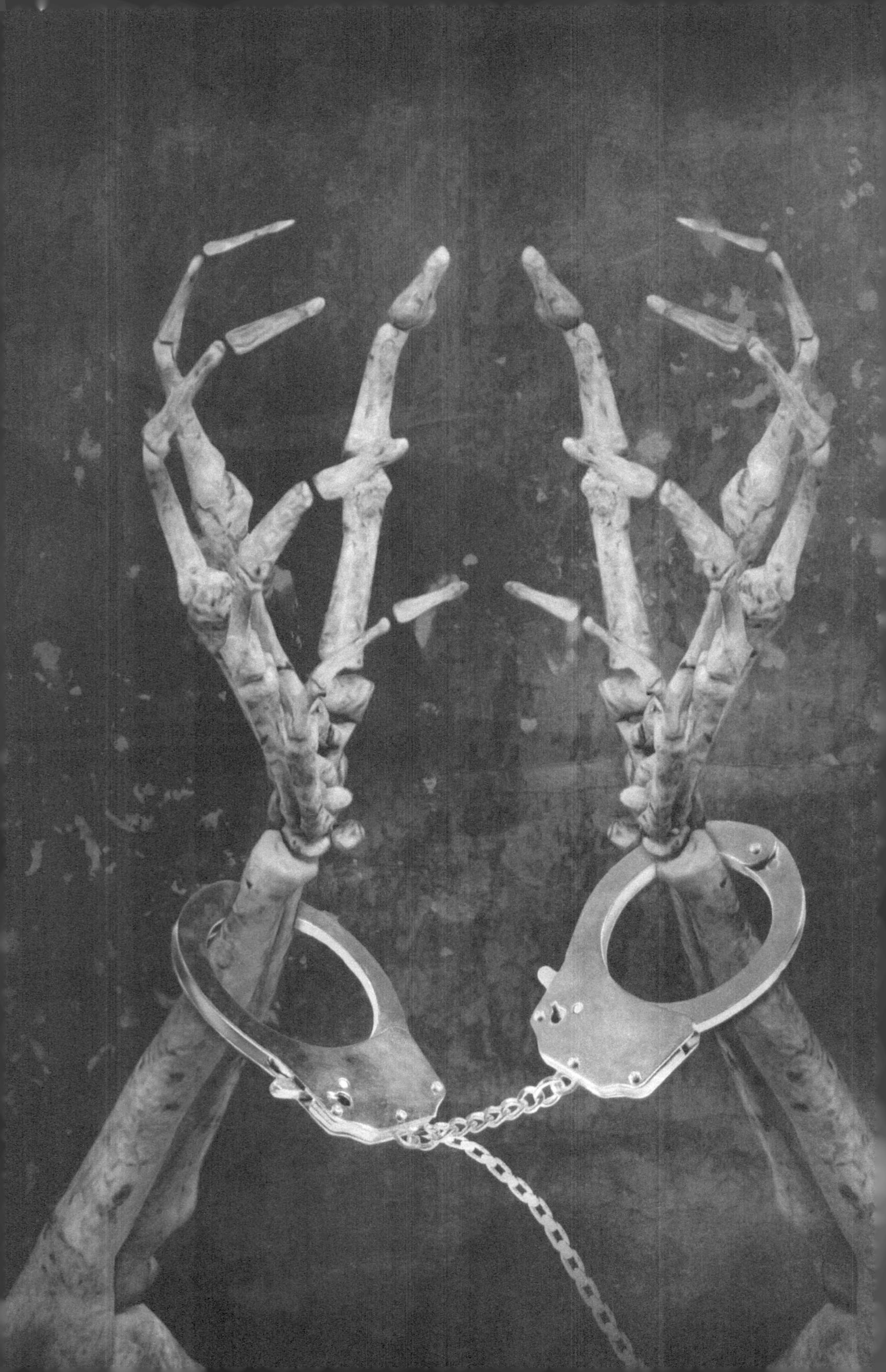

CHAPTER 10

MINA

Damon turned slowly to stare at me. "You've never—"

"I've never seen him before," I repeated. "Whoever Hammer is, it's not him."

"That's a matter of opinion." Enzo placed his hands behind his head and grinned at us, completely shameless. "I've been called very similar. Damon, what the fuck are you doing here?"

Angelina slid off him and onto the floor on the opposite side of the bed to scoop up a shirt and pull it over her head. Enzo's shirt, by the look of it. It fell to her knees, the sleeves down to her elbows.

"What the hell?" she demanded. She placed her fists on her ample hips and glared at us. She was a younger version of her mother. Dark hair, dark eyes and a pissed off expression on her face.

Damon ignored them for a moment. "You're absolutely certain? Think back carefully. You were drugged at the time."

I frowned and thought, but ultimately shook my head. "It's definitely not him."

For one thing, Hammer was blonde and Enzo had dark hair, like his brother. Hammer had a slim build and Enzo was muscular. Even if he'd dyed his hair and bulked up, Enzo looked nothing like Hammer.

Even his face shape was different. His voice wasn't one of the ones that haunted my nightmares.

Thank fuck, because I really hadn't wanted to kill Damon's brother.

Damon closed his eyes in relief and turned back to the pair, arms crossed over his chest as he lounged against the door frame. "Do you want to put that away?" He nodded at Enzo's still erect cock, which was in full view.

"Nope," Enzo said easily. "How about you fuck off so we can finish what we started?"

"Nope," Damon repeated. "If we can find you, then Carlos can. He wants you killed for some reason." He nodded toward Angelina.

She groaned in frustration. "How many times do I have to tell my brother to fuck off? I am not marrying Salvador! I am not marrying any man my brother chooses for me. Especially Salvador. I'd rather marry Hades."

Enzo glanced over at her. "Hey!"

She rolled her eyes at him. "I don't want to marry Hades either, fuckwit. I'm just saying he's better than Salvador." She shook her head at his apparent obtuseness.

"Everyone is better than Salvador," Gianni said, although he clearly had no idea who Salvador was.

Neither did I, but I could make some assumptions. Anyone who wanted to buy a woman, or marry her against her will, was immediately on my shit list. Even after a handful of minutes, I knew it would take a certain type of man to fulfil her needs. Someone with balls of steel.

Angelina turned to Gianni and raised her hands. "Right? Tell my asshole brother that. And tell him I'm not coming back. He and my mother can go right to hell. I'm staying with Enzo." She nodded like that settled the matter, once and for all, although she must have known it wouldn't make the situation go away. Nothing about her suggested she was naïve, just frustrated and determined to get her way.

Enzo finally rose from the bed and moved to stand beside her. His cock had finally softened enough to hang heavy between his thighs. "Exactly. Angie and I are getting married and there's not a fucking thing Carlos can do about it."

"He can have you killed, *fuckwit*," Damon said. "Do you really think someone like Carlos is going to let her go that easily? Because he won't. He'll keep coming after you until you're dead."

Enzo lifted his chin. "Then we'll go somewhere no one can find us."

"Like here?" Damon gestured around with one hand, without unfolding his arms. "It wasn't that difficult to find you."

Considering how easy it was, both of them should be more worried than they were. What must it be like to be so carefree and sure of yourself? It would be nice until it got them both killed. Or worse.

"My mother told you I was here, didn't she?" Angelina's eyes snapped with anger.

"Yes, and if she told us, then who knows who else she's told," Damon said. "There could be people right behind us." He jerked his thumb towards the road.

"We should get out of here," Angelina said. She started to gather up her clothes.

Enzo didn't move. He nodded towards me. "Who's she? Why was she supposed to know me? Who the fuck is Hammer?"

He didn't look worried, but he also looked as though he wouldn't move until he got some answers. In that, he reminded me of his brother. They also had the same firm jaw and blue eyes, the same fierce independence. No wonder they clashed, they were a lot alike.

"Mina DiMarco," I replied. "We were given the wrong information. We were told you were someone else. We came to kill him." I saw no reason to pull punches. People like this heard worse on an hourly basis, they wouldn't flinch.

"You're not going to kill him?" Angelina stopped, still crouched behind the bed.

I would have bet anything she had a gun. She'd use it, depending on what I said next. Assuming she could aim before I embedded a blade between her eyes. Which was unlikely, so I replied calmly and honestly.

"Not unless you gave us a reason to, then no. I think we can help you instead."

"With a threesome?" Enzo's gaze grazed up and down my body. "Sounds good to me."

Angelina threw a shoe at his head. It bounced off his cheek and fell back to the floor.

She swore at him in Spanish while he chuckled.

He spread his hands and shrugged. "Sorry, baby, another time maybe."

Reuben shot daggers at him with his eyes. For a moment I thought he may order one of us to kill Enzo after all.

I put a hand on his bicep to remind him I wouldn't have taken up the offer, and Enzo was joking around. I doubted Angelina would share anyway, even if I was interested.

"We can help by getting you out of here," Damon said. "We'll take you back to the house and sort something out from there. You'll be safe from Carlos, and Angelina's mother."

Enzo clenched his jaw. For a moment I thought he'd refuse. He glanced at Angelina who nodded.

He exhaled and nodded. "Fine. We'll go with you. For now. Only for Angie's sake. I know what Salvador would do to her if he got his hands on her. He's a fucking slug."

"He's a fucking slug who'd get me pregnant and keep me that way," she said bitterly. "Then fuck around with whoever he could get his dick into."

"He sounds charming," Gianni said sarcastically.

I murmured my agreement. It sounded to me like Carlos was trying to kill the wrong man. "Maybe we should let them get dressed." I stepped away from the doorway.

"I don't mind who sees me naked," Enzo said pleasantly. "But if you keep looking at my woman, I'm going to have to shoot your eyes out."

As if any of my men were leering at her in any way. I knew all of them better than to even glance at them to check. They weren't interested in another woman. They wouldn't stare at one.

"Bro, none of us wants to see you naked," Gianni said. "No offence or anything."

Enzo grinned. "None taken, bro." He turned around and bent over, baring his ass to all of us.

I grimaced and stepped into the darker part of the corridor so I couldn't see him anymore.

"This all begs more questions than it answers," Reuben said. He slipped an arm around me.

"It does," I agreed. "Why did Martina think Enzo was Hammer? And if she knew he wasn't, why tell us he was?"

"Where is the real Hammer?" he added to the list of questions.

Gianni went one further with, "*Who* is the real Hammer? And can he sing 'Can't Touch This'?"

"And why send us after my brother?" Damon leaned against the wall, his hands in his pockets.

"To stop Carlos from getting to him?" I suggested. "Why would Martina give a shit?"

Damon shook his head. "I have no idea." He turned his head towards the bedroom. "Enzo, why would she?"

Enzo strutted out, fully dressed in torn jeans and the T-shirt Angelina was wearing a few moments before. He gave me a wink before turning to his brother. "Because I'm smoking hot and awesome?"

Damon snorted. "That's a matter of opinion and doesn't answer the question. Why would someone like Martina get involved? Stepping in between you and Carlos, I mean."

Enzo looked down at the floor and shuffled his feet. "I might have done her some favours in the past."

"Must have been some hell of a favour," Gianni said. "We might have shot you before checking that you were who we thought you were."

Enzo looked up and gave Gianni a lopsided smile. "The favours didn't always go the way they should have. I never said she was looking out for me."

"She set you up?" Angelina emerged from the bedroom, dressed in leggings and a crop top, her dark hair wound in a messy bun.

I envied the way she looked, comfortable in her own skin. I was getting more confident in myself, but some days I still wanted to peel off mine and step out of it.

She had an effortless beauty, and an attitude that gave absolutely no fucks. She was exactly the kind of person I wanted to keep away from men like Kurt. If Salvador was anything like him, the further away she was from him, the better.

Right now, Angelina looked ready to tear Martina apart, if she tried to get Enzo killed. It was easy to see why Carlos described her as a wildcat. She was all of that and more.

"Can you blame her?" Enzo shrugged. "If it wasn't for me, she wouldn't be on Carlos' radar. She was doing good at lying low and dealing out her information. Now..." He didn't elaborate on what he did to piss her off. He didn't need to. Revealing someone like that to anyone else was a good reason for that someone to want you dead. We'd be doing Martina a favour if we killed him, but we wouldn't. We owed her absolutely nothing. Less than nothing, since she'd given us information that was completely useless and self-serving. Clearly she had no idea who or where Jase or Hammer were.

"I see you haven't changed," Damon said dryly. "Still causing trouble."

Enzo rolled his eyes. "I see you haven't changed either, big brother. Still being a judgemental prick."

"We could always inform Carlos of your whereabouts," Reuben said. His gaze slid from Enzo to Angelina and back again. He wasn't bluffing. He had neither time nor patience for their bullshit.

Enzo looked like he was ready to lunge at Reuben, but Angelina grabbed his arm and held him back.

"Don't be a fucking idiot. Attacking Reuben Brantley will get you dead. Did you hear their offer to help us, or do you need your ears cleaned?" She let go of his arm and grabbed his earlobe to pull him closer to her. Speaking loudly she said, "*Don't. Do. Anything. To. Get. Killed.*"

He winced. "Okay, okay. I'll be nice. As long as they are."

"We're always nice," Gianni said. "But I think we should get out of here before someone else shows up."

Reuben nodded. "Let's go."

I slipped into the lead as we headed to the front of the house. No one said a word. No one complained when I held my hand to stop them.

"What is it?" Reuben whispered.

"Someone else has already shown up," I whispered back.

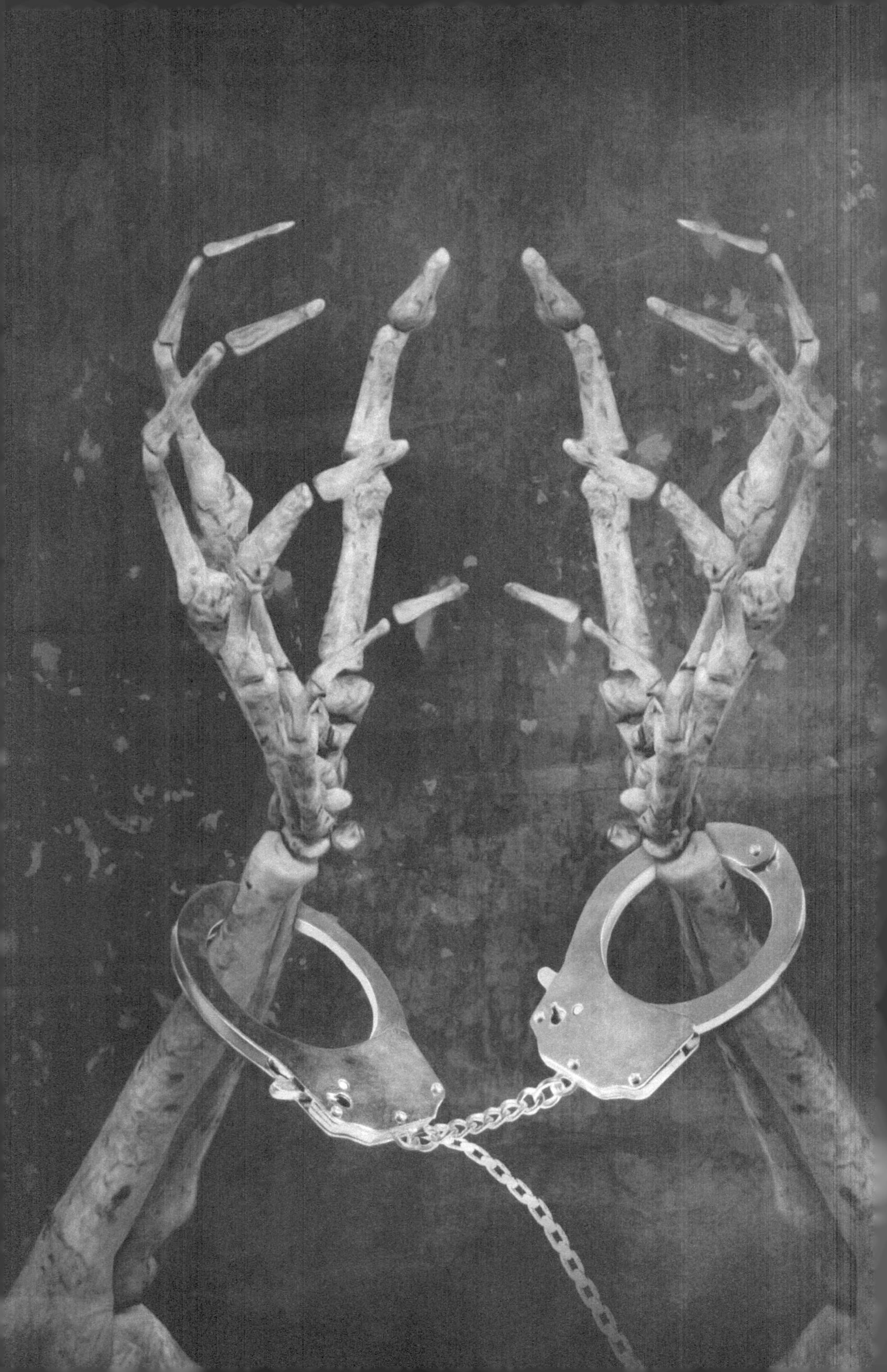

CHAPTER 11

GIANNI

"It's party time," I said under my breath.

Damon glanced at me like I lost my mind.

I grinned back. We both knew he enjoyed this shit as much as I did.

He shook his head and pushed past us all to the front of the house. He teased open the space between two curtains and peeked outside.

"Fuck," he said softly. "There's four cars out there. All facing the front of this place. They're not making any effort to hide. They want us to know they're there."

"I'm going to kill my mother." Angelina marched to another window and yanked open the curtains. She glared outside before unlocking and sliding the window open. "Fuck off, Carlos!" she shouted. "We don't want any of what you're selling."

Carlos stepped out of the vehicle and onto the front lawn. He held his hands behind his back like they might just have a pleasant conversation.

"I'm not leaving without you, hermana," he called back. "I won't touch Enzo if you just get your ass out here."

"Bullshit, *hermano*," she spat. "The moment I'm inside that car, he's dead."

Damon pulled out his phone and started to tap on the screen, giving orders for our people to get themselves here for backup. As awesome as we were, we were boxed in here.

"I'll check the back," Mina said. She slipped away down the corridor to the back of the house, moving silently. If I couldn't see her silhouette in the light from the bedroom, I wouldn't have known she was there. She was beyond incredible. My heart swelled with love for my gorgeous little assassin.

She returned a couple of minutes later. "There's people waiting for us to sneak out that way. At least another eight of them."

"Nothing we can't take care of," I said. "Right, boss?" I glanced over to Reuben.

He seemed to be weighing up his options. I had a feeling fighting our way out was at the very bottom.

"Boss?" I pressed.

"If they want her that badly..." he said slowly.

"I won't let you hand her over." Enzo's hands were in fists, ready to take a swing.

"Don't do anything you'll regret," Damon warned. "We're on your side. No one wants to give Angelina to Carlos." He turned his face toward Reuben, wanting agreement.

Reuben didn't agree, but he didn't disagree either. Top of his agenda was us getting out of here alive. Whether or not that included Enzo and Angelina was less important to him.

"We're going out the back." Enzo grabbed Angelina's hand and started to lead her that way.

"Last chance, Angelina," Carlos called out. "Otherwise, I might be forced to do something drastic." He gestured to the car behind his.

The door opened and one of his men pulled Bianca out onto the street.

Angelina stopped and stared in horror and disbelief. "You'd kill my mother?" she called out the window.

Carlos shrugged. "She's not my mother."

"She raised you," Angelina hissed. Her eyes shone with tears. "You're the devil himself."

Carlos raised a gun to Bianca's temple. "I'll count to ten. One."

"Angelina…" Enzo said softly.

"Two."

Angelina shook her head. "She's my mother."

"Three."

"I can't let you go," he pleaded.

"Four."

"I can't let him kill her." She wiped tears from her cheeks.

"Five."

"But I love you." He pulled her to him and held her tight.

"Six."

"I love you too." She squeezed him, but pulled away. "But she's my mother."

"Seven."

Angelina stepped over to the door, unlocked it and wrenched it open. "Stop!"

A shadow slipped past me. Past Angelina.

Mina pulled out a knife and aimed it. She threw with deadly precision, the knife slamming into the gun in Carlos' hand. It flew out of his grip and clattered onto the road.

Bianca dropped to the ground and rolled under one of the cars.

"Fucking hell." Carlos rubbed his hand.

"The next one goes into your brain," Mina said coldly. She already held another knife in her hand. I hadn't even seen her pull it out.

"This is none of your business," Carlos said, trying to pretend he wasn't rattled.

She could have killed him, but she hadn't. She was smart enough to know that would provoke a war between the Brantley family and the Vipers. That would get ugly and bloody very quickly.

Although, getting in the middle of a transaction like this also might. In my opinion, it was totally worth it. I was with Mina, women were not possessions.

"I'm making it my business," Mina said. "Enzo is family. That makes Angelina family. We take care of family. Tell Salvador to look elsewhere for a wife."

"There's a shit ton of dating apps out there," I said helpfully. "Or he could try one of those dating shows. Maybe— Asshole Wants a Wife. I'm sure that's a thing. If it isn't, it should be. The ratings would go through the roof."

"We aren't done," Carlos said, his tone icy. He nodded to his men and climbed back into the car.

Bianca rolled out from under the one she was hiding under, and bolted for the door.

Angelina grabbed her hand and pulled her inside. They both stepped back, growling at each other in Spanish. Something along the lines of, "How the fuck could you let him bring you here? You knew what he'd do. He's an ungrateful piece of crap." And so on.

We all waited until the cars pulled away before closing the door and collectively exhaling.

Enzo shoved his hands in his pockets and shuffled his feet. "Thank you," he said to Mina. "Those are some sick knife skills."

"I don't like bullies." She slipped her other knife away. "If I was you, I'd take his warning seriously. He will come for you again."

"They will," Damon said, stony faced. "The only reason he left now was that he doesn't want trouble with us. If we weren't here, this would have ended differently."

"We would have handled it," Enzo said. His voice held more confidence than his eyes did.

"Let's go," Reuben said. "We've wasted enough time here." He didn't bother to hide his irritation at Enzo and his continued stubbornness. He waited until Damon opened the door and stepped out again, before he followed him, leaving the rest of us to fall in behind.

"It's going to be a tight fit," I remarked as seven of us headed out to the SUV. "Mina, you can sit on my lap."

She leaned over to snatch up her knife from the road and tuck it away. "Better than being in the boot."

I caught her hand and pulled her to me. "First of all, we'd never put you in the boot. Second of all, the way you dealt with Carlos was hot as fuck." I whispered in her ear, "When we get home I'm going to fuck your pussy with my tongue until you scream."

"Is that a promise?" she asked. Her voice was husky, like throwing a knife at Carlos turned her on as much as it did me.

Death and violence were an addiction neither of us needed, or wanted, help for.

Lucky for us we had the jobs we did, or we'd get our rush by doing things which were more illegal than the things we already did.

"You can bet your cute little ass it is," I said. I cupped her ass cheeks and squeezed, while pulling her closer still. "I can't wait to have the taste of you on my tongue."

I pressed my quickly growing erection against her leg. I wanted to push her up against the SUV and fuck her, here and now.

I kissed her mouth, thrusting my tongue between her lips as though it was my cock pounding into her pussy. Her mouth was warm, her plush lips tasting faintly of coffee and something sweet that was uniquely Mina.

"Get a room," Enzo called out.

My hands still on Mina's ass, I flipped him off with two fingers. "You can talk. We've all seen your cock, remember?" The guy had absolutely no shame. Not unlike me. Life was too short to care about shit like that.

"Only because you broke in for a look." Enzo grinned.

Damon shook his head at all of us and raised the seats in the third row of the SUV. He gestured for Enzo and Angelina to sit back there. "Don't fuck in the back of my SUV."

"That hadn't occurred to me until you suggested it." Enzo grabbed Angelina's hand and pulled her into the back of the vehicle.

"We'll make a stop at the Vipers' headquarters to leave you there if you do," Reuben said.

That was both a threat, and a promise. I suspected he wouldn't lose much sleep over it.

On the other hand, Mina was right. Damon's brother was family and we took care of each other. Reuben would tolerate Damon's brother, even if he, and Angelina, pushed him too far.

"Don't you fucking dare," Angelina hissed.

Apparently Reuben didn't intimidate her. Or maybe she knew Mina would never let him do that. Women's intuition and all that.

"Have some respect for the boss," Damon told her. "What happens to you now is up to him."

She gave him a look that suggested she didn't agree, but she flopped back against the seat and fell silent.

I followed Mina into the car, where she settled between me and Bianca.

Bianca looked weary and more than a little pissed off.

"I thought I raised Carlos better than that. He really would have shot me." She rubbed her temple where he'd had the barrel of the gun pressed.

I got the impression she might shoot him the next chance she got. That was her prerogative. If Vipers wanted to kill Vipers, that was up to them. As long as they left us out of it.

"I wouldn't have let that happen to you." Angelina leaned forward over the seat in front of her, and kissed her mother's cheek. "Even if I had to marry Salvador. But now, thanks to Mina, I can marry Enzo."

Bianca groaned. "Can't you find yourself a nice boy?"

"I'm nice," Enzo said. "You just need to get to know me."

She looked as though that was the last thing on Earth she wanted. He was better than Salvador, whoever he was, but apparently not by much.

I had a sneaking suspicion she'd have to get used to him. He wasn't going anywhere if Angelina had anything to say about it.

I caught Mina's eye and grinned. The three of them made our lives look easy and peaceful. For a while, they'd taken my mind off Kurt Lasalle. Now, I wondered if he had a hand in all of this somehow. Like he'd set this up to distract us. I wasn't sure how, but if he had, it worked.

"You think Kurt paid Martina to do all of this, don't you?" Mina asked softly. "The fact she was pissed off with Enzo was an added bonus."

"The thought crossed my mind," I admitted. "If I had to bet, I'd say if we went back to her house, she'd be long gone by now."

"Without doubt," she agreed. She looked tired too. But something else. Satisfaction at keeping Angelina away from her brother and a life she didn't want. She seemed to have made it her mission to save women from a dark fate, even if she had to do it one woman at a time.

"I'll send the twins to check anyway," Damon said. "She might have left some sign behind."

We all knew that was unlikely. People like her knew how to disappear without a trace. At this point, she didn't matter all that much. What mattered was, what was Kurt up to while we were looking in a different direction?

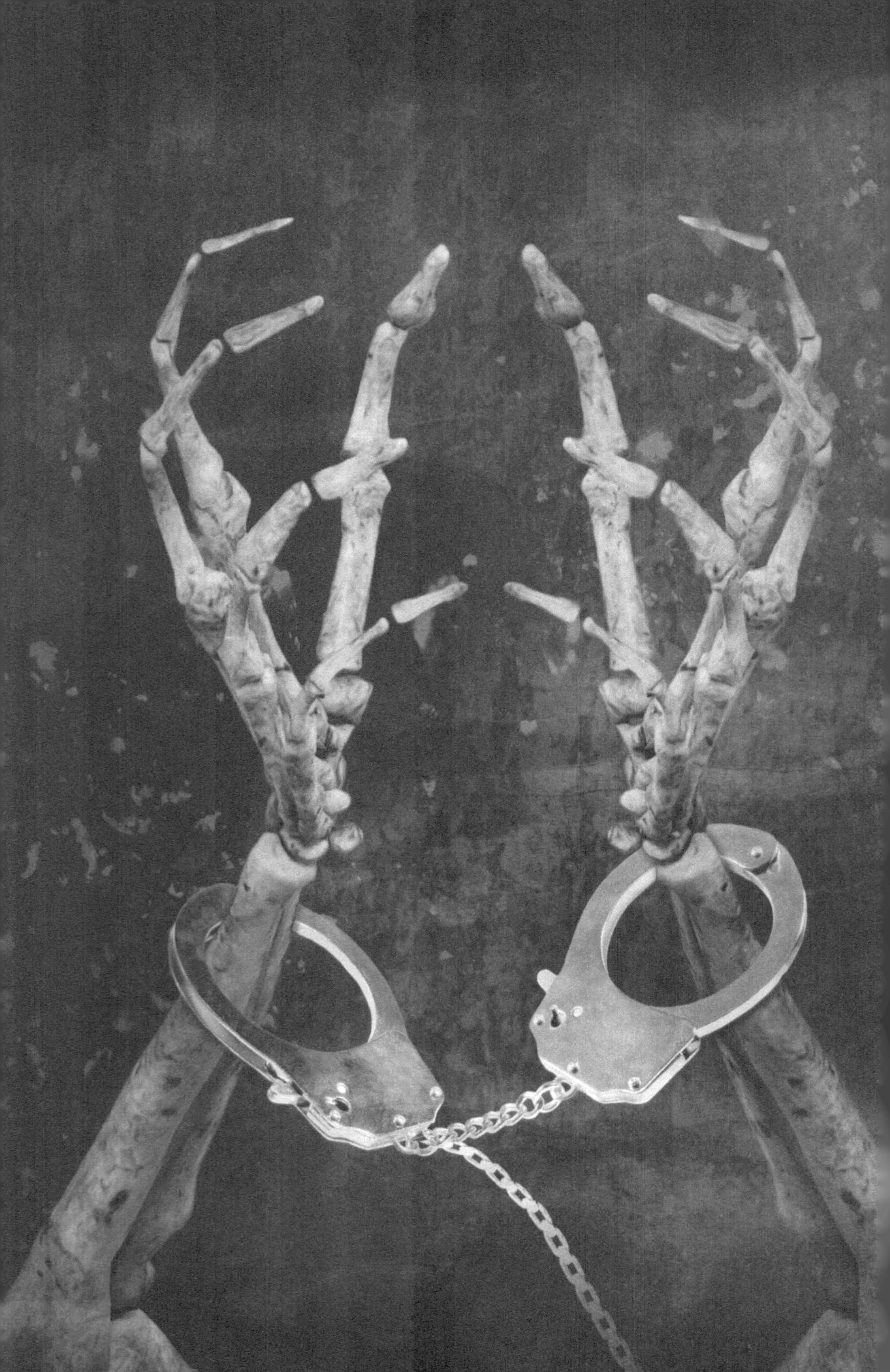

CHAPTER 12

MINA

Damon directed Enzo and Angelina to a room in the house, where they promptly disappeared, closing the door behind them. Bianca, with several rolls of her eyes, disappeared into a room on the other side of the corridor.

She muttered something that sounded like, "Far enough away that I don't have to listen to them fuck."

Damon grimaced and headed back down the stairs.

I followed him, watching the tension in his shoulder and back. He looked stiffer than a column of stone. Hard, but not brittle. Nothing about him was fragile, in spite of Enzo pushing his patience to its limits.

We reached the lower level as the twins returned.

"Just as you said, there's no sign of Martina," Hunter said. "The entire house was empty."

"Personally, I'm impressed at how quickly she cleaned the place out," Parker said. "It couldn't have been more than a handful of hours."

"She had help." Reuben stood with his hip against the kitchen island, a glass of whiskey in his hand.

"Probably lots of it," Gianni agreed. "The question is, from whom?"

Reuben shook his head. "It doesn't matter now. I'll have Caleb keep an eye on the chatter about her. She'll turn up sooner or later."

"People like her always do," Hunter said. "Like a proverbial bad smell."

"Like you two?" Gianni teased.

"Exactly," Hunter said, not rising to the bait. "They can't keep people like us down. Right, Park?"

"Right," Parker agreed. "On a scale of one to a hundred, how much did you piss of the Vipers?"

"Nothing we can't handle." Reuben took a sip of his drink. "They know we could squash them if we wanted to. Or cut them off from our supply of goods."

The second one would hurt them worse than the first. They could fight off an attack, but not being able to get shipments would bring them to their knees within weeks, if not days.

Reuben could sell contraband elsewhere, but if no one would sell to the Vipers, they were fucked.

"I'm sorry I missed all the fun," Hunter said. "Did you really throw a knife at Carlos Jones?"

"Yes, I did," I said. "And I'd do it again. I will if he keeps trying to sell his sister."

"He's probably going to claim you tried to kill him, but missed," Gianni said.

"Of course he is." I shrugged. A man like him wasn't going to let the truth get in the way of his...manly reputation. He'd lie to save face.

No doubt everyone there, those who worked for him, would agree with his claim.

I didn't give a shit, we knew the truth. If his ego couldn't deal with that, that was his problem. I knew the extent of my abilities.

"If Mina wanted to kill him, he'd be dead," Reuben said. "If that needs to happen in the future, then it will. It might be a good idea to consider replacing him with someone we can continue to work with. I don't need anyone with an ego his size creating trouble for us."

"I'll look into who might potentially replace him," Damon said.

Reuben nodded. "Do it."

Hunter lounged against the island, on the opposite side from Reuben. "Parker and I have been talking to some people. Casually mentioning Kurt keeping a woman in his basement, like you asked us to."

One day, someone might mention that basement and I wouldn't shudder, but it wasn't tonight.

"And?" I prompted.

"And people believed it," Parker said. "Mostly, they're speculating on who it was. We also circulated the information that someone knows who the Sparrow is, and that the information was for sale."

"We might have also slipped in a rumour that the Sparrow kept a woman in their basement," Hunter said. "Sooner or later, people are going to start comparing notes and coming to conclusions. It won't be long before they realise that one and one equal three. Then, the shit will hit the proverbial fan."

"Good work," Reuben said. "Keep spreading those rumours. The sooner we can push this to a conclusion, the better. Any further information and the whereabouts of Kurt Lasalle?"

The moment the words passed his lips, my phone vibrated in my pocket.

I had the ringer turned off, because no one had any reason to call me. The number was new and the only people who had it were in this room.

That is, the only people who *should* have it were in this room.

"Let me guess, telemarketer?" Gianni asked.

I pulled out my phone. As expected, the screen said 'unknown number.'

I knew exactly who it was before I pressed on the screen to accept the call. I put the call on speakerphone and held the device on my palm.

We all waited in silence for the caller to speak.

"What fucking game are you playing, Mina?" Kurt's voice echoed through the kitchen. "You think people are going to believe I'm the Sparrow? Yes, I heard the rumour your little twin friends are trying to spread. "

"We're not little," Parker whispered.

"People will believe what they want to believe," I said coolly. "Although, most people who've met you don't need an excuse to want you dead. You seem to have that effect on people. Probably because you're a slimy prick."

He laughed. "Is that supposed to hurt my feelings, bitch? You need to work on your insults."

"It wasn't an insult, it was an observation," I said.

"An accurate one," Damon said.

"Sounds like the whole crew is there," Kurt said. "Hi guys. Long time no see. Don't worry, I'm working on rectifying that as soon as possible. Did you have fun on the side quest I sent you on? You knew that was me behind that, right? Martina was paid well to give you that false lead. Don't bother trying to find her, she's long gone. In the meantime, I put some plans into place. It's only a matter of time before you're back where you belong. On your back, under me."

Reuben, Damon and Gianni all growled softly.

The twins looked murderous.

I swallowed to keep from throwing up my last meal and said, "You're cocky for someone who won't be alive much longer."

He laughed again. "Threats? That's fucking adorable. You can't even find me. I could be right under your nose and you wouldn't have a clue. By the way, nice aim on that knife you threw at Carlos. I could tell you were aiming for his gun, not for him. Bravo." He clapped slowly.

My blood went cold. Kurt was watching? Of course he was. The question was, where was he watching from? Another house, or a camera? Would he have dared to get close enough to watch in person?

"You should have come out and said hello," Gianni said. "But you wouldn't, would you? You're too much of a fucking coward. I'm looking forward to seeing how tiny your cock is, right before I slice it off." He made a slicing gesture with his hand.

"More threats?" Kurt sneered. "I had no idea how pathetic you all were. Disappointing, really. Still, it'll be easier to replace the Brantleys when people realise how much more competent I am."

"You said 'fucked up in the head' wrong," Gianni said.

Kurt snorted. "Please, you're embarrassing yourself now."

"Did you actually want something?" Reuben asked. "It seems to me all you're doing is wasting our time. Making idle threats and pretending you have power and contacts you clearly lack. No one in this room is fooled by your bullshit."

"Reuben Brantley himself," Kurt said derisively. "Does Mina moan when you fuck her? She has the best moans. She has spread her legs for you, hasn't she? I'm sure she has, she loves nothing more than being fucked. Especially when she's restrained. I recommend chains, but rope would do too."

Reuben's fingers tightened around his glass, so tight it shattered in his hand, sending a spray of whiskey onto his sleeve and the floor.

"You'll moan when we're done with you," Damon said darkly. "You'll beg us to kill you." Before Kurt could respond, he leaned over and ended the call.

"Have I mentioned recently how much I really, really hate him?" Gianni said. "He's such a shithead. Actually, that's an insult to shitheads. He's worse than a shithead."

"He really is," Hunter said. He looked like he wanted to live up to his name and hunt Kurt down personally and drag him here by his balls.

Parker looked similarly furious. "He must have missed the part where pissing off a member of the Brantley family was a really, really bad idea. People who do it tend to live to regret it."

"Yes, they do," Hunter agreed. "What else can we do? It's not fair for this oxygen thief to keep living any longer than necessary. Another hour is too much."

"Short of knocking on every door in Dusk Bay…" Damon rubbed his forehead with the heel of his hand. "We're doing everything we can think of."

No one suggested actually going door-to-door. That would be time-consuming and ultimately pointless.

Kurt was likely moving around, and wasn't dumb enough to open a knock on the door. He'd have someone to do that for him. Someone to take the bullet if one was aimed at him. No, we'd have to be smarter than that.

"Mina, can I have your phone?" Parker asked. "I can at least try to trace wherever he called from. I couldn't last time, but it's worth a try."

I nodded and handed him my phone. "Just don't go poking around in the apps in there."

He grinned. "I wouldn't dream of it. And I won't look at your photos either, just in case there's a dick pic from Reuben." He stuck out his tongue in playful disgust, his eyes shining with amusement.

Reuben gave him a look that was drier than a martini, before raising his hand in front of him. His palm was red with blood from the imploding glass. Indifferent, he walked over to the wet bar on the side of the room and poured himself another drink, this time a double.

"She's more likely to get a dick pic from me," Gianni said.

Parker grimaced. "That's just as good a reason not to look in her photos. No offence. You're almost as much a big brother to me as Reuben is."

"How am I supposed to take offence when you finish with something like that?" Gianni stepped over to give Parker a hug.

Parker hugged him back. "I know what to say to avoid getting shot."

"So far," Damon said. He smirked at Parker.

Parker grinned. "I'm going to fuck up at some point and I know that, but in the meantime, I'll keep trying to be smooth. It's gotten me this far. I might even live to be as old as Reuben."

"Not if you call me old." Reuben downed the contents of his glass in one gulp and poured another.

Both twins chuckled and fist bumped at the expense of their oldest brother. If they weren't giving him hell, they wouldn't be themselves. Even if it scored them dark looks from time to time.

"I'll get this back to you as soon as I can." Parker nodded towards the phone in his hand. "And I'll change the number to one that'll be harder for him to get a hold of."

I shook my head. "Don't bother. The cockier he gets, the better chance he'll make a mistake. He already did by reminding us he was watching tonight. We know he's still in Dusk Bay. We know to look out for something. Something big."

"He could be trying to convince us he's doing something when he's not," Damon said.

He didn't look like he believed that any more than I did. Something was coming and, whatever it was, we had to be ready.

If not, I might have to take a leaf from Angelina's book and step out the front of the house before someone else paid the price for me.

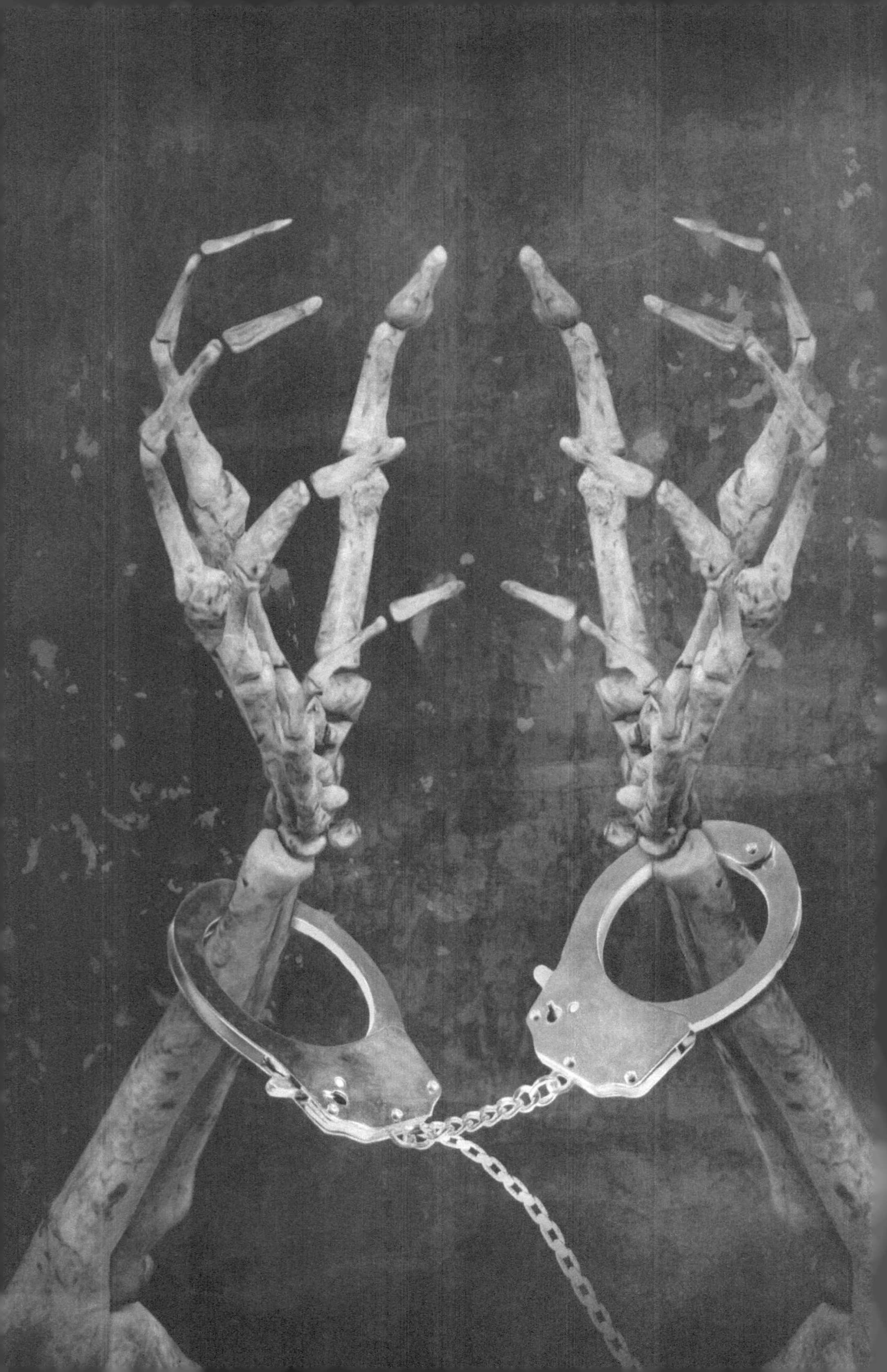

CHAPTER 13

MINA

My hair still damp from the shower, I stepped out of Reuben's ensuite and into his bedroom.

All three of my guys stood beside the window, talking in hushed tones. They stopped the minute they saw me and stared with open hunger in their eyes, like three lions sizing up a delicious deer. Trying to decide which bit they'd feast on first.

Not long ago, that deer's instinct would have been to flee into the forest. Now I stood my ground, letting them appraise me. Admire and want me.

Making me want them.

"Did I miss something?" I asked lightly.

I combed my fingers through my hair. Healthier than ever, dark waves hung down to my shoulders. Now I was eating properly and keeping clean, it was growing quickly. My scars would never disappear, but my skin was healthier too.

At some point, I might get past the urge to shower two or three times a day. After being filthy for so long, I loved being clean. I couldn't get enough of standing under, or soaking in, hot water. It was the ultimate luxury. Sometimes it really was the little things in life that mattered. I didn't care if we lived in a tiny house, as long as we had running hot water. I promised myself I'd never wash in cold again. Not if I could help it.

"No. You didn't miss anything important." Reuben's tone made it clear that whatever they were talking about, they wouldn't elaborate.

Not long ago, I would have been insecure about them keeping something from me, but now I trusted that if I needed to know, they'd fill me in. They might have been discussing nothing more important than the weather. Making small talk while they waited for me.

All right, I suspected it was something more than that, but still not vital. Not more important than us spending this time together.

Reuben moved towards me, took my hands to pull me to him. He kissed my mouth, softly at first, but quickly deepening.

Every time he touched me, he held back less and less. So did I. What used to be terrifying, was becoming as comfortable as it was natural. More and more, I could let go of my inhibitions. I could be myself around them, like I never could with anyone else.

In the corner of my eye, I watched Damon walk over to the door. I thought he was leaving, but he closed it and turned the lock, to give all four of us privacy from the rest of the house.

A shiver of excitement passed through me. In the back of my mind, I still struggled to get my head around the fact three incredible men wanted me, but I pushed the insecurity aside. They'd all made it abundantly clear how they felt. It was time for me to accept and embrace everything they wanted to give to me. Including themselves.

Gianni moved to stand behind me. His hands were firm on my shoulders before starting to massage them, his long fingers working out all the knots. Gradually, he moved his hands down my arms, down my sides, to my hips. He held them cupped in his palms while pressing his erection into my side.

"The things you do to me," he whispered. "Since I met you, I feel like I'm hard all the time. No one has ever made me feel like that. Not even Damon."

Damon grunt-laughed. "Same here."

I broke off my kiss with Reuben to grab Damon by the front of his shirt and tug him in for a kiss. I needed him to know he was very much wanted.

My feelings for all three of them were equal. I needed all of them as much as each other. When it came to intimacy, I wanted Damon to put his insecurities aside like I was trying to do. Put them aside and let go.

Surprised at first, Damon quickly rallied and kissed me back, his tongue probing into my mouth. Sliding against mine. He tasted of whiskey and spontaneity. Like he understood my desire for him to let me in more. He wanted me to know he was trying.

I gave him that back with my kisses. I was also trying. Together, we could do this.

We explored each other's mouths for a minute or two before we were forced to come up for air.

I sucked in a breath and laughed at the headiness of being kissed so thoroughly. When Damon started to let go, he didn't hold back. He'd put everything into the kisses. Everything and then some.

"My turn." Gianni gripped my chin and turned my face so he could kiss me.

Beside us, Damon and Reuben looked at each other warily, before they came together, hands on each other's shoulders, mouths pressed against each other.

I moaned at the sight in the corner of my eye, and the feeling of Gianni's lips on mine.

The rest of the world evaporated, and all that was left was the four of us. Maybe the world burned down around us, because we were so hot we ignited it. I was that aroused, I wouldn't have been surprised. My panties were so drenched, it was about to trickle down the insides of my thighs.

I found myself lying back on Reuben's bed while all three of them jostled to help me out of my silky sleep shorts and singlet.

After hearing Kurt's voice again, I needed this. I needed to feel wanted and safe and loved. I needed to be touched and to touch. To remind myself I was Mina DiMarco and I was stronger than anything he ever did to me.

All three of my incredible, sexy guys shed their clothes. Shirts, pants, socks and underwear flying. I was quickly surrounded by bare, hot muscle.

As he'd promised, Gianni scooted down until his face was between my legs. Dark eyes on me, he teased my clit with his tongue and fingers. He thrust his tongue inside, and tasted all around my pussy.

Reuben lay beside me running his hands and mouth up and down my body and lavishing attention on my breasts.

Damon watched us for a while, the smallest hint of uncertainty in his eyes.

I gave him a smile of encouragement as he looked at Reuben's cock, while trying not to look at it.

Reuben was also looking at him, speculatively. Not unwelcoming. Not insistent either.

Gianni's gaze swivelled over to Damon, watching intently as the other man lowered himself so Reuben's cock was right in front of his face. His tongue swiped over his lips before he tasted Reuben's head with the tip of his tongue.

Reuben shivered, but didn't pull away.

Encouraged, Damon swirled his tongue around Reuben's tip before taking him into his mouth and starting to suck.

"Good boy," Gianni said before lowering his face back to my pussy and lapping at me more firmly.

Damon managed an eye roll without losing his rhythm.

Reuben and I both rolled our hips in time with each other. He kept one hand on my breast and held my hand with the other, our fingers laced. His grip tightened the closer he came to coming.

"Be a good girl and come with me," he said breathlessly.

I moaned in response. "I'm so close."

"Me too." He forced the words out.

I squeezed his hand hard and came, grinding myself against Gianni's mouth while I saw stars. My ears were filled with the pounding of blood, and the sound of Reuben as he too orgasmed.

For the longest time, there was nothing but bliss and the pleasure of knowing he was feeling the same thing at the same time. That he was squirting his cum into Damon's mouth. That Damon was tasting the salty release that must have coated his tongue.

We sagged back, side-by-side on the mattress.

I lay puffing lightly, catching my breath.

Damon slid his mouth off Reuben's cock and swallowed.

"Just when I think you couldn't get hotter, you do," Gianni said to all of us. He snaked an arm around the back of Damon's head and slammed his mouth down onto the other man's. Letting Damon taste my release from his lips.

Damon groaned. He grabbed Gianni's arm and kissed him like the world was about to end.

They finally broke off and Damon scooted on the bed until his cock was in front of my face.

Gianni rolled me onto my side and gently parted my legs. He gripped my hips, positioned his cock and slid himself into my pussy.

I closed my eyes to savour the feeling of him inside me, his piercings already massaging me.

I opened my eyes again, and my mouth, to take in Damon's cock.

We let Gianni set the rhythm, as he thrusted into me with deep, even strokes.

Reuben moved around to the other side of me so he could slip his hand between my legs and tease my clit with the tips of his fingers.

I was right, the attention of three men at once was incredible and compelling. I'd never felt so full, spoilt or loved in my life. These three men, who would kill without a second thought, fucked me like I was a queen.

I felt like one.

Their queen.

"Good girl," Reuben said. "You take both of their cocks so well. You like being filled like this, don't you? You like it when we fuck you."

I could only respond to him by smiling with my eyes, my mouth was too busy sucking and teasing Damon's cock with my lips and tongue.

"You feel amazing," Gianni said, thrusting slowly.

"Fucking amazing," Damon agreed. "Fucking perfect."

"Fucking ours," Reuben said. "Always. I love you, Mina DiMarco."

I slipped my mouth off Damon's cock long enough to say, "I love you too, Reuben Brantley." I smiled and went back to sucking.

Between Gianni thrusting inside me and Reuben's fingers, I was pushed all the way to the edge and over again. This time, even more intense and all-encompassing than before.

Every single part of my body was on fire with pure heat and pleasure. Nothing existed but that, and a shower of fireworks in my otherwise darkened vision.

"Good girl." Reuben's voice was barely audible over the blood in my ears. "You come for us so beautifully. So fucking gorgeous."

I came back down to reality, quickly catching my breath without stopping sucking.

My whole body went on tingling, but I wanted Damon and Gianni to feel good like I just had. I wanted to give that to them.

"I want both of you to come inside her," Reuben said. "Show her you love her. Show her she's ours."

"Yes, boss," Gianni said, his voice strained. "Just about to… Come… Inside her…" He thrust more frantically before groaning and coming inside my body.

Damon was only a couple of moments behind, thrusting into my mouth, all the way down to my throat.

I gagged, but went on sucking until he exploded in my mouth. A blast of warm cum shot into my throat before I swallowed it down.

"Good girl," Reuben said. "Take every drop. It's all for you. All for our beautiful woman."

Damon slipped out of my mouth and sagged down in a corner between Reuben and the wall.

Gianni, panting lightly, stayed buried inside me until his breath finally slowed.

"I could stay here forever." He sounded sleepy. "My cock doesn't want to leave your pussy. He might just live there forever."

In spite of that, he gradually slid out of me and held me close. "I love you."

"I love you too," I told him. I snuggled up to him and glanced over to Damon.

"You're still a distraction, but I also love you," he said with a grunt.

I smiled. "You're still an asshole, but I love you too." He wasn't that much of an asshole anymore, but I couldn't resist ribbing him. What were boyfriends for, after all?

"Let's get you cleaned up," Gianni said. "Then, maybe round two, in the shower."

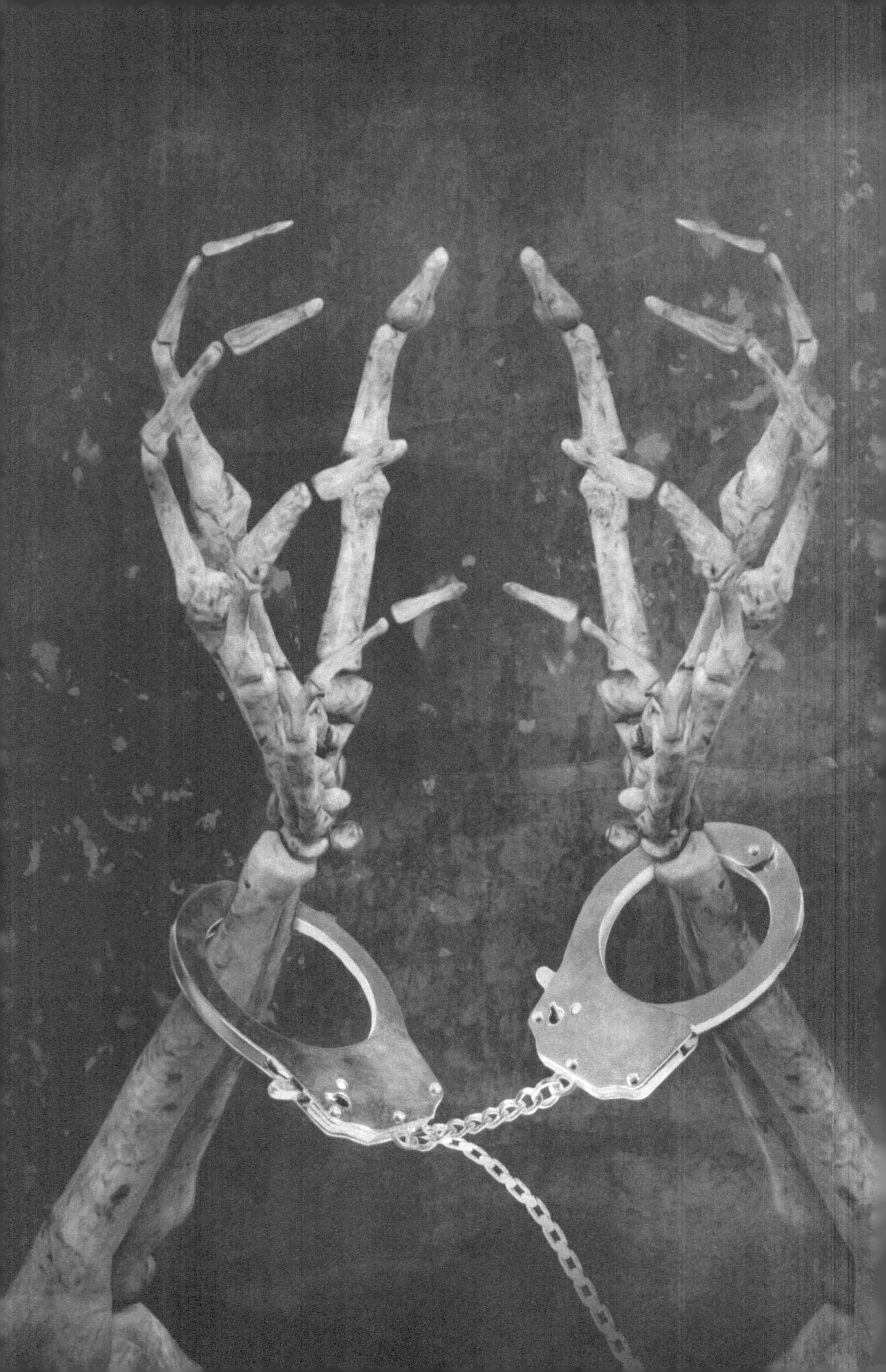

CHAPTER 14

MINA

"He's not looking so good." Gianni looked sideways at Leon Graves. "I guess hanging from a chain for a week will do that to a guy."

"I guess so," I agreed with no shred of remorse.

Leon was pale, and his wrists chafed from the cuffs around them. Heavy circles surrounded his eyes, and bags hung underneath. He couldn't have had much sleep between the position he was chained in, and the constant barrage of loud, metal music.

He looked all but broken, and the only place Gianni touched him was in his calf. As torture went, it was clearly effective.

"I told you everything I know," Leon said. "Please…" There was no hint of hope in his eyes anymore. Nothing but the desire for all of this to end.

"Martina was a bust." Gianni briefly told Leon about our meeting with her, and about Enzo and Angelina. And the phone call from Kurt. "So you see, we're back at square one. Reuben doesn't like being at square one, Leon. Especially when you were the one who guided us there. We need more information. Better information. Who exactly is this Jase? Who is Hammer?"

"I don't know," Leon whined. "I swear. I've told you everything I can think of. Please…"

"Everything you can think of?" Gianni echoed. "I guess you better think about things you haven't thought of yet. Otherwise, I might have to find some different music to play for you. What about some kid's music?"

"That would be evil," I remarked. "I've heard some of it since... I came home. It would drive anyone crazy."

"Exactly." Gianni grinned. "Can you imagine hearing 'climbing goat, goat, goat,' over and over? Or the next chorus, 'fainting goat, goat, goat.' I guess whoever wrote that has a thing about goats."

"I think they have a thing about earworms," I remarked. "Excuse me if I stick to Bobby Sparkle."

Gianni snapped his fingers. "We could play that and pretend we're at a school disco."

Leon groaned. "You're both out of your fucking minds."

Gianni crouched down in front of him. "That's not a nice thing to say about my woman, Leon."

Leon raised his chin and almost managed to look defiant. "Why don't you go on and kill me then?"

He sucked in a ragged breath and spoke in a hoarse voice. "Kurt enjoyed raping her. I enjoyed watching it. I enjoyed every moment of it. I was hoping he'd let me do it too. I wanted to stick my cock in her mouth and make her suck it."

I pushed down the spike of anxiety at the memories his words evoked.

"I was just about to tell Gianni I thought you'd outlived your usefulness." I stepped closer. "But for that, you can live for a while longer." He deserved to suffer a little more for bringing all of that up. A lot more.

His head flopped back down and he groaned softly. Frustrated that his attempt to provoke us into killing him had failed miserably.

His next words came out in a pleading rush. "Jase's last name is Andrews. Jason Andrews. He was an old friend of Kurt. Hammer's real name is Wade. I heard Kurt call him that once. I don't know what his last name is, I swear. They might be brothers, I don't know."

Gianni glanced over to me questioningly, but I shrugged. Neither name was familiar. Leon might have made them up in the moment, to give us something.

I pulled out my phone and sent off a message to Damon to put his contacts onto finding anyone by those names.

"That wasn't so hard, was it?" Gianni asked. He gave Leon a shove, just enough to force him half a metre sideways, and put more pressure on his wrists.

Leon screamed. "Fucking hell. Please, for fuck's sake, I don't know anything else."

"What about Kurt's addresses in Dusk Bay?" I asked. "You must have some idea. Where were his minions supposed to take me?"

"I don't know." He shook his head and winced.

"I don't believe you," I said. "I might reconsider letting you live for longer if you can give us more."

"On my laptop," he said finally.

"We got it from Clarissa, but haven't been able to get into it yet," Gianni said. "You can imagine what that did to the twins' egos. Especially Parker. He prides himself on that shit."

"I can tell you how to get in," Leon said eagerly. "There's more information on there. Most of it is encrypted. You'll need my help to access it. If you let me go, I can—"

Gianni said. "Tell us how to get in. If that works, we might decide to go easier on you."

Leon exhaled, long and ragged, but started to explain.

"I'd be impressed if he wasn't a toad," Parker said. He lounged over the kitchen island, Leon's laptop open front of him. "I've never seen encryption like this. He must have developed it himself."

"Is there anything useful on there?" I asked. As far as I could tell, computer code was another language. One the twins were apparently fluent in, but that made little sense to me.

"That depends on your definition of useful," Parker said. "There's a shit load of records of transactions. Money coming in and out, goods being moved around. That should help us find some of the shipments he stole from us. And from the Bell family." He glanced at Hunter, who didn't quite meet his eyes.

"What about addresses?" Damon asked. "In particular, in and around Dusk Bay?"

"Several," Parker replied. "Nothing that stands out."

"Anything near Demons' Arena?" I asked.

"A couple of them," Parker said. "By the way, no luck on tracing Kurt's phone number." He pulled my phone out of his pocket and handed it to me. "He's a slippery motherfucker."

"Yes, he is." That wasn't news to any of us.

I put my phone away and waved toward the laptop. "Any indication of a connection between Kurt and those addresses?"

"Those addresses being on here suggests there's a connection," Parker said. "There's nothing concrete. Nothing is labelled 'Kurt's main residence,' or 'Kurt's place of business.' You think they would have tried to be more helpful, but apparently not." He flipped the laptop off.

"Send them to me," Damon said. "I'll see what our people can find out."

"Tell them to be on their guard," Reuben said. "There's a good chance Kurt will expect us to check out each location for ourselves. Which is why we won't. We won't walk into any traps."

"Kurt probably gave those addresses to Leon, knowing we might find them," I said.

Reuben was right, that was a trap waiting to happen. And probably the exact reason why Kurt mentioned watching me throw the knife at Carlos. He was hoping to draw us to him. We needed to find a way to turn that back on him.

"He really screwed Leon over," Gianni remarked. He didn't look even slightly sympathetic. "He used him to try to lure Mina, knowing if we got to him first, he could turn it to his advantage. I'd be impressed, if he wasn't such a complete and utter prick."

"Kurt or Leon?" Hunter asked.

"Yes," Gianni replied with a smile.

Hunter grinned. "Both sounds about right."

While Parker continued to go through the laptop, I stepped over to Damon. "Any luck on finding Jason Andrews, or Wade?"

He rolled his lips. "We've discovered Jason Andrews is a very common name, as is Wade. I have my contacts looking for brothers called Jason and Wade, who might work for Kurt. Or be an old friend of his. If they even exist, they'll be found."

"They exist," I said. "Or, they used to."

I'd thought about them often, but I still couldn't clearly picture their faces. Just vague details about their build and hair colour. Their voices were more vivid than their appearances. But I knew if I met them again, I'd know them immediately.

"Either way, we'll find out." He put a reassuring arm around me, his large hand squeezing my shoulder. "We're closer than we were when we just had the nickname, Hammer."

"Yeah, I know we are," I said.

We weren't close enough, but Damon was doing the best he could.

I knew I wasn't alone in my frustration. Kurt had been playing games with us for weeks, and it was getting exhausting. Every time we seemed to be getting somewhere, we took a step back. Or several.

I pictured him laughing at us as he toyed with our strings, like we were his puppets. Tweaking and making us dance to his tunes.

Fuckhead.

I wanted to punch the smug smile off his smug, asshole face. Right before I sliced of his cock and balls and made him eat them. And then—

"Bingo, motherfucker," Parker said suddenly.

"What is it?" Reuben leaned over his shoulder.

"It's an encrypted conversation between Leon and Kurt," Parker said. "Kurt telling Leon when to arrive in Dusk Bay and where to go. It goes back a lot further than that. There are details of meetings between them, including addresses of the places they met up. Kurt telling Leon who to speak to. A number where he can be reached."

My heart started racing. "Any chance you can trace that number?"

"There's every chance I'm going to try," he agreed. "In the meantime, I'll send all of this to Damon. This could help narrow things down."

"Only if it's legit," Damon said.

"Considering the layers of encryption, we weren't meant to find this," Parker said. "I don't mean to toot my own horn, but someone less skilled than me wouldn't get in." He tapped the tip of his finger on the island, beside the laptop. "We definitely weren't meant to see this. I'd bet my trust fund on it."

"If you lose that bet, I'm not sharing," Hunter told him.

Parker flashed him a grin. "I won't lose." He turned back to the screen. "All of this goes back before Kurt took Mina." He squinted. "By the look of it, Kurt had all of that planned for weeks. Maybe even months." He frowned deeply.

"What is it?" I asked.

"It seems like Leon is the one who found out about your father's attempt to take down the Brantley family. There's messages in here of him telling Kurt all the details. He must have been pleased with himself, because he didn't delete what I'd consider to be fucking damning evidence. Smug prick. He was very sure no one was getting past his encryption. I love being underestimated. Especially when it helps to fuck people over. There's enough chain in here for him to hang himself."

"Yeah," I said vaguely.

I'd known Leon was a snake, but now I knew he was the one who gave Kurt the weapon to get to me. He was as much to blame as Kurt was. They were in all of it together. Right from the start.

"How did Leon find out?" I asked.

"It seems he stumbled upon some transactions that didn't add up. He looked into it and found evidence that pointed straight to Mina's father," Parker said. "I get the impression Leon and Kurt were pretty tight. Assholes of a feather and all that shit. He ran straight to his bestie to spill the tea. And Kurt used that information to his own advantage. Leon gave him an opportunity and he took it. Some close friend Kurt turned out to be. The first chance he got, he threw him right under the bus and into our basement. With friends like him, who needs enemies?" He turned to Hunter and they both shrugged.

"What do you want to do?" Gianni asked me.

I became aware of all of their eyes on me. My tongue slid across my lips. "I think we should let him go. Leon Graves, we should unchain him and let him out."

"Why would we do that?" Reuben asked.

"Because I think he can lead us to Kurt," I said.

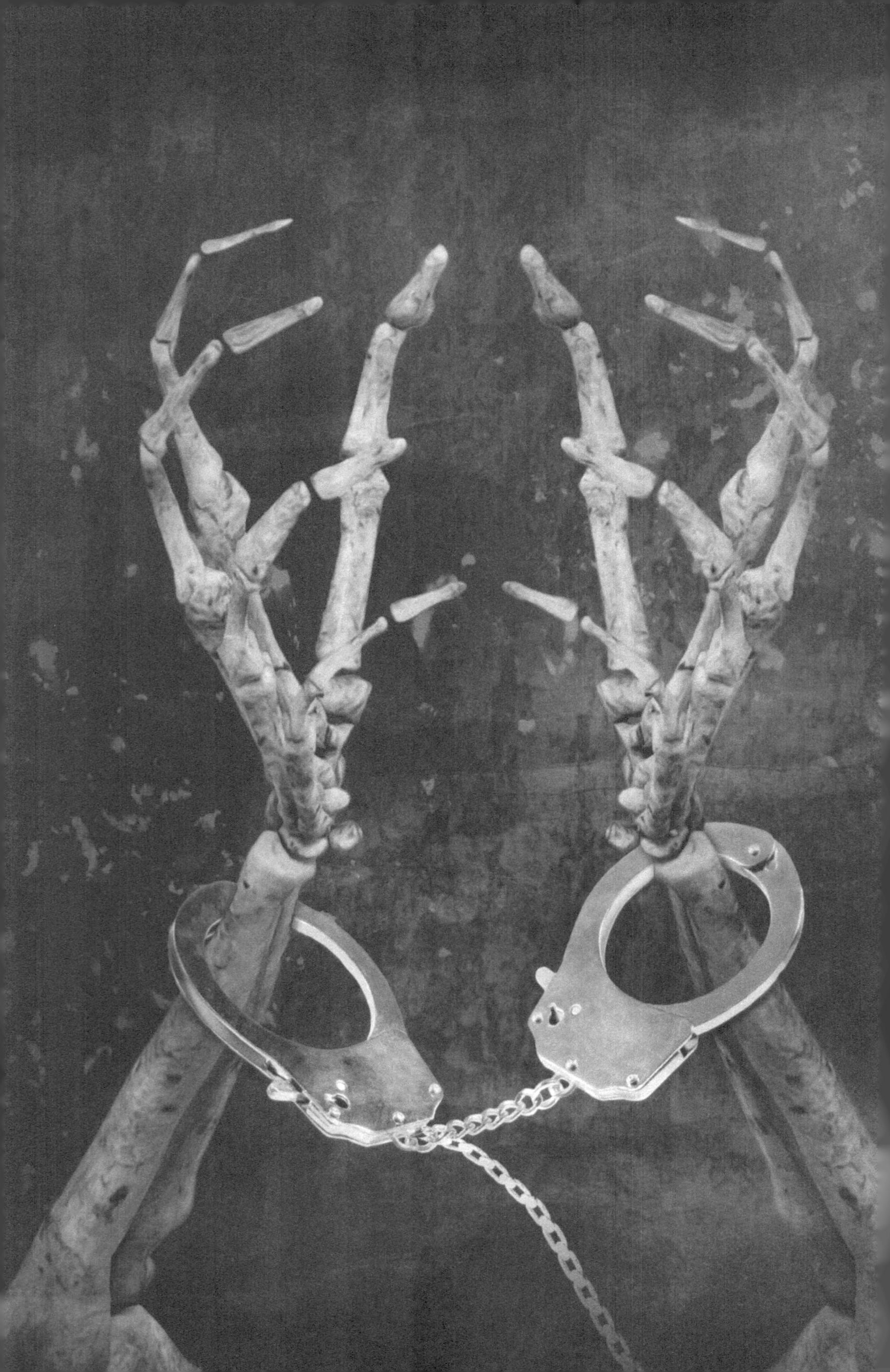

CHAPTER 15

GIANNI

I leaned my shoulder against the wall and watched Leon eat his bowl of soup.

He stopped every now and again to dip in a chunk of bread, before stuffing it into his mouth. The whole time, he kept half an eye on us.

Unfortunately, his food wasn't poisoned. Not even with a handy laxative. I suggested it, but no one seemed to like the idea apart from me. I put it aside for potential future use on Caleb instead. It might help to get the stick out of his ass. Or on the twins, just for shits and giggles.

We all ate from the same pot of soup made by Terry. And the same loaf of freshly made bread. Personally, I would have given Leon stale bread and maybe a glass of dirty water. Between Terry's pride and Mina's insistence we treat him well, I held my peace.

For now.

I wouldn't have minded if he choked on that bread. We'd been too nice to him as far as I was concerned. We'd even stopped to treat the knife wound in his leg. And of course, slip in a tracking chip. Asshole wasn't getting off that easy.

"How long have you known Damon?" Mina asked Angelina. She was chewing on a piece of bread covered in a thin layer of butter. She still half closed her eyes while she ate, as though everything was pure heaven. Granted, Terry's bread was that good, but when you're virtually starved for so long, even substandard food would taste amazing.

I made a mental note to let Terry have a night off and make her my family's special carbonara recipe. I prepare it with a secret ingredient I don't share with anyone. If I did, I'd have to kill them. That's how secret it is.

Angelina shrugged and slurped her soup. "A few years, I guess. Ever since Reuben took over as head of the Brantley family. I used to have the biggest crush on him." She slid a sly glance toward Enzo and Damon.

Enzo glared at Damon like he might carve out his brother's heart out with the spoon in his hand.

"Me too," I said to break the tension.

Damon wouldn't have been interested in Angelina in that way anyway. Especially given her relation to Carlos. Carlos would have come after him instead. Nothing Damon couldn't handle, but a complication he neither needed nor wanted.

I got the impression he thought of her as something of a little sister. To be honest, I was starting to think of her in the same way myself. She had more balls than most of the men I knew. Enzo would certainly have his hands full with her. And vice versa. Their lives together wouldn't be boring.

Hopefully it wouldn't also be short.

Damon shot me a glance before returning to his meal.

"Who is Salvador?" Mina asked.

I'd been wondering the same thing myself. Damon worked closer with the Vipers than I did, which wasn't saying much. They were secretive when it came to outsiders. Just like we were. Let people in on your secrets, and they tend to use them against you. Or mess up perfectly good carbonara. That was a crime if there ever was one.

"Salvador Briggs is my brother's right hand," Angelina said. "At least, that's what he's angling for. He's about fifteen years older than me." She made a face like that made him incredibly old.

The age difference in age between Mina and I was about the same.

And that between her and Damon and Reuben. Although, Mina was mature for her age.

I wouldn't wish for Angelina to grow up quicker, as she had. She had plenty of time. I hoped.

Reuben slid her a glance, suggesting he wasn't as engrossed in his own meal as he looked. Of course not, he was always paying attention. Nothing got past him.

People were more likely to let down their guard when they thought someone wasn't listening, even when that someone was him. It was a good way to learn any number of things.

'Observe, listen and absorb,' might be his motto. Along with 'anyone who got in his way was dead.' Or wished they were. Sometimes, he liked to bide his time, but he always fucked back sooner or later. Usually way worse than anything inflicted on him.

"He needs to keep his hands to himself before someone cuts them off," Enzo said. "If he touches Angie…"

Once again, he gripped his spoon like he'd use it as a knife.

"You're so hot when you get angry and possessive." She leaned over to kiss his cheek.

He melted immediately.

"Just then?" he asked, the dimple in his cheek showing. That dimple would have gotten him into a lot of trouble over the years. And probably got him out of just as much.

No one could resist guys like him. Guys who were much prettier than me. Luckily, I could get by on my charm and personality. And lack of remorse when people who pissed me off ended up dead.

"No, not just then." She socked him on the arm teasingly. "Other times too, but don't let it go to your fucking head."

He grinned more broadly. Clearly, he was head over heels for the woman.

I hoped they'd find a way to get their happy ending.

In the meantime, my attention returned to Leon. Like Reuben, he was pretending not to listen. He was probably taking in every word, but he'd learn nothing important from us. All he got so far was a couple of crushes, and the weather forecast for the rest of the week.

"This soup is really good," Leon said. "Much nicer than the food in the basement." He glanced at Mina, as though maybe he wasn't referring to our basement.

To her credit, she didn't stab him in the neck with a butter knife, or even look angry. She was completely composed and calm. Ready for him to try to provoke her. Ready, also, to pretend she wasn't ready to slice him into pieces for his part in her imprisonment.

"We take good care of our guests," I said. "You've been helpful to us, so there's no reason to be anything but nice. Right, Damon?"

Damon grunted and went on eating.

"That's Damon for, 'you're absolutely right, like always, Gianni.' With a little bit of, 'how did you get so wise?' As a matter of fact, I wonder that myself some days. But here we are."

Damon and Leon both snorted. Then glared at each other.

"See how well we're getting along?" I asked.

I briefly wondered if I could change everybody's mind and, instead, tie rocks to Leon's ankles and throw him off the cliff. The only person in the room who didn't want that was Leon. Frankly, if the rest of us did, then he didn't get a vote.

Unfortunately, right now, neither did I. I'd just inserted the tracking chip as ordered and hoped like hell the plan went the way it was supposed to.

"It's all rainbows and lollipops around here," Parker said from the other end of the table.

"And sunshine and bunny rabbits," Hunter agreed, sarcastically. "Are you almost finished?" He glanced at Leon's bowl. "Reuben wants us to drive you into the city. After that, you're on your own. If it was up to us, you'd walk there."

"True story," Parker said. "But thanks to you telling us how to get into your laptop, we're that much closer to pinning down Kurt."

Leon glanced at him, visibly worried we got into the heavily encrypted information he'd tried to hide.

Every single person sitting at this long dining table had perfected the art of the poker face a long time ago.

Parker had closed those files and assured us Leon would never know we were in there.

All we'd told Leon was that he was actually helpful, and we'd decided we got all we could from him, and couldn't be bothered to kill him.

We also all knew he wasn't that stupid. Of course we wouldn't just let him go and that was that. Leading us to Kurt was a faint hope at best. But with the tracking chip embedded in his leg, we could take him back anytime we wanted to. He'd get that one way trip off the cliff, soon enough.

"Yes, I'm finished," Leon said finally. "Let's go."

If I didn't know better, I'd think he was worried we'd change our minds. Okay, I'd be worried about that too, if I was him. People like us didn't show mercy. He knew we were up to something, if not what. He'd go to ground the second he could. And we'd be watching every move.

The twins leapt to their feet and Hunter hurried to grab the keys to the SUV.

"Drive safely," I called out behind them. "And Leon." I waited until he turned back to say, "Be good."

He looked as though he wanted to sneer, but instead he nodded and hurried after the twins.

"Is anyone counting down?" I asked.

"I am." Damon had his phone in his hand and was watching the app that tracked the SUV. "It won't be long."

Enzo and Angelina glanced at each other.

"Is there anything we can do?" Angelina asked. "I mean, you helped us, so it's only fair."

Enzo looked at her funny. "What the hell? We need to get the fuck out of here."

"You're not going anywhere," Damon said without looking up.

Enzo glared at him. "You can't—"

"Yes, we can," Reuben said. "You can help by staying here. We'll need you. And anyone else we can get."

"What are you expecting?" Enzo asked.

"It's time," Damon said without answering his question. He rose to his feet "Enzo, Angie, stay here and listen to Caleb's orders. He should be down soon." He nodded towards the stairs. "If all goes well, we won't be long."

"What the fuck?" Enzo insisted.

Angelina actually looked excited. "You have enough weapons for us?"

"We have plenty." I placed my hands on the table, to either side of my empty bowl and pushed myself up before moving to stay beside Mina. "Are you sure you won't stay here, boss?"

"We've got this," Damon said, his worried gaze on Reuben.

"I'm coming," Reuben said simply, and that was that.

"Are you sure you don't need—" Enzo started.

"We've got this," Damon said again before unlocking and opening the door to the garage.

"If we don't come back in an hour, send help. And don't open the door to any strangers," I said.

"We won't," Caleb said as he hurried down the stairs. "Go." He actually looked concerned. Whether it was for his own safety, or for Reuben and the twins', I didn't know.

He might have even been worried about me, which was sweet, but unnecessary. I had no intention of dying tonight.

No, my plans included Mina's pussy and Damon's cock.

I followed them and Reuben out the door and into the other SUV.

"Are you all right?" I asked Mina after she secured her seatbelt.

She glanced over at me and nodded. She was already in assassin mode. No smiles or laughs now, just stoic professionalism. She was never hotter than she was right then.

"I'll be better when this is done," she said.

"Everything is in place," Damon assured her, speaking over his shoulder. "It won't be much longer."

"I know," she said. "I've just been waiting a really long time for this."

I laced my fingers in hers. "You have. But everything ends tonight. By the time the sun rises again, Kurt Lasalle will either be dead or regretting every single one of his life choices."

"I can't fucking wait," she whispered.

"Neither can I," I agreed. "Neither can I."

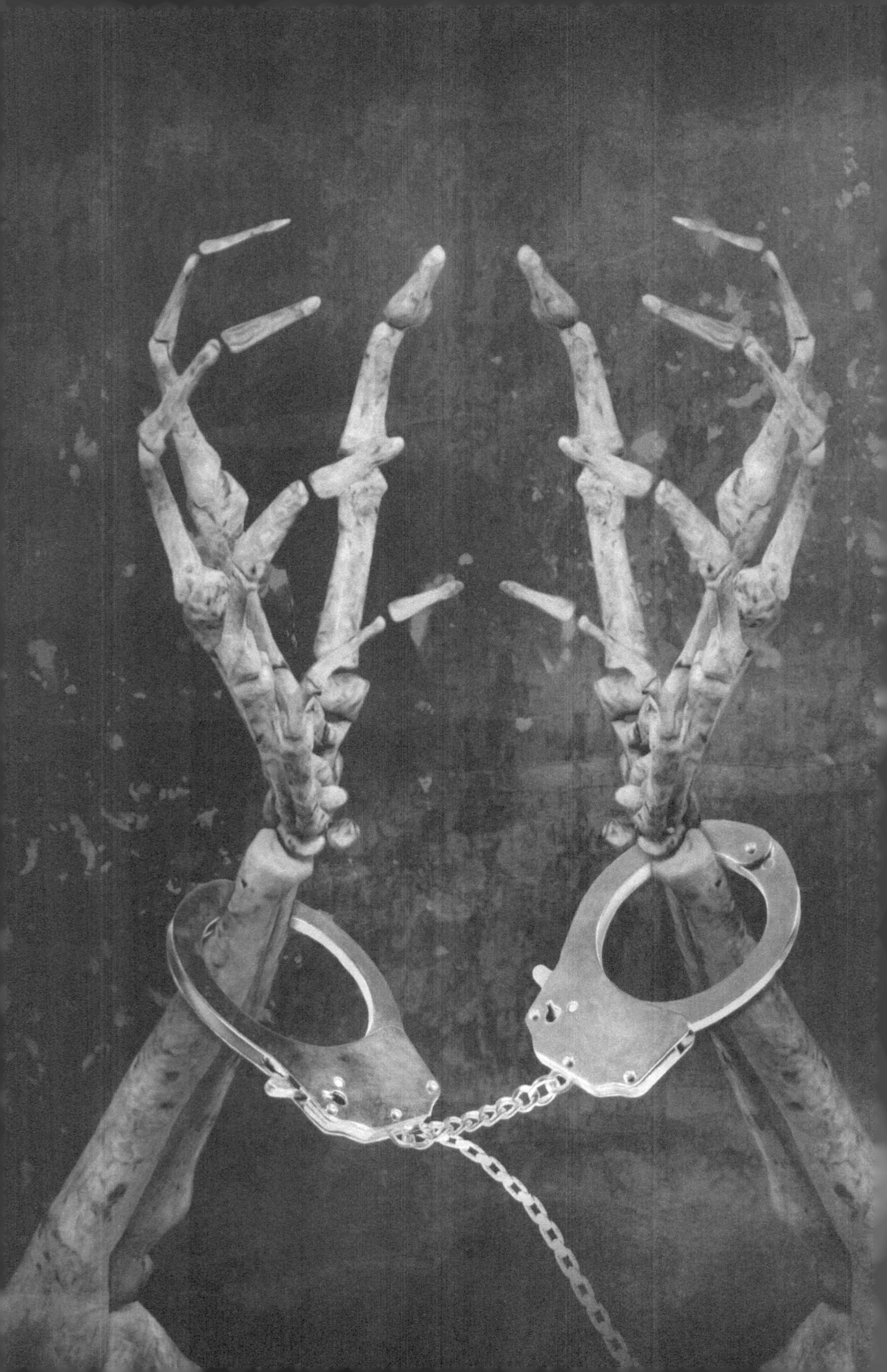

CHAPTER 16

MINA

"Where are they?" I leaned as far forward as the seat belt would let me and peered over the front seat. Damon had connected the tracker in his phone to the dashboard of the SUV, and glanced down at it every so often for directions.

"About another kilometre away," Damon said.

"Stop a hundred metres away," Reuben said. "We won't get any closer without being seen." He pointed at the map, and a street beside the flashing light that indicated the stopped SUV. A smaller flashing light showed the whereabouts of Leon Graves. One transposed over the other.

"Got it, boss," Damon said. He slowed the SUV a few moments later and pulled over to the side of the road.

I followed my three men out of the vehicle and down the otherwise empty suburban street. Shivers slid slowly up and down my spine.

I didn't need to, but I checked my knives and gun anyway. In the corner of my eye, I saw Gianni do the same. Then Damon. Only Reuben seemed calm in spite of everything.

I drew on that, using it to buoy my nerves. Anxiety wasn't useful. If I ever needed to be composed, it was now, tonight.

We reached the corner of an average looking street, lined with trees.

On a normal day, nothing much exciting would happen here, not even in Dusk Bay.

A dog barked as we walked past one house. A TV was on in another. It sounded like they were watching some kind of game show. The kind where people answered trivia questions in return for cash prizes.

Gianni enjoyed one which involved a huge machine dropping discs like an arcade game, if the questions were answered correctly. He was good at pop culture questions and I was good at geography and history. Mostly, I think we were both mesmerised by the machine sliding back and forth, pushing the discs forward.

Through the trees, the lights of the first SUV were visible, along with three other vehicles, facing it. Three figures sat in ours, while several people surrounded it. They each had guns pointed at the windows.

"Good luck with that," Damon muttered.

I glanced over at him and nodded. All of Reuben's cars had bullet-proof glass. No one was shooting Leon or the twins, but they couldn't shoot out either.

"Can you make out Kurt?" Gianni whispered.

I squinted, but shook my head. "Not yet."

I wasn't sure if he'd come in person, but I hoped he would. Caleb had put out the word that Leon told us everything except Kurt's whereabouts. In addition to that, he'd put out the suggestion we were moving Leon to a different location. Somewhere likely to get more information from him.

It seemed Reuben had someone working for him, who had different torture techniques to force information out of people. When Gianni spoke of Ice Miller, he spoke with admiration. It took a lot to impress Gianni, so these techniques must be very efficient.

Shame Leon wouldn't end up there.

All of this, in the hope it drew Kurt out to save Leon or kill him.

Judging by the presence of the armed people around the SUV, that was exactly what we achieved.

"I'm going to go around behind the other vehicles," I said. "If he's here, he might be inside one of them."

Reuben nodded. "Gianni, go with her. Damon, signal the twins that we're ready." He pulled out a gun.

Shit was about to get very real.

Gianni and I circled back and slipped between two of the houses.

That meant climbing over fences and dodging a very feisty dog. He looked like a cross between a Jack Russell terrier and a fox terrier, with a fan tail and a face that said, 'give me cheese,' rather than, 'I want to bite your face off.' He even let Gianni give him a pat, before rolling over onto his back and offering me his belly.

"You could use some work on your guard dog skills, buddy," I whispered. "But you're very cute."

The dog wagged his tail, got back up and ran off back inside when someone called his name.

"See, even dogs like you," Gianni said. "Dogs are very good judges of character."

"He liked you too," I pointed out. I gripped the top of the fence and pulled myself up, thankful for the strength I'd finally managed to regain.

"I rest my case." Gianni grinned and pulled himself up beside me. "When this is over, we should talk Reuben into letting us get a dog. We could train it to bite Caleb."

I managed a soft laugh, but we couldn't have done this without the help of Caleb. He was a prickly prick, but he knew how to get things done. That was exactly what we needed right now.

"It would probably bite Damon instead." I dropped down off the fence onto the grass.

"I see no problem here," Gianni said. "Damon would probably enjoy it."

"I suspect you'd enjoy it more," I said lightly.

Okay, thinking about biting Gianni was a distraction I didn't need right now. I pushed it into the back of my mind for later.

We slipped across the next backyard and over another fence, before dropping down in the bushes beside the street. We were twenty metres behind the enemy vehicles.

"Can you see anyone inside?" Gianni asked.

I squinted. "I don't know. I need to get closer."

"*We* need to get closer," Gianni corrected.

"It'll be easier for one of us to go undetected," I said. It was a losing battle, but I was going to try to fight it anyway, to keep him safe.

"Maybe, but I'm not letting you go by yourself," he said firmly. He didn't put his foot down often, but when he did, there was as much chance of budging him as there was changing Reuben's mind, or Damon's. Or mine, for that matter.

I was about to rise, when the sound of gunshots rang out through the quiet of the evening.

The dog barked a couple of times, but that was the only indication anyone in any of the houses noticed. They must have assumed it was a backfiring car or someone else's TV.

A shout sounded close by, followed by another, then footsteps running toward our SUV.

"That's our cue," Gianni whispered.

I stayed in a crouch for a few moments longer.

Reuben, Damon and the twins were capable of taking care of themselves, and I was torn. I wanted to see if the person in the back of the vehicle was Kurt, but should we deal with his people first? If it was Kurt in there, we'd get another opportunity, sooner or later. But if my men died in the process… None of this would have been worth it.

"Reuben would want Kurt taken care of," Gianni whispered.

I shook my head. "Not at the expense of family. Killing him isn't worth losing them. We need to go back. We have to help them."

Another shot rang out, followed by a cry of pain. One that was cut short by another gunshot.

The blood froze in my veins.

For the first time in my life, I was unable to move.

It wasn't indecision, it was fear. This was my plan and so much could go wrong. It might already have gone to hell. If it had, it would be my fault. I could have let them kill Leon, or done it myself.

Instead, I'd come up with a plan to try to get Kurt's attention. To get him to come to us. My guys, the twins and Caleb had all filled in the blanks, but it was my idea.

If they died, their blood would be all over my hands. Seeping into my skin. Soaking my soul, like the blood of that little girl.

So much blood it would turn black and flow through the streets.

It threatened to wash over me and drown me, filling my lungs full until I couldn't breathe. My head spun.

"Mina." Gianni gripped my shoulders tight enough to bruise.

I wanted to flinch, but I couldn't even do that. My mind took me right back to the first moment when I woke up in that cage.

I was cold, bare. A tight strap around my ankle. I hurt all over. The insides of my thighs were sticky. I tried to sit up, but I bumped my head on the bars of the cage.

I winced and rubbed my head. What the hell was going on? Was this some kind of prank?

It was dark. My eyes took a while to become accustomed to the gloom. While they did, I felt around me, trying to figure out where I was and how I could get out.

A cage?

The cage was locked. It wasn't long enough to let me stretch out fully, or high enough to let me sit up. I had to curl up to get... Not comfortable. That wasn't happening here, there wasn't room. I couldn't lie flat. I was coiled like a spring instead.

There weren't bars underneath me, just concrete. The cage must have been bolted to the floor. The floor was cold and hard.

How had I gotten here? The last thing I remembered was my father bringing me a drink of... Was it lemonade? He had a strange look on his face, but talked to me about nothing in particular until I drank it all down.

I couldn't remember anything else. Nothing until I woke up alone.

Outside the cage, a door opened and someone stepped inside.

My blood turned cold.

"Mina," Gianni said insistently. "Come back to me. We need you right here, right now. You're not locked up in that cage anymore. No one will do that to you again. I promise. But we need to move. Come on, sweetheart. Come back to me."

I blinked a few times to clear my vision and my mind.

Where was I?

Still on a suburban street, an SUV parked nearby. Gunshots. Shouts. *Shit.*

Could I have chosen a worse time to freak out and lose my mind in the shadows of the past? Anyone could have crept up behind me and I wouldn't have known. I tried to remind myself that wouldn't have happened, but I was so lost in the memory… There was no guarantee.

"I'm here," I whispered. "I'm sorry, I don't know what happened."

"What happened was, you're still human," he said gently. "But we need to decide what to do. Do we see if that's Kurt, or do we help the others?"

"I need to see if it's Kurt," I said finally. My guys were not going to let themselves get killed. They weren't. I had to have faith in that. But I needed to know. If we were this close to him and didn't even try, then we'd taken this risk for nothing.

"All right, let's go." Gianni dropped his hands from my shoulders, to wrap them around my fingers. "Unless you'd like me to go first."

"Not a chance," I said. Whatever happened to me, the flashback, it was gone now, replaced with efficient assassin mode.

I might let myself fall apart later, but for now I couldn't. I had to be Mina fucking DiMarco, the Sparrow, for a while longer.

We slipped through the darkness, moving slowly and silently towards the vehicle. A couple of metres away, I stopped again.

"What the hell?" I whispered.

In the back of the car was some kind of dummy. It was propped against the seat, high enough to look like a person. As far as I could tell, it had no face, but that wasn't what had me staring.

Sitting around where a person's chest would be, was a phone. The screen was on, showing a visual of our house here in Dusk Bay.

I couldn't tell who held the phone, but it was pointed at Kurt, who sat on the couch, a gun in his hand. Beside him was Enzo, Angelina and Caleb. They all looked pissed off. Their mouths were covered with duct tape.

Same with the fourth person on the couch with them.

Kurt's gun was pointed at the temple of my sister, Rose.

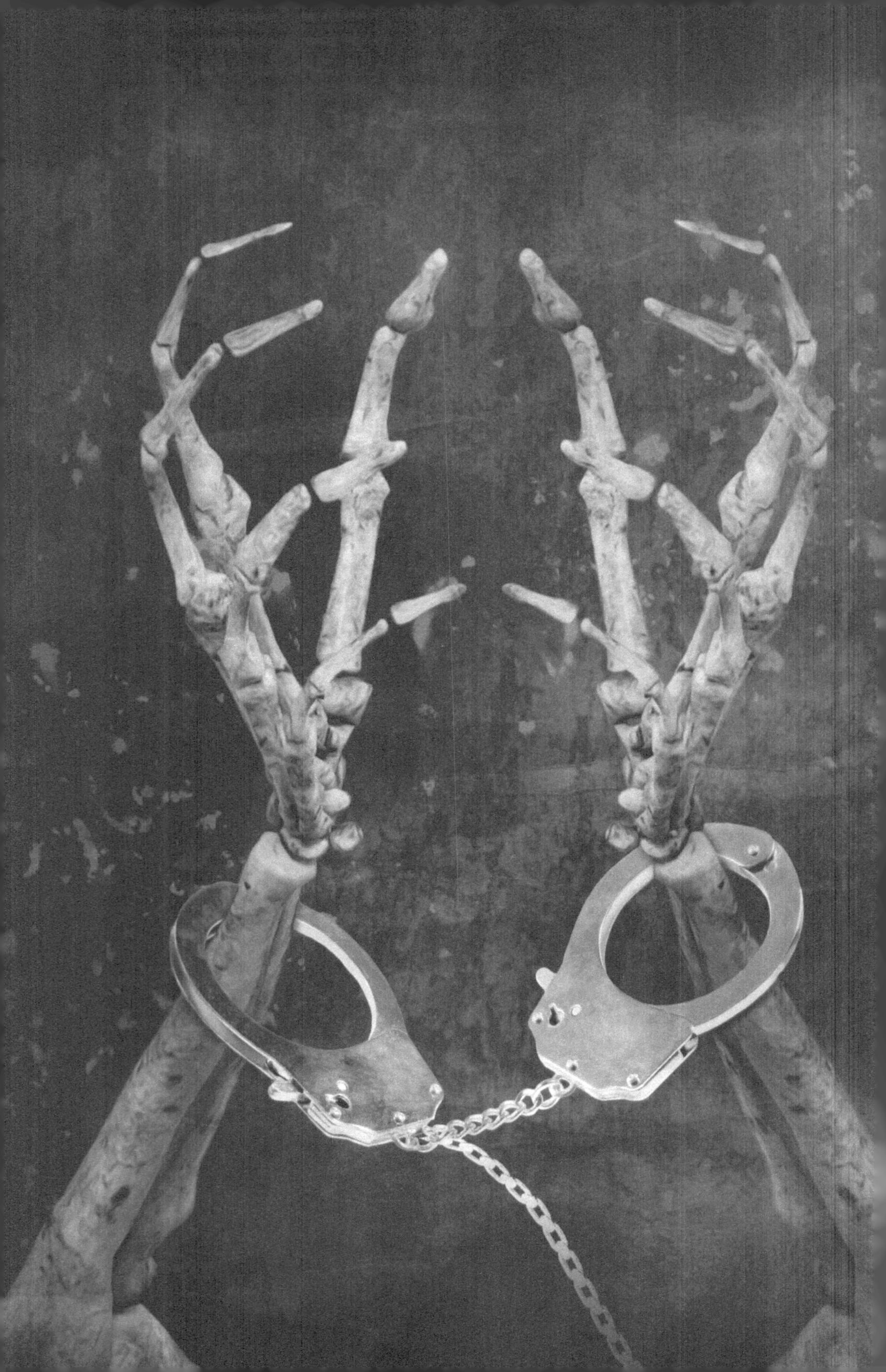

CHAPTER 17

MINA

"We need to get back," I said urgently. I darted away from the SUV, back to the shadows. "Now."

Gun in hand, I trotted in the direction of the gunshots, leaving Gianni to hurry to catch up.

Several of Kurt's minions still surrounded the SUV, their backs to the vehicle while they exchanged shots with Damon and Reuben. Two lay dead near the front tyres. The others were way too alive for my taste.

I preferred subtle and quiet, but when Kurt put a gun to my sister's head, all bets were fucking off.

I raised my gun and took out two of them with two shots before they even knew I was there. I ducked behind their second vehicle before they could turn and return the favour.

"We need to get away from these vehicles," Gianni said as he crouched beside me.

I glanced at him and nodded.

Another gunshot rang out. Another minion fell to the ground, Damon taking advantage of the distraction I provided.

That left ten. Too many for comfort.

I rose high enough to peek through the window at our vehicle. I caught a glimpse of the twins, both looking like they were waiting for an opportunity to push out of the vehicle and join in the gunfight. Both were frustrated they'd been designated with the task of keeping Leon inside the vehicle and stopping him from joining his 'friends.' If you could call them that.

I ducked back down, pulled out my phone and dialled a number. A couple of moments later, Daze's voice came down the line.

"Hey, Mina, what's up?"

"Just wondering if you're up to anything right now," I said lightly. "We could use a little help, if you're not busy."

Gianni rose and took a shot at one of the minions who'd turned his back at the wrong time. "Fuck." He dropped back down. "I missed."

"Are you having a party without me?" Daze sounded slightly miffed.

"You could say that." I peered around the side of the vehicle and took a shot at the closest set of ankles. "I know it's short notice, but if you'd like to hang out for a while, you're more than welcome. I've texted you the address."

She laughed. "We're on our way. That's only a couple of minutes from here. Later, we might have words about you having a gunfight in my neighbourhood." She ended the call.

I smiled and pushed my phone back into my pocket.

"We just need to hold them off for a little while." I thought for a minute. "Are you ready to be a distraction?"

"If it involves you, I'm ready for anything," he replied. "Even a quickie while we wait."

I grinned at him and shook my head before scooting over to the other end of the SUV. "On the count of three?"

"Three works for me." He scooted up behind me, close enough to place a hand on the small of my back.

I whispered the words to count us down, before we rose and broke into a run. We swerved as we bolted to where, if I guessed correctly, Reuben and Damon were crouched behind a stand of trees.

Shots rang out behind us, but none connected. Somehow, we managed to make it to the trees and behind the thick trunks without being shot.

"Long time, no see," Gianni said to Reuben and Damon. He briefly filled them in on what we saw on the phone in the back of the car.

Predictably, they both looked pissed off as hell.

"We need to get the twins out of here," Reuben said.

Before I could tell him backup was on the way, two dark sedans pulled up behind our SUV. Both were packed with people.

The doors swung open. Daze was the first out. She ducked behind the door, a gun in her hand. Ric was right behind her. Followed by her two other boyfriends and six others, split between the vehicles.

"This really is a party," she called out.

I smiled. "That's what I thought."

One of Kurt's minions called out orders and several split off to approach the newcomers, a couple trying to get off shots before they were fully out of the sedans.

"Fuck off." I recognised my cousin, Phoenix DiMarco, who landed a bullet right between the eyes of one of the enemy.

"Good shot." One of his companions patted him on the shoulder.

I squinted. Was that... I'd have to wonder about that later.

In the corner of my eye, I caught a couple of the minions heading back to their SUV.

"It seems like not everyone wants to join the party," Gianni remarked.

I hummed my agreement. "Spoilsports."

They slid inside and turned on the ignition.

The SUV exploded with a burst of flame and a shower of metal and glass.

"That was meant for us," I said softly.

"As they say in the classics, suck shit." Gianni grinned.

"Seven left," Reuben said.

Apparently the twins had enough of sitting tight. The front doors of the SUV swung open and they all but jumped out, taking out two of the men around them in the process.

"Five left," Damon said. "And they're outnumbered."

Evidently, the minions realised that too. They dropped back behind one of the remaining SUVs.

"I think they're reconsidering their life choices," Gianni said.

"I would be too," I said.

The other two vehicles might be rigged to explode. They had to decide if they could outrun us or not. Considering we had three vehicles which probably wouldn't explode, we had the advantage.

Reuben nodded to Damon and gestured for us to stand and join Daze and the small army she brought with her.

"There you are." She turned to me and grinned. "Thanks for the invitation."

"Thanks for coming," I said. I glanced back to see Reuben talking to a man around his age.

"Aidan Draeger, head coach of the Dusk Bay Demons," Gianni supplied. "Along with a bunch of the first line players."

That explained the presence of my cousin, and his friend, Coast Riggs, the team's centre. I should have suspected a team owned by Caleb would be made up of people like us.

Aidan gestured for his players to circle around and surround the remaining enemy. He didn't look impressed at being dragged out in the middle of the night.

I turned my attention back to where the minions still huddled. Every so often, one would rise and try to get off a shot, but they missed every time. None of our return shots connected either.

I chewed my lip. Something about this felt off. What would I do if I was—

"Tell everyone to come back," I said quickly. "Now."

Aidan looked at me, confused as to who the hell I was, and why I was giving orders, but Reuben nodded.

"Do it." He showed no sign of hesitation. He trusted my instincts completely.

Aidan shrugged, but called out the order for his players to trot back behind us.

"What's going on, Coach?" Phoenix asked.

"Hell if I know," Aidan said with a grunt. He glanced at me again.

I looked back, completely unflinching. I was right about this. Without a hint of doubt in my mind.

Phoenix squinted at me. "Are you—"

His words were interrupted when the other two SUVs simultaneously exploded.

Flames burst from the top of them and spread to either side, instantly incinerating anyone within a few metres. If any of our people were still there, they would have been killed along with Kurt's minions.

"Well, shit," Coast Riggs said. "I feel like we just won the playoffs."

"We might as well have." Aidan looked at me again, this time with grudging respect and a curt nod.

I nodded back and turned away from him, to Reuben. "We need to get home."

"Yes, we do," he agreed.

"I have so many questions," Phoenix said, staring at me.

"I have answers, but not right now," I told him. We had one more piece of unfinished business to take care of here. Then we needed to get home before Kurt could pull any more of his bullshit. Bullshit I was getting thoroughly tired of. We all were.

Whatever happened, this ended tonight.

My back straight, I marched over to our SUV and wrenched open the door.

Leon Graves was still inside, curled up around himself as though he hoped we'd forget about his existence. Or bracing himself in case this vehicle exploded too.

"Mina," he said when he saw me. "So good to see you're still alive. We were on our way to the city when those other vehicles stopped us. They told us to get out, but Hunter and Parker insisted we stay here."

"They saved your ass?" Gianni came up behind me and placed a hand on my shoulder.

"I… I guess they did," he said.

"Very heroic of them," I said dryly. "Maybe we should give them a trophy."

"I'll take a trophy," Parker said, appearing on the other side of the SUV. "Can we have one each though? Having to figure out a way to share with Hunter would be a pain in the ass."

"I should be offended, but Parker is right," Hunter said. "We're good at sharing lots of things, but not a trophy. Remind me to tell you later about the time we played hockey as kids. Shit got ugly."

I snorted softly. "You don't need a trophy. Not from me anyway. I'm sure you're good at gathering your own."

Leon stared at me for a moment before realising I wasn't talking about a metal trophy. He let out an awkward laugh. "I'm sure there's still a few trophy heads attached to bodies out there. Can you believe Kurt sent all those people to get to me?"

"No, I can't," I said. Because he hadn't. Some of them were for Leon, but the rest were for me and my men.

"He doesn't get a trophy for world's best friend." World's worst would be more accurate. Kurt Lasalle was good at looking after his own ass while not giving a shit about anyone else's. He hadn't changed a bit in all the years I'd known him. He was a narcissistic psychopath who used people to get what he wanted. There was nothing and no one he wouldn't step on, kill or shove aside.

Leon laughed awkwardly again. "No, he won't. So… If you can't guarantee my safety from Kurt…"

"I don't give a shit about your safety, Leon," I said coldly. "I know you were the one who found out what my father was doing. I know you were the one who told Kurt. You gave him the ammunition to use against my father and me."

Leon's face paled. "I don't know who told you that—"

"You did," I said coldly. "Parker found your most encrypted files. Files you should have deleted. Messages between you and Kurt."

He looked genuinely confused. "I swear, I didn't have anything like that on the laptop."

"I saw it myself," I said with a slight edge of uncertainty. Either he was lying through his teeth, or this was another one of Kurt's setups.

"I wouldn't have left something like that on that," he insisted. His voice was high with panic. Clearly terrified we'd throw him back in the basement. Chain him up and leave him to rot.

"You're not denying that you were the one who told Kurt," Gianni pointed out.

Leon's hesitation was all I needed.

I raised my gun and shot him right in the centre of his forehead.

"We need to get home. Before he lays a hand on my sister."

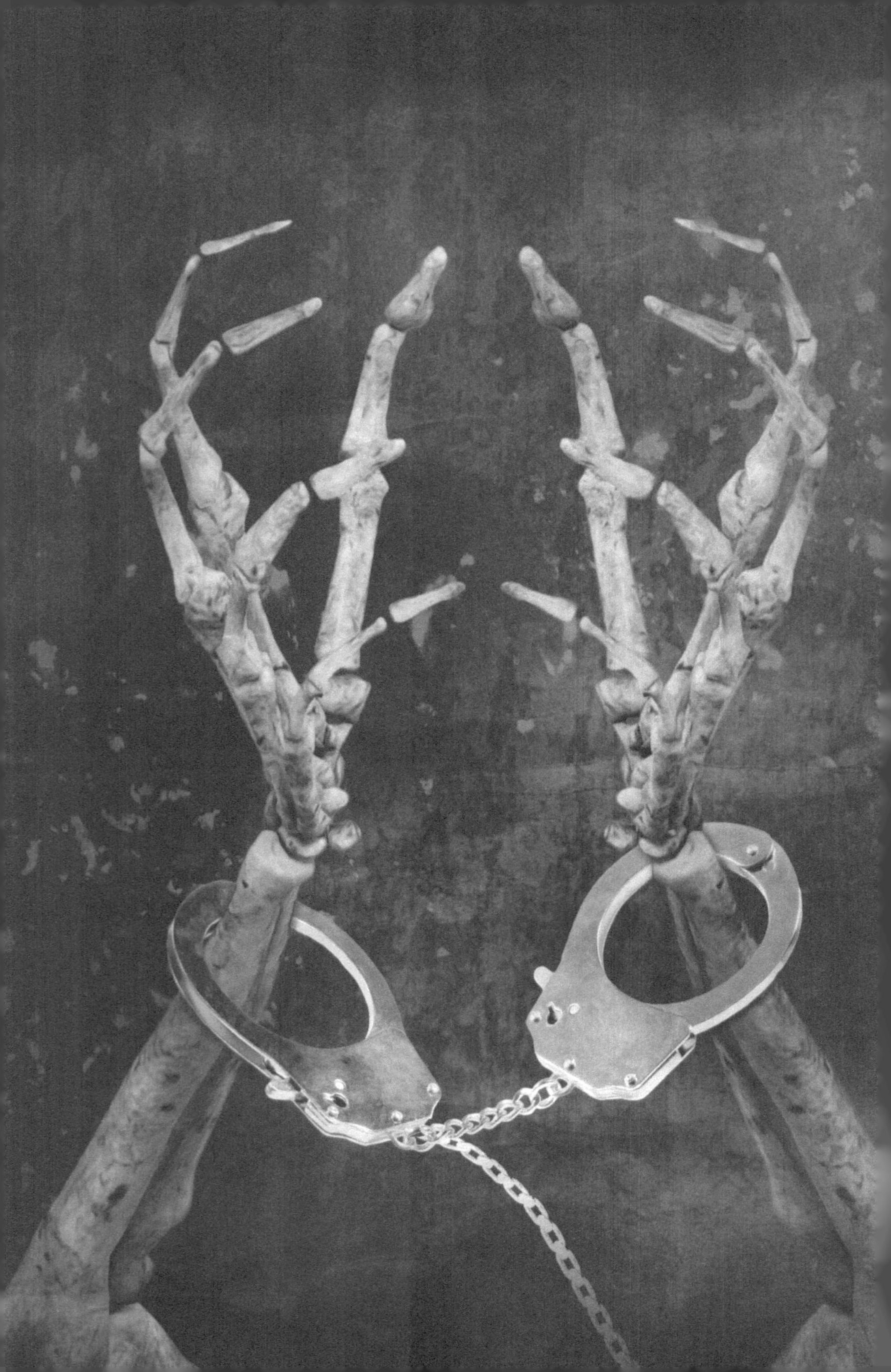

CHAPTER 18

MINA

The ride back was tense as fuck.

I sat in the back seat with Gianni, while Damon, as usual, drove. Reuben sat beside him, his back straight, shoulders stiff.

No one said a word. We were all thinking the same thing. How had Kurt managed to get inside, much less alive? How had he taken my sister? When? Had he…

I bit my lip. I didn't want to think about what he might have done to her.

"She'll be okay," Gianni said.

I nodded, but I wasn't so sure. Kurt was just as likely to kill her to get a reaction out of me. And kill Caleb to get a reaction out of Reuben. He'd probably be amused at provoking Carlos too.

I glanced back to the other two sedans behind us. The twins drove in front, in the other SUV, making a cavalcade of dark vehicles.

How many people did Kurt have with him?

Did we have enough? We had to. My sister's life might depend on it.

The twins slowed about half a kilometre from the house and pulled to a stop.

Damon stopped right behind them.

"What are you doing?" I insisted. "We don't have time to wait." The time it would take for us to walk, or even run, the extra kilometre could be time we needed to help Rose.

"We're not waiting," Damon said calmly. "There's more than one way into the house."

I should have anticipated that. The Brantley family wouldn't have a house here in Dusk Bay that didn't have a secret back door.

"But if Kurt knows where it is—" I started.

"He won't," Damon said. "The only ones who know about it are us and the twins. The rest of Dusk Bay is just about to find out."

Reuben let out a breath of annoyance at that, but he'd also do whatever was necessary to save my sister and get Kurt out of his house.

We all climbed out of the cars and, in quiet ranks, followed the twins onto a property beside the road. We swished through high grass to a massive water tank.

"No one ever suspects the water tank," Hunter said ominously.

I gave him a funny look, but followed him around to the rear of the tank.

It was Damon who pulled out his phone and tapped on the screen.

Without a sound, a door in the side of the tank started to rise. If I didn't see it with my own eyes, I never would have guessed it was there.

I tapped the side of the tank. "It doesn't sound hollow."

Damon smirked. "Of course not. That would be too obvious."

"The insides are lined with concrete," Reuben said. "Pipes take the water that lands on the rim of the tank down to our house. Simple but efficient."

I thought back to Clarissa and her hidden trapdoor. She'd love this, if she knew about it. Another secret door that didn't lead to Narnia.

"How many of these things do you have?" I asked. "Secret passageways and things like that."

"None we're going to discuss in front of anyone else." Damon jerked his head towards Daze, Ric and Aidan. And all the people they brought with them.

"I'll fill you in on all of them later," Gianni said. "You should know about all of them, just in case."

I nodded. We had to get through this first.

I let Gianni take my hand as we stepped through the door, into the tank.

Hunter and Parker both had the lights on their phone, showing the way.

The inside of the tank was massive, but like Damon said, lined with concrete. That made it seem a lot smaller. Small enough to make me anxious. This was exactly the kind of space that reminded me of Kurt's basement.

The same flashback that came over me while we were crouched in the bushes threatened to sneak back into my mind. Memories clawed back at me, trying to suck me back into the past.

That nightmare was my present for so long, putting it behind me was never going to be easy, but I couldn't let it get to me now. This was when I needed to be strong, for Rose's sake. And for mine.

"You've got this," Gianni said, his voice echoing. "I have to confess, this place gives me the creeps too, but we can do it. We can't let it get to us."

"I'm with Gianni," Hunter said. "This place is creepy as shit, and I know creepy as shit."

"Some people say you *are* as creepy as shit." Parker grinned.

"Some people can fuck off, and so can you," Hunter said to his twin. "I'm not creepy, I'm awesome."

"You pronounced 'awful' wrong," Gianni teased.

"The next time we need someone used as bait, the answer is no," Hunter said to no one in particular. "Gianni volunteers instead."

"Keep your voices down," Damon snapped.

I noticed he didn't tell us to be completely quiet. I suspected he was as creeped out by this place as the rest of us. Only Reuben looked unruffled. On the outside anyway. I doubted too many people would enjoy being in a place like this.

No one but spiders and people like Kurt, and Leon Graves.

And the cockroach that ran past my left shoe. I shuddered, but didn't flinch.

This time.

We fell into silence after that anyway. Lost in their own thoughts.

The ground dipped before the tunnel led to a set of steps. Two by two, we stepped down them, slowly and carefully.

After those, the tunnel widened, becoming slightly more comfortable before we headed up another set of stairs. If I had to guess, I'd say we must be close to the house.

It already felt like we'd been walking forever. Maybe forever and a day or two.

Enough time for a million thoughts to tumble through my mind. Chief amongst those was, how had any of this happened?

We were keeping tabs on Rose. The house should have been secure. So many questions and, like too many times before, there were no answers. Not yet.

We reached the top of the second set of stairs and stopped in a wide, rectangular room.

There, Damon gestured for us to halt.

Behind me, Aidan gestured for his players to do the same.

"Where do we go now?" I glanced around, but couldn't see a door leading out.

For half a heartbeat, I started to panic. Maybe there wasn't a way out. We might have come all this way only to end up stuck in the end of nowhere. This might have been someone's plan. To bring me here and—

I shook my head. Those thoughts were ridiculous. There was no way in the world that would happen. No one here would have allowed it, especially me. This was nothing but the past trying to get to me again.

I told it to fuck off, into a corner of my brain for now. I'd deal with one asshole at a time.

Parker turned off the light on his phone and tapped on the screen. "We could do with better connectivity in here, but this will have to do."

Damon nodded and pulled out his own phone.

I stared at them, confused until Parker said, "Got it."

He turned the screen to me, and showed camera footage of inside the house. "Now we just need to find where they are. And how many there are."

I nodded and waved for him to get on with it. Stopping to explain might be a waste of time. Time we couldn't afford to lose a moment of.

"He's still in the living room," Damon reported. "Rose, Angie and Enzo are still alive. Caleb too."

I peered over his shoulder.

Sure enough, they were still sitting on the couch, looking as though they hadn't moved since we saw them last. Kurt was pacing back and forth, gun still in his hand. He was surrounded by several other people.

I caught a glimpse of two of them and sucked in a breath. Sweat sprag out on my palms and under my arms. "That's Jason Andrews and Wade."

"Are you sure?" Gianni asked.

The angle wasn't good, and they were half turned away, but I was certain.

"It's them," I said softly.

"Good, then we can kill three birds with one stone," Gianni said. "Four, if you count Leon."

"There are people in the kitchen too," Parker said. "They don't seem to be anywhere else. None have shown themselves down to the basement."

"Yet," Hunter said. "I can see that place getting really full, really soon."

"Bring it on," Gianni said. "I've always wondered exactly how many people we could fit down there. Although, I was thinking about a party."

"Are you saying this isn't a party?" Daze asked. "Looks like one to me."

"It sounds like your boyfriends need to show you a good time more often," Hunter remarked.

"Don't even think about it," Ric growled. Hilton and Gunnar looked equally unimpressed.

Typically, Hunter just grinned. No one would have bought that he was interested in Daze anyway. He was just trying to lighten the mood.

That lasted approximately three or four seconds before Reuben spoke.

"Where's Terry?"

Damon glanced up from his phone and shook his head. "I can't see any sign of him."

His expression was grim. They would have gotten past Terry over his dead body.

That was exactly what we were all afraid of. I'd become fond of the gentle, silent giant, not just for his cooking. He had a way of conveying his thoughts without words. He didn't put up with any shit from anyone and I admired that about him.

He was as much a part of my family as my men or my siblings. Or Daze and her boyfriends. Or anyone currently in this secret bunker, who'd come when I called. Every single one of them had dropped whatever they were doing and raced to help us.

For that, I'd always be grateful. Assuming I lived long enough to have much in the way of gratitude.

"It looks as though we have equal numbers," Parker said. "Approximately. There's still a handful out the front, along with their cars. The majority went inside with the asshole."

Reuben nodded. "Nothing we can't handle. They know we're coming, but they don't know where we're coming from."

"Chances are, they're expecting us to pull up out the front of the house and take on the people outside," Hunter reasoned. "They'll think we're complacent, after taking care of only a handful of assholes. They'll expect us to walk in through the door so they can ambush us."

I nodded my agreement at his assessment. Based on the placement of people, that was logical. It sounded like something Kurt would do. He'd make sure he was surrounded by a lot of people who would die while he made a run for it.

Fuck that.

"Maybe some of us should turn up out the front," Aidan suggested. "We can deal with them, and provide a distraction."

"A distraction is a good idea," I agreed. I met Damon's eyes and smiled.

He offered a faint smile in return. His version of a grin. Neither of us would hear or say that word again without thinking of each other.

Reuben nodded. "Four of you go. One for each car. Let them think we're all turning up at the front. Parker."

"On it," Parker said. He frowned in concentration and tapped at his phone screen. "There. The cameras out the front of the house are on a loop. Assuming they don't realise it too soon, anyone Kurt has monitoring will just see what's out there right now."

"Good job," Reuben said. His gaze followed Aidan, Phoenix, Coast and another one of the players back down the tunnel. "We'll give them five minutes, then we go inside."

Hunter rubbed his hands together. "Time to fuck some shit up."

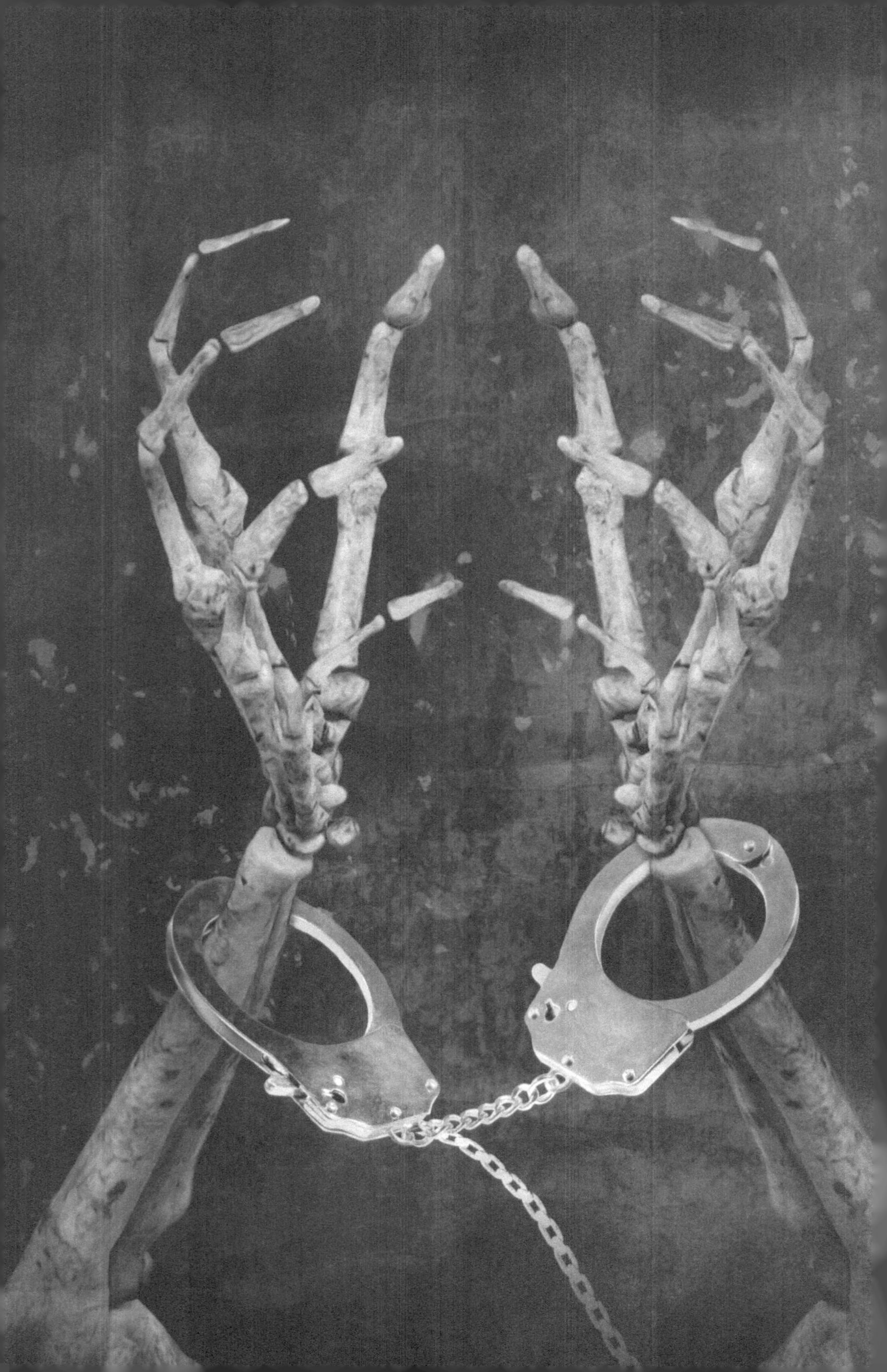

CHAPTER 19

GIANNI

"We need to split up," Reuben said before we unlocked the door leading into the house. "Hunter, Parker, Daze, you all go left, toward the kitchen. The rest of us will go right, around to the back of the living room. If we're careful, we can come up behind them. We'll try to surround them and take them all out."

Hunter raised his phone and pointed the light in the direction of a fuse box on the wall. "I'm ready to blow the lights."

"I'm ready with the knives." I squatted and opened a box that lay on the ground beside the door. Stored there for just this eventuality. It was full of blades and guns.

I handed out knives to anyone who didn't already have one. Mina, of course, was already armed with several. Could she get any hotter? She looked like some kind of angel, dressed in black and armed to the teeth. My kind of woman, through and through.

"No guns until you have to," Reuben added. "Once they know where we are, do whatever you have to do. Until then, be quiet. Let's not jump through the door and announce our presence."

I smiled.

I couldn't imagine Reuben jumping through the door and shouting out, "Heeeere's Reuben!" The twins, certainly, but not him.

"Got it, boss," I said. "Stealth mode. A trillion points to anyone who ends Kurt."

"Infinity points to anyone who helps us catch him alive," Mina said softly.

"What could we do with infinity points?" Hunter asked.

She gave him a bland look. "You can swap it for a Maserati."

"Fuck yeah." He offered Parker a fist bump. "I can't wait."

"You'll have to wait, that's my infinity points and my Maserati," I told them both.

I didn't give a shit about either of those things. What I really wanted was for us to get out of this alive. Preferably in one piece. A car, no matter how sexy, meant nothing in comparison.

I knew they agreed with that sentiment. They weren't shallow enough to really give a shit about an expensive vehicle. That wouldn't keep us from making jokes about it. Only our deaths would put a stop to that.

"Game on." Hunter grinned. "One Lasalle coming up."

Daze cleared her throat.

"One *male* Lasalle," Hunter corrected. "Have you ever thought about changing your name?"

"Have you?" I asked him.

Being a Brantley came with a lot of responsibility. And a metric fuck ton of expectations, especially from Reuben. Although, they were lighter than the ones Reuben put on himself.

"Can we focus?" Damon snapped. His expression was tighter than I'd ever seen on him before. I couldn't say I blamed him. In spite of the banter, I was tense myself. A shit ton of things could go wrong. We just had to make sure they didn't.

Somehow.

Reuben nodded at Hunter. "Kill the lights."

Hunter opened the fuse box and turned one switch at the same moment Damon opened the door.

For a split second, the house was illuminated, before it fell into complete darkness.

The curtains were closed, blocking out any moonlight and most of the starlight. The only illumination was the flashing of various electrical devices, like the front of the microwave oven, and the keypad for the air-conditioning system.

I hadn't realised how bright they both were. Even from here, I could make out the one in the microwave.

Voices muttered in surprise as we slipped off in the directions Reuben ordered us to go.

I stayed beside Mina, close enough for our arms to touch as we moved through the darkness.

We had the advantage that we knew this place better than the enemy, but I had no illusion this was going to be easy.

At this point, it had already stopped being fun. Trust Kurt Lasalle to suck the joy out of the people around him. I added that to the ever-growing list of reasons to hate him.

Another factor in our favour was that we'd stood in near total darkness for about twenty minutes. Our eyes didn't need time to adjust.

The same couldn't be said for the first two of our enemies we snuck up behind and dispatched silently. A quick slash to the throat and we lowered them to the floor.

I pictured the expression on Reuben's face at the idea of blood on the hardwood, but it couldn't be helped. Better their's than ours, anyway.

A low grunt sounded from the direction of the kitchen. That was quickly followed by another.

Mina grabbed hold of my wrist and pulled me to the side. Lucky she did, because I almost walked into another one of our enemies.

Instead, I grabbed them from behind, my hand over their mouth, my knife across their throat. They tried to cry out, but the sound was muted by my fingers and their quick death. Still, it was enough sound to inform others of our presence.

I lowered them to the ground and winced. I'd have to ask Reuben if we could put up speakers around the house. Music, when played loud enough, would mask anything and everything. We could have stomped through the house and never been heard.

That was an oversight. Something I hadn't considered before and I could kick myself for it now. In retrospect, it was obvious, but at least we could fix it later.

I hoped.

Light from a phone flashed out across the room in front of us. The living room.

"I know you're there, Mina," Kurt called out, taunting. "I know that you know I have your sister here. And Reuben's brother. And Damon's brother. How cosy all of this is. It's up to you whether they live or die."

I've always found it ironic when people said shit like that. The only one responsible for their deaths was him. It was past time he took responsibility for his own actions.

I made a note to tell him that later. Right before those actions led to his death.

"What do you want, Kurt?" Mina called back. Her fingers curled around my wrist, drawing me with her while she stepped forward. Reuben and Damon moved along slowly behind us.

"The same thing I've always wanted," Kurt said. "I want all the power and influence the Brantley family has, and I want you."

Reuben snorted softly. An articulate expression of 'fuck that' if I ever heard it. He always did have a way of quietly conveying what he was thinking.

"Why?" Mina asked. "From the look of things, you have plenty of power and influence. There are women out there who are attracted to things like that. I'm sure you could find someone more than willing to be a part of your life. Why do you want me?"

"Because you belong to me," he stated, like nothing could be simpler. "I own you. Every millimetre of you."

"Why me?" she pressed harder. "Of all the women in the world, why do you want me?"

"We're wasting time here, Mina. And I'm running out of patience." The light flashed again, presumably Kurt turning around in a circle, trying to figure out what direction we might jump out from. "I'm going to start killing in a minute. How many die, depends on you."

A short grunt of pain came from the direction of the kitchen. My heart thudded in my chest. It sounded like one of the twins.

"Parker!" Hunter's harsh whisper was like the crack of a whip through the darkness.

Fucking hell.

Fucking hell.

Mina's fingers trembled. Her intake of breath was sharp, horrified.

"One of them is dead," Kurt sounded amused. "How many more are you going to allow to die? Hunter is surrounded, as is your sister. All I need to do is say the word. Or, you can hand yourself over to me. Reuben can step aside and give me the keys to his empire. That's all it takes for the rest of the people you care about to walk away."

Mina swallowed audibly.

"You can't," Damon whispered. "We're not—"

His words were interrupted by gunshots from outside the front of the house. Someone shouted and everything fell quiet again.

I pictured the scene outside in my mind, but couldn't draw any conclusions. Aidan and the Demons might be dead, or they might not.

I'd like to think they were more difficult to kill than that, but only time would tell. All I could do for them was to send good thoughts and hope like hell they made it through. The team needed them. The hockey team as well as us.

"What choice do I have?" she asked. "You can't all die for me."

"Enough of this bullshit," Kurt snapped. "Kill the other twin."

A shuffle sounded from the direction of the kitchen before silence fell once again.

Mina's breath was a soft sob. "I have to. It's the only way."

"I won't let you—" I started.

"You can't *stop* me," she said. "This is what I have to do. I need to do this for all of you. Forget about me."

There was conviction in her tone, but a heavy dose of fear. Yes, she would do this for us. She'd give up the rest of her life and spend it caged and chained so we wouldn't die, but the idea of going back to that life was the worst, most inconceivable nightmare possible. The fact she'd even consider subjecting herself to that again, just for us, made me love her even more.

She was, without a doubt, the most incredible woman I'd ever met.

I pulled her to me and brushed my lips over hers. "We will never forget you. Never." I held her tight like I might be able to change her mind if I held her for long enough.

"You have to let me go," she insisted.

"Who shall I kill next?" Kurt mused in a singsong voice. "I guess I could start with Angelina. She doesn't have any family here to stick up for her. Although…her death might be enough to convince you I'm serious."

Enzo let out a roar of protest from behind his duct tape.

"I think he's volunteering to go first," Kurt said. "How touching. Is that something Damon would do, too? Give up your life for the woman you think you love? Even while knowing she belongs to someone else? I bet Reuben would do the same thing, wouldn't you Reuben? And Gianni. So heroic for a bunch of criminals."

"Hey, everyone, I found the pot," I called out. "First of all, yes, we would die for Mina, because she belongs to us, not you. Secondly, you're the kind of person who gives the word 'criminal' a bad name. And coward. And asshole. And…" I could have gone on for hours.

"Sticks and stones," Kurt sneered.

"Breaking your bones would be my pleasure," Damon growled.

"Ah, there's Damon," Kurt said. "I changed my mind, I think your brother can die next. Then maybe Reuben's other brother. It was Caleb who helped to spread the rumour I was really the Sparrow, wasn't it? Do you realise that made it difficult for people to trust me? Some of them even thought they might turn on me. Instead, all you did was force my hand tonight. But don't worry. Before I came here, I put out word of who the real Sparrow is. Along with some damning evidence about something she once did. People were only too happy to believe the truth."

"I didn't kill her," Mina said softly.

"Yes, you did," Kurt contradicted. "The same way you just killed Hunter and Parker. The same way you're about to kill Enzo and Caleb if you don't hurry up and give yourself to me. I'm going to be generous and give you two more minutes. Then I'm done fucking around. Time starts… Right now."

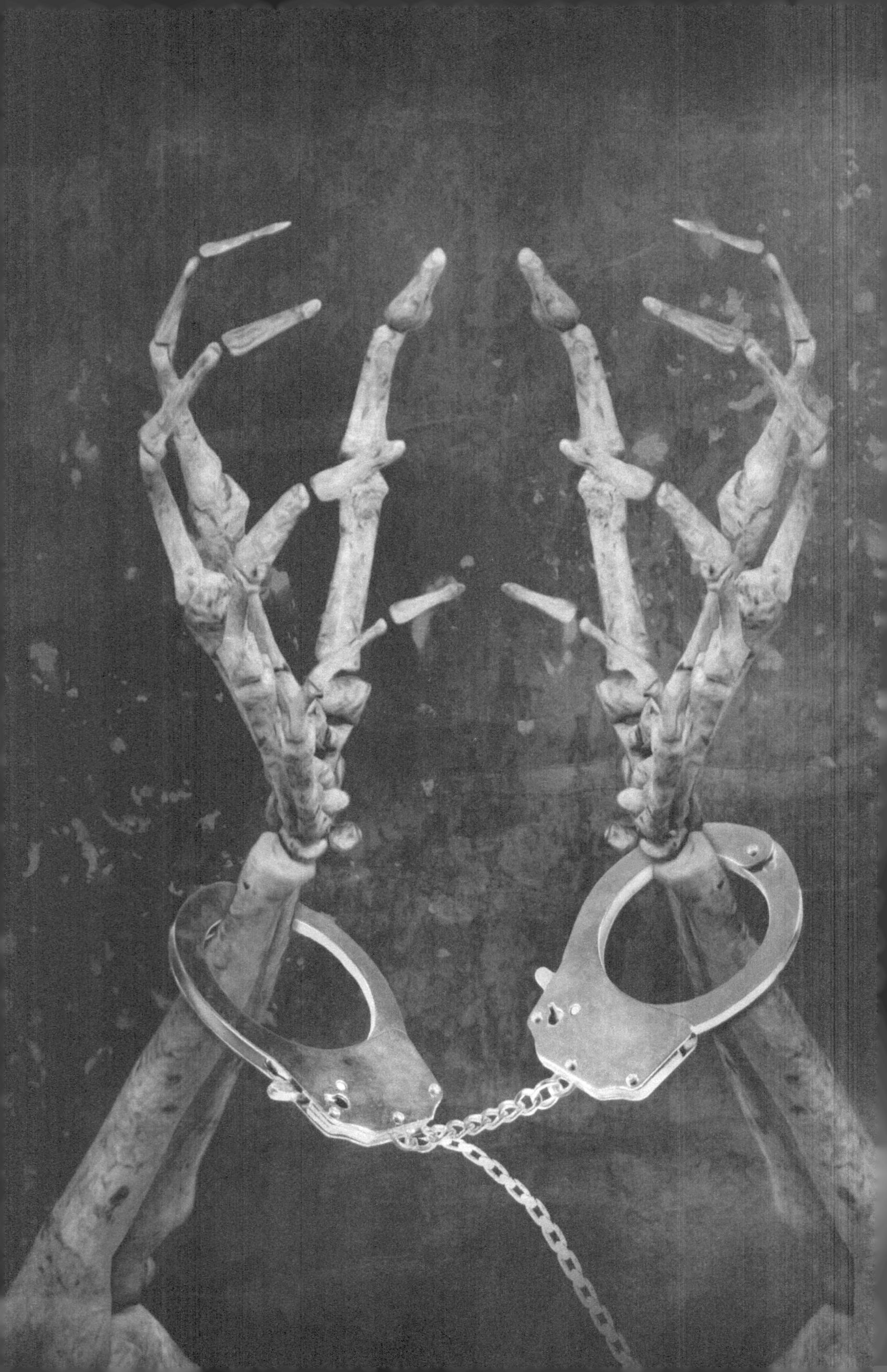

CHAPTER 20

MINA

I sank against Gianni for a few moments.

This could be the last time I got to see any of them. These few moments weren't enough. It never would be. All three of them had saved me in so many ways. They got me out of the basement and they gave me my life back. They gave me themselves and their hearts.

Now it was time for me to give back to them.

I could hardly believe that the twins were dead, they'd been so full of life.

They had to be the last. I couldn't let anyone else give up their lives for me. No matter how willing they were to sacrifice themselves. I knew all three of them would fall on their own swords for me. I loved them for it.

For so long, I hadn't thought myself capable of love, or worthy of being loved. They taught me how wrong I was. They showed me what it was to give everything and live every day to the fullest. For that, I'd always be grateful. Their love was what I'd hold on to when I was back where Kurt put me. For however much longer I lived, I'd hold on to that. It might be the only thing that kept me sane.

I pressed my ear against Gianni's chest and listened to his heart racing. I never knew anyone could have a heart as big as his. He'd contradict me, but I didn't deserve him. That was an argument we'd never get to have.

"I love you," I whispered. "All of you."

Before they could respond, I tore myself away from them and headed towards the living room.

"Mina." Reuben's whisper sounded devastated.

I had to force myself not to look back. If I did, I might change my mind.

I couldn't. People would die.

I stepped through the cased opening, into the living room.

At that moment, the lights came back on. I squinted against the glare.

Rose was in the same place she was sitting when I saw her on that phone.

How long ago was that? It felt like hours. Weeks.

It couldn't have been more than an hour.

She conveyed a dozen thoughts with her eyes. Frustration at having been taken. Anger at Kurt. Heartbreak that I'd consider giving myself up for her. Fear for me. And an insistence that she would also have offered herself in my place. She would have died for me.

All I could give her was conviction that I wouldn't let her. The world had lived without Mina DiMarco for five years. It could live without me again. It couldn't live without her.

My brothers would mourn her loss, while they went on thinking I was happily married, off in the suburbs somewhere.

They say ignorance is bliss. Never knowing what happened to me, could be theirs.

Caleb's eyes were also on me, his irritation clear. Not at me specifically, just in general. He tried so hard to be like his oldest brother, even now. He hated being bound and powerless. Just like Reuben would.

I hoped he'd find his own way at some point. He needed to step out of Reuben's shadow and be his own man. Maybe then, he'd be happy. Or at least, less unhappy.

Angelina and Enzo sat close together, their shoulders touching. Both looked as though they could shoot daggers out of their eyes if anyone touched either of them.

Angelina was as protective of Enzo as he was of her. If anyone doubted their feelings for each other, they wouldn't if they saw them like this. At least now they may get a chance at a happily ever after.

Finally, my gaze slid to Kurt. He'd lost weight since I saw him last, but he was still the same smug, hateful asshole I'd known for so long. He'd forced us to play his game and now we were at Checkmate.

Knight takes queen.

"You're looking well," he said smoothly. "Hand over all your knives." He nodded to one of his minions to step over and take them from me. "If she tries anything, kill her sister first."

Of course he'd plan for what would happen if I threw a knife and embedded it in his loathsome head. I considered doing it anyway, but several of his minions moved closer to Rose, ready to carry out his orders. I could kill him and a couple of them, but not before they got to her.

She growled in the back of her throat and gave Kurt a death glare, which he ignored. His gaze was fixed on me. Waiting for me to act.

I sighed and reached for my knives, handing them to the closest asshole, hilt end first.

I contemplated using one on myself, stabbing one into my own heart. Ending the pain before it began all over again.

If I did that, Kurt would kill everyone here. The only way they walked away from this was if I left with him. He knew I knew that. It increased his smugness level by at least double.

Asshole.

"That's all of them," I said finally.

"Make sure," Kurt ordered. He looked extremely amused at the idea of one of his men touching me, checking for any hidden weapons. I suspected he might be more amused at the thought of killing his man after he touched me, even though he'd done it on Kurt's orders. He was nothing if not fucked up.

His minion approached me carefully before quickly patting me down. "Nothing else there, sir." He stepped away from me quickly.

"Good," Kurt said. "Get a couple of cable ties and some duct tape and bind her."

The minion nodded. "Yes, boss." He hurried over to the couch to grab up both.

"In case you were wondering, Leon Graves is dead," I said. I glanced around, but saw no sign of Jase or Wade. I presumed they were in the kitchen. They might have been the ones who killed the twins. Grief flared inside me, white hot devastation, and burning hate for the hands that took their lives.

I hoped my men would catch up to them and return the favour. Long, slow and painful, preferably.

Kurt shrugged. "He outgrew his usefulness anyway. But he was helpful in bringing you back to me."

A couple of his assholes moved behind me to grab my arms and pull them behind my back. One of them held them, while the other fastened the cable tie around them.

Another tore off a long section of duct tape and raised it to my mouth. I pressed my lips together and let him stick it to my face.

"Much better," Kurt said. "I'm sure you'll agree we have a lot to catch up on. Don't worry, I'll keep plenty of my people here, to make sure no one follows us. If they try, they'll be dead too. In a few hours, we might let them go, one by one."

He walked past Rose, close enough for her to kick him. She looked like she was about to, but I shot her a warning look. I hadn't done all of this only for her to provoke him into killing her. She had to understand that. This was my choice. My sacrifice. It would be for nothing if any of them got themselves killed for me.

His minions stepped back as Kurt approached me. "I like you like this," he said. "Bound and gagged is a good look for you." He took the second cable tie and held it in his hand. "We'll leave this until you get into the car. I could have you carried, but it's much more fun to see you walk voluntarily. Knowing your place."

He turned around, smiling at everyone in the room like he was about to receive his own trophy. When he turned back, his expression was darker.

"I only have two regrets in life. One is leaving you for Reuben to find. The other was not breaking you. I won't make either mistake again. When we're done, you'll never want to be away from me again.

Your biggest regret will be going with them when you did. You should have stayed there and waited for your owner to come and get you. Like the bitch you are." He pinched my chin between his thumb and forefinger. "You. Should. Have. Waited."

I looked back at him, unflinching. Maybe he could break me and maybe he'd kill me instead. I'd never give up until I provoked him to end my life. Whatever it took.

He released my chin and backhanded me across the face so hard I staggered back against his minions. Two of them grabbed me at the last moment before I fell.

Rose growled.

I shot her another warning look. I knew she was trying to be the big sister I needed, but right now I needed her to be inconspicuous. I needed her to hold her peace, for both our sakes. If Kurt killed her, it would be one step closer to him breaking me. I couldn't allow that to happen.

"We've wasted enough time here," Kurt snapped. "Let's get out of this dump. You, stay behind and kill them if they try anything." He waved a hand at several of his assholes.

They nodded and moved to stand around the couch, and the corridor where my men still stood.

"The rest of you come with me," he ordered. He grabbed my arm and pulled me towards the front door of the house.

I glanced back at my sister, giving her a silent apology and trying to tell her I loved her.

Her eyes widened slightly.

Before I could turn back, a loud clang echoed through the room.

Kurt's grip on my arm loosened before his hand fell away. His eyes rolled back in his head and he started to fall to the floor.

He landed with a thud heavy enough to make me wince.

Eyes wide, I looked up from where he lay.

Terry stood with his hands around the handle of a heavy frying pan, a satisfied look on his face. He nodded to me and then actually grinned.

He must have lain in wait for Kurt before smashing him over the head with the pan.

The front door burst open and Aidan and his players poured inside. A couple of them were bleeding from what appeared to be bullet wounds in their shoulders, but they only appeared to be grazes. Not enough to slow them down or stop them from playing.

Coast Riggs was grinning like he'd never had so much fun in his life.

My guys appeared from the corridor, heading towards me at a trot. All three of them were frowning, but relieved to see me still standing. They were at least as relieved as I was to see them.

They were the most beautiful sight I'd ever seen in my life. So much so, my heart might burst out of my chest.

On the other side of the room, Daze and her guys appeared followed by—

I blinked a couple of times to make sure I wasn't seeing things.

Hunter and Parker were right behind Ric. They were both covered in blood, but didn't seem to be badly hurt. Like the Demons centre, they were smiling like they were having the time of their lives.

Thank fuck.

I couldn't have been more grateful they were both still alive. I was so sure…

For half a second, I thought maybe I was dead and this was some kind of afterlife. But the tear that trickled down my cheek felt real enough. That was followed by another one.

"Take them all," Reuben ordered. He gestured towards Kurt's men, who were stepping back away from the couch and looking as though they were trying to find somewhere to run to. They had nowhere. One by one, they started to toss their weapons to the floor.

In moments, all of the minions were surrounded and I found myself in Reuben's arms, where I sagged and silently wept.

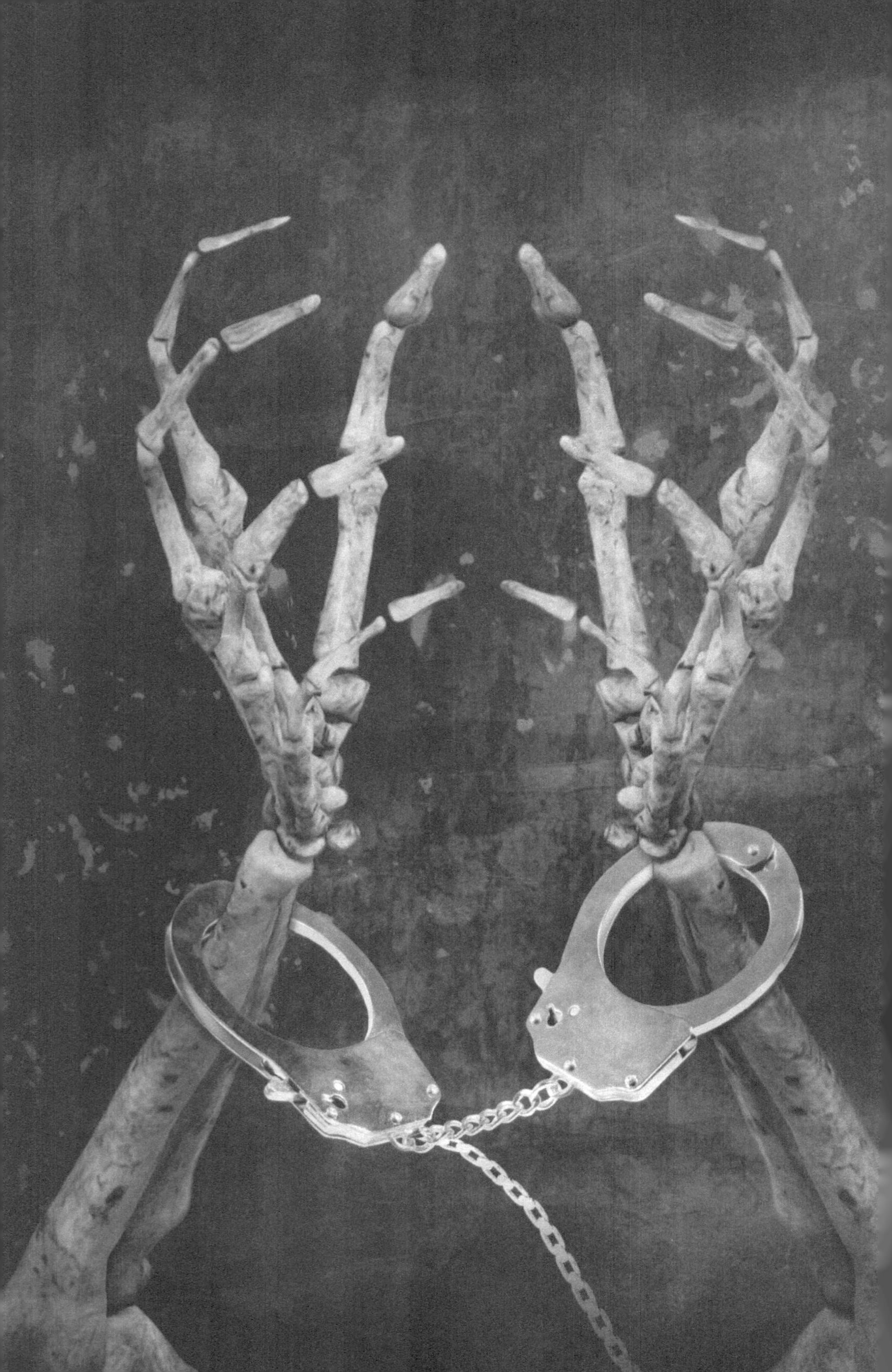

CHAPTER 21

MINA

I handed Rose a cup of steaming tea Gianni made and lowered myself down beside her. "Are you okay?"

She offered me a smile. "I should be asking you that."

I shrugged. "I'm fine." After a moment I added, "More or less."

I sipped my own tea and winced at how hot it still was. "How did he—"

"I got a frantic phone call from a friend, asking for help," Rose said. "Turns out she had a gun to her head. When I got there, I was over-powered. He brought me here and convinced one of the staff to open the door. That's everything I know until you showed up."

Damon sat down on the other side of me. In his hand, he held what looked like a triple whiskey. He and Gianni, with help from the twins, had taken Kurt down to the basement. "He's still alive. For now. Terry and his frying pan knew just the right place to connect."

I managed a small smile for the gentle giant. If it wasn't for him, things might have worked out very differently.

"According to the twins, he hid out when the asshole showed up." Gianni sat on the floor beside my feet and placed his own cup of tea on the table.

"Are you talking about us?" The twins approached before squeezing onto one of the chairs together.

"I'm glad you're both alive," I told them.

"Us too," Hunter agreed. "We found Jase and Wade in the kitchen. One of them went for Parker."

"Hunter warned me just in time for me to turn around so he could fall on my knife," Parker said cheerfully. He leaned into his twin and grinned.

"And Parker gave me the opportunity to dispose of the other one," Hunter said. "We were going to come and help, but that's when we saw Terry. He was waiting for the right moment, so we waited with him. If anyone deserves a trophy, it's him."

Gianni grinned. "Terry is the real MVP here." He waved over at Terry, who was in the kitchen making sandwiches with Daze and a couple of the Demons. "He deserves a raise, right, boss?"

We all turned to Reuben, who was standing off to the side of the room, talking to Caleb. I couldn't hear what they were saying, but Reuben was clearly worried about his younger brothers. All of them. And as relieved they were alive as I was.

Reuben nodded. "He does. Double." After a moment he amended that to, "Triple."

"And a Maserati," Hunter said.

Terry raised his eyebrows, but didn't look like he'd decline if a fancy car turned up at the door with his name on it. Personally, I'd give him just about anything he wanted right now. I had a suspicion he wouldn't ask for much anyway. He seemed to enjoy a simple life.

"Aidan and his boys took care of everyone at the front," Gianni said. "A couple of them gave them trouble, but they won't give anyone any trouble anymore."

"Neither will any of the ones inside the house," Damon said darkly. "Some of them were quick enough to turn on Kurt. The rest will be dealt with in the morning."

Reuben patted Caleb on the shoulder and came over to join us. "We have some work to do to seize the rest of Kurt's assets, but Caleb is going to get a start on that tomorrow. You two can help." He nodded to the twins.

They responded with identical grimaces, but ultimately shrugged and nodded in return.

"Whatever it takes to tear him down the rest of the way," Hunter said.

"And make an example for anyone else." Reuben sank into a chair and rubbed his forehead. "We also need to destroy the access from the water tank. Too many people know about it."

"I'll put that on the to do list for tomorrow," Damon said. "I've already ordered a cleanup on all of those exploded SUVs. People will start asking questions if we leave them as they are."

"Let them ask questions," Gianni said. "We can give them honest answers. It was all Kurt Lasalle's fault. He got too big for his boots and decided to come after us. But, because we're awesome, we won."

"We did, didn't we?" I asked. "It's over." I couldn't begin to get my head around it. After everything we'd all been through in the last few months, we finally had Kurt. He'd never touch any of us again.

Rose put her arm around me and held me carefully. "Yes it is. You're finally free to live your best life. Just like you always were supposed to."

I placed what was left of my tea down on the table in front of me and hugged her back. "I'm sorry you got dragged into this. You deserve better."

"We both do," she said firmly. "I saw the expression on your face. You would have gone through with it. You would have gone back with him to save all of us. You must have a uterus of steel. Like balls of steel, but a lot stronger."

"I would have," I agreed. "I couldn't see any other way out. He would have killed all of you without a second thought. He would have laughed at the expression on my face while he did it. He would have reminded me of it, over and over again until I broke."

"Just like he did with that girl?" Rose asked gently.

I was too tired to hide my surprise, or pretend to be confused. "Just like that."

"Her name was Jana," Rose said. "I heard the rumour about Kurt being the Sparrow, and did some digging. According to my sources, the Sparrow was on a job, and Jana died. The thing is, my sources confirmed that Kurt Lasalle was there that night, to do something else. I figured the Sparrow must be someone else."

"I guess that's possible," I said evasively. Most of the people in the room knew the truth, but not all of them. Those who didn't know didn't need to. I was relieved that my sister did though. I didn't want to keep any more secrets. Not from her.

"Who the hell are your contacts that you can find out something like that?" Caleb asked. He'd moved to stand behind the couch.

She glanced back at him and smiled. "I'll tell you mine if you tell me yours."

He grunted and moved away. Apparently not everything was smoothed over yet.

Hunter whispered something to Parker, which made him laugh.

"You think?" Parker looked at Rose, then over to Caleb.

I snorted and looked at Rose myself.

She looked amused. "I don't know who'd kill who first, me or him."

"You'd be adorable together," Hunter told her.

"How much did you bet that my sister would get together with your brother?" I asked bluntly.

Both twins grinned.

"We'll never tell," Parker said. "Twin privilege."

"I don't think that's a thing," Damon said.

"If you two don't have anything better to do than speculate on other people's love lives, then I better give you more work to do," Reuben said dryly.

"We have plenty to do," Hunter said. "We can multitask. Right, Park?"

"Right," Parker said. "In fact, we have to go and do some of those things right now." He managed to ease himself out of the chair without tipping it over and sending Hunter sprawling.

I stood too and gave them both a hug each. "Thank you."

"For what?" Hunter asked. "We were just doing our jobs."

"You were being the best younger brothers I ever had," I said. "The only ones, but still the best."

"I guess that makes Rose our big sister too," Parker said. "Which means she can't get together with Caleb. That would be weird."

"It totally wouldn't," Hunter argued. They headed away up the stairs, friendly banter following them the whole way.

Rose shook her head. "Those two are a pair."

"Pair of clowns," Gianni said, but in an affectionate way.

"A pair we thought were dead," I said softly. My heart had broken for a little while. Seeing them alive… I couldn't put it into words.

If they'd died, they would have left a huge hole in my wonderful, found family. A hole no one would have been able to fill. No one I ever met was quite like the Brantley twins.

The younger brothers I never had. The younger brothers who'd always have my back and I'd have theirs.

"Pair of cockroaches then," Gianni said jokingly. "Always underfoot, but virtually impossible to kill."

Damon grunted a laugh. "That sounds about right. Just don't tell them that, they might start to think they're invincible." He didn't need to remind us that none of us actually were.

I suspected we all felt very mortal right now. I certainly did.

If not for Terry…

I'd have to try to think of a way to thank him for what he did. Him and his frying pan. He'd succeeded where guns, knives and technology had failed. Sometimes the simple, old-fashioned methods worked the best. I, for one, would never look at a frying pan the same way again.

Thinking about the kitchen brought my mind back to something I'd tried hard not to think about. Something I had to face, whether I liked it or not. There were still a couple more demons I had to put to rest.

I licked my lips. "I need to see Jase and Wade. I need to be sure it's them and that they're really dead."

If I didn't see with my own eyes, I'd never fully believe it. I'd never put them behind me. In the back of my mind, I'd always wonder if they were still out there, coming for me.

Fuck that. I wasn't going to live my life in fear of them. Not when there was no need.

"Are you sure, sweetheart?" Gianni asked gently. "I know you're not scared of death, but…"

"I'm sure," I said. "I need to do this now." I'd hesitated long enough, drinking tea and talking instead. Filling in the moments before I faced those ghosts.

I left Rose on the couch and walked with my three men, to the side of the kitchen, where a row of bodies lay. Mostly faces I didn't recognise. Several men and a couple of women. None whose deaths I'd mourn. They made up their minds when they worked for Kurt. They wouldn't get any sympathy from me.

I walked down to the end of the line and saw two faces I did know. Both already pale, and splattered with blood.

Jase had a gaping wound in his chest. His clothes were soaked with his blood. His eyes were half open, staring like he wanted to give me nightmare fuel even after he was gone.

Wade lay beside him, a smaller wound in the side of his neck. His clothes were also soaked with his blood, but his eyes closed, making him look almost peaceful. He might have fooled me, if I didn't remember the way he looked when he was alive. Not to mention the things he'd done.

"That's them," I said. "That's all of them. Leon, Jase, Wade and Kurt. And my father."

"Kurt isn't dead yet," Gianni reminded me. "But that's just a formality we can rectify any time you're ready." He looked like he was looking forward to doing just that.

Of course he was; so was I. We all were.

I had no doubt they'd give me first choice, otherwise they might resort to rock, paper, scissors to decide who ultimately took his life. Even Reuben looked keen to get his hands dirty himself, just this once.

"You might want to hold off for a little while," Damon said. "I have a surprise for you. Something I think you'll like."

"It can wait until morning," Reuben said. "We all need rest first."

No one bothered to argue with him. What I needed right now was a quick shower and a long nap.

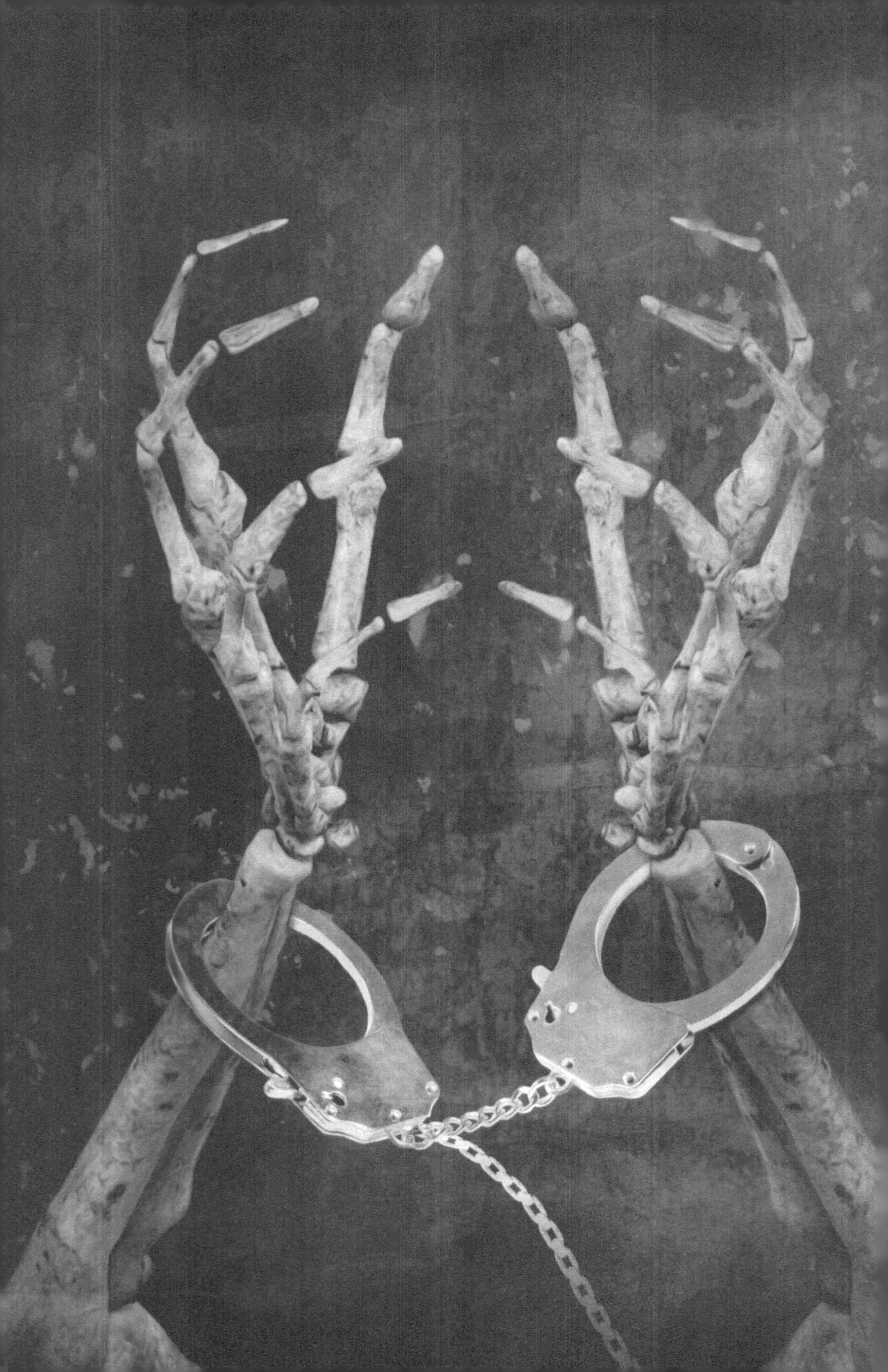

CHAPTER 22

MINA

"Don't ask if I'm all right," I told my men as they followed me into Reuben's bedroom.

"Were we going to do that?" Gianni asked. He turned back around to face the other two, his hands spread to either side.

"Yes." Damon stepped around him, into the room. "That's exactly what we were going to do." He looked at me questioningly.

"I'm fine," I said with a sigh.

I touched my mouth, where the duct tape was adhered. Taking it off had sucked like a bitch, but it was better than having it on there. The cable tie only needed a snip with a decent pair of scissors. Being restrained by that was worse than the tape over my mouth.

If anything was going to give me nightmares, it was that.

All three of them looked at me sceptically.

"I'm *fine*," I insisted. "Tired, relieved and okay. And in need of some hot water."

"I'll turn it on." Gianni hurried to the ensuite to turn on the shower.

"I'll help you in." Damon nodded for me to raise my hands, before gripping the hem of my T-shirt and pulling it over my head.

Reuben undid the clasp of my bra. I dropped my arms to let it fall to the floor.

Damon undid the front of my jeans and they both worked them down my legs and off my feet.

"Thank you," I said graciously before stepping towards the shower. Gianni was already naked, and ready with the body wash. All I had to do was step under the delicious warmth and let it wash the night away.

"Turn around," Gianni said.

I turned to face the water and let him rub body wash all over my back before massaging it into a lather. I closed my eyes and enjoyed the way his hands felt on me, and the occasional brush of his erection against me.

"You're so tense," he said. He worked out the knot in one of my shoulders while Damon and Reuben stripped off and joined us, using the shower head on the opposite wall.

They moved around each other carefully, not quite touching while they washed, but both with erect cocks.

"It's been a long night," I pointed out.

"Very long." He pressed the head of his cock against me deliberately.

I reached around behind me to grip his length and run my hand up and down from his head to his balls. "Very long and very hard."

He moaned softly. "Accurate." He rinsed the last of the body wash off me and his hands, before shampooing my hair and turning me around to rinse that off too.

While I washed it away, he slipped his hand between my legs and rubbed it back and forth over my pussy.

It was my turn to moan.

After all we'd been through for the last handful of hours, he still got me going. His touch and the sight of the other two men, virtually dancing around each other.

Finally, Damon grabbed a bar of soap and started to wash Reuben's back. That was all he did, but the intimacy was both endearing and arousing.

If I ever doubted the way they felt about each other, I didn't anymore. They went way beyond being boss and employee or even brothers. I wasn't sure when they'd crossed that line, but they had. They'd become something much more. Something deeper.

"Cute, aren't they?" Gianni asked. He let his feelings for Damon show on his face. He cared about him, wanted to be physical with him, but I wasn't sure if they'd ever have a deeper relationship. His heart was with me.

Reuben and Damon, their hearts were with me, and with each other.

"Very cute," I said breathlessly.

Cuter still when Reuben turned around and kissed Damon, while Damon slowly pumped Reuben's cock. Okay, maybe cute wasn't the word. Smoking hot might be more accurate.

Gianni sank to his knees in front of me and gently parted my legs, just far enough to be able to tease my pussy with his tongue.

"Why are you always so delicious?" he asked.

I assumed that was a rhetorical question, because I couldn't respond with words. Just a groan as he slid a finger inside me, then another.

I kept my eyes half open, watching Reuben and Damon become more bold with touching each other. They both had their hands curled around each other's cocks. Reuben's touch was more tentative than Damon's. Like he'd imagined doing this, but never thought the moment would come.

I was the next to come, my head back under the hot water as I rolled my hips, increasing the friction as Gianni fucked me with his tongue and hand.

The world exploded in fireworks, and something I'd never experienced before. A true and absolute sensation of letting go. I held absolutely nothing back, not one drop of blood, not one beat of my heart. Heat roared through my body like an inferno, engulfing me, burning me down to my core before I was reborn from the ashes.

In that moment, my past was finally behind me. I could be the woman I was always meant to be. Fully, totally free, belonging only to these three men, and to myself.

Finally, I drifted back down to reality, panting lightly.

I waited until Gianni pulled his fingers out of me to pull him to his feet and wrap my leg around his waist. I positioned the entrance of my pussy against his cock and nudged him with my heel on his ass.

He obliged by sliding slowly and carefully into me, my back pressed against the side of the shower.

"Why do you always feel incredible?" he said breathlessly. Another rhetorical question, because after that we only communicated with thrusts, rolls of our hips and moans.

His piercings massaged my insides and drove me all the way back to the edge, holding me there for the longest time while he thrust into me with slow, deliberate, savouring strokes.

I sensed he felt my epiphany. Maybe he experienced it too.

Where before we felt like time was limited, now we knew it wasn't. We won, and now we got to enjoy that wonderful, beautiful victory.

The only sound in my ears was the roar of blood and the delicious sound of three men close to coming. Was Gianni waiting for Damon and Reuben? If he did, he timed it to perfection.

Almost simultaneously, all three men reached their orgasm, grunting, groaning and thrusting hard and fast.

Reuben and Damon spilled themselves into each other's hands and Gianni into my body. The hot water from the other shower head quickly washed away the pearly cum, from their fingers, but the sight of it was something none of us would ever forget.

It wasn't just release, it was acceptance.

Love.

It meant everything and it was arousing as hell.

I tipped my head back and closed my eyes, letting Gianni's piercings hit me at exactly the right angle. The friction from them was fucking incredible. The gift he gave me by having them was next level.

I came for a second time, along with them. The shower was awash with steam and bliss. My whole body was alight with pleasure, even more intense and powerful than the first time.

It was like nothing I had ever experienced before. A rush of moisture gushed from me, drenching Gianni's cock even more.

"Good girl," he managed to say, his words strained as he was still coming down from his own orgasm. "You fuck so beautifully. Not like anyone else I've ever met. So perfect. So fucking ours."

"So yours," I agreed when I was finally able to speak again. "So yours. You're all so mine."

I was the luckiest girl in the world.

Maybe I had to go through what I went through in order to end up here. In which case, maybe it was worth it. If this was the light at the end of a long, pitch black tunnel, then I was happy to bask in every bit of that glow.

Reuben and Damon exchanged soft looks. They didn't say the words out loud, but we heard and understood. They were so each other's too.

"Let's get out of here," Reuben said finally. "It's past time for us to get some rest." He didn't look as though he regretted taking the time to shower first. Partly because he would have been as dirty as the rest of us and partly because he'd taken this next, huge step.

"Good idea, boss," Gianni said.

"Yeah, good idea." Damon looked like he didn't know if should address Reuben as boss or something else. Evidently, that was a conversation for later. He stepped out of the shower and started to dry himself before tossing a towel to each of us as we stepped out with him.

"This feels like it was always meant to be this way." Gianni dried himself and wrapped his towel around his waist. He grabbed another to start drying my hair. "All four of us. We all had dysfunctional families, to some extent, but we all found each other and now we're family."

"We are," Reuben agreed. He too finished drying and wrapped his own towel around his waist. He seemed lighter as well. Like he'd spent years carrying the weight of the world on his shoulders and now he was sharing that weight. With us and with his brothers.

In spite of his stoic exterior, I suspected this was a relief for him. He had been raised to take over the family, but that was an enormous job for one person. His pride had stopped him from delegating as much as he should have. Maybe now he'd do more of that. After all, the twins did need to be kept busy. And I suspected Caleb would appreciate more responsibility.

I wondered if I could convince Reuben to step down as head of the family and hand it over to one of his brothers. Probably not, but I'd do what I could to lighten his load.

"And family looks after family," Gianni said. He put the towel aside and picked up a brush to start on my hair. "Especially when they're the family you choose. That's the best kind of family."

"They certainly make more sense than people we're related to by blood," Damon said dryly. It seemed as though he and Enzo still had some work to do. Hopefully they'd sort things out. I had a feeling they both needed each other more than they realised.

Which reminded me, there were some conversations I needed to have. Asher was at the top of that list. But that list could wait until tomorrow. For now, I want to snuggle up with my incredible men, and get some rest.

I didn't bother with a towel. Once I was dry and brushed, I padded over to the bed and climbed in, laying in the centre.

Gianni crept under the covers on one side and Reuben and Damon on the other. They all shuffled over closer to me and each other, close enough that I felt their presence, warm and solid.

After so much death tonight, I felt very much alive.

So loved.

The next day wouldn't be easy, but we'd get through it. Together.

I closed my eyes and listened as one by one, they drifted off to sleep. Gianni started to snore slightly.

A smile on my lips, I drifted off as well. Into a sleep full of dreams, which bordered on nightmares. None as terrifying as the ones I used to have. Those gradually retreated to the back of my mind, ready to be forgotten.

Finally.

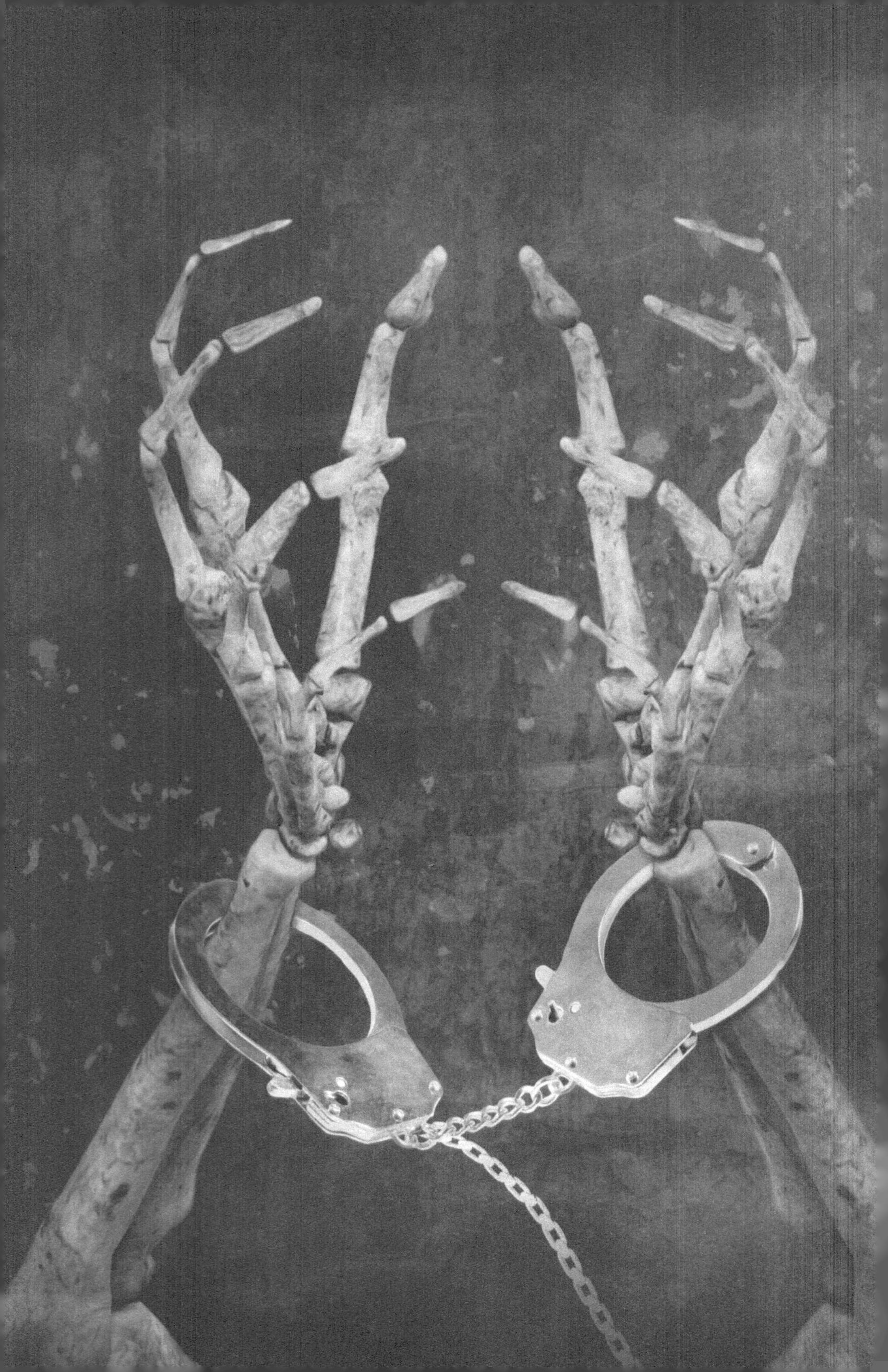

CHAPTER 23

MINA

"Are you going to make me close my eyes?" I asked.

They hadn't suggested blindfolding me, but Damon and Gianni looked cagey as fuck. Even Reuben was watching me for my reaction as they led me down the stairs to the basement.

After a long night, we all got a few hours of sleep. Fitful and full of dreams, but much-needed sleep.

"You could," Gianni said. "You trust us not to let you fall or walk into anything, right?"

"Of course I do," I said. "I'm just curious what's going on. You didn't kill him yet, did you?"

"Absolutely not," Gianni said. "We wouldn't kill him without you knowing about it. No, we've gone to great lengths to ensure he enjoys his time with us for as long as we want him to. And when I say enjoy, I mean… Why don't we show you?"

Gianni stood behind me and placed his hands on my shoulders.

Damon nodded at me to close my eyes, and put his hand on the door handle.

I exhaled playfully, as though annoyed with them, but closed my eyes and let Gianni steer me forward, one step at a time.

The first thing I noticed was the tang of blood, mingled with sweat. The rattle of something all-too-familiar. A soft, pained groan.

"Okay, open your eyes," Damon said.

I hesitated for a moment, before opening them and staring at the sight in front of me.

On the floor, in the corner of the basement was a cage. It was big enough to fit a large dog, but not big enough to comfortably fit a large human.

Kurt was hunched up inside, both ankles circled with manacles attached to chains on the wall behind the cage. His hands were free, gripping the bars of the cage as he stared at us.

"Surprise," Damon said blandly. "I figured he could use a taste of his own, sour medicine."

"You did this?" I looked up at him.

"It's been in the works for a while." He shrugged. "But yes, I did this."

I wrapped my arms around his neck and pulled him down for a kiss. "I love you. This is the perfect surprise. You knew exactly what I wanted, when I didn't."

It hadn't occurred to me to do to Kurt what he did to me. Although, in retrospect, it should have. He deserved exactly this.

"Damon is so thoughtful," Gianni enthused. "I have to admit, I was just thinking chains. The cage is…" He mimed a chef's kiss.

"It was inspired," Reuben agreed. "We should have had one of these down here already."

"No one else has quite fitted one as well as he does," Damon said modestly. "I'd suggest it's because he's a dog, but that would be an insult to dogs."

"It certainly would." I stepped closer to the cage. So, this was how it felt to look at someone the same way he looked at me for so long. He looked sad and pathetic. Scared, but still with a hint of defiance. Somewhere, in the back of his mind, he was still convinced he was in the right. That maybe I came to let him out and we could live our lives together.

He must have been out of his fucking mind.

"Mina," he said softly. "I was hoping you'd come to me. I know you missed me as much as I missed you. You and I, we belong together."

I crouched down in front of him. "You must be delusional. You have been for a long time. I'm sorry you never got the help you clearly needed. If you had, we might not be here now."

"You can help me to get help," he said. "I can get better and we can be together."

They were just words, he seriously didn't think anything was wrong with him. He didn't seem to grasp the concept of what he did to me was fucked up. Had Terry hit him so hard he'd broken something in his brain? He was always a little unhinged, but this was new, even for him.

"I don't want to be with you, Kurt," I said bluntly. "I never have. That was why you had to cage me, remember?"

He frowned. "Cage you? I would never do that to you, Mina. I love you." He reached his hand out towards me.

I shifted away and glanced back at my guys. They all looked as doubtful as I felt.

I turned back to Kurt. "What was the last thing you remember?"

He looked even more confused. "I remember... We practised this morning. You're getting so good at throwing me over your shoulder." He actually looked proud. "Then we went to... You had a job. I waited outside. I shouldn't have been there, I know that. I just like watching you sneak in and sneak back out. You're incredible to watch. Oh, I was thinking about this the other day. I think Fiori is the perfect name for you."

I stood and stepped away, my blood cold. "I remember that conversation. My father was trying to encourage me to choose something else." I shook my head as I thought back. "Fiori. It's Italian for flower. My mother was obsessed with flowers."

"Right," Kurt said. "Fiori. But he didn't like it. He said it was the name of a car."

"It was," I said. "A Subaru. He didn't want me to have the same name as a car." This whole conversation was surreal. I hadn't thought about any of this for years. At least seven or eight.

Kurt chuckled. "I'm sorry I teased you about that. You're right, flower would be perfect. You always were a beautiful flower." He cocked his head at me.

I swallowed down the small breakfast I'd managed to eat before the guys brought me down here. I glanced at them again. I didn't know what to think. In his mind, it was like the last few years never happened. Like he never laid a hand on me.

"What are they doing here?" Kurt asked. "Why am I in this cage?" He kicked his feet, rattling the chains. "Is this some kind of prank your brothers are pulling on me? No offence, but it's not funny." He was starting to become agitated.

"It's not a prank," I said quietly. "You held me in a cage for five years. Just like this one."

"I would never—" he started.

"You raped me. So many times I lost count." I leaned back against Reuben as he stood behind me, his hands on my upper arms.

Kurt's eyes widened. "Mina! I would never do that to you. I know it's going to take some time for you to turn to me, but you will. When you do, you'll willingly give yourself to me. Why would I force myself on you?"

He looked horrified. Not as horrified as I felt. Those moments ran over and over in my head on repeat, hard as I tried to ignore them and push them away. I could still feel him on top of me, pinning me down, pushing himself into me. Thrusting.

I swallowed hard. "It was what you did. You even had one of your friends video you raping me. I saw it. They saw it." I jerked my head towards my guys.

"Yes, we did," Damon said coldly.

Kurt gaped before sinking back to the back of the cage. "I wouldn't do that. I wouldn't do that. I wouldn't do that." He said it over and over at least a dozen times, while shaking his head.

"What the fuck do we do now?" Gianni asked. "He's still the same asshole."

My tongue swept over my bottom lip. He was, but at the same time, he wasn't. Terry must have hit him extremely hard.

In Kurt's mind, he hadn't harmed a hair on my head. Maybe, like this, he was harmless. Defenceless. Could we actually kill him like this? If we didn't, then I had no idea what we'd do with him.

"You could let me out of here," Kurt said pitifully. "Whatever I did, I'll make it up to you. I swear. Whatever you need me to do, I'll do it. If you think I need help, I'll get help. Just please..." He crawled back to the front of the cage and gripped the bars again.

"Please, let me out of here." He looked like he was going to burst into tears.

Something I'd never seen him do. Something I never would have thought he was capable of.

Reuben stepped forward, crouched down right in front of Kurt. "No," he said simply. There was an air of absolute finality in his tone. It didn't matter what I said, Reuben was absolutely not letting him walk away. Never.

Kurt's expression changed like a switch was flipped. He snarled at Reuben and tried to take a swing at him. He couldn't reach through the bars, Reuben was just out of reach.

"Reuben motherfucking Brantley," Kurt growled. "You think you're so fucking better than everyone else. You and your asshole sidekicks and your slut." He glared at me, teeth bared.

"It was all an act," I said softly.

Of course it was, he'd always been a good actor. He must have figured this was his only chance. If he appealed to my humanity, maybe, just maybe, I'd go soft on him. At least I had some humanity left. He had none, not even a tiny bit.

The grin he gave me was brutal and nasty. "You almost bought it, stupid bitch." He raised his voice to a high-pitch. "Mina, Mina, I never touched a hair on your fucking body. I *sweeeear.*"

He closed his mouth and smirked. "You would have let me out, wouldn't you? You would have let me walk out of here. I would have come straight back for you. You would have been the one in the cage again. Like the stupid bitch you are. Fucking slut. You spread your legs for the first man that came along. Didn't you? *Didn't you?*"

"At least we know what to do next," Gianni said. "Let's see how long he lasts in that cage. I'll tell Terry to save some scraps to feed him every few days. Maybe some water here or there. What about some country music thrown in for shits and giggles?"

Kurt jerked his legs against the chains. "Fuck off. Get it over with and kill me. You know you all want to."

He lifted his chin, as though daring me to grab another length of chain and wrap it around his throat. Tempting, but that would be far too easy.

"All the more reason to leave you alive," I said. "Because you want to die, just like I did. And it gives us something else to look forward to, when we get bored."

I yawned playfully, my hand in front of my mouth. It was past time I had some fun with this asshole. He'd had the upper hand for long enough. Now it was my turn.

"Fucking bitch!" he snarled.

"Sticks and stones, Kurt," I said. "Sticks and stones." I turned around to leave, but then turned back. "Gianni, do you think Terry will let me borrow his blowtorch later? I have a favour to repay."

Kurt glanced down at his chest and shook his head. He started to plead and went on pleading as we left the basement, closing the door behind us.

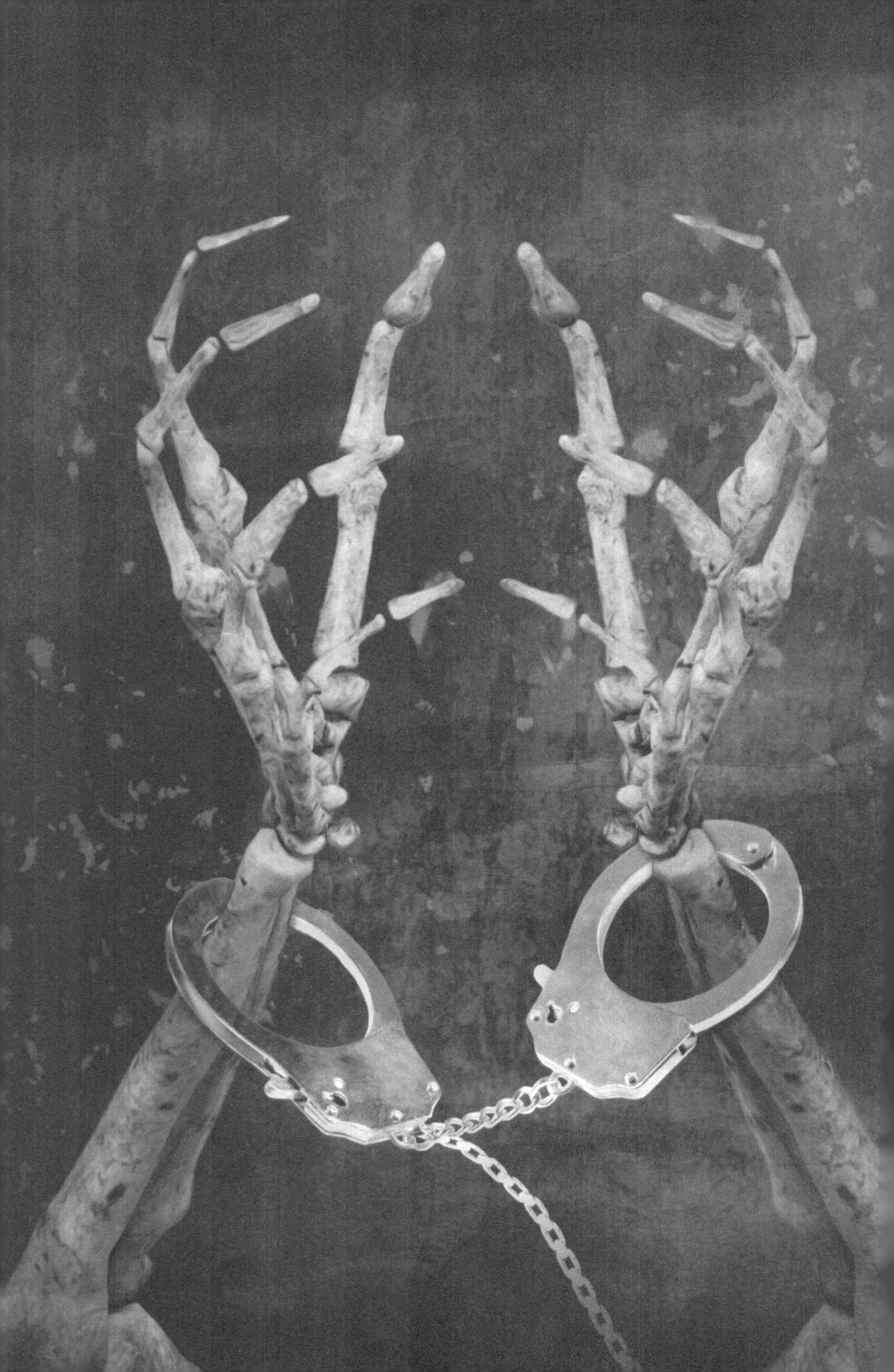

CHAPTER 24

GIANNI

"This is the life." I laced my fingers together and placed my hands behind my head. I leaned against the back of the outdoor lounge and gazed out at the view.

"It could be worse," Damon agreed. He sat down beside me and copied my pose.

"It has been worse." Mina sat on the other side of me, her legs crossed. She wore black leggings and a dark purple T-shirt with the logo of Bobby Starlight, her childhood favourite pop star, on the front. She wore her brown hair tied back in a ponytail.

For the first time since I saw her in that cage, she looked like a woman who was almost twenty-four, not so tired and world-weary. Not quite carefree, but we'd work on that.

Reuben sat on the edge of the lounge, lost in thought. His polo necked shirt looked new. It might have been hanging in his wardrobe for years, but he hadn't let himself relax enough to wear it. It wouldn't last long, but it was good to see him take a rare day off.

Mina uncurled and walked on her knees to place her hands on his shoulders. She started to massage them lightly, her upper body pressed against his back. "You should get a professional masseuse."

He dropped his chin down to his chest. "Why would I need one when I have you?"

She laughed, soft and husky. "Because I'm not a professional. Although, maybe now I could be. I could go back to school and get myself a day job. Something to keep me busy between contracts."

"If you need the money—" Reuben started.

"I don't," she said quickly. "I just want to do something interesting with my life. Maybe not masseuse. I wouldn't mind learning about technology and how to use it the way the twins do. Then you wouldn't have to call on them all the time for things like that."

Reuben grunted. "It keeps them busy, but if you want to study, you can. Any university would be lucky to have you. Brutham Academy has an excellent computer science department. The campus is a long way from here or Sydney. For a number of reasons, they don't do external study."

"You're on the board of Brutham," I pointed out. "They'd open a campus here in Dusk Bay if you insisted on it. And funded it. We could live here during term time and back in Sydney when Mina isn't studying."

"You could go back to school too," Damon said. "Learn how to do something useful."

I flipped him off. "Ha fucking ha. I'm very useful." I rolled onto my side to face him. "If I went back to school, it would be to teach. Psychological torture one-oh-one."

He turned his face until his nose was almost touching mine. "You're an expert at that. I feel psychologically tortured right now." His eyes shone with humour, his equivalent of laughing.

"The only thing you're suffering from right now is the suppressed desire to fuck me," I said. "An issue I'm happy to rectify any time."

His eyes were immediately darker.

Nail, meet head.

I lay perfectly still. He'd either make the first move, or he'd shift back away from me. Whatever he'd do was fine with me. I wouldn't put any pressure on him to...

The thoughts flew out of my head when he moved closer, brushing his lips over mine.

Then I was kissing him back, deepening the kiss before rolling onto my back and pulling him with me. His upper body lay across mine, growing erection pressing into me.

I slipped my hands up the back of his shirt and over his firm, scarred skin. Every centimetre of him was warm under my palms. With every caress, I wanted to feel more of him.

He groaned and pushed his tongue between my lips, like he was thrusting into me.

I was so hard by now, I'd be lucky if I didn't lose my load in my track pants. I managed to whisper his name right before I undid the front of his pants and pushed them down so I could palm his cock.

I raised my hips so he could pull down my track pants and do the same to me. His hand was hot and firm around my length. His fingers explored my piercings with fascination.

"Did they hurt?" He broke off our kiss to look down at my cock.

I glanced down too, marvelling at the way his hand fit around me. "A little, but it's completely worth it."

"It definitely is," Mina agreed. She and Reuben were watching us with heated expressions. He gripped her hips and pulled her over to straddle his lap. His hands slipped up the front of her T-shirt so he could palm her breasts. She pulled her T-shirt off over her head and threw it aside. She wasn't wearing a bra.

"So fucking gorgeous," Damon whispered.

"I know I am." I pulled him back in for another kiss. He grunt-laughed against my mouth, but kissed me back.

I grabbed the back of his T-shirt and pulled it up over his head. He did the same for me before we both shimmied the rest of the way out of our pants.

Mina discarded hers, before helping Reuben out of his. She placed her hands on his shoulders and lowered herself down onto his length.

"If you want to…" I raised my eyebrows at Damon.

He swallowed visibly and nodded before pushing himself up off the lounge and heading inside. He returned a minute or two later with a tube of lube in his hand. He gestured for me to lie on my side and opened the tube to squirt some lube onto his fingers.

Eagerly, I lay still while he applied the cool lube to my rear hole.

Tentatively, he pressed a slippery finger inside and worked it around to spread the lube and relax my muscles. He added a second finger, which made me quiver with pleasure and anticipation.

"Have you ever been fucked here?" he asked.

"Not recently," I said. "But yes. Please... I need you inside me."

He lay down behind me and pressed the tip of his cock to my entrance. "I don't want to hurt you."

"Yes, you do," I said teasingly.

He hesitated for a moment before bringing his hand down hard against my ass cheek.

My eyes widened and I almost came on the spot. I groaned. "More of that. Please."

He slapped my ass a couple more times, harder each time. Stinging, but perfect. After the third slap, he pushed himself inside me. Slowly at first, stopping to let me stretch and get used to having him inside me.

"That feels so good," I said.

"You're so fucking tight," he groaned. He pushed himself all the way inside me and lay still for a while.

I savoured the way he felt inside me, while watching Mina bouncing on Reuben's lap, her breasts bouncing with her.

"Good girl," I told her. "You're making him feel so good, with your perfect pussy."

Reuben's hand was between her legs, massaging her clit while she rode him. "She's a very good girl," he agreed. "The best." His voice was strained, attention split between looking at her in front of him, and watching Damon fuck my ass. Not with any jealousy, just with fascination and approval that I was making Damon feel good.

Damon snaked a hand over my hip to grip my cock. He pumped it at the same time as he thrust into me.

I moaned. "Fucking hell, I'm going to come."

"Me too," he said. "Can I..."

"Come inside me," I said. "Please. Fill me with your cum." That threw us both over the edge, coming hard and fast with each other. My balls clenched tight before exploding in his hand, covering his fingers with pearly, warm cum. At the same time, he filled my ass with his.

Reuben and Mina came moments later, him grunting while she tipped her head back and screamed out his name. I'd never get enough of watching her come. Him either. They were both hotter than hell. Sexy, smart and incredible. And mine.

Damon slumped down behind me, puffing lightly. "That was amazing."

"I told you you liked me," I teased.

He actually laughed softly. "Maybe I do. Don't tell anyone, or I'll have to kill you."

"My lips are sealed," I said. "Until the next time they're on your cock."

He groaned. "You're going to make me hard again." He carefully slid out of me.

I rolled over to face him and grinned. "Sorry, not sorry. Making people hard is part of my job description. It's on Mina's as well." She'd been doing that since we met. "See, I do have useful skills."

"Possibly." He lightly kissed my mouth before rolling onto his back and exhaling.

I propped myself up on my elbow and looked out at the view. "I know we have to get back to Sydney tomorrow and back to work, but we can enjoy this for a while longer, can't we?"

"This is why I bought the place," Reuben said. "So my family could enjoy the peace of the ocean." His arms were around Mina, her face pressed against his chest. He was running his hand up and down her bare back, just lightly, lovingly. Like she was cherished. Like he could sit with her like that forever and never need another thing.

I couldn't remember having ever seen him look content before. He did now. Holding her like that, he looked as though he'd come home to someplace he'd wanted to be all his life.

I knew he'd loved her for a long, long time. Now he had her, he wasn't letting her go. Neither were Damon and I.

She was the piece of the puzzle that completed all of us. The sun the rest of us circled around. The centre of our universe. Our beautiful, badass assassin.

"And we do," I said. "I love my job, but it's nice to stop and smell the sea air once in a while."

Not for too long though. I'd get bored if I wasn't running around getting shot at, shooting people and slitting throats. Those were the things that made life worth living. Especially doing them with the people I loved.

"That reminds me." Mina raised her face reluctantly. "I've come to the conclusion that the Sparrow is too burnt. After the rumours we spread and whatever Kurt said about me, the Sparrow needs to die. Figuratively," she added quickly.

"What are you saying, sweetheart?" I asked gently. "You're going to give up being an assassin and become a hacker instead?" That would also be hot. Whatever she did, would be.

"No," she said. "I want to keep working as an assassin. But I want to build a new name. I want to use the one I would have chosen for myself if my father hadn't insisted. Fiori."

She looked shy, as though she thought we might laugh, but if we did she was ready to deal with us. She wasn't taking shit from anyone, not anymore. She was so fucking strong, so beautiful it almost hurt. So incredible.

I'd never laugh at anything she ever wanted to do. Whatever she did, we'd support her, every single moment. The same way she'd support all of us.

"Flower." I smiled. "That's absolutely perfect. Just like you."

She smiled back and my heart never felt so full. I couldn't have been more proud of her. This new name was going to be even more successful and feared than the Sparrow. I couldn't wait to be on the sidelines, cheering her on. Maybe she'd even teach me some of her assassin skills.

She was so fucking perfect.

So fucking ours.

EPILOGUE

MINA

Voices came from Reuben's library.

I knew they were here, and why, but knowing that and stepping into the room, were two different things. I'd waited so long for this, but now I was paralysed.

I could let Asher go on living in his happy bubble, without ever seeing me. The selfless part of me wanted to do that. The realistic part of me knew he'd find out about me sooner or later. The longer I waited, the more hurt he'd be, knowing I was here all along.

I stopped outside the library door to listen to him and Zeke talking to Reuben. They'd brought their girlfriend, Abbie. Them and the twins were discussing something that took place at the end of Wolf Venom's world tour.

I knew the details, but was more interested in listening to my brother's voice than what they were talking about.

The twins were currently defending themselves to Zeke. I liked Zeke, but I couldn't help bristling slightly at his accusing tone. The twins could take care of themselves though, so there was no need for me to stab Reuben's rock star brother. If Reuben wanted him stabbed, he could have the twins do it.

I placed a hand on my swollen belly and held my breath.

At a break in the conversation, I took a few heavier steps forward, so everyone in the room would know I was there.

"You can come in," Reuben called out to me.

The nerves almost got the better of me, but I forced myself to step inside.

Asher's eyes widened the moment he saw me. He pushed himself out of his chair and gaped. His gaze slid to my pregnant belly. The first thing out of his mouth was, "Whose baby is that?"

I swallowed hard and tried to conjure the words. When they wouldn't come, it was Reuben who filled the heavy silence.

"Mine," he said. "And Gianni's, and Damon's."

Asher blinked a couple of times before putting his arms around me and giving me a careful hug. "I missed you. I'm super confused right now, but I missed you."

I hugged him back and laughed softly. "I missed you too."

I hugged Zeke when he also rose to embrace me. I smiled at Abbie, who was looking at me and Reuben like she was wondering what I saw in him.

I tried not to bristle at that too, but I knew Reuben hadn't made their lives easier for the last little while. Hopefully we could start to change that today.

I sat down beside Reuben, my hand on his. "It's a long story." I took a deep breath and started.

"Six years ago..."

Thank you for reading. Please leave a review before you go!

If you want to read more about Mina's brother, Asher, you can find him in Saving Abbie.

For Daisy Lasalle's story, you'll find that in Dark Daze.

Hunter and Parker, and their girlfriend, have their own story, Brutal Academy.

If you'd like a light-hearted scene of Gianni and Mina, stealing a pop star's underwear, read the bonus scene here.

Next up is a rugby RH series, Ruck Boys. It starts with Filthy Ruck.

ABOUT THE AUTHOR

Maggie Alabaster writes reverse harem romance.
She lives in NSW, Australia with one spouse, two daughters, one dog, and countless birds.

Sign up for Maggie's newsletter! Sign Up!
Join Maggie's reader group! Join here!
Follow Maggie on Bookbub! Click here to follow me!
Check out Maggie's website- www.maggiealabaster.com

ALSO BY MAGGIE ALABASTER

Ruck Boys

Filthy Ruck

Sparrow and the Mafia Kings

Possessive

Ruined

Corrupted

Pucking Dark Hearts

Pucking Hearts Collide

Pucking Forbidden Hearts

Pucking Hardened Hearts

Dusk Bay Demons

Puck Drop

Breakaway

Power Play

Brutal Academy

Book 1 Heartless

Book 2 Cruel

Book 3 Vengeful

Court of Blood and Binding

Book 1 Song of Scent and Magic

Book 2 Crown of Mist and Heat

Book 3 Sword of Balm and Shadow

Book 4 Whisper of Frost and Flame

Dark Masque

Book 1 Bait

Book 2 Prey

Book 3 Trap

Saving Abbie

Book 1 Pitch

Book 2 Pound

Book 3 Session

Book 4 Muse

Book 5 Rhythm

Book 6 Encore

Novella Venomous

Saving Abbie books 1-4

Saving Abbie books 4-6 + Venomous

Ruthless Claws

Book 1 Ivory

Book 2 Crimson

Book 3 Elodie

Harmony's Magic

Book 1 Summoned by Fire

Book 2 Summoned by Fate

Book 3 Summoned by Desire

Shifter's Vault

Book 1 Discarded

Book 2 Deceived

Book 3 Disgraced

My Alien Mates

Book 1 Star Warriors

Book 2 Star Defenders

Book 3 Star Protectors

Academy of Modern Magic

Book 1 Digital Magic

Book 2 Virtual Magic

Book 3 Logical Magic

Complete Collection

Summer's Harem

Book 1: Shimmer

Book 2: Glimmer

Book 3: Flicker

Complete collection

Short reads

Taken by the Snowmen

Jingle All the Way

Also by Maggie Alabaster and Erin Yoshikawa

Caught by the Tide

Book 1–Pursued by Shadows

Book 2 Pursued by Darkness

Book 3 Pursued by Monsters